NIGHT. SLEEP. DEATH. THE STARS.

A NOVEL

Joyce Carol Oates

4th ESTATE • *London*

4th Estate
An imprint of HarperCollins*Publishers*
1 London Bridge Street
London SE1 9GF

www.4thEstate.co.uk

First published in Great Britain in 2020 by 4th Estate
First published in the United States by ecco in 2020

1

A catalogue record for this book is available from the British Library

ISBN 978-0-00-838107-3 (hardback)
ISBN 978-0-00-838108-0 (trade paperback)

Set in Fairfield LT Std
Printed and bound in Great Britain by
CPI Group (UK) Ltd, Croydon

MIX
Paper from responsible sources
FSC™ C007454

This book is produced from independently certified FSC™ paper to ensure responsible forest management.

For more information visit: www.harpercollins.co.uk/green

Night. Sleep. Death. The Stars.

NOVELS BY JOYCE CAROL OATES

With Shuddering Fall (1964)

A Garden of Earthly Delights (1967)

Expensive People (1968)

them (1969)

Wonderland (1971)

Do with Me What You Will (1973)

The Assassins (1975)

Childwold (1976)

Son of the Morning (1978)

Unholy Loves (1979)

Bellefleur (1980)

Angel of Light (1981)

A Bloodsmoor Romance (1982)

Mysteries of Winterthurn (1984)

Solstice (1985)

Marya: A Life (1986)

You Must Remember This (1987)

American Appetites (1989)

Because It Is Bitter, and Because It Is My Heart (1990)

Black Water (1992)

Foxfire: Confessions of a Girl Gang (1993)

What I Lived For (1994)

Zombie (1995)

We Were the Mulvaneys (1996)

Man Crazy (1997)

My Heart Laid Bare (1998)

Broke Heart Blues (1999)

Blonde (2000)

Middle Age: A Romance (2001)

I'll Take You There (2002)

The Tattooed Girl (2003)

The Falls (2004)

Missing Mom (2005)

Black Girl / White Girl (2006)

The Gravedigger's Daughter (2007)

My Sister, My Love (2008)

Little Bird of Heaven (2009)

Mudwoman (2012)

The Accursed (2013)

Carthage (2014)

The Sacrifice (2015)

A Book of American Martyrs (2017)

Hazards of Time Travel (2018)

My Life as a Rat (2019)

A Clear Midnight

This is thy hour, O Soul, thy free flight into the wordless,
Away from books, away from art, the day erased, the lesson done,
Thee fully forth emerging, silent, gazing, pondering the themes
thou lovest best.
Night, sleep, death and the stars.

—**WALT WHITMAN**

CONTENTS

III. *UNTITLED: WIDOW*

IV. THE STARS

V. GALÁPAGOS

In memoriam Charlie Gross, first reader and beloved husband

Prologue

OCTOBER 18, 2010

Why? Because he'd seen something he had reason to believe was wrong and it was within his power or at any rate it was his moral obligation to rectify it, or to make that effort.

Where? Returning home on the Hennicott Expressway at approximately 3:15 P.M. of that day. Just beyond the grimy and graffiti-defaced overpass at Pitcairn Boulevard where in the early 1970s a ten-foot chain-link fence had been erected when high-school-aged youths rolled heavy rocks down upon motorists bound for the northern suburbs causing the death of one motorist and the injuries of others and considerable damage to their vehicles.

From where? A luncheon meeting of the trustees of the Hammond Township Public Library at the downtown, central library which John Earle McClaren (at that time mayor of Hammond, New York) had helped to rebuild in the mid-1990s with a capital campaign of several million dollars; since then, John Earle—"Whitey"—had not missed a meeting of the trustees in fifteen years.

Driving his vehicle, a new-model Toyota Highlander, in the right lane of the three-lane highway at a speed neither above nor below the fifty-five-miles-per-hour limit. This caution in the light of his having consumed a single glass of white wine at the luncheon (though John Earle did not seriously believe that he was driving under the influence of alcohol or that his driving, perceived by any neutral observer, might be so interpreted).

Seeing then, just before the exit at Meridian Parkway (which would have had him safely home in the house on Old Farm Road in which he'd lived so happily with his dear wife for most of his adult life, within twenty minutes), a Hammond police cruiser parked at the side of the road with its red light flashing, and another vehicle parked close by; (two) uniformed police officers pulling a (young?) (male?) (dark-skinned?) individual from his car, shouting into his face and slamming him repeatedly against the hood of the car. Slowing his vehicle to get a better look, and shocked at what he seemed to be seeing, now braking, daring to stop just beyond the police cruiser, John Earle climbed out of his vehicle to approach the officers who were continuing their manhandling of the dark-skinned young man though it was clear (to John Earle) that the young man was not resisting them unless you called trying to shield his face and head from their blows "resisting"—boldly calling out, "Stop! Officers! What are you doing!"—brazen-seeming, fearless, summoning something of his old mayoral authority in this new century, in this uncharted place (scrubby inner-city Hammond in which a stricter and harsher police presence prevailed, little-known even to white citizens as knowledgeable as John Earle McClaren); and there followed then an excited exchange which John Earle would not recall clearly afterward as he would but vaguely recall that the dark-skinned man was of slender build, very frightened, not an African-American but (seemingly) a young Indian, in a suit, white shirt torn and blood-splattered, wire-rimmed glasses knocked from his face.

Both police officers shouted at John Earle—"Get back into your fucking car and get the fuck out of here, mister"—and John Earle dared to continue to advance—"You're beating a defenseless man. What has he done?"—fired with adrenaline, heedless, insisting he *would not leave*—"I want to know what this man has done. I am going to report you for excessive force." Forgetting that he was sixty-seven years old and had not been mayor of Hammond for a quarter-century. Forgetting that he was (at least) twenty pounds overweight, easily winded, and taking a powerful medication for high blood pressure. In his vanity assuming that since "Whitey" McClaren had been a popular moderate-Republican mayor with a skill for political compromise, that he'd been a civic-minded citizen, a well-to-do local businessman, a poker-playing friend of the late Hammond police chief and longtime contributor to the Police Benevolent Association who believed (and had said so often, publicly) that police officers have a difficult and dangerous job and need public support not criticism—the officers might recognize him, and relent, and apologize. But this did not happen.

Somehow instead it has happened, John Earle is on the ground. On his back, on the filthy pavement. Broken glass, stink of diesel. Once you are down, you are down. Not likely you will get up of your own accord. The police officers have slammed into him, incredibly, unbelievably, such force, such fury and such seeming hatred, with their gloved fists and bodies. He is stricken with shock, as well as physically stunned. *Never in his life has Whitey McClaren been treated so roughly, so without courtesy! A man other men like and admire . . .*

Trying to rise. Oh but his heart is pounding—hard. A booted foot strikes his soft belly, groin. John Earle who is such a stoic he often eschews Novocain at the dentist's is now writhing in pain. John Earle who is so often heedless of fear, caution—now terrified. In the three-piece Black Watch plaid suit purchased years ago for a relative's wedding which he wears to trustees' meetings to show respect for the gravity of the occasion. *The American public library is the bedrock of our democracy. Our beautiful Hammond Library of which we are all proud.* But unwisely he'd tugged at his necktie when he'd left the luncheon, that pale blue silk Dior tie given to him by his wife, which might've impressed the officers otherwise, but now he's looking slightly disheveled, harried and flush-faced—(*is* he drunk?—not possible, a single glass of white wine)—and the officers might've been impressed by the Toyota Highlander (not an inexpensive vehicle) but which, he could kick himself now, he hadn't gotten around to taking to the car wash out on Route 201 in weeks, and it's coated in a fine film of dust; and so none of this has worked out to John Earle's advantage, and prevented what is happening from happening in quite the way it is happening, like an avalanche, if you are positioned below the loose-sliding rocks; as, if John Earle McClaren had identified himself properly, boastfully, claiming to be a friend of the police chief, knowing the police chief by name, might've forestalled the officers' fury though possibly not for already it is being shaped, rehearsed—*Interfering with law enforcement, endangering the safety of law enforcement officers, resisting arrest, aggressive assault.*

But what has happened to John Earle, that he is lying on the ground? One of the loud-shouting officers crouches over him holding a Taser in his right hand, is it possible that the officer has Tasered the defenseless, unarmed, supine white-haired older man—not once but a half-dozen times in a frenzy of indignation—and has caused the fallen man's heart to flutter, and stop, and flutter, and stop—is this possible? Dr. Azim Murthy, a young resident physician at St. Vincent's Children's Hospital, lately of Columbia Presbyterian, New York City, has been a witness to the violent Taser assault who, though he speaks English almost fluently in normal circumstances, has virtually forgotten his English now, in a state of animal panic. Dr. Murthy will claim that the police officers had so frightened him, confused him, he could barely comprehend what they were shouting into his face, which they interpreted (he supposed) as refusing to comply with their orders; he had no idea why they'd forced him to pull his Honda Civic onto the side of the highway since he had not been speeding, why they'd dragged him from the car with such force that his left shoulder was dislocated; no idea why they were demanding to see his ID, and so when, in great pain, he began to remove his wallet from his coat pocket, this was (evidently) a wrong move, for one of the police officers shouted obscenities at him, grabbed him and flung him against the hood of his vehicle; slammed his face against the hood, lacerating his forehead and breaking his nose; threatened to "light him up"—(with what Dr. Murthy in his terrified state had no idea was a Taser, and not a firearm); at this point Dr. Murthy, twenty-eight years old, born in Cochin, India, moved to New York City with his parents at the age of nine, was convinced that the unaccountably furious policemen would murder him, for what reason he had no idea; Dr. Murthy did not want to think that they'd stopped him on the Hennicott Expressway because of the color of his skin which with some pride he did not think resembled "black" skin—though certainly you would not mistake it for "white." True, the officers might have surmised from Dr. Murthy's suit, white shirt and necktie that he was (probably) not a drug dealer, or a "thug," and would (probably) not be a threat to the well-being of one or either of them if they took him into custody without extreme force; though very frightened, weak-kneed, Dr. Murthy was determined to behave as if he were not "guilty" though he wasn't at all sure what he might be guilty of, or what the enraged police officers hoped to charge him with. Drugs? Murder? Terrorism? Dr. Murthy was uneasily aware of a surfeit of mass murderers, random snipers, shooters, and "terrorists" in the United States in recent times, dominating news headlines and cable TV so you might surmise that the Hammond police officers were but reasonably on the lookout for such individuals who carried with them, on their person and in their vehicles, arsenals of weapons; very dangerous persons whom law enforcement might be tempted to shoot on sight. The homeless, the mentally ill, with or without (visible) weapons might be considered dangerous to law enforcement also, but Dr. Murthy did not resemble a mentally ill person, or a likely mass murderer; the tincture of his skin, olive-dark, like his very dark eyes, might have suggested, to the suggestible, a "terrorist"—but by this time the police officers had examined Dr. Murthy's laminated ID card from St. Vincent's Children's Hospital which identified him as a staff physician—AZIM MURTHY, M.D. Nor were there weapons, drugs or drug paraphernalia on his body or in his Honda Civic as the officers would subsequently discover.

In their police report the officers would claim that Dr. Murthy's vehicle was "weaving" in traffic; when the police cruiser came up close behind him, flashing its red light, the alarmed driver increased his speed as if to "escape" the cruiser; grounds for suspecting drugs in the vehicle, or inebriation in the driver; and so they stopped him, for public safety; according to both officers the driver was immediately "resistant"—"shouted at them in a foreign language obscenities, profanities"—"made threatening gestures"; for officer safety they had to drag him from behind the wheel of his car, as he resisted they were obliged to use force, in an effort to handcuff him they had to use "maximum" force; at which time another vehicle pulled off the Expressway, a "suspicious-looking" Toyota Highlander driven by an individual whom the officers believed to be an accomplice of the man being arrested; an individual who presented a "clear and present danger" to the officers by shouting at them, waving his fists, threatening to shoot them and seeming to be reaching inside his coat, as if for a weapon—again for officer safety this individual had to be overcome, thrown down, Tasered with a stun gun (fifty thousand volts at twenty-five watts) and handcuffed.

This "aggressive and threatening" person, initially believed by the police officers to be an accomplice of Azim Murthy, subsequently identified as John Earle McClaren, sixty-seven, of Old Farm Road, Hammond, New York.

As it would turn out neither Azim Murthy nor John Earle McClaren had a prior police record. No drugs or weapons would be found in Dr. Murthy's Honda Civic or on his person, and no drugs or weapons would be found in Mr. McClaren's Toyota Highlander or on his person. No connection between the two men would be established. It happened that Tasers were used on both men—for reasons of "officer safety"—but Dr. Murthy did not lose consciousness or lapse into a coma as John Earle McClaren did, perhaps because he was forty years younger.

I.

The Vigil

OCTOBER 2010

Wind Chimes

A light chill rain but she doesn't want to come inside just yet.

Gusts of wind, a sound of wind chimes.

So happy!—at the faint, fading sound of the wind chimes hanging from several trees at the rear of the house.

Is it selfish, she wonders. To be so happy.

Something about the wind on this October afternoon, rich ripe autumnal smells, wet leaves, a grainy sky, wind chimes with a distinct silvery tone, that makes her almost faint with yearning as if she were (again, still) a young girl with her life before her.

All that you have, that has been given you. Why?

She has been (carefully) pouring seed into bird feeders, that hang from a wire above the deck. Corn, sunflower seeds. In nearby trees the birds are waiting—chickadees, titmice, sparrows.

It is such a small task. Yet it is crucial to her, to execute it correctly.

Realizing then that she has been hearing, from inside the house, a ringing phone.

Lightning-Struck

He'd been electrocuted—had he? Struck by lightning?

Not once. More than he could count.

All he can remember—torso, throat, face. Hands, forearms lifted to protect his face.

Bolts of electricity. Stunning, burning. Sizzling flesh he'd smelled—(had he?).

Mistake. His mistake.

Not a mistake: had no choice.

NOT A MISTAKE. BLUNDER, MAYBE.

What's a blunder but a soft sort of mistake.

Words uttered without thinking. Actions recklessly undertaken like you've forgotten your age (what the hell's his age?—not young). Clumsy footwork taking you somewhere you'd never intended to go, Jesus!—and now can't turn back.

Whitey wants to argue. Plead his God damn case.

BUT SOMEHOW, WHITEY IS MUTE. Tongue too large for his mouth, gluey sensation in his throat. Can't speak?

Lightning-bolt struck his throat. Burnt out his vocal cords.

He, John Earle McClaren—"Whitey"—all his life the very reverse of *mute.*

Could speak, for sure Whitey would protest. Could summon words, syllables, sounds articulated by (damp, not dry) tongue, (damp, not dry) interior of mouth, however the miracle of speech is executed, *if he could remember how*—Whitey would plead his case not to a jury but to the electorate, see how he does at the polls. Whitey McClaren would be vindicated!—he is sure.

It hurts! Heart hurts.

Some kind of shunt or clamp in the heart or (maybe) where the heart used to be, now there's a pump.

Iridescent-silver wire threaded through—(what is it?)—(an artery?)—and through the artery and into his brain strangely shaped and textured like a walnut.

Smell of burning flesh, hair. Sizzle-smell.

Skull-bone. Skin-flap.

NOT WONDERING WHY IT'S SO NUMB in this place where he finds himself in a kind of tight-wrapped body-bandage, so dark, and why so silent, tremulous reverberating silence with a quick-pulse like falling water beneath—not wondering, yet.

Not wanting to think that once you've been struck by lightning you are finished.

Point he's trying to make: a blunder should be fixable, not lethal, fatal.

God damn blunder not *the last thing Whitey McClaren will ever do on this earth*.

The Cruel Sister

"Oh. Oh *no*."

Passing by an upstairs window of her house on Stone Ridge Drive and happening to glance out, and down.

Seeing—what was it?—a shiny-yellow-clad figure on a bicycle frantically pedaling up the long gravel driveway to the house. Shiny safety helmet and jutting elbows and knees like a large insect awkwardly riding a bicycle and the bicycle itself singularly ugly, rusted and mended with black tape.

Something so urgent about this creature, something so desperate, you did not want to know what urgency so propelled it, what desperation, you wanted only to shrink back against the wall to hide, not to hear footsteps on the front porch, a loud rapping at the door and a faint cry—*Beverly? It's me . . .*

Could it be?—(quickly Beverly had stepped away from the window hoping not to be seen)—her brother Virgil?

Her younger brother, by five years. Her vagabond-brother, she thought him. Whom she had not seen in—how many months? A year? Virgil McClaren who had no cell phone, no computer, no car—with whom she had no way to communicate except through their parents, unless she wanted to write him a letter and put a stamp on it which no one ever did anymore.

Of course, it was Virgil. On the bicycle he'd boasted was too old, too ugly for anyone to steal. Who else!

That silly slick-yellow raincoat. Wouldn't it be awkward, riding a bicycle while wearing an actual coat?

Had to be bad news. Why else would Virgil bicycle so frantically to see *her*?

Now he was knocking at the door below. Rude, loud. Not taking time to ring the doorbell as a polite visitor would. *Bev'ly? H'lo*—expecting her to drop everything she was doing, or might conceivably be doing, run downstairs to see what on earth he wanted.

Beverly's heart beat rapidly in opposition. *No I will not. God damn I will not run downstairs to you.*

If Virgil had had any sense or good manners—(which, being Virgil, he did not)—he'd have found a phone to use, to call her. To call first. Oh why couldn't Virgil *behave like other people*?

Beverly stood very still, listening in disbelief. Was Virgil trying the door? Actually turning the doorknob, to see if the door was locked?

Of course, the door was locked. All doors, windows. Locked.

However Virgil lived—(Beverly had an impression of a slovenly commune, persons like himself sharing a ramshackle old farm property that never had to be locked or secured since there was nothing worth stealing from it)—Beverly and her family lived very differently in Stone Ridge Acres where no property was smaller than two acres and all of the houses were four- or five-bedroom Colonials with landscaped lawns.

Not a gated community, it was not. Not a "segregated" community. Virgil was always saying it was, and that was why he wasn't comfortable there amid myriad yellow signs and warnings—SLOW 15 MPH, PRIVATE ROAD, NO WAY OUT.

Virgil must have known that Beverly was home, he continued to call to her, and rattle the door.

(But—how could he be certain? To see Beverly's SUV behind the garage he'd have had to bicycle back there. Or maybe he'd seen her at the upstairs window, peering down at *him*?)

It was too much like a child's game. Hide-and-seek. One of their games, that had left them excited and sweaty.

If the door hadn't been locked, Beverly wondered if Virgil would have dared to enter the house. Probably yes. He had no respect for boundaries. He had no private life, he often said, whether boastfully or simply truthfully, and didn't think that others should have "private" lives, too.

Beverly recalled how, if Virgil hadn't been able to find his big sister, he would cry for her plaintively—*Bev'ly! Bev'ly!*—until she couldn't bear it any longer, the child's fear and yearning, and stepped out of hiding to run to him.—*Here I am, Silly-Billy! I was here all along.*

How happy it had made her, to be so wanted. And to so easily placate the frightened child.

But not now. The hell with Virgil, now. Too late by too many years.

She didn't want his bad news. She didn't want his agitation, his emotion. Too late.

The more Beverly hardened her heart against Virgil, the more adamant she was he had wronged *her.*

And she was not going to bail Virgil out if he was in debt, or desperate. Not her!

Making her way to the guest room at the rear of the house, and into the bathroom beneath the slanted roof. Quickly—door shut and latched behind her as if there was a serious possibility that Virgil might come looking for her.

What is wrong with you? What has happened to you? Hiding from your own brother?

Actually it felt good to be hiding from Virgil. Felt good to be behaving as selfishly as Virgil behaved, and without apology.

But why was she panting? Was she *panicked*? As if this really was a game of hide-and-seek played with their old ferocity.

In the bathroom mirror a flushed face like a blowsy peony. Was that *her*?

The toilet lid, not plastic but wooden, covered in soft fuzzy pastel-pink, was down. Feeling weak, Beverly sat.

She was thirty-six. Her legs had grown fleshy, like her thighs, belly.

Not that she was an overweight woman, she was not. Steve still called her *my gorgeous wife. My Olympia.* (Sometimes, meaning to be exotic, he'd called her *my odalisque*—but Beverly wasn't sure she wanted to be one of those.) Standing too long, especially when she was tense, made her legs ache.

Hearing him—where, now?—at the side door, that led into the kitchen?

Beverly? It's Virgil . . . But really his voice was too faint, she couldn't hear.

The wild thought came to her: maybe Virgil had "snapped"—there was a good deal of "snapping" in the U.S. today—and had come to the house with a firearm, to slaughter her . . . Maybe the Zen Buddhist peace-lover had imploded, and was revealed as murderous.

Bev'ly? Hello . . .

A few more seconds and the knocking ceased.

Intensely she listened, hearing only the blood beating in her ears.

Was it safe? To emerge from the bathroom?

Her brother hadn't forced his way into the house, had he?—hadn't crept up the stairs, and was approaching her hiding place with the intent to—accost her?

What relief: no one.

At a front window she saw Virgil in shiny yellow bicycling away, out the driveway and along Stone Ridge Drive. As suddenly as the threat had appeared, it was disappearing.

Trembling! Her hands! Why on earth was she . . .

Why hidden from her brother when he'd needed her. Had something crucial to tell her.

"Oh, *why*!"

QUICKLY THEN, downstairs to check if Virgil had left a note stuck into the door. Front door, side door. Nothing.

And this too was a relief. (Was it?)

And quickly then calling their mother.

Oh why didn't Jessalyn answer the phone? That was not like Jessalyn, if she was home.

Five rings, a forlorn sound.

Then Whitey's solemn voice mail clicked on.

Hello. This is the McClaren residence. Unfortunately neither Jessalyn nor Whitey—that's to say, John Earle—John Earle McClaren—can come to the phone at this time. If you will leave a detailed message, complete with your phone number, we will call you back as soon as we are able. At the sound of the beep.

Beverly left a message:

"Mom? Hi! Sorry to miss you. Guess who was just here just now—on that ridiculous bicycle of his—Virgil . . . I was upstairs and couldn't get to the door in time so—he went away looking miffed. Any idea what is going on with him?"

Wanting to say *what the hell is going on*. But Beverly's phone voice to her mother was her good-daughter voice, bright-glittering like bubbles on a stream beneath which, if you looked closely, you'd see sharp-edged rocks and rubble.

Hung up. Waited thirty seconds. Called back.

No answer. She was sure that Jessalyn should be home.

John Earle McClaren's computer-voice recording like something out of a mausoleum.

If you will leave a detailed message . . . At the sound of the beep . . .

But by this time, late afternoon, Jessalyn should have been home. Beverly was the only person apart from Jessalyn who knew her mother's weekday schedule virtually hour by hour.

Through Jessalyn she kept tabs on Whitey's (much busier) schedule. He'd had a Hammond Public Library trustees' meeting that day, downtown at the library.

Whitey had a cell phone, in theory. But he rarely took it with him. He didn't want personal calls, and he didn't want interruptions at the office.

Beverly called her sister Lorene at North Hammond High, where

Lorene McClaren was principal. Had to leave a message with a secretary, of course; Lorene would never answer her own phone and if she had, she'd probably have been rude—*Yes? What do you want, Bev?*

"Just tell her—'Please call Beverly immediately.'"

There was a pause. Beverly could hear the secretary breathing.

"Oh."

"'Oh'—? What?"

"You are a relative of Dr. McClaren? She is out of the office for the rest of the day . . ."

"'Rest of the day'—why?"

"I think—I think—I think Dr. McClaren said—there is a 'family emergency.'"

Beverly was astounded. "'Family emergency'? What kind of—'family emergency'?"

But the secretary was sounding frightened, as if she'd revealed too much. She would pass on Beverly's message to Dr. McClaren, that was all she could do.

Family emergency. Beverly was frightened now.

Called her father's number at McClaren, Inc. And here too a secretary informed her that Mr. McClaren was out of the office.

"When will he be back, do you know?"

"Mr. McClaren didn't say."

"This is Mr. McClaren's daughter Beverly. I need to reach him. Can you give him a message . . ."

"Yes, ma'am. I will try."

Oh, why didn't Whitey carry a cell phone! Though Whitey did use a computer he was of the generation of Americans who were quietly waiting for the "electronic revolution" to go away.

Hurriedly then Beverly left the house. Jamming her key into the SUV ignition. She'd had time only to grab a corduroy jacket, her oversized purse, cell phone. It was crucial to get there—to the house on Old Farm Road.

There was no direct route. There was only a circuitous route. Long ago Beverly had memorized every turn, every intersection, every four-way and two-way stop, every blind corner and landmark of the slightly more than three miles between Stone Ridge Drive and Old Farm Road.

Fumbling with her cell phone trying to call her younger sister Sophia, who worked in a biology lab and (probably) had her cell turned off. Trying to call (again) Jessalyn who might now be home. And Lorene on Lorene's cell phone—which was virtually always turned off.

Even Thom seventy miles away in Rochester—their *big brother.*

No one answered. All the phones went at once to voice mail.

It was eerie, unsettling. Like the end of the world.

Like the Rapture—and only Beverly left below, of the McClaren family.

In an emergency Whitey could be tracked down. Of course. During the day he would check in at the office for messages.

He'd said that he hoped to retire at the age of seventy—but that time was coming faster than he'd anticipated. No one believed that Whitey would retire before seventy-five. Or ever.

Your father's secret is, he has to *keep in motion.*

Jessalyn had said this, admiringly. For Jessalyn was the still point in the McClaren family about whom the others revolved.

Their beautiful mother with the soft voice and unfaltering optimism.

Pleading now into the silence, "Mom? Aren't you home? Pick up? Please?"

Family emergency—what could that mean?

Someone should have called Beverly. For it seemed that someone must have called Lorene.

Bitterly Beverly resented it, whoever had failed to call *her.* In fact, Lorene should have called her. Might've had her secretary call her.

As a little girl Beverly had tormented herself with the question: Which of her parents did she love best? If there were a car crash or an earthquake or fire which parent would she hope would survive to take care of her?

"Mommy."

Immediately came the answer, unhesitatingly: *Mommy.*

All the children would have answered *Mommy.* When they'd been younger, at least.

They'd loved Mommy the most. Everyone who knew their mommy loved her. Yet, it was their father whose respect and admiration they sought, precisely because John Earle McClaren's respect and admiration were not easy to attain.

Their mother loved them without qualification. Their father loved them, with many qualifications.

There was Whitey McClaren, good-natured and approachable. But there was John Earle McClaren who was capable of looking at you, forehead creased and eyes narrowed, as if he had no idea who the hell you were and why you were daring to take up his time.

In the McClaren family, sisters and brothers contended for the father's attention. Each family occasion was a test of some sort from which you could not exclude yourself even if you'd had an idea how this might be done.

Like gold coins Whitey might toss at you with that special dimple-Daddy smile that signaled *Hey kid. You know, I love you best.*

"Oh. God."

She thought too much about this. She knew.

It wasn't that Whitey—their father—was *rich,* that was the surprising fact. If Whitey hadn't a dime, if Whitey were in debt, they'd have felt the same way about him, Beverly was sure.

Like dirty water the memory washed over her: that birthday dinner she'd given for Virgil. Tried to give, and been rebuffed.

The first time she'd realized that Virgil didn't love her. How rude, how indifferent he was, she counted for so little in his life. How embarrassing it was, to be so snubbed.

Poor Beverly!—she tries so hard.

Poor Mom!—the teenagers made mouths at one another, dangerously close to laughing, under their mother's very nose.

A place at the beautifully decorated table—Virgil's place—empty.

Like a missing tooth, an emptiness in the mouth which the tongue seeks, irresistibly.

"I spoke with him. Just the other day. I made it a point to—remind him. And he'd seemed . . ."

Jessalyn had laid her soft, calming hand on Beverly's tremulous hand. Telling her not to feel bad—"It's just a misunderstanding, I'm sure. Virgil would never—you know—be deliberately *rude*."

Like one positioning to deliver a *coup de grâce* Lorene leaned forward on her elbows to smile cruelly across the table at them. "'Would never'—what? You're always making excuses for Virgil, Mom. Classic maternal 'enabler.'"

"'Enabler' . . . Well, I think I know what that means."

But Jessalyn sounded uncertain. No one ever criticized *her*—she could not see, comprehend, somehow.

"Yes! An 'enabler' is one who 'enables' another individual to persist in addictive and self-destructive behavior. An enabler invariably 'means well' and her well-meaning can precipitate catastrophe. No one can dissuade *her*."

Lorene spoke with zest. She was never so much in her element as when she was pointing out the flaws in others; her zinc-eyes glittered.

Her face was an unsentimental elf's face—plain, small as if squeezed together, *tough*.

The other McClarens were intimidated by Lorene when she was most herself. Even Whitey preferred to stay out of the fray.

Sophia suggested driving over to Virgil's cabin. She would volunteer.

Lorene said irritably: "That's exactly what he *wants*. All of us jumping loops for *him*."

"Jumping through hoops, I think you mean."

"Don't be flippant, Sophia. If there is anything that grates the soul, it's adolescent flippancy—I am surrounded by it every day, and it's destroying me. You know exactly what I mean, and you know that I'm right."

At last Whitey spoke, somewhat reluctantly.

"Sophia, no. You will not drive over to get your brother. That would be approximately fourteen miles round-trip—you are not his keeper. Nor will we further interrupt this meal. Lorene is correct: we should not 'enable' Virgil to behave rudely."

Lorene smiled, triumphant. Never too "mature" not to brighten when your parent corrects a sibling in front of everyone.

Beverly too rejoiced, inwardly. Her position, exactly! A family is a battleground, constantly shifting allies and enemies.

At the other end of the table (Beverly saw) Jessalyn pressed a hand to her heart, in silence. She was trying to smile, bravely. Obviously it pained her to hear the father of her children speak harshly of any of the children.

For any displeasure the father takes in their children has to be the mother's fault, somehow.

Well, perhaps not entirely! That is an outmoded notion.

And yet—unavoidably, it did seem to be so. Like a table at a tilt, if just a very subtle tilt, the blame would roll down to Jessalyn's end, where Jessalyn would put out her hand gently and unobtrusively to arrest it.

(Did Beverly feel that way, too? When Steve complained of the children?)

(You could not just shout at the man: *They are your children, too! Whatever their faults, you are half to blame!*)

"But, Daddy, what if something actual has happened to Virgil?" Sophia asked; and Thom said, with a wink, "Nothing 'actual' ever happens to Virgil. Haven't you noticed?"

Thom, named for an older brother of Whitey's who had died in the Vietnam War, had long been designated his father's heir. In his late thirties he was still the aggressively competitive boy, smartest of the children, or in any case the most charismatic, very good-looking and sturdily adult-male, with a cruel, cutting smile. Even Jessalyn was fearful of his sarcasm though never in memory had Thom turned his wit upon either of his parents.

"We will eat this delicious meal which Beverly has prepared, without Virgil. If he joins us, we will welcome him. If he does not, we will not. We will begin."

Whitey spoke somewhat flatly, not with his usual ebullience. The exchange had begun to annoy him, or to weary him. Beverly glanced at her father covertly.

He was an imposing man, big-boned, with the fatty-muscled build of a former athlete. In his mid-sixties he'd begun to lose height and so it was startling to his children to see him, and to realize that he wasn't any longer as tall as they expected; though each time they saw him was a surprise, for they could only imagine him as he'd been when they had been growing up—well over six feet tall, weighing well beyond two hundred pounds. In repose his lined, boyish face was affable, big and broad with the look of an old coin, somewhat worn, of a faint coppery hue as if heated blood beat close beneath it. His eyes were wonderful eyes—quick, alert, wary, suspicious and yet good-natured, humorous—crinkled with laugh lines. When he'd been quite a young man his brown hair had turned a remarkable snowy-white, and had become his most distinguishable feature. In any crowd you could pick Whitey McClaren out immediately.

Though Whitey was not so easy to know, as people wished to think. His genial demeanor was a kind of mask that did not suggest the gravity of his soul; his playfulness, prankishness, was a way of hiding from others his intense and brooding seriousness, that was not always so very nice.

In his innermost heart, a puritan. Impatient with the foibles of the world. In particular, impatient with so much talk of his younger son.

Seeing him frown, Jessalyn caught Whitey's eye. The length of the table between them, but instantaneously Whitey's expression changed.

Whitey darling. Don't fret! I love you.

It never ceased to amaze Beverly, how her parents could *connect.*

She was envious, perhaps. They all were.

Jessalyn said, "Whitey is right! If Virgil shows up he won't mind at all if we begin dinner before him."

They began. They ate. The meal, passing for Beverly in a buzzing blur, was to be pronounced a *great success.*

Beverly laughed as if delighted. Well—she was delighted.

Is this my life? Reduced to this? Humored by my family.

Humored, pitied by my children. Not a model for the girls!

But—better humored (and pitied) than not.

"MOM? HELLO . . ."

Nothing so unnerving as walking into a house that is unlocked—and, seemingly, empty.

A house that should not be unlocked. And should not be empty.

Beverly would long recall entering the house on Old Farm Road that afternoon. As it would come to be recalled—*that afternoon.*

Her parents' house was more familiar to her than her own house yet, empty, made unfamiliar as in a distorted dream.

"Mom?"—her voice, confident elsewhere, thinned in this house to the voice of a frightened girl.

Well—no one appeared to be home. Beverly had entered into the kitchen, by the side door that was the door most frequently used.

That the kitchen door was unlocked did not mean that Jessalyn must be home; for Jessalyn often neglected to lock the door when she left the house, to Whitey's displeasure if he knew.

"Mom? Dad?"—(but it was less likely that Whitey would be home, if Jessalyn were not home. It did not seem probable that Whitey *could be home* if Jessalyn were not home).

Bad news. Family emergency. Unmistakable. But—what?

Of the McClaren daughters it was Beverly who worried the most. You never get over being the oldest girl.

Their father had chided her: "It doesn't do anyone any good to be always imagining the worst case scenario."

Worst case scenario. As a girl she hadn't quite known what it meant. Through the years the phrase had echoed in her memory as Worst Case Scenario.

Of course—(Jessalyn also understood)—Beverly imagined the Worst, in order to nullify its power. The Worst could never be exactly as you imagined it—could it?

Daddy stricken with a stroke, heart attack. In a car crash.

Mommy ill. Collapsed. Among strangers who had no idea how special she was. Oh—where?

Nervously Beverly went to check the front door—locked.

In all, there were several entrances to the McClarens' house at 99 Old Farm Road. Most of these were kept locked most of the time.

The house was an "historic landmark" originally built in 1778, of fieldstone and stucco.

In its earliest incarnation it had been a farmhouse. A square-built stone house, two stories, to which a Revolutionary War general named Forrester had retired with his family and (according to local histories) at least one African-American slave.

By degrees the Forrester House, as it came to be called, was considerably enlarged. By the 1850s it had acquired two new wings, each the size of the original house, eight bedrooms and a "classic" facade with four stately white columns. By this time the farm property consisted of more than one hundred acres.

Through the early 1900s the village of Hammond grew into a fair-sized city, on the banks of the Erie Barge Canal, and began to surround the Old Farm Road farms. By 1929 much of the Forrester farmland had been sold and developed and by mid-century the area known as "Old Farm Road" had become the most exclusive neighborhood in Hammond, suburban yet still partly rural.

The elder McClarens had come to live in the Forrester House at 99 Old Farm Road when Thom was just a baby, in 1972. Much of early family lore had to do with fixing up a somewhat neglected property—about which the younger children knew little except these tales.

Why, if you were to believe their father, Daddy himself had painted many of the rooms of the house, or struggled to wallpaper the walls in comic-epic struggles. Paint that dried too bright—"eye-glaring." Floral wallpaper strips not-quite-precisely matched so that you felt "like one-half of your brain was separated from the other."

Mommy had chosen most of the furnishings. Mommy had "single-handedly, almost" created the several flower beds surrounding the house.

All of the McClaren children had grown up in the house, that no one in the family called the Forrester House. All of the children loved the house. So many years—decades!—Jessalyn and Whitey McClaren had lived here it was scarcely possible to imagine them elsewhere, or to imagine the house inhabited by anyone else.

Upsetting to Beverly, to imagine her parents seriously old, ill. Yet with a part of her mind Beverly imagined one day living in this beautiful house, to which she would restore the original name, with an historical plaque beside the front door: FORRESTER HOUSE.

(Whitey had removed this plaque as pretentious and "silly" as soon as they'd moved in. Hadn't General Forrester been a slaveholder, like his revered comrade George Washington? Nothing to boast about!)

The Hammond Country Club was close by, to which she and Steve might belong, though the elder McClarens had never joined. Whitey hadn't wanted to waste money on a country club since he rarely had time for golf, and Jessalyn hadn't approved of the membership requirements—at the time, in the 1970s, the Hammond Country Club had not yet admitted Jews, Negroes, Hispanics, or "Orientals."

Now, individuals from these categories could become members if they were nominated, and if they were voted in. If they could afford the application fee, and the dues. So far as Beverly knew, there were indeed Jews—a few. Probably not so many African-Americans, Hispanics. But a number of Asians? Yes. Half the roster of Hammond physicians.

Most nights, when Beverly dreamt, it was of the house on Old Farm Road she dreamt. Sometimes the house was the setting for the dream, and sometimes the house was the dream.

But, wait. This was not a good sign: newspaper pages scattered on a kitchen counter. Unlike Whitey who pored over newspapers in finicky detail, reading virtually every page, Jessalyn only read through the paper, turning pages quickly, often without sitting down. Usually the front-page news upset her, she had no wish to read it in detail and absolutely no interest in staring at photographs of wounded, dead, suffering human beings in faraway disasters. In any case Jessalyn would not have left newspaper pages scattered in the kitchen, as she would not have left dishes in the sink. Yet there were newspaper pages in the kitchen, and there were dishes in the sink.

Jessalyn had had to be surprised by something, and had departed the house suddenly. Whatever had happened, or had been revealed to her, it had been *suddenly.*

Beverly had checked: Jessalyn's car was in the garage. Naturally, Whitey's car was gone.

Since she wasn't in the house Jessalyn must have departed in someone else's vehicle.

Beverly searched for a note. For how often her mother had left notes for one or another of the children to discover, when they'd been growing up, even if she'd gone out for a very brief time.

> *Be back real soon!*
> ♥♥♥ *Your Mom*

It wasn't just that Mom was "Mom"—to be precise, she was "Your Mom."

For as long as Beverly could remember there'd been, on a wall behind the breakfast table, a cork bulletin board festooned with family snapshots, graduation photos, yellowed clippings from the *Hammond Sun-Ledger*—less frequently changed since the McClaren children had grown up and moved away.

When she'd prospered in high school Beverly had quite liked the family bulletin board in which Bev McClaren had been displayed to advantage in snapshots, newspaper photos and headlines. *Varsity Cheerleaders Choose Captain: Bev McClaren. Senior Class Prom Queen: Bev McClaren. Most Popular Girl Class of '86: Bev McClaren.*

So long ago now she could barely remember. Felt not pride but a dislike for the bright-smiling girl in the pictures. In the strapless pink-chiffon prom dress like cotton candy, she'd had to tug up, hoping no one would notice, all night long. Damn strapless bra cutting into the flesh of her underarms and back. In the photo looking both glamorous and bereft for the tall handsome prom king beside her had been scissored out for whatever unforgivable transgression Beverly could barely recall.

In more recent photos Beverly was fleshy-faced but still attractive—if you didn't look too closely. Her hair was highlighted to a radiant blond she'd never had as a girl. (She'd never needed as a girl.)

Of course, she'd never dare to wear anything strapless now. Anything that showed the bunchy flesh at her upper arms, and at her knees. Her teenaged children would erupt with horrified glee if they'd seen. Their mother might draw admiring glances from men in the street, at least men of a certain age, but she could not impress *them*.

When they'd been girls, Beverly had been *the good-looking McClaren sister*—(maybe, in some quarters, *the sexy one*)—while Lorene had been *the brainy one*. Sophia was too much younger to have competed.

In high school Lorene McClaren cut her hair short, "butch" style, wore wire-rimmed eyeglasses and a perpetual scowl. Not a bad-looking girl but nothing soft-edged about her though there'd been boys—(Beverly had always been astonished)—who'd found Lorene attractive, who had not seemed so impressed (indeed, Beverly had been baffled) with Beverly. Every picture of Lorene on the bulletin board showed a scowling smile, or a smiling scowl, through the years; it was remarkable, how relatively unchanged Lorene appeared. *Face like a pit bull and personality to match*—so Steve had said, meanly. But Beverly had laughed.

And there was Sophia. Wanly pretty, delicately boned, with a look of perpetual concern. It is hard to take seriously a sister nine years younger than you are.

Virgil—where was *he*? Beverly didn't see a single picture of Virgil, come to think of it.

The bulletin board was festooned with numerous pictures of Whitey.

Family snapshots, public photos. Here was Daddy presiding over a birthday cake blazing with candles, children tucked about him, and here was dignified John Earle McClaren, mayor of Hammond, in black tie, commemorating an anniversary of the opening of the Erie Barge Canal locks at Hammond, on a barge with local and state politicians.

Playful Whitey, silly Daddy, stiff-backed John Earle McClaren shaking hands with Governor Mario Cuomo of New York State on a stage banked with giant gladioli like sinister upright flower-swords.

But where was Jessalyn, among this profusion of snapshots and photos?

Beverly was dismayed: there appeared to be no pictures of Jessalyn except in group shots in which she was a small, peripheral figure. Beverly holding a baby, Thom with a toddler straddling his shoulders, Jessalyn looking on with a radiant-grandmother smile.

No pictures of Jessalyn alone. And no pictures of Jessalyn at all that were less than twenty years old.

"As if Mom doesn't exist."

So long Jessalyn had been the perfect wife and mother, invisible. So happily living for others, she scarcely lives at all.

Her husband adored her of course. When they were young the children had been embarrassed seeing Daddy kiss Mommy's hand, hug Mommy and burrow his face against her neck in a kind of rough play that offended them to have to witness. How mortified they were, seeing their parents greet each other with something like tenderness!—it did not seem right, in persons so *old*.

Yet, Whitey took Jessalyn utterly for granted as they all did. He didn't know it, and Jessalyn didn't know it. But it was so.

They'd tried to convince their mother to spend money on herself, not just presents for other people.

But, but—what would she get for herself? Jessalyn had stammered.

Clothes, a new car.

She had more clothes than she could wear in a lifetime, Jessalyn protested. She had fur coats. She had a new car.

"Don't be silly, Mom. Your car is *not new*."

"Your father oversees my cars, as you know. I need a car only to drive a few miles, and back. It isn't as if I am a *world traveler*."

World traveler—they'd laughed. Jessalyn was very funny at times.

"And why do I need new clothes? I have such beautiful clothes. I have a mink coat your father insisted upon giving me that I never wear. I have ridiculously expensive jewelry—to wear in Hammond! And shoes—far too many shoes! But I am *just me*."

Not that they were laughing at her. Their laughter was tender, protective.

It was so, Whitey was the one to oversee household expenditures. He'd insisted upon a lavish kitchen renovation a few years ago, which Jessalyn had resisted; he was the one who became obsessed with granite counters, Spanish tile floor, recessed lighting, state-of-the-art stainless steel stove, refrigerator, sink. Beautiful as something in a glossy magazine, and very expensive.

"Just for us? *Me*? I'm not even a serious cook . . ." Jessalyn had stammered with embarrassment.

Whitey was the one who oversaw the exterior of the house—the condition of the roof and chimneys and driveway, snow removal, landscaping, care of shrubs and tall aging trees. Jessalyn's idea of reckless spending was buying flowering plants for her garden, wind chimes for the deck, the "very best" wild-bird seed, the kind that contained dark sunflower seeds amid the more common corn kernels, to attract fancier birds like cardinals.

Yet Whitey often said, with an air of protest—*It's not like we're rich. We are not.*

It had become a joke within the family, and within the McClarens' circle of friends.

We're not rich! Jesus.

With an expression like Groucho Marx's. *Not rich! Not us.*

In fact, how rich were the McClarens? Their neighbors assumed that the McClarens had as much money as anyone else on Old Farm

Road. Within the Hammond business community, it was understood that McClaren, Inc. was "profitable." But this was a sensitive subject the children never wished to discuss as, growing up, they would not have wished to discuss their parents' sex lives.

Beverly winced, considering. No!

Still, it was known that, as a young man, Whitey McClaren had been given the responsibility of the McClaren family business to run, a commercial press in (evident) decline; within a decade Whitey had managed to double, treble, quadruple the company's size and profits by dropping old-time, small-scale printing jobs (menus, calendars, flyers for local businesses, material for the Hammond Board of Education) and specializing in glossy brochures for professional schools, businesses, pharmaceutical companies. Unskilled in what he called "high tech"—(anything to do with computers)—Whitey had cannily hired a young staff skilled in computers and digital publishing. He'd begun a line of school textbooks and YA books with a Christian slant, which had proved unexpectedly successful.

Thom, the eldest, had been (tacitly) selected by their father to work with him at the press even before he'd graduated from Colgate with a degree in business administration; it was Thom who directed Searchlight Books, with headquarters in Rochester.

How is the business doing, Thom?—Lorene might inquire through clenched teeth; and Thom would reply with a disingenuous smile—*Ask Dad.*

Yet you could not, really. You could not *ask Dad*.

Whitey had invested in real estate, and he was a co-investor in several shopping malls, that had prospered as the downtowns of old, industrial cities (Buffalo, Port Oriskany) had faded. Though on principle he didn't "believe" in most pills and drugs which (he was sure) were no better than placebos, he'd purchased stock in the pharmaceutical companies for which he published his lavish brochures.

While other investors had lost money in the Wall Street debacles of recent years, Whitey McClaren had prospered.

He hadn't boasted, however. Whitey never spoke of money at all.

None of the McClaren children wanted to think about their parents' wills. Or even if they had wills.

"Hello? Steve . . ."

After several tries Beverly had managed to get through to her husband at the Bank of Chautauqua. Before Steve could interrupt she told him excitedly that she was feeling desperate, she was at her parents' house and no one seemed to be here—she had no idea where anyone was and before this Virgil had bicycled to their house but had gone away again before Beverly could find out what was wrong . . .

"It isn't a great time to talk, Bev. I'm headed for a crucial meeting . . ."

"But, wait—this is crucial too. I think that something must have happened . . . I don't know where anyone is."

"Call me back in a few hours, OK? Or—I'll call you." Steve was a senior loan officer at the Bank of Chautauqua who took his work very seriously, or gave that impression to his family.

"No, wait—I told you, I don't know where anyone is."

"Probably nothing. They'll explain. See you tonight."

How like Steve to respond to an anxious call from his wife with all the nuance of a boys' sports coach. You blink back tears, the man hands you a stick of gum.

Oh, she hated him! She could not depend upon him.

So often it was like this. Steve brushed her away as you'd brush away an annoying gnat. Not angry with her, nor even irritated, just—it's a gnat.

Always Beverly was suggesting to Lorene how wonderful it was to be *married*. To have a *family*. She could not bear her sneering younger sister to know how Steve disrespected her, so often.

Married seventeen years. Sometimes she wondered if that was a few years too long.

The ungrateful husband would miss her, she thought, if she didn't come home to make supper. All of them, her dear family, would miss her then.

Trailing through the house. *Bev? Mom?*

Nothing in the kitchen? No food being prepared?

Another time, Beverly tried calling Lorene. Futile to try Lorene's office, Beverly could never get past Lorene's assistant, so she tried the cell phone, also usually futile, but this time, unexpectedly, Lorene answered at once.

"Yes? Hello? Oh—Beverly . . ."

Lorene was sounding anxious, distracted. Saying she was at Hammond General in downtown Hammond where their father was undergoing emergency surgery for a stroke.

The initial surprise, Lorene had answered her phone. For Lorene *never answered her cell phone.*

But what was Lorene saying?—*Daddy has had a stroke?*

Beverly fumbled for a chair. Her nightmare come true.

She'd tried to nullify bad news by anticipating it. So often, she'd tried this superstitious ploy. Her father stricken, her mother, both parents—*family emergency.* Somehow, she had not—quite—believed that the Worst Case Scenario could ever occur.

"Calm down, Beverly. He isn't dead."

"Oh my God, Lorene—"

"I told you, calm down. Stop that wailing! Daddy has been in surgery for almost an hour. He had a stroke driving home on the Expressway but he'd been able to pull over to the side—thank God! Police officers saw his car there and called 911—looks like they saved his life."

Beverly was trying to make sense of this. She was badly shaken and could not hear her sister's voice clearly.

Except she did hear Lorene say: "Everyone is here at the hospital except you, Beverly. And you live the closest."

And: "I tried to call you, Beverly. On the way to the hospital. But your phone doesn't seem to be working."

Was this an accusation? Which phone? Beverly tried to protest but Lorene said, "Thank God for those police officers. Thank God Daddy was able to park the car at the side of the road, before losing consciousness."

"But—is he going to be all right?"

"'Is he going to be *all right'*—" Lorene's voice swelled in sudden fury. "How can you ask such an inane question? Do you think I can predict the future? Jesus, Beverly!"—pausing then, to say in a calmer voice, as if someone with her (Jessalyn?) had admonished her, "They did an fMRI—they think the stroke was not 'massive' and it's a good sign, Daddy is—almost—breathing on his own."

Almost breathing on his own. What did that mean . . .

"I—I—I'm just so—shocked . . ."

Beverly was feeling light-headed. But she must not faint!

"We're all shocked, Bev. What the hell d'you think?"

How she disliked Lorene. The *brainy middle sister* who'd always been too certain of herself, bossy, smug. Not for a moment did Beverly believe that Lorene had made any actual attempt to call her, on any phone.

"Is Mom there? I'd like to speak with Mom, please."

"All right. But don't upset Mom with your hysteria *please*."

Fuck you. I hate you. Beverly was eager to console her mother (who had to be frantic with anxiety) but, as it turned out, Jessalyn seemed determined to console *her*.

"Beverly! Thank God you called. We were wondering where you were. Virgil tried to contact you—he said. There is good news—I mean, the doctors are 'optimistic.' Whitey is receiving the very best care. His friend Morton Kaplan is chief resident here and Dr. Kaplan arranged for Whitey to be given the fMRI at once, and taken into surgery—it all happened so fast. By the time Lorene and I arrived. We've been assured that Whitey has the very neurosurgeon available, the very best neurologist . . ." In a slow careful voice Jessalyn spoke like one making her way across a tightrope, who dares not glance down. Beverly could imagine her distraught mother smiling a ghastly smile. For how like Jessalyn McClaren it was, to assure others that all was well.

Jessalyn had enunciated "Morton Kaplan" as if the syllables possessed magical properties testifying to Whitey McClaren's connections with the Hammond medical elite—exactly as Whitey would have done in such circumstances.

"It's a miracle, Beverly—what they can do today. As soon as Whitey arrived at the ER they did a 'screen' of his brain—there was a blood vessel that had ruptured the surgeon is going to repair . . . Oh sorry, Lorene tells me it's *scan*. A *brain scan*."

Beverly shuddered at the thought of her father subjected to neurosurgery. His skull drilled open, baring his brain . . .

"Mom, do you need anything from the house? Any clothes?"

"Just bring yourself, Beverly! And pray for Dad! We are hoping that he will wake from the surgery sometime tonight, and he will want all of you here if he does. He loves you all so much . . ."

Pray for Dad. It wasn't like Jessalyn to speak this way.

Lorene took the phone back from their mother whose voice had begun to quaver and told Beverly yes, good idea, bring things for Whitey, underwear, toothbrush and toothpaste, comb, toiletries—one of Jessalyn's sweaters, the hand-knit heather cardigan, she'd come away dressed too lightly; she'd run out of the house when Lorene drove up, and they'd gone at once to the hospital.

Reproach in Lorene's voice. As if she were scolding subordinates at the high school.

Hastily Beverly packed a small suitcase upstairs in her parents' bedroom. Her hands were shaking. Her eyes were filling with tears. *Dear God let Daddy be all right. Let the surgery save him*. Except at such desperate times Beverly had not much use for God.

Who knew how long Whitey would be hospitalized! Days, a week—even if the stroke was minor, it would (probably) require therapy; it would require rehab. Maybe bring a (flannel, plaid) nightgown of Whitey's, he'd hate hospital attire and insist upon his own bedclothes. Poor Whitey, how he hated to appear *weak*.

Jessalyn would insist upon staying with Whitey as much as possible and Beverly was determined to stay with her.

Dear God. Please!

Hurried from the house. But then, at her car, remembered that the kitchen door wasn't locked, and hurried back to lock it.

Remembered to leave a light on downstairs. Two lights. To suggest that someone was home, the beautiful old stone Forrester House with the steep-slanted slate roof set back from the road at 99 Old Farm Road wasn't empty, vulnerable to invasion.

"GRANDPA WHITEY IS SICK. WE'RE at the hospital with him."

"Oh." The girl's voice was small as a pinprick. Her usual sarcasm had vanished in an instant.

"We don't know how serious it is. We don't know when he will come home."

Brianna had called Beverly on her cell sounding peevish and exasperated. She'd been waiting for forty minutes at a friend's house for Beverly to pick her up and bring her home and—(how was it possible?)—Beverly had totally forgotten.

"I'm sorry, honey. It's an emergency. You can defrost something from the refrigerator for supper. OK?"

"Oh, Mom—gosh."

Beverly had not heard her teenaged children speak so solemnly to her, so respectfully, in a very long time. A sensation of giddy relief washed over her.

She wanted to hug the girl. Oh, she loved Brianna!

Even the bratty ones, you love. Especially the bratty ones because no one else is going to love them like their mother.

A little later, Beverly's cell phone rang again. She left the Intensive Care room to take the call in the corridor.

Again, it was Brianna. Asking, anxiously: "Should we come to visit Grandpa?"

"Maybe, honey. But not right now."

"Is it a—heart attack, Mom?"

"No. It's a stroke."

"Oh. A stroke." Again the voice went small, frightened.

"You know what a stroke is, don't you?"

"Y-Yes. Sort of . . ."

"Grandpa has had neurosurgery. He's still unconscious."

"How sick is that?"

"How *sick*? We really don't know, honey. We're waiting."

Very sick. His brain has been bleeding.

Not so sick, Grandpa is "improving."

"Is Granma Jess OK?"

"Granma Jess is OK."

Beverly heard herself say in her heartening-mother voice: "You know Grandpa Whitey, he'd never complain. Except he'd hate to be cooped up in a damn old hospital bed and he'd want to come home right now."

It was a breathless outburst. Beverly steeled herself for the girl's response—*You are so full of shit, Mom! What d'you think I am, a little kid you can bullshit like that?*

But Brianna said, in a rush of words, bravely, "T-Tell Grandpa we love him. Tell Grandpa *get well soon and come home*."

Beverly could all but see tears shining in the girl's eyes. Oh thank God after all she was a *mother*.

IT WOULD BE SEVEN HOURS and forty minutes before Beverly returned to her own house on Stone Ridge Drive, to her sober-faced husband and teenaged children who'd waited up for her past midnight.

Whitey was out of surgery and in Intensive Care, still alive if not (yet) conscious; the prognosis was "guardedly optimistic"—his condition was "critical, but stabilized."

How did Whitey *look*? Well—not like Whitey.

Yes, you could recognize him. Of course! But (maybe) Whitey wouldn't have recognized himself.

Very bruised, battered-looking. Welts in his skin like burns—his face, neck. For (police officers had reported) he'd crashed the Toyota Highlander at the side of the Expressway, and the air bags had "burnt" him.

Alive. Dad is alive.

Still alive! We love him so.

Before returning to her own home Beverly had driven family house with the others to see their mother to bed— everyone was there, all five McClaren children—Bev *wanted not to be with them*—and she was now staggering tion. Yet her brain felt perversely clear to her, bright-lit, as i hosed clean, a terrible instrument of clarity.

She needed Whitey in her life, desperately. They all did most of all.

Without Whitey to give a sort of anchor to her life—wh her life? And an anchor, a *rightness* to her marriage. Steve feared his father-in-law in about equal measure and wit as a presence in their lives, without the support and app her parents, Beverly's own family, including even the child loved, would not seem altogether—(Beverly hesitated to *worth it.*

Oh but she didn't mean any of this. Just—tired, and sc

Pleading with God to *Let Daddy be all right. Oh please!*

NEXT MORNING AT 6:30 A.M. as she was hastily leavi Beverly happened to notice, blown against the side of t scrap of paper. Grunted to pick it up, and saw to her mort it was a note from Virgil after all.

Must've stuck it in the door, and it had fallen out.

DAD IN HAMMOND GENERAL

THINK IT'S A STROKE

WHY'D YOU HIDE FROM ME BEVERLY

DESPERATION & HOPE

YOUR BROTHER VIRGIL

Still Alive

Hey! *Let me explain.*

But it isn't clear: What can Whitey explain?

Problem is this burning sensation in his throat. No voice. Eyesight all blotched. Like someone has rubbed ashes into his eyes.

And—breathing? *Was* he breathing?

Something is breathing for him. Like force-feeding. Pumping air into his lungs in an ugly chuffing like a bellows.

What happened was . . .

. . . struck by lightning.

Confused memory of his vehicle bouncing, jolting along the shoulder of the highway. Potholes, the kind you don't see until it's too late, God damn you can ruin a tire that way but you won't know it immediately, the air will hiss out slowly and one day (soon) the (not cheap!) tire will be flat.

Trying hard to remember why he'd stopped. Leaving the highway at a high speed (?). Trying to remember what happened next.

Trying so hard, the effort is hurting his brain.

(But why assume that something actually *happened*? Maybe this condition he's in is just—*him*.)

(Always liked to take the contrary position, if there was one. Even as a kid. Schoolteachers, smiling and shaking their heads at Johnny McClaren—long-ago as grade school. Flattering to Whitey all his life to be told he sounds like a lawyer. Except he isn't a lawyer.)

Last memory has to be a face: glimpsed at a distance, as in a telescope in reverse.

Dark-skinned face. Dusky-skinned.

Stranger's face. He thinks.

(Or were there more than one of them?—*faces.*)

Face recognition at birth. He'd read. Infant's neurons "fire" at the sight of a human face.

Because survival can depend upon recognizing a human face. Does depend.

Is that true at the end—also?

End? Of what?

Can remember, must've been junior high, reading *Scientific American*. "Steady-state universe."

Well, that was comforting. Never had to wonder what had come before the universe, or what would come after. Universe just *was.*

Made more sense than that God had "created" the universe in a few days like a stage magician pulling things out of hats. Even as a kid he'd never taken that seriously.

But then, the big bang was—(how'd you phrase it?)—*discovered.*

So the universe isn't "steady"—isn't a "state"—but erupted out of nothingness at a point before time began and is still exploding outward billions of years later. Are its components rushing away from the center, and from one another, forever and ever?—or just for a fixed time?

Not a theory. He thinks. Proven fact: Hubble telescope.

Jessalyn laughed and pressed her hands over her ears. *Oh, Whitey! It makes me dizzy to think about that.*

Think about—what?

Eternity.

This was a surprise to Whitey. Hadn't expected to hear his young wife utter such a word, and the expression in her face suddenly serious—*pained.*

Hadn't known that's what they'd been talking about—*eternity.*

In fact he'd just been talking. Something out of the newspaper. Like

Whitey McClaren, every crazy thing sifts through his brain and awakens some spark there.

It was like her, though. The young wife. Say something to her, any random remark, off-the-top-of-his-head, in Jessalyn it acquired meaning, gravity.

Other girls he'd joked with. Liked to laugh.

But with Jessalyn Sewell, you didn't. Not much.

Hearing himself say *What the hell, maybe we should get married* and another girl might've laughed knowing it was, or maybe was not, not-serious but Jessalyn lifted her beautiful eyes to his—*Yes. All right.*

That look, piercing him to the heart. He'd felt it—actually: not a mere figure of speech—beneath his breastbone. Tough muscle-heart, pierced with certainty.

For he'd known (hadn't he) from the start. Only one person like Jessalyn Sewell in his life who could make John Earle McClaren a better human being not (merely) accept him as he was, who could love him for what he might be, his deepest self. In this individual the gravity required to keep Whitey McClaren's helium-soul from drifting up into the clouds, and lost.

Funny he's having such difficulty talking now, he who'd always been an easy talker. Never shy even as a kid. *Oh Whitey! He can converse with anyone. Strike up a conversation anywhere. Any stranger.*

But that had not happened, had it. Feeling the chagrin, the hurt, of an obscure rebuff.

Kick in the stomach, groin. That kind of rebuff.

Whoever it had been, they hadn't liked him. Hadn't been charmed by him. Problem is, he's *old.*

Problem is, he's *cold.*

Teeth chattering. Feels like bones chattering. That chit-chit-chittering noise the long-billed long-legged herons made, sends a shiver up the spine.

Problem is, some careless person (attendant?) has left a window open here.

Wherever *here* is.

Rushing wind. Rain-splatter flung like tears.

From where he's lying, where the bastards have pinioned him, and with this God damn respirator down his throat, can't move to reach the damned window to shut it.

He has glimpsed her—his wife. The young wife, face lit from within.

His dear wife. Has he forgotten her name?

Wife—the word is a burr in his throat.

Can't speak. Words like thorns. Trying to cough up the thorns, to clear his throat to speak.

Has forgotten—*speak.*

Reaches for her hand—but he is being pulled from her.

Darling?—I love—

The wind is rushing, can't hear.

It is so tempting, to give up!

So tempting, so tired. His legs heavy . . .

Not like Whitey McClaren, to give up. *God damn he will not.*

Never a good swimmer, his legs are too heavy. But he is swimming now. Trying.

Wind-buffeted waves. Very hard to swim against. Swift current. Cold.

Barely, keep afloat. Just—his head—uplifted, at tremendous strain. *One breath at a time.*

Swimming wasn't his sport. Hadn't the right body-shape to cut through the water. Too *inward.* Throwing you back on your own thoughts, not good.

Football was his sport. Running, careening together, tangling legs, head-butts, piling-on . . . *Tackling:* that word, he'd loved.

Loved the sweat-smell, his own and the other guys'. And the dirt-smell.

Swimmers stink of chlorine, too clean. Up your nostrils. Christ!

Touch another guy in the pool, brush legs, what the hell . . . Repulsive like lizard-skin.

Harsh clean chemical-smell in this damned place: antiseptic.

Germ-free. Bacteria-free.

What did his scientist daughter say: *Life is bacteria, Daddy.*

The kids, how'd they grow up so fast? Turned his back, there was Thom moved out of town. Beverly, pregnant. Slap in the face but no, not right to think that way.

You know better, Whitey. Please.

You can't possibly be jealous of your own son-in-law.

And now grandchildren. Too many! Names slipping from him like water through outspread fingers.

Christ, life is a struggle. Anybody who tells you anything else is a liar.

The greatest effort—*breathe* . . .

Pushing, shoving. Trying to get free, to breathe. Shouts of strangers in his face, booted feet kicking. Two of them.

Had that been real? *Had* it?

Electrocuted. He'd stepped, or fallen, onto a wire cracking electricity . . .

His face. Throat. Afire.

Is he—*dead*?

Not possible. Ridiculous.

But in this rough-rippling current, a dark wind. Frantic exertion of arms, legs. His strong shoulders, or shoulders that had once been strong only days ago. Arms like frantic blades propelling him upward.

Can't give up. Can't drown. Love you so . . .

Oh God, love you all.

The Handclasp

It is a late hour, she is very tired.

Love you so, darling. We are all right here.

Saying his name. Many times saying his name certain that though unresponsive, he can hear her.

Numbly her lips move. Almost inaudibly.

Yet she doesn't doubt, her dear husband can hear her.

Doesn't doubt, her dear husband is aware of her.

How old he looks! Poor Whitey, vain about his age since (at least) fifty. And now—sixty-seven.

His handsome face now scarcely recognizable. Skin like creased parchment. Bruised, swollen where he'd struck the steering wheel or the windshield thrown forward in the crash.

Stroke preceding the crash. Or—had the stroke followed the crash?

Possibly, she has been told. Possibly, she has forgotten.

Police officers arrived at the scene, called 911, saved Whitey's life.

Scene of the accident. No witnesses.

ER physician saying it looked like burn-wounds on the patient's face, throat, hands. Scorch-marks on his clothing they'd had to cut away.

Speculating the air bag had exploded, bruising and battering. Acid may have splattered out of the air bag which sometimes happens.

Air bag injuries can be considerable. If you are small-boned, slender, a child, elderly, don't sit in the passenger's seat. Exploding air bags can kill.

Can you hear me, darling? You are going to be all right . . .

Leaning close, scarcely daring to breathe. All the strength of her being is required to keep her husband with her.

Holding his (right) (bruised) hand. But his hand is not holding *hers.*

First time in memory, she is sure. First time in fifty years Whitey's large strong warm hand has not grasped *hers.*

If he knew, he would console her. Protect her. All I've been meant to do on earth, Jess—take care of *you.*

Joking but serious. Every other word out of the man's mouth a joke, but serious too. Easy to misunderstand such a person.

Still alive. He is still alive.

Not sure of the extent of the stroke, just yet. What it will mean.

Which areas of the brain are affected, contiguous with the stroke-region.

She has heard the word—*stabilized.* She is certain that she heard this word and that she has not imagined it.

After surgery. Repairing (broken) blood vessels. Brain shunt to drain liquid. Catheter threaded into the brain through a hole in the skull. A second catheter subcutaneous, traveling down into Whitey's abdomen, draining away there. The shunt is the life-saver.

Bargaining with God. *Please God let him live. Please God we love him so.*

She is very cold. One of her daughters has pulled a sweater onto her shoulders, that keeps sliding off.

Blood has drained out of her face. Her lips are cold and numb as death.

Holding his hand. Cannot give up his hand. No matter how tired she is, how dazed. For (she is certain) that his hand can feel hers even if it does not exert any strength and remains limp in her hand and alarmingly cold.

If she releases his hand, it will fall heavily onto the edge of the bed.

Not like Whitey McClaren, a *cold handshake.*

Not like Whitey McClaren not to squeeze his wife's hand in his, bring it to his chest in a protective gesture that pulls her forward, awkwardly.

But he does not. The hand does not.

Hours she has been at his bedside. A high bedside, surrounded by machines.

How many hours coalesced into a single hour like something gigantic growing exponentially—iceberg, snow-mountain.

The larger the object, the more surface-area. The more surface-area, the most rapidly the object will grow.

It is not a quiet place. Even the Intensive Care Unit which you would expect to be quiet is not.

He will sleep, he will rest. He is exhausted.

He will be himself again—when he has rested.

Someone has told her this. She has half-listened, she has wanted to believe. It is comforting to her, that every nurse, every medical worker, every physician she has met tonight, has been so very kind.

The Intensive Care nurses are particularly kind. She will remember their names, *Rhoda, Lee Ann, Cathy,* she will want to thank them once the vigil is over.

Of course she has visited many relatives, friends in the hospital in her lifetime. She is not young: sixty-one. She has seen many people die, and most of them elderly and infirm—as her husband is not.

Not elderly, at sixty-seven. Not infirm!

Whitey has not been in a hospital for decades. He'd boasted. Appendicitis when he was thirty, once in the ER when he'd broken a wrist in a fall (in fact, he'd lost his footing on steps, carrying a heavy suitcase: an accident). Good to avoid hospitals, Whitey liked to joke. People die in hospitals all the time.

Edgy laughter, at Whitey McClaren's jokes.

She smiles, recalling. Then wonders why she is smiling.

Something slipping from her shoulders. One of her daughters catches the thick woolen sweater before it falls to the floor.

Oh, Mom. You're exhausted. It's not helping Daddy, or any of us, wearing yourself out like this.

Let me drive you home. We will come back in the morning.

Daddy will be all right, Mom. You heard the doctor—he has "stabilized."

She is thinking: if they could die at the exact same moment, then it would be—well, not good; but nowhere near as bad as if one or the other dies first.

Terrifying, to think of Whitey dying first. How will she endure, the remainder of her life without him!

Yet worse, if she dies first, and Whitey is bereft . . .

Hiding his face against her throat. In his big, damply-hot arms. Stricken with love for her, clumsy in speech that is sincere and not joking, bantering. Oh. I love you.

She tells the children: if they stay at the house during the emergency, Whitey would like that. When he comes home.

(Maybe tomorrow? Day after tomorrow? Considering that his condition has *stabilized.*)

Strange, the daughters are not girls any longer. Beverly, Lorene. Well, you could say that Sophia is still a "girl"—could be mistaken for a girl in her early twenties. Younger.

(She feared for Sophia who did not seem to be maturing as the other girls had. There was a schoolgirl earnestness about Sophia, a defiant sort of naivete, that worried her mother even as [she sensed] it annoyed the older sisters.)

(And how old is Sophia? Tried to recall when Sophia had graduated from college—Cornell, after transferring from Hobart Smith.)

(Oh, it is confusing, frightening: which year this is, which month; how old they are all becoming, like heedless tobogganers rushing downhill through the blinding-white snow of their own, finite lives!)

Still, managing to smile. At the nurses, at the girls' strained faces, at poor dear Whitey whose swollen and distended mouth can't smile in return at her.

(And where is Thom? He'd been here earlier. And Virgil.)

(Well. You don't expect Virgil to stay in one place for long. What has

Sophia said of her brother—*Attention deficit disorder. Given a spiritual spin.*)

No wonder the boys aren't here. Somewhere in the hospital probably, but not right here.

Both Whitey's sons were frightened. Seeing their father so helpless-seeming, somehow *crooked* in the high hospital bed amid a tangle of beeping machines and a powerful smell of disinfectant, and his face burnt-looking, battered and swollen; his eyes not exactly shut but not open, and not seeing. Dread word *stroke.* Dread words *Intensive Care, respirator.* Thom's eyes had misted over as if in pain and Virgil's eyes had narrowed to slits as if a bright light were shining into his face.

With a mother's sharp eye she'd seen how each son swallowed hard as a way of not sobbing aloud.

Terror of a (grown, adult) child seeing his parent so diminished.

You want to spare them such shocks. Fleeting thoughts through her life as a mother, if she could hide away somewhere, when mortally ill. If she could prevent their seeing, their knowing until it was all over—*fait accompli.*

Her own mother had sent away her children, in her final days. Vanity, desperation. *Don't want you to see me like this.*

But John Earle is not mortally ill, in fact. The facial injuries have nothing to do (it seems) with the stroke and are (it seems) superficial.

Angry red swellings on his face, throat, hands. As if some creature had sunk its beak into him. How many times?

She would wonder what has caused these curious injuries. Except in her distracted state she is capable only of smiling.

Smiling as an act of will. Smiling as an act of courage, desperation.

Giving Whitey's hand a gentle squeeze as you urge a child. *Darling! We are all here, or almost. We will stay until they make us leave.*

(Was that so? Would the hospital make them leave? Intensive Care? When the day shift ends?)

It is just a coincidence. She thinks.

Tried to bring up the subject with Whitey, the other day.

The Subject. No!

Of course, Whitey reacted with his (usual) panicked joking. Making a (comic) fuss over the coffee machine. Pretended not to hear.

Just the two of them now in the sprawling house on Old Farm Road that had once been the very center of—everything! You could count on a pack of kids occupying the premises at any time. Five children, five sets of friends. (Well, that wasn't accurate perhaps. By the time Virgil was old enough to bring friends home, Thom was too old to wish to bring his friends home; not to mention those girlfriends of Thom's he hadn't dared bring home.) How many for supper? *How many?*—Whitey pretended to be exasperated but (really) he'd loved the house bustling with life.

Those years. You'd think would go on forever. Parents of the kids' school friends calling the McClarens to see where their children were, and usually they were there, at the sprawling house on Old Farm Road.

And now, where?—where had all those kids, all that noisy life, scattered?

Last to leave home had been Sophia, who'd had only two or three close girlfriends. And Virgil, who'd had a motley assortment of friends, weird friends, who'd come and gone, and seemed not to count. So the diminution, the loss, had been gradual, not abrupt.

Why on earth is she wiping tears from her eyes! It is not like the children's mother, to alarm them.

For after the terrible shock of the emergency, after the hours of surgery, Whitey was *all right*.

Thinking what they need are children who live in distant cities and will come to visit them, bring their grandchildren and *stay*.

It's a fact: when your children live nearby they never stay in the house any longer. Visit, yes. Come to dinner maybe. For a few hours.

Then they go home. Their *home* is elsewhere.

She is trying to explain this to Whitey. How sad she is, how frightened, their *home* is slipping through their fingers.

(Is this a joke? Squeezing her husband's limp cold fingers trying to galvanize them into life.)

What an odd-matched pair. Jessalyn so quiet, and Whitey so— Whitey.

Yet often when they're alone together it is Jessalyn who speaks to Whitey earnestly and persuasively, at length. No one would believe how in her quiet voice Jessalyn explains to her husband how he should reconsider a decision he has made impulsively. She will say *Darling, please just listen. I think you need to reconsider . . .*

Whitey has never disagreed with Jessalyn. He has never argued with her. Though Whitey McClaren can be curt and dismissive with others he has never so much as interrupted his wife in fifty years.

In fact he loves to be corrected by her. Chagrined, humbled by her. It is delightful to him, to be proved wrong by his dear wife.

Well, all right. Now you put it that way, I guess—you are correct.

She is his best self, he tells her. His bright angel.

Of all the world, she was/is his salvation. Not in the next world but in this. Only Jessalyn could make of John Earle McClaren the person he was meant to be—so he has told her as he has told others.

Is it rare, that a husband can be so assertive in his dealings with others, yet so compliant in his dealings with his wife? Of course, the harsh term *dealings* does not quite apply.

He'd fallen in love just once in his life. Seeing Jessalyn at seventeen. Shy, soft-spoken, *demure*.

But frankly very pretty. John Earle had stared and stared at her face, her smooth-plaited hair. Her breasts.

She'd seen. That *helplessness* in a man's face. A boy's face. No one can moralize, no one can legislate.

Might as well call it *love*.

Their first time, holding hands. Johnny Earle had seemed embarrassed. He'd wanted to hold Jessalyn's hand—tight; but (he said) he hadn't wanted to "mangle" it.

She'd laughed. She had never, ever forgotten—*mangle*.

You can mangle my hand now, darling.

She'd been slower to fall in love with John Earle McClaren whose personality was so strongly defined, even in his early twenties. But eventually, she had fallen in love. She had *not resisted*.

Wishing he would grip her hand hard—yes, now.

But it is not Jessalyn's way, she is resolved. To burden another with your need for them.

Better to be the one to take the other's hand. Firmly.

As for so many years—an inexhaustible span of time, she'd thought—she had gripped a child's hand, often the hands of two children, crossing a street, in a public place, on a flight of stairs—*"Chick-chick!"* had been her signal, in an undertone, a cheerful sound, a sound to alert the child, yes it is necessary, Mommy wants your hand.

Without hesitation, the child lets you take his/her hand. Nothing quite so wonderful, that trusting grip.

Her terror had been that one of the children would slip from her grasp and run into a street, or—in some other way manage to kill or maim herself when for a fleet moment Mommy had not been alert.

Mom? We're taking you home now.

We'll be back first thing in the morning.

Jessalyn is reluctant to leave Whitey's bedside. Oh, how can she abandon poor ravaged Whitey! When Whitey's eyes flutter open, the first face he sees should be hers.

Of course, I'm here. I will always be here.

Stares at her watch confused for a moment if it might be morning, not night. And where exactly is this place?

Whitey seems to take up less space in this hospital bed than he does in their bed at home where the mattress sags comfortably on his side. Each night sleeping with Whitey has been an adventure: Whitey sprawls, sighs, turns restlessly in the night, flings an arm over her, or an arm in her direction; wakes, or seems to wake, with a clicking sound in his throat, but sinks back into sleep at once like one sinking beneath the surface of water, deep, deeper while Jessalyn lies beside him in a trance of wonderment, in awe that sleep comes to her husband so easily, that must be caught, as in a flimsy net, by her.

But in this bed, on his back, clamped in place, poor Whitey seems—well, smaller. Diminished. It is what the man has been fighting for all of his life—not to be *run down*.

His breathing has become so arduous, the strain so extreme, Jessalyn wants to crawl into the bed beside him to hold him and help him breathe, as often she holds him in the night, in their bed, as he sinks in a series of twitches and missteps into sleep; but the bed is too narrow, this would never be allowed by the hospital staff.

Oh, what is she thinking! Thoughts rattling in her head like dried seeds in a clay pot. Or—loose coins, rolls of adhesive tape, spools of thread in one of the kitchen drawers swiftly opened.

So sleepy! She sees what appears to be loose macaroni, that has fallen from a box onto a kitchen shelf . . . This is wrong. It is not like Jessalyn to be so careless a housekeeper.

Newspaper pages scattered on the counter. Dishes soaking in the sink, she'd been about to rinse and put into the dishwasher.

Pouring seed into the bird feeders. Exacting, trying not to spill too much, which draws squirrels. Whitey's feud with resident squirrels—*Go on! Get the hell out of here! Damn you!* They'd laughed at Whitey exasperated chasing squirrels who fled scarcely a few yards before stopping, squawking at him, shaking their enormous tails like livid jeering rats. Sophia had said *Oh Daddy, the squirrels are hungry, too.*

Another feud of Whitey's, Canada geese on the back lawn. Each day, more Canada geese. Nothing enraged Whitey McClaren like Canada goose droppings.

Go on! Get the hell out of here! Go back to Canada where you belong and take your crap with you.

He'd enlisted the boys to help him. Long-legged Thom, rushing at the geese with a hockey stick, laughing.

Short-legged, six years old, Virgil trailed behind.

Where will Thom stay the night? In his old room, at the house?

And Virgil—where *is* Virgil?

Too many McClarens to fit into the Intensive Care room. A limit of two visitors. The rest are waiting outside in the hospital corridor—(she wants to think that's where they are).

Even in the surgical waiting area Virgil had been too restless to stay in one place. She'd seen him pacing in the corridor. Talking with one of the night nurses. Fascinated to observe Virgil (too thin, shoulders bowed as if to minimize his height, dark blond hair tied back in a ponytail, skimpy beard—how exasperated Whitey would be, to see him in this public place!—and wearing loose-fitting overalls, embroidered Indian-looking shirt Whitey would categorize as *hippie,* his usual chewed-looking leather sandals) speaking with a stranger, seemingly an admiring stranger, whatever could he be telling her?—as the nurse (a woman of about Virgil's age, or a little older) blinked at him, nodding, smiling as if she'd never encountered anyone so *eloquent*.

Virgil's bullshit—Thom has a way of sneering.

That is cruel. Unfair. You don't always know what Virgil is getting at but Virgil certainly does, and Virgil takes it all very seriously.

Scrub my soul clean.

Effort of a lifetime.

Only Jessalyn knows how Virgil antagonized Whitey a few years before by suggesting that people like him should double-tithe. *You can't spend your money, Dad. You just keep re-investing it.*

Of course, Virgil doesn't know how much money the elder McClarens donate to charitable organizations each year. Virgil has no idea.

What had hurt Whitey was the tactless phrase *People like you.*

Jessalyn had been hurt, too. What does it even mean—*People like you*?

Wanting to plead even now, on Whitey's behalf—*We are not perfect people but we are living the best lives we know how to live.*

And Virgil would smile his maddening-Virgil smile without needing to say *But that best isn't good enough, Mom. Sorry.*

Has Whitey squeezed her hand?—Jessalyn's heart pitches forward.

"Whitey? Oh—Whitey?"—so excited, she is feeling faint.

The handknit heather-colored sweater has fallen to the floor. The eldest daughter is gripping her shoulders to steady her.

But no, possibly Whitey has not squeezed her hand. Possibly she'd imagined it . . .

Mom! We'd better take you home. Now.

We'll be back first thing in the morning . . .

Has something been decided? The middle daughter, the bossy one, high school principal, has taken Jessalyn firmly by the arm.

Daddy is doing really well. He looks better—his color is much better. You know Whitey— . . . "never say never."

The daughters laugh together. Jessalyn hears herself join in, weakly.

"Never say never"—it is indeed an expression Whitey uses often.

Feeling so very tired, a watery sensation in her brain, knees like water, trembling with cold, Jessalyn supposes she has no choice, must give in. Abandoning Whitey to this terrible place—(if he wakes, whom will he see?—what?)—she stoops to brush her lips against his (slack, chill) cheek, dares to approach his shuddering breath.

Love you, darling! Praying for you.

How Whitey would wince, and laugh. *Praying for me? Must be bad news.*

In a confiding voice a nurse is urging the McClaren daughters—*Take your mother home.* Jarring to hear *your mother* spoken as if she (Jessalyn) were not even present. Is this a presage of being elderly, elderly and infirm?—gently-but-firmly "walked" along a corridor and your every movement scrutinized for if you falter, if you appear dizzy, in danger of fainting strong (i.e., younger) arms will seize you and support you; and Jessalyn McClaren is not the sort of person who causes a disruption in any quasi-public place, has always been the most courteous, the most obliging, the least assertive of persons, a lovely woman, a beloved woman, wife, mother, grandmother, trying not to feel panic at the prospect of her husband *not home.*

Just a single night. Unthinkable.

The Vigil

One by one they'd moved away from the house on Old Farm Road to become adults in the world beyond the McClarens.

And now, this harrowing succession of days in October 2010 when their father was hospitalized in the aftermath of a stroke, and their vigil was a flimsy shared raft on a choppy river, and their eyes did not dare lift much above the level of the river for fear that the dark, surging waters would engulf them, they found themselves returned to the house each night as if to the safety of dry land.

Yet it was strange to them, it was eerie and unsettling, the house had changed so little since they'd left, and they had changed so much.

Or, the house had not changed so much, and they had scarcely changed (inwardly, essentially) at all.

"I'LL STAY WITH MOM TONIGHT."

"No. It's fine. I live close by, I can stay with her."

"I drove her to the hospital, so I'll stay, and drive her back to the hospital in the morning. It's just easier."

"Why's it *easier*? I should drive her tomorrow."

"You'll just upset her. You're always so *grabby*." Meanly, Lorene made a gesture with both hands as if tugging at a cow's teats.

Stung, Beverly objected: "You'll have to go to work—won't you? They can't function at the high school without the 'She-Gestapo'—can they?"

Lorene cast her sister a look of sheer savagery. It must have been,

Lorene knew of her *She-Gestapo* reputation at North Hammond High but had not known that the others knew.

"Of course I'm not going to work tomorrow. Not as long as my father is in Intensive Care!"

Eventually it was determined that, except for Beverly, who felt that she must return home to her family that night, they would all stay at the old house with their mother.

"Just in case. We'd better."

Jessalyn was given no voice in the matter. She didn't know whether to be touched by her adult children's solicitude, or to feel oppressed by it. Why were they speaking of her as if she weren't even present? Seeming to think that she shouldn't be alone in her own house as if she were very elderly, or very unstable.

Jessalyn protested, weakly: she could drive herself to the hospital in the morning. She would meet them there. "The nurse said—seven A.M. Certainly, I will be all right tonight . . ."

"Mom, *no*. Daddy would never want you to be alone at such a time."

None of them would listen to her. Jessalyn was forced to see how they were all taller than she was, and loomed over her. When had this happened? Even Sophia, the youngest.

In their faces, defiance. Though they were exhausted, and anxious, this opposition was thrilling to them, that they might overcome their mother's wishes in the service of protecting her. She opened her mouth to protest but felt too tired, suddenly.

And it would be comforting, certainly—to have someone stay with her.

She would tell Whitey—*The children took over. They were so protective of me. You'd have been proud of them.*

Dear Whitey! He was always looking for ways to be proud of his children, and not annoyed and irritated as he was so often with Virgil.

Yes of course Virgil was with us. Every minute.

When the terrible news had come that afternoon, for several hours her brain had shut down. But now that Whitey appeared to be *holding his own* she was collecting things to tell him.

It was a cheering phrase, especially out of the mouths of the Intensive Care nurses who, presumably, knew what they were saying.

Holding his own. You had an image of Whitey gripping something tightly, a rope perhaps, a rudder. Holding himself steady even as the floor shifted beneath him.

He would want to know—everything! How he'd been discovered in his car on a shoulder of the Hennicott Expressway, or (possibly) he had tried to get out of the car, and collapsed and fallen onto the pavement. How Hammond police officers had discovered him—unconscious. How they'd called 911 and an ambulance had come (within four minutes, it was claimed) and brought him to the very best emergency medical facility within one hundred miles.

Saving up things to tell Whitey. Nearly forty years.

Mostly these were things about which no one else would care in the slightest. Every small, inconsequential, fascinating tidbit to tell her husband who, like most men, pretended to disapprove of gossip but relished it. As he saved up things to tell her.

Darling, I was so lonely! But I could hear your voice—I could hear our children's voices—though I could not answer you—and I could not see you . . .

She had faith, her husband would tell her where he'd been. As soon as he was returned to her.

"I'LL TAKE YOU UP to bed, Mom. Come on!"

As soon as they were at the house. Switching on the kitchen lights.

Beverly reached for Jessalyn's hand, and would not release it, though Jessalyn protested, "Don't be silly, Beverly. I can 'take' myself to bed, thank you."

"You're exhausted. You should see yourself—your face is white as *wax*."

Beverly insisted. For she was going home, soon. But Lorene insisted, also. And Sophia could not bear to be left behind.

Six of them, entering the kitchen. So many McClarens, you'd expect a festive occasion.

Jessalyn continued to protest faintly as the sisters accompanied her upstairs. Their voices lifted like the cries of birds, lightly chiding, melodic. In the kitchen Thom and Virgil were left behind with each other.

They resented their sisters, perhaps. Not entirely consciously but—it was so, in a time of crisis, in a time of emotions, in a time when (physical) comfort was required, *daughters* took precedence over *sons*.

"Want one of Dad's beers? Ale?"—Thom opened the refrigerator and took out two bottles of dark brown ale. Virgil shrugged—*No.*

"Oh, I forgot. You 'don't drink.'"

Stiffly Virgil said, "Yes. I do. Sometimes. But not now."

It was awkward for the McClaren brothers to be alone together.

Neither could have said when they'd last been alone together in this house or anywhere.

Rare for them to think of themselves as *brothers*.

In their parents' house, in the kitchen, it was impossible not to expect to hear their father's voice. Whitey would have been surprised and pleased to see them if (possibly) somewhat mystified, at this hour.

Jesus! What the hell are you two doing here? Sit down, let me get you something to drink . . .

But Whitey was shrewd enough to know that his sons, who had so little in common, would hardly be together in his kitchen at this hour of the night unless something in the family had gone terribly wrong.

Thom was drinking ale, out of the bottle. Whitey's German ale, so bitter Thom winced as it went down. He'd found an opened jar of cashews in the cupboard.

Virgil was drinking orange juice, he'd found a carton in the refrigerator.

The silence between them was strained. Yet neither wanted to speak of their father, just yet.

Seven and a half years separated them. For Virgil, a lifetime.

If Virgil shut his eyes he could make out the shadowy, elusive figure of his elder brother Thom always in silhouette, his back to Virgil and moving away.

He'd adored his big brother, as a child. But no longer.

Now, Virgil was wary of Thom. He understood those sidelong glances, scowled greetings and mock-friendly remarks—*How's it going, Virg?*

Virg wasn't a name, wasn't a diminutive, only just an ugly sound.

Thom had grown distant to Virgil, living now in Rochester. Virgil scarcely knew his brother's wife and children—(two young children? three?). Casually it was said that Thom was Whitey's "heir"—obviously, Thom would be Whitey's successor in the family business.

(Whitey had never tried to hire Virgil to work for him. Well maybe, a long time ago, when Virgil was in high school, and Whitey had asked if he'd like to help out writing advertising copy since, it seemed, judging from published work of Virgil's he'd seen in a student literary magazine, Virgil "had a way with words." Fifteen, Virgil had stared at his father with a wounded look murmuring *No thank you!* as if Whitey had asked him to commit an outrage.)

Just a glance at Thom McClaren, tall and rangy-limbed, sandy-haired, handsome face now just perceptibly beginning to thicken, in his late thirties—(Virgil often stared, when [he believed] Thom wasn't aware of him)—you could see that Thom was one of those persons who feels very good about himself, and his self-estimate is (largely) shared by those who gaze upon him.

So Virgil thought. A sliver of envy pierced his heart.

"HAVE SOME. I don't want to eat these all alone"—Thom pushed the jar of cashews in Virgil's direction.

Cashews were Whitey's weakness. The children had laughed at their father insisting their mother hide nuts, cookies, chocolates in the kitchen in places where he couldn't easily find them.

But when Whitey ate a handful of nuts, he'd begin coughing. That was a giveaway, Daddy'd been eating nuts . . .

Half-consciously the brothers were observing that something was wrong in the kitchen. Their mother was so fastidious a housekeeper, you'd never expect to find newspaper pages scattered on a counter, or dishes soaking in a sink. Especially since her children were gone and the cheerful disorder of those years was only a memory.

Thom recalled when he'd been a boy in the household and one of his duties was to sweep the kitchen floor after dinner, each night.

Another duty, to drag out the trash containers early Friday mornings.

For these tasks and a few others, Whitey had paid him ten dollars a week. But Jessalyn had always given him a little more—"Just in case you need it, Tommy."

They'd grown up in a well-to-do household. No disguising the fact that the McClarens had money—you didn't live in one of the beautiful old houses on Old Farm Road if you didn't have money. Yet none of the McClaren children had felt what's called *entitled*.

At least, Thom didn't think so. *Not him.*

All this while, with the maddening care of one trying not to draw attention to himself, Virgil was collecting the scattered newspaper pages which he shuffled together and stuffed in the paper-recycling bin, without so much as glancing at a headline. Thom recalled with scorn how, in Virgil's Oberlin days, and after, his hippie brother had evinced a visceral horror of what he might discover in the newspaper by accident—he'd thought it "obscene" to look upon the suffering of strangers in photographs.

Too restless to sit still Virgil rinsed the dishes in scalding-hot water and placed them in the dishwasher one by one with such exaggerated care, Thom's patience was tested.

"Sit still! For Christ's sake."

Thom resented it, as his sisters did, that Virgil seemed to have become closer to their mother than any of them, in recent years. Because

Virgil lived nearby, came often to the house (on his damned bicycle) when Whitey was away, probably more often than Thom and his sisters knew.

Not asking for money from Jessalyn, probably, because that wasn't Virgil's way, but surely accepting money from her, for that was certainly Jessalyn's way.

D'you think Dad knows?—Beverly would ask; and Thom would say, *Well. We can't ask him.*

In the darkened window above the sink Virgil saw his own, dark reflection. And beyond his shoulder his handsome, elder brother sprawled in a chair, drinking from a bottle.

The wonder of an older brother, to a younger. The adolescent male body, utterly fascinating, captivating, to the younger brother, knowing himself inadequate in every way.

Glimpsing Thom part-clothed, or naked—how Virgil had stared.

Swallowing hard. Even now. His brother's supple, lean-muscled body. His brother's careless grace. Wiry hairs growing in his brother's armpits, on his chest, legs. At his groin.

His brother's penis.

The very word, forbidden to murmur aloud even in privacy—*penis.*

And other, similar forbidden words, *cock, dick, balls*—Virgil trembled to recall the spell such words had upon him, for years.

A lifetime. If you are the younger.

As if he sensed Virgil's thoughts Thom dared to rummage in a coat pocket for—what? A pack of cigarettes.

Dared to light a cigarette!

"Hey. C'mon. Mom will smell the smoke in the morning."

"I'll air out the kitchen."

"They'll smell it upstairs right now. Come on, Thom!"

"I said, I'll air out the kitchen."

"Well." Virgil registered his displeasure with a shift of his shoulders. "Well, *I will.*"

It wasn't like Virgil to provoke his brother. He'd had too many unpleasant consequences in the past. The lateness of the hour was a kind of unraveling.

Thom said, exhaling smoke: "Dad smokes. He still does."

"Dad *does*?"

"Nobody's supposed to know. Especially Mom. Not as much as he used to, but at least once a day. In his office. I've seen the ashes." Thom paused, for there was a kind of luxuriant satisfaction in knowing something about their father that Virgil didn't know. If Virgil made a prissy remark about Whitey smoking, with his high blood pressure, and having had a stroke, Thom planned to spring up from his chair and smack him on the side of the head.

But Virgil was wary, and kept his distance. Chewed his lower lip in silence, preoccupied with arranging sponges on the rim of the sink.

Their mother had two (synthetic) sponges for kitchen work: one for rinsing dishes, the other for wiping counters. The former was always kept on the left, the latter on the right. Over a period of a week or two, the counter sponge was discarded, as used-up; the left-hand sponge was moved to the right, and a fresh new sponge removed from its cellophane wrapper.

Tonight, the left-hand sponge was bright yellow; the right-hand, purple. Virgil took care not to mix them up.

In Virgil's household which was, to a degree, a communal household, in which no one took particular responsibility for keeping things clean, one large (natural) sponge sufficed for long periods of time. Eventually the sponge was discarded because it began to shred, not because it had become singularly ugly and filthy.

How dismayed Jessalyn would be, to see the way Virgil lived. It was his responsibility to shield her.

Once Sophia had dropped by the ramshackle old farmhouse, and happened to see the sponge in Virgil's sink, which she hadn't identified immediately as a sponge. "God! That looks like liver cirrhosis," she'd said. "But I suppose it must be something else."

They'd laughed together but Virgil had understood his scientist-sister's dismay. Disgust.

But life is teeming with pathogens we can't see, Virgil thought. Surrounding us. Inside and out.

"Of course, he's trying to quit. That's why he's gained that weight in his gut, he needs to work off."

Thom was still talking about their father. Their father's surreptitious smoking. To which Thom was privy, and Virgil was not.

It was giving Thom a coarse sort of pleasure to know that he was making his brother jealous (a little, at least) and making him uncomfortable (secondary smoke inhalation—Virgil was trying not to cough). Boastfully Thom said, "Dad confides in me. I give him good advice—get back into the gym and just quit. Lots of guys his age and older work out and some of them are pretty impressive." Thom laughed as if what he was saying was true, or true in some way. He liked it that Virgil would be imagining him and their father conferring together so intimately, and not just on matters of business.

"But don't tell Mom. About Dad smoking, I mean."

Virgil wanted to retort, if anyone should tell her it's *you*. Certainly Dad's doctors would want to know.

Insane to be thinking about smoking. Anyone in their father's condition. Was Thom *smiling*?

Virgil's heart was hurting. He'd been made to think of their father in Intensive Care, his breathing done for him by a respirator. And maybe Whitey would never breathe again on his own.

He could not bear it, if his father died. Without having loved him.

Without having said, just once—*Virgil, I am proud of you. For being the person you are and knowing it isn't what we do but what we are.*

Not what people say about us but what we say of ourselves.

Whitey hadn't touched Virgil in—how long?—could not even guess. Laying his hand on Thom's shoulder, greeting Thom with a pumping handshake, that lit-up look in his face—so different from the way he greeted Virgil.

No handshake. (But that was all right: Virgil wasn't one to *shake hands*. Silly social custom springing from primitive masculine anxiety.)

No hugs. (The way Whitey hugged his daughters!)

Regarding Virgil, Whitey's characteristic manner was stiffness, apprehension; a wary smile, narrowed eyes. *What will this son of mine do to embarrass me next.*

Some feelings, you can't hide. Though a parent should try harder than Whitey did.

On the cork bulletin board in a corner of the kitchen was a display of snapshots and cards. Years, decades. Overlapping newspaper clippings, school programs, class photos. Jessalyn was always adding new things but was reluctant to take anything away. A glossy photo of Hammond mayor John Earle McClaren shaking hands with the governor of New York State and both men stiffly posed smiling into the camera. In 1993 their father had looked so ruddy and so *young*, it was painful to see.

Virgil disliked the family bulletin board. Too many snapshots of his big jock-brother Thom who'd been a high school athlete. And too many pictures of Beverly glamorous as a face on a billboard.

Family pictures, he didn't mind so much. Even weddings, newborn babies. The McClaren family together with arms linked smiling at the camera in a backyard, on a beach. Somewhere.

The earliest photos of Virgil were of a beautiful little child with pale blond hair, luminous blue eyes. Virgil had seen to it that these had been removed from the bulletin board, years ago.

In high school Virgil had started hiding pictures of himself beneath others' pictures, or removing them entirely. Excepting one of Virgil at about age ten, clutching his mother's hand with a look of stricken adoration.

His young self, Virgil didn't consider exactly *him*. All children are innocent of vanity and even homely children are beautiful. That begins to change by about age thirteen.

Embarrassed, Virgil saw that his mother had tacked up several newspaper photographs of scrap-metal sculptures of his, exhibited at a recent arts fair. Virgil hadn't even known that these pictures had been published in the Hammond weekly paper; he scarcely remembered the sculptures, which had all been sold at the fair.

(What's the secret of selling all your work? Virgil was asked. The answer was, Just keep lowering prices.)

(Was Virgil touched to see these pictures on the bulletin board in his mother's kitchen? He had not the heart to remove them.)

"Some great things there, that Mom has saved. My kids can't believe how young we all were, once."

Thom spoke lightly, as if relenting. Seeing that Virgil was looking at the bulletin board and wanting to be nice to Virgil, for once.

Thom continued: "I've got a corkboard in our kitchen, too. Not as big as this. It's a great idea, I think. For the kids especially. So much gets forgotten otherwise." He paused, considering. "I guess you've seen it? Or no, maybe not."

No. Virgil had not seen the damned corkboard in Thom's house in Rochester. He had not ever visited Thom's house in Rochester.

Thom opened another bottle of dark German ale. He'd finished most of the cashews. Christ! The interior of his mouth stung with salt.

It was too quiet. Where the hell were the sisters?

Thom resented them running off with their mother and leaving him with Virgil when they knew how Thom felt about Virgil.

But it wouldn't seem right for Thom to have gone upstairs. It was a matter for the sisters—putting their dazed mother to bed. Not for him. And Virgil would probably follow him like a stray dog.

"It's good, maybe."

"What's good?"

Virgil had spoken so belatedly, Thom had no idea what the hell he was talking about.

"Forgetting."

"'Forgetting'—what?"

In the bright kitchen lights the brothers' faces were too clearly delineated. Like high-definition TV, you're forced to see more than you care to see.

Virgil lowered his eyes, shyly. Yet there was stubbornness in every action of Virgil's, even the self-effacing. Thom knew, and lay in wait.

"Guess we should go to bed. There's only a few hours to sleep before we need to get up."

Waiting for Virgil to say something, for Virgil had become very quiet since examining the bulletin board.

"I haven't slept in this house since—Jesus, I don't know when." Thom tried to think. Last semester of college? Last summer, after graduation? His old room had been dismantled years ago, for other purposes. "What about you, Virgil?"

Virgil seemed startled. Lost in his own thoughts.

"I guess—I don't need much sleep."

"Don't you!"—Thom sneered.

God knew, he was making an effort with Virgil. He was almost forty years old—not a kid any longer. Father of an eleven-year-old. His siblings who'd never had children (Lorene, Sophia, Virgil) had no idea how rapidly time passed when there were children in your life, to measure yourself against.

It was true, Thom disapproved of Virgil's *lifestyle*. (Like Whitey, he had no idea what Virgil's *lifestyle* might be; like Whitey, he did not wish to know.) However, he owed it to their parents to try to get along with Virgil.

Still, it maddened him to see Virgil's wispy beard, scruffy dirty-blond hair tied back in a ponytail with a length of twine. A slight stoop of Virgil's shoulders though he was only thirty-one. Slovenly embroidered shirt, frayed and paint-stained overalls, open-toed sandals. (And Virgil's toes were knobby and unsightly.) What roused Thom to particular indignation was that look in Virgil's warm blue eyes of infinite compassion, understanding, sympathy—a *swimmingness* of feeling.

Looking in those eyes, you were in danger of drowning.

Sometimes, Thom said to Beverly, with whom he shared family preoccupations, Virgil makes me want to punch him in the mouth. Except he'd just forgive me, and then I'd want to kill him.

Beverly had laughed, though she'd been shocked. She liked to hear such terrible things from her revered elder brother but she would not have wished to share her own feelings about Virgil for she knew that such feelings sprang from what was meanest in her, and furthest from the family love and loyalty their parents had tried to instill in them.

But Beverly had laughed, feeling as if Thom had tickled her.

Who's he think he is, the Dalai Lama?—Beverly had said wittily.

At last, footsteps on the stairs. But it was only one sister—Beverly.

Disappointing, Beverly was going home. Lorene and Sophia had gone to bed upstairs in their old rooms.

No, Beverly didn't want a drink. Thanks but *no.*

Thom saw, his sister was looking disheveled, fattish. Not much like the radiant high school girl in the snapshots. And shiny-eyed, teary. (Had she been crying? Christ!) Refused a bottle from the refrigerator but she did take a swig from Thom's and wiped her mouth with the back of her hand as a man might have done.

"We put Mom to bed, finally. She wouldn't remove all her clothes, she says she's afraid of the phone ringing and we'll have to drive to the hospital and she wants to be prepared. It's so strange—she speaks so *calmly.* It's like Dad is instructing her—you know, how Dad is always telling her what to do. And how weird it is, to be in that bedroom, and know that Dad isn't there. We stayed with her a while until it seemed that she was asleep (unless she was just pretending, to get rid of us) and we crept out and shut the door and I'm going home now, I am absolutely wrung dry."

"Why don't you stay here, too? It's late to drive home."

"No, I just called Steve. They're waiting for me. I need to get home. I'll stay tomorrow night if—if Dad is still in danger . . ."

Beverly was looking frightened, haggard. *Still in danger* had scared her.

Abruptly Thom unwound his long legs from his chair, rose and hugged Beverly with a muffled sob. Beverly grabbed him tight.

"Hey, c'mon. Dad will be just fine. You know Whitey McClaren—he'll outlive us all."

Looking on Virgil stood uncertainly a few feet away as if waiting for Beverly to detach herself from Thom and next hug *him*.

But Beverly only just said, to both brothers, at the door—"Good night!"

"YOU ARE ONLY AS HAPPY as your least happy child."

(Someone had said this. Or had she heard it on TV.)

(Was it a silly platitude? Was it true? Painfully true?)

Whitey didn't think of it that way. Not Whitey!

"It's more like we give them life, we set them free, like little boats on a river. We prepare them for the journey but once they're twenty-one, let's say, it's up to them to make the journey by themselves. And our children are long past twenty-one."

Whitey spoke so sensibly, she knew he must be correct.

Yet, she did not agree. She had to object.

Not an hour passed but that Jessalyn didn't think of each of her children. It did not matter that they were "grown up"—"adults." In some ways this made them more vulnerable. As they'd spun out in ever larger concentric circles from her.

Like bases on a baseball field. First base: Thom. Second base: Beverly. Third base: Lorene.

(In her imagination, still children. But Thom lanky-long-legged, a baseball cap pulled low over his forehead so you couldn't see his eyes.)

But there the metaphor broke down. For there was Virgil, and there was Sophia. The babies! Their mother had spent fewer years thinking about them for the simple reason that they'd been in her life for fewer years. It was eerie how, in a dream, though there were children, *there were not enough children* for she'd forgotten one or two, or, worse yet, they had not been born.

This was an unspeakable horror to her. As it was senseless, ridiculous.

How Whitey would laugh at her, if he knew! How the children would laugh.

And Virgil would quote some ancient Greek curmudgeon-philosopher about how it is better not to have been born at all—ridiculous!

"Maybe a mother feels differently. I do feel that they are my responsibility and always will be, if I am their mother."

"Well, darling—that's silly. That's *you*."

Whitey kissed her lips, that felt slightly cold. His own lips always felt (to him) slightly over-warm.

Adding: "I hope you don't think that I am your responsibility, too."

Jessalyn drew away from her husband, just slightly stung.

"Of course! Of course I feel that you are my responsibility, darling. 'In sickness and in health.' Any wife would feel that way about her husband."

"Not any wife, dear. But you're very sweet to say so."

They were sitting close together, hands clasped together.

Jessalyn thought, with a kind of wild elation—*But I will have to outlive him, to care for him. I cannot ever leave him even to die.*

AND NOW. In the bed, alone. Her side of the bed.

How strange it is, in this bed, alone: without Whitey beside her.

Exhausted and dazed, seemingly wide-awake, and her eyes wide-open (though in fact her eyes are closed) sinking into a dark perilous place—fearful of what she will see there.

Nothing. There is—nothing.

Gusts of wind, against the darkened windows. Skeins of rain slapping against the glass and a sound of wind chimes almost inaudible, she strains to hear, faint and fading, silvery, the most frail beauty. She strains to hear.

"Heir"

Of the McClaren family it was only Thom who knew.

Without being certain what it was, he *knew.*

Mistaken identity. All charges dropped.

It was all very upsetting. Confusing. His father had evidently been "arrested"—or rather, his father had been "taken into police custody"—for having allegedly "interfered" with a police arrest at the side of the Hennicott Expressway.

But then, his father had "collapsed"—not inside the Toyota Highlander but at the side of the Expressway—and police officers had called 911.

Somehow, there had been a "mistake" in "identifying"—someone. (Whitey McClaren?) A mistake by—*whom*?

Thom was being assured, all charges had been dropped.

In the light of a "further investigation"—"substantiating by 'witnesses'"—all charges had been dropped.

All this, or as much of this as he could absorb, Thom was informed on his cell phone, in a corridor outside his father's room in the Intensive Care Unit at Hammond General Hospital. Cell phone reception inside the hospital was poor, the voice at the other end was continually breaking up. *Hello? Hello?*—Thom cried in exasperation.

The call was from a Hammond police lieutenant who'd seemed to be acquainted with Whitey McClaren, or at least to know who Whitey was, and may have known Thom McClaren, also. (Had they gone to high school together? Middle school? The lieutenant's name had a vague teasing familiar sound.) In a conciliatory voice the lieutenant informed Thom that his father's 2010 Toyota Highlander had been towed from the Expressway to the police auto pound and that Thom could pick it up the next day. In his distracted state Thom had not thought to demand *What the hell did you do to my father* but only rather to stammer a question or two about the procedure of picking up the vehicle for he knew that Whitey would be anxious about the Highlander, where it had been taken and who had been driving it.

Thom would need to come to police headquarters first, to pick up authorization papers. He would need his ID.

Confused, Thom had thanked the lieutenant who expressed the hope that his father was "doing OK" at the hospital.

"Yes, thanks. I guess—he is."

But after the connection was broken Thom stood in the hospital corridor as others passed around him, white-clad medical workers, attendants pushing gurneys, or laundry carts, visitors like himself in ordinary street clothes, looking pained, lost. Trying to hear again those words whose significance had eluded him—*Mistaken identity, charges dropped.*

"DAD'S CAR. WHERE IS IT?"

"At the police auto impound. I'll pick it up tomorrow."

"They towed it away?"

Lorene was urgent, anxious. Her interrogatory manner was grating to Thom.

"Of course. They wouldn't leave it at the side of the Expressway."

"How badly is it damaged? Did they say?"

"My impression is, just minor damage. I think I'll be able to drive it home."

"If you want me to drive you there, or drive with you and bring your car back . . ."

But no, Thom would take a taxi. He insisted. He didn't want to involve anyone else. The impound lot was in a derelict neighborhood south of the Expressway and he could go there directly from the hospital, next morning.

Thinking how it was like Lorene to posit her offer in a subjunctive mode—*If you want me* . . . So that the onus was on Thom, to say yes, or to decline.

Not that Lorene wasn't generous, in the time of a family emergency. Not that Lorene did not *care.* But there was the (subtly reproachful) assumption on her part that Thom, as the eldest, was responsible for their father's vehicle, as the others were not.

Since you're Dad's favorite. Dad's "heir." These accusatory words were not uttered aloud.

How differently Beverly reacted when she learned about the Toyota—immediately she'd offered to drive with Thom, in his car or in hers, so that he could drive their father's car back home. "You can't go *alone,* Tommy. What if, in that neighborhood . . ."

Laying her hand on his arm, pleading.

Tommy was a kind of claim. Their old, easy intimacy, eldest sister and elder brother.

But Thom preferred to go alone. He *did not want* to take this brief trip with either of his (older) sisters. In this family crisis he'd have enough of them.

Nor would Thom tell the others what he'd been told on the phone. Certainly, he would not tell Jessalyn. *Mistaken identity. Charges dropped.*

Collapsed.

"WHO? WHAT NAME? 'McCLAREN'—THAT'S YOU?"

Finally, the authorization papers were found. Payment of sixty-five dollars required.

Leaving the scene of an accident. Abandoning vehicle in no parking zone. Keys in ignition.

These had been checked. But the checks had been crossed out and initialed. What was this? At the bottom of the form, an unintelligible scrawl of a signature.

Ordinarily Thom would have demanded to know before he paid a fee or a fine but now, a taxi waiting outside, and Whitey in critical condition in the hospital, he hadn't the heart to protest.

He did ask to speak with the lieutenant who'd called him. But he didn't remember the lieutenant's name—*Calder, Coulter.* Impassive and unhelpful as a (leaden) toad in a garden, the desk sergeant could offer no assistance.

At the hospital that morning Whitey was showing signs of coming into consciousness. His eyelids fluttered, his left eye appeared to be in focus. His bruised lips moved, soundlessly.

The fingers of his left hand. But not his right.

Toes of his left feet. But not his right.

"Whitey? Oh, Whitey! We're right here . . ."

Jessalyn, tireless. Caressing Whitey's hands which were cold, stiff.

She'd slept a few hours, she'd said. She'd had time to dress carefully, brushing her hair. Makeup, lipstick. For Whitey.

Wearing a strand of pearls Whitey had given her for one of their anniversaries, his favorite of his many gifts to her. On her ears, matching pearls.

Happiness in her eyes. Seeing that Whitey seemed to be reviving.

Thom wanted to caution his mother—*Don't expect too much.*

Their parents' love for each other had been so strong, you felt it as excluding you. Even Thom, the eldest, had not escaped this curious sort of jealousy.

The prognosis for Whitey was *good.* You did not want to inquire too closely what *good* might mean, post-stroke.

He'd paid the fee. The fine. Whatever the hell it was. And at the impound a heavyset individual who appeared to be in charge wasn't very friendly, frowning suspiciously at the authorization paper, and at Thom McClaren's driver's license.

"You're thinking that I'm here to steal a car? My father's car? And why'd I do that? How'd I even know the car was here, if my father had not told me?" Thom was furious, suddenly.

The strain of the vigil. How many hours. He hadn't slept well the night before. He was one who required hours of sleep, steady, consoling. He could not bear his life, if he could not sleep. His father's stroke was a devastation. He saw that the heavyset man was staring at him and he realized—he was like an animal that has been weakened, injured. Other animals sense its infirmity and will turn against it.

"OK, sorry. I guess—you have to be careful. I'll find it."

Surprising, a large number of the impounded vehicles were new models and in good condition. You had to wonder what had happened, that these vehicles had ended up *impounded.* Some of them looked as if they'd been in the lot a long time.

Automobile graveyard. Had to figure, some of the owners of these were no longer living.

Trouble was, Whitey's Toyota Highlander was that obscure earthy-brown-gray, a neutral hue that fitted in with its surroundings like camouflage. Mid-sized SUVs common as sedans, or nearly. Expensive vehicles, hundreds of thousands of dollars here in the Hammond police impound lot.

Finally, Thom located his father's vehicle in a farther corner of the lot. License plates matched.

Examined it outside and in. Not so clean and shining as Whitey's vehicles usually were but no evident dents or scrapes in the chassis. No cracks in the windshield.

"That's strange . . ."

He'd been told—at least, he thought he'd been told—that the vehicle had been in an accident on the Expressway. The air bags had detonated and injured his father and yet—it didn't look as if the air bags had detonated.

He asked if any "repairs" had been made to the Highlander and was told no.

Hardly likely, that Hammond police had "repaired" his father's car.

Later, at home, at the house on Old Farm Road where he would be staying another night at least, he called Hammond police headquarters another time and asked to speak to Lieutenant—was it *Calder, Coulter?—Coleman?*—(could've kicked himself, he had not heard the name clearly, and had been too distracted at the time to ask).

No one there by that name.

"Well, is there a lieutenant in the Hammond Police Department with a name similar to that?" he asked, trying to be patient. Courteous. "This is about an incident on the Hennicott Expressway on October 18, 'mistaken identity'—'charges dropped'—'John Earle McClaren of 99 Old Farm Road, North Hammond'—"

Put on hold. Waited.

The Seed

In the twilight before dawn, the first, tentative cries of birds.

Ghostly-white birch trees emerging out of mist.

Sloping hills of their neighbors' property, where horses grazed.

Each McClaren child had a particular room, a window, a singular view from a window, that meant *home*.

IN A FAMILY OF FIVE CHILDREN, one is invariably the *baby*.

One is the *eldest,* with nearly the status of an adult.

It is like a footrace: the eldest is first, then the next-born, then the next-, and the next. And the last.

And each of them thinking, staring out a window—*Why, this is home! I've never left.*

TRUE THAT THE McCLAREN CHILDREN LEFT home in a timely fashion but the fact is, none of them went far.

Of the five only Thom was living in a city other than Hammond; and Thom lived (with his wife and children) in Rochester, seventy miles away. As head of the textbook division of McClaren, Inc. he was in constant communication with his father.

Beverly, Lorene, Sophia—the McClaren daughters—lived within a radius of eight miles of the family home.

Virgil had traveled the farthest—as far north as Fairbanks, Alaska—as far south as Las Cruces, New Mexico. In his twenties he'd disappeared for weeks, months at a time without letting anyone know where he was except belatedly, when they received postcards indicating he'd already moved on. He liked, as he said, to *drift*—"Like cottonwood seed."

So vain, he was without vanity. As an infant is without vanity, enthralled by its own mere being.

"A seed is meant to take root and grow. It's meant to turn into something larger and more significant than a damned *seed*."

To mitigate the exasperation of his words Whitey laughed, or tried to; and Virgil said, frowning, "But what do you mean by 'mean,' Dad? Why would you assume that anything in nature exists for any purpose other than itself?"

"Why would I assume—what?"

"Well, Dad, see—that's your fallacy. In this case."

***FALLACY.* A RISKY WORD TO TOSS CASUALLY AT WHITEY McCLAREN.** The others listened, keenly. Even Sophia who was usually Virgil's ally was hoping that their father would rebuke her annoying brother.

It did not go unnoticed among the McClaren siblings that Virgil was never (seemingly) hurt by their father's remarks. Virgil was apt to smile his small stoic smile, and stroke his wispy beard; sometimes he laughed, a wincing sort of laugh, of the kind a household pet might laugh when, not meaning to hurt, someone stepped on his tail.

"It is not a 'fallacy' to believe that we are here on earth to be *of use*. That's just common sense!"—Whitey had begun to speak impatiently. His face had begun to tighten and to flush. Like most public men whose social manner is unfailingly genial and good-natured, whose seduction of an audience is achieved through frankness and directness, or the appearance of these, he could not easily bear opposition.

"But what does it mean—'of use'? What kind of use, for whose use, at what price to the user, and to what purpose? There is utility, and there is 'uselessness'—that's to say, art." With naive urgency Virgil spoke, leaning forward on his skinny elbows and seemingly unaware of his father's mounting irritation.

"Art is *useless*?"

"Well. Lots of things that are useless are not 'art'—but yes, 'art' is not a *useful* thing. If it was, it wouldn't be 'art.'"

"Bullshit! Plenty of useful things can be beautiful if they are beautifully designed. Buildings, bridges, cars—airplanes, rockets—glassware, vases"—Whitey spoke excitedly, stammering—"and I'd include our books, the books we design and print, they are first-rate products, they are *useful* and they are *art*."

Virgil said: "Beauty is not 'art'—not necessarily. Beauty and art are two different things, and usefulness and 'art' are two different things . . ."

"I said—bullshit! You don't know what the hell you are talking about, you've never *worked*. How can you have the slightest idea of what life is, what 'usefulness' is, if you've never worked at a real job?"

Jessalyn intervened, gently: "Now, Whitey. You know that Virgil has had a number of jobs. He has had—"

"—part-time jobs. 'Helping out.' 'House-sitting.' 'Dog-walking.' But nothing permanent, or *real*."

This was unfair! And inaccurate! Virgil drew breath to object but a warning glance from his mother quieted him, as surely as if she'd laid a restraining hand on his arm.

How frustrating to Whitey, he could not—quite—win any argument with his wily youngest child though he knew, indeed everyone knew, that *he was in the right*. Whitey had only himself to blame (he conceded) for agreeing to name his younger son after some airy notion of Jessalyn's and not some more traditional name: Matthew, for instance.

Not likely, Whitey thought, that he'd have such frustrating exchanges with a son named Matthew, as he never had with a son named Thom.

HE'D ALWAYS BEEN A DREAMY CHILD. A lonely child. A stubborn child. In school, evasive. Among children his age, elusive. Among his older siblings, a *baby*.

At the age of eleven Virgil fell under the spell of William Blake whose poetry he discovered by chance in one of his mother's old college anthologies crammed into a bookcase.

A *robin redbreast in a cage puts all of heaven in a rage.*

Oh! Virgil felt something like a current touch him, coursing through his body and leaving him weak.

Some are born to sweet delight.

Some are born to sweet delight,

Some are born to endless night.

His mother's handwritten annotations on the page had intrigued Virgil, also. He had not ever considered his mother as a girl, a student, leaning over a book, taking notes in a classroom and pondering this very poem.

That dreaminess in Virgil, you could see it in Jessalyn too, when she believed that no one was observing her.

It had been Jessalyn who'd suggested the name "Virgil"—(had she had a high school teacher with that name? a handsome young man, a lover of poetry?)—and Whitey had not objected, for Jessalyn so rarely evinced wishes of her own.

(Whitey had regretted the name afterward. Half-seriously he'd thought that maybe Virgil's troubles had begun with "that name.")

WHEN AT THE AGE OF ELEVEN Virgil asked Jessalyn about William Blake she'd seemed at first not even to know who "William Blake" was—all that, the world of poetry and books, had been long ago. She'd had only a vague memory of "Auguries of Innocence," and *Songs of Innocence and Experience*. When Virgil showed her *The Norton Anthology of English Literature: Volume* 2 she'd seemed baffled by the very book which she doubted was hers until Virgil showed her the name inside the front cover—*Jessalyn Hannah Sewell.*

Wistfully she'd said, "Well, yes—I do remember now. I remember something."

Soon then, Virgil discovered the intoxicating poetry of Walt Whitman, Gerard Manley Hopkins, Rimbaud, Baudelaire. His first attempts at writing were imitations of these poets, as his first attempts at art were imitations of Matisse, Kandinsky, Picasso (color plates in *European Art Masters,* another book he'd discovered at home). The precocious boy read, or tried to read, the *Iliad,* the *Odyssey,* Ovid's *Metamorphoses, Great Dialogues of Plato.* He gave up soon with *The Aeneid,* by his namesake Virgil.

He acquired a battered old upright piano and insisted upon teaching himself. From a relative he acquired a battered flute.

He composed music, to accompany his poetry. He considered his art a "visual" form of music.

It was exhilarating to think of himself as mythic, oracular. If he had to think of himself as "Virgil McClaren" he felt trapped and suffocated. The meaning of life wasn't a narrow personal identity but an impersonal, higher self. The great aim of his life was to *scrub his soul clean.* His poetry and his artworks he began to sign without a last name, just *Virgil (March 2005), Virgil (Sept. 2007),* etc.

After he'd dropped out of Oberlin, and after he'd drifted about the country for a year or two, Virgil returned to North Hammond to live in a rented farmhouse with a shifting contingent of other, self-styled artists and activists of diverse ages. (Was this a *hippie commune?*—Jessalyn wondered uneasily.) Their ideal, Virgil said, was to live "morally blameless" lives without exploiting other people, or animals, or the environment, acquiring what they could of food and services through "barter" and not currency; it was rumored that they made nighttime raids on supermarket Dumpsters and local landfills. Once, Virgil had brought back a scarcely battered Formica-topped kitchen table with four matching chairs, that turned out to have been discarded from his sister Beverly's household. (Beverly was incensed that her brother was turning into a "scavenger" but Virgil hadn't been embarrassed in the slightest.)

Virgil's little sculptures made of paper, scrap metal, twisted pieces of wire, rope, twine, tinsel were displayed on the front veranda of the farmhouse. By degrees he acquired a reputation at local arts and crafts fairs where *Virgil* works sold well for they were priced very reasonably, or for "barter." Occasionally, Virgil won an award (though no money was likely to be involved). The local community college hired him to teach art—an actual, *paying job*—(and if he'd persevered, the possibility of a permanent hire, with benefits)—but after two semesters Virgil decided to quit, on the principle that (1) he was (probably) taking work from another artist, who needed the job more than he did, (2) he preferred free, open days, with no stifling restrictions, and (3) he preferred a yearly income so low, he didn't have to pay taxes.

Jessalyn had been delighted when Virgil accepted the teaching job, and dismayed when he'd quit. "Jesus! When will he be able to support himself," Whitey fretted.

"Darling, I think Virgil does support himself, to a degree. With his artwork."

"His *artwork*! It's junk—literally. Not marble, or aluminum, or steel, or"—Whitey's voice trailed off, uncertainly—"alabaster. *Scrap-metal.* What can that be worth?"

"Art isn't a matter of material, I think. It's what the artist does with the material." Jessalyn tried to speak enthusiastically. "For instance, Picasso . . ."

"Picasso! Are you serious! Picasso *would not be living in North Hammond, New York.*"

"Well—Virgil is also influenced, he says, by that hermit-sculptor who made little boxes—Joseph Cornell? And there are other examples of what Virgil calls 'outsider art'—where the artists don't show their work in galleries."

"'Galleries'—what a joke! Virgil is lucky he can show his work at the local mall, or at a 4-H fair with the cows and hogs. I guess that's what 'outsider art' is—not picky."

"He's exhibited his work at the library downtown, and at the college. You know that."

"Well, yes—I guess that's an achievement: an exhibit *indoors* and not out in the rain." Whitey was fuming, reveling in his very unfairness.

"Have you ever even looked at his sculptures, Whitey? The five-foot rooster he gave us, in my garden—it's funny but really quite beautiful. And ingenious, the way he coated actual feathers with some kind of preservative, and—"

"Our son has no insurance! No benefits! He's 'living off the land'—like a pauper."

"Don't be silly, darling. We can take care of him if it's ever necessary. He knows he can depend upon us."

Jessalyn spoke with more confidence than she felt. Whitey flared up in anger.

"He *knows*? And how does he *know*? Is that what you tell him?"

"Of course not. Virgil never asks for money—for himself. In fact, sometimes, if he has money, he gives it away . . ."

"'Gives it away.' Jesus!"

It was particularly infuriating to Whitey that their son gave away money, small amounts to be sure, but more than a near-indigent like himself could afford, to such charitable organizations as a local animal rescue, a "green acres" wildlife sanctuary, environmental protection groups, the ACLU. Virgil was an occasional activist with Beasts of the Suburban Wild, an animal rights organization that intervened on the behalf of animals subjected to experiments in research laboratories; to Whitey's consternation Virgil had been photographed, with a dozen other protesters, picketing Squire Laboratories, one of Whitey's pharmaceutical clients. (Fortunately the picketers hadn't been identified in the newspaper, nor was the photograph very clear.)

There was a philosophy behind this behavior, Virgil had tried to explain to Jessalyn. (Virgil dropped by the house at unexpected times. Or rather, since Virgil only dropped by when Jessalyn was likely to be alone, and Whitey was nowhere near, there had to be some element of the expected to his visits, but being Virgil, committed to spontaneity and taking each day as it came, he did not alert his mother beforehand.) "Extreme altruism"—was that it? Jessalyn had thought that you might start with a moderate sort of altruism, before working up to extreme, but there was no trying to convince Virgil, who would never do anything moderate if he could do it to an extreme.

Jessalyn hadn't mentioned any of this to Whitey, for she didn't want to provoke her excitable husband any further.

"What I think, Jessalyn, is that you are 'enabling' our son. As Lorene says. You have infantilized him, he will never grow up."

"Whitey, that's unfair. Virgil is far from being an 'infant'—he's probably the most socially conscious, intellectually engaged person we know. He just 'marches to a different drummer' . . ."

"Wait. Who said that?"

"What?"

"'Marches to a different drummer'—who said that about Virgil?"

In the midst of his disapproval of their son, Whitey was suddenly, inexplicably, smiling. Jessalyn was astonished.

In fact, it was Virgil himself who'd said, one day, with the air of one quoting a famous remark: "'If a man does not keep pace with his companions, perhaps it is because he hears a different drummer.'"

Jessalyn had asked Virgil who'd said this—(she'd thought that the remark was a brilliant one: she was determined to remember it)—and Virgil had said, with a shrug, "What does it matter who 'said' what, Mom? The important thing is, *it got said.*"

Now Jessalyn told Whitey she wasn't sure. It was just something she'd heard about Virgil, or maybe someone like Virgil.

"The important thing is, darling—*it got said.*"

SHE DID WORRY ABOUT VIRGIL. She worried, with a mother's obsessiveness, about whether he was *happy;* whether he would ever *find anyone,* who would make him *happy.*

Growing up he'd had numerous friends but never any close friends. So far as they knew, never any girlfriend.

Unlike Thom who'd had girls pursuing *him*.

How they were all living out on the farm on Bear Mountain Road, Jessalyn had no idea. Was it a *hippie commune* as in the 1960s, or was it just a large ramshackle house with shifting tenants? They grew organic vegetables, fruit. They kept chickens, and sold eggs. (Not the jumbo eggs Whitey liked [for his poached eggs] but malnourished little brown eggs, the shells shockingly dirty. Jessalyn felt obliged to purchase these eggs from Virgil whenever he brought a carton or two to her, but she used the eggs in ways that disguised their origins.)

Jessalyn knew that Virgil smoked "dope" (as he called it offhandedly) or rather that he had smoked "dope" years ago; whether he did now, in his more "organic" phase, she could not ask. With his disarming frankness Virgil would have told her possibly more than she wanted to know.

So too, she didn't feel that she could ask about Virgil's romantic life. If "romantic" was the word. She had certainly seen him in the company of women but whether these were romantic liaisons, she doubted. There was so little of *possessiveness* in Virgil, it didn't seem likely that he was anyone's *lover.*

(How possessive Whitey had been, when they'd first met! Those first months, before they were married! No one who'd seen them together, who'd seen how Whitey had looked at Jessalyn, could have doubted how he felt about her, and what their relationship was. The recollection made her shiver.)

But with Virgil, you never knew. Young people behaved differently today. They were well into the "new" century—the twenty-first century—and Jessalyn supposed old ways were just fading out no matter how people (like Whitey McClaren) disapproved.

Still, Jessalyn wished that Virgil would fall in love, and that someone would love him. She didn't dare wish that he might get married and have children like her two oldest children—for Virgil that might be a stretch. But she could hope.

A very pretty girl with a small, triangular face, stunted and malformed body, shaved head that glinted metallic-blue—this was Virgil's friend Sabine, a fellow artist whom Jessalyn had met by chance in Virgil's company, in a North Hammond shopping center. Astonishing to look up and see her son pushing what appeared to be a petulant, bald child in a wheelchair! The two were headed for Home Depot.

"Mom, hello! I'd like you to meet my friend Sabine."

Jessalyn had to lean down, to shake the girl's small limp hand. Sabine stretched her mouth in a grudging grimace of a smile.

"Hello! Is it—'Sabine'? That's a beautiful name . . ."

So banal a remark, Sabine couldn't be troubled to respond. She folded her thin arms tight across her thin chest in a way to suggest how barely contained was her impatience with Virgil, how strong her wish to escape into Home Depot.

But Virgil had no radar for social cues. Or, if he did, he was blithely indifferent to his friend's restiveness.

Sabine was a "new arrival" at the farm, Jessalyn was told. She did "fantastical carvings" with natural wood. She had advanced degrees in computer science, statistics, and psychology; she'd published a book of poetry at the age of eighteen.

"I love poetry," Jessalyn heard herself say, foolishly. "That is—when I can understand it."

"It was Mom who introduced me to William Blake," Virgil said, peering (fondly?) down at the top of Sabine's bare, bluish head, "—even if she didn't exactly understand Blake."

"Do *you* understand Blake?"—Sabine glanced upward at Virgil with a startlingly quick smirk.

Virgil laughed, as if Sabine had said something witty.

Jessalyn wasn't sure if the smirk on Sabine's lips was sarcastic or affectionate or some mixture of the two, an intimate exchange that pointedly excluded her.

"Oh, you should come visit us, soon," Jessalyn said, though the pained expression in the girl's face made it clear that such a visit was not probable; like a runaway trailer truck on a steep incline she blundered on: "Some Sunday, Virgil? Bring Sabine to dinner?"

"Well, Mom—I'm not sure. Sabine is a *vegan* and also can't tolerate gluten . . ."

Sabine glared at Jessalyn as if daring her to reiterate her invitation which of course Jessalyn did, if somewhat uncertainly. She could look up recipes online. She could make special dishes for Sabine. With forced enthusiasm Virgil said, "Thanks, Mom! Sounds wonderful."

Biting her tongue not to say *What about next Sunday? Or—the Sunday after that? Please.*

Silent, Sabine continued to hug herself, tight. She might have been sixteen, or thirty-six. The squeezed-together little face was misleading. Her legs were skinny as sticks and her feet were the feet of a young child, in pink sneakers with checked laces. Even her teeth were child-sized.

"Well, Mom—great to see you. G'bye!"

With a look of relief Virgil pushed his friend away in the wheelchair as Jessalyn stood gazing after them.

She would tell Whitey—what? Impossible that she would fail to share this glimpse of Virgil with her dear husband, as she shared so much with Whitey, the very detritus of a day's life; yet, she could not think how to suggest to him the teasingly ambiguous nature of Virgil's manner with Sabine. Clearly they were very close friends, yet—how close? Could this peevish shrunken little Sabine be their son's *lover*?

Jessalyn felt chagrin, thinking such thoughts. No, she didn't want to *envision*.

In the end she'd told Whitey only that she had run into Virgil at the shopping center, with a fellow artist from the farm. Impulsively, she'd invited them to dinner.

"Good!"—Whitey was nodding, without having quite been listening.

"The friend is a girl. Quite pretty, and quite young."

"Really! Good."

"She's a *vegan*. And she's allergic to gluten."

"Well. Most of the young people are, these days."

"And she's in a wheelchair."

"In a *wheelchair*? Do you know why?"

Carefully Jessalyn told Whitey that she didn't know. But she didn't think it was anything "really extreme" like cystic fibrosis or—what was it?—Lou Gehrig's disease . . .

"Well. I'm not surprised."

"What do you mean, 'not surprised'?"

"I don't *mean* anything. Except it's like Virgil to take up with someone like that."

"'Someone like that'—? You don't even know the girl!"

"I don't know the *girl*. That is true. But I know our son and his predilection for wounded things. Broken and crippled things."

"Whitey, that's a terrible thing to say. 'Crippled' is considered crude today. People say 'handicapped'—"

"Actually, people say 'challenged.' But I'm not being critical of the girl, I'm just commenting on our son." Whitey was becoming flush-faced as if his temperature were rising. "Remember the dog he brought home when he was ten? Missing a leg! If there'd been another dog, missing two legs, Virgil would have brought home *that dog*."

"Oh, Whitey. You're being ridiculous."

"If there was a blind child within a ten-mile radius, that child would be Virgil's friend. I think he actually went out bicycling to look for those signs—CAUTION BLIND CHILD IN NEIGHBORHOOD. Even his favorite teachers had something wrong with them, like the math teacher with the wooden leg—"

"—not *wooden leg*. They're made out of something light and synthetic like plastic today, and they're called 'prosthetic limbs'—"

But Whitey was just being funny now. When he was upset, he'd never acknowledge it. Jessalyn let him go on.

So long as no one heard but her.

Though later when they were lying in bed in the darkness sifting through the events of the day as if casting a wide, fine-meshed net Whitey said suddenly, "You said she was a pretty girl? And she was a *girl*?"

"Of course she was a girl, Whitey! Her name was Sabine."

Jessalyn considered. "Her name *is Sabine.*"

BUT MONTHS PASSED, and Virgil didn't bring Sabine to the house as he was always promising. "Soon, Mom! It's just a kind of busy time right now. We're planting."

Or, "We're harvesting."

It was not helpful to pin Virgil down. For really you could not pin Virgil down.

If she pressed him Virgil would stay away from the house altogether. Or he would agree to come to dinner and never show up. And that would irritate Whitey. (Though Whitey didn't have to know, always.) And since Virgil had no phone, there was no way to easily contact him.

Eventually Virgil's replies became more clearly evasive. He was still saying "yes" but there was a hurt look in his face that Jessalyn wished not to acknowledge.

Finally asking him, "Are you still seeing Sabine?"

"Yes. Every day. We share a household, Mom."

Virgil spoke with pained patience. She saw, up close, how his forehead was furrowed with fine, near-invisible lines—her younger son! His teeth were discolored, faintly. His eyes were furtive.

Badly Jessalyn was wanting to ask—*But are you in love with her? Is she in love with you? Are the two of you—together?*

The moment passed. She could not ask. And Virgil would not volunteer to tell her.

He'd bicycled to the house that morning, a weekday. Of course, Whitey was away.

Mother and son were outside in Jessalyn's garden, at the side of the house. When Virgil came to visit he was never idle. Weeding, hoeing, watering, clearing away storm debris from the lawn, helping in the kitchen—Virgil took pleasure in every sort of household task so long as he wasn't expected to do any task and especially to show up at any particular time.

"Is her health—all right?"

"Why wouldn't it be? It's a condition she has, not an illness. Not a *curse*."

He'd been yanking weeds from a patch of Shasta daisies, and was smelling of his body.

It was one of those days, Virgil asked if he could take a shower at the house. God knew what showers and tubs were like at the farmhouse on Bear Mountain Road . . .

After Virgil washed his hair Jessalyn volunteered to comb out snarls for (it seemed) Virgil could not be trusted to comb snarls out for himself. His hair fell to his shoulders, beautiful hair Jessalyn thought, wavy, with coppery highlights; it was hair very like her own, as his eyes resembled hers. It made her laugh, to be so maudlin and so foolish.

Though she dared not pry into her son's personal life she retained still a mother's prerogative regarding the general cleanliness and grooming of her (adult) children.

Later, straddling his bicycle, that Beverly's teenaged children marveled at as the ugliest bicycle they'd ever seen, and loved to post on Facebook, Virgil said, with a bright smile, as if he'd only just thought of it, "Maybe Sunday, Mom. I mean—Sabine. Dinner here. Sunday after next. OK?"

AND IS THAT SABINE, with Virgil now?

Jessalyn has found herself staring at a tall, slope-shouldered young man on the far side of the café—the young man's fair, fawn-colored hair has been pulled back into a ponytail, and he is wearing farmers' overalls, and a black T-shirt beneath.

So this is where Virgil has been!—in the hospital café.

(Hiding away, as Beverly says.)

Jessalyn doesn't want to stare. It is always an awkward matter, coming upon one of the children when he/she doesn't know that you are there, and (certainly) you have no intention of spying on them . . .

In the hospital café, at a table near floor-to-ceiling plate glass windows, silhouetted by bright, mildly dazzling light, her son Virgil and a girl, or a young woman, whose face Jessalyn can't see clearly—(but is this person *bald*? is she wearing a little knitted cap of the kind chemotherapy patients wear, or is her hair just cut very short? It isn't even clear from where Jessalyn is positioned that the girl is in a wheelchair, or merely in a chair)—in what appears to be an earnest conversation.

Jessalyn's eyes flood with tears in even mild light. Indeed, she can't trust her eyes. And her view of the couple in the café is blocked by other people.

"Here's a table, Mom!"—Beverly has her elbow, firmly.

Jessalyn is feeling shaky. She has not left Whitey's bedside for several hours. Knows it is ridiculous, superstitious, but fears that something terrible could happen to her husband if she is not present . . .

Mom has forgotten to eat, has she? Beverly has been scolding her.

Won't do Daddy any good if you're sick, too. Mom, please!

That morning when they'd arrived at Whitey's room soon after 7:00 A.M. it was to discover that his bed was gone—Jessalyn gave a little cry and almost fainted . . .

But Whitey had been taken downstairs to Radiology for tests. A nurse hurriedly explained.

Beverly said curtly: "For God's sake, you should place some sort of notice on the outside of the door! You must scare visitors practically to death all the time."

But to Jessalyn she said, "Mom, don't be so *upset*. We can figure that Dad is being 'tested.' The neurologist told us yesterday afternoon he'd ordered an fMRI for today."

Was this so? Had she known? Jessalyn was too agitated to remember.

Seeing the empty space where his bed had been. White walls, ceiling. A look of such absence, she'd been unable to comprehend what it might mean.

"They would have notified us if—if—there'd been some radical change in Dad's condition. They wouldn't have just cleared out the damned room."

Beverly spoke with such vehemence, you might have thought that was exactly what she'd expected the hospital staff would do.

When after forty minutes the patient was wheeled back to the room, IV lines attached, eyes still (lightly) closed and face (seemingly) slack it did appear that there was a subtle change in him. Jessalyn stared, and smiled—Whitey's skin definitely looked less waxen, his lips less blue. As if blood and heat were flowing back into him.

And he was off the respirator now, breathing through an (unobtrusive) oxygen tube.

Though his every breath had to be monitored to determine what degree of oxygen he was drawing into his lungs, yet the miracle was *he was breathing on his own.*

The neurologist had told them, the previous day, that Whitey's reactions were improving. Very slowly, but improving.

You could see, grasping Whitey's hand, that the fingers quivered in a way they had not previously. Almost, you could feel that the fingers were trying to squeeze in acknowledgment, recognition.

Hi! Hello! I am here.

Sometimes, Whitey's eyelids fluttered as if he were waking from a deep gluey sleep. You could catch a glimpse of his (bloodshot) eyes—one, the left, seemed (almost) in focus.

"Whitey! Darling, can you hear me?"

"Hey Dad, hi! It's Beverly . . ."

It was exhausting, such hope.

For it seemed to them, the McClarens, that their beloved Whitey was struggling beneath the surface of an element like water, transparent, yet palpable, trying to forcibly thrust himself into wakefulness—but growing exhausted suddenly, sinking back.

"Dad? Hi, it's Thom . . ."

"Daddy? It's Sophia . . ."

It was crucial for them to continue to talk to him, they were told.

Yes (perhaps) (possibly) he could hear them. Though he was (still) unresponsive yet that did not mean he wasn't *hearing.*

Softly, Virgil played his flute for his father. Unless this was a new woodwind instrument he'd carved for himself, and painted robin's-egg blue. A breathy sound like whispers, so faint and unobtrusive it seemed to have virtually no melody.

"What is that tune, Virgil? I can almost recognize it . . ."

"It isn't a 'tune.' It's breath—my breath. Pure sound before it becomes subjected into music."

Did Whitey hear Virgil's breath-music? Jessalyn stared at his lips which seemed (she thought) to move—or nearly.

The good news was: damage to Whitey's brain appeared to be "not extensive" but "localized." He'd had a hemorrhagic stroke involving a major artery in the region of the cerebellum and swift surgical intervention and intravenous treatment within three hours of the stroke had almost certainly saved his life.

They were shown the fMRI video. Fascinating, appalling, to peer into the interior of Whitey's head, to see how ghostly the brain is, its textures blurred so that you saw only the shadowy pulsing of blood. And what a curious sort of eagerness in that pulsing, like life!

(Like the living fetus in the womb. If the fetus were a soul, bodiless but pulsing with life.)

No dark, gnarly tumors or blood clots. But there was a shaded and striated area of damage: "deficit."

Jessalyn felt light-headed, staring. For where was her husband, where was the man she knew, in this—X-ray?

The fMRI was not an X-ray machine, they were told. Its images were formed by establishing a "magnetic field" and "pulses of radio waves"; it did not involve radiation and so was not dangerous unless the patient was wakened by deafening thunder-claps inside the machine, that earphones could not suppress, and was thrown into some sort of seizure.

Did that happen often?—Jessalyn asked, alarmed.

Not often. Statistically.

She could not bear to think that Whitey was frightened, or subjected to pain. That he had no idea what had happened to him or where he was or—what would happen . . .

Sophia, who knew something of the latest imaging machines from her neuroscience courses at Cornell, described how the patient was trussed up in a kind of cylinder and "inserted" into the interior of the machine for about thirty minutes, to determine injury to the brain's functions. The technology was miraculous—Sophia thought—for it could prove that a stroke victim was still brain-alive, still-conscious in a part of his brain, though outwardly paralyzed and nonresponsive. How many individuals, paralyzed by strokes, had been wrongly diagnosed as in a "vegetative" state and left to die . . .

In Whitey McClaren's case, definitely the patient was *brain-alive, responsive.*

He'd suffered the trauma of the stroke, and of a probable seizure. He'd suffered the trauma of anesthesia and surgery. He was being treated intravenously for vascular occlusion and his vital signs were being closely monitored.

Most stroke victims require extensive rehabilitation, therapy. In Whitey's case, if and when he recovered sufficiently to be transferred to a stroke therapy rehabilitation center, it would be a matter of—well, many weeks—months . . .

When would my husband be able to come home, Jessalyn knew it was futile to ask, for how could Dr. Friedland reasonably answer such a question, yet, she heard herself ask, a frightened wife's query, and the doctor said with disarming frankness that he had no idea—though maybe in a day or two, he would know more.

And where was the rehab center?

Excellent stroke rehab facilities in Rochester. Not the nearest but the best.

Seventy miles, approximately. Eventually Whitey could be an outpatient, and live at home.

Live at home. Good news!

But an odd way of phrasing it—*Live at home*. Somehow, there was something ominous about these words.

(And is he with Sabine? Are the two—*together*?)

Jessalyn doesn't tell the others that Virgil is in the café. They have not noticed him, amid a crowd of customers.

At about ten o'clock that morning Virgil had arrived at Whitey's room. He'd played his flute for a while, and it had seemed that, just possibly, Whitey was hearing the breathy, sweet sounds . . . Then a nurse interrupted, needing to draw Whitey's blood from his poor bruised arm, and Virgil had quickly retreated.

"Mom? Try to eat this. And this mushroom quiche, we can share."

Beverly is humming under her breath. The consultation with Dr. Friedland this morning was so—encouraging!

Jessalyn understands, the children are terrified of losing their father. When a father has been so *strong* . . .

She is only half-listening to Beverly. And there has come Lorene to join them, but Lorene (as usual) is frowning into her cell phone.

Thom should arrive soon, he has said. And Sophia is upstairs at Whitey's bedside, contentedly working on her laptop, processing data for a project at Radcliffe Research Partners.

Is that Sabine? Sitting at a table with Virgil, silhouetted in a bright haze of sunshine?

Jessalyn wants to think so. Little Sabine in her wheelchair exhibited a strong enough will, Virgil's flightiness might well be held in check.

(But why would Sabine be here at Hammond General Hospital? Surely not to accompany Virgil.)

It makes Jessalyn uncomfortable to think of her youngest son's sexuality, if that's what it is—his intense, seductive, yet (she has always thought) unconscious manner; his soft-modulated voice, his way of leaning forward and listening closely, staring you in the eyes . . .

Your son is so—unusual, Jessalyn!

It's obvious that he is an artist, or a poet—someone special.

Strange that, often, Virgil attracts girls and women without seeming to be attracted to them, himself.

Sabine had seemed different, somehow. In the brief moments Jessalyn had seen the two together, Sabine had impressed her as the more willful of the two.

Not nice of Whitey to have asked if Virgil's friend was a *girl*.

(And what if Virgil's friend in the wheelchair had been a young man, what difference would that make?—Jessalyn wanted to confront her husband.)

It is not her business, Jessalyn tells herself. She *must not* interfere with Virgil's life, even to wish for him a happy and fulfilling life, a "normal" life with a companion, love . . .

She has seen how awkward Virgil is with men of a certain type—men like Thom, or Whitey. That kind of aggressive male, who takes for granted his masculine authority. Half-consciously Virgil has learned to shrink from Thom, to try to avoid Thom's scrutiny. Jessalyn doesn't want to think that Thom might have bullied his much-younger brother when he'd been in high school . . .

And she has many times seen how Virgil shrinks from Whitey's gaze. His father's (harsh) judgment.

She has wished that Whitey could love Virgil as he did the other children. Thom he'd adored as (one might as well concede) a small-scale version of himself, even as a toddler; the girls he'd adored as *girls*.

When Thom was newly born Whitey had regarded him, the tiny infant, with an expression of intense love, bafflement, wonder and awe. He had never expected to be so "crazy" over a baby!—he'd claimed. He marveled at the fact that, though the baby had been born at one of the busiest times in Whitey's life, when as a relatively inexperienced CEO of a small, struggling company he'd had to finesse business deals that might have fallen through, and precipitated bankruptcy, Whitey had spent hours just *staring* at the baby.

Yes, he'd tried to "diaper" the baby. That had not gone so well.

That love, for the firstborn, had been profound for Whitey. Jessalyn had realized what a good, kind, responsible man she'd married. And the girl-babies, Whitey had loved deeply as well, though his paternal infatuation had not been so intense. Even Lorene, the most independent-minded of the five children, from childhood the most contentious, did not seem to present any threat to her father's authority, as (evidently, inadvertently) Virgil does.

The child least loved by one parent will be most loved by the other.

(Who said that? A wise man like William Blake? Walt Whitman? Or, Jessalyn herself?)

"Mom, hi!"—Thom has arrived, stooping to give his mother a kiss on the cheek.

In his usual robust mood Thom pulls over a chair to the table and joins them. How tall, how handsome her oldest child is—blunt-jawed, with Whitey's slightly recessed eyes, Whitey's way of swooping at you. Impossible to believe that Thom is in his late thirties, he is so boyish and energetic.

Yet: Thom's hand, gripping Jessalyn's briefly, is surprisingly cold.

He is fearful of the hospital, Jessalyn knows. Fearful of how Whitey will look when he enters his room.

Quickly Thom is assured: the latest fMRI results are very encouraging. It looks as if Whitey will be discharged to a stroke rehabilitation center soon . . .

(Is this what Dr. Friedland told them? Jessalyn tries to recall the neurologist's exact words but cannot.)

At last, on the far side of the café, Virgil and his companion (clearly not Sabine) are on their feet. The shapely-bodied young woman is hardly a girl but Virgil's age at least, in a white lab coat, one of the medical staff whom Virgil has befriended.

A young doctor? A therapist? Her hair has been cut very short—but she doesn't have a shaved head. She is no one Jessalyn recalls having seen before. Virgil has been meeting people in the hospital, even sketching some of the medical staff. He has roamed about the corridors sketching what he sees—(Jessalyn hopes, with permission). It is like Virgil to strike up such acquaintances, if but fleetingly.

The young woman touches Virgil's arm lightly as she turns to leave. Virgil smiles after her—then turns aside, resumes his seat at the table, takes up whatever she has left on her plate, and eats it with his fingers; happily content to be alone, and to open his sketchbook.

Immediately, Virgil has forgotten the woman. You can see.

Scrub his soul clean he'd said. Jessalyn has no idea what that could possibly mean.

“Evidence”

“Thom! What on earth are you doing . . .”

On his iPhone Thom was taking pictures of their father’s (visible) injuries. Small, circular wounds on his face, throat, hands. Even his arms were bruised, burnt-looking, though he’d been wearing shirtsleeves, coat sleeves, at the time of the “accident.”

“You’re violating Daddy’s privacy, Thom! You know how sensitive Daddy is, he hates to appear weak or sick, he certainly won’t want anyone seeing how ravaged he looks right now . . .”

It was unfortunate, Thom’s bossiest sister had walked into the room. He hadn’t expected anyone for a few minutes at least. Whitey was deeply unconscious and “peaceful”—unaware of anyone in the room (Thom was sure); breathing slowly, rhythmically, not erratically as before but with a raspish sound like stiff paper being crinkled.

“I’m talking to you, Thom. Don’t just ignore me!”

Thom ignored her, and continued taking pictures. An older brother isn’t required to justify actions to any younger sibling and that does not alter with age.

Lorene tried to snatch the iPhone from Thom’s hand and he snatched it away from her, and gave her a little shove.

“Quit it. You damn bully.”

“You—mind your own business.”

“Daddy is my business . . .”

How swiftly they reverted to childhood. Adolescence. The two strongest-willed McClaren kids, whom *no one could push around*.

"Daddy is our collective 'business.' Keep your voice down, he might hear you."

"Keep *your* voice down, you're standing right over him."

Thom had not wanted to tell anyone about the situation, yet—*the situation* is how he thought of it.

Their father's injuries not (seemingly) the consequence of the stroke.

Not from a car crash.

Not from an air bag.

Thom had taken a dozen pictures which he now mailed to himself. Shutting off the phone then, and slipping it into his pocket.

"I—I just don't think—under the circumstances," Lorene said, not quite so bossy now, her voice faltering, "with Daddy so helpless, and looking so *old*—I just don't think it's *nice*."

"All right. I'm sorry."

"You know how sensitive he is. How vain . . ."

"No one will see the pictures, I promise."

"Then why are you taking them?"

"Just for the record. For me."

ALREADY HE'D BROUGHT UP *the situation* to Morton Kaplan.

Saying he had reason to suspect that his father's injuries hadn't been made by air bag detonation, or any kind of crash—"I'm thinking maybe—stun guns? Tasers?"

"Taser? You mean, police?"

"I'm thinking, maybe. Yes."

Kaplan did not seem so impressed as Thom might have expected. Not so incensed as you'd think an acquaintance of Whitey McClaren might reasonably be.

Even after Thom showed him the iPhone pictures the doctor seemed doubtful, like one who will have to be convinced.

"But why? Why would the police do a thing like that, to a man your father's age, who'd had a stroke while driving his car?"

The Swimmer

Help me. Give me your hand.

He is begging. For he can see them—just barely.

Beneath the surface of the water he is a shadowy figure like a shark.

Moving slowly, laboriously. Arms and legs like lead.

Their voices he can hear, at a little distance.

He can't speak, his throat has been soldered shut.

An agitation of all his limbs but with difficulty for the water is gluey-thick.

He has never been a confident swimmer. Now too late.

Yet, he is able to breathe. Only just barely.

They have drilled a tiny hole in his throat. They have inserted a very thin straw. Through this straw, just enough oxygen flows to his brain to keep him alive.

But no, that is mistaken. Instead, the tiny hole is in his trachea. It is a hot acid substance that is being injected.

An oxygen tube in his nostrils. Very light, plastic.

IV line directly into his heart. A steady pumping.

His skull they'd opened. He'd heard the drill. Smelled burning bone. A flap of skin. Blood noisily sucked through straws.

Hopes that by this time they have removed the old, contaminated blood in all his veins. (He'd heard the pumps, like straining septic pumps, through the night.)

(And the night is perpetual. What you'd suppose might sometimes be day is in fact *night*.)

So tired! But—he will not give up . . .

At last—(or is it again)—he is approaching the water's surface. Churning light-dazzling surface through which he must break . . .

On the other side, their faces. Voices.

Whitey. Darling!

Dad.

The Party

"Mom, and Sophia, ride with me."

"Wait! Mom is riding with *me*."

"Mom rode with you this morning. She's said she wants to ride back home with me now . . ."

"Mom and I have things to talk about."

"Mom and I have things to talk about."

QUICKLY IT HAD HAPPENED, she'd become a person who is *taken places*—a passenger.

A person discussed in the third person: *she, her. Mom.*

"LET ME FEED YOU SOMETHING, please! I haven't turned on the stove for days . . ."

In the refrigerator were eggs, bacon. In the freezer, Pacific Northwest smoked salmon, Whitey's favorite. And frozen whole grain bread from the Farm Market.

She was very tired. In fact, her head was reeling. Yet there she was—(poor, desperate Mom)—all but begging.

Such pleasure it would give her, in this time of strain, to prepare a meal, not a lavish meal, not even a proper supper, but a kind of midnight-breakfast, for them. *The children.*

And who would most enjoy such an impromptu meal at the sprawling old house on Old Farm Road?—who would delight in setting out his favorite cheeses, provolone, cheddar, Brie, with his favorite Swedish crackers?—taking out a six-pack of dark German ale from the refrigerator, passing around tall glasses?

Smiling, to think of Whitey. Exactly the sort of family gathering without planning, without fuss, that would make her husband very happy.

"Mom, no! We wouldn't hear of it."

"You sit down, Mom. We'll feed *you*."

Planning ahead, Beverly had brought several frozen pizzas to the house earlier that day. Despite Jessalyn's protests they would devour these like ravenous children.

Insisting that Mom sit down, please.

She was not to wait on them.

"Mom, *no*."

"But—"

"We said, Mom! *No*."

When Whitey was discharged from the hospital, and came home, she would prepare all his meals—of course. She would nurse him, as much as he needed. Gratefully!

Possibly, the stairs would be too much for Whitey, at first. That was a distinct likelihood for (it seemed) he had lost the ability to move his right leg—(temporarily, it was hoped). Therapy would restore his ability to walk but that would take time.

Already she was planning to convert the first-floor guest room at the rear of the house into a room for Whitey. There was a door that opened out onto the redwood deck. There was a floor-to-ceiling window that overlooked the creek at the foot of the hill.

She too would move into this room—of course. For Whitey did not like to sleep alone, ever.

Those days he'd been out of town on business, or politics. Overnight in Albany, New York City. Calling her to say how he missed her.

Keep waking up during the night thinking something is wrong—what's missing? My dear wife.

It had been a hopeful day at the hospital. Whitey was being treated with a combination of drugs to reduce his high blood pressure and the vascular occlusion. Another drug, to stabilize his heartbeat. The broken artery in his brain had been surgically repaired. His blood work and vital signs were near-normal—heart, lungs, liver, kidneys. He had regained a tenuous sort of consciousness that emerged and faded and emerged again like a weak radio station and he was able now to swallow liquids, carefully spoon-fed to him.

Swallowing reflexes had returned. This was a good sign!

Soon, a diet of easily masticated food—"mechanical soft."

Still, the words *vascular occlusion* had a harrowing sound.

Very hard to leave the patient. Now that he was conscious at least part of the time, and making an effort to speak . . .

But today had been a good day for soon, it seemed, Whitey would be able to speak above a hoarse hissing whisper. Soon, his words would be intelligible.

His "good" eye was ever more in focus. (It was not clear if his ravaged right eye could "see.")

Certainly, Whitey recognized his wife. His dear wife.

Several times he had seemed (almost) to be smiling at her, with half his mouth.

It will take time. There are sometimes setbacks.

His good eye swimming in tears focused on her face until the vision seemed to fade, the light to go out, whatever inside had been seeing her vanished like an extinguished flame.

She was reminded of holding an infant in her lap.

Her children, in the first weeks after birth. Her grandchildren.

That rapt stare of the infant. The eye that seems to be all iris, staring.

Greedy to know, to learn. In awe of all that there will be, to be stored inside the brain.

Leaning to kiss the infant's hot little brow.

Leaning to kiss the husband's (just slightly overwarm) brow.

Love you love you love you

Surest communication with a stroke victim (the nurses said) is touch.

Healing takes time. Therapy requires time.

How long? Impossible to say.

It filled her with horror to abandon him. To seem (to him?) to be abandoning him in that place, in that bed and in that room where he would be alone until in the morning she could return, to take his hand in hers, to kiss him.

But they were not allowed to remain overnight in the Intensive Care Unit and it was crucial (they were told) for them to maintain their own well-being, to sleep each night.

Damn hospitals breeding grounds for germs, viruses. What do they call them—staph infections.

Keep me out of God damn hospitals!

(She smiled, hearing Whitey's voice. How vehement he often was, meaning to be funny!)

(Were they observing her, smiling to herself? Were they wondering why?)

Pungent odor of dark German ale. Melting cheese, pizza dough.

Beneath, a smell of—was it cigarette smoke?

But none of the children smoked any longer. And Whitey had quit, years ago.

Not easy for Whitey to quit smoking. Poor Dad!

Those Cuban cigars, Jessalyn had not liked. No.

She had never asked him pointedly to stop smoking. Only just not to smoke his cigars in the house.

'Course not, darlin'. Cigar smoke is not an easily acquired taste.

It had evolved into a kind of joke between them.

Many things had been jokes between them: Jessalyn's habit of keeping things clean and tidy, Whitey's habit of letting things fall where they would.

Jessalyn's way of driving—"defensively."

Whitey's way of driving—"offensively."

The subject of Whitey's Toyota Highlander came up. Thom was saying he'd examined the vehicle and near as he could tell, there had been no "crash." The air bags had not been "detonated."

What's that mean?—Lorene asked.

The edge of the table was rising. A sudden sharp blow, against the side of her face.

"Mom! For heaven's sake . . ."

". . . help her up. We'd better get her to bed."

She was protesting she was all right but they ignored her. Trying to lift her for she could not seem to arrange her legs beneath her, that she might rise from the table.

Something had fallen over. A fork had clattered to the floor.

One of them taking her hand. "Mom? Lean on me."

As once she'd taken children upstairs to bed in this house. Slipping her fingers through the children's fingers when they would allow her. Tugging at them as they balked wanting to stay up later, with the other, older children.

Someday soon, they were promised. They could stay up as late as nine o'clock.

No, no!—they did not want to stay up until nine o'clock *someday soon* but *that very night.*

Now, she could not recall the children. Might've been Thom, might've been Lorene. Stubborn strong-willed children.

Recalling with a smile how their father would seize a misbehaving child, lift him (or her) into the air, legs thrashing. Set him (or her) onto his shoulders, for a "daddy-back-ride."

Like a flock of geese, trying to herd them. Their children!

Individually each had been tractable enough. Whitey agreed. But together, you could not keep them all in focus. Like those large white waddling geese, you might try to herd along a path.

As you kept one or two of the geese moving in the correct direction, one or two others would drift off in the wrong direction.

"You are staying the night, I hope?—you aren't going to drive home at this hour . . ."

"Yes, Mom. We're staying the night."

She could relax, then. All of them in the house, beneath the roof. Safe.

On the stairs she was trying to walk unassisted but they held her secure as if they did not trust her.

She was trying to explain to them that, when Whitey came home, they would both sleep in the downstairs guest room, but they seemed scarcely to hear her, helping her undress, urging her into bed.

Wanting to take a hot bath but she was just too tired. Smelling of her body probably but too tired, in the morning perhaps . . .

She'd been waking early. That was the problem.

Fell into a deep delirious sleep but woke after two or three hours in the utter darkness listening to her lone heartbeat.

Trying to recall the distinction between a CT scan and an MRI. The distinction between an MRI and an fMRI.

The precise names of the (very expensive) drugs being dripped into Whitey's veins to reduce the terrible *occlusion* that threatened to kill him.

On a sheet of paper she'd written down—words . . . No idea how to spell them, not wanting to ask the neurologist.

(But where was the sheet of paper? She was sure she'd lost it.)

(No. It was in her purse, somewhere. She could retrieve it another time.)

(At the hospital she'd broken into a cold sweat convinced that she'd misplaced her wallet. In it were credit cards, insurance cards, driver's license, twenty- and fifty-dollar bills Whitey had given her to put in her wallet "just in case"—she'd hurried back to a restroom to see if the wallet was there but had not found it. And then, searching through her purse another time, amid crumpled tissues, folded sheets of paper, the cell phone Whitey had purchased for her which she rarely used—she'd found it. *Oh God thank you.*)

"Is this your nightgown, Mom? You're still wearing *this*?"—Beverly treated her with such bemused tenderness you'd think that Jessalyn was (already) an invalid.

What was wrong with Jessalyn's old floral-print flannel nightgown? It was Whitey's favorite nightie of hers no matter how thin it was becoming.

The daughters were glancing around the room. This was their parents' bedroom—the "master bedroom" that had been a place of some mystery to them when they were growing up for (they'd sensed) they were not welcome in this room unless invited inside.

It was a large room with filmy white curtains that, in warm weather, when the windows were open, stirred and rippled in the breeze like something living and had made Sophia (as a child) hurry past the room without wanting to glance inside for the sinuous movement of the curtains made her uneasy.

Sophia was hanging back now, as her older sisters fussed over their mother. She'd grown to dislike Lorene, and she was finding Beverly grating, so overblown, so *emotional*. They were trying to appropriate their mother's anxiety, to make it something within their power to alleviate. She felt a rush of resentment for them, pure rage.

Her older sisters had always intimidated Sophia. Lorene in particular had bullied her. Beverly had been so *fleshy* . . . Sophia winced to recall Beverly's brassieres, the size of the "cups," repulsive to Sophia who was so much smaller than Beverly, yet objects of surreptitious fascination like the sisters' "periods" that were crudely kept secrets of great embarrassment to Sophia.

Just shut up about it! Please.

Did Jessalyn know? Could Jessalyn guess, how her youngest daughter was intimidated by her sisters?

Terrible to think, unless it was amusing, how the old, established patterns of childhood prevailed into adulthood.

"Mom, you made up your *bed*. The room is so *neat*."

But why was this surprising? That Jessalyn took time every morning to carefully make this bed, to tuck the sheets in neatly and smooth the white satin spread regardless of whether she'd slept by herself and regardless of the family crisis?

The girls were laughing at her, tenderly. She didn't want to think that their eyes were wet with tears.

It was so, like a sleepwalker Jessalyn *kept things clean in the household. In order.* Picking up Whitey's clothes where he'd flung them, setting his shoes in a row, in his closet. Socks, underwear. Car keys, wallet, cell phone, pocket address book—things Whitey was always misplacing. And now that Whitey hadn't slept in this room for several days the spaces that were normally his, comfortably cluttered, askew, now unnaturally clean, were a rebuke to her who prized a trivial matter like neatness so highly.

Thinking of a remark of Louisa May Alcott that had struck her, years ago—*When will I have time to rest? When I die.*

When will the house be perfectly clean and in order? When—the husband dies.

Crucial not to faint. Not while the girls are here.

Lie down quickly in the bed, position your head carefully, not too high on a pillow. Blood will rush into the brain and restore consciousness.

"Mom, good night! Make sure you *sleep*."

One by one they kissed her. Switched off lights, left the room.

Drifting off to sleep hearing voices downstairs. Far away, in the kitchen.

The comfort of voices. At this lonely time.

She was holding his hand in the dark. His fingers gripping hers. In this bed. In the dark.

Sounds like a party, downstairs. Who is it?

Who do you think, darling? The kids.

The kids! They sound happy.

Yes—maybe. They are trying to be happy.

But why aren't we with them, Jessalyn? Why are we up here? Let's go downstairs and join them.

Whitey restless and excited, swinging his bare legs out of the bed, impatient, perplexed, why are the two of them hidden away upstairs in bed like elderly invalids when the kids are downstairs in the kitchen eating pizza (unmistakably, Whitey can smell pizza), drinking his ale and beer, as if they'd never left home and yet: fact is, when they'd lived at home, the kids had never hung out together in the kitchen at such an hour, they'd had their own friends, they were the wrong ages to socialize together, it is strange, unnatural, that they are together now, what is it, what has brought them back home, some kind of God damn *wake*?

Whitey, on the verge of being incensed with her, demanded to know.

Mutant

Virgil! Where the hell are you *always going*."

Maddening to them, the responsible McClaren children, how at the hospital Virgil was always disappearing.

He'd arrive with the others in the morning, visit with Dad maybe ten-fifteen minutes. Play his ridiculous flute. (As if, in the condition he was in, poor Dad wanted to hear a God damn *flute*.) Then you'd look around, and Virgil was gone.

Later he'd appear like nothing was wrong, he'd been here all along.

(Somewhere in the hospital? Sketching in his *artiste's* book? "Making friends" in his hippie-hypocrite way?)

When Virgil did sit in the lounge with the others, couldn't sit still for more than a few minutes. Couldn't bear the TV (CNN "Breaking News"—nonstop). If you tried to talk to him about something serious he'd answer with a vague Virgil-smile and a few seconds later excuse himself and disappear.

Only if Sophia particularly pressed him would Virgil have a meal with her in the café downstairs. Rarely with his older sisters and virtually never with Thom if he could avoid it.

Even with his mother at the hospital Virgil behaved strangely. You wanted to strangle him, sometimes!

His dishwater-blond hair, tied back in a slovenly ponytail, was unwashed and matted. His long skinny bony feet, in sandals, looked coated with ash. His clothes were ridiculous—hippie-farmer overalls, rumpled pull-over jerseys. And the sketchbook! And the hand-carved "flute"! Yet, maddeningly, young and not-so-young women often glanced at him with small smiles of interest, expectation.

Excuse me! Are you—?

(Beverly and Lorene were astonished to overhear an attractive young woman ask Virgil if he was *that artist Virgil McNamara—who lives in Hammond and makes animal sculptures*?)

(How incensed they were that Virgil replied with his usual faux-modesty—*Just "Virgil." Yes, that's me.*)

Certainly it was Virgil who evinced the least worry or concern about their father. If he couldn't avoid a conversation about Whitey with his mother, his brother, his sisters he would manage to deflect it onto other matters—an environmental activists' organization with which he was involved, Save Our Great Lakes; an animal rights' organization preparing to picket a research laboratory in Rochester where rabbits were being used in cruel experiments testing the safety of cosmetics, Mercy for Animals. Virgil's mind seemed to fasten, like a hungry boa constrictor, upon any crisis other than the family crisis at hand.

With the others he'd listened to Dr. Friedland speaking at length about Whitey's condition and the physical therapy he would have to have to restore "cognitive" and "motor" skills that had been impaired by the stroke; he'd listened, or given the impression of listening, to the doctor speak of how Whitey would need support in every way, emotional, and also literal—help in walking, talking, eating and drinking, hours of practice each day, both in the rehab clinic and at home. When he came home.

Everyone asked—when would Whitey come home? Except Virgil.

Everyone had questions for Dr. Friedland. Except Virgil.

Especially Sophia with her background in biology and neuroscience had questions to ask about their father's medical treatment—(the others were impressed with the youngest sister, who knew so much that they didn't know, and could articulate her questions so intelligently; much of the time Sophia was *the quiet one,* easily overlooked).

And then, when they glanced around—Virgil had slipped out of the doctor's office and vanished.

"HE DOESN'T CARE AT ALL that Daddy is seriously ill."

"It isn't real to him . . . I think that's it."

"All that's real to Virgil is Virgil. *That's* all."

"MAYBE HE HAS 'RESTLESS LEG SYNDROME.'"

"Is that a joke, or is that real?"

"What? 'Restless leg syndrome'—a joke—I think."

"No, actually—I think it's real. 'Restless leg syndrome'—you read about it in the newspaper—is some kind of neurological impairment."

"Are you sure? It sounds like a joke."

"I swear, Steve has it, or something like it—'restless leg'—he's always *twitching*. Especially in his sleep . . ."

"That's what Virgil has: a 'neurological impairment.' Part of his brain is missing."

"Don't be silly! You always exaggerate. Virgil is just spoiled, lazy . . . Mom has spoiled him."

"Don't blame Mom! She has not spoiled Virgil, *he has spoiled himself*."

"Some part of his brain is missing—the part that is sensitive to social cues. He's like—one of those"—(Beverly hesitated, uncertain of the clinical term she was seeking: not *asparagus,* though she knew it resembled *asparagus*. But if she uttered the word, in this context a silly word, the others would laugh at her, and the point she was trying to make about their brother, a point with which [she knew] they concurred, would be lost)—"autistic persons. Except he's a high-performing autistic. He lacks empathy with people he should feel empathy for, like his family, and he has empathy for the wrong people, total strangers—and animals! He understands that our father had a stroke and that he might have died but it isn't real to him the way it's real to us."

These smug, cruel words made Sophia squirm. For the past several minutes she'd been resisting the impulse to press the palms of her hands over her ears. Now, she leapt to her feet: "You're all too judgmental! Virgil cares for Daddy in his own way. You don't like Virgil because you don't understand Virgil. Deep in your hearts you're jealous of him."

Sophia hurried from the room. Thom, Beverly, Lorene stared after her astonished.

In a lowered voice Beverly said with a grim smile, "*Her,* too."

"DADDY WOULDN'T MIND in the slightest."

"Are you kidding? Daddy would *love this.*"

That night, drinking Whitey's Johnnie Walker Black Label whiskey in the kitchen of the house on Old Farm Road.

They weren't bothering to microwave pizzas tonight. They'd eaten in the hospital café earlier that evening, in shifts. In the cupboard they'd discovered boxes of cereal, *Wheaties, Cheerios, Rice Chex,* they were devouring in handfuls, like nuts. Remains of Whitey's favorite cheeses, the last of the Swedish crackers. A jar of peanut butter, eaten with spoons as they'd never dared eat it when they were children in this house.

"Did you know, there's a specific phobia about peanut butter?—'fear of peanut butter sticking between teeth.'"

"No! You made that up."

"I *did not*. Why'd I even think of anything so weird?"

"There are all kinds of phobias. Claustrophobia, agoraphobia—everybody knows about them. But there's 'equinophobia'—fear of horses. There's fear of spiders, cockroaches—"

"There's fear of dogs, sex, blood, death . . . Anything, you can add 'phobia.'"

"That's right. Anything."

Flatly Thom spoke. The topic had worn itself out.

Jessalyn had gone to bed almost as soon as she'd come home from the hospital. Sophia had slipped away to curl up in her old bed beneath a comforter, removing just her outer clothing and shoes. And

Virgil, the exasperating one, had neither found a place to sleep in the house nor joined them at the kitchen table for a late-night whiskey but had chosen to wander about outside in the dim cold light of a quarter-moon.

"What d'you suppose Virgil is doing? Communicating with extraterrestrials?"

They laughed, in scorn. Though uneasily.

(Swallowing whiskey that burned wonderfully as it passed down her throat and into the region of her heart Beverly wondered: Who knew? Their brother resembled an extra-terrestrial himself!)

(Thinking of, what was it, a movie she'd seen as a teenager—*The Man Who Fell to Earth*? Eerie-eyed, epicene David Bowie as an extra-terrestrial being with some sort of doomed plan for—whatever, she'd forgotten, or had found too confusing at the time to comprehend.)

"I can't figure out where he sleeps. Maybe in the basement, on the sofa."

"His old room . . ."

"He avoids that. He said."

"Why?"

"Christ, who knows *why*. Ask Virgil."

"I find my old room comforting. I guess. Though it's strange to wake up in the morning and realize—like a ton of bricks it hits you—*I'm not a kid any longer, I have kids.*"

"Jesus! Yes."

"Remember, at school, kids would ask us if we were Catholic?—five kids."

"That isn't such a lot . . ."

"It *is*. At our school it's getting to be unusual if there are *two siblings* in a family, let alone five."

To make her point, Lorene paused. Beverly bristled knowing you were supposed to think *More than two siblings, lower-class. Could be black, Hispanic, poor-white but bottom-line, uneducated.*

She and Steve had more than two children, in fact more than three children, which Lorene knew. But damn if she'd let her sister rile her at this hour, *she would not*.

"Mom used to say, very pleasantly, in that way of hers that's dignified—'No, we are not Catholics. We just like children.'"

"We're the largest family on Old Farm Road . . ."

"Mostly everyone else here is *old*. Our neighbors haven't had children at home for years."

"Well, Mom and Dad don't have children 'at home' now either. Though I don't think of them as *old*."

Thinking of poor Whitey. Fact was, since the stroke, Whitey was indeed looking *old*.

"Still, it's pretty clear that Sophia was an accident."

"And Virgil."

In the way of older siblings secure in the belief that they were *wanted* by their parents they laughed together conspiratorially.

"Virgil's more than an accident, he's an aberration."

"What's it called?—mutation . . ."

"Poor Mom! You ever get the feeling, Daddy blames her for how Virgil turned out?"

"Daddy *does not*. What a—an inappropriate thing to say. Daddy would never blame Mom for anything she did or—didn't do."

"He didn't want her to work, though."

"He never said she couldn't—I'm sure."

"Well. Mom had wanted to teach, she has a degree in education and was taking graduate courses in something fancy like 'comp lit' . . ."

"Taking care of Daddy is a full-time occupation. Not to mention five children and this house."

"Everyone envied us, our 'perfect' mom."

"I think Mom *is* perfect."

"A perfect 'mom'—yes. No question."

Lapsing into silence then as Thom splashed more of the amber liquid into their glasses, and they drank.

— ∞ —

"Hi, Dad."

Shyly he spoke. He had yet to become accustomed to approaching his father *in bed*.

(Had he ever? Even as a young child? Been invited to approach his father *in bed*?)

(The parents' bedroom, off-limits. Even if Virgil had wished to explore that part of the house he would not have dared. No!)

(Though now, as an adult, visiting Mom, he might wander anywhere in the house he wished, his mother would neither know nor care, outside in her garden, or in another part of the house oblivious of what Virgil was up to. *You know, I trust you.*)

(But Jessalyn would never say to any of them, *You know, I trust you*. For it was understood that their mother loved them and trusted them in all things.)

"It's Virgil, Dad. Hi."

So awkward! His tongue felt swollen in his mouth.

So strange to approach his father *in bed* and to come so close. For in life, Virgil and Whitey would not ever find themselves *so close*.

In normal circumstances Whitey would draw away from Virgil half-consciously. In normal circumstances, Virgil would keep a discreet distance from Whitey. All this was accomplished without conscious negotiation, awareness. (How many inches, minimum? Twelve, twenty?) No handshake, no hearty hug.

But these were not normal circumstances of course. In a hospital there are no normal circumstances. Virgil had noted, with alarm, how the floor of a hospital room is susceptible to sudden shiftings, disorientations. You believe that you are standing upright until you are not.

On the hospital stairs more than once he'd been just slightly dazed, dizzied. Avoiding the elevator though (he knew) the others were annoyed by him, eccentric behavior, yes but no behavior is actually *ec-*

centric but rather *purposeful*. How'd he tell them, who disliked him anyway, that he did not want to crowd into an elevator with them, breathing their exhaled breaths, pressing close, Thom, Beverly, Lorene, even Sophia, even Jessalyn, *no thank you*.

Elevator claustrophobia is just family life, condensed. To the size of an elevator.

He'd brought his flute. Without the flute, what would he do with his hands? What would he *do*?

In the cranked-up hospital bed the sixty-seven-year-old patient was neither obviously asleep nor was he obviously awake. He was neither obviously aware of his visitor seated uneasily near him nor was he unaware. His ravaged face was ruddier than Virgil recalled, and his eyelids quivered almost continuously as if he were debating, arguing with himself. His mouth too quivered, damp with spittle. Almost you might think that he was about to speak at any moment as it seemed that, at any moment, the not-quite-focused right eye would sharpen to attention, and *see*.

Clearly, some violence had been done to this man's head. His thinning gray hair had been shaved unevenly, exposing his pale, mottled scalp.

Beefy arms, stippled with bruises and mysterious wounds like infected insect bites. What Virgil could see of his father's torso, fatty-muscled, gray-grizzly-haired, inside the loose-fitting white hospital gown, this too was stippled with the mysterious wounds though they were less evident here, or had begun to fade. Virgil did not want to think of how a catheter was draining urine from his father's body in a slow stream into a plastic container beneath his bed even as the IV dripped liquids into his veins as in some bizarre Rube Goldberg machinery meant to make you smile at—what?—the vanity of human existence, or its ingenuity?

Or, desperation.

Please don't die, Daddy. Not yet.

Too many flowers in this room. Heavy, potted mums and dyed-looking hydrangea on the windowsill. Fruit baskets covered with crackling cellophane no one had yet unwrapped. *Get well* cards. Please, no.

Yet more bizarrely, well-wishers had brought gifts for the "convalescent"—hardcover books of the kind (*The Butterfly Effect: How Your Life Matters; Blink: The Power of Thinking Without Thinking; A Brief History of the Universe*) Whitey McClaren was always reading, or trying to read. It seemed to Virgil particularly ironic that such books were brought to the stroke-victim who would have difficulty learning to "read" again in the most elementary way.

On the wall just inside the door, the hand-sanitizer. All medical workers, all visitors, were instructed to sanitize their hands whenever entering the room.

The first time he'd entered his father's room in Intensive Care, Virgil had been instructed (by Sophia) to sanitize his hands—"Here, Virgil. Always remember!"

In his distracted state at the time he'd scarcely noticed the sanitizer. It was like Virgil to think, not entirely consciously, that routine behavior prescribed for others was not inevitably prescribed for him.

Yet, he'd washed his hands briskly in the disinfectant. He'd felt like a boy washing his hands to please his mother—a boy *again*—and in that way safe.

But only in that way. And so, not really *safe*.

"Remember, Virgil. Each time."

Looking anxious, Sophia had made a gesture with her hands as if washing them. Virgil had nodded—*Of course*.

Now drawing a deep breath. Lifting the flute to his lips. Positioning his fingers, and beginning to play.

Earnest, breathy notes—so airy, you couldn't define them as flute-sounds. (In fact, the instrument was Virgil's approximation of a flute, carved by him from elderberry wood.)

Virgil had tried to explain to his family, it wasn't conventional music he wanted to play for his stricken father, or not music exactly, but something else, a communication special to Whitey from him, from Virgil, for he feared that actual music would be too complicated for the stroke victim to absorb like a damaged eye confronted with too much stimuli.

Something like a prayer—*his* prayer for Whitey.

Jessalyn had seen to it that Virgil had time alone with his father each morning. The others had resented him, perhaps. But Jessalyn had held firm; she knew that Virgil would be shunted aside by his older siblings, and would never dare assert himself to their father. For this Virgil was grateful to his mother—for this, and so much more!—but uneasy too for intimacy made all transactions too significant, too important, intimacy is always close-up. He felt most comfortable at a little distance.

It was he who'd pushed Sabine from him. Not Sabine who'd pushed him. Though, physically, *literally* you might've interpreted it otherwise, as (possibly, though not probably) Sabine might feel free to interpret it. If.

These thoughts went through his head, as he played the flute for Whitey. His tongue still felt swollen, and his fingers felt awkward, yet the flute-sounds were beautiful (in Virgil's ears at least) and (he thought) were making an impression on the stricken man, whose bruised eyelids fluttered with a new urgency, and whose lips seemed to be straining to speak even as, with his (bruised, wound-stippled) left hand, very slowly, with what appeared to be enormous effort, he reached toward Virgil, lacking the (evident) strength to lift his hand but pushing it along the bed, and spreading his fingers as Virgil had not seen him spread his fingers since the stroke, and his mouth moved as if in a spasm, and to his astonishment Virgil heard "Vir-gil"—unmistakably, the first coherent word Whitey McClaren had uttered in these several days in the hospital.

Vir-gil.

Virgil stared at his father, transfixed. He was not certain that he'd heard what he had heard. The flute slipped through his fingers and clattered to the floor.

Then, he burst into tears.

The Return of Whitey

H'yeh."

All he could manage for now. But smiling with half his face and his (bloodshot, tearful) left eye clear and in focus and *seeing*.

For this, they rejoiced. That left eye *seeing*.

And he could move his head—he could *nod*. With some calculation, deliberation, intensity—*nod*.

And he could move—(not exactly "use")—his left hand almost normally or (maybe) almost almost-normally and nothing was more thrilling to them than to approach his room, and enter the room, taking deep breaths before entering in anticipation or in apprehension of what they might see (for each visit was both a re-visit and an entirely new, terrifyingly new visit) but there he was, their Whitey, almost-again-Whitey, sitting up now in the cranked-up bed, pillows behind his back, head lifted of its own (seeming) volition, (some degree of) muscular coordination restored, that "alertness" of being we take for granted in ourselves and others, that constitutes "life"—"livingness"—"sentience"; most wonderfully, to arrive with no expectation at all to see how with the assistance of a nurse's aide Whitey is holding, or seems to be holding, in his tremulous left hand, a small container of orange juice, and is sucking liquid through a straw.

Unfathomable to calculate the effort of (firing) brain neurons, coordination of myriad nerves in the left arm and hand, muscle and tissue, bone-joints, each required in tandem with the others to produce *sucking liquid through a straw.*

SHE KISSES HIM, she weeps with relief.

With the terrible strain of relief, that feels like blinding light in a dark-adapted eye.

The Blessing Stopped

Thom determined: his father didn't remember what happened to him that day. Didn't remember the stroke and didn't remember what preceded the stroke and what followed the stroke. When he'd awakened in the hospital, in this room and in this bed, hearing Virgil's flute, he'd been utterly baffled, astonished—*How'd the hell he get* here? Though at the time lacking the ability to express this astonishment.

Only after he was told that he'd been returning home from a trustees' luncheon at the library when he was stricken did Whitey seem to think yes, he did remember—something.

"The library, Dad? You remember—you had a meeting?"

Nodding *yes*. But not with certainty. So that Thom was inclined to think that his father was really remembering another, previous meeting at the library, not the last meeting, shortly before his stroke.

The Hammond Public Library trustees had luncheon meetings every other month. Very likely, Whitey was conflating these.

Whitey's long-term memory had not been seriously affected by the stroke, so far as anyone could determine: he recognized faces, he seemed to know names, he'd been made to understand where he was, in Hammond General. But he seemed to have no memory for events that must have occurred just before the stroke, like getting into his car, driving on the Hennicott Expressway, braking to a stop . . .

Whitey didn't remember a "stroke"—of course. All he could say when asked what he did remember was a stuttering syllable—"B-B-Bl'k."

"'Black,' Dad?"

"Yy. B-B-Bl'k."

Whitey's good, left eye awash with tears his family interpreted as tears of triumph, that he was able at last to speak to them.

Not in the presence of his family, nor within hearing of any of the medical staff, Thom asked Whitey if he remembered Hammond police officers? Possibly being flagged down for a traffic stop?

No. He did not.

A police siren? Police cruiser pulling up behind him, beside him?

No. He did not.

Pulling off the Expressway, braking his car on the shoulder of the road . . .

No. He did not.

If Whitey wondered why Thom was asking these questions he gave no sign. He'd become, since the stroke, not only slow-speaking but slow to become impatient, even curious. The old Whitey would've asked why the hell was Thom asking him these questions about cops but the new, post-stroke Whitey exuded an air of childlike trust and infinite patience.

You had the feeling (Thom thought) that the poor man was begging *Please don't abandon me. I don't know how to answer you but I am still Whitey, please don't abandon me.*

Often it wasn't clear if Whitey was actually hearing, or comprehending, what was being said to him. But he'd learned to smile with half his mouth, eagerly. He'd learned to nod his head in an arc of an inch or two—*Yes.*

Or—no.

As, in the prime of his life, Whitey McClaren had never acknowledged being sick if he could avoid it. Severe colds, flu, bronchitis and even, one winter, ambulatory pneumonia and a high fever. His stoicism was bound up with masculine pride, vanity. *Never show your enemies any weakness* had been his mantra since high school football days.

His children had laughed at their father, Whitey was so stiff-backed about what people thought of him. Macho vanity, the girls thought it. But loved him anyway.

Thom understood. Of course. A man doesn't show his weakness to other men.

What Virgil thought, Thom didn't know and didn't care to know.

Several times Thom had spoken with doctors in the hospital about his father's mysterious wounds. He was deeply suspicious that these were wounds consistent with stun-gun shots which meant that his sixty-seven-year-old father might have been hit with charges as high as fifty thousand volts of electricity!—enough to fell a heavyset man in the prime of life.

Enough to fell a steer, before slaughter.

But the wounds were fading amid myriad bruises precipitated by frequent blood work and anti-coagulant medication. Except for the pictures Thom had taken on his cell phone, which would be difficult to substantiate. The Hammond PD claimed to have no record of John Earle McClaren being stopped by law enforcement officers on October 18.

The family was vastly relieved that Whitey was better, and improving daily. Wasn't that all that mattered? If he didn't recall what had happened to him, wasn't that a blessing? After five days on the critical list he'd been transferred from Intensive Care to Telemetry, and was scheduled to be transferred directly from Telemetry to a rehabilitation clinic at University of Rochester Medical Center, possibly as soon as the following week. All this was very good news.

Exhausted by the hospital vigil Thom had not mentioned his suspicions to anyone in the family. He'd held off contacting a lawyer. Whitey seemed to have been hospitalized already for weeks rather than days and the ordeal—the vigil—had not yet ended. Perhaps it would never entirely end.

Thom had not encouraged his wife to drive to Hammond, to visit her father-in-law. The more visitors Whitey had, the more distracting and exhausting it was. Thom was eager to return to some semblance of his own life in Rochester; he'd tried to keep up with work at the publishing house by way of telephone calls, emails. He had a reliable assistant. But he was eager to return, for there was much that had to be overseen by him, in person.

Possibly, best to let his suspicions go, for now. Since Whitey was going to be all right.

For maybe Thom was mistaken after all. He had not been thinking clearly for some time. Possibly, Whitey had somehow banged himself up as his vehicle lurched to a stop. He'd struck his face against the steering wheel, the windshield. He'd climbed out of the car and collapsed and cut his face on gravel.

This Thom knew: Whitey would be very reluctant to initiate any sort of adversarial claim against the Hammond PD for he'd been proud of his relationship with the police when he'd been mayor. He had invariably taken the side of the police in disputes with citizens even when (as Thom recalled) it was likely to assume that police officers had committed misconduct and had violated the civil rights of civilians.

They have a tough job. Out there making split decisions. Could cost them their lives. Not good to second-guess our brave law enforcement officers.

These were Whitey's words, precisely. And that grim truculent look of Whitey's. In the parlance of politics, *doubling-down.*

You took a public position, and dug in your heels. You took a position that drew strength to you, from the strength of an ally whom you would protect and defend whether he deserved it or not just as, one day, *quid pro quo,* your ally would protect and defend you whether you deserved it or not.

The Steady Hand

"Sophia! You have the steady hand."

Praise in the form of a jest. Or has it been a jest in the form of praise.

Praise and jest commingled, in a kind of caress.

Though it is indisputably true. Everyone in the lab would agree. Of Alistair Means's several skilled and trusted assistants at the Memorial Park Research Institute it is Sophia McClaren who displays the steadiest hand in the laboratory: injecting the tiny rodents, decapitating the tiny rodents, dissecting the tiny rodents.

AND YOU HAVE THE MOST BEAUTIFUL HANDS, *Sophia. But you know this.*

You, the young unmarried and (so far as one can guess) unattached female research assistant whom I single out for the sort of praise no one can—quite—decode: (frankly sexual) (congenial, friendly though also sexual) (congenial, friendly and not sexual at all) (each of these) (none of these).

BRAINS REMOVED FROM TINY SKULLS, examined under microscopes. Exquisite tiny organs "harvested"—"isolated"—rendered as "data."

All that is, is rendered to "data."

What is not "data," is not.

Fiercely proud, wants to be proud, Sophia McClaren has the steadiest hand.

And yes, it is a beautiful hand—long slender fingers, nails always very clean, unpolished and evenly filed.

She is aware of him observing her. His eyes moving on her, and lingering. And that sensation of excited warmth that rises in her, from the pit of her stomach into the region of her heart, when he speaks to her, when he is kind to her, asking after the *family emergency* that had kept her out of the lab for nearly a week.

Quickly she tells him the emergency is over. The crisis. The hospital vigil.

One of her parents?—he asks.

She hesitates before telling him yes, her father.

"But he's better now?"

"Yes. Better now."

There is a pause. It is up to Sophia (she supposes) to supply more information.

But she doesn't want to utter the word *stroke*. For then she will be obliged to provide further information—*hemorrhagic stroke, aphasia, partial paralysis*.

He says, awkwardly, "Well. If you need anything . . ." Pausing as if he has no idea what to say next.

Sometimes, his manner with his assistants is brusque, jocular. Not conversation but banter quick, deft and of no more significance than a swift Ping-Pong volley, to get talking out of the way, before settling into the day's serious business.

But now, Means is hesitant, regarding Sophia. He has noticed the bruise-like shadows around her eyes, the pallor of her skin, a frantic elation in her voice. *Oh yes! Better now. We are all—so relieved*.

It is not like him to stand so close beside her. As if unaware (is he?) of what he is doing.

Sophia shifts her position, just slightly. She feels that sensation of excited warmth another time.

She hears herself tell her supervisor that she is very grateful to be back. She has missed the lab, she has missed their work.

Not wanting to say—*I missed you! I miss the person I become, in your presence.*

"Exactitude. That's what we miss, when we are out of the lab and in the 'world.'"

His Scots accent is faint but unmistakable though he has lived in the United States for many years.

"'Exactitude.' Yes."

Sophia has never heard any scientist speak in quite this way. But it is true, Means has named it. *Exactitude*—the precision of assembling evidence, methodically accruing "data"—what is missing in life, in what's called the world.

Another time Means asks Sophia if he can be of help, somehow. If (for instance) she needs anyone to drive her—anywhere . . .

"Thank you. But I guess—no. I have my own car . . ."

It is the most insipid statement. Sophia has no idea what she is saying.

Suddenly, they are very awkward with each other. They are not quite able to look at each other. Means bares his teeth in a fleeting smile as he turns away with a wave of his hand.

It is an extraordinary exchange, in these circumstances. Yet, it is ordinary, banal. Sophia must not make too much of it.

She is weak with relief, that something terrible has not happened—yet. Exhausted from nights of half-sleep and suffused with gratitude for her good fortune that includes now Alistair Means's kindness to her at this fraught time Sophia thinks—*I will love him. This man.*

OUR YOUNGEST DAUGHTER SOPHIA, *she's a Ph.D. research scientist at Memorial Park, on an A-list team working on a cure for cancer. Jesus, we're proud of her!*

She has overheard her father boasting shamelessly of her. She has wanted to laugh, and she has wanted to press her hands over her ears and run away.

Of course Whitey has exaggerated her position at the Institute. He has exaggerated (Sophia has always thought) all of his children's accomplishments (except Virgil's, of which he seems scarcely aware). You would almost think that John Earle McClaren looks at his family, his "offspring," with something like astonishment. *These are—mine. How has this happened?*

True, Sophia McClaren is one of a team of researchers involved in a massive experiment but she is only an assistant to the principal investigator, one who follows instructions and not (yet) one who helps devise the highly complicated science.

Smartest of the kids and hardest-working but I worry about Sophia, she takes after her mother, believes the best of everyone and is too trusting, doesn't know the first thing about protecting herself.

Hearing this Sophia wanted to protest, that is not true! She is plenty protective of herself, she believes. In ways her dear unsuspecting parents could never guess.

She has never allowed herself to fall in love, for instance. The very cliché—*fall in love*—brings a smile to her lips.

She has never allowed herself to become *too close* to another person, beyond her family.

Friends from high school have drifted off. Perhaps it has been Sophia's fault, perhaps not. Most of them have married, have become mothers. It is enough Sophia can do, to muster up interest in, affection for, her nieces and nephews, her parents' grandchildren of whom she (sometimes) feels rivalry, just a little, observing her parents with them; she has no interest at all in her friends' children. How boring, babies! Nor are Sophia's girl-cousins with whom she'd been friendly through adolescence of much interest to her now that she has embarked upon a career in science.

To these cousins, Sophia's seriousness and sobriety are *boring.*

Yet she has always sought the admiration of others. Especially, she has sought the admiration and approval of her parents. Their unquestioning love for her has kept her young, she thinks. Perhaps too young.

Though she is no longer a girl, she is still a daughter.

It is a relief to Sophia, the McClarens have no idea what her research actually involves. Nor do they understand that Sophia has deferred her Ph.D. (at Cornell) in order to work in a laboratory funded by a pharmaceutical company.

Maybe this is a mistake, Sophia isn't sure. Deferring her adult life, in a sense. Always she has been the very best student, the most valued intern, the "indispensable" assistant. It is a role that fits her tight as a glove. At twenty-eight she could easily be mistaken for twenty, or eighteen. Emotionally, she isn't so much young as untried, untested.

But Alistair Means has made it clear that he has a very high opinion of her.

Sophia has fallen under the spell of the Lumex project. Her own dissertation project at Cornell is overly theoretical, she thinks. Her own research, her own ideas, are not so attractive to her as those of others with more authority, in truth she is frightened (a little) at the possibility of being mistaken, squandering months and years of her life on a project of her own devising that might very well (for this is the nature of science!) come to nothing. The Lumex project is here, now. *Seeking a cure for cancer. Specific kinds of cancers.*

She can live in Hammond, within a few miles of the house on Old Farm Road.

In Ithaca, at the edge of the vast Cornell campus, she'd felt lonely, isolated. There, her work had not seemed sufficient to her, to give meaning to her life.

So badly Sophia wants these experiments to yield results! Powerful chemical compounds that will shrink cancerous growths, or kill cancerous cells before they take root. Drugs to counter the injurious effects of cancer chemotherapy. Cancer treatments customized to individual cancers . . .

Whitey's pride in her will be confirmed, one day. She is willing to wait a long time.

It is a relief, how each day Whitey is improving. He has regained (almost) the use of his left hand and he is regaining (by degrees) the ability to speak. He can make his (labored, valiant) way now, with assistance, into the bathroom close by his bedroom, though his right leg yet dangles useless, like his right arm. Next week he will be transferred to the Stroke Center at the University of Rochester Medical Center.

Haltingly he speaks. With much difficulty he speaks. Spittle on his lips, an effort of heart-straining valor as he tries to move his (paralyzed) right arm hanging limp onto the bedclothes.

". . . c'pse am. J's h'ngs t'ere."

Of the observers only Sophia can decipher her father's words:

"'Corpse arm. Just hangs there.'"

Whitey does not seem disconsolate, uttering these attempts at words. More, his battered face conveys an air of genial resignation.

The McClaren children have returned to their own lives. Thom has returned to his family and work in Rochester and keeps in close contact with Jessalyn. Lorene and Sophia have returned to work and drop by the hospital each evening. Jessalyn is always there, at Whitey's bedside, and Beverly is often with her. At unpredictable times Virgil shows up, to play his flute which Whitey quite likes.

No one is sleeping over at the house on Old Farm Road now. Though Beverly has offered to stay with her Jessalyn has insisted that she return home to her own family at night.

Family emergency Sophia called it. Explaining why she'd had to be away from the lab for what has seemed a very long time and not only a few days.

Indeed it is something of a shock, to return. Driving the interstate in another direction, north and not south into downtown Hammond. Stepping out of bright October sunshine into the fluorescent-lit interior of the research lab where no ventilator is powerful enough to entirely carry away the sour smells of bodily wastes, animal misery and terror, death.

It is a morning of decapitation and dissection to which she has returned. A test for Sophia's steady hand which she does not intend to fail.

Walls of cages. Timorous, shivering little rodents. Nervous chatter. Some of the specimens are bloated and hairless, some are anorexic, shriveled. Some appear to be robust, even manic. Most others are enervated. The tiny bodies of some are riddled with tumors that may have shrunken, or may not have shrunken. All to be discovered that very day, and rendered into "data."

Tiny rodents, injected with diverse strains of cancerous cells. In stages, following a complex algorithm devised by Alistair Means, the rodents are injected with "anti-cancerous" pharmaceutical compounds and, in time, in carefully calibrated stages, dissected to determine if the cancerous tumors riddling their tiny bodies have shrunk. If there are side effects—(of course, there are side effects)—these are duly noted. The Lumex project has been a highly complicated sequence of overlapping experiments involving thousands of laboratory animals over the years, in process long before Sophia McClaren was hired as an assistant.

Slipping on latex gloves. Tight-tight, can't breathe, the glove that is your life, you learn to breathe inside it.

Some of the mice are decapitated with a small, razor-sharp device. (Sophia wonders who was the inventor of such a device. Who patented the ingenious guillotine, who manufactures and profits from it.) Most are dispatched with a lethal injection from a very thin needle.

Strange, the tiny creature scarcely resists. It is a consequence of the *steady hand,* perhaps.

In the experimental lab, precision is the highest form of mercy.

A swift injection into the belly. A final spasm, final squeak, lifeless.

Now, the scalpel . . .

Her work is thrilling to her. At least, it is thrilling to perceive from a little distance. *The end does justify the means. You must believe this.*

Consider the battery of drugs involved in her father's post-stroke treatment. All of these drugs, FDA approved, had to be tested initially on animals. Induced strokes in primates (marmosets, monkeys) from pinpoint to massive. Anti-coagulants, coagulants.

Psychosurgery: incisions in primate brains, removal of parts of brains, halving of brains. Induced paralysis, spinal cords severed. Can a mutilated brain "repair itself"? Can brain cells undergo "neurogenesis"?

It is now forbidden by United States law to experiment on living persons without their consent. Though in the past researchers often conducted such experiments among captive subjects in prisons, orphanages, mental hospitals. Especially vulnerable were mentally ill or developmentally challenged persons whose families gave researchers permission out of naivete or desperation.

Sophia McClaren would never have participated in such experiments, had she been a young scientist in those years. She wants to think so.

Proud of you, honey. Such important work you are doing.

Sophia's eyes fill with tears of gratitude. Tight-gloved hands unfaltering as the tiny creatures spasm and die between her fingers and the smell of their small deaths lifts to her nostrils.

"SOPHIA?"—THE VOICE IS LOWERED, unexpectedly close.

She glances around, startled. Feels a flush of heat in her face. How long has Alistair Means been standing there just a few feet away, why has he approached her so quietly . . .

"Excuse me. I'd like to check your data, if I may."

"Yes! Of course."

She stands aside. She watches his fingers move rapidly over the keyboard. His concentration shifts to the computer screen, he leans forward, frowning.

It is late afternoon. Hours have passed swiftly, Sophia is scarcely conscious of how tired she has become.

So many miniature death-spasms on this utilitarian counter-top, so many miniature tumorous organs "harvested." Her eyes ache from squinting. Her head aches from the strain of leaning forward to record data on the computer, hunching her shoulders.

Whatever Dr. Means sees on the computer screen, he is (at least tentatively) pleased.

"Thank you, Sophia."

He does not always call his assistants by their first names, Sophia has noticed.

His way of enunciating her name—*Soph-i-a.* She wants to think this is a tender sound.

Means is not like other men Sophia has known, at the Institute and elsewhere. Men who make it clear that they are attracted to her and who (therefore) exert pressure on her, however obliquely, however genially, to respond to their interest in her.

She cannot decode Alistair Means. Perhaps it is entirely her imagination, his "interest" in her. Perhaps it is entirely unconscious on his part, and he has no idea how frequently, in Sophia's presence, he seems to be staring at her. In her more subdued emotional mood she cannot decide if she is truly attracted to the man, or feels nothing more for him than admiration for his intelligence, his reputation, and his zeal as a scientist. Perhaps she feels a subordinate's ignoble hope of advancing her career, through him. She isn't sure, even, that she trusts him.

It is believed that Alistair Means is a "brilliant" research scientist. Yet, to his staff at the Institute, Means is something of a riddle.

At times he is friendly, affable. At other times, brusque to the point of rudeness. He is gentlemanly, courteous, patient, kind. He is not at all patient—his fingers drum with irritation when you try to speak to him. He is stiffly formal, and rarely smiles. Oh yes he will smile—when you don't expect it.

He is generous with young scientists. He is (sometimes) not-so-generous with his colleagues.

He has an eye for women. *He rarely notices women!*

But here is an uncontested fact: Alistair Means arrives each weekday morning at the Institute in a sport coat, a white shirt, a necktie; not once has he been glimpsed in jeans or khakis or any sort of casual attire. Perversely, he never wears dress shoes, only just a pair of badly worn moccasins or a pair of badly worn running shoes. With white socks.

In the lab, he wears a clinician's white cord coat. He goes through a box of latex gloves within a few days. Indeed, Dr. Means has a medical degree though he has never practiced medicine; his Ph.D., in molecular biology, is from Harvard.

He has published more than three hundred papers in his highly specialized field, Sophia has learned. He has been a mentor to a number of young scientists scattered across the country at the most distinguished research centers.

He has also been known to "terminate" young scientists and staff members, without explanation.

Or maybe—(for this is all conjecture)—these are rumors circulated by those who were terminated with good cause, and are embittered.

Alistair Means is in his early forties but looks older. His thick, wavy, steel-colored hair has begun to recede from his forehead and there are distinct lines, like opening crevices, in his cheeks; his jaws are covered in a short-trimmed beard much grayer than his hair. His posture is very straight, perhaps because he is not a tall man. Out of a kind of aggressive courtliness he behaves like a man of another, earlier era: he was born in Edinburgh and was brought with his family to the United States as an adolescent. His accent is faint but unmistakable though he has lived in the United States for more than thirty years.

That slurred, melodic accent!—how subtle an accent *is*. Sophia finds herself entranced by the peculiar music of her supervisor's speech, quite apart from what he is saying.

Before Memorial Park, Means taught molecular biology at Columbia and Rockefeller University; for the past seven years he has headed the Memorial Park Research Institute, which has received millions of dollars of funding under his auspices, much of it from pharmaceutical companies like Lumex, Inc. The rumor is, despite a very high salary Means is absurdly frugal: he drives a not-new Honda Civic, he lives in a single-bedroom condominium in an undistinguished neighborhood in North Hammond. Sometimes, he even bicycles to work, a distance of nine miles.

When Sophia was new to the lab Alistair Means had seemed at times scarcely to know who she was. (Though he'd hired her himself.) She'd been conditioned not to smile at her supervisor and not to say *Good morning, Dr. Means!*—for he seemed startled by such effrontery from his staff and rarely responded in kind.

Is he married? *Was* he married? In any case it is rumored that Means is estranged from his wife/ex-wife and his (near-grown) children who live in a distant city. He has never been seen frequently with any woman, at the Institute at least. If he has male friends, he is rarely seen with them; his closest associates are his post-docs, who are all male, youthful heirs.

Sophia has encountered her supervisor on the grounds of the Institute, where he is likely to be walking alone, staring at the ground before him distracted and frowning, lost in thought and oblivious of his surroundings. Sometimes, he stops to take notes. Sophia has been surprised to see him bicycling along the highway, against traffic—not on a battered bicycle like Virgil but on an English racer.

She has watched him, and felt a wave of tenderness for a man who seems so alone, unaware even of his aloneness.

What is he thinking about? she wonders. His work, his life? His family?

But Alistair Means has no family, has he?—Sophia thinks this must be so.

Smiling to think—*But I have more than enough family, for two!*

NEXT DAY, AT HAMMOND GENERAL, visiting Whitey, seeing a white-coated older doctor making his rounds, she finds herself thinking of Alistair Means.

It is the first time she has thought of Alistair Means outside the Institute.

Is this a good sign, or not such a good sign? Sophia does not want the stress of more *hope* in her life.

Tempted to confide in her mother that she has met a man, at the Institute, in whom she is "interested"—but no, that would be a mistake, for Jessalyn would be too happy for her and really there isn't likely to be any future in Alistair Means.

In recent years Sophia has become such a solitary person, the idea of love blossoms in her imagination as it could not in actual life. Takes root, emerges, blossoms and effloresces. Petals fall to the ground, bruised.

Her actual encounters with men have been awkward. She is all elbows, almost literally. A man's mouth on hers—her breath is sucked away. She feels a rush of excitement but simultaneously a counter-rush like the palm of a hand pushing against her chest, hard. She laughs inappropriately, and too loudly.

Her unease in her body seems to have begun when she was ten or eleven, keenly aware of slightly older girls, her older sisters.

Am I expected to look like—that? My God.

To the neutral eye Sophia McClaren is poised, thoughtful. She smiles readily, she is as gracious as her mother Jessalyn McClaren, whom she superficially resembles.

Is she considered a beautiful young woman, or—not-so-beautiful? She is very vain—her mirror-reflection makes her wince for it is not how she wishes to appear. She is shy to see herself. Her eyes are too large, and set too deep in their sockets—her expression is stark, startled, owl-like, yearning. Her hair is stiff with static electricity, the hue of something burnt. Her hands move nervously like laboratory creatures that climb over one another in desperation. Her clothes swim on her slender body, a size or two too large. Yet, she is detached, distant. Irony numbs her like Novocain.

Oh, impossible! If a man's eyes move onto her, Sophia wants to hide her face.

Better yet, stick out her tongue. *Don't look at me! Please.*

She knows, Jessalyn is concerned for her. All the old, tiresome clichés, the concern of a mother that her daughter find a companion, or a lover; be found by a companion, a lover; marry, have children, perpetrate the race—these clichés live and thrive in Jessalyn McClaren, like germs in a petri dish.

Mom!—I think I am falling in love.

But no. Ridiculous. She is not a schoolgirl.

Besides, all talk among the McClarens is of Whitey's condition. His transfer to a rehabilitation clinic in Rochester which is scheduled for Tuesday of the following week. His therapy will mean a massive overhauling of Jessalyn's life. Weeks that Whitey will be a patient in the clinic in Rochester, followed by weeks—months—when Whitey will be an outpatient. So long as Whitey is in the clinic, Jessalyn will stay with Thom and his family; the clinic is only four miles from their house. When Whitey returns home, Jessalyn will be his primary caretaker. She has been online learning about the post-stroke therapy he will be prescribed, which is grueling and relentless but (almost) guaranteed to "work miracles." She is planning to take a training course at the local community college—Life after Stroke: A Learner's Manual. It is the most enthusiastic Jessalyn's children have seen her in recent memory.

"Mom, you should have been a nurse!"—Beverly said, marveling; but Sophia said, reprovingly, "No. Mom should have been a *doctor*."

Whitey has visitors, a steady stream of visitors, now that he is off the hospital's critical list. His room is filled with flowers, gift baskets, books, even crudely cute stuffed animals, every surface taken, parts of the floor. Those nurses who had not known that John Earle McClaren had once been mayor of Hammond have begun to see that their "Mr. McClaren"—"Whitey"—is a very popular man.

("Before your father is discharged maybe I could have his autograph?"—one of the nurses asks Sophia.)

It's a relief for the McClaren children to be returning to some semblance of normal life. Only Jessalyn is at the hospital from morning to night; the others drop by when they can, or telephone. Sophia is annoyed that, whenever she visits, Beverly is always there; she even eats with Whitey and Jessalyn, for visitors can arrange to buy meals. Gaily Beverly says, "Steve is accusing me of 'abandoning' my family—as if he'd ever noticed me when I was at his beck and call."

Does Beverly really not like her husband?—Sophia wonders. Loves him, but doesn't much like him? Resents him? And does not seem to trust him. Why are some marriages so *strange*?

She has not thought that she wants to be married. Even her fantasies of Alistair Means do not include marriage. She would not want to marry a man less devoted to her than Whitey is to Jessalyn; yet frankly, she would not be capable of being so devoted to any man as Jessalyn is to Whitey.

In sickness and in health. In death do us part.

But wait, this doesn't sound right. *At death do us part?*

To death—do us part?

It is the most extraordinary of vows. Who in her right mind could conceive of such an extravagant promise . . .

Like squeezing into a sleeping bag with another person, and zipping the bag up. Forever!

So long as Sophia has her parents to love her, she doesn't really need the love of another person. No lover, no husband, could compete with Jessalyn and Whitey who ask so little of her, only just that she remain their daughter.

A silken cord, of a kind. So wonderful to have a family *close-knit* as theirs! She'd said to Virgil, "We don't actually have to *grow up*. We are spared having to start families of our own."

Virgil didn't think this was funny. A prim Virgil-face and scolding words.

"Well. Mom and Dad won't be around forever."

"'Forever' is a long time, Virgil. I don't plan ahead that far."

Recklessly Sophia spoke, as if her profligate words were untrue.

FRIDAY AFTERNOON AT 5:00 P.M. Alistair Means is giving a presentation at the Institute—"The Evolutionary Role of Mutations: A Theory."

Everyone in the lab will be there of course. All of Means's associates and staff. It is the first day of a three-day conference at the Institute and Alistair Means is one of the featured speakers.

Visiting professors, graduate students and post-docs have come to Memorial Park for the conference. There are papers on molecular biology, neuroscience, psychology. Sophia has never seen so many people streaming into the large auditorium in which Dr. Means will speak, that can accommodate five hundred.

He has invited Sophia to dinner after the lecture in the Institute dining room—"A dinner in my honor," he has said. It is the first time that Alistair Means has invited Sophia anywhere.

She is conscious of the occasion. Its significance. (Maybe.)

She tells him she can't come to the dinner. Then, seeing the look in the man's face, of disappointment, and raw hurt, quickly she says that yes, she can come to the dinner but will have to leave early—"They will expect me at the hospital to see my father. If I can get there by eight-thirty . . ."

She feels a pang of guilt, she'd come late to the hospital the day before, also. Working late at the lab. But she has seen her father every evening this week.

So wonderful to Sophia, to hurry into Whitey's room and to see his face light up at the sight of her. His mouth moving—*S'phi*.

Always, Jessalyn jumps up to hug her. Mother and daughter embrace tightly.

It is astonishing to Sophia, how she'd taken her father for granted, all of her life. At times, exasperated with him. Embarrassed by him. *Daddy exaggerates so. Oh, I wish Daddy wouldn't!*

Now, it is so precious to her, to see that he is alive. To see that he recognizes her and can pronounce her name, or nearly—"S'phi."

The previous day, she and Jessalyn helped Whitey walk in his room under the supervision of a therapist. Slow, painstaking-slow!—but Whitey is determined, he will regain the use of his legs.

He has been running a mild fever for the past day or two. His skin is flushed as if with excitement, hope. His eyes beam a faint yellow. His breath has a chemical smell.

So many drugs are dripping into his veins. Sophia has been keeping a precise medical log.

Jessalyn says the nurses have assured her, the fever is nothing to worry about. But of course, Jessalyn is worried.

Alistair Means's subject—mutations, DNA, gene "editing"—is fascinating to Sophia, for her dissertation touches upon these. In her father's hospital room she downloads articles on such subjects, one of them by Alistair Means, that appeared in *Science* a few months before. It is comfortable to use her laptop in the room even with the TV blaring overhead (poor Whitey craves news even when he has difficulty understanding it, the TV people speak so rapidly). Usually, Jessalyn watches TV with Whitey, or pretends to watch. Her eyelids droop with exhaustion but the look of severe strain and anxiety has mostly faded from her face.

The night before, Whitey signaled for Sophia to turn off the TV. With some effort he'd said to her what sounded like *Wh's d'ng*—after several repeats Sophia deciphered this as "What are you doing?" She tried to explain, speaking slowly and clearly: Lumex, Inc. manufactures a drug that, taken within forty-eight hours of chemotherapy, mitigates some of its more severe side effects, like a plummeting of white blood platelets. This medication, which is a very complex chemical compound, and very expensive, the Institute lab is trying to improve, and Sophia is involved in the "trials."

She doesn't hesitate to speak of cancer to her father since (thank God) it isn't cancer with which he has been stricken.

Whatever she'd told Whitey, he had seemed eager to hear. His way of straining forward, regarding her searchingly, reminds her of an infant's intense staring at the adults who are leaning over it, trying to make sense of the mysterious sounds that erupt from their lips with such seeming ease and spontaneity.

But Sophia had been baffled by *Ys, ys—wy.* She'd looked to her mother who said, "Whitey is saying, 'Yes, yes—why?'"

Why?—what? Sophia has no idea.

"WITHOUT MUTATIONS THERE IS NO EVOLUTION. Without random errors in DNA, there is no evolution. Yet most mutations in the DNA are harmful, and lead to dead ends—the inability of the life-form to reproduce itself."

A paradox, Sophia thinks. The applicability to human life is all too obvious and yet, as Whitey would say—*Why?*

It is late Friday afternoon, in late October. Not yet 6:00 P.M., but the sky has darkened like a stain introduced into a clear solution. Amid the audience of several hundred in the Institute auditorium Sophia sits, second row center, with coworkers from the lab. She is listening intently to Alistair Means who speaks just a little too rapidly, his words sometimes lost in the Scots burr, as if he were thinking aloud, reasoning to himself in a manner both abstruse and excited. There is an argument here, in fact several arguments, theories posited to explain the connection between mutations and evolution—that is, between alterations in DNA and the success (or failure) with which organisms move their DNA into the next generation.

Sophia observes Alistair Means with the air of an attentive schoolgirl. It is her safest, most trustworthy pose: it leaves her mind free to ramble about, undetected.

He is too old for her. Of course.

Whitey would not approve.

Yet: she finds him attractive. Very.

The precision of his speech, the way in which he flails his hands about, as if he is thrilled with what he has discovered, and must suppress his excitement, to a degree. Here is *exactitude,* but also *aliveness.* Nothing is so sexually stirring to Sophia as an intelligent, rigorously intellectual person, who tells you things you would not have ever thought to tell yourself, in a way uniquely his own.

Too bad, Means's sport coat looks rumpled. His necktie is of a neutral hue. The cuffs of his white shirt do not show beyond the cuffs of the sport coat. Sophia smiles to recall the many times that Jessalyn has stopped Whitey on the way out of the house, to straighten his tie, or suggest that he change his shirt, or put on another pair of shoes.

Jesus, Jessy! What would I do without you.

Sophia wonders if Alistair Means would be grateful. It is very hard to imagine tugging at this man's sleeve, suggesting that he change a tie or a shirt.

Sophia glances about, to see how others regard the distinguished man. She wonders if there is another woman in the audience who feels for Alistair Means something more than intellectual admiration.

(There are not many women at the Institute. Less than 10 percent and of these, most are junior appointments.)

In any case individuals at the Institute who might be romantically involved with one another would do their best to keep their relationships secret. For a supervisor to be involved with an assistant would be unprofessional, and risky.

She, Sophia, clearly feels something for Alistair Means, or for the occasion, for she is wearing dressy clothes today, appropriate for a semi-formal dinner; not her usual jeans, not her usual cotton shirt and pull-over sweater, but a skirt of soft dark lavender wool with a knitted top and tiny wooden buttons. Her hair has been attractively fluffed-out. Her eyebrows have been plucked and thinned, given a little arch.

Her mother would see what this meant, instantly.

Oh, Sophia! Who is he?

Some of what Means is saying is familiar to Sophia, for it has origins in the lab. That you can induce stress in all creatures, even bacteria. That stressed rats have a higher mutation rate than rats that are not stressed but this does not (self-evidently) seem to be a result of natural selection, more likely an epiphenomenon of stressful environmental conditions like extreme heat or cold, dehydration, physical trauma.

The great variety of species and adaptations on Earth at the present time is a consequence of random errors that have increased the propagation of gene copies; the paradox, that natural selection would seem to reduce the frequency of mutations to zero, which would then reduce genetic variation to zero, and bring evolution to a halt.

The greater the change in environment, the greater the pressure on the organism to "adjust." The old adage *Better safe than sorry* has no applicability to evolution nor even, Alistair Means says, with a rueful smile, to human life though it is an adage that has itself survived.

He is projecting slides onto a large screen. Densely specific, graphs and statistics. His talk, spirited in its generality, turns now to the arid precision of molecular biology, a computational science that holds little interest for Sophia. Only fleetingly is she able to understand—where the environment changes rapidly, natural selection must favor a higher mutation rate; no matter how many bad mutations, there is a greater likelihood for enough good mutations to assure the species' survival among other species competing for the same food and territory.

Have there been animal species that acquired near-zero mutations? If so, these died out because they failed to adapt to environmental change.

Sophia has been listening so intently, there is a crick in her neck from leaning forward in her seat. Badly she wants to understand—she wants to understand *him.* But the points Means is making are becoming increasingly impenetrable to her, as the computational statistics on the screen are unreadable to her; she is disappointed in the turn the talk has taken, which others can follow, but not Sophia. She feels a pang of dismay, like one who flounders in a rough sea, trying in vain to grab hold of a lifeboat, breaking her fingernails in the effort. In the lifeboat are the survivors, and she is not one of them.

Wait! Please don't leave me behind—the plea springs from her, silently.

Still, she will attend the dinner. In Alistair Means's honor.

As his guest, she will attend. In the Institute dining room, in which she has never yet dined, though she can't stay through the entire dinner, as she has explained.

It will be *their first dinner together.* Sophia wonders if it will come to be, in time, a kind of anniversary.

The lecture has ended. Much applause!

Questions are being raised. Sophia listens to these too, frowning, eager to understand. To a degree, she does understand. She is feeling less dismal. She is feeling, for the moment, hopeful. For forty minutes Alistair Means fields questions—thoughtfully, courteously, brilliantly. He makes every effort not to be impatient, even with aggressive questions. Even with pompous, rambling questions. She is proud of him. Surreptitiously she checks her cell phone which has been turned off for nearly two hours. She is surprised to see several calls.

She hears—*Sophia? Dad is very bad. Please come as soon as you can.* It is Beverly's voice, agitated.

And another, also from Beverly—*Sophia! Something happened, it looks like Dad might not make it. Where are you? Can you get here?*

On her feet, dazed. Oh, what has she done? Why has she gone to Means's lecture instead of the hospital? Pushing her way into the aisle. *Excuse me! Excuse me!* Alistair Means has come forward from behind the podium, to shake hands. He sees Sophia in the aisle. In the flush of well-being at the success of his talk Means may well imagine that Sophia McClaren is hurrying to him, with these others, to shake his hand and congratulate him; instead, to his surprise, Sophia seems not to see him. She has turned away, to ascend the aisle. "Sophia? Is something wrong?"—Means calls after her but she ignores him. She is indifferent, rude. It is clear that she is determined to make her way out of the auditorium, out of the Institute building, out of his life.

Going Home

G*ood news! We're taking you home.*

So eager to get dressed he fumbles thrusting his foot into the place where you put the leg, the trouser, off-balance and his dear wife laughs at him—*Oh, darling! Let me help you.* Often she kisses him for no reason other than she loves him. Slips her arm around his waist to support him.

She kisses him to calm him. If his temper flares up.

He is trying to make his way *down.* It is a cautious matter, to make your way *down.*

Fearful of stumbling on the flat things you step on, that go down, he has forgotten the word for what they are, it is not *star,* it is not *stays,* you step down on them going down, one foot and the other foot, very carefully.

Going *down* he can grip a railing. He can hold tight. One foot and the other foot.

Sees to his surprise that his feet are bare. Where are his socks and shoes?

He is not sure what he is wearing, that fits him loose like a gown. And his legs bare, and the hairs stirring.

He has fallen to the foot of the things-that-go-down. He has fallen onto his back.

He is fearful of moving, he is fearful that his spine has shattered.

They are calling to him—*Johnny! Johnny come here!*

Often he falls. He is such a little boy! His legs are so short. He has scabs on both knees. He falls but not hard for quickly he scrambles to his feet. He crawls on hands and knees. He makes funny barking noises like a puppy. He *is* a puppy, wiggles his little bottom like wiggling a tail, his parents laugh loving him so.

But first, he has to give away these damned flowers. Perfumy smell in the room like a funeral parlor. What do you think this is, a damned funeral parlor?

Damned crank-up bed is not a casket. Not yet!

For you, with my sincere gratitude. Thank you.

His favorite among the nurses. Polish girl. Blue eyes. Always smiling. *Call me Whitey, that's my God damn name.*

Is he imagining, she caresses his face? His face is hot-mottled and raw. His eyes are those swirling little fruits in the slot machines. When the swirling ceases they are not lined up evenly, why he can't fucking *see straight.*

He is very tired, giving away these potted flowers. They are bright gaudy colors as in a coloring book. There is too much to give away—someone will have to help him.

Baskets of fruit, beginning to rot. Balloons in flat pillow shapes, floating to the ceiling.

Is he imagining, the Polish girl had slipped her cool hand inside the nightshirt? Caressing his fatty torso, the stark nipples, hair-clusters across his chest and at his groin where no one could see.

She could not see. Legs curled up beneath her in the chair with arms, a blanket pulled over her.

But now, this morning there is good news. *He is going home.*

His dear wife has brought him this news. Her eyes are bright with tears, she is very happy.

He isn't sure where he has been. But now, *he is going home.*

There is only one thing wrong, that makes him sad. He had promised her he would protect her but now, he is not so sure.

She has been removing his things from the closet. He had not known there was a closet in this place. Taking out his suit?—he had no idea that his suit was in this place. The three-piece plaid suit he'd been wearing that day, tight at the waist, had cost more than he'd ever paid for any article of clothing.

But that was a long time ago. Can't remember how long. The lightning-bolts striking his body. His face. The explosion. The collapse. He has been slip-sliding since then. On the icy sidewalk he'd fallen, hard.

Johnny?—she is calling to him, anxiously.

He has not heard that voice in so long, he is numbed at first with happiness so vast he cannot comprehend it—confuses the sensation with fear, that fear of slipping-down, falling-down-hard, *hurting*—(for he is often crying, his child's heart is easily wounded though it is also [as his parents are relieved to see] easily healed).

Except his feet are tangled in these damned bedclothes. Fishhook in his arm, in the soft skin at the crook of his elbow, he tears out.

That voice! It is *her voice*.

He is running to her, it is a bright happy day, his feet are bare in stubby tufts of grass. *Are you my Johnny-boy? Darling come here.*

His legs are too short, he is going to fall. Biting his lip to keep from crying if he falls, if his short legs fail him, but he has not fallen for Mommy catches him, under his arms, covers his face with kisses quick and wet like little fishes, that tickle. He is not afraid now. So happy his heart is filled with love to bursting like a child's balloon blown big, tight and wonderful-shiny.

II.

The Siege

OCTOBER 2010—APRIL 2011

"What Did You Do with Daddy?"

In a panic she wakes. Where are the children?

In a clumsy little pack they'd been with her a moment ago lurching and surging about her legs. Small children, chattering excitedly, it must have been many years ago. The mother was herding them across a wide windy cobblestone street, a kind of boulevard in a foreign city (she'd had an impression of singularly ugly equestrian statuary) with traffic streaming by in a blur of exhaust.

The sky was smudged. The air was of the hue of old, faded documents.

This was a time in the mother's life when she was often anxious. For she was a young mother, and understood that the gravest danger is to lose a child.

At the same time, something was tangled about her (bare) legs. The pillow beneath her head was damp. Her hair was matted, sticky. There was a night-side to the mother's life, that tormented her.

Where had the children gone, so suddenly? Slipped away from her as she'd tried to grip their little hands and with deft movements of her elbows tried to both herd and shelter them with her arms.

Always the danger is, you will forget one of them.

The horror is, one of them *will not be born*.

Not so worried about the oldest child—Thom. For he is the only one of the children who has been *named*.

The youngest children are easily confused with one another. Their faces are soft-wax, pliable and undefined.

Where is the father?—she does not know.

It is important to keep this fact from the children. They must not know that Daddy is missing. They must not know that Mommy has no idea where Daddy is or where their hotel is in this (unnamed) country and that Mommy has lost her handbag containing passports, documents, travelers' checks, wallet.

Her hope is that the children (who are lost) (temporarily) will be at the hotel when she returns. Her hope is that Daddy is there, with the children. Indeed, she is telling herself that that is obviously where the children are, for otherwise she does not know where they are.

Her heart is lacerated from their small, sharp claws scratching through the thin much-laundered fabric of her nightgown.

The husband would gather the nightgown in his fists, he would inhale deeply the softly clean soap-smell of the nightgown, after a laundering, and the softly clean soap-smell of her hair, and he would weep with happiness, in love of her. *She will try to remember this. The small coin of her only happiness.*

Ah, a church bell ringing! Church bells.

A cathedral. A cathedral square. Splotched sunlight but still the sky is smudged like newsprint.

Bells, chimes. Stirred by the wind . . .

Eagerly she thinks *But it has not yet happened, then.*

Then suddenly, they are in an open, crowded square. They are together at a table that is too small for them. Not Daddy, Daddy is not here, but the children are here, tired and vexed and squabbling together. It is not strange to her (at the time) that the children are approximately the same age except for Thom, the firstborn, whose face she can see distinctly, who is older. But Thom is tormenting his baby brother, which is bad of him, and the oldest girls are pulling the youngest girl's hair because it is beautiful curly chestnut-brown hair.

Oh, where is the father, to restore order?

Now something terrible has happened, the table has been overturned. The children are hiding from their mother, beneath the table. Their voices are furious, pleading—*Mommy what did you do with Daddy! WHERE IS DADDY!*

She realizes that the children are doll-sized—too small. The youngest are made of that flimsy paper that lines gift boxes. Still, their cries of accusation are earsplitting.

Her heart is racing with dread. The children are furious with her, they will never forgive her, Daddy is lost and will never return home.

The Strong One

Sure you can do it, darling. Who else?

The kids are devastated, clueless. You must take care of them. Never lost a father before.

In the guise of comforting their mother they came to her one by one, to be comforted.

For she was the strong one. Of course.

For Whitey's sake. All of her effort, the desperate motions of her heart that lifted her, just barely, from the sweat-sopped sheets of the bed she crawled into, the interminable hours of the day like a great roaring sewer, were for *him*.

Tight and taut as a drawn bow she felt to them where they feared she would be soft; strong, protective, she felt to them, her arms like great feathered wings shielding them; the beat of her heart consoling and not frantic like the beat of their hearts. *Can't believe Daddy is gone. Can't believe we won't see Daddy again.*

In her arms, they wept. Holding them, comforting them, she did not allow herself to weep, not much.

They did not understand, she was not (yet) a widow. For Whitey was still very present. Whitey would not abandon her just yet.

Close beside her, observing, judging. Shrewd Whitey-comments no one else could hear.

Fact is, the kids depend upon you, Jess. This is tough on them. Even Thom, don't let him fool you.

They'd been concerned for their mother imagining she would collapse. Like something made of paper, Beverly had thought. Like cotton candy.

Gossamer. A spiderweb. Beautiful in design but lacking strength. In their ignorance they'd thought they would console her. In their vanity.

How many times she held them, those first days. She did not speak much. She did not utter familiar words. She did not say *But we will all be together in Heaven*—though almost, in the misery of the moment, they wished she might say such a thing, in comfort; as a child is comforted by familiar words devoid of all meaning.

But she could only murmur to them what sounded like *Oh I know, I know.* And hold them tighter.

There was no need to think of Whitey, just yet. Whitey remained too close, at her side. He had not abandoned her. As Whitey had been bossy in life (she smiled to think) so Whitey would be bossy in death. Of course! Who could think otherwise, who knew Whitey McClaren? Hardly one to stand by passively while others made decisions that involved *him.*

Whitey who'd been devastated by his own father's death, when they'd been married only a few years. Whitey who'd needed to be comforted by his young wife.

And his young wife shocked by the degree of his grieving, the commingling anger and sorrow.

No adult is anything but a kid, when a parent dies.

She'd known then what she had only suspected beforehand: that her husband was not so strong as he appeared to others, not so sure of himself. Like a big tree with shallow roots, in soft soil, susceptible to rough winds, vulnerable.

There was Whitey looming close. That way Whitey had of leaning over her, needing to be physically near.

Sometimes she'd been (just slightly) discomforted by this habit of his, which seemed to be half-conscious.

Nudging against her, now. Of course, he would not abandon his dear wife.

All I know is, I love you. As long as we have each other, I am OK.

JOHN EARLE McCLAREN BORN FEBRUARY *19, 1943. Died October 29, 2010.*

Death certificate. Stiff paper, single page, seal of the State of New York.

"You will want to duplicate this many times, Mrs. McClaren."

It would become a reflex, stiffening at the sight of the name—*John Earle McClaren.*

Each death-document, each form of the seemingly endless forms she was obliged to fill out and sign.

Jessalyn McClaren, wife.

Blinking tears from her eyes. Quickly, that no one could see.

None of this was very real to her. That was her secret—none of this was very real at all.

For one thing, *Whitey* was the man she knew not *John Earle McClaren.*

There was no *John Earle McClaren,* in fact. His parents and relatives had called him *Johnny.* He'd been *Johnny* through much of high school but then, when his hair began to bleach out, to lose color, to become so strangely white, one of the sports coaches started calling him *Whitey* and his (guy, jock) friends took *Whitey* up. The name would prevail through decades.

Jessalyn had the idea, Whitey didn't greatly love the name as an adult. He'd outgrown it the way he'd outgrown his North Hammond High sweatshirts and varsity jacket. *Hey Whitey!*—an actual term of opprobrium if shouted from a passing car in downtown Hammond.

In a racially tense era, not the most appropriate of nicknames for a white man.

Yet *Johnny Earle* hadn't sounded right, either.

Best to call the man *darling, dear. Daddy, Dad.*

Days after the death she could not—yet—bring herself to speak of him in the past tense. Could not say *passed away,* still less *died, has died.* With the logic of a child or of one who has not completely wakened from a confusing dream she had begun to think of him as *Whitey-who-is-not-here.*

Decoded as *Whitey-who-is-somewhere-but-not-(evidently)—here.*

Like a toddler's steps. Halting, hesitant. Grabbing for support—anything.

Still she comforted the children, who'd grown so tall, arms and legs so long, she could not easily embrace them any longer. *The kids* as Whitey called them.

It was baffling to them, that after the vigil at the hospital, after their father's struggle, after their rallying-together and the bond of their dread that their dear father would die and their (premature) relief that he was recovering, their dear father had after all died; as a virulent staph infection ravaged the badly weakened man, driving his temperature up, up—causing his blood pressure to plummet—and his heart to seize, in fibrillation.

In the early evening of his twelfth day in the hospital. The evening of the very day they'd made specific plans for Whitey to be transferred to the Rochester clinic.

The change had come over him swiftly. Fever licked at him like flames. You could feel the terrible heat coming off his skin. Sicker and sicker he'd become, Jessalyn had cried for help. Soon he was delirious, unconscious.

Only Jessalyn and Beverly had been with him at the time. Soon, they were barred from the room.

Others were expected that evening but had not yet arrived and by the time they arrived, Whitey would be gone.

She hadn't been able to hold his hand, at the end. She hadn't fully comprehended that this would be the end. It had seemed to her that the crisis was an interim and not an end.

It was her hope he'd been in a deep sleep. A coma. As she'd been assured.

Had not known he was alone. No idea where he was, what was happening. Intubated, and his poor straining heart shocked into beating after it had ceased beating, but he hadn't known she was not there.

So swiftly the staph infection had swept through both his lungs, into his bloodstream, there'd been no time for Friedland to come to the hospital. No Morton Kaplan.

Not even Whitey's favorite nurses who'd so flattered him he was their handsomest, best patient were there, at the end.

No idea, she was assured. Your husband could have had no idea what happened to him.

Staphylococcus. Flesh-eating bacteria. Swarming into the lungs. No effective antibiotic. No way to stop.

WONDERING NOW where Whitey *was*. What Whitey had become. If Whitey had disappeared into a pinprick, a tiny point of light somewhere inside his brain, and that tiny point of light now extinguished.

Unless: The tiny light was never extinguished but passed into another state? Invisible to the naked eye?

PASSED AWAY. *In his sleep.*

A merciful death as deaths go . . .

But wait: Wasn't Whitey getting better? Wasn't Whitey scheduled for therapy in Rochester?

What the hell happened to Whitey McClaren?

SEEMED LIKE, his father had died as soon as he, Thom, had returned home.

Turn around and drive back to Hammond—no other option.

Helping to plan the next step: cremation.

Advising his mother, she should request an autopsy from the hospital before it was too late.

Urging the stricken woman, she must request an autopsy.

Jessalyn shuddered with revulsion, horror. An autopsy—she could not—*no.*

In his living will, in all his directives, Whitey had requested cremation. *No nonsense* he'd liked to say.

In fact, Whitey had been reluctant to think about such matters. One of those persons (busy, distracted) who pretends to have no time to draw up a will, has to be talked into it, finally succumbed at quite an advanced age—late fifties.

Whitey would not want an autopsy, Jessalyn was certain.

She wanted to respect his wishes. She said.

Thom understood that his mother was in an acute state of shock. And Thom himself, having driven back to Hammond in a haze of dread, was not thinking clearly.

Yet (Thom believed) Jessalyn should request an autopsy. He felt strongly about this though he did not want (yet) to explain his reasons.

Trying to enlist his older sisters but neither would support him, in appeal to their mother.

Only halfheartedly, despite being a research scientist, Sophia supported the idea. But Sophia would not insist—*If it upsets Mom . . .*

Even Virgil seemed distressed by the prospect. As if cremation were not more extreme than an autopsy!

So, Thom persisted. Explaining to their mother that an autopsy would be needed if there were a lawsuit of some kind . . .

Frantic Jessalyn pressed her hands over her ears. Literally, she would not hear him.

Telling him she could not bear the thought of poor Whitey subjected to an autopsy after all he'd endured.

Her (beautiful) (bloodshot) eyes were showing white above the rim. Her lips were wet with something like spittle. Always so carefully groomed, never without makeup in any public place, his mother was looking disheveled, distraught. How shocked Whitey would be, to see his wife in such a state.

To Thom's astonishment Jessalyn began to scream at him—*No! I said no! You can't do such a thing to your father.*

(WHEN HAD JESSALYN McCLAREN LAST SCREAMED at anyone? Not within memory. Possibly, she'd never screamed at anyone.)

(Afterward Jessalyn would not recall screaming at Thom. She would not even recall Thom putting pressure on her about the autopsy.)

(Nor would Thom recall Jessalyn screaming at him.)

NOT FOR WEEKS, even months afterward would they be capable of uttering the terrible word *died*. It was just not possible.

Not Thom, and not Beverly. Not even Lorene, the most practical/least sentimental McClaren, could quite bring herself to utter the blunt flat stark final-sounding word *died* preferring instead the softer *passed away.*

In fact, Lorene would further soften the utterance—*Passed away in his sleep.*

(Was this true? Had Whitey died *in his sleep*? Strictly speaking this must be so, since he had not been conscious for hours before his death. His immune system had been so ravaged by the infection, he'd sunk into a deep—"unresponsive"—comatose state.)

Sophia had difficulty speaking of the death at all. From friends she received calls to which she barely listened. At the house on Old Farm Road she was silent while her sisters talked endlessly. In the kitchen, preparing meals with their mother, Beverly and Lorene did all the talking as if their grief was not genuine to them if it was not aired aloud, displayed. How could Jessalyn bear them! Sophia's old dislike of her sisters flared up leaving her trembling.

"Can't you be quiet about Daddy? Nobody wants to hear you."

The sisters were stunned by this attack. Sophia could not bring herself to look at their mother.

"For God's sake, Mom doesn't want to hear it. You could just *stop talking* for once."

Running from the kitchen to take refuge in her old room upstairs.

AT THE TIME OF THE death Virgil had been elsewhere (of course: that was Virgil) but next day he was with his family and seeing how their mother smiled blindly he'd understood—*This is not real to Mom. Not yet.*

He was fearful of his mother. Fearful for her, and fearful of her.

Beverly had hugged him, fierce and hard. Beverly had wept and wetted his neck. He'd had all he could do not to recoil, feeling his sister's breasts against his chest, like springy foam rubber, *please no.*

Lorene at least had not hugged him. Squeezed his arm at the elbow, a gesture of commiseration, brisk, no-nonsense, eyes wet with tears that might've been tears of exasperation as well as grief. *Oh Christ. Oh shit. This wasn't supposed to happen. God* damn.

Lorene, tough and sexless as a turnip. Even Virgil who knew nothing about women's fashions could see that Lorene's pants suits were defiantly outdated, in dark berry colors, olive, mud-brown.

Improbably for a woman high school principal her hair was razor-cut short as a Marine's. Her fierce face was sharp as something carved with a knife but her small mouth glistened bright-blood-red, just to throw you off your stride.

Growing up, Lorene had been Virgil's friend sometimes, in league against their big swaggering brother. Other times, she'd picked on Virgil as much as Thom did, making him cry.

He'd learned: you can't trust them. Older brother, sisters. You just can't.

Since that night in the kitchen Virgil and Thom had avoided each other. After the death Virgil had seen, or imagined he'd seen, in Thom's face an obscure rage at *him.*

In the kitchen, drinking Whitey's whiskey. It gave Virgil a small thrill of insight, his brother was a *drinker.*

Back in high school Thom had started drinking. With his jock-friends, showing off to one another. At Colgate, in the big-deal fraternity the name of which, cryptic Greek letters, Virgil could never recall out of disdain and disapproval. *Sexist pigs* Lorene had called them but

Thom had bristled *Bullshit. You don't know fuck-all. Dekes are the good guys.*

Virgil had long ago ceased wondering why his older brother disliked him. Still it was a puzzle to him, why his father hadn't seemed to like him except at the end, what was to be the end of his father's life, in his hospital bed listening to Virgil playing his flute and something like love in his face.

T'ss g'd. L'k t'ss.

Virgil had drawn close to his father to hear better. What did these whispered sounds mean, uttered with such effort?

Jessalyn could usually decipher what Whitey was trying to say. And Sophia. But not Virgil, usually.

At the house, following the death, Virgil had drifted off from the others. He'd felt—oh, what had he *felt*?—he did not know if he was sick with grief, stunned and baffled with loss, or whether—(but this was unexpected)—he was feeling *airy, aerated.*

Never would he see his father again. Never again, that pinch at the corner of Dad's eyes, the tug of Dad's smile, the (almost palpable) hesitation before Dad greeted him. *Virgil. How's it going.*

In Whitey's home office, in a farther corner of the house. As a child Virgil had not been allowed in this room except if Whitey invited him inside but that had rarely happened, as Virgil recalled. *I don't want you kids messing in here. A shut door means stay out.*

The surprise was, Whitey's big desk and adjoining table were clean. Neatly ordered as if he'd known that he would not be returning.

On the desk was Whitey's big state-of-the-art console computer with a dark screen. Idly Virgil wondered what Whitey's password might be.

He could never hack his way into his father's computer. Virgil hadn't the computer skills, Sabine was more skilled than he.

Not that he wanted to hack into Whitey's private life. If his father had secrets, better not to know.

If Virgil had secrets, better that no one knows.

Barely Virgil could hear his family in another part of the house, his sisters' voices.

They were nowhere near. They would not know . . .

Swiftly Virgil moved. Stealthily Virgil moved. Twenty years and more he'd craved to do this, unobserved. And now—*Whitey will never know.*

Opening desk drawers. Just to see.

Nothing of evident interest: documents, folders, envelopes, stamps.

In a lower, deep drawer: bank records, checkbooks. Stock printouts.

If he'd had more time he might have studied these records. But he did not want to know how much money his father had, really. There was something repugnant about such knowing. And so many documents, he'd have had to pore over them, and this would be degrading.

He'd thought, when news came of Whitey's death—*He won't remember me in his will. Of course.*

He was determined not to care. He *did not care.*

On a corner of Whitey's large handsome desk was a paperweight. A heavy, triangular rock of about the size of a man's fist, pink-gleaming, glittering. Quartz? Pink feldspar? Possibly it was a gift to Whitey, with a sentimental meaning; possibly, Whitey had acquired it on his own, and so it surely had a sentimental meaning.

Virgil crammed the rock into a pocket. No one would ever miss it.

"SOMETHING BAD HAS HAPPENED to Grandpa."

The grandchildren had known that Grandpa Whitey was very sick for they'd been taken to visit him in the hospital. Almost, they had not recognized the ravaged man in the bed who breathed funny, and smelled funny, and when he tried to talk to them, talked funny so that they could not understand him.

"Grandpa has gone away . . ."

These were weak, faltering words put to the younger grandchildren, who had not a clear idea what "death" was. But the older grandchildren were frightened too. It was alarming to them, to see the faces of adults streaked with tears. They were very still biting their lips waiting for this awkwardness to stop.

"Grandpa has p-passed away . . . He loved you so much!"

This was making them feel bad. Like bad children. But—it was not clear what they had done that was bad, exactly.

The older grandchildren had known Grandpa Whitey the longest time—all their lives! And so, they knew him much better than the younger grandchildren.

To them, Grandpa Whitey had long been the only "old" person who made you smile and laugh and did not scold, ever. Grandpa Whitey behaved sometimes like a child himself, bossy and unpredictable, sometimes cranky but always funny. Grandpa Whitey was so unlike other grandparents, he was *fun*.

But now, Grandpa Whitey had passed away. And *passed away* was not fun but scary. And *passed away* became boring after only a few minutes.

For there was nothing for the grandchildren to do or say about *passed away*. There was nothing to look at about *passed away*.

Passed away was a kind of special language only the adults could speak to one another. The grandchildren could not participate in this speech. Only the very young grandchildren asked silly questions that were unanswerable—"Where did Grandpa *go*?"

The older grandchildren rolled their eyes, in misery.

It was a sad, subdued time in the grandparents' house on Old Farm Road following the "cream-ation" (a mysterious event which none of the grandchildren had attended and of which they were told very little). The grandchildren grew restless at having to be so still, and so quiet. They were forbidden to run outside. They were forbidden to run on the stairs. Their skin itched, they'd been made to wear "good" clothes. Their nostrils itched to be picked. But you *could not pick your nose* at such a time. *Gross!*

You could not even *laugh*. For there were adults all over and the adults outnumbered the children.

It was strange to them, all these adults—and no Grandpa Whitey.

That would take a while to absorb—no Grandpa Whitey.

There was plenty to eat for Grandma Jessalyn made the very best food but still, at this sad, subdued time you were warned not to *stuff your face like a pig* or *spill food all over your nice clean clothes.*

The older grandchildren drifted together on the farther side of the buffet table. They were making an effort to talk about Grandpa Whitey without the adults present. It was not possible to talk about Grandpa Whitey and how bad they felt that he had *passed away* with any adult listening for to speak of Grandpa Whitey with any adult listening, especially Grandma Jess, or Beverly who was always blowing her nose and sniffling, was very awkward, and made the words sound wrong.

Oh, what was there to *say*? It was hard even to cry, none of it seemed real.

Already Grandpa Whitey was on the far side of a ravine. Grandpa Whitey was walking away. Limping away. You could see only his back—the back of his head. They'd been made to visit Grandpa Whitey in the hospital and were frightened by the change in him, and so they did not wish to recall that person, who'd been (almost) a stranger to them, but the other Grandpa Whitey, before the hospital.

They did not ever utter the word *stroke.* They did not think—*stroke.* This was an adult term, an old-people's clinical term, it would never apply to them.

The grandchildren were all cousins! The oldest was seventeen and the youngest was six.

Some of the grandchildren were allies. Some of them were rivals.

Beverly's older children knew to resent (sort of) their cousins because their cousins' father (Uncle Thom) was more important to Grandpa Whitey than their mother was; at any rate, this was what their mother believed, and *grumbled all the time about.* (Brianna's words.) For Uncle Thom was some sort of partner with Grandpa Whitey, while Beverly had nothing to do with the family business.

(Were Uncle Thom and his family *richer than* Beverly and her family? Was that it?)

Among the grandchildren/cousins were shifting alliances. The older children preferred one another's company (even if they did not always "like" one another) for no one is so boring as a younger brother or sister or cousin.

The older grandchildren/cousins went to different schools in different districts of North Hammond except for Brianna (Bender) and Kevin (McClaren) who went to North Hammond High but were in different classes: sophomore (Brianna), senior (Kevin).

Lanky-limbed shock-haired Kevin was saying how for his tenth birthday Grandpa Whitey had taken him to a secondhand bookstore in downtown Hammond where there was an entire wall of comic books in cellophane wrappers; Grandpa Whitey had seemed to know a lot about comic books, and talked with the proprietor for a long time, and bought old copies of *Action Comics, Flash Comics, Batman, Superman, Spiderman* to give to Kevin. It had been a surprise to Kevin that Grandpa Whitey knew so much about comic books, and cared about them, and really great of Grandpa Whitey to buy these "rare" comics for Kevin though (as Kevin admitted) he didn't know exactly what he'd done with the comic books, had to be in his room, somewhere; in a drawer or a closet where one day he'd discover them unopened in their cellophane wrappers though yellowed and torn, returning home from college and a pang of loss would sweep through him like a kick in the gut—*Oh. Grandpa Whitey.* Wiping his eyes with the edge of his hand.

Surreptitiously Brianna checked her cell phone another time. Had the message she'd been waiting for all day come, at last? No.

Shit.

"PUT THAT CELL PHONE AWAY. So rude!"—Aunt Lorene hissed into her bratty niece's ear.

Quickly, abashedly Brianna shoved the phone into a pocket. How had anyone seen?

"At such a time! Your grandfather has just *passed away* and you are on that damned phone. For shame."

Brianna's eyes welled with tears. Brianna swallowed hard, and shrank away in shame.

Kevin shot her a covert look. *Better you than me!*

All of the grandchildren disliked and feared their Aunt Lorene who saw through sham good-behavior-in-the-presence-of-adults. Not even the youngest of her nieces and nephews were spared Aunt Lorene's piercing raptor-eye: she knew children's secrets and such secrets disgusted her for often they had to do with fibbing, nose-picking, going-to-the-bathroom-in-some-slovenly-way, failing to adequately wash hands, staining underwear, pajamas, sheets.

Staining sheets. Adolescent boys, Aunt Lorene knew so thoroughly, with such disgust, disdain, and yet bemusement, it was (almost) pointless to greet her in a normal voice, to smile and say, trying not to stammer, *H-Hi Aunt Lorene . . .* For Lorene knew, knew all, and did not forgive, as she knew, arguably, even more of adolescent girls and their nasty, dirty, sheet-staining habits, their *time-of-the-month* stains, smells, *faux*-cramps calculated to get them excused from gym class. Worse yet, girls' slutty clothes, makeup, and fingernails painted the most lurid colors—dark purple, bright blue.

Lorene spoke darkly, in a lowered voice: "The least you kids could do, at such a time, is pretend to mourn your grandfather—*at least.*"

Beating them about the heads with a broom, it felt like. Even Kevin who was five feet, ten inches tall flinched.

Laser-eyed Aunt Lorene. She'd look you in the eye and whatever you'd been hoping to pretend, that worked with other adults, Aunt Lorene totally ignored, seeing *you.*

Brianna dared to stammer: "But we do m-m-miss Grandpa . . ." Her voice was so low, Aunt Lorene could pretend she hadn't heard.

It was strange, the older children could remember when their aunt hadn't been so mean to them. When they'd been little: Beverly's children, Thom's children. Little nieces and nephews, she'd seemed actually to like. She'd been an almost-silly doting aunt for years. She'd bought them "educational" toys—lots of books—but then, about the time they started school, she began to grow wary; she'd said it was the time children learn to "dissemble"—they are not born with that facility, but acquire it, at about the age of six. Ironic that she'd liked Kevin and Brianna so much when they were babies but couldn't seem to stand them now that they were teenagers.

(Did it have to do with sex?—the older grandchildren wondered. Or was it just with kids' bodies, that Lorene found repulsive?)

And now it was worse. Today. Aunt Lorene seemed anxious, angry. Her short-cut hair lifted from her head like an indignant jaybird's crest. Her mean mouth quavered. As if Grandpa Whitey *passing away* was not something the principal of North Hammond High had expected and had no idea how to factor into her no-nonsense life, like discovering filth on her hands in a public place with nowhere to wipe it.

AUNT SOPHIA THEY LIKED. Aunt Sophia was OK.

Though not-young Sophia looked *young.* Usually Sophia wore jeans, white shirt not tucked-in, no belt. Hair tied back so her long pale earnest face was exposed. Never wore makeup, no color on her mouth. Even at the house on Old Farm Road after their grandfather had *passed away* Aunt Sophia was unadorned, stark and staring and sincere in her grief. You did not feel, seeing Aunt Sophia, that she would suddenly crouch over, grab you in her arms and start bawling into your terrified face.

The older smarter grandchildren were impressed by an aunt who was a scientist, how smart Sophia was (and not sneering-smart like Lorene) in a way that seemed casual as if everyone should know what "mitosis" is—"natural selection"—"dark matter." Any school question you had, especially math or science, Sophia would know and explain it so you could understand at least at the time she told you, and she never laughed at you or showed impatience but might murmur *Good! Now you have it.*

But how did Grandpa Whitey *pass away*? Hadn't Grandpa Whitey been *recovering*?—thirteen-year-old Alice (McClaren) had to ask her aunt Sophia for there was no one else to ask, who would not make her feel terrible for asking; and Sophia started to explain, weakened immune system, influx of deadly bacteria, "staph" infection, but then Sophia went silent and began to choke up as if she could not continue.

Quickly then Sophia turned away. Alice was left to stare after her feeling *just terrible*.

HOW MANY HUGS FROM GRANDMA JESS, how many whispers—*Grandpa loved you! Grandpa will miss you.*

IT WAS NOT THE FIRST death in her life of more than six decades. Hardly!

She was tired, yes. She was very tired. Yet: the house was her house and it was a beautiful house fragrant now with the most beautiful flowers and she was determined to be the *hostess*.

The duty of a hostess is to make all guests feel at ease, and welcome; to make all guests happy to have come to your house, and reluctant to leave.

"Oh, please don't leave yet. It's early."

And: "You know how Whitey loved parties."

This was not a party, was it? Just family, relatives, very close and very old friends.

They were serving Whitey's very best liquor. Whitey's best wine, beer and dark German ale. Some of the visitors were so devastated, it was scarcely possible to keep their glasses filled.

And Whitey's favorite mixed nuts with a prevalence of cashews, and those awful-tasting peas, Whitey ate by the handfuls—*wasabi*?

A buffet of Whitey's favorite dishes—poached salmon with dill, chicken pasta salad Provençal, those little spicy meatballs served with toothpicks. Swedish crackers, cheeses.

The impromptu gathering at the house on Old Farm Road was not a memorial for the deceased (there would be a proper memorial in December to which hundreds of persons would come to recollect, to mourn, and to honor John Earle McClaren) but an occasion for remembrance. For those who'd loved Whitey McClaren and wished to comfort his widow and children.

Not that Jessalyn McClaren was a "widow"—not yet. In the woman's fine-boned face was the look of someone who has been struck very hard and very decisively on the skull, the skull has shattered, yet has not fallen into pieces, just yet; the watery, just perceptibly bloodshot eyes hold firm, fixed.

"Whitey would be so happy to see you here! Please, let me fill your glass . . ."

The McClaren children, all grown up. Looking dazed, disoriented. Even the eldest—Thom. And poor Beverly, face swollen with grief. Though none of them could have been totally surprised that their father, nearing seventy, had died of complications following a stroke.

For so the obituaries said—*Complications following a stroke.*

(One glance at Whitey McClaren, you could guess the man had high blood pressure. Thirty pounds overweight at least, drank too much, ate too much red meat and fried onion rings, smoked.)

(Still, it was a shock. Such a great, generous guy. Nobody quite like Whitey McClaren—an honest politician! Always so *alive*.)

"Please don't be upset. You know how Whitey loved you all . . ."

She was smiling. She was determined to smile. Her lips were parched, finely cracked. But she'd done something desperate—smeared red lipstick on her mouth that, in the waxy pallor of her face, looked bizarre as neon.

Also, her hair that had never seemed to be lusterless and lank and faded had been brushed back flat against her head showing the stark outline of her skull in a way sobering and sad to see.

Poor Jessalyn! How will she live without Whitey to take care of her . . .

Yet aloud in chiming voices they marveled at how "elegant" she was in black silk, a black lace shawl tight around her shoulders, stone-colored shoes. Pink-toned pearls Whitey had given her for an anniversary, a double strand rising and falling with her quickened breath.

No one knew: she'd lost so much weight in a week, she'd had to use a safety pin at the waist of the black silk skirt that fell to mid-calf, to secure it.

No one knew: since the cremation that morning when she'd come close to fainting she'd been light-headed, nauseated, running to the bathroom every half hour, bowels like scalding-hot suet . . .

Demeaning facts, Whitey had no need to know.

Much in her life recently, Whitey had no need to know!

However, she was going to be all right. She was determined.

Comforting others: she was good at that.

McClaren relatives. Neighbors on Old Farm Road. Whitey's high school friends in their late sixties, early seventies looking shaken and sick and scared like divers on a high board with no choice but to follow a disastrous dive—*If there's anything I can do, Jessalyn. Let me know.*

Mr. Colwin, the kids had called him. Mr. and Mrs. Colwin who'd lived next door to the McClarens on Old Farm Road until Mrs. Colwin who'd been a nice lady died, and Mr. Colwin was left alone, and Jessalyn and Whitey invited him to dinner, how many family dinners, Thanksgivings, Christmases, included Leo in their parties, poor Leo Colwin, so long retired no one could remember what his profession had been, living now in a retirement village in East Hammond, wearing an old-man zip-up olive-green cardigan riddled with moth holes, old-man moccasins with little tassels, so shaken by the news of Whitey's death he'd clung to Jessalyn's hand for so long, Virgil (who scarcely left his mother's side all evening) was beginning to think he'd have to intervene.

If there's anything I can do, Jessalyn. Let me know.

Mr. Colwin, arriving hungry. Haunting the buffet, impossible to avoid him.

Just beyond the drinks table the impertinent question was being asked: Would Jessalyn be selling the house now?

Beautiful old Revolutionary War–era house with several acres of land—two-three million at least. Of course it wasn't an ideal time to talk now—but—if . . .

Stiffly Thom said no, he doubted that his mother would be selling the house anytime soon.

Stiffly Beverly said, no! Absolutely, her mother would not be selling the house anytime soon. (And when Jessalyn did want to sell the house it would not be put "on the market" but would be sold privately.)

If there's anything I can do. Please let me know.

A property like this needs to be brokered in just the right way.

Terrible shock!—but Jessalyn had the children who were devoted to her, rallying around her, that was a comfort. Without the children, unimaginable.

The cremation had been that morning, early. You wouldn't call it a "ceremony" exactly.

Just the family had been there. No young children (of course).

The ashes—(it was not possible to say *Whitey's ashes*)—were in an urn that looked like antique masonry but was made of some cheap synthetic material like compressed cardboard, with a very tight lid.

Heavier than you'd expect. But not *heavy*.

They would take the urn to be buried in the cemetery in North Hammond which was both a churchyard (behind the Presbyterian church) and a municipal burying ground where McClarens had been buried dating back to 1875.

In a single burial plot, you can fit two urns. Easily.

No. No plans for the memorial yet.

Probably in December, before Christmas.

Still, the doorbell kept ringing. Why were people coming so *late*?

Thom had had enough. Jesus! It was 9:20 P.M. The day had begun for the family at 6:00 A.M. (Half these people hadn't been invited. Who the hell had invited them? Every time the damned phone rang his mother was inviting someone else to the house. What would Whitey say—*Jessalyn! Lock the God damn door and turn out the lights.*)

In a room off the living room there was Mr. Colwin in a chair, legs asprawl, looking sickly-white as if he'd had a faint, and one of the neighbor ladies fussing over him. *Who the hell invited* him?

Upstairs in a guest bathroom smelling so strongly of lavender soap you could hardly breathe there was shock-haired Kevin producing a joint out of a baggie for Brianna, the cousins giggling together and the door locked behind them.

Maybe open the window? Great.

Downstairs they were keeping a sharp eye on Jessalyn.

How many times hearing their mother say in a voice of wonder how surprised Whitey would be, if he could see them all together like this. "He'd say, 'What's this? A party in the middle of the week? Why wasn't I invited?'"

"DO YOU KNOW WHO DIOGENES IS?"

Impulsively Virgil spoke. They were outside at the rear of the house: Virgil's breath steamed faintly about his mouth.

"*Is*? Don't you mean *was*?"

"*Was,* then. Who Diogenes *was*."

"Some old, ancient Greek philosopher who's been dead a thousand years."

Thom spoke carelessly, with an air of contempt. But Virgil persisted: "More like two thousand. *More* than two thousand."

It was late. The air was cold and wet and smelled of rotted leaves.

The last of the guests had departed finally but none of the McClaren children wanted to leave the house on Old Farm Road just yet.

They were wandering in the frost-stubbled grass behind the house that resembled a ship in the dark, looming high above them, only a few lights burning.

They were drunk. Drunk*en*. Even Sophia who never drank had had several glasses of Whitey's white wine over several hours and had to concede, it was *delicious*.

Lorene said, lighting a cigarette borrowed from Thom—(rare for

Lorene, with a harried, inexpert striking of a match), "Diogenes was a 'stoic' about whom lurid tales were told such as he went about naked in just a barrel, or was it a bathtub . . ." She paused, considering. "Or no, that was the 'Eureka!' man, in the bathtub, what's-his-name . . ."

"Archimedes."

"What?"

"*Who.* 'Archimedes'—the one in the bathtub, who discovered the law of gravity."

"No. Wait." Sophia objected, laughing. How ignorant her siblings were! It endeared them to her, somehow—they seemed so much more American than she, so casual and careless about things that should matter but clearly did not. "You must know that it was Newton who discovered the 'law of gravity.'"

"So what did Archimedes discover, then?"

"Many things! But you are thinking of the mathematician calculating that the volume of water displaced by an object must be equal to the volume of the object—supposedly, his own body as he stepped into a bathtub."

"Somehow, that seems obvious." Beverly, who'd been silent, brooding, spoke suddenly. In the house she'd kicked off her tight-fitting high-heeled shoes after the last guest had left and now she was wearing a pair of Whitey's old boots. Her breath steamed about her mouth as if she were panting. "I mean—you lower yourself into a bathtub, the water spills over. Why is that a great discovery?"

Lorene said, bemused: "You think you'd have discovered whatever it was Archimedes discovered, Bev? Two thousand years ago?"

Beverly persisted: "It's like Steve getting water all over the bathroom floor—not from a bathtub but from the shower. How's he do it? Like, the volume of his actual body, in water. Though there are shower curtains—of course. But with Steve, they're on the *inside* of the tub . . ." Beverly's slurred voice trailed off, she seemed confused by what she is saying.

"We were talking about inventions, Bev. Discoveries."

"Well. I couldn't discover anything *invisible*. Math, or physics, germs . . ."

But *germs* was a blunder. If Beverly were trying, in her clumsy way, to be amusing, entertaining.

For it was *germs* that had killed their father. Though called by the fancier name *bacteria*.

Of the McClaren children, only Lorene was considered witty, even when she wasn't. When Beverly made an effort to be funny, the others frowned, resisting.

Sophia was the earnest schoolgirl, Lorene the sardonic schoolmistress. Thom was the bossy one, whose sarcasm could be construed as funny, if it wasn't directed at you. Virgil just *was*.

Were we always like this?—Sophia wondered. Or are these the roles we settle into, when we are together?

In her schoolgirl fashion Sophia was explaining that Archimedes' discovery allowed for a new way of measuring volume. That was why it was important. But the bathtub story—"Eureka!"—was probably apocryphal.

"'Apocryphal'—'apocalyptic'—who gives a damn?"

Lorene laughed coarsely. It was clear that Lorene had had too much to drink.

"I mean, who gives a shit? Seriously."

It was high school speech, *shit*. Any sort of brainless profanity, obscenity. Fascinating to Lorene, and repugnant, how sub-literate the high school students were when they spoke to one another, or sent their idiot text messages. Even the smart ones. Since becoming a public school teacher, and then an administrator, Lorene had begun to speak in a patois of a kind, not her own speech, a cruder, crueler speech meant to entertain and alarm. The others detected in their sister, who'd once been relentlessly upbeat and vigorous, like a marcher so close behind you the toes of her boots nudge your heels, a kind of angry despair they did not want to acknowledge.

"Whoa!"—Thom steadied Lorene as she stumbled. On her feet were ankle-high black leather boots.

"Fuck you. Hands off." Lorene giggled, exhaling smoke in steamy little spurts.

All this while Virgil had been easing away from them. Not in disapproval or repugnance but obliviousness, Virgil's maddening obliviousness, as if he were alone.

Beginning now to run down the hill in long strides to the stream that bordered the McClaren property, swollen from recent rains, sparkling and glittering in the muted light of a quarter moon.

They looked after him. What was it about Virgil that so *annoyed*?

"Did you see him tonight? Acting like Hamlet's ghost."

"It's all an act. He doesn't care about Daddy at all. It's all just 'illusion'—'world of shadows'—Buddhist crap. Things slide off him like—what's it—oil off a duck's back."

"'Oil off a duck's back'?—what's that mean?"

"The duck's feathers are oily, I think. Water slides off the duck's feathers like oil."

"He brought that damned flute with him. He actually intended to play it."

Why Virgil hadn't played his flute wasn't clear. They'd seen Jessalyn speaking with him, no doubt encouraging him, for Virgil was one of those persons who requires being urged to do something he fully intends to do; yet, mysteriously, perhaps perversely, Virgil hadn't played the damned flute after all.

Sophia said, "Well—it's kind of nice to hear. There's a haunting sound to it . . ."

"Oh, Christ! It isn't *a real flute*. It's some thing with holes in it he carved, and a real flutist—"

"—flautist—"

"—would laugh in his face. Everything Virgil does is *amateur*."

This was true. This was irrefutable. And everything Thom did, and everything Lorene did, and everything Sophia did, was *professional*.

Beverly, who resented Virgil as much as the others, but was stung by their disparagement of *amateur*, said, in defense of their brother:

"The fact is, Dad liked Virgil playing the flute. Or whatever it was. If those were Dad's last days it was kind of wonderful, not that anyone realized at the time, that he seemed to be enjoying Virgil's music that he wouldn't have listened to for five seconds when he'd been well."

"Poor Whitey didn't have much choice, he was a captive audience."

"No. Daddy did enjoy Virgil's flute. Mom was grateful, she has said so."

"Bullshit. Mom would say *anything,* you know that."

"What do you mean—'anything'? Mom never lies."

"Mom never *lies*—from her perspective. But much of what Mom says, or believes, is just not true."

"And you know this—how?"

Beverly turned a face of fury on her tall swaggering brother. God, she was fed up with Thom! Ever since Whitey was hospitalized Thom had assumed authority within the family; as head of McClaren, Inc.'s textbook division, Thom had naturally assumed authority over the entire company.

As majority stockholder in the family business. Never forget that!

Next day, Whitey's will would be read at the law office. Beverly felt a pang of dread. She knew that Whitey had loved her very much, more than he'd loved Lorene, for instance, and more than he'd loved Virgil, obviously; but Thom was the firstborn, and had always been special to his father.

As for Sophia, she seemed too *slight,* somehow. Though Beverly knew that Whitey was proud of their young sister, she couldn't think that Sophia mattered to him quite so much as Beverly did, who'd provided him and Jessalyn with beautiful grandchildren.

(At least, Whitey and Jessalyn thought the Bender children were beautiful, or had been so, as babies.)

Overhead, the wan fading moon in an inky-black sky.

Here below, somewhere in safekeeping in the house, their father's ashes in a faux-stone urn with a tight, tight lid.

Down at the stream where they'd played as children long ago Virgil was squatting, back to them. On the far side of the stream was a dense stand of fir trees and beyond that, a lightless sky.

"*Do* you think Mom will sell the house? I hope not."

"Of course, eventually. Whitey couldn't face selling it but Mom is more practical. She'll do the sensible thing . . ."

"Which is? Give the house to *you*?"

"Nobody is giving the house to anyone! That's ridiculous"—Beverly was hurt, stung.

"And where would Mom live, if she sold the house?"

"She could buy a smaller house. She could buy a condominium. She has widow-friends, they've all downsized. There's that beautiful 'retirement' community, what's it called—Ten Acres. Mr. Colwin lives there. They can play bridge together! This was coming anyway, selling the house I mean, even if Daddy had—hadn't—had a s-stroke . . ."

"Mom could live with us. Brooke would like that, I think."

"To help with the kids? With the housework? Sure, Brooke would love that."

"What the hell are you saying, Beverly? I wouldn't treat my mother like a servant. We have servants."

We have servants. How smug this sounded! Smirking Beverly had no need to say a word.

Ridiculous anyway: all Thom and Brooke had were maids who came once a week, a nanny to help with the younger children, meals, and cleanup. How was that *servants*?

Deftly Lorene intervened: "What's he doing down there? Wading in the water?"

They stared at their brother, a shadowy figure some fifty feet away that might have been, if they hadn't known it was human, a vulture or a buzzard, very still hunched at the water's edge.

"Did you see him tonight? Acting like Hamlet's ghost."

"You said that before—but did Hamlet have a *ghost*? I think the ghost was supposed to be Hamlet's father . . ."

"He was hanging over Mom every minute. Hardly let anyone near her."

"Poor Virgil! I think this has hit him hard . . ."

"It has hit us all hard. Jesus!"

"Yes, why 'poor Virgil'? He didn't love Dad. He'll just move in with Mom."

"Of course! He'll move in with Mom. You are one hundred percent correct. He'll pry all of Dad's money out of Mom that he can, to give to his ridiculous charities . . ."

"Oh, no he won't. He *will not*."

"You know Mom, she's so—"

"—so not at all—"

"—firm. Stern."

"I've said it: enabling. Our brother is a kind of addict, a hippie-bullshit-addict, and our dear mother has *enabled him*."

"We can talk to her. We can be stern with her. We can just make it clear to her, what Whitey would wish."

Sophia stood a little apart, not wanting to listen to the urgent lowered voices of the others. Wanting to protest—*But I could move back with Mom, too. Virgil and me both. Why not?*

Soon then Virgil came loping back to them like a greyhound, his eyes furtive and shining. In an ecstatic voice he said:

"It's like I could feel the spirit of our father—almost . . . The 'creek,' he called it. So beautiful, and peaceful . . ."

Virgil was wearing a long dark-leather jacket buttoned to the throat, badly frayed and cracked, that gave him the look of a priest of another era—Dostoyevsky, Russian Orthodox, impassioned and deluded. Like most of his clothes the leather jacket was both dramatic and silly, like a costume. And like a costume, purchased at a secondhand shop.

With the long buttoned-up jacket Virgil wore brown corduroy trousers of the kind he'd worn in middle school, sandals with dark socks. Beverly perceived with a shiver of repugnance how the nails of both Virgil's big toes were beginning to poke through the dark socks.

There he stood, before them. Shivering with a kind of excitement, they chose to ignore.

"Should one of us stay with Mom tonight? I can."

"*I* can."

"Mom doesn't want us to 'baby' her, she has said . . ."

"It's hardly 'babying,' to spend the night in the house. She won't even know, I think she's gone to bed by now."

"Yes, but is Mom able to *sleep*?"

The question hovered about them like a soft, silent moth. Not one of them had been *able to sleep* in any normal way since their father's hospitalization.

"She has sleeping pills. I think she's been taking them."

"She really doesn't want us 'babying' her—she has said."

"D'you think it's real to her?"

"No."

Beverly gave a little, choked sob. "Oh, God. What is Mom going to *do*? They've been—they'd been—married forty years . . ."

Sophia said, uncertainly, "Well—look . . . People die every day, and their families survive. Somehow."

Not what she'd meant to say, or what she was feeling.

"I mean—Mom has plenty of widow-friends. They have all survived, somehow."

Again, this was not right. Sophia persisted, trying to be exact.

"It just happened sooner than we expected, and we're—we're surprised. In stress experiments, with lab animals, some are devastated and demoralized by stress and give up right away but others—(it's genetic, that's the point of the experiment)—learn to adjust, and can survive—to a degree." Sophia paused, stricken with horror. What was she saying? Were the others staring at her in disgust and dismay? Blindly she continued:

"We haven't had time to adjust. Mom didn't have time. It all came too fast. We were expecting Daddy to *recover*."

How reasonable this was! How primly Sophia spoke, for one whose head was swirling, and how hopeful she was, that her impatient sisters and brothers would take her seriously for once, and not dismiss her as *the baby*.

(And was Sophia a *virgin*? Beverly and Lorene discussed this possibility, often. Beverly thought yes, Lorene thought no. Each had persuasive arguments that could not persuade the other.)

(Sophia's brothers had no opinion on the subject of her virginity and would never have discussed it with anyone.)

With a grim sort of satisfaction Lorene said: "Well. Stress kills."

Furtive-shining-eyed Virgil said: "About Diogenes?"

"What about 'Diogenes'?"

They'd all been hoping that Virgil would have forgotten whatever he'd meant to tell them. Just—*no*.

But: unbelievably then, with no mind for how hurtful, how wounding, how crude, how stupid, how offensive and unforgivable his words were to his grieving sisters and brother: "Diogenes had the right idea about death. How over-seriously we take it. How we *fuss*. The body is just 'material'—a thing that is sloughed off. Essentially, a human corpse is garbage. Diogenes proclaimed that when he died he wanted his body tossed over the city wall for scavengers to eat." Virgil paused, smiling. That smile struck them like a draft of cold rank air.

"Virgil. For heaven's sake . . ."

"Asshole. Go away."

The look in Virgil's face, disingenuous, yet defiant, arrogant, you wanted to slap it off, how inappropriate such remarks were, their father only just *passed away*.

Their dear father who'd become, in a matter of minutes, a *body*.

Stubbornly Virgil said, "How is Diogenes not correct? He called himself a 'cynic'—(*cynic* is Greek for *dog*)—but what he says is not at all cynical, it is absolutely true. If you believe in the soul, as Diogenes did, the soul is immortal—the body is trash. The soul does not decay, the body decays."

"Will you please shut up?"

Thom threatened to grab hold of Virgil. As the sisters tried to intervene, Thom pushed Virgil, hard.

Virgil protested, trying to duck. But Thom was too strong, and, though he'd been drinking, and was very tired, too quick for Virgil whom he grabbed in a headlock, as he'd done when they were boys, when Thom was a big boy, and Virgil was a puny little boy.

Beverly cried, "Thom! Don't! This is crazy."

"*He's* crazy. He doesn't care what damn fucking stupid thing comes out of his mouth."

With a grunt Thom threw Virgil to the ground. Heavily Virgil fell in the frost-stubbled grass, on his side, and for a moment could not move. Adrenaline rushed through Thom's veins like liquid fire, delicious.

Virgil lay stunned, frightened. His big brother had hurt him. His ears rang. A thin line of something dark and liquid ran from one of his nostrils and tears welled in his widened eyes.

Sophia pleaded, "Thom, come on. Virgil was just talking . . ."

"Nobody wants to listen to his bullshit."

"What if Mom hears you? For God's sake . . ."

Angrily Thom staved off his sisters' restraining hands. Virgil had managed to get to his feet and cowered in front of him.

"Don't worry, I'm not going to hurt you. Christ! Think I'd kill *you*."

The fury was spent. As quickly as it had flared up, it subsided.

Like a kicked dog Virgil ran limping toward the house. He would go crying to their mother, Thom supposed. God damn him!

His sisters were fearful of Thom, also. Standing a little apart from him as he stood spread-legged, breathing hard, his heart kicking in his chest like a crazed thing.

Hiding from his sisters' eyes the hot elation in his face.

IN THE POCKET*, the triangular rock.*

Even as he fell he was reaching for it. Removing it, with some difficulty.

On the ground, and then on his knees. And on his feet grabbing at his brother who loomed over him flush-faced and brute in drunkenness, rage. And swinging the rock at the bully-brother, striking the astonished man on the side of the head, above the left eye, drawing blood, drawing a cry of pain, and leaping from his brother as he staggered—leaping from the women who were screaming at him—

Virgil, no! Virgil!

IN THEIR BED on her side of the bed.

Thoughts come to her in slow floating monosyllables like broken clouds.

Here is the surprise: she is still alive.

It is the first, the most profound of the many surprises the widow will endure. *Still alive.*

Wakefulness unending like a Sahara glittering and glaring in a hot blinding sun. So many people plucking at her needing to be consoled.

To escape this terrible wakefulness you would do a desperate thing.

In the bathroom on the sparkling-white counter she has laid out the pills. Some of these are her pills, and some of these are Whitey's pills. Some of them are reasonably new, some are old. The oldest, dated 1993.

Powerful painkillers following root canal work (Whitey's). Fifty-milligram pills so large she'd have to cut them in two, possibly in thirds, with a serrated knife, to swallow them down with water.

And so many: the little plastic container is almost full.

Out of the medicine cabinet, out of a cupboard in the bathroom, how many pills? Fifty, eighty, one hundred?

Varied sizes, colors. Fascinating to behold.

Maybe you don't need them, Jess. Not tonight.

It is true. She is very tired and believes that she can sleep without medication.

She'd had one, two, possibly three glasses of wine this evening. Each glass taken up, set down and forgotten in the excitement of greeting new guests, being embraced, kissed. How much she'd actually drunk could not be calculated.

Just come here, Jess. Settle in right here with me.

As always he wraps his arms around her. Their limbs tangle together. His jaws slightly stubbly, needing shaving.

He is a big man. Even horizontal he seems to loom above her.

Always he will love her. Protect her. He has vowed.

It is not Whitey's voice exactly but a voice of great calm and consolation assuring her *The widow is the intermediary between the dead husband and the living world. Without her, he is lost.*

The Last Will & Testament of John Earle McClaren

To my dear wife, and my dear children, my estate to be divided accordingly . . .

Well, the *dear children* were stunned. They were incensed. They *could not believe what Whitey had done.*

He'd left them each equal bequests! He'd left Virgil as much as he'd left *each of them.*

He'd left Virgil as much as he'd left Thom (who was his right-hand man) and he'd left Beverly (who'd scarcely worked a day in her life and was married to a bank officer) as much as he'd left Lorene and Sophia (who'd had to work all their lives).

How was it fair, Beverly fumed, for Whitey to leave her sisters (who were unmarried, had no children, no one except themselves to provide for) as much as he was leaving her, the mother of children? Didn't Whitey know, had Whitey forgotten, how expensive children are today?

How was it fair, Lorene fumed, for Whitey to leave Thom (who'd already taken over the McClaren family business, with a sharp increase in salary) the identical bequest he'd left *her* (who'd toiled for years on a public educator's salary)? How was it fair to leave fat, frowsy Beverly, who had a husband to support her, anything at all?

Thom was disbelieving: that his father had left Virgil *anything at all*.

Sophia too was stunned by her father's bequests, but for different reasons. She would not have thought that he would leave her so much money, as well as shares in McClaren, Inc.—the equivalent of five years' salary at the Institute (before taxes).

Oh Daddy, I don't deserve this! She wasn't getting a Ph.D. at Cornell as her family believed. She wasn't really a scientist, just a lab assistant following the instructions of her supervisor. She had no *integrity*. Her poor deceived father had had no idea.

She would have thought that Virgil, with virtually no source of income, should have been left more than any of them. But this was not something she'd have dared to say aloud.

Virgil alone of the McClaren children hadn't showed up at the lawyer's office. To Sophia he'd said: "Why should I come, to be humiliated? I know what Dad thought of me." In the final, post-stroke week of his life Whitey had been receptive to Virgil as he'd never been previously; but Virgil knew that his father's will had been drawn up years before. Sophia said, "But, Virgil, how can you *know*?" and Virgil said quietly, "I know."

Sophia saw the hurt in her brother's eyes. She would not pursue the issue. But thinking now, in the aftermath of the disclosure of the will, that in Virgil's Buddhist renunciation of desire as in his resignation to something like perpetual defeat there was something complacent, even smug. And mistaken.

"**BUT WHY WOULD DAD DO** such a thing? 'In trust'—*why*?"

The other surprise of Whitey's will didn't involve bequests to his children but the arcane stipulations of a trust he'd established for his widow.

Apart from property jointly owned by Mr. and Mrs. John Earle McClaren, which under state law automatically reverted to his widow upon his death, Whitey seemed to have made elaborate financial arrangements for the bulk of his estate to be held "in trust" for Jessalyn. More surprising still, Artie Barron, Whitey's lawyer, whom Thom and the others knew only slightly, was the executor of this trust.

"Excuse me, Mr. Barron—why did Dad do this? And why *you* as executor?"

"And when did Dad do this? We didn't know anything about it . . . Mom, did you know?"

Slowly Jessalyn shook her head as if she didn't know the answer to the question. Or—had she not heard the question?

Since she'd been seated beside him, by Artie Barron, at the polished mahogany table, Jessalyn had been very still, and very quiet. Her children had noted that her eyes were red-rimmed and raw-looking; where usually Jessalyn smiled whenever you caught her eye, now she smiled without looking at you, a twitch of a smile, wan and fleeting.

As the terms of the will were being read by Barron in a clipped, precise voice, as a metronome might speak if a metronome could speak, Jessalyn listened with the polite attentiveness of a deaf person hoping not to be discovered that she isn't hearing a thing.

Barron asked Jessalyn if she understood the terms of the trust her husband had established for her. Like one addressing a convalescent he leaned forward into Jessalyn's wavering line of vision.

"I—I think so." Then, seeing how they were all looking at her with concern and pity, "Yes. Of course."

Thom said, "Mom? Do you understand what this 'trust' is?"

"Not in detail, no. But—overall—I know what a 'trust' is . . ."

"If you like, Jessalyn, I can explain more thoroughly. Either now or at another time that is convenient for you . . . I could come to your house, if you wish. It wasn't clear to me that your husband had not informed you, or anyone in the family, that he was establishing a trust . . ."

"Or that he was choosing you to execute it. No. No one told us."

"No one told us."

Beverly spoke sharply, glaring at Artie Barron for whom she felt animosity as if (though this was unfair, it was quite natural) blaming him for the *equitable* nature of her father's bequests to his children as well.

Jessalyn was thinking how, last time she'd been in this sumptuously appointed room at Barron, Mills & McGee it had been to sign Whitey's and her wills several years before. How she'd had to plead with Whitey, to get him to come to the law office; before that, even to consider making a will.

He hadn't opposed her, that was the problem. Whitey had never said *no* to Jessalyn in their married life. (Or, almost never.) She smiled recalling his habit of just forgetting what they were talking about. The effort of remembering fell to *her.*

How many times Whitey had said *Oh I know, darling—I know I should. But this week is crazy-busy, I can't make time. Next week . . .*

In the carpeted room Whitey's voice was almost audible. Jessalyn half-wondered if anyone else could hear.

. . . remind me again, will you? Thank you, darling.

But the lawyer—(what was his name: Barron)—continued talking in his dogged wearing-you-out way and would not be interrupted. (*His meter is on and ticking: "billable hours"*—Whitey would say.) You could see that Barron had had plenty of experience contending with unwelcome surprises and disappointed heirs. Thom had asked how much salary he would be receiving as executor of the trust and Barron was giving a masterly evasive answer.

Jessalyn smiled. What had Whitey said after they'd completed their wills and left this office?—*What's the difference between a school of piranha fish and a school of lawyers?* She didn't remember the comical answer but she remembered laughing; she always laughed at Whitey's jokes. She did remember Whitey's grim quip—*Joke's on us. Guess how much those damned wills cost.*

He'd taken her hand. They'd walked hand in hand to the parking lot.

Had Whitey's fingers been cold? Maybe . . . Or maybe she was misremembering.

Words were flying about her now. *Trust. In trust. Executor. Salary. Purpose?* She saw how words were dangerous as flung rocks. Laid down in layers like rocks, unwieldy and ill-fitting, no sooner set in place than loose and wobbling.

Tasting something dry in her mouth, like the husk of an old dead thing: beetle, a portion of a shrugged-off snakeskin.

She was close to vomiting, and felt the blood rush from her face.

Shakily she rose from her seat at the polished mahogany table. One of the daughters began to rise with her but Jessalyn signaled for her to stay seated. *Please.*

She was just going to a restroom, she said. No need to follow her.

But standing so quickly had made her light-headed. In the adjoining room which was a kind of lounge something like an old trolley swung toward her through a doorway, bringing chaos with it. An electric trolley, propelled by overhead rails, a most remarkable clatter and racket, on its rails flying white sparks. But how could such a trolley be *indoors*? Her eyes widened in panic. She shrank, ducked. The receptionist would claim later that Mrs. McClaren had cowered like a poor shelled creature, a turtle, retracting its head, in terror of annihilation.

"AS I UNDERSTAND IT, Whitey worried that your mother would give money away. He thought that she was 'soft-hearted'—'insufficiently skeptical.' He worried"—here Artie Barron lowered his voice, confidingly, with a glance around the table to make sure that no one was present who should not be present—"that your brother Virgil would appeal to her for money, for 'hippie' organizations he belonged to, and that she wouldn't be able to say no. It wasn't that Whitey didn't trust her, but he was concerned for her well-being. The amount of money Jessalyn will receive monthly from the trust is generous, and she can give away some of it if she wants to, but there wouldn't be the temptation to give too much away, since she will need it to live on. There's no possibility of your mother giving away, for instance, ninety percent of your father's investments."

"Mom isn't so naive, that she'd give away 'ninety percent' of anything. That's an insult."

"—it is an insult. Poor Mom!—she's always had to be urged to buy things for herself . . ."

The sisters spoke excitedly. Artie Barron maintained a calm level so-reasonable tone, like a man leveling cement with a trowel.

"Well, that's what your father seemed to be saying. He deliberated over this for weeks when we were drawing up the terms. He told me he'd lost sleep over it. He thought that your mother was just too good-hearted, and that people would take advantage of her as soon as—if—something happened to him." Barron's voice faltered, as if politely.

Now Thom recalled an awkward conversation he'd had with his father months before, a vague sort of exchange, baffling at the time. Whitey had professed concern about Jessalyn being "taken advantage of" if something happened to him.

In their exchanges, the possibility of death could only be couched in oblique terms. *If something happened to me. If Jessalyn was left alone.*

Whitey had said extravagantly that he wasn't much worried about McClaren, Inc.—Thom was doing more than half the business now, and could "easily" take over; but Whitey did worry about Jessalyn, his dear wife.

Thom had said that Jessalyn would hardly be alone; he and his sisters would take care of her, if any sort of care was needed.

(Whitey hadn't seemed to notice that Thom had failed to mention Virgil.)

But Whitey hadn't been assured. Whitey had seemed strangely fixated on the possibility that, if something happened to him, Jessalyn would have to be protected.

"You kids have your own lives. You have your own children. I've got to provide for Jessalyn. She wouldn't have a clue if she was left—alone."

He'd been fretting. Something on his mind. Maybe he'd gone to a doctor, Thom had thought.

"Is there any advantage to a 'trust'?"—Sophia had to ask, for no one else was asking.

"Yes! Certainly. A widow is protected against what used to be called 'fortune-hunters'—and a widow is protected against spurious lawsuits against her estate, instigated by unscrupulous persons who want to take advantage of a woman whose husband has just died. The 'trust' is a legal protection against marauders."

It seemed obvious here that Barron meant *well-to-do widow.* Whitey had fretted that his dear wife was not temperamentally capable of dealing with a large inheritance.

Beverly said, hotly: "We can protect our mother against marauders. We don't need a 'trust.'"

Lorene objected: "Enough of this talk of 'protecting' Mom. Jessalyn McClaren isn't an invalid. She's been taking care of her husband for all of their married life, frankly—*she's* been the strong one, not Dad. We are all amazed—she's handling Dad's death very well . . ."

"Very normally, we think."

"*Very* normally."

"Except—"

"—yes, well—"

"—it's clear she doesn't seem to—exactly—grasp that Dad is *gone.*"

There was a pause. Lorene had surprised herself with her words—*Dad is gone.* Her plain pale tough-elfin face crinkled and with no warning she burst into tears.

Such an astonishing sight, bossy stiff-backed Lorene bursting into tears in the law office of Barron, Mills & McGee, Beverly could not stop herself from crying as well; and of course, in her tremulous state, Sophia broke down also.

Jesus! Thom and Artie Barron exchanged a look of manly consternation.

A READING OF A WILL IS TURBULENCE: after it is *read,* small quakes and ripples remain as in any agitation of the air, water, or earth.

Needing a drink, badly! Thom spoke in jest, hoping one or two of the others would say *God, yes,* on our way home, great idea.

Swollen-eyed Beverly licked her lips. (Thom saw.) But no . . .

Lorene, no. Sophia, no. And Jessalyn, of course—*no.*

Fuck he'd have to stop for a drink by himself, then. Maybe better, anyway.

Was he drinking *too much*? If no one to gauge, what is *too much*?

In Thom's car driving Jessalyn back to the house on Old Farm Road they tried to gauge their mother's feelings.

(But did Jessalyn have *feelings*? She was so selfless, stoic—you could never tell what she was thinking, let alone *feeling*.)

Was she upset about the trust? Did she even understand? Had (maybe) Whitey told her of his plans, and she hadn't (quite) been listening? (For Jessalyn had so little interest in finances, she sometimes pressed her hands over her ears when the subject came up. Any discussion of income taxes made her heart flutter.)

The McClarens had never lived extravagantly, not even showily, as others did, who had not nearly as much money as they had, with the result that they'd saved a good deal of money without being quite aware of it. Whitey's investments, like his business risks, were conservative, with a low yield, but even a low yield adds up, in time.

Except for the trust Whitey's will had not been unconventional. Equal bequests to his heirs, a scattering of other, smaller bequests to individuals and to charitable organizations to which he and Jessalyn had been donating for years, nothing out of the ordinary, or so it seemed.

No mysterious names, no unexpected beneficiaries. No bastard child or second family! Nothing to baffle or upset them in the wake of his passing.

This was a relief, at least. (Wasn't it?)

On the matter of the trust, the widow didn't seem to have any opinion. Whatever her husband had wished, that was his wish: she'd always deferred to him in financial matters. That she could not easily put her hands on hundreds of thousands of dollars, millions of dollars, for whatever purpose of her own, didn't concern Jessalyn; she would no more have thought of it than she'd have thought of running away to—Tasmania, the tip of Argentina, the Galápagos or Antarctica.

She had to laugh, the children seemed so incensed on her part. Yet (she guessed) they would be more incensed if she had inherited a good deal of money, and decided to spend it at once.

"You're not upset, Mom? That's good."

"I've told you dear—*no*."

Why did they keep asking her! How could they be so unfeeling! Investments, property, insurance, McClaren, Inc.—damned "estate"—"trust"—the remainder of her life—what did these mean to her, now that her husband was gone?

Staring at her hands, that smarted as if she'd been scrubbing them with disinfectant, abrading the tender skin.

AT THE HOUSE they would've come inside with her but Jessalyn said with a quick, forced smile that she was very tired, and thought she would lie down for a while.

But—they could stay at the house with her, if she wished. If she wanted company.

If she wanted to discuss the will, later. The "trust." The future.

No, no!—she insisted, she was fine.

"If you're sure, Mom . . ."

". . . sure you're feeling all right . . ."

All but pleading with her. Coercing her. Were they afraid that she would harm herself, if left alone? Do something stupid like falling down the stairs, breaking her neck? Drinking the rest of Whitey's whiskey, falling into a stupor?

How powerfully it came over her, she wanted no more of this.

Though *widowhood* had scarcely begun she was exhausted, and could bear it no longer.

"Just go home. Please. You have your own lives. I can take care of myself. It isn't lonely here—this is Whitey's house. Thank you!"

One breath and then another, darling. You will get through it.

Taser

Thom's father was already on the ground and incapacitated, Azim Murthy was saying.

"They were firing point-blank. Your father wasn't 'resisting.' He didn't even seem to be conscious, he'd stopped pleading with them . . ."

It was early November. Out of nowhere and in the very week Thom McClaren decided to file a complaint with the Hammond Police Department Civilian Review Board, Azim Murthy appeared in his life.

He'd learned that Mr. McClaren had died, Dr. Murthy said. He'd seen the obituary in the Hammond paper. "I am the only witness who knows what happened."

As it turned out Dr. Murthy had actually come to Hammond General Hospital in the late afternoon of October 19 to learn if a man—"late sixties, white-haired, heavyset, Caucasian"—had been brought into the ER following a stun-gun assault by police officers; but his contacts at the hospital hadn't been able to help him, not definitively. A patient named John Earle McClaren, sixty-seven, had been brought into the ER by ambulance at about that time, a stroke victim who'd been in a car crash and not (evidently) a victim of assault.

Dr. Murthy had taken down the information, however. He'd suspected that the "stroke victim" was in fact the man he'd seen assaulted by police officers at the edge of the Hennicott Expressway.

"I was the reason your father stopped. He was protesting two police officers beating me. He was a very brave man, he saved my life. But the police beat him savagely when he intervened. They knocked him down, and kicked him, and shot him with 'stun guns.' Even after he was unconscious they kept on. They were like maniacs. Before that they'd shot me also with the electric charge—for no reason. They'd stopped me on the highway claiming that I was 'driving recklessly'—'changed lanes without signaling'—the reason was they'd thought I was a young black man—(this is what my lawyer has told me)—and they wanted to search the car for drugs or whatever else they could find, that they'd thought a young black man might have in his car. When they saw who I was—that I was not an 'African-American'—they were furious. They did not pay any attention when I tried to tell them that I am a doctor, and where I worked. They did not even look at my ID or driver's license. They pretended to be thinking that I was 'under the influence'—'driving recklessly.' When they couldn't find any drugs in my car they were more angry. They shouted at me to put my hands over my head and to get down on my stomach, on the ground. No matter how I obeyed them they kept shouting like insane men. I was trying to shield my face and head—I was begging them not to hurt me—this was interpreted as 'resisting arrest.' They kept shouting at me. For no reason then, except that I was writhing on the ground in pain, they fired their stun guns at me. The electric shock is awful—paralyzing. I thought I would die. I thought my heart would stop. I could not breathe. I have never felt anything so painful. It's like a convulsion—being shocked to death. You cannot breathe. About this time your father pulled his vehicle off the highway, and shouted at them to leave me alone. So they turned their attentions to him. It saved my life that he came. I couldn't see all that they did to him but I could see that they threw him down, and were kicking him, and firing their guns at him point-blank. They were shouting—always shouting. The same two or three things—'get down'—'get down'—'fucker get down'—even if you are already down. They handcuffed me and arrested me and took me to the precinct but your father they left behind for an ambulance to pick up—they saw that he'd had a heart attack or a stroke . . . They seemed scared then, that they might have killed him. I was in so much pain, and terrified of what they might do to me, I didn't really know what happened to my 'rescuer' at the time. I am not proud to recall, I was in such bad shape I could not think of anyone but myself—I was not thinking clearly. I was in fear of my life. I am not born in this country but I am a U.S. citizen. I was in fear that I could be deported for some reason. I had never been arrested for anything before—I'd never been dragged into a police station. I'd never even been stopped in my car by police. I thought that I might be killed—beaten or shocked to death. It wasn't like movies or TV, I was not allowed a telephone call. But eventually, at about four A.M. for no reason I could comprehend, I was released. I was not in good shape by that time. I was badly beaten and had many aches and bruises and the shock wounds hurt very badly. But I was very happy to be released. There were no charges against me, I was 'free to go.' Someone was feeling sorry for me, or worried about me, that I would die in the jail cell. So I was allowed a phone call, and called for help, for someone to come pick me up and take me to the ER at St. Vincent's Hospital (which is my place of work) where I was examined for face and head injuries and sprained ribs and pictures were taken of my wounds. They said, you have been beaten, we will call the police but I begged them *no!*—I wanted only to go home. Even now I am not in good shape but I know that I am very fortunate to be alive. I am a resident physician at St. Vincent's and work very hard. I do not tell my family of my troubles for they would be terrified more than me. Since the attack I have not slept more than a few hours each night and I have many pains and headaches. I have been told that I was 'profiled' as a black man—that was the cause of the arrest. It was a nightmare and made all the worse that another, innocent man—your father—was killed by these madmen. I have filed charges against them. I know their names—I will give you all the information my lawyer has found out for me. I will testify against them for assaulting me and for a 'false arrest.' I will testify against them for what they did to your father who did not resist them and was unarmed. They are murderers!"

So astonished was Thom by this torrent of words from a young Indian man whom he'd never met before and of whom he'd known nothing, he had to ask Azim Murthy to repeat what he'd said, and to speak more slowly.

Painful to listen to Murthy speak, and to think of poor Whitey so assaulted at the side of a highway, unable to defend himself and alone. Essentially it was what Thom had suspected: his father had not died a natural death, his father had been murdered.

"YOU HAVE GROUNDS FOR BRINGING criminal charges against the police officers, and you have grounds for a multimillion-dollar civil suit."

Thom was meeting with a Hammond litigator named Bud Hawley, a former associate of Whitey's. Hawley had made inquiries at the Hammond PD and learned that indeed there'd been an arrest by police officers of "Azim Murthy" on October 18, 2010, on charges of "reckless driving," "disorderly conduct," "suspicion," "disobeying a police officer's command," and "resisting arrest." These charges were subsequently dropped.

There was no record of a second man having been apprehended at about the same time and at the same place on the Hennicott Expressway. There was no record of a second man forcibly restrained, beaten and Tasered into unconsciousness; but there was a Hammond General Hospital record of sixty-seven-year-old John Earle McClaren being brought into the ER by ambulance that afternoon, believed to have suffered a stroke while driving on the Hennicott Expressway, and having sustained injuries when his car slammed into a retaining wall.

The officers' names were Schultz, Gleeson. Both were patrolmen who'd been with the Hammond PD for years. Questioned by Azim Murthy's lawyer about the arrest of Murthy on charges the lawyer characterized as "spurious and unfounded"—a consequence of "racial profiling"—the officers had insisted that the young Indian doctor had been driving recklessly, which was why they'd stopped him; they had every reason to suspect that he was driving under the influence of drugs or alcohol; they insisted that *he* had threatened *them*; despite warnings he'd advanced upon them and appeared to be reaching for a weapon (in his coat pocket); he'd had to be forcibly restrained for reasons of clear and present danger to officer safety.

When Murthy "continued to resist" they'd had no choice but to fire their stun guns at him a "minimal" number of times.

These statements, seemingly memorized, were sullenly and even defiantly given under the guidance of an attorney for the Hammond PD union who insisted that his clients had not acted in any way in violation of Hammond PD protocol.

"Shooting a man point-blank with a stun gun, not once but several times, after he has been thrown down and handcuffed and is clearly unarmed—that isn't 'in violation' of Hammond PD protocol?"

To which the reply was a reiteration of *clear and present danger to officer safety.*

The presence of the second man, later identified as John Earle McClaren, was established only after protracted questioning by Murthy's lawyer. Initially Schultz and Gleeson denied knowledge of McClaren but, confronted with Murthy's deposition, they acknowledged that a second man had appeared at the scene of the arrest: McClaren had pulled over onto the shoulder of the highway with the intention, it had seemed to them, of interfering with the arrest of Murthy; the officers had believed that McClaren was an accomplice of Murthy, and so had to defend themselves against him.

McClaren, too, had "threatened" police officers, advanced upon them "despite repeated warnings"; made a "threatening" move for his waistband, or his pocket; had to be "forcibly restrained" with a stun gun fired no more than two or three times.

This was an era before police videos. No one had recorded the incident(s). Only twenty-eight-year-old Azim Murthy, himself badly traumatized from having been assaulted, could testify against the police officers.

A preliminary hearing was held at the bequest of Murthy's lawyer in one of the smaller courtrooms at the Hammond Township courthouse. A township judge presided. Thom was not present: he would be told of the proceedings only afterward. And hearing his lawyer explain the legal situation as he saw it Thom became increasingly agitated. *But they killed my father. They precipitated the stroke. He never recovered from the stroke. They are his murderers.*

IT WAS NOT POSSIBLE to locate a Hammond PD arrest report on John Earle McClaren for October 18, 2010. If there'd been an arrest there would have been a report; if there'd been an initial report, it must have been destroyed.

Bud Hawley would file for a subpoena to be allowed entry into the Department's computerized records. But very likely, this record too had been altered following the instruction of someone in the Department.

Thom had evidence, as he saw it, of Taser burns on his father's face, throat, hands. He'd taken numerous pictures on his cell phone and he'd sent these pictures to Bud Hawley immediately, in case something happened to his phone. He had a copy of the hospital report which noted "burn-like welts" on his father's face and body which had been initially and inaccurately attributed to lacerations presumably caused by a car crash—(which crash had not in fact occurred).

The police officers had lied about a "car crash." They'd lied about John Earle McClaren stricken at the wheel of his vehicle, jolting to a stop on the highway shoulder. Their newer account was that McClaren had stopped his vehicle at the side of the road with the "express intention" of intervening in an arrest. They'd had to admit that yes, they'd fired their stun guns at McClaren, felling him, but only for purposes of "officer safety." They'd fired their guns only before, not after, having handcuffed McClaren.

They would change their stories several times about what had happened to McClaren. In the final version, after they'd had to subdue the fallen man, and handcuff him, he'd seemed to have "some kind of fit"—"like, an eliptetic fit"—so they'd called 911.

Eliptetic?—epileptic?

Or maybe a heart attack, stroke.

Some pre-existing condition he'd had, that wasn't caused by the arrest.

But why had there been no charges made against John Earle McClaren? Or, if charges had been made, why had charges been dropped? (Nullified by a lieutenant at the ninth precinct, the officers' immediate superior.) Bud Hawley would claim, on Thom McClaren's behalf, that the "arrested" man, Thom McClaren's father, had been left on the shoulder of the highway unconscious, scarcely breathing, having suffered a stroke after being violently assaulted by the officers; he'd been picked up by medical workers and brought to the Hammond General ER where his life had been saved.

Eventually, McClaren's injuries led to his death. Complications following a stroke precipitated by Hammond police officers in an unprovoked assault of an unarmed, unresisting man of sixty-seven.

FIRST, A COMPLAINT FILED with the Civilian Review Board. Following that, a suit filed against the police officers Schultz and Gleeson and the Hammond PD charging homicide incurred in the commission of reckless endangerment of human life.

Homicide was an extreme charge, Hawley knew. In bargaining, the charge would be lowered to manslaughter (voluntary). There would be ancillary charges of excessive force, police misconduct.

Thom understood: justice was on his side. But Thom also knew: prosecutors, judges, juries were reluctant to find police officers guilty of the most extreme examples of malfeasance.

How humiliated Whitey would be! Worse even than the physical injuries, the blow to his pride. For he'd been proud of his relationship with the Hammond PD which had been very carefully, very diplomatically forged when he'd been mayor two decades before.

Whitey would have wanted the police officers disciplined, fired. Possibly he'd have wanted to press criminal charges and send them to prison. But he wouldn't have wanted to collect money from the city of

Hammond for that meant taxpayers, not the police department. Only if the criminal case was thwarted would Thom consider a civil suit.

While Whitey had been mayor of Hammond a large settlement was made to the family of a young Cambodian man who'd been shot and killed by police officers at the conclusion of a cross-county high-speed chase. Three squad cars, six police officers had given chase at a speed of over eighty miles an hour on country highways. The fleeing "suspect" had ended up in a cornfield in an overturned vehicle. No drugs had been found in the vehicle, no firearms or contraband of any kind, just children's clothes and toys. The "suspect" had been twenty-seven years old and the father of young children and he'd died in a fusillade of Hammond PD bullets.

It had not been one of the episodes of which Whitey McClaren had been proud in his two-term mayoral career. He'd tried to mediate between the intransigent chief of police on one side and the publicity-seeking attorney for the grieving family on the other.

Finally, after more than a year, and much unfortunate media attention, the city settled with the litigants for an undisclosed sum (one million, five hundred thousand dollars); the officers involved in the high-speed chase and shooting were suspended from the force, and allowed to retire with benefits.

There'd been no question of a criminal trial. There'd been no grand jury. The prosecutor had not pursued the case.

A tragic situation. We cannot risk such a tragedy again.

Whitey had spoken as firmly as possible. He'd given numerous press conferences. He'd chastised the police officers but he had never—quite—criticized the police department as a whole, and he had never directly criticized the chief of police who (he'd wanted to think) was his friend.

He would not have wanted his son to pursue this case. Thom supposed.

And there'd been no autopsy. Thom should have insisted, when Jessalyn demurred. He should have told her why he wanted an autopsy, why an autopsy was necessary, for he meant to bring suit against the Hammond police. But he'd been reluctant to upset his mother further, he'd given in to the emotions of the moment.

"If you'd thought you might be going to sue, you should certainly have insisted on an autopsy, Thom."

"I couldn't persuade my mother. I tried."

"You should have explained to Jessalyn how urgent it was."

"Jesus! I tried."

At the time he'd been too tired. His brain had not functioned clearly.

And now, too late. No physical evidence, only an inconclusive medical report which the defense would attempt to undermine, and the testimony of the young Azim Murthy.

STILL, THOM HAD NOT DISCUSSED the situation with his sisters. He had no wish to confront their wild, unpredictable emotions. He had no interest in discussing it with Virgil.

When finally he spoke with Jessalyn, bringing up the subject of a police assault against Whitey as carefully as possible, Thom saw how Jessalyn stiffened, her eyes showed fear. For a wild moment, a moment of sheer pathos, he understood that his mother was thinking that there'd been some mistake, some hospital confusion, Whitey had not died after all.

She does not want to hear. She does not want to know. Why are you tormenting her?

But he saw no alternative. He took pains to explain: Whitey had not had a car accident as they'd been led to believe, he hadn't been stricken while driving and injured in a "crash." He'd been injured, probably, by police officers discharging stun guns at him, when he'd stopped on the highway to intervene in their beating of a young Indian-American physician.

This assault had precipitated the stroke. As the stroke, after a week in the hospital, had weakened his immune system, and precipitated an infection that had carried him off.

Carried him off. These words had come to Thom out of the air.

Jessalyn asked Thom to repeat what he'd said.

She seemed to be listening, intently. Her bruised eyelids blinked rapidly as if she were having difficulty seeing Thom's face.

"Dad's stroke was caused by the police. It was an unprovoked assault. They attacked him. We have a witness. We are going to bring charges."

(What did Thom mean, *we*? He had not yet enlisted any other McClarens in his mission.)

Jessalyn said, in disbelief, stammering: "Oh, but—why would they do such a thing? Your father was—Whitey was—you know, Whitey was so—" Thom supposed she was wanting to say *well-liked*.

Her eyes filled with tears of shock and pain. Her voice quavered. He hated himself, to be upsetting his mother in this way. Yet he saw no alternative.

"Because they're ignorant, stupid. Because they're racists. They'd stopped the Indian doctor because they'd thought he was a young black man. So, when Dad tried to intervene they turned on him."

Thom paused. He took his mother's hand, and held it tight. Such cold, slender fingers! He had not wanted to see how Jessalyn had lost weight, these past several weeks.

"They didn't know who he was, Mom. They didn't recognize Whitey McClaren. He hasn't been—hadn't been—mayor for a long time, Mom."

"Oh but why, did you say? Why did they hurt him?"

It was like trying to reason with a child. Patiently Thom repeated how Whitey had stopped on the Expressway to intervene. He had seen two cops beating a dark-skinned young man at the side of the road, he'd saved the young man's life.

"He's a doctor at St. Vincent's—'Azim Murthy.' He was born in India, in Cochin. He has said he will testify for us. If—when—we bring charges."

Jessalyn's hair, that had once been smooth and glossy, a beautiful faded auburn, was now dull and without luster, brushed back flat against her head. Too bluntly, her skull seemed outlined. Her watery eyes were overlarge in her wan face. Her son felt a thrill of something like fear of the woman, even revulsion, fleeting, terrible.

She was pleading, protesting. "But—Whitey wouldn't want any trouble, Thom. It will look so, so awful in the newspapers—on TV—he will be so *shamed*. He'd call the police officers 'hotheaded kids'—he was always making excuses for them. Do you remember? Poor Whitey! He was so sorry he'd been talked into going into politics. He'd said he had been manipulated by people he'd thought were his friends. Everyone said, 'Whitey, the police have to be disciplined,' and Whitey said, 'Our hands are tied. The union is too strong. It brings mayors to their knees. I don't have a strong enough political base to fight them or believe me, I would.' He wept in my arms sometimes. Oh—what am I saying? Your father was so brave. He worried so much. People thought he was so strong, and bossy, they had no idea how much he cared, how he feared failing, he'd hated those lawsuits settled with taxpayers' money while the police department paid nothing, not a cent . . ."

Wildly Jessalyn spoke as Thom had never heard his mother speak before. Gripping his hand so hard it hurt. He listened but did not hear her say *no*.

WHEN BUD HAWLEY ASKED THOM if he should pursue the case Thom said, "Yes." He thought for a moment and said, "Fucking yes."

The Beneficiary

In a pocket of the oversized khaki jacket grown grimy with time he carried his father's death.

Many pockets in the khaki jacket (purchased at a church rummage sale for nine dollars) and of these some were zippered and others, larger, snapped shut.

Sometimes he kept his father's death in the long vertical pocket on his right thigh where you might put tools, a small claw hammer for instance, if you were a carpenter. Sometimes he kept his father's death in a left-hand pocket at waist level into which he could slip his hand if his hand was cold or was feeling lonely in which case his father's death was a jolt to him, a reminder—*Yes. Here.*

Sometimes the death was kept in an inside pocket, against his heart. In which case he was reminded of it too often—*Yes. Here. Where else?*

He'd have liked to leave his father's death somewhere not in a pocket of the khaki jacket but (for instance) on a closet shelf, in a drawer in his work bench amid paintbrushes, stained rags. He'd have liked to leave his father's death at a distance except there was the fear—(he felt this fear as if it were outside him, like a chill pelting rain)—that the death might become misplaced, lost.

Essentially his father's death was unwieldy, obtrusive. There was no place to keep it that was not in some way wrong.

THE LAST MORNING in Whitey's hospital room, he hadn't known would be the last.

The last day. He'd departed mid-afternoon for the farm. Planning to return in the morning with his elderberry flute to play for his father.

Thinking—*If Dad recovers will he remember me like this? Or—the way he used to think of me?*

There was much unsaid between them. Unspoken, unasked. He had not (yet) the courage to ask his father the crucial questions of his life for he had not (yet) the courage to comprehend what these questions might be.

Why didn't you love me, if you love me now?

Do you love me now, if you didn't love me before?

Abruptly then, rude as a page ripped from a book, it had ended. The news had come to him: he would not ever see his father alive again.

He would not ever ask those questions. His father would never grope for the words with which to answer.

IT WAS A COWARDLY GESTURE, to run away. Not a gesture of freedom, independence, "artistic integrity." But he'd run away.

And when he returned to the cabin behind the farmhouse on Bear Mountain Road one of his friends who lived in the house came down the hill to bring him an armful of mail.

Mail for *Virgil McClaren*! That hardly seemed possible.

In fact all but two or three of the letters were mass circulars, advertisements. He hadn't troubled to have his mail held at the post office nor even to make provisions for someone to keep it for him.

It was like Virgil to just disappear. Anyone who knew him, knew this. There was no question of being annoyed or exasperated, still less of being alarmed. The friend had known Virgil for several years now but would not have claimed to be an intimate friend and would not have been greatly surprised if Virgil didn't quite recall his name.

Abruptly after his father's death Virgil had departed. After the impromptu gathering at the house on Old Farm Road when he'd seen family, relatives, neighbors and friends beneath his parents' roof for the first time in memory and (he was sure) for the last time. And later behind the house after the guests had departed he'd seen a look of pure hatred in his brother Thom's face as Thom seized him in a headlock and threw him onto the ground while their sisters looked on in astonishment.

He'd realized—*Now that our father is gone there is nothing to keep him from killing me.*

He'd fled. He'd taken just a few changes of clothes, an extra pair of boots. He'd taken the pink feldspar rock he'd found in his father's desk, whose veins glittered in sunlight; this, he placed on the dashboard of the vehicle where he could see it easily. He'd vowed he would not see Thom again.

The hospital vigil had ended. Whatever had been between them had ended.

For several weeks he'd been away. In a borrowed vehicle he'd driven almost aimlessly. In the Adirondacks and into northern Vermont, New Hampshire, Maine. The season's first snow had fallen in Maine while in Hammond there remained an autumnal warmth to the days, an air of the unreal and precarious. He had not wanted to call home, he had not wanted to hear the voices of his family.

He felt guilty, to have abandoned his mother at such a time. They might have commiserated together. He should certainly have called his mother, and Sophia. To the others he had no idea what he might say.

He was sure as he'd told Sophia that their father would not remember him in his will. Of the McClaren children, Virgil was the least cherished by Whitey for (so far as he could recall) Whitey had never once been proud of any accomplishment of Virgil's.

Virgil, you are exaggerating! Dad loved you.

He knew, Jessalyn would assure him in this way. Sophia would assure him.

But he did not want to be assured by them. He did not want to be humored, like a child.

No wish to be humiliated in front of the others. Of course he'd kept away from the law office on the day his father's will would be read, by hundreds of miles.

AMID THE THIRD-CLASS MAIL WAS a single letter in stiff cream-colored stationery. *Barron, Mills & McGee LLP.*

He'd discovered the envelope at once. But did not rip it open at once.

Telling himself this could have nothing to do with him personally.

And so as he quickly skimmed the letter, squinting at the legal terminology, and then seeing the figure, surprised, and then shocked—his brain seemed to go blank.

"Virgil? Something wrong?"—the friend who'd brought his mail down to the cabin stood watching him.

Something wrong? No words with which to answer.

Virgil was staring at the stiff sheet of business stationery, that shook in his hand. He was sitting on the floor of the cabin near a wood-burning stove into which, less than an hour earlier, he'd inserted firewood, to light a fire, warm up the cabin cold as a refrigerator—he'd sat down abruptly as if his legs had given out beneath him. It didn't seem that he was altogether certain where he was as his friend's dog Sheffie wetly nuzzled his face.

"Virgil?—is it bad news?"

Seeing the notification of the sum of money his father had bequested him, how many thousands of dollars, more money than he'd ever had in all of his life—Virgil could not reply.

God! Whatever he'd expected, or not expected, he had certainly not expected *this*.

"N-No. Not bad news . . ."

His throat was constricted. He'd expected nothing and he'd wanted nothing. He'd prepared himself for nothing.

Almost he'd felt joyful, giddy. While he was away from Hammond and out of reach of his (grieving) family. The expectation of nothing is such freedom.

Ashes to ashes, dust to dust. Nothingness.

In that way (he'd told himself) he needn't have mourned his father. They had parted ways, that was all. In the last week of Whitey's life they'd been "close"—that was true. But the diminished father in the hospital bed had not been Virgil's true father, he knew.

But now the situation wasn't so clear. Virgil had no idea what to think for the will predated the hospitalization, the stroke, his father's final illness. The will had to be the *true father.*

He was thanking his friend for bringing the mail. He was joking that it was the most mail he'd had in years, and most of it would go right into the wood-burning stove.

Except the single, singular letter from *Barron, Mills & McGee LLP.* That, Virgil would not burn.

Briskly he forced the letter back into the envelope. Could not—quite—bring himself to tell his friend that his father had remembered him in his will, and so generously. There were not the words for this.

His friend (fellow artist, substitute middle-school teacher) offered to stay with Virgil if Virgil was feeling upset about something and Virgil insisted that wasn't necessary.

His friend's dog continued to nuzzle wetly against him. How comforting this was! Virgil hugged the big coarse-furred shepherd mix round the neck. He shut his eyes tight against tears as the dog continued to thump his tail against the bare floorboards quivering with joy at being so hugged.

"OF COURSE DAD LOVED YOU! Dad loved us all."

He'd had to call Sophia. Had to speak with Sophia. On a borrowed phone, had to speak with his sister who would not chide him or scream at him as he deserved.

Sophia's words were sweetly damning. Astute, irrefutable.

"You confused Dad not approving of your life with Dad not loving you. I tried to explain but you never listened. Oh, Virgil!"

Virgil did not protest. He was feeling a strange pulsing glow.

He was hearing that faint, murmurous buzz. In Maine he'd stayed with a beekeeper, a woman friend with a dozen beehives from which she harvested honey, and the sound of the bees came to him now, mixed with the excited beat of his blood.

Loved you were loved all along loved. You.

"You know, Dad left us all the same amount of money. Exactly the same. And he left most of his estate in trust, to Mom . . ."

Loved you as much as the others. All along?

Not possible.

Possible?

Not.

"Virgil? Are you there?"

Yes. Still there.

"Have you called Mom yet?"

Not yet.

"She will want to hear from you. Shall I tell her that you're back?"

No. Yes. Thank you.

"D'you want to come over for supper? Come to Mom's? I can meet you there?"

No. Not yet.

"Or—just us? I can drive out to your place, I can bring something for supper?"

No. Not yet.

I am not ready to see you. Yet.

"Well. Welcome back, anyway. From wherever you were."

Sophia spoke carefully. Of course Sophia was much exasperated, very likely she was disgusted with her irresponsible brother, but she would not betray such emotions over the phone.

"Next time you disappear let me know at least where you're going. Or Mom."

OK. Will do.

"Want to know what they're going to do with their inheritances?"

They meant the older brother, sisters. Between Sophia and Virgil, *they* did not require explanation.

"Thom is going to 'plough the money' back into McClaren, Inc. Beverly is going to use the money for home repairs—she says their house is falling down around their ears. Lorene is going to take a 'much-deserved vacation' in December. And I—I'm not decided."

Silence.

"So—what will you do with Dad's money, Virgil? Give it away?"

Give it away.

OR MAYBE, keep it for himself.

Greedy, selfish. Glutton. The Virgil McClaren no one knew, no one had guessed existed. Certainly not Dad.

Keep the money for himself. No more secondhand rummage-sale crap.

Art supplies, a place of his own. Instead of renting, Virgil's own *studio.*

Instead of the ugly bicycle no self-respecting kid would wish to steal, a pickup truck. Instead of borrowing others' vehicles like a beggar, his own.

(Happened that he knew a Dodge pickup for sale, very reasonably priced. Perfect for hauling scrap-metal sculptures to art fairs.)

(Yearning to travel—where? Southwest. High arid deserts, enormous skies that dwarfed individuals and their guilt. Out of here. When?)

Also: could use the money to repay others he has owed for years.

(Jessalyn? Repay *her*? Jessalyn wouldn't accept money from him. Especially the money Dad had left him. How perverse that would be! He would only upset her, if he tried.)

Realizing then: inheritances are taxed.

Of course, he hadn't thought of this. The actual sum of money he would receive as John Earle McClaren's beneficiary would be much less than the sum cited in the will.

Hadn't paid income tax for years. State, federal. And then, when he'd been an adjunct at the college, his income was so low, he'd had to pay less than five hundred dollars.

How out of touch Virgil was with the much-vaunted *world of reality.*

Then it came to him, out of nowhere, out of the smell of woodsmoke in his nostrils: how exactly his father had died.

He, Virgil, had not always washed his hands thoroughly when he'd come into Whitey's room. Much of the time he'd simply forgotten—so focused upon Dad, and playing his flute for Dad. With the half-mindedness of a twelve-year-old boy he'd ignored the sanitizer on the wall. He had not even seen it. Such scruples of cleanliness applied to other people but not to *him.*

Or: he'd believed that his father was tough, resilient, not weak, not easily *made sick.*

They'd called it a *staph* infection. Virgil knew of something called E. coli. A common bacterium found in the earth, particularly on farms, near manure. Animal waste. Sewage. The rich farm soil on Virgil's boots, sandals. Always a faint odor of manure at the farm that quickened and thickened in damp weather though the last cows had been gone for years. You tracked it everywhere. And horseflies, everywhere. E. coli is powerless to infect the healthy but merciless with those whom illness has weakened.

First visit to the Intensive Care Unit Virgil had been shown the hand sanitizer on the wall just inside the door of his father's room. *Like this. Be sure always wash your hands thoroughly.*

How grimly, how briskly, how determinedly they'd all been—washing their hands in the strong-smelling disinfectant.

Yet, Virgil had been careless. Not-clean hands, dirt beneath his nails. Grimy khaki jacket. Mud-splotched boots. Entering his father's hospital room with his flute beneath his arm like a character in a fairy tale privileged and free of commonsensical restrictions.

In this way he'd infected his father.

In this way he'd killed his father.

And, unknowing, his father had rewarded him . . .

Terrible to realize. The horror of it washed over him like filthy water. *You, Virgil. You are the one.*

AT DAWN waking to suffocating woodsmoke in the cabin.

"Oh, God!"—had to save himself, worthless murdering-self, throwing off bedclothes, stumbling to the door barefoot and outside into cold rain-splotched wind he might have hoped, if he didn't know better, would forgive him.

The Widow's Orgy

"Oh, Mom. What on earth have you *done*."

Poured out all that remained of Whitey's opened bottles of high-quality whiskey, gin, vodka, bourbon into the kitchen sink so that hours later the kitchen still reeks of a most giddy orgy.

(But the pills upstairs in the bathroom cabinet, which will remain her most precious secret, she keeps.)

The Shaking Hand

Hurry! Must not be late.

Where once she was out of bed and eager to drive to the Institute never later than 7:30 A.M. now she can barely force herself to open her eyes for fear she will see the black toad-shaped thing squatting on her chest.

And the taste of something black, dank, toad-like in her mouth.

And a heaviness like lead in all her limbs. That numbness she has injected into laboratory animals, to desensitize them against the pain she would next inject into them with her admirably steady hand.

Yet, she is eager. Badly she needs to return to work in the exacting rigor of the lab after too long away.

Glamor of *exactitude*. While actual life is soft, flabby, formless, unmeasurable.

She'd intended to return soon after her father's death. No more than three days. But it had seemed necessary to spend time with her mother at the house on Old Farm Road, to accompany Jessalyn to the law office of Barron, Mills & McGee, to the Hammond Township Probate Court, to other appointments falling under the blunt and punitive-sounding rubric *death duties*.

Worriedly Beverly had said *Keep an eye on Mom.* For Beverly had her own family life to which she must return.

And Lorene had said *Give me a call right away if something seems wrong.* For Lorene had her own professional life to which she must return.

Thom, too, expected Sophia to keep a *close eye* on their mother. As the new CEO of McClaren, Inc. he was much distracted by work: company headquarters in Hammond, Thom's home and family in Rochester, a grueling commute.

And Virgil?—vanished for nearly three weeks.

(Finally, Sophia had driven to the farmhouse on Bear Mountain Road to seek out her brother when he'd failed to appear at their mother's house for several days in succession. She'd known that Virgil had no intention of meeting at the law office of Barron, Mills & McGee for the reading of the will but she hadn't quite realized that he'd planned to leave Hammond altogether. Friends of his informed her that Virgil had borrowed a car to drive "somewhere upstate" with no clear notion of when he'd return. The shock was, she hadn't been so very shocked.)

When she'd told Jessalyn that Virgil had driven away somewhere by himself Jessalyn had seemed to understand. *Oh, I know! Virgil needs to be alone with his father.*

DRIVING TO THE MEMORIAL PARK Research Institute along the familiar route.

Except: death makes of all that is familiar, unfamiliar.

For instance: driving a road which, last time you'd driven it, had seemed very ordinary, not-memorable; but now, the shadow of death upon it, you see the road as irrevocably altered. *Never again can you drive this road as it had been, before the death.*

Trying to recall the last time she'd driven on Federal Road which would have to have been the day of Alistair Means's lecture: the day the news had come to her.

Sinking sensation in the heart, seeing so many calls gone to voice mail.

"Oh Daddy! I miss you."

Inside a car it is permissible to talk to oneself. No one will hear, no one will suspect. No one will care.

How Whitey had loved to talk while driving! Lifting both hands off the wheel at times, to gesture.

To Whitey, talking *was* gesture.

Sophia smiles, recalling. Hairs at the nape of her neck stir as she hears again Whitey's voice alternately playful and serious telling one of his long involved tall tales . . .

Strongly the impulse comes to Sophia: turn the car around, drive back home to Old Farm Road.

A mother is her caring. A mother is her children, her husband.

Did she want to emulate Jessalyn? Did she want to *be* Jessalyn?

Her parents had an ideal love. An ideal marriage. It will be hardly possible to emulate such a marriage, for their children.

It is a beautiful thing, Sophia thinks. To so live for others. To so live in others. She is fearful of the inclination in herself, to revere her mother.

In all creatures self-survival is the highest instinct. Yet, in the mother, another instinct emerges: the protection of the young.

She wants to have children, someday. As Jessalyn did.

Or—does she?

For the time being, she will be a loving and protective daughter.

Smiling to think how her mother has been planning to sort through Whitey's clothes, to donate to Goodwill. Also shoes.

Well, she will need help! Whitey was famously reluctant to throw away old shoes claiming he might have use for them one day.

Once you've broken in a pair of shoes it's like old friends, can't just toss them out into the trash.

And Jessalyn would say *You don't mean you'd want to toss away your old friends, Whitey, do you?*—and Whitey would say *Hell yes.*

What is awful about death: no more laughs.

No more words. No more Whitey. Just—

If Jessalyn tries to do the sorting alone it will never get done.

Sophia will ask Jessalyn if she can take some of Whitey's neckties for herself. Her favorites of his ties. (Some of the ties, of course Sophia had given her father herself.) She has a vague notion she might—someday—give these ties to a man with whom she has fallen in love.

SOPHIA? IT'S ALISTAIR. Just wondering how you are.

Wanting to call him back but could not. Why, why not, can't bring herself, out of fear, why?

Give me a call to let me know how you are. Please.

A stranger's voice, mesmerizing. Again and again she plays it. But she could not call . . .

Eager to return to the lab and to her true life (as she would call it: *not* the daughter-life) but as she approaches the Lumex lab building the leaden sensation returns in all her limbs. *So heavy!*

And inside the building, the surprise of the air. The odor.

Making her way along corridors. Familiar route but she turns a wrong corner into a cul-de-sac with a single ominous door. EXIT EMERGENCY ONLY.

Opening the heavy lab door and a sick-sinking sensation spreads in her like nausea.

"Sophia! Hello."

"Good to see you, Sophia . . ."

Smiles to show she's fine. Bravely smiles.

Avoiding conversation. Not just now. Coworkers' eyes on her grave, sympathetic. Curious.

To some of these, with whom she works closely, Sophia has sent emails of explanation. *Death in family, I am very sorry. Will catch up promise.*

(She supposes that they know: her father has died. Possibly they know who her father is. Was.)

(She isn't sure how much they know of Alistair Means's interest in her. If they know, they will be scathing, pitiless.)

So long she has been away from her computer. The machine is suspicious of her and rejects her password.

Then, allowed into the program, Sophia clicks onto columns of recorded data. So many columns! So many miniature deaths. Like ether wafting from the screen, suffusing her with nausea.

Another unpleasant surprise: the steady hand is not so steady this morning.

Fumbles to pull on a Latex glove. Sticky inside-out skin, repulsive to the touch.

Not far away from Sophia's work-area, walls of cages. Animal misery. Near-inaudible chittering of (tumor-ridden, doomed) creatures. No quantity of disinfectant can dispel their odor.

Still, she is determined to work. She will *catch up.*

Except: away so long from the lab, she seems to have forgotten what it is like. Faces of coworkers, fluorescent lights, chittering of the doomed, their smell.

No avoiding her supervisor, she supposes. As soon as he realizes that Sophia McClaren has returned to the lab at last.

If he says *Please accept my condolences, Sophia. I am sorry for your loss.*

Cannot bear the words. Not again. No!

It is a fact, no one knows how to speak in the face of death, grief. She has seen even the elderly hesitate, not altogether certain what to say about Whitey.

Preparing the (toxic) solution. So many times she has prepared it but today something seems wrong. Like a pianist suddenly made aware of single notes, thus unable to play. Fumbling with the syringe, the *steady hand* not so *steady.*

Frightening to Sophia, to be trembling like this. The smell is overwhelming. She is faint but she cannot give in. Prepping the first of the lab animals to be injected prior to dissection.

Slowly, gradually, like erosion it is the fate of the small lab animals to disappear from their cages as they are converted into data.

And data into graphs, statistics. "Science."

And "science" into pharmaceutical patents, sales and profits.

Enormous profits for Lumex. Billions.

Damned proud of you, Sophia. That kind of work you are doing—for mankind . . .

How vivid her father's voice is! But his eyes, she sees that his eyes are closed.

Her hand shakes. This has not happened before.

Oh God—she drops the syringe with a clatter that must reverberate through the lab. In her tight-clenched left hand the small creature is very still as if such stillness were a proven way of outwitting death.

Should have told Whitey—*No. Don't be proud of me. I am not worthy of your pride. I have deceived you.*

The Latex gloves are on. Tight, tight.

Too tight to breathe, ribs squeezed, heart squeezed and pinched but she will prevail, she will not disappoint her admiring elders.

Dr. Means has praised her also. His eyes on her warm, yet calculating at their first meeting, when he'd hired her to assist him with the Lumex experiments.

Suddenly, abruptly as if making a decision after he'd looked through her résumé, asked her a few questions—*All right! Good. "Sophia McClaren." Can you start on Monday?*

So happy, she'd wanted to seize the man's hand and kiss it.

Well—almost.

And now she is thinking—"No."

Returns the creature to its cage against the wall, squirming now in her fingers, excitedly squeaking with the possibility of life, more life however tumor-ridden, however fleeting, more life! *All creatures yearn to persist in their being*—Sophia recalls from a philosophy course.

It is Spinoza who speaks. Speaks to *her.*

Tearing off the Latex gloves, that are so repulsive. Throws them into the trash.

Hurriedly now packing her things. Into a cardboard box. She has been in the lab less than an hour, after so many days of absence and now—leaving? Going home?

If packing her things, not planning to return?

Her supervisor comes to speak with her. Beneath his Scots accent is a voice of faint disbelief, incredulity, the bafflement of a man accustomed to being treated with the utmost civility if not deference, made to deal now with an individual who confounds him.

He wants her to come with him so that they can speak in private. In his office. Sophia demurs, doesn't want to come with him but wants to leave. Now.

But why—why *now*?

Because it is impossible to breathe in this place. Impossible to endure.

He insists, she should come with him. He touches her arm.

Not hard. Not forcibly. Not with any particular familiarity or intent—but Sophia feels the touch, and with a flicker of dislike, recoils.

And he sees. (Of course, he sees. Nothing escapes the scrutiny of Alistair Means!)

Sophia isn't listening closely to him. She is listening to the tiny squeaks, the panicked chattering. Creatures who know: it is their execution day.

In her arms most awkwardly she carries the cardboard box filled with items she has cleared from her cubicle, such banal items, embarrassing that Means should see—coffee mug in need of scouring, flattened box of tissues, near-empty tube of toothpaste, small blue tube of medicated lotion she rubs into her hands that chafe from the Latex gloves.

Goodbye! Can't breathe in this place, have got to leave.

In the parking lot he catches up with her. He is breathing audibly, his breath steams. His forehead crinkles with disapproval of the headstrong young woman he'd hired to assist him in this crucial set of experiments. Is she actually walking away from him? From what he has provided her? *Is that what she is doing?*

Alistair Means is now nothing like the fluent and genial lecturer at the podium, engrossed in fascinating material, thoroughly informed, confident. The research scientist who'd expertly fielded questions, graciously accepted applause. Instead he is an incensed middle-aged man staring at Sophia as if, if he dared, he'd reach out to grab her like a recalcitrant daughter, give her a good hard shake.

"You might regret this, Sophia, if you quit. I assume that you're quitting. You can have more time off, if you need it . . . You know, I tried to call you."

He is part-pleading, part-accusing. They have gone too far, Sophia thinks. He will never forgive her.

"Look, what the hell is wrong? You can't make a decision in your present state. A decision that will affect your career. I think we should talk about this . . ."

Oh, it has become a comic scene! Sophia has clumsily managed to unlock her car door. She has managed to slide the box into the backseat. She sees that her supervisor is upset on her behalf and perhaps he is also annoyed, angry. For she is behaving emotionally, she has lost control. A science of exactitude is hostile to a loss of control.

"I just don't want to kill animals anymore. I've killed enough for you, I think."

— ∞ —

It is the end. What relief!

No more Lumex experiments. No more miniature deaths at her fingertips. And she'd never known, never made inquiries, ashamed to even consider making inquiries, if Alistair Means is divorced, or still married; if he has a wife, children.

If his interest in her is genuine, and not that of a sexual predator.

If her interest in him is genuine, and not that of an ambitious young woman calculating to advance her career.

That night Means calls, and leaves a message *Sophia. I'm outside at the curb. I really think we need to talk this over. Your future. The future. Will you let me in?*

In this way, it begins between them.

Sleepwalker

She has become a sleepwalker. The sleep is her life, through which she glides numb, unseeing and unfeeling like a species of undersea life so minimal it isn't clear if it is, in fact, "alive."

One breath at a time, Jess. You can do it.

THE SLEEPWALKING BEGAN in her husband's hospital room. When she'd been summoned at last. *Mrs. McClaren we are so sorry.*

Seeing Whitey, so very still. His eyes not entirely shut (so you might imagine that he was peering out, slyly, the "good" eye at least) and his mouth just slightly open (so you might imagine he was about to speak) though twisted, one side just perceptibly higher than the other, a paralytic tic she didn't think she'd noticed before, exactly—(though of course she must have noticed. Many times).

The shock was, they'd detached the machines from him. Detached him from the machines. The IV line had been withdrawn. The monitors had been disconnected. Keenly she felt the insult, the wound, why had they *given up.*

This was the shock: what was different about the scene. What was missing.

"Oh, Whitey . . ."

The other, this too was a shock. That Whitey appeared to be asleep yet was not (you could tell) asleep—not breathing.

But (her brain scrambling to comprehend as an animal scrambles, claws at a pebbly hillside in terror of falling) the more profound shock, the first glance, stepping into the room and in that instant, this shock was the missing machines, the missing IV line, for they had *given up.*

She could not comprehend this. After so many days, it had seemed like weeks, months—he'd been in their care, he had been entrusted to them. And now, they had *given up.*

Kissed him, trying not to break down into helpless sobbing. For he would need her to be strong as always.

Leaning over Whitey. Awkwardly stooping to press her face against his face. The shock of it was, this was the shock, how quickly his skin was cooling.

YET THERE WILL COME, a dozen times a day, the husband's car in the driveway!

Waiting for him to enter through the kitchen door—*Jess! Darling! I'm home.*

As if—(she smiles to remember)—she would not know that the husband was home. Or that it was he, Whitey, who was *home.*

Thirty-seven years! It is like peering over the edge of a great chasm, trying to see to the very bottom of the Grand Canyon, to the beginning of time.

Elation, happiness. Usually, she would hurry to the husband, even if she was far away upstairs she would hurry to him, and they kissed in greeting.

(But what did they say? All lost.)

Instead, she hears her heart thump like—what?—an old, dingy tennis ball being batted about, negligently—in the silence of the house that tastes like ether.

Selfish woman! Think how much happiness you've had, did you imagine it would go on forever?

What a fool you are.

Very still the widow stands, transfixed. Not paralyzed exactly—rather more numbed, leaden—like a mannequin that has lost her nether limbs but hasn't (yet) fallen over.

Hearing this voice which is not Whitey's voice (of course) but the voice of a stranger speaking calmly, contemptuously.

ONE OF THE NURSES, TELEMETRY. Rhoda?

She'd been so kind to them. So considerate. Bringing a blanket for Jessalyn who'd been shivering, the hospital room was so cold. *Whitey is our favorite, your husband is a very special person we can tell.*

We love Mr. McClaren! He is a sweetheart.

When Whitey was discharged they'd bring a gift for Rhoda. For the other nurses too (maybe) but something special for Rhoda.

Yet Jessalyn saw how Rhoda detached herself from them: patient, family. Chilling to realize how Rhoda had seen many patients die, had witnessed how much suffering, the dying, the surviving, the wife who clings in desperation at the husband's unresponsive hand, the (adult) children horrified by the sight of the diminished, dying father, unspeakable, no one can speak of it. This is where words fail, insubstantial and silly as soap bubbles.

When one day Beverly asked Rhoda if her father might be able to drive his car again in a few months the nurse had seemed to hesitate, to restrain herself before saying, with her bright practiced smile, "Oh it's possible. Oh yes."

"Dad is a great driver. He loves to drive . . ."

Inanely Beverly spoke. With such hope, and loud enough so that Whitey a few yards away would have no difficulty overhearing.

". . . taught us all to drive, and Mom too . . . Didn't he, Mom?"

"Oh, yes! Whitey was a wonderful driving instructor . . ."

Such inane conversations. Such hope.

Filling the void like those wispy white seeds—cottonwood? Willow. All we have to keep us from being sucked into the void, such exchanges. Clutching at one another's hands.

Seeing the favorite nurse outside the hospital, briskly walking in a parking lot. Calling out, lifting a hand to wave—*Hello!* And there came Rhoda's gaze turned onto her, and Rhoda's quick smile though (it would seem obvious to Jessalyn afterward) Rhoda'd had no idea who she was—*Hi! Hello!*

When Whitey died, the favorite nurse had been nowhere near.

When Whitey died, of course they forgot the favorite nurse.

Never gave another thought to bringing gifts for the nurses, all such intentions ended abruptly as if a massive murderous wave had rushed along a beach sweeping aside all in its path.

Now in a patch of winter sunshine in her silent house silent in her sleepwalker-trance Jessalyn recalls with a pang of regret—the nurse who was so nice to them, in Telemetry, what was her name?

OH WHAT WILL BECOME OF US?—many times she'd asked, pleading, gripping his hands, when no one else was near and Whitey himself was asleep and could not hear, still less reply. *Oh what?*

The vigil, then. They had not understood that the siege was yet to come.

I DON'T THINK SO. NO.

Please no but possibly she hadn't spoken aloud.

Pleading with them *please no please not so soon* but it was their way of grief and it was a legitimate way of grief, she understood. Not her way but their way, that must be honored. Busy, busyness, phone calls and emails, text messages, a swirl of plans for the memorial in December like a dust storm in which she dared not breathe for the swirling particles would lodge deep in her lungs and suffocate her.

John Earle McClaren—"Whitey" McClaren—must be mourned publicly as by a marching band. The widow could not bring herself to march in the band but she could not (she knew) protest the band for (she guessed) Whitey himself would have enjoyed it for had not Whitey McClaren many times in his life participated in the memorials of others, fallen friends, comrades, relatives? Very publicly he'd marched. He'd displayed his emotions, grief. Of course Whitey had.

You can be sincere in public. It is not insincerity (the widow chides herself) to grieve in public.

The elder children: Thom, Beverly, Lorene. These would march at the very head of the band.

McClaren relatives scattered through New York State, New England, the Midwest. Old friends of Whitey's, newer friends, poker buddies, high school and college classmates, business associates and business rivals and directors of charitable organizations to which Whitey had donated—all had exalted statements to make about beloved Whitey McClaren and these statements made publicly from the pulpit of the beautiful old stained-glass St. John's Episcopal chapel made available to the McClaren family for the solemn occasion.

The widow alone did not speak. Seated at the very front of the chapel where (if she'd wished) she might have turned to survey those many who'd gathered to publicly celebrate her husband crowded into the five hundred seats of the chapel.

On an organ were played a selection of Whitey's favorite songs—*"Battle Hymn of the Republic," "Oh Shenandoah," "If I Had a Hammer," "Blowin' in the Wind," "Sounds of Silence."*

Like one embalmed the widow endured the ceremony, and the reception that followed, and the dinner hosted by Whitey's oldest Hammond friends. For one is obliged to eat, even amid sorrow. And no one enjoyed food more than Whitey McClaren. Food and drink.

Once joking if he'd been an ancient Egyptian pharaoh he'd have insisted on a supply of oysters Rockefeller in his "pyramid."

What a beautiful memorial. The most beautiful memorial. What a beautiful human being.

At last the widow was allowed to depart. Though the dinner had not yet ended.

Poor Jessalyn! Hardly said a word all evening.

Do you think it's sunk in yet?

Taken home by her daughter and her daughter's husband who would have come upstairs with her and undressed her and tucked her into bed like an invalid except no, politely she thanked them but no, please good night, thank you and go away. Please.

And upstairs, in the bedroom, feeling her life flowing back into her as if a tourniquet had been released.

Where were you, Jess darling? I've been waiting.

THE WIDOW IS THE ONE to whom the worst has happened.

Yet perversely, the widow exhausts herself with *waiting.*

Waiting for him to come home.

How many times a day. An hour.

Thinking of the husband as *he, him.* Cannot think of him in the past tense, a being that *was.*

Waiting for his voice that comes to her (only) when unbidden.

In the night in the dark in the bed in a stupor of exhaustion, sleeping pill(s), the widow is happy at last like one who has skidded down a steep hill treacherous with rocks, still alive if but barely but no longer awake, all consciousness obliterated, what relief what joy sinking into his arms and the warmth of his embrace coursing through her.

Jess, darling! I've been missing you.

BEVERLY COMPLAINED that when Jessalyn came for dinner at their house she was distracted most of the time and kept rummaging through her purse to see if she'd lost her keys—car key, house key—or her wallet—*So annoying!* And she'd only looked happy when it was time for Steve to drive her back home *like she's desperate to get back to that house where something, someone is waiting for her.*

"MRS. McCLAREN?—JUST SIGN HERE."

". . . sign here."

"Here, please . . ."

"Sign here, Mrs. McClaren. Thanks!"

"If you would, please—sign here . . ."

"Also here, and here. Now here . . ."

"Mrs. McClaren?—just a few more pages . . ."

"And here . . . Thanks!"

". . . one more, here . . ."

". . . here . . . Just initials, please!"

Not clear if the widow had actually read the documents. If she'd glanced through the investment house portfolio, seventy-five densely printed pages.

If she had any idea how much *Jessalyn and John Earle McClaren* owned in investments, property, bank accounts. How much the printing business *McClaren Printing, Inc.* was worth.

Certainly it seemed clear that the widow had no idea that her husband had savings and "money market" accounts with several banks in his name only, each of about $500,000.

How little she knew of his financial accounts. *Their accounts.*

"None of it matters much. But thank you."

Sam Hewett looked at Jessalyn McClaren with surprise. The widow had spoken apologetically, yet with an air of willfulness.

Whitey McClaren's "team" (as he'd called them) from Merrill Lynch Wealth Management would come to the house several times a year. They would meet in Whitey's home office and at some point during their negotiations Whitey would call to Jessalyn—*Jess? Need you in here for just a few minutes to co-sign, hon.*

She might be in the kitchen, or in the garden. Out back on the deck, watering potted geraniums. Upstairs, in one or another room doing whatever it was she was doing, the wife of the house.

Jess? Darling? Please come.

If they'd explained what it was she was signing, Jessalyn did not exactly listen. Never read what she was signing. Fifteen, twenty pages of dense-printed type. She'd laughed, feeling giddy. Whitey might take her hand, indicating where to sign.

"Just sign here, Mrs. McClaren."

Beneath *John Earle McClaren, Jessalyn Hannah McClaren.*

Hewett wasn't sure he'd heard correctly. The widow spoke so softly.

"None of—what—doesn't matter, Mrs. McClaren?"

"Oh, well"—Jessalyn seemed embarrassed to have spoken at all—"everything."

Trapped inside a drum the widow can hear hammering on the outside of the drum, trapped and struggling to breathe inside the drum but if she can endure it she can't be hurt by the hammer and eventually (she knows: this is her solace) she will sleep.

In this sleep, the husband awaits her. *Jess darling! Come here.*

Eyelids began to close even as her hand continued to sign the documents.

"Mrs. McClaren? Jessalyn?"—Sam Hewett was distressed.

He'd been Whitey's personal accountant for twenty years. Like the wealth management team he'd been coming to the house on Old Farm Road several times a year and at these times he'd met Jessalyn McClaren, if but briefly.

Thinking now, the poor woman probably wasn't sleeping well at night. After a trauma the brain can become hyperactive. Brain chemicals needed to shut down neuron firing to allow sleep are depleted and so neurons continue to fire, like strobe lights flashing.

Sam Hewett knew something of grief. Though not (yet) what it would be to lose a spouse of nearly forty years.

Touching to Hewett, how Jessalyn McClaren was making an effort to behave as she'd always behaved. Smiling at her visitor in mimicry of her old, lost wife-self, one of those beautiful older women who wear pearls, nice cashmere sweaters, not a hair out of place though in fact (Hewett was surprised to observe) poor Jessalyn wasn't so well-groomed that afternoon, rumpled woolen slacks and gray cardigan fitting her so loosely you'd think (Hewett did think) the sweater might've belonged to Whitey. Hair matted, limp, without body or luster. And no pearls. No makeup, not even lipstick, white thin-looking skin, blue veins at her temples, evasive watery eyes.

Doesn't want anyone looking at her. Like a raw, awful wound.

Poor woman! Must be over sixty, and her life over.

Eyelids closing, can't stay awake. Pen slips from her fingers.

Hewett would report: you hear of widows who sicken and die after their husbands die. That's what happened to my grandmother after my grandfather died. They'd been married like sixty years. Granma just went out like a candle burning and dripping and nobody even noticing until it's *out.*

Hope that isn't happening with Mrs. McClaren.

Fell asleep at the table where we were doing her accounts and tax documents. Signing papers. Signing checks to U.S. Treasury, New York State Division of Taxes. Laid her head down on her arms and shut her eyes and I had a hard time waking her, it was scary. But when I suggested calling one of the daughters to come over she begged me no, please like she was scared of the daughters, or anyone, finding her out.

All that money, that estate, and the house was freezing—must've had the thermostat set at 66 degrees Fahrenheit.

Like Granma too, after my grandfather died. Hoping to save money by saving on heat.

LET US HELP YOU, MOM.

She has laughed, I am not helpless, to need *help.*

Determined to make her way alone, so far as she can. Discovering much she hadn't known, hadn't guessed. Aloneness.

One of us could live with you. Help out.

How to explain to them, can't explain, she is not alone exactly. A widow is never alone.

Waiting for him each day. Each day a steep flight of stairs to climb . . .

Nearing dusk the waiting intensifies. A crisis is imminent.

Headlights of vehicles on Old Farm Road visible for miles if she positions herself at one of the upstairs windows.

Stares into the distance. Until her eyes begin to ache.

There! Those lights . . .

A childish excitement suffuses her. For a fleeting moment, she can think—*Whitey?*

It is only a fleeting moment. But it is a moment.

Buoyed by hope when you know there is no hope. A small cork in befouled water, bobbing amid sewage, unsinkable.

IT WILL BE A WHILE. *But you can wait.*

I'm waiting. Hey—I love you.

TOLD HILDA WHO CAME to clean the house each Monday morning that she was going away for the rest of the winter, would call when she returned.

(Whitey had insisted on the house being cleaned "top-to-bottom" each week. Insisted he did not want his "dear wife" to pick up after him.)

(Jessalyn had laughed. *Of course* a wife would pick up after such a husband, profligate in his usage of the house, oblivious of the swath he cut through the household on any ordinary day.)

She pressed into Hilda's hand a thank-you card, which contained a check for twice the usual payment—"And Mr. McClaren thanks you, too."

WHY?—SHE'D NEVER FELT COMFORTABLE giving orders to anyone.

She would know the house intimately, now. Just the widow, and the house.

RARELY IS THE WIDOW ALONE. Even outside the safety of her house the widow is not alone. Keenly she feels this, it is making her very self-conscious.

Searching for her (lost) (misplaced) keys. Car key, house key.

It has become an obsession, searching for these keys.

Or, wallet. Cell phone.

Or, when she is out of the house, fearing that she will lose/misplace her handbag containing keys, wallet, cell phone. Any and all of these.

Fearing that she will lose the car. (That is, where she has parked the car.)

Observed in the grocery store. Futility of pushing a cart up and down aisles. A robotic activity, and a smiling face overseeing.

Observed pushing her cart outside and into the parking lot. Observed in pelting icy rain.

It isn't clear who is observing her. Judging her. Whose voice, that assails her.

Why would you do such a stupid thing. Are you not thinking, why are you not thinking.

Do you hate yourself so? But why?

Hating/hurting yourself will not bring him back.

Bags of groceries she lifts with difficulty from the shopping cart to set into the trunk of the vehicle. She is stubborn, she will continue until the last of several bags has become soaked and ripped, groceries spill out onto the parking lot in a sodden tumble *Oh Whitey please, let me die. If you love me* but stooping in the icy rain to pick up groceries to set into the trunk, how embarrassing each item, mandarin oranges, three unattached bananas, cartons of yogurt, cartons of cottage cheese, small loaf of multigrain bread, cans of soup, each item a gesture of pathos *Must be, someone wants to live. Someone is desperate to continue to live, if she is feeding herself. Pathetic!* For of course you continue with the widow's ridiculous life, a Möbius strip that has no end.

Her face is wet. The widow's face is often wet. But in the rain the widow's advantage is that you can't tell if the widow is crying.

AND IN THE CEMETERY, she has become lost.

A day in early winter slipping to dusk. Impulsively she has decided that it is imperative to visit Whitey's grave.

Desperate to be there. The first time, when the ashes in the urn were buried, she'd been too distracted to fully comprehend.

Whitey had not instructed them to scatter his ashes in some romantic place like a river, a lake, a canyon. Hadn't wished to think that far into the future, also wasn't the type to take himself so seriously.

Self-importance embarrassed him. Worst thing Whitey could say of someone—*He's full of himself. Christ!*

Cremation he'd wanted. Not a formal burial. But he had not elaborated. *Enough, let's get it over with.*

And here is the problem: the (temporary) marker provided by the crematorium is so small and so resembles other small utilitarian markers in the cemetery, the widow becomes confused in the waning light, and loses her way. She and the children have ordered a beautiful granite gravestone of respectful proportions that will bear the stately carved words

BELOVED HUSBAND AND FATHER
JOHN EARLE MCCLAREN

but this stone is still at the stonemason's. In the meantime the widow seems to have mis-remembered the (temporary) marker as larger than it is, easily two or three times larger, and so keeps missing it. Her feet in impractical shoes sink in the spongy earth. Her nostrils pinch with a sharp smell of sodden-leaf rot and the futility of such acts of desperation. For always the widow is seeking something that is lost, that is *not-here*.

Trying not to panic. Oh, how can she be *lost*!

It is not like Jessalyn McClaren, who has always been the person who knows the route, took time to write down the address, has an idea where to park, knows precisely when. Certainly she knows that the grave marker is nearby. She is certain.

Descending a muddy hill. Rain-flattened grasses, slick mud of the hue of offal, and as badly smelling.

Trying to cross a patch of muddy grass, a shortcut to a graveled walkway. Her ankle turns, she falls suddenly, heavily.

In the cold muck, sobbing.

Whitey! Please let me come to you, I am so tired.

A fellow visitor to the cemetery, on his way out, sights her. Possibly (she will think afterward) the man had deliberated whether to acknowledge her, a drunken-seeming woman, a confused woman, a heartbrokenly sobbing woman who has slipped in mud, has fallen in mud, graceless.

But he doesn't disappear. Gallantly he comes to her, and helps her to her feet. This touch—this sudden physical contact—from a stranger—is overwhelming to Jessalyn, like an unexpected eclipse of the sun.

A relief, he seems to be no one who knows her. No one whom she should know.

"Here. Try these . . ."

The gallant stranger provides tissues for Jessalyn with which she can wipe at her muddied clothes. Standing at a polite distance he does not assist her.

Through tear-dimmed eyes she sees: he is a man not-young, not-Caucasian, with a swarthy creased face and kindly eyes, a drooping Brillo pad of a mustache. He wears a tweed jacket with leather patches at the elbows and on his head a dandyish hat like a Stetson. He is tall, angular, wary and alert as if he fears that Jessalyn will collapse again into the mud, and he will be obliged to haul her out.

He asks if she is all right? His manner is oddly formal, wary—he calls her *ma'am*.

Jessalyn wonders: Is he afraid that the white lady will panic and begin screaming?—is he afraid of *her*?

Embarrassed, she assures the gentlemanly mustached man that she is not injured—she is just a little muddy. "But, I guess—I'm lost . . ."

"Lost?"

"I mean—I can't find the g-grave that I am looking for."

She tries to laugh, this is such a ridiculous predicament.

With something like pity the man regards Jessalyn. A woman wandering lost in this small cemetery, which can't cover more than two or three acres?

Politely he asks which grave she is looking for and she tells him—"The grave of 'John Earle McClaren.'"

There, it has been said: THE GRAVE OF JOHN EARLE MCCLAREN.

The mustached man does not seem to register how profound this utterance is for Jessalyn. He does not seem to register that the muddied woman standing before him may well be the widow of the deceased who has become lost searching for his grave.

Nor does he seem to register that *McClaren* is a name of some local significance. No?

"Well. Let's see what we can do for you, dear."

Dear. The widow feels the jolt of this casual word like a caress that is unexpected, though (perhaps) not unwanted.

Dear. As a kicked dog would feel when it is stroked, and not further kicked.

The mustached man is carrying something like a pack, out of which he takes a flashlight. One of those pencil-thin flashlights with surprisingly strong beams.

"What does it look like? The grave stone."

"Oh, it doesn't look like anything, really," Jessalyn says apologetically, "it's just one of those little, temporary markers that are all over the cemetery. You know, the funeral homes provide them, or—the crematoriums." Pausing, stricken. Of course, Jessalyn knows to say *crematoria* except the word seems pretentious uttered in this place, to the mustached man in the Stetson hat.

Is he touched by her air of apology, her distractedness, so thinly masking the most profound despair? Is he amused by her muddied clothes, expensive tasteful clothes, a black cashmere coat, impractical leather shoes?

Of course, he must have guessed that Jessalyn is the widow. *Widow* has become her essence.

Shining his narrow laser-beam of light along the lumpy ground he leads Jessalyn past rows of grave stones and grave markers. Some of the grave markers are very old—faint, carved dates as long ago as the

1880s. Some are covered in a scabrous-looking moss. Jessalyn is trying to keep up, following close behind the mustached man. She sees that he is taller than she by several inches—taller than Whitey. Beneath the Stetson hat cocked at a rakish angle his hair is a tangle of gray and silver, as long as Virgil's hair. She wonders if he knows Virgil: if he and Virgil know each other. (But he had not seemed to know the name *McClaren.* Though she is the least vain of persons Jessalyn is mildly hurt by this.)

"Sorry, dear—am I going too fast?"

"N-No. I'm fine."

Dear. No one has called her *dear* since Whitey.

Not drunk but why is she stumbling, can't seem to keep her balance on this uneven ground, the harsh fresh wet air is making her light-headed. Since the ordeal of the vigil and the *passing-away* and its aftermath she has lost her sense of what it requires to be *upright*—how to walk without swaying and stumbling.

A neurological problem, perhaps. *Deficit*—that dread word.

How quickly it can happen: *stroke, deficit.* Each morning the widow wakes astonished and guilt-stricken that it has not (yet) happened to her.

The mustached man offers Jessalyn his arm but she pretends not to notice. She is stricken with shyness, doesn't want to come too near to him.

"Ma'am? Over here?—did you look here?"

Darting like a snake the laser light moves along the ground. Jessalyn's eyes follow with a kind of dread.

"There—that's it . . ."

How small the grave marker from the funeral home is, how meager, a dull pewter-color—JOHN EARLE MCCLAREN 1943–2010.

Is this—*this*—all there is, she has been seeking so desperately? As if her life depends upon it?

She feels a moment's vertigo. *How small it's all.*

"You'll be all right now, ma'am? Don't stay long, it will be dark soon."

The mustached man speaks in a kindly voice, with a faint, very faint accent. Is he—Hispanic? Middle Eastern? Jessalyn has not failed to notice how he glances about as if seeking someone else, a companion of Jessalyn's perhaps, who will be responsible for her. She has the impression—oh, she is embarrassed!—that he is eager to escape her.

"Thank you. You've been very kind. But I'm fine now—I won't get lost again."

What a foolish thing to say!—*won't get lost again.*

Jessalyn tries to laugh but the sound comes out unconvincingly.

No matter, the tall kindly mustached man has turned away, walks away.

At the gravesite, churned earth. Some sort of earth-digging machine must be used in the cemetery though (possibly) Whitey's grave is shallow, containing only an urn: a strong-armed gravedigger wouldn't have much trouble using just a shovel.

Here is something jarring: Whitey's grave abuts another grave with very little space between.

How did this happen? Did someone miscalculate? Whitey's near-neighbor has a large square-cut slab of ugly stone carved with the name *Hiram J. Horseman*—about which Whitey would surely make a sardonic remark.

Actually it is Housman not Horseman. Look again, darling.

Jessalyn looks more closely: the name is *Housman. Hiram Housman.*

Neighbors in the cemetery though strangers in life. So far as Jessalyn knows.

"Oh, Whitey! It is all so—futile. Isn't it!"

Silly to have come here when Whitey, her Whitey, is likely to be back in the house if he is anywhere. He is not *here.*

The harsh wet open place inhabited by strangers—grave stones of strangers—is not a friendly place for Whitey, or for her.

Yet Jessalyn lingers at the grave. Nowhere to sit here, nowhere to rest or lean against for she cannot lean against, still sit on, the gravestone of *Hiram Housman*—that would be disrespectful.

She'd meant to bring flowers. Oh, she'd left flowers in the car . . .

Her heart thuds with disappointment. A widow is one who forgets, who leaves the flowers in the car.

(Oh God—where are her keys? In her handbag? Blindly, frantically she rummages for her keys amid wads of tissue.)

(Why does she never remember to empty her handbag of used tissues? It is a fact, she cannot remember to do this.)

Now it is becoming dark. Seriously dark. Jessalyn rouses herself to leave the cemetery.

Here is one good thing: it is far easier to make one's way out of a cemetery than to make one's way in. Small pathways lead to a single wide graveled walkway at the center of the cemetery, which leads to the parking lot behind the church.

Exiting the cemetery the widow halts, and thinks; begins walking again, and again halts—for what did she lose? What has she left behind?

Searching through her handbag, and through the pockets of her coat . . .

Near the entrance gate the mustached man in the Stetson hat seems to be waiting. She is embarrassed to see him, she'd thought that he had vanished. He is being helpful—gentlemanly—aiming his beacon of light onto the graveled path, as Jessalyn approaches. Oh, she wishes he'd left her alone!

Feeling just slightly fearful as she approaches him. Telling herself it is not because he is Hispanic, or—Mediterranean?—*it is not because of this.* But she is alone, and the mustached man though kindly-seeming is a stranger. She has no other way to exit the cemetery unless she wants to abruptly retreat (which she certainly can't do, he is watching her) and walk a considerable distance back toward Whitey's grave, and even then, in the gathering darkness—oh God, she would never find her way out.

Why is this man waiting for her? Has he been lingering? Is there no one else in the entire cemetery—no one? Jessalyn feels her heart begin to pound in apprehension.

She has already thanked the man but nervously thanks him again—tells him again that he is *very kind*. But as she hurries past him to her car he addresses her—"Ma'am?"—and her heart leaps in fear of him. "What—what do you want?"

"Your glove, dear. Is this your glove? Found it on the path."

It is her glove. Soft black leather, muddied. With abashed thanks she takes it from him.

Driving home she hears the soft, caressing word—*dear*. Not a word she can trust, she thinks. Not ever again.

"OH, MOM! YOU HAVE LARYNGITIS! Sounds like you have a terrible cold."

Relief. They'd thought that their mother had simply ceased speaking because words pained her too much.

DEAR. FINGERS GRIPPING HER ARM at the elbow, not hard, but forcibly enough to lift her, steady her.

Ma'am. Are you all right.

She wonders why the tall mustached man had been in the cemetery. Why had she not been more polite to *him*.

He too had been visiting a grave. Probably.

And at that hour. And alone.

PHONE RINGS! LEO COLWIN.

Leo Colwin is not discouraged if Jessalyn McClaren neglects to return his calls.

Leo has sent flowers *For dear Jessalyn, fondly your friend Leo.*

Since that terrible day in October courtly Leo Colwin has sent Jessalyn flowers each week, usually roses, but occasionally lilies, gardenias, eventually tulips and daffodils and narcissus whose fragrance makes Jessalyn feel faint, it is so beautiful and might, like all sweet fragrances, be confused with something more abiding and more significant.

For dear Jessalyn, fondly your friend Leo.

Of Leo Colwin, widower, one of the first in the McClarens' circle to lose a spouse, it is frequently said—*What a sweetheart! What a dear, lonely man.*

Low-keyed was Whitey's word if Whitey was intending to be polite. *Boring as hell* if not.

Leo Colwin is retired from a family-owned local business, something to do with estate management. He is well-to-do but not wealthy. He has adult children, at a distance. Stoop-shouldered, gentlemanly, soft-spoken and always clean-shaven, neatly (if not stylishly) dressed—suit from the English Shoppe, white shirt, handkerchief in lapel pocket, decent shoes. With no wife to scrutinize him Leo must scrutinize himself and sometimes overlooks crucial details.

Jessalyn sees, and bites her lower lip. *I will not play the wife-role with Leo Colwin! No.*

"Leo? Let me fix this."

Straightening his polka-dot bow tie. Now he looks less like Red Buttons.

But the thin graying disheveled hair like a crooked cap on his head—*no.*

And seeing that he has cut himself (blindly?) shaving beneath his chin, a thin-oozing thread of blood—*no.*

Leo Colwin has arrived to escort Jessalyn to a wedding anniversary party at the home of friends. Jessalyn can't recall having agreed to accompany Leo and suspects it was her daughters who made the arrangement without her consent figuring it would be too rude of Jessalyn to demur, and Jessalyn McClaren can be counted on never to be rude, and this is true, the widow is trapped in graciousness like an insect in honey, too demoralized to buzz or flutter her wings in protest.

"Jessalyn! It's so—so—seeing you is so—"

Courtly Leo Colwin, eyes behind bifocals swimming in tears. Impulsively Leo takes Jessalyn's hand, a cool limp unresisting hand, and lifts it to his lips to kiss.

(*Kiss?*—Jessalyn is stunned.)

(*Kiss?*—Whitey just laughs. To him, Leo Colwin is a straight white old-style Republican, decent and trustworthy, fair golfer, un-argumentative. *Christ! Boring as white bread.*)

"—I am so deeply—so moved—grateful—" Leo stammers and goes silent, what a mercy.

Poor dear Maudie, Leo's wife. A few years older than Jessalyn and not a close friend but much-admired. Tragic death, one of the unspeakable cancers—cervical, uterine. Driving to the party Leo speaks fondly of Maudie as Jessalyn listens, or half-listens. Enough simply to incline your head at a certain angle, a man like Leo Colwin will be encouraged to think you are listening intently.

She'd liked Maudie, more than she'd liked Leo who'd been hard of hearing even then, years ago.

"This year would be our fifty-second anniversary, if Maude had lived." Leo pauses, to let the significance of this remark sink in. "I'd never thought of, you know, remarrying . . ." Leo pauses again, as if now he has said too much.

Stepping into a familiar house, the house of friends—there is that moment when, as you cross the threshold, you have a panicked impulse to glance down, to see if the elevator shaft opens before you, into the bowels of the Earth.

"Oh, Jessalyn! Thank you! Thank you for coming, it can't be easy . . ."

Because it is the Bregmans' fiftieth anniversary? Because Jessalyn and Whitey didn't make it to their fiftieth anniversary? Is that why it *can't be easy*?

(Whitey nudges her—*You can do it, sweetheart. Don't be ridiculous.*)

Yet: to see Jessalyn McClaren by Leo Colwin's side, and Whitey McClaren nowhere near, well—that's a shock. The widow suggests the absent husband, the husband-who-has-vanished. The widow is beautifully dressed at least—silky black, simply cut, long sleeves to hide her thin arms and wrists, long skirt almost to her ankles, beautiful black shoes and around her neck a single strand of translucent pink-toned pearls.

Oh, look!—Jessalyn's hair has turned *white*.

How quickly it has happened, within a few months of Whitey's death all pigment has faded from Jessalyn's hair. From behind you would not recognize the poor woman.

Does the widow frighten them? Even the close friends? Especially the close friends? A widow is a sign of what-lies-ahead, the missing husband, their own mortality.

Which husband will follow her husband? Which of you?

Jessalyn feels a sensation of such sorrow, such dismay, such despair she can't bring herself to greet her friends who seem blithely unaware of what misery awaits them.

It's a party, a *celebration*. Of course they are blithely unaware.

Whitey nudges her. *Lighten up. Get a drink. Ditch Leo.*

Leo hurries off to fetch drinks. It is just slightly easier to breathe, without Leo Colwin looming over her.

In any gathering, in any public place, invariably there are some who have not seen the widow since the husband's death and who feel a compulsion to hurry to the widow to take her hands in theirs and declare how badly they feel, how sad, what a shock and what a loss.

How (guiltily) sad the widow is made to feel, being the cause of another's sadness!

How much more merciful for all if the widow wore a mask, or a bag over her head, to spare the emotions of others.

"Of all people! Whitey was so filled with, with—*life* . . ."

Soon then Jessalyn McClaren is seen to have disappeared.

The expression on poor Leo's face! Must be, Leo Colwin is in love with Jessalyn.

You think? So soon?

It's not soon for Leo. Maude's been gone how many years—five, six . . .

Well, it's soon for Jessalyn.

Oh, Jessalyn. That woman will never remarry.

She was just standing there. At the very end of the hall, in that kind of spare room. There was a mirror but she wasn't looking into it. She didn't seem to be looking at anything. Her face was like a mask, what a beautiful woman Jessalyn is, for her age, or any age really, and that white hair is gorgeous, I hope if I ever have to have white hair it will look like Jessalyn McClaren's. But her skin did look waxy. You could see she wasn't well. Sometimes after a trauma like losing a husband a woman will become ill—shingles, even cancer. The first signs come a few months after the death. It did seem strange, she didn't seem to notice me. I didn't want to frighten her so I spoke softly—"Jess? Are you all right?"—and her eyes moved onto my face like the eyes of someone who is sleepwalking and has no idea where she is.

Then she shivered, and laughed, and said something apologetic like she'd gotten lost looking for a restroom, or maybe she was looking for her coat and didn't want to interrupt or intrude anywhere. Her voice was hoarse and cracked as if it hurt her to speak, as if she was losing her voice, and I said, "Do you want to go back to the party, or would you like to just stay here and I could stay with you, or I could go away if you'd prefer that," and Jessalyn was smiling at me without seeming to hear me, it was strange and disturbing and the only thought that came to me was I'd better hurry and find Whitey, Whitey needs to know how strangely Jessalyn is behaving, but then I realized that Whitey wasn't with us, we would never see Whitey McClaren again; and finally Jessalyn said, with no idea what she was saying but wanting only to be agreeable—"Oh thank you. Yes."

"SOMETIMES I FORGET, WHITEY—we are all still alive here."

PROMPTLY NEXT MONDAY MORNING the deliveryman brings a lavish bouquet in crinkly cellophane, two dozen red and cream-colored roses with a note written in Leo's own hand—

For dear Jessalyn, from your loving friend Leo

(IS IT RUDE OF JESSALYN, she has ceased thanking Leo for the flowers? At first she'd emailed him a terse *Thank you!* after each bouquet but this only encourages Leo to write back to her, and to send more flowers.)

THE (ELDER) DAUGHTERS ARE INCENSED! Their beloved widowed mother is not behaving as they expect her to behave.

Beverly complains that Jessalyn doesn't answer the phone when she calls, has to call three, four times—*Mom, pick up! Please.*

Lorene complains that Jessalyn is behaving foolishly, shortsightedly—she has told Hilda not to come clean the house any longer, as if she, Jessalyn, could keep up that house by herself. *Daddy would be chagrined, he didn't want his wife to be a housemaid.* Both sisters are concerned how it will reflect upon them, if people in North Hammond learn that Whitey McClaren's widow has cut back on the upkeep of her property as if (could it be?) she is worried about money.

Yet more upsetting to the sisters is that their mother is reported to be declining invitations to occasions (dinner parties, receptions, museum openings and concerts, bridge nights) to which sweet lonely widower Leo Colwin might escort her.

What do you think Mom does alone in that house all day?

Maybe Mom isn't alone. Maybe Daddy is there.

I KNOW YOU MEAN TO be kind but please don't invite me to dinner.

Not comfortable eating with others (and not just because she'd rather be home with Whitey) but because, and this is embarrassing, and not something Jessalyn has told anyone including her daughters, when she tries to eat an actual meal instead of intermittently through the day spoonfuls of yogurt, pieces of fruit, dry cereal or toast, she is often stricken with stomach cramps like dysentery and her bowels transformed into hot scalding watery feces.

Not very romantic. Not what you'd think a widow's life is like.

Nothing that Whitey need know, either! Let's spare poor Whitey.

IT IS A FACT, a widow must keep certain secrets from her (deceased) husband.

A marriage is based upon carefully calibrated revelations and secrets: for each revelation, a secret.

Before they'd married Jessalyn had understood: Whitey must be spared.

Random facts or speculations that might worry him, cause him to fret, to feel distress on Jessalyn's account, or anger, or dismay—these Jessalyn took care to keep from Whitey.

Complications with pregnancies, she'd kept from him. No need for the husband to know except if the husband needs to know. (Her obstetrician, a woman, agreed.)

The false positive she'd had a few years ago, mammogram.

Unfortunately the radiologist had called the house and left a message which Whitey had heard. *Please call for an appointment, diagnostic mammogram.*

When Jessalyn walked into the house she saw Whitey's face clammy-pale, sick. Listened to the voice mail and assured him that a "diagnostic" mammogram was commonplace, at least 30 percent of mammograms required a second mammogram, all women know this, nothing to be alarmed about truly.

(Was this so? Thirty percent? Jessalyn had no idea, she'd made up the statistic.)

But Whitey wasn't to be so easily consoled. Whitey was frightened for—*What if?*

She'd had to comfort him. She'd had no time to think of herself and indeed, she was not much worried.

"I have to spare Whitey. Whatever it is."

She conferred with the elder daughters. She would have a biopsy as soon as possible if the mammogram indicated that one was needed and in this event, they needed to keep the news from Whitey; if the biopsy was negative, Whitey need never know there'd been one—"He would just fret, and be distracted at the office." If the biopsy was positive and

Jessalyn did indeed have cancer they would have to consider how to break the news to Whitey, or how to spare him knowing exactly what was wrong.

"How on earth?"—Beverly was shocked.

"Well—we can do it."

No need to tell anyone else, either—Thom, Sophia, Virgil. If they needed to know, they could be told but until then, why?

"The less information given to people, the better, on the whole," Lorene said, practicably; for, as a high school administrator, Lorene did not believe in "open disclosure" and had been inclined, since middle school, to conspiracies and artfully withheld information. She thought it wasn't a bad idea, keeping Whitey *in the dark*—"If you're seriously sick Whitey will have to know, of course. But until then, until there's actual surgery, radiation or whatever, better for him not to know—no one should utter the word 'cancer.' He'll just make himself and all of us anxious."

"Well, I'd tell Steve—I'd want my husband to know." Beverly spoke with a grim sort of complacency, a near-imperceptible emphasis on *my* meant to signal (Lorene had no doubt) that Lorene could not lay claim to any such *my*.

"You'd want your husband to be anxious—unhappy."

"What does that mean?"—Beverly was incensed.

"What I said. You'd want Steve to be anxious—unhappy on your account. But Mom isn't like that, Mom loves Dad." Here, emphasis was upon *loves*.

Quickly Jessalyn intervened: nothing was more distressing to her than the sisters quarreling as they'd done (constantly!) as teenagers.

In fact the diagnostic mammogram had showed something shadowy, small as a pea in Jessalyn's left breast. There'd been a biopsy that very day and a (non-malignant) cyst was removed. All Whitey was told was that the mammogram had been "negative."

"There never was any possibility of a malignancy. It was just an error in the X-ray, that happens all the time."

Whitey's relief was visible. His stiff-set face had seemed to melt and his eyes brimmed with tears.

Had to walk quickly out of the room, to hide his emotion from her but soon after she'd heard him whistling, and then on the phone talking and laughing with a friend.

How fragile, the man's world. He'd constructed it with her at its core. She could not betray him. She could not undermine him by a thoughtlessly uttered truth.

Even Whitey's own medical condition following his stroke, she'd had to misrepresent to him as much as possible.

"How much does your husband want to know?" the neurologist had asked; and Jessalyn had said, "No more than he needs to know, Doctor. But you can tell me."

HOW SHE HAS GROWN to dread and fear a ringing phone!

No matter who, it isn't the one.

No matter the voice, will not be the voice.

Too-jingly sound of a cell phone doesn't upset her as much since Whitey rarely called her cell phone; Whitey had disliked cell phones and electronic "gadgets" with keyboards too small for his broad stubby fingers.

(Jessalyn never knows where her cell phone is. Lost somewhere in the house for days at a time.)

Mom, give a call back please!

Mom, are you all right? Where are you?

Mom, if you don't call back I'll have to come over . . .

Quickly then Jessalyn calls back. She has grown to dread the (adult) children dropping by the house just to "see how you are . . ."

To anyone who will listen Beverly worries about Jessalyn adjusting to life without Whitey. *She* herself is having difficulty adjusting to life without Whitey.

Upsetting to Beverly that Jessalyn seems withdrawn, even reclusive. Doesn't express much enthusiasm about spending time with her younger grandchildren as she'd used to, *before.*

Lorene says, You just want Mom to babysit for you, for free.

Beverly says, That is not true! Mom loves the kids, she always has.

Lorene says, Hmmm.

Beverly says, Oh what's that mean?—*hmmm*?

When Lorene doesn't reply, adding, vehemently, Of course Mom has babysat for us, *for free*. You can't imagine Mom taking money from us for spending time with her grandchildren, can you?

In the maddening way of a younger sister Lorene laughs snidely as she hangs up the phone.

"WHITEY? COME LOOK!"

At the feeder, on fluttering wings, a lovely little bird with a pale red breast. Gray feathers, dun-colored. A modest bird she knew Whitey would like, if he took time to notice.

"I think it's a house finch . . ."

If he was home, if he was home and not on the phone, if he was home, not on the phone, and not busy in his home-office Whitey might come when she called him. *Oh Whitey, come look!*

Though (secretly: she knew) Whitey didn't care overmuch about birds. He'd humored her for how many years, confusing chickadees with sparrows, grosbeaks with robins, titmice, catbirds, wrens, warblers . . . He could identify a (red) cardinal, a blue jay, "some kind of blackbird" and those strangely stately, prehistoric-looking waterfowl that dwelt in the marshes beyond the creek—"great blue herons."

He'd humored her though (probably) he'd thought it was a waste of time, or silly or eccentric. She'd overheard him remarking to a friend how his wife took "lots of things seriously, no one else would give a damn about."

He'd laughed, fondly. Whatever reply the friend had murmured, Jessalyn moved quickly away not wanting to hear.

At the window she makes a movement that frightens the little birds away from the feeder on the deck. Like the shadow of a predator heron, her uplifted hand.

NOW THERE IS NO ONE to humor her.

Well, there are the (adult) children. Grandchildren.

Seeing in their eyes how they pity her, and fear her. The emptiness in her. How they glance nervously behind her, to the side of her—*Someone missing? Gone where?*

Friends whom she has known longer than she has known her children. Women friends especially, with whom she has grown up. And several of these widows like herself—"young" widows. Fascinating to Jessalyn, and appalling, how some of these women have learned to refer to their (deceased) husbands as having *died*—so casually uttered, you would think they are referring to a houseplant having *died*.

Almost greedily their eyes moving onto her—*Now you are one of us.*

Hands gripping hers—*Yes it's bad now, Jessalyn. But it will get easier.*

And Jessalyn stiffens thinking—*But I don't want it to get easier!*

As if Whitey is listening. (Yes, Whitey is easily wounded, thin-skinned.)

Will Jessalyn continue to live in her "beautiful" house?—or will Jessalyn sell the house? Jessalyn parries these questions with the skill of a middling Ping-Pong player.

Object is not to win, just to get the volley over.

In a whisper a friend, a sister-widow, tells her not to pay any attention to what people tell her, keep the house, keep everything exactly the way it is, especially don't give anything away, you will regret it.

In a whisper another sister-widow tells her to move out of the house, too many memories in the house. Go away, Caribbean for a week in February, Dominican Republic—("Come with me, my daughter and son-in-law rent a house, a big house on the beach, no one will bother you, just rest, heal in the sun, Whitey would want that").

It's true, Whitey would want her to be happy. But—how?

Barely can Jessalyn's friends wait until she's out of hearing, excusing herself to use a restroom, before speaking of her in lowered voices.

She used to be so beautiful! Poor Jessalyn.

Her face looks so strained . . .

Really? I don't think so—I think she's looking remarkably good.

But her hair has gone white! Almost overnight . . .

Such a gorgeous white, she doesn't have to do a thing with it, I envy her.

She has lost too much weight. That doesn't suit her. Whitey would be appalled, he didn't like skinny women—he'd say . . .

She can't eat. Did you see?—just pushed food around on her plate.

I was the same way—for a while . . . I must have lost twenty pounds . . .

That, I envy. But—

She isn't drinking. That's good.

But how tired she's looking! And her fingernails . . .

What about her fingernails?

Didn't you see them?—split and broken.

That's some kind of malnutrition symptom. I was the same way . . .

Did you hear—Whitey didn't leave her much money? Some kind of complicated "trust"—

Oh why would Whitey do such a thing, he adored Jessalyn—

—but she has inherited the house, hasn't she?—isn't that state law—

—half of the husband's estate, usually—

Maybe Whitey had money secreted away somewhere, you know—in foreign banks—

—Whitey was the type! So shrewd . . .

But he adored Jessalyn, I always thought—didn't you?

Well—Whitey was a secretive type, essentially.

No! Whitey McClaren?

It isn't "still waters run deep" but bossy friendly men like Whitey McClaren who really "run deep"—you think they are all on the surface, but they are not.

And you know this—how?

Let's just say, I knew Whitey McClaren. For something like fifty years.

"MRS. McCLAREN?—THANKS."

Eagerly she has handed the valet-parking attendant her card. How badly she wants to leave this place, and return to the safety of the house on Old Farm Road!

Left her friends in the restaurant. Never (dared) return from the restroom where she'd narrowly escaped a bout of vomiting, diarrhea.

At a trot the boy disappears into the vast parking garage attached to the Riverside Hammond Hilton that both rises above the surface of the concrete earth and descends beneath it.

In a chill wind she waits. *A widow is one who waits for something that has already happened to un-happen.*

She is shivering, waiting. In a cloth coat too light for the sub-zero wind off the Chautauqua River.

(Where is her car? Where has the boy in the uniform gone? Has he forgotten her? Has he disappeared, with her car?)

Since Whitey *passed away* such breaches in civility have become frequent. If the widow shuts her eyes she may open them in another time, minutes later, or hours or days later. Often—once she leaves the safety of her home—she finds herself marooned.

Could not face them, knowing how they spoke of her: the newest widow in their circle.

Dreading their pity of her, like a cold paste. Yet more, their well-intentioned sympathy like something prying beneath her fingernails from which she wanted only to flee.

She knew: the women spoke of her husband casually, familiarly, as if they had a right to him. Knowing Whitey McClaren in ways (inescapably, she supposes: Whitey had grown up in Hammond, as she had not) she did not know him, or Whitey did not allow himself to be known.

Feeling a shaky sort of triumph that she'd succeeded in staving off a humiliating physical attack in the rosy-wallpaper restroom. Refusal to acknowledge the sickly-pale face swimming in the mirror she has no wish to confront away from the safety of home where (should he seek her) Whitey would have a difficult time finding her.

When the parking attendant fails to return with her car the widow seeks the car herself in the vast drafty echoing parking garage that appears to be deserted.

Rows of vehicles, and no human beings.

"Whitey? Help me . . ."

Ahead then she sees something: not human, not upright and vertical but sub-human, horizontal: a dog of about moderate size, or a large thick-furred cat, a feral creature, moving away from her with a kind of mocking slowness, not scurrying in panic . . . Oh God: is it a *rat*?

It disappears beneath a vehicle. Her heart is pounding absurdly, in fear that the creature is a *rat*.

For a moment she stands paralyzed. It is a measure of her derangement that she feels she should not cry again *Whitey? Help me* so soon again, Whitey would be dismayed.

Seeing then, some distance away, a figure that might indeed be Whitey: of the same approximate height, breadth, not heavyset so much as thickset, a man of late middle age, in a windbreaker that resembles an old navy blue windbreaker of Whitey's, headed away from her and (seemingly) oblivious of her. His hair is a mangled-looking grayish-white, not so white as Whitey's hair had been. But Whitey's hair was always cut, trimmed.

(Is this the parking attendant, grown older? Not in his uniform?)

(*Is* this Whitey, in a confused memory she has forgotten, intruding now into consciousness like something carved of wood that, forced beneath the roiling water, cannot be kept from surfacing?)

She follows the man in the navy blue windbreaker. She will not let him out of her sight. In impractical high heels, expensive beautiful silly shoes Whitey had liked her to wear, and bare-headed, shivering, eyes damp with moisture but determined not to lose the figure lurching ahead of her who (she sees now) is glancing back at her over his shoulder, with an inscrutable expression.

Wildly she thinks—*Is this Whitey, somehow?*

If not Whitey, Whitey's emissary. For in life Whitey had been unable to operate without assistants, helpers, right-hand men who'd worked for him, very loyal, to whom Whitey was loyal in turn, remembering many of them in his will.

She'd teased him, he'd made of his wife one of his assistants. Whitey hadn't laughed at first. Often he was easily wounded, his skin was notoriously thin. But then came around to seeing the humor in Jessalyn's remark, and the truth.

A wife is the assistant a man has married.

The man in the windbreaker has left the parking garage. She sees that he is walking with a limp. She follows him into a vacant lot strewn with rubble, making her way between crumbling walls, broken concrete, her high heels stick in the earth, she is in danger of twisting an ankle and injuring herself . . .

At last the man turns, crouching inside a part-crumbled wall where the wind isn't so strong.

"Ma'am? You needin' help?"

A homeless person. He is older than she'd guessed. His face looks stained, his eyes are jaundiced. His lower jaw is missing teeth. Except that it is caked with filth and missing a zipper his windbreaker resembles Whitey's longtime windbreaker ordered from L.L.Bean. His filth-stiffened trousers are too long, bunched at the ankles as if he has lost height, he has been unwell.

Seeing him, such sorrow in his face, and his jaws covered in stubbly whiskers, Jessalyn bursts into tears.

IT IS A SIEGE. She is under assault from all sides, she cannot relax her guard, she dares not sleep. Even if Whitey sleeps, gripping her in his strong arms, easing his weight on her like a great warm slab of earth, she dares not sleep.

A HOMELESS PERSON SHE'D BROUGHT HOME!—to their precious childhood house. The McClaren children were astonished and alarmed.

Their mother was apologetic, chastened. She would acknowledge:

she'd met the man downtown near the Riverside Hilton where she'd gone to have lunch with friends; she'd brought him home to feed him, to allow him to take a bath for he was "very filthy" and "not looking well" and somehow it happened (she was trying to understand why) that this needy person who'd appeared to be soft-spoken, unaggressive and grateful for her kindness became by degrees aggressive and wild-eyed, and began ranting incoherently about religion, the federal government, "rich people"—by which time Jessalyn realized that he might be dangerous, and locked herself in Whitey's study to call for help.

It was Beverly and Steve's number Jessalyn called, reasoning that they lived closest to her; she did not want to call 911, for she did not want the homeless man arrested. By the time Beverly and Steve arrived the man had fled the house taking with him an armful of random items: a pair of Whitey's winter boots out of a closet, an antiquated BlackBerry found in a kitchen drawer, a handful of loose change from a pewter dish on a kitchen counter where for years Whitey had unloaded his pockets of stray coins.

(These coins Jessalyn would take away as they accumulated. But after Whitey's death she had not touched the pewter bowl which the homeless man had emptied into a pocket.)

With a flashlight Steve searched the property including the three-car garage attached to the house, and an old fieldstone barn that had once been a stable, and found no one, nothing.

Still, as soon as she'd stepped inside the house Beverly could tell that an intruder had been there, by his *smell*.

She wanted to call 911 and report the theft—"A dangerous person in the neighborhood."

Jessalyn insisted that the homeless man had not been dangerous really, he'd just gotten excited, and confused. Inviting him home had been her idea, not his—"I don't want the poor man to be punished for a mistake of mine. I'm sure he's far away by now . . ."

"Mom, how can you say that? You have no idea where this person is. You said he was 'raving, ranting'—"

"I've told you, it was my mistake. If we call the police he might be arrested, or—worse."

"He should be arrested! If he's a madman—"

"He's *homeless*. That would drive anyone mad, I think."

"Oh Mom, what are you saying? *What would Whitey think about this?*"

In the end they didn't call 911. Steve insisted upon spending the night in his mother-in-law's house in case the homeless man returned while Beverly drove to their home, indignant and too upset to sleep, as she would complain the next day.

What was most worrisome, Beverly told anyone who would listen, but first of all her sister Lorene and her brother Thom, was that their mother didn't seem to realize the gravity of the situation, how reckless she'd been. "Mom seemed embarrassed, and kept apologizing to us—as if that was the point, not that she'd brought a madman into the house who could have killed her but that she'd made a mistake, disturbing us when we'd just gone to bed. *That* was what she felt bad about."

"Did you see this 'madman'?"—Lorene wanted to know.

"I smelled him! You'd call it a *feral smell*."

It was Lorene's instinct to disagree with her overwrought older sister but in this case, possibly Beverly was correct.

"Well. We'd better keep a closer check on Mom."

"*We?*—I'm the one who calls her two or three times a day—I'm the one who drops by if I don't hear from her. *You're* the one who's too damned busy to give a damn . . ."

Beverly spoke heatedly for some seconds before realizing that her infuriating younger sister had broken the connection.

When Thom heard news of the homeless man he drove immediately to Jessalyn's house to do a thorough search of the property, bringing with him a baseball bat. Jessalyn greeted him apologetically, and accompanied him as he searched the house, the garage, the old fieldstone barn, and every corner of the property where an intruder might be lurking. "Thom, I'm so sorry! It was a mistake of judgment—mine. It was not the poor man's fault." Jessalyn was out of breath trying to keep up with her incensed older son who brandished a baseball bat as if he'd have liked to use it. "It will never happen again, I promise."

At the foot of the McClaren property, in the tall, scruffy grass at the creek, Thom discovered what appeared to be the remnants of a kind of crude camp, where someone might have been sleeping.

"Jesus, Mom! What would Dad be thinking!—you know how anyone trespassing on his property upset him, even Canada geese."

And next evening Thom returned again to search the property with a flashlight, afterward patrolling Old Farm Road as dusk deepened to night, finding no one suspicious in the vicinity except, at the intersection with Mill Run, a mile away, a lone figure, a disheveled-looking individual walking with a tote bag over his shoulder, who might have fitted Jessalyn's vague description of the homeless man.

Rare to see anyone on foot in this part of North Hammond, walking on the roadside, who was not obviously a jogger or a young person. This had to be the *homeless man*.

Thom braked his vehicle to a stop, rolled down his window and told the astonished man that he'd better get the hell out of this neighborhood, and never return, or he'd regret it.

"That way. That way is the city limits. Go on—get going. Back to hell where you came from."

With the baseball bat Thom pointed. He was breathing heavily, his eyes glared in their sockets. Seeing his face the disheveled man asked no questions, backed away, turned and began to run limping into the night, until Thom could see him no longer.

A (DECEASED) HUSBAND WISHES *to return to his (still-living) wife but lacks the proper body, for his body has been cremated. Is it a possibility, if not a probability, that he will use for expediency's sake another (male) body, that bears some resemblance to his own?*

Before the answer is revealed she has been awakened by something slapping her face: tall wet grasses sharp as blades.

WHITEY'S MUCH-BATTERED COPY of Arthur Koestler's *The Sleepwalkers: A History of Man's Changing Vision of the Universe,* Jessalyn has brought into bed with her into the nest she has made of bedclothes, comforter, quilt. One of the key books of Whitey's life (to hear him tell it) to which Whitey would frequently allude; he'd liked to quote the opening sentence of the densely printed book—"'We can add to our knowledge, but we cannot subtract from it.'"

Was this an optimistic perspective, or—not? Jessalyn had never doubted the veracity of the oracular words (of 1959) as Whitey had declaimed them. Now, she isn't so sure. A single, singular stroke in the brain can subtract virtually all the knowledge of a lifetime, so patiently acquired. And how much more swiftly knowledge is subtracted than acquired.

Jessalyn thinks: it isn't difficult to imagine that entire societies, civilizations, might suffer strokes of another kind, obliterating history, knowledge, memory as in a cataclysm of the Ice Age. She had never spoken of such matters with Whitey who hadn't seemed comfortable discussing "serious" issues with her, his dear wife; though she'd often overheard him talking of such matters with his men friends and acquaintances.

Whether Whitey had read the entire five hundred–plus pages of *The Sleepwalkers* Jessalyn didn't know. She would never have asked for the question would have been too private, prying.

The bookshelves of Whitey's study are crammed with reference books: encyclopedias, histories, history of science, philosophy and cultural criticism, such titles as *Cosmos, A Brief History of Time, The Perfect Storm, The World's Wisdom, The Battle for God, The Greatest Generation, Team of Rivals: The Political Genius of Abraham Lincoln, The Selfish Gene, The Purpose Driven Life, The Art of Happiness, A Short History of Nearly Everything, Chaos: Making a New Science.* Each year Whitey spoke of taking off the entire month of August just to lie in the hammock right here at home and read, to hell with the business, to hell with trying to make money . . . Somehow, he'd never managed to accomplish this. After only a few days away from the office he became restless, bored, and irritable, and had to return to work.

They'd laughed at him, dear Whitey. Now Jessalyn thinks it wasn't funny but sad.

She'd tried to read Koestler's *The Sleepwalkers* at least once before but she'd never gotten beyond the first few chapters ("The Heroic Age"). The effort of that earlier reading, when she'd been a young woman, with young children clambering for her, in a (near-chaotic) household returns to her now, as she lies in the halo of light inside the darkness of the (empty) house trying to read *as if reading will save her.*

The theme of *The Sleepwalkers* does seem interesting: great scientific advances are made as if intuitively, more than "rationally"—at least, Jessalyn thinks this is the theme of the densely printed book. It's a vision of history in which the individual is a conduit of forces far greater than he can comprehend. He didn't know what the hell he was doing 100 percent of the time (Whitey liked to say) but he knew what had to be done, what was *the right thing.*

But it is difficult for Jessalyn to concentrate. The euphoria she feels at having survived another interminable day is fading. Insomnia has made her apprehensive of lying in bed, though this bed is the only place in which she feels safe; her brain feels ravaged, hyper-alert as if she were in the presence of actual danger. (Could the walls of this familiar room melt away? Is there an infinite darkness beyond, from which Whitey had shielded her?) Yet, perversely, she is very tired, and finds herself reading and rereading the same sentences without comprehension.

Finally, her eyelids are shut. She has not the strength to open them. The heavy book slips from her hands into a kind of abyss, a beautiful darkness.

Darling. His arms close about her, to shield her.

"I CARE FOR YOU, JESSALYN. Very much."

Gentlemanly Leo Colwin has a faint tremor in his left hand, which he tries to hide. Jessalyn feels an urge to take his hand and hold it between both her hands, to give solace to the man, to comfort.

"I hope you know . . . I hope you are not surprised, or—displeased."

Displeased. What a silly word, Whitey sneers.

Jessalyn has no idea how to reply to Leo Colwin. Her face burns with embarrassment.

Poor sap. Tell him something. Don't make him wait.

"I—I didn't know, Leo." Awkward pause. (Are there pauses, Jessalyn wonders, that are *not awkward*?) She sees that Leo's hand is trembling and looks away. (What to say to the man that is neither discouraging nor encouraging!) "Thank you."

Thank you! Whitey laughs.

But Leo Colwin seems encouraged. Leo Colwin is not one to be discouraged by another's muted response.

In his sweetly smiling way Leo reminisces of their "first meeting"—"how many years ago"—introduced by mutual friends "who have since passed away . . ." Jessalyn is only half-listening. She is recalling Maude Colwin with whom she'd been friendly if not exactly friends; Maude, an attractive and accomplished slightly older woman who'd allegedly given up a promising career as an attorney to raise a family in suburban Hammond and who one day unexpectedly confided in Jessalyn—"Please be kind to Leo if something happens to me, he will be utterly helpless without a wife."

The McClarens had included Leo in so many family dinners, the grandchildren had assumed he was a relative. *Please don't seat me next to Uncle Leo, he always asks the same old dumb questions about school he doesn't remember he always asks.*

Jessalyn has the uneasy idea that her own daughters, Beverly and Lorene, though perhaps not Sophia, are hoping that she and Leo Colwin will become a *couple*. How practical, how expedient, what a relief for the (adult) children of both, to know that their surviving parents are taken care of and will not be a vexation to them, at least not for a while.

Jessalyn is sure that she has overheard Beverly and Lorene whispering together about Leo Colwin—*Just the perfect gentleman. Dad would be so relieved.*

(But how would Whitey feel, really? Jessalyn wouldn't want to inquire.)

It's understood by the young that no one of her or Leo Colwin's age could possibly have sexual feelings any longer. Very barely, romantic feelings. The (adult) children would shudder at just the thought, as attractive as the proverbial scratching of fingernails on a blackboard.

She herself feels like a lamp that has been unplugged. Just—nothing there, anesthetized and numb.

Sometimes, in sleep or the twilight of near-sleep, taken unaware, she feels a sudden small leap of desire, or of hope, in the pit of her belly—*Whitey! I love you . . .*

Fleeting as a match that is struck and almost at once goes out.

"Well, Jessalyn! Did you give any more thought about—"

An upcoming event to which Leo might escort Jessalyn. Has she forgotten?

Leo is not an aggressive person—he is, as all say, a very kind, very considerate person—yet Jessalyn feels oppressed by his earnestness as by a large upright sponge pressing too close. His persistent smile, his myopic gaze, his rounded shoulders and monotone-voice drain the widow's already diminished energy. Each time they meet he has memorized a joke to tell her as if "cheering up" the widow is a task he takes very seriously.

"'What do you get when you cross a dyslexic, an insomniac, and an agnostic?'"—(Leo waits for Jessalyn to respond but Jessalyn just smiles to indicate she has not the slightest idea)—"'Someone who lies awake at night wondering if there is a dog.'"

Jessalyn isn't sure that she has heard the joke correctly, or is it a riddle, the word *dyslexic* drew her attention, for Whitey'd often said that, as a child, he'd been dyslexic, to a degree, which had made his teachers think that he wasn't very smart, or wasn't trying very hard, or was naturally restless, impatient—*deficit attention disorder before it became trendy.*

Or: is it *attention deficit disorder*?

Jessalyn is smiling blankly. Leo chuckles, and repeats the answer: "'Someone who lies awake at night wondering if there is a *dog*.'"

"Oh, I see. 'Dog.'" Jessalyn doesn't quite see but laughs obligingly.

"'Did you hear about the dyslexic KKK chapter?—they go around killing gingers.'"

Jessalyn is startled. Is this funny? *Gingers?*

Leo thinks the "joke" is funny, baring his teeth in a hoarse, heaving laugh.

It is late: nearly 11:00 P.M. Leo has brought Jessalyn home from a dinner party given by mutual friends—(is there a communal plot, Jessalyn wonders, throwing widow and widower together nearly every weekend?)—and Jessalyn seems to have invited him inside the house out of politeness perhaps for Leo is invariably reluctant to leave her—"Alone in that big house."

Is he planning to move in? Sap.

But Whitey is amused, not worried. To Whitey who'd been, for most of his life, what you'd call a *full-blooded alpha male,* a timorous ectomorph like Leo Colwin is no serious rival.

Really it is time (for Leo) to leave. Frequently he has mentioned that he is "usually in bed by nine-thirty P.M.—and up at six A.M." (Why do people imagine that their sleeping habits are of interest to others?—Jessalyn has wondered.) She is conscious of being rude in not offering her guest a "nightcap"—(silly term! what does it even mean?)—but (should she be obliged to explain to him) in a fugue of panic soon after Whitey passed away she'd poured all of Whitey's alcoholic beverages out in the sink fearing that in her deranged state she might begin to drink and so succumb to a slovenly pitiable death. (Whitey's store of good, moderately expensive wines, kept in the basement, Jessalyn has not touched: Whitey would be devastated if she behaved so rashly, and would never forgive her. She wants to think that someday she might give a dinner party, and need wine; she will certainly have family dinners like Thanksgiving and Christmas and in any case it's too much effort for her to open a bottle of wine, for the purpose of drinking it herself.)

But Leo isn't showing signs of leaving just yet. He has begun to recount to Jessalyn his history "in politics"—running for class office in high school and college—("came close to winning class president in my senior year at Colgate, and was elected vice president of our Sigma Nu chapter"); his stint in the U.S. Army ("Intelligence, stateside"); his early work-experiences ("thought I'd try New York before going into our business here, but that didn't work out so well"). Leo's marriage, children, grandchildren are elided over, glimpsed like landscape from a speeding train.

Jessalyn wonders if Leo is hoping to establish himself as a worthy rival to Whitey. Or maybe Leo senses Whitey's presence in the house and is boasting of himself for Whitey's benefit.

Boring as an old shoe.

In his case, an old moccasin.

(This is cruel: Leo Colwin favors moccasins with tassels. So far as Jessalyn knows he has several pairs, all comfortably worn.)

Jessalyn thinks it is not quite true, as Maude foretold, that Leo is helpless without her. He plays golf at least twice a week, with other, older male friends at the East Hammond Hills Golf Club; he is "always welcome" (he claims) at his children's homes; he is a "deacon" in his church, the First Episcopal Church of North Hammond; he attends local functions—concerts, exhibits, fund-raisers. Like the McClarens, he is a donor to local arts and charitable organizations: you will see his name, like theirs, listed on programs, in columns of print beneath *Sponsors.* But since his wife passed away Leo has become a becalmed sailboat. *The wind has gone out of his sails, for sure!*—a jocular expression Whitey often used.

"Well—I think—"

"Yes, well—"

Time for Leo Colwin to depart! Jessalyn is suffused with happiness.

She sees her guest to the door. (Does she imagine it, or is Leo as relieved to be leaving, as she is that he is leaving?) At the door he hesitates as if he has something more to say, or as if he is about to kiss her. Jessalyn stiffens, for she has forgotten how to "kiss"—even her handshakes have become quick, ineffectual. *Don't touch me, please! Go away.*

Yet she is smiling, weakly. Since girlhood Jessalyn has been too cowardly not to smile in such situations.

Good manners must always trump instinctive revulsion: that is the first premise of society.

"Jessalyn, I—I hope you weren't offended by—what I said earlier . . ."

No. Yes. Please just go.

"—always there has been this 'rapport' between us, I think—since we'd first met—our spouses were so sociable, gregarious—*we* are more introverted—two of a kind. I'd always thought."

"Yes."

"Yes? You'd thought so, too?"

Jessalyn has no idea what the conversation is about. She is so eager for Leo to leave, she will agree to anything.

"Well—good night! Dear Jessalyn."

At the last moment Leo veers, or Jessalyn veers, so that his lips only brush her forehead.

"Thank you, Leo. Good night!"

HOW HAPPY THE WIDOW IS, to be alone!

Euphoria courses through her. Alone. She is *alone.*

In this house, in this bedroom that is her sanctuary. In this bed that is her nest. No one to speak to her as if she's a convalescent. As if, as a widow, she is something *other.*

No one to gaze at her with doggy adoring eyes. No one to expect her to behave sensibly.

Whitey would say—*Tell them all to go to hell.*

At her bedside, a small stack of Whitey's "wisdom" books. Along with *The Sleepwalkers* are *Into Thin Air, The Tipping Point: How Little Things Can Make a Big Difference, A Brief History of the Universe.*

But Jessalyn isn't ready for bed just yet. Easing her gentlemanly suitor out of the house, shutting and locking the door behind him, scarcely waiting until he was in his vehicle before switching off all the outside lights—she is feeling too exhilarated.

She crosses the room to Whitey's closet, which she has not (yet) emptied. Her daughters have volunteered to help her sort through his clothes to give away to Goodwill, which Jessalyn knows is a very good idea, certainly a practical idea, but she has not gotten around to it yet.

Not yet, not yet. Soon.

Not soon. But—sometime.

Presses her face against one of Whitey's sport coats. An old well-worn camel's hair coat, worn thin at the elbows.

His clothes are beautiful to her. How can she bear to part with them!

In the bathroom, in the cabinet, the pill containers, lined up. The widow checks them not once not twice but several times a day. Her precious cache! These are her rosary. Her consolation. She would shake out a dozen pills in the palm of her hand this very hour and swallow them down eagerly with mouthfuls of lukewarm water but Whitey would be upset with her.

Not yet, not yet. But—soon.

— ∞ —

"Yes, I will. Today."

(A widow talks to herself not only for companionship but also to give clear instructions. What is clearly articulated is likely to be executed.)

Bravely, Jessalyn has decided to sort through Whitey's clothes.

Not with her daughters but alone. For the widow is happiest alone.

Yes I love my daughters but they talk, talk. Never cease talking because they are terrified of silence.

Whitey's closet dense with clothes. So many!

Since his *passing-away* Jessalyn has not been able to examine her husband's things. Thom had located for her the relevant legal papers in Whitey's files including IRS tax documents and other financial records, numbering in the hundreds of pages, but Jessalyn has not wanted to search Whitey's desk drawers, shelves, boxes in his study and in the basement—it is not something a wife of Whitey McClaren would have done while he was on the premises and so she does not feel comfortable about doing it now.

His privacy. His life. Must not violate. No.

(Also: Jessalyn is [perhaps] afraid of finding something that will upset her. Amid the accumulation of nearly four decades, there must be something.)

Beverly and Lorene are eager to undertake the task, with her. Sophia would join them too. But no.

Too much emotion. Turn the faucet on, can't turn it off.

Please understand, I am not ready.

Soon after Whitey's *passing-away* she'd looked through photo albums in a trance of disbelief: that what had existed so naturally in the world now existed no longer, and was irretrievable. Of course it had always been Jessalyn who'd tended the family albums as she'd tended the bulletin board in the kitchen—others were enthusiastic and helpful, but only temporarily; the wife and mother of the household understands that she alone is the proprietor of memories, no one cherishes them quite as much as she does, and no one understands how perishable they are, quite as much as she does.

In her numbed state she'd brought the albums into bed with her, into the nest of bedclothes, pillows, comforter, where she could lose herself in the contemplation of so many years in which (here was proof!) they'd all been happy . . . And Whitey had been *so handsome,* even when clowning for the camera, or scowling, she stared and stared at him and did not ever want to look away.

It is the astonishment of her life, if she surveys her life from the perspective of a small single-prop plane flying overhead: that Whitey McClaren had loved *her.*

Of all of the world—*her.*

Randomly inserted into the photo albums were cards she and Whitey had given each other, birthday cards, Valentine's Day cards, some of them handcrafted by Jessalyn in her young-wife phase, countless cards over the years, *happy birthday to my dearest wife, happy birthday to my dearest husband, love to my dearest wife, love to my dearest husband*—some of these dating back to a time when Jessalyn's handwriting so differed from her present handwriting, the cards might have been from another person named *Jess.*

Love, Your Jess.

Love, Your Wifie Jessie.

She'd forgotten too how Whitey would sign a card with just his initial—*W.* As if he hadn't liked his name—"White-y"—(it did sound droll, flippant) but had been trapped inside it. Poor Whitey!

(And was she *Jess,* or *Jessalyn*? *Jessie?* She had liked her name well enough though as an older teenager she'd wondered if, named *Hilda, Hulga, Mick* or *Brett* she might've felt less of an obligation to be "feminine.")

She had not told anyone that by chance she'd come across, in a pocket of one of Whitey's coats, a few days after his death, a birthday card he'd bought for her, but had not yet signed: one of Whitey's typically large, lavish, expensive cards with shiny rose-colored *Happy Birthday to a Wonderful Wife.* (At a glance you could see which cards were from Whitey, and which from Jessalyn—these were smaller, less showy and less expensive, made from recycled paper.)

This cheery birthday to a *wonderful wife* Jessalyn has positioned atop a bureau in the bedroom. Also on the bureau are framed photographs of Whitey: young, not-so-young, middle-aged; smiling cautiously, smiling broadly; alone, with Jessalyn and/or children at various ages. (She has not intended it but she has included not a single photograph of Whitey at the office, Whitey in his professional mode, Whitey McClaren as mayor of Hammond. As if he'd never lived such a life, what he'd have called with a commingling of ruefulness and pride his *public life*.)

Until this morning Jessalyn has done little more than glance into Whitey's bedroom closet. It is a large, walk-in closet—larger than her own closet in a farther corner of the room. A mist comes into her eyes as she opens the door and a light switches on like an eye opening.

So often he'd said *Jess, have you seen my—?* Sincerely bereft, baffled, searching through the closet unable to find a favorite shirt, sweater, only Jessalyn could locate it.

She smiles now, recalling. For not once (she is sure) had she failed to find the elusive article of clothing.

Newer clothes, favored clothes, are within easy reach. Sport coats, shirts, hangers bearing neckties . . . Whitey was notoriously reluctant to discard anything including even those ridiculous ultra-narrow ties men were wearing decades ago. He'd never wanted to toss out anything that "might come back into fashion, someday"—nor would he concede that he'd grown forever out of the clothes of his earlier, leaner self—tuxedo, moth-eaten three-button pinstripe suit, floral-pattern shirts, hearty Scots wool sweaters he hadn't been able to squeeze into for years.

D'you think this is too tight, Jessalyn?

Yes, Whitey. I'm afraid so.

*Well—*is *it too tight? What d'you think?*

Yes, I think it's too tight, dear.

But, well— It's too tight, or too short?

Too small, Whitey.

D'you think it shrank? At the dry cleaner?

Yes. Shrank.

Damn dry cleaner! I should sue.

Jessalyn wipes her eyes, recalling.

Here is Whitey's most recent suit, which they'd brought home from the hospital: Black Watch plaid, lightweight wool, with a vest. Not Jessalyn's favorite suit of his but Whitey who was usually reluctant to shop for clothes had been enthusiastic about the purchase, and so Jessalyn had assured him it was very "handsome"—"unusual"—even as she'd exchanged a glance with the salesclerk in the three-way mirror.

"The one thing I do not want," Whitey said, "is a conventional suit. A 'traditional' suit. Three-button pinstripe, or gray flannel."

"I don't think that three-button suits are available any longer," Jessalyn said. "There is no danger."

Whitey told the salesclerk that he had Scots ancestors and the McClaren tartan wasn't Black Watch but he wasn't sentimental or patriotic, he liked any kind of plaid provided it was on the dark side and "dignified."

Jessalyn and the salesclerk had laughed together quietly. Whitey hadn't noticed. How she'd loved him, her husband, his innocent vanity and obliviousness.

The suit, badly torn, dirtied, bloodied, damaged, has been hanging in Whitey's closet in a plastic bag, as Thom had instructed. "Don't have it dry cleaned, and don't throw it away," he'd told Jessalyn. For the damage to the suit wasn't caused (Thom has said) by an accident in Whitey's vehicle but by an assault by police officers.

(Jessalyn has not heard from Thom in weeks about the legal action he is planning to take against the Hammond Police Department; she is not sure that she'd ever quite understood what Thom is, or was, planning, with Whitey's lawyer-friend Bud Hawley. *Misconduct? Excessive force? Assault? Manslaughter?* It will not be good for them—for any of the McClarens. Her mind shrinks from such upsetting thoughts as her sensitive eyes shrink from too-bright sunshine.)

In any case, Jessalyn wouldn't give away Whitey's favorite suit. Proudly Whitey had worn the suit for special occasions though the waist had grown tight and the trousers a little long—"Am I getting shorter, Jess? Jesus! It feels too soon for that."

"My dear, handsome husband," she'd said, laughing. On her toes to kiss his cheek. "My Black Watch husband."

He'd worn it on that day. The last day of his life as Whitey McClaren.

Such vanity! His, and her own.

Weakly she shuts the closet door. She isn't strong enough after all for the tasks that await her.

FOR MY SAKE *you have got to keep living.*

If you give up I am lost utterly.

She would not give up. She would not abandon her husband a second time.

(PHONE RINGING: BEVERLY'S PETULANT VOICE *Mom? Mom! I know you are home will you PLEASE pick up.*)

(*Mom, if you don't answer or call back within ten minutes I am getting into my car and DRIVING OVER THERE.*)

(Hurriedly then Jessalyn calls back her daughter with a feeble excuse, she'd been outside and had not heard the phone ring, she'd been vacuuming . . . *Yes I am fine, dear. No need to come over just now.*)

EACH WEEK, flowers from Leo Colwin.

Promptly on Monday at about 11:00 A.M. The familiar delivery truck barrels up the long driveway, familiar burly deliveryman, ringing doorbell, Jessalyn remains upstairs observing from behind a curtain until the deliveryman briskly departs having left the bouquet on the front stoop.

She will bring the flowers inside, eventually. Though sometimes she forgets.

"Mom? There're flowers out here, I'll bring them inside . . . What's the card say?—*To My Dearest Jessalyn, Love Leo.* This is so sweet!"

Often, flowers from the previous week are still on the kitchen table in an identical glass vase from the florist's. Over the weeks, now months, the flowers have changed from roses, mums, carnations to amaryllis, daffodils, tulips, daisies, hyacinth, (Easter) lilies.

Such a sweet man, Leo Colwin. So wonderful, the two of them (widow, widower), longtime friends, seeing each other, giving comfort to each other—"Daddy would be happy, I think."

To this Jessalyn makes no reply. Sees her hands moving in homemaker ways, familiar and comforting (to the daughter if not to the mother), fussing with the previous week's flowers which are (admittedly) past their bloom, bruised petals beginning to fall on the counter and on the floor, bending the flower stalks in half in order to shove into a trash container with a certain restrained zest; emptying out the old, now smelly water into the sink. Feels her mouth tug in a small triumphant smile. There! Gone.

"I think—Daddy would be happy . . . About Leo . . ."

But now Beverly isn't so sure. Glances about as if (Jessalyn understands, Jessalyn glances about in this way a hundred times a day in this house) Whitey were in the very room glowering at her.

"He always loved—people . . . Going out, friends, making new friends, even people he didn't like—Daddy kind of *liked*. Y'know? Those old feuds of his, going back for years, remember how upset and sad Daddy was when some old enemy"—Beverly hesitates—"*passed away* . . ."

Beverly speaks a little too heartily. The silence in the widow's house is palpable as a sweet-smelling gas.

At such times (unscheduled visits, *dropping in to check on Mom* like a social worker checking on a suspect client) Beverly is over-cheerful, over-loud, over-inquisitive, over-vigilant taking note of (for instance) the stacks of unread/unopened mail (sympathy cards, letters) in a wicker basket on the kitchen table, untouched for weeks, about which she'd chided Jessalyn before—"We could open them together, Mom. I think it would do you good, to know how people l-loved Daddy . . ."

Jessalyn blinks at her daughter. *Why on earth*—her expression seems to ask—*why would that do me good?*

". . . it's just polite to at least see what your friends have written. Some widows—people—reply to sympathy cards . . ."

Beverly speaks haltingly like a person with something foreign in her mouth, small sour seeds or nettles. Each clumsy word is a surprise to her yet she cannot seem to stop speaking.

Beverly is hoping that Jessalyn will invite her to stay here for the rest of the day. Or maybe—for the night. Such solace in the house on Old Farm Road, she can find nowhere else in the world.

Her husband has become impatient with her moods. Her children are impatient, embarrassed. *Jeez Mom. Get hold of yourself.*

She will run away to her old home! Her old, girlhood room still containing a bed, a dresser and a mirror once her closest companion.

It is a fact: no one is so *interested in you* as that reflection in the mirror.

"Is there anything of Whitey's left?—I mean, to drink? Did you pour it all out?"

Yes. All out.

"Oh, Mom!"

But I am not the mother, just now. Please understand.

Beverly will retreat from the house on the Old Farm Road wounded, annoyed; disgusted with herself, she'd really wanted a drink!—and disgusted with Jessalyn, or disappointed with Jessalyn, pouring out the remains of Whitey's expensive whiskeys for what desperate reason Beverly doesn't want to consider. Five minutes after she leaves the house she pulls over to park at the side of the road, eager to call Lorene and leave a voice mail of martyrish complaint *I've tried to tell you, our mother is unhinged by grief, she has not been herself in months, she is almost rude to me, Daddy wouldn't recognize this woman in old clothes, not even clean clothes, her hair is every-which-way, wild-looking,* white—*Daddy would be shocked she'd let her hair go* white, *he'd always been so proud that Mom was so young-looking. It was noon, and Mom hadn't gotten around to putting on makeup, or proper shoes—she was in bedroom slippers. She won't let me help her with the sympathy cards or with Whitey's clothes. She didn't want to come out grocery shopping. She just looked blank when I invited her for Sunday dinner with the kids. It's beyond normal grief, normal grief is shared. And she scarcely seems to care that poor Leo Colwin is in love with her, such a sweet man, such a gentleman, and Leo has money, he isn't after her money like some other man might be, her women friends are calling me to say they feel exactly the same, Mom doesn't have time for them, Mom doesn't answer the damned phone, Mom is taking Leo Colwin for granted, her behavior is going to drive him away and then what? Mom is turning into some wild-white-haired old eccentric woman! Imagine, Jessalyn McClaren of all people! I think we will have to have an intervention, damn it Lorene this is serious! Don't you dare not call me back.*

SNOWFALL. AND IN THE MORNING, animal tracks close beside the house.

Jessalyn discovers them when she goes outside, onto the rear deck, to put birdseed into the feeders. Not myriad animal tracks but a single, singular creature (of about the size of a dog) that made its way up the steps and across the deck, approaching the house as if to peer inside the plate-glass sliding doors.

And elsewhere, in loose powdery snow at the sides of the house, as if the creature was seeking entry, blindly.

LATELY, the tremor in Leo Colwin's left hand has been more pronounced. Jessalyn feels sorrier for him, more kindly disposed. She'd expected to be caring for Whitey after his hospital discharge and had prepared herself emotionally for a period of rehabilitation; so now, cheated of this experience, which she has imagined as a romantic adventure, she is likely to find herself gazing after wheelchair-bound or obviously incapacitated older men when she sees them, with an air of yearning. Unfortunately such men are invariably tended by their wives who would not wish (would they?) to give them up.

Just as well, sweetheart. I'd have been an impossible bastard in a wheelchair, you'd have ended up hating my guts.

"Oh, Whitey! No . . ."

Jessalyn is stricken at the thought. No no *no.*

She'd acquired pamphlets, books with such no-nonsense utilitarian titles as *The Stroke Caregiver's Handbook, After a Stroke: Support for Patients and Caregivers, Stroke Recovery: Tips for the Caregiver.* She'd researched night school courses at the community college nursing school.

And Leo Colwin is indeed a very nice man. Though she has no more feeling for him than (for instance) she'd have had for a mannequin discarded in a trash heap she can see that he is an attractive man for his age, a generous man, often "witty"—as her daughters are always saying, *a gentleman.* And how touching it is, he likes *her.*

Often, Leo speaks of his "residences." A two-bedroom condominium in Hammond's most prestigious retirement village overlooking the Chautauqua River; a "camping lodge" in the Keene Valley, Adirondacks; an "almost-Gulf-front" condominium in Sarasota, Florida. Leo is one of those local residents who take an interest in Revolutionary War history of the region and so admire the Forrester House—as he calls it; clearly, Leo would like to live in such a house, with its General George Washington connection.

Where others ask the widow out of idle, cruel curiosity if she planned on selling her house Leo Colwin asks with a look of apprehension, pain—"You don't plan to sell your house, Jessalyn, do you?—I hope not." Nervously he grips both hands to keep them from trembling.

Jessalyn wonders if Leo had Parkinson's? Or is his tremor only "benign"—not a symptom of something beyond itself? She is feeling more kindly disposed to him; within a year or two, he might require some sort of wifely care.

Widow, widower. Match made in Hades!

It is touching to Jessalyn, that Leo dresses with such apparent care for their evenings together at dinners in the homes of mutual friends, invariably seated next to each other—"Here, Jessalyn! Here's your place card, right next to me." (Peering nearsightedly at the place cards as if there might be some terrible mistake or confusion, as if Jessalyn might be at the farther end of the table, as a wife might have been positioned, out of earshot.) That Leo wears once-elegant, now lightly moth-hole-ridden J. Press flannel jackets, polka-dot bow ties (at which Whitey, who disliked most neckties anyway, would sneer), reasonably sharp-creased trousers that match, or nearly match, his jacket. On his feet, not always but often, tasseled moccasins with black socks. Always he sports a handkerchief tucked into his lapel pocket and in his lapel is a small mysterious pin of intersecting triangles (pyramids?) that identified the wearer as a member of a secret fraternal order to which (so far as Jessalyn knows) John Earle McClaren had not belonged. (Though Whitey, contemptuous of all such "secret" organizations, excepting the Order of the Arrow commemorating his particular Eagle Scout status as a boy of fifteen, might have been inducted into Leo's organization for purely professional reasons and discarded the pin without even mentioning it to his family.)

Leo's flat blank-colored hair is thin but meticulously barbered. He smells of a faintly astringent shaving lotion, cologne. He has always been a Republican, Jessalyn knows, though not so flexible a Republican as Whitey (who'd voted for Obama) who'd liked to goad Leo Colwin and others with: "A Republican is an individual who hires someone else to do his dirty work for him—cops, military, lawyers."

Leo firmly believes the less government, the better. Regulate decent, family-owned businesses?—why? He'd disapproved of the Clintons. He disapproved of "rabble-rousing" by any politician. He "had doubts" about women in high public office or in the judiciary. Once, Whitey described him as "an old-school white Anglo-Saxon Protestant Republican vintage 1950"—Leo laughed glowingly, flattered.

Now Leo is saying to Jessalyn, in the hesitant voice you might use with a convalescent, "Dear Jessalyn, I—I am wondering if you've given more thought to . . . what I'd suggested . . ."

What has Leo suggested? Jessalyn has no idea.

". . . our losses, our lives . . . so much in common, 'rapport' of many years . . . donated to Whitey's campaign for mayor . . . My children admire you so, Jessalyn! They are delighted that we are 'seeing each other' . . . they both say, 'Please tell Mrs. McClaren hello for us!'"

As Leo speaks in a rapid excited voice Jessalyn has a vision of the (adult) Colwin children, whom she scarcely recalls, has not seen in years, gazing at Leo and her with intense interest. *Please! Please take over the care and feeding of our dear lonely father.*

To dampen her suitor's interest Jessalyn tells Leo that she did not inherit Whitey's estate, exactly. That is, Whitey left her money in a "trust" that pays her a fixed sum each quarter; if she applies for more money it would have to be at the discretion of the estate executor, a lawyer-friend of his.

She wouldn't be able, she warns him, to acquire a million dollars easily, let alone five, ten million—"Whitey has seen to that. One of my daughters says his will is like a 'foot-binding.'"

The sardonic remark was Lorene's, and it had been received by all who'd heard with dismay. Jessalyn is surprised to hear herself repeat it now.

Leo draws in his breath. Is he surprised?—shocked? At the lurid image of *foot-binding,* or at the conditions of Whitey's will?

Is he disappointed that Jessalyn doesn't have access to large amounts of money, or is he sympathetic and embarrassed on her account, that her husband so little trusted her good judgment?

"Oh, dear Jessalyn. That is—too bad . . ."

Leo takes Jessalyn's hand in his, to comfort her.

Leo is quiet for a while, thinking. Then—"A trust can be broken, Jessalyn. I wouldn't consider that trust binding, only just temporary, with the proper lawyer." Leo speaks firmly, almost with exhilaration, as Jessalyn has rarely heard him speak.

He wants Whitey to hear. He is challenging Whitey!

In life the men had not been competitive. Leo had so far trailed behind Whitey, neither man would have considered the other a worthy rival. And so this (belated) challenge is somewhat out of character for Leo.

That night as he is about to leave Jessalyn's house Leo grips her shoulders and stoops awkwardly to kiss her on the lips—a lukewarm rubbery kiss that makes her want to laugh shrilly like a twelve-year-old.

"Good night, dear Jessalyn!"

"Good night—Leo . . ."

Quickly then shutting the door, locking it. What has she done? What is happening to her? She hopes that something has not been tacitly decided between her and Leo, of which she is but vaguely aware. Rubbing at her lips, that feel numb. She has a vision of swirling water, foam and froth on its surface, and something borne in its current, a living thing, a body, helpless as it is swept along—where?

That night lying awake waiting for a sardonic and witty remark of Whitey's to conclude the evening. But nothing.

"WINTER SQUASH."

"*Butternut* squash."

Virgil has brought her a large butternut squash, oblong-shaped, like an Indian club, graceless, with a hard rind, dirty-cream-colored. In her hands it feels heavy as a heart.

"Oh, Virgil! Thank you. It's beautiful . . ."

Virgil laughs at her, this is such an untruth. Jessalyn has to laugh as well, at herself.

Famously gracious Jessalyn McClaren. Confronted with a singularly ugly large vegetable as with a singularly ugly baby, Jessalyn can only exclaim *Beautiful!*

"You don't have to cook it, Mom. You don't have to do anything with it. It's from our farm, I guess you could say it's 'ornamental.'"

"I know perfectly well what a butternut squash is, Virgil. I've made butternut squash, roasted, with almonds, cinnamon, and brown sugar. You used to love it. Whitey, too."

By *you* Jessalyn means the children. The collective *you.*

"Well. I can't stay for supper, in any case . . ."

"Did I invite you?"—Jessalyn gives Virgil a little pinch.

Virgil is smiling but not so sure of himself now. Does he want to leave or—stay? Every hour of Virgil's life seems to be so mediated.

Jessalyn's younger son, the son who sets her heart aflutter (with worry? exasperation? dread? love?) is standing in her kitchen, hasn't removed his oversized jacket, nor the knitted cap on his head, that looks like something purchased at a rummage sale. (It is.) Virgil's still-adolescent skin is unevenly flushed from the cold, his eyes are watery and evasive. His fair-brown beard is sparse, wispy, but longer than Jessalyn recalls; the (darker) hair on his head is tangled and straggly over his (worn, not-very-clean) collar. Though Virgil lives only a few miles away from the family home it has been some time since he has visited Jessalyn.

Why?—no reason. Jessalyn knows better than to ask.

You can't call Virgil, his siblings complain. Virgil can't call *you.*

(Of course, if Virgil wanted to call, he certainly could. No problem borrowing a phone. But Virgil has been inconsiderately reluctant to own a phone, for in that way he would be making himself accessible to his family.)

Since he'd moved out at the age of nineteen it has been Virgil's habit to drop by the house at unpredictable times. Of course, being Virgil, he will fail to come if he has (vaguely) promised he will. So annoyed was Whitey at his son's "hippie" behavior, Jessalyn rarely mentioned to Whitey when Virgil visited the house, or failed to visit. She hadn't considered it duplicitous exactly, rather more protective of both Virgil and Whitey.

A mother protects a son against the father. Is this, Jessalyn wonders, something like *classical*?

She has given up hoping that Virgil will reform—"re-form" for Virgil would require considerable effort, like a pretzel untwisting itself.

Except today Virgil has surprised his mother. Glancing out the window in the late morning, seeing what appears to be a Jeep making its way along the icy driveway Jessalyn is baffled: Who on earth does she know who owns a Jeep?

Not even Thom owns a Jeep. And Thom is, Jessalyn supposes, a Jeep-type.

But it is Virgil, looking both embarrassed and (covertly) proud.

"Hey, it's secondhand, Mom. A bargain. So I can get around in the winter without having to borrow a vehicle."

As if he expects Jessalyn to accuse him of something. What?

Jessalyn thinks that the purchase is eminently practical. Sensible. Good for Virgil, to be using the money his father had left him for a good cause. Next, he might purchase a cell phone. Make a dental appointment. *Mature.*

Virgil is perpetually embarrassed about money. He has few needs himself, it seems; but he has often strongly hinted that he "needs" money for one or another charitable organization—Green Space, Mercy for Animals, Save Our Great Lakes—which Jessalyn has usually provided.

(Of course, without telling Whitey. This has involved strategic transferences of money from their checking account.)

"How are you, Virgil?"—Jessalyn asks lightly. (For this is a question that must be asked lightly by a mother, put to an adult child.)

Virgil winces, or almost. Wishing to say, Jessalyn supposes, *Oh who cares about* me? *Virgil doesn't "exist."*

"Are you sure you can't stay for dinner, Virgil? I could prepare this butternut squash."

"Well. I guess—not."

His mouth twists as if he would like to say *yes.*

(But why on earth can't he say *yes*? This is so like Virgil!)

Jessalyn doesn't persist as she would have once done—*Are you sure? Why do you have to rush away?* Too often she has seen her son's harried look. He is like a wild creature that has been only partially tamed, wary of a collar around its neck, a tight leash.

Once Virgil has established that he isn't staying for dinner—once his mother has accepted this—he is noticeably more relaxed. Unzips his jacket, drapes it on a chair. Beneath he is wearing paint-stained bib-overalls over a long-sleeved flannel shirt with soiled cuffs. But even the unlaundered musty scent of her son is precious to Jessalyn, flooding her with pleasure, relief.

Virgil is too shy to ask his mother how she has been. Dreading to hear an obvious answer.

I am in despair. To breathe is to feel pain. Will you release me, let me go? I am so lonely without him.

No, Virgil can't possibly ask such a question. His heart behaves strangely when he thinks the very words *Dad, Daddy. Gone.*

Jessalyn tells Virgil it's good to see him! She has been thinking of him.

Well. Virgil has been thinking of *her.*

Impulsively Jessalyn hugs her son. The flood of pleasure is too strong to resist. Like a teenaged boy Virgil stiffens, just slightly; holds his arms out, limp and uninvolved as scarecrow arms. But (to Jessalyn's relief) he doesn't shrink away.

How bony he has become! And how tall, taller than she remembers. He dreads her speaking of Whitey, she understands.

Quickly she says, before Virgil could be expected to mutter an apology for how long he has stayed away from her, "I'm really doing well, I think. I'm starting my volunteer work again, at the library. And the hospital, next Monday. I think it's time."

There is a pause. (Is it true, about the volunteer work? Jessalyn has returned for a half-day at the local branch of the township library, where she checks out books and DVDs and, upon occasion, reads to pre-school children during Story Hour. But she will probably not return so soon to Hammond General Hospital where she volunteers at the information desk and where every minute of every hour will remind her of entering a room on the fifth floor to see Whitey's motionless body in death. Eyes not entirely shut, mouth slightly open. *Oh dear God.*)

"Tomorrow I'm going to sort through Dad's clothes, and shoes. I think it's time." (Is this true? Maybe.)

Virgil asks if she wants help?

Please say no—his eyes beg.

"Thank you but I don't think so. I mean—I'm not sure when I will actually get to it . . ."

Her mind has gone blank. She feels as if she has been shaken—literally: lifted, shaken like a doll so that her teeth rattled and her brain knocked against her skull. (What had she been thinking of just now?—it's gone.)

In the awkward silence Virgil asks if he can have something to drink. Helps himself to grapefruit juice from the refrigerator, poured into his old, favorite turquoise glass that is the last remaining of a set of twelve, from Target.

(Whitey always insisted that Jessalyn make household purchases at the best stores. Jessalyn never disagreed but made many purchases at Target, Home Depot, JCPenney, about which Whitey never knew. *What great glasses!*—he'd surely exclaimed.)

Jessalyn spoons out (plain, low-fat) yogurt into a bowl. Slices a banana, sprinkles the yogurt with muesli and cinnamon, sets it before Virgil, who begins to eat hungrily.

Hands him a paper napkin. Distractedly, he tucks it into his shirt-front.

Care and feeding of a son. A boy.

Shy, backward, Virgil will find it hard to thank his mother. *Why* is he so strange? Jessalyn's heart is suffused with love for him, and fear for him. He seems to crave affection—and care—even as he shrinks from it; even as a child he'd been like this, amid the (mostly) loving McClaren family. Virgil can be charming, even seductive, with women, and with men, for whom it isn't likely that he can feel anything much—he can be quite playful, extravagant. She has seen women and girls stare after him in public places, his homely-handsome face radiant with feeling, energy quivering in all of his limbs. She has seen men stare after Virgil, too.

She'd wondered—sometimes. When Virgil was in high school. His notable lack of interest in girls, sex.

Unless Virgil's interest was hidden from her. Surreptitious.

Most of the time Virgil gives the impression of (resentful) restraint. Like one hobbling in an ill-fitting shoe who nonetheless insists upon wearing the damned shoe to spite—what?—the shoe, or the self-wearing-the-shoe?

Or, the parental authority, that pushed the shoe upon him?

Jessalyn asks if Virgil would like a little more to eat and Virgil hesitates—*no? yes?*—as if the decision should not be his own. She laughs, and replenishes the yogurt-muesli mixture.

True, the mother has "enabled" the son to persist in such behavior—Lorene is quite correct. (Without guessing that Lorene's own prickly, sharp-elbowed personality has got to be the consequence of "enabling" as well on the part of both parents.) But what is the alternative, exactly?—Jessalyn has never understood.

If Whitey had been more accepting of Virgil, less judgmental—that would have made a difference. Jessalyn couldn't allow Virgil to feel *less loved* than the other children.

No need to indulge Thom, for instance. Thom has been fully capable of indulging himself.

It is a pleasure to Jessalyn, to see Virgil eat in her kitchen. She believes that she doesn't want "company"—she prefers to be alone with Whitey, that's to say her grief. But of course, Virgil is the exception.

He'd fled Hammond after his father's death—Jessalyn had fully understood.

Her other children, certainly the girls, surely Thom, would think to ask Jessalyn how well does she eat these days; does she prepare actual meals, or eat just haphazardly (out of a yogurt container, for instance, with a spoonful of muesli sprinkled inside)—but it would never occur to Virgil to ask.

The mother is strength. You do not question strength.

"And how is—is it 'Sabine'?"

Virgil shrugs, frowning. As if he knows very well that Jessalyn knows very well the name is "Sabine."

"Well. She's all right. As far as I know."

"Is she still living at the farm?"

"Sometimes."

Jessalyn wants to ask—*But do you still see her? Are you a—couple?*

Jessalyn has not given up the fantasy of Virgil falling in love, being married. Finding someone (oh, almost anyone!) who will love him and care for him as his mother does. *So I can die happy.*

(But what a foolish idea! Whitey would be furious if he'd heard. Foolish notion to tie her happiness to another's well-being, and then to feel that her life has been used up satisfactorily, in such a way.)

Don't think it—Jessalyn can hear Whitey muttering.

"You never brought her to dinner . . . That would have been fun."

"Doubtful, Mom. Sabine isn't into what you'd call 'fun.'"

Virgil laughs with a kind of vindictive mirth.

Jessalyn supposes that this is true. She remembers another of Virgil's girlfriends, or rather girls-who-were-friends—what was her name—

"'Polly.'" Virgil volunteers the name ruefully.

"Oh yes, 'Polly.' Whatever happened to *her*?"

Polly had been a heifer of a girl, stern-faced, difficult. A veterinarian's assistant with buzz-cut hair, in denim and hiking boots and with an eagle tattoo on her left wrist at which, during an awkward Sunday dinner, Whitey had stared in amazement (as he'd explained afterward) not at the tattoo so much as at the size of the wrist, as large as his own. *Man. That was a big gal.*

Virgil and Jessalyn laugh together, recollecting. The Sunday dinner is far enough away to laugh at, the prim way in which Polly had castigated the McClarens for eating meat—"You are putting in your mouths something that was *once alive*. Just as *you are alive*." Polly had glared at them as if they'd been monsters.

Virgil had apologized to his guest: "I should have warned you, Polly. I guess I forgot."

Polly! The McClarens had to stifle their laughter, this was the least *Polly-like* person you could imagine.

Feeling the responsibility of the hostess, as well as the responsibility of being Virgil's mother, Jessalyn had stammered apologetically to the glaring girl: "We are—just—really just—ordinary people . . ."

How lame this sounded! Jessalyn's voice trailed off guiltily.

"Don't apologize, Mom. She's the rude one."

Thrilled at a dinner table quarrel for which she could not possibly be blamed Lorene had intervened in a sharp snide voice.

Polly retorted to Lorene: "I'd rather be *rude* any day, than *carnivorous*."

"Well. I'd rather be *carnivorous* than *rude*."

Polly shoved herself from the table, incensed. Despite the quarrel (which had flared up within the first several minutes of the meal) Polly had managed to eat a hot buttered biscuit, a large serving of yams, and mushroom stuffing; her jaws were grinding even as she charged out of the room. Virgil had had no choice (he'd explain afterward) but to run after her.

All this while at the farther end of the table Whitey had looked on more surprised than offended. Didn't utter a word to their brash guest, which wasn't like him, except in the aftermath of Polly rushing from the room, and Virgil close behind her, he couldn't resist an amused chuckle—"Some folks could use a lesson in old-fashioned good manners."

Turned out that the heifer-girl hadn't been a girl after all but a woman older than Virgil, twenty-six at the time. She worked with him at the Chautauqua Living Farm and was in charge, according to Virgil, of hogs and oxen.

Jessalyn and Virgil laugh together, recalling Polly. Jessalyn thinks that it's mean to bond together over poor unattractive Polly—but bonding with her son is the crucial thing.

In mimicry of Jessalyn's plaintive words, about which Whitey and the others had teased her for years, Virgil says in a falsetto voice, "'We are just—really—ordinary people . . . Forgive us.'"

That comical voice! Jessalyn wonders if this is how Virgil hears her.

"I didn't actually say 'Forgive us.'"

"Yes, you did. Didn't you?"

"I did not. Whitey made that up."

Whitey was always *making things up.* Half the family stories sprang from Whitey appropriating an unexceptional event and giving it a grandiloquent turn.

But once Whitey had appropriated an event, it was very hard to reestablish it as unexceptional.

"How funny, to be in charge of hogs and oxen. But if you needed someone to tend them, Polly would be your choice." (Jessalyn is drawing Virgil into laughing at Polly again. Is this a betrayal of sisterhood?) She asks what became of Polly but Virgil only shrugs ominously as he had when she'd asked about Sabine.

No idea, Mom!

For a long moment they are silent. Mother and son pondering the long-ago girl- and woman-friends of Virgil's.

Virgil asks Jessalyn if she has any work for him to do today, any household repairs, he has brought tools out in the Jeep. It's customary for Virgil to fix things around the house and on the property, if he can, whenever he drops by. Jessalyn is touched that Virgil will work hard at such tasks for her, so long as he isn't expected to do them; like Whitey she has wished that Virgil would support himself at least partially as a handyman or carpenter, at which he is surprisingly skilled. But no, Virgil is an *artiste* and a Buddhist, he doesn't work for hire and most waking hours of his life are reserved, as he says piously, for art or meditation.

Virgil's talent for household repairs had impressed Whitey, who wasn't handy himself. But he'd rarely praised Virgil without giving an ironic little twist to his words—*Our son the handyman. Good he can earn his keep if he has to.*

Virgil takes pride in his handyman/carpenter tasks. Screwing in a drawer handle that has fallen off, repairing a leak in a faucet, changing a burnt-out ceiling light far too high for Jessalyn to risk changing herself, on a stepladder—he is prepared now to leave, and yet lingers in the kitchen staring at the bulletin board. (Jessalyn has noticed: not a single snapshot of Virgil remains on the board. How sad this is! But she is determined to say nothing.)

Virgil studies a newspaper photograph of Whitey, one of the older, frayed clippings. Jessalyn doesn't have the heart to come closer, to see which one it is.

Though in fact she has memorized the bulletin board. Shut her eyes, she can reproduce it piece by piece and year by year.

"You're sure you don't need help sorting through Dad's things?"

"Yes! I mean, I am sure."

Jessalyn shudders at the thought of sharing such an intimate task even with a son.

She wonders if that is it: she doesn't want to share Whitey with anyone else. Each article of clothing she will touch, stroke, contemplate . . .

Oh what has become of us?

Virgil drifts restlessly about the downstairs of the house. He has put on his jacket but has not zipped it up. The knitted cap has been stuffed into a pocket. A child who doesn't know if he wants to go outside or stay inside.

She will not beg him to stay. She is not lonely!

(Almost) she hopes that Virgil will leave. For it is always a relief when the (adult) children leave, you no longer need to plead (secretly) with them to stay.

Easier on them, and easier on the widow.

In the front hall Virgil discovers Leo Colwin's most recent bouquet. One of his most opulent, a dozen white and yellow roses, beginning to wilt. Jessalyn set the flowers on a table and forgotten them, and has not freshened the water in the vase for days.

"People still sending flowers for Dad?—I guess they really l-liked, loved him . . ."

Jessalyn tells him yes. Oh yes.

Virgil asks who'd sent these?—Jessalyn says she isn't sure.

(No need to tell Virgil about Leo Colwin. Jessalyn is not proud of her relationship with Leo Colwin. Too timorous to hurt the man's feelings, God knows she may end up married to him out of sheer lethargy and cowardice, a vague wish to placate and to please. Virgil has probably not heard of this shameful impasse, his sisters don't confide in him. This is fortunate!)

Virgil has drifted into the living room which has become a deserted place recently. Even the dust motes in the air look thicker.

From the farthermost window Virgil calls that there is an animal by the creek, by the dock—"Looks like a young fox."

Foxes locally are not so uncommon and must be quite common over on Bear Mountain Road where Virgil lives. Yet Virgil sounds excited, boyish.

By the time Jessalyn hurries to the window the creature is too far away for her to see clearly. To her eye it doesn't have the oddly ungainly, loping gait of a fox.

Coyote? Wildcat—lynx?

Swiftly, it has disappeared into a neighbor's property thick with pine trees.

"I used to look out my window in the night, toward the creek. Remember the screech owls?—sounding like babies shrieking. It made my blood run cold, to hear them hunting in the night and early dawn. Rabbits and other birds, we'd just see matted fur and feathers, bloodied feathers, a few bones . . ."

Is that how he remembers his childhood home?—Jessalyn wonders, dismayed.

Virgil confides in Jessalyn that he has been having trouble sleeping lately—"Thinking about things. It's like my brain is on fire."

Jessalyn doesn't want to say *I know*. Doesn't want to appropriate her son's sleeplessness as if it were a variant of her own.

"When I'm awake, I'm OK. When I lie down, try to fall asleep, it's like a World War Two war movie, aerial bombardment . . . I was thinking maybe I could sleep better, back in my old room in this house. It's like stepping into time, into something blank like an elevator shaft when there's no elevator, coming back to this house. But I guess it isn't a good idea. In fact, I know it isn't."

Virgil's eyelids have grown heavy. His words have slowed. In a corner of a sofa he curls up like a child, leans his head onto his arms, falls asleep within a minute or two as if exhausted. When Jessalyn hears him in the hall bathroom it is hours later, nearing dusk.

Virgil appears in the kitchen, which is the warmest room in the chilly house. He is looking excited, his voice quavers with urgency.

In his sleep, he tells Jessalyn, Whitey appeared to him! This was the first time it had happened.

He'd opened his eyes (in his dream: he was still asleep) and there was Whitey sitting on the sofa, looking at him.

"I said, 'Hi, Dad, what're you doing here,' in this voice like a kid's voice, to disguise how astonished I was, because I didn't want Dad to know that he wasn't alive; so far as Dad knew, he was alive, like always. You know how Dad was—he didn't like surprises unless they were his own! But whatever he said to me, I couldn't hear. It was like he was speaking but the words were lost. I could see his mouth moving and I could hear something, but not actual words. So I said, 'We were wondering where you were, Dad,' and my throat was choking, I was trying not to cry because that would tip him off, that he was dead; and it was important to keep that from Dad, not to demoralize him. And when I woke up, I could not move for a long time. It is an ontological paradox, Mom—I was given to understand. That was the meaning of the dream, that I would understand this . . . Dad explained it to me except not in actual words but in a feeling like music. The kind of music I was playing for Dad? Did you hear? You heard! Not music but breath, air waves. Vibrations. If a spirit could move through space it would move in that way—ripples. Dad explained it to me, without needing to say a word. I think it was from one of Dad's books he was always reading, you know?—out in the hammock, and we'd sneak up on him and he'd have fallen asleep. But see, Dad was trying. Most people don't. He'd look through my college books sometimes, I saw him. But he wouldn't ask anything. Plato, Aristotle, Spinoza—he'd wanted to know. He was not an ordinary man but he masqueraded as an ordinary man, that was Dad's way. He'd never wanted to be a businessman, he said. Not to me, not personally, but I knew. Thom was the anointed one—Thom *is.* But it was me Dad spoke to, just now. Telling me what we need to know. If you and I are *here,* Mom, it isn't impossible that Dad is not also somewhere that is, for him, *here.*" Virgil has been speaking excitedly, Jessalyn hasn't been able to follow.

Virgil adds: "Or, as we would call it *here, there.*"

What is her son saying? He has never spoken to her in his life, in such a way. (Is Whitey speaking through him? Is this possible?) Jessalyn is listening with all her strength.

"The absent are *there,* while we are *here*. The *hereness* of the absent is described as *thereness,* but only from our perspective. Think of Daddy traveling. He could be in Australia, he isn't *here*. If he's in Japan, you don't encounter him *here.* His *thereness* is a property of his being elsewhere relative to you, who are *here*. But if he were *there,* you would not experience him *here*. And so, Daddy not being *here* is not an essential quality of his existence but only of your experience of his existence. Do you understand, Mom?"

Jessalyn stares at her son whose face is suffused with emotion, like one entrusted with a great, consuming vision, that has squeezed itself inside the too-small space of his brain.

She is astonished by him, confused. But there is something consoling in the mad cascade of her son's words, she will long cherish.

Smiling wanly, shaking her head. "No. But I will try."

So it happens, Virgil stays for dinner after all. Possibly, he will stay the night.

With much pleasure, for she has not prepared any meal in some time that involves even the stove top or the oven, Jessalyn prepares roasted butternut squash, tomato bisque soup. In the toaster oven Virgil defrosts and toasts several slices of multigrain bread from a loaf that has been in the freezer since last October. They eat together in the warm kitchen whose windows look out upon the night, vivid with reflected, antic-seeming light. Almost, Jessalyn thinks, judging from the window reflections, there is a family gathering here, a festive occasion.

"If we were eating meat we could put leftovers out on the deck, for the fox, or whatever it was," Virgil says, with an odd air of wistfulness. Jessalyn has no idea how to reply to such a curious remark that comes out of nowhere, and fades into nowhere, inexplicably.

"IT IS AN HEIRLOOM, YES. But it wasn't *hers*."

Only in a hushed voice does Leo Colwin say *her, hers.*

Meaning *My late wife. Maude.*

He has placed it on a table, in front of Jessalyn. In such a way that it is not possible for her to fail to identify it.

". . . sapphire, edged with tiny diamonds. White gold that's worn a little thin. At a jeweler's they can 'size' a ring, you know . . ."

Of course, Jessalyn knows. She is staring at the exquisite ring—she has never seen so large a sapphire, close-up. She must suppress the impulse to push it back hurriedly at Leo.

Am I supposed to try it on?—Jessalyn wonders.

"Would you—like to—try it on? Just to see if . . ."

Leo Colwin is so nervous, both his hands are trembling. Jessalyn feels a tremor growing in all of her limbs.

"I—I don't think so, Leo— I . . ."

But Jessalyn has spoken softly, and Leo is hard of hearing.

Slips it onto her finger, middle finger of her right hand not third finger of her left hand. Stares in a paroxysm of embarrassment.

(But where *is* Whitey? She has been dreading his scorn since Leo Colwin first arrived in brass-button navy blue sport coat, tasseled moccasins, bow tie and lapel pin, to escort her to a dinner party.)

"Beautiful! I thought it would be."

Jessalyn's fingers have become so thin, she has had to remove her rings, which Whitey had given her, for safekeeping. And so now her hands look thin, bare, bereft; it's no wonder Leo Colwin has thought of pressing this ring upon her.

Slips it off her finger, to push back across the table to him.

"But it's for you, Jessalyn. A token of our friendship . . ."

"I don't think so. It's much too . . ."

". . . a memento. For you."

"But no, Leo. It wouldn't be right."

"'Right'—why not? What else can I do with it?" Leo speaks plaintively, as if Jessalyn is becoming unreasonable.

Jessalyn can only repeat that it doesn't seem right to her, not just yet.

"'Not—yet'? Another time, then?"

"Well . . ."

"In a few months? Would that be more appropriate?"

"I—I don't know, Leo . . ."

Tenderly, Leo picks up the ring. It is indeed a beautiful object, that stirs in Jessalyn only a detached, chilly admiration—no interest and no desire.

Leo returns the ring to a small felt-lined box which he slips into an inner pocket of the brass-button coat. "You are right, Jessalyn. It may be too soon—for you."

It is March now. Jessalyn dreads dripping eaves, the first crocuses and snow flowers pushing through the hard earth close outside the house on Old Farm Road.

YOU ARE ONLY AS HAPPY *as your most unhappy child.*

Is this true? Jessalyn wonders if it is a statement of resignation and defeat or a goad to action and change.

If it means that you will never be happy if a child of yours is not happy; or, you must do all you can to ensure that neither of you is unhappy.

"WELL. I QUIT MY JOB."

Sophia utters this fierce blunt astonished pronouncement as soon as she steps into the house. Her white skin glares, her eyes blink rapidly with a kind of shrinking defiance.

"Oh, Sophie! Why?"

Mother, daughter embrace. It is always a surprise to Jessalyn, her children are so *tall*. Even the youngest daughter.

Sophia is trying not to cry, Jessalyn knows. For Jessalyn too is trying not to cry.

Whenever the children step into the house the first thing that comes to them is *Where is Whitey? Why is just Mom here?*—she sees it in their faces. In the quickness with which they smile to disguise their terrible unease.

Sophia is edgy, anxious. She is also very excited. She has much to tell Jessalyn and will measure it out over the course of several hours with the precision of a scientist. Of the children, Sophia has always been the one to *take pains*.

"Oh Mom. Look at *you*."

In fact, Mom rarely does. If she can avoid it.

Sophia laughs, Jessalyn laughs. What is there to say about a widow who has *let herself go in grief*.

"Your hair is beautiful, though. If you'd just comb it. Such a stark *white*."

Jessalyn gathers that her stark-white hair, growing untidily onto her shoulders, carelessly parted for expediency's sake in the center of her head, has become a subject of much excited debate among Sophia's sisters and (female) relatives. Some are of the opinion that Jessalyn should have her hair "colored"—the soft, silvery-brown hue it had been before last October; some, a smaller number, are of the opinion that it should be left white. *What would Whitey say?*—is the question.

Mostly, this question is unvoiced. But Beverly and Lorene have voiced it, tactlessly Jessalyn thinks.

"You seem to have gotten shorter, Mom! What on earth are you wearing on your feet?"—Sophia, long indifferent to clothes and shoes, with a patrician sort of intellectual disdain, stares at the flat, scuffed slippers on her mother's bare bluish feet with something like horror. "It's freezing in here. You should at least wear wool socks, like me."

Jessalyn's feet are sockless but this is just an oversight. She'd forgotten about socks or stockings hours ago at dawn dressing with a sleepwalker's vagueness in the wool slacks she'd been wearing every day for the past week, pink cashmere sweater beginning to fray at the cuffs, Whitey's gray cardigan several sizes too large for her with the cuffs rolled up.

"I will, dear. I'd meant to. There is just so much to think about, I get easily distracted."

Sophia looks at her, alarmed. *So much to think about? After so many weeks?*

She has assumed that the widow's life is over, perhaps. Even Sophia whom Jessalyn adores. Of course, the widow understands: to all others, a widow is *de trop*.

"It's been a siege," Jessalyn explains. "I have to defend myself, so much is attacking me." Seeing that Sophia continues to look alarmed, and perplexed, Jessalyn adds quickly, "But I have it under control, really. Please don't worry. Don't look *concerned*. I've filled out all the forms, I think—probate court, 'death duties.' I've met with Whitey's team and Sam Hewett and signed papers and checks. I have a dozen copies of the death certificate. All I need to do—(Sam Hewett said there was no urgency)—is register Whitey's Toyota Highlander in my name at the Motor Vehicle, and finish sorting through Whitey's clothes and shoes for Goodwill."

"Oh. I see. Well—I can help you, Mom. We could start tonight with Dad's clothes."

"Maybe not tonight. But soon."

"As long as I'm here . . ."

"Soon."

Since early adolescence Sophia has had faint, bluish shadows beneath her eyes. Hers is an odd, angular sort of beauty as if glimpsed through a subtly distorting lens. She'd often been too tense, too excited, to sleep: preparing for high school exams, writing papers that required extraordinary feats of concentration. Late in the night Jessalyn would discover a bar of light beneath Sophia's door and linger in the hall wondering if she should knock, or whether she should pretend she hadn't seen. (Usually, she pretended she hadn't seen. Whitey would have been adamant that Sophia turn out her light, go to sleep like a good girl if he'd known.)

Mother and daughter prepare a meal together in the warm-lit kitchen as (in fact) they had rarely done in the past. At family dinners Beverly had long assumed the role of Mom's principal helper.

Remains of the immense butternut squash Virgil had left, which Jessalyn reheats in the microwave oven. Sophia remarks how good this is, with cinnamon, brown sugar, a dollop of yogurt—"You used to make this, didn't you? When we were kids?"

Over their meal Sophia tells Jessalyn that she has decided to leave Memorial Park. She has a temporary job with another biology lab in Hammond—"Much smaller, and I've taken a salary cut. Daddy wouldn't approve at all, I think."

"But why did you leave Memorial Park, Sophie? We'd thought you were happy there . . ."

"I was, for a while. I guess. It was flattering to be hired by—the director of the Lumex trials. But then, after Daddy passed away it suddenly wasn't possible—I couldn't come back."

"But why?"

"Well, I guess—I'd lost my lab skills."

"'Lab skills'—?"

"Couldn't bring myself to torture and kill animals."

Jessalyn is looking blank. Sophia sees that her mother's fine, newly white hair has been not very evenly parted in the center of her head, as if she'd drawn a comb through it quickly with eyes averted from a mirror. (And her eyes seem to be chronically moist, a condition Sophia diagnoses as "dry eye"—perpetual tearing, as tear ducts cease to function normally.)

"Lab animals. Research animals. They're bred for experiments. They have no life outside of experiments. You must have known, Mom. I'm sure that Daddy did."

Did she know?—Jessalyn has no idea. Like Whitey's financial documents, Wealth Management and IRS forms she'd signed without reading, eyes averted.

What Whitey knew, or didn't know, had never been clear to her. Vaguely it did seem (how could it be otherwise) that Beverly had put pressure on Steve to get married earlier than they'd planned, for (obviously) Beverly had become pregnant earlier than they'd planned; vaguely it did seem that Lorene had had some sort of breakdown the Thanksgiving weekend of her senior year at Binghamton when she'd refused to come home and wept over the phone. (Lorene! Weeping! Lorene had scarcely wept, since.) Thom had gotten into some sort of trouble at Colgate, perhaps not Thom personally but his fraternity Delta Kappa Epsilon, and Whitey had been one of the fathers who'd contributed legal fees to help out—exactly how much, exactly why, Jessalyn hadn't been told for Whitey wouldn't have wanted her to worry.

Money is the solution to most problems. Worry just gets in the way.

Mostly he'd wanted to be proud. Pride sometimes depends upon not looking too closely.

"Experimental animals are 'sacrificed.' In the interests of science. There wouldn't be modern medicine without it. I understand this but—I can't do it any longer."

Sacrificed. Jessalyn seems to be considering this word.

"Not dogs or cats, Mom. Not monkeys. Rats, mice."

As if rats and mice didn't suffer quite as much as larger animals, ounce for ounce! Sophia laughs mirthlessly.

"Stroke victims' treatment wouldn't be possible without animal experimentation. Neuroscience has mostly worked with primates—brains closely resembling human brains. Blood-clotting, hemorrhaging. Brain surgery. At least I never did anything like that—I don't have the training. Never opened up a monkey's skull to take slides."

Sophia speaks with a fascinated sort of dread as if she is thinking of someone who'd done just this. She laughs again, a harsh sort of laugh, and her eyes snatch at Jessalyn's with a kind of defiance.

"My life came to a kind of halt. After Dad. Now I have to—I am trying to—make a new way . . ."

She is in love with someone. Someone has come into her life.

Jessalyn smiles encouragingly. But Sophia will measure out the news of her life methodically, warily.

It is a mother's prerogative to touch a child: Jessalyn exercises this prerogative with restraint and discretion. Lightly brushing wisps of hair off Sophia's forehead which feels heated, slightly damp. *Your daughter is in a fever state. Crazily in love.*

Since the age of eleven Sophia has had a habit of frowning. Furrowing her beautiful forehead. The fine white creases disappear now, or nearly; but will not always disappear.

Fine white creases in Jessalyn's forehead, she has noticed more prominently in recent months.

Jessalyn's heart aches with yearning, she wishes she could absorb her daughter's excitement and anxiety into herself, to soften it, nullify.

After cleaning up the kitchen they decide to put on heavy coats and to walk about the property. By moonlight!

Jessalyn takes a flashlight. Whitey's big old flashlight, kept for decades on a shelf near the kitchen door.

The snow of late winter has partially melted, and has refrozen. The air is sharply cold and very still. Jessalyn can't recall walking with her youngest daughter, her dear, most-loved daughter, in such a way, in years, perhaps ever: just the two of them, impulsively clutching mittened hands.

A hike in the snow-crust. Down the hill to the partly frozen creek. To the small dock which Whitey persisted in calling the "new dock" though it is at least ten years old.

"Thom thought that someone might have been camping here a few weeks ago. You can't see anything now with this snow, but Thom imagined he'd seen something."

"Why would anyone camp *here*? I doubt it."

Sharp-eyed Sophia, with her scientist's skepticism! Jessalyn adores her.

Sophia takes the flashlight from Jessalyn to peer more closely at the snow-crusted creek bank. There are faint, trampled footprints here as well as on the dock. A scattering of animal prints. A short distance away in a tangle of broken ice, what appears to be a blood-tinged clump of fur or feathers, the remains of a predator's prey.

Sophia tells Jessalyn about the work she'd been doing at the research institute for the past two years: injecting mice with cancerous cells and then with a sequence of chemicals to block the cancerous cells, impede their growth, shrink tumors.

"I don't miss the Lumex project, though I do miss some of my coworkers. I think they all hate what they're doing—but it's 'science.' Serious science, which will have results. I'm grateful to have another, reasonably well-paying job. I'm thinking about returning to graduate school . . . My field is moving so rapidly, I have to move with it or be left behind."

"How can you be 'left behind'—at your age? That doesn't seem possible."

"Time moves more rapidly in some areas of science than in others. The field can change in months, even weeks. It's very easy to be left behind at any age."

Yes, Jessalyn thinks. It is very easy to be left behind at any age.

Sophia has been speaking distractedly. As if she is thinking of something else.

Wanting to ask Sophia what it is, what has happened in her life, but no. That is not Jessalyn's way, to pry.

"Your father would be very happy to know you're thinking of returning to graduate school. Such good use for the money he left you."

Shouldn't have said this. *Good use for the money* sounds crass, too intimate.

"Do you think Daddy had that in mind? My returning to Cornell?"

"Yes. Probably."

This is an answer to encourage Sophia. It is not exactly a lie for Jessalyn does not lie to her children, or to anyone.

Though thinking how Whitey (obviously) divided a sum of money into five equal shares for their five children, methodical and fair-minded and with no particular intention for the use of this money. Saying to Artie Barron the equivalent of *What the hell. Divide it up. Let's get this over with.*

Their wills had been drawn up together. Like going to the dentist together, root canal work—Whitey had been tense, solemn. Jessalyn hadn't known the details of Whitey's will and the details of her own have become vague to her.

Just can't think of it. Can't imagine a time when you are not.

Pointless to try, then. Fuck it! (Whitey laughs. Whitey gripping her hand.)

Sophia is shining the beam of the flashlight out onto the creek. Swift blackly-running water bearing on its surface shards of ice. In and out of splotched moonlight. (What is that faint sound? A screech owl in the distance?) Jessalyn has to rouse herself to realize where she is, shivering in the cold inside one of Whitey's old down jackets.

The widow wakes to find herself in unexpected places.

"What did Daddy think of me?"—Sophia asks.

"What did he think of *you*? Your father loved you."

"But—did he think of me? Apart from being his daughter?"

Jessalyn is mildly shocked. She has no idea how to reply. Sophia is too smart to be humored as Jessalyn might have humored the others.

"He thought you were very intelligent, and very beautiful. He worried that you worked too hard and didn't take enough time for yourself."

That summer Sophia remained in Ithaca assisting in her professor's lab, returning home only once or twice, and briefly. *It's like she has married someone hostile to us.* Whitey had felt slighted.

Not good to speculate how any family member feels about the others, or would feel if they were not related. Not likely that Sophia would be visiting a sixty-one-year-old widow living alone on the Old Farm Road, a woman lacking a Ph.D., with embarrassingly little knowledge of the science that is Sophia's life; a woman whose education is in tatters, a precious fabric ravaged by moths. Indeed, Jessalyn McClaren is surrounded in Hammond by individuals like herself, well-to-do, well-intentioned, obliviously clad in the rag-remnants of their long-ago education.

In the siege she has lost everything, she thinks. Navigates herself through each day like one in a skiff, in a treacherous current.

You can do it, Jess. Hang on!

But, Whitey, I am so tired.

Your daughter is here for God's sake. Isn't that Sophia?

So tired, Whitey.

Jess. Jesus!

"Mom? Are you all right?"

"I—I am. Yes."

Hasn't been listening to Sophia. (Almost) has forgotten that Sophia is here even as Sophia is speaking to her of matters of urgent importance.

(What have they been talking about? Jessalyn can't remember.)

"We'd better go back, Mom. All this ice. Watch out you don't slip."

Shining a beam of light onto the path they'd taken down from the house, in the snow.

And on the deck at the rear of the house, animal prints like hieroglyphics it is imperative for the widow to decipher.

Inside the house, preparing to leave, at last Sophia asks about Leo Colwin. She is not so happy about Leo in her mother's life as her sisters are: the memory of Whitey takes precedence, for her, over more practical concerns.

"Leo is a friend. He has been very kind but he makes me feel like a convalescent, or someone missing a limb . . ."

Jessalyn's voice trails off weakly.

"Beverly says he's in love with you."

Jessalyn stammers no, she doesn't think so.

In love! What a charade.

As if she could be *in love* with someone who is not her husband.

"Mostly I remember Leo Colwin coming to our family dinners and just sitting there, and smiling. He was always saying 'thank you' when we passed bowls of food around—as if you had to say 'thank you' every time—he was so *grateful*. You and Dad were very generous to him after his wife died. Beverly says it was obvious the poor man was in love with you."

"That's silly. How could it be 'obvious' if no one noticed?"

"Beverly noticed. I think I did too . . . The way he'd look at you, at Thanksgiving here."

Jessalyn is embarrassed. She wants to ask, Did Whitey notice?—but of course, Whitey would never have noticed.

Jessalyn begins laughing. And Sophia too, laughing until tears spring from her eyes.

Then, Sophia is in Jessalyn's arms, and crying.

"Honey, what is it? Has someone—are you . . ."

All Jessalyn can do is hold her daughter. Until the sobbing subsides, and Sophia wipes her eyes with a tissue.

You would think Sophia's heart is broken but no. Sophia surprises Jessalyn by saying she is happy.

"So happy, Mom—it makes me afraid."

Jessalyn thinks—*Dear God, let him not be married.*

So quickly this thought comes to her, it's as if the thought has been hovering in the air, a mother-thought, like a large clumsy moth.

Sophia is abashed at having said so much and will not say another word. Whatever has happened in her life, whoever has entered her life, is now drawing her away. She has been happy with her mother for several hours and now it's time to return to the other who will make her happy also, or happier. The other who has not yet been named.

"Good night, Mom. I'll call you in the morning . . ."

Jessalyn follows Sophia to the door. She does not want her daughter to leave just yet.

If Sophia will not confide in her just yet, she will confide in Sophia.

Gently Jessalyn takes Sophia's hand in hers. She tells Sophia that there is something Whitey would like them to know.

"I'm not sure if I can explain. I'm not sure if I understand, myself. Whitey wants us to love him but not to miss him. Not grieve for him. *That,* he certainly doesn't want. You remember Whitey was always saying, '. . . like pouring money down a rat hole.' That's to say, a waste of time."

Sophia looks at Jessalyn with alarm. What is Jessalyn saying? Just as Sophia is about to leave? And in that earnest, eager voice that is entirely out of character.

"You see, Sophia, if I am *here*—in this house—and nowhere else—all other places are absent of me—and people would say, where is Jessalyn? Yet, I am *here*. So it isn't impossible to think that Whitey is not also somewhere else that would be, for him, *here*."

"Oh, Mom. What are you saying?"

"Whitey was away from the house often. During those hours, he wasn't *here;* he was *there*—at the office, or—wherever. And if I was *here,* he was *not here*. So now I am *here* and he is absent from *here*. Except sometimes, of course—Whitey *is here*."

Sophia would think that Jessalyn has been drinking but she knows that Jessalyn has not been drinking. It is worse, Jessalyn has been *thinking*—stumbling through the illogic of a primitive philosopher just discovering quasi-paradoxes of being, existence, nothingness and the (limited) capacity of language to express these.

"All we can know about Whitey, at a given moment, is that he is *not here*."

Sophia doesn't want to say *Yes. Daddy has been cremated, his ashes are buried in the earth.*

Sophia tells Jessalyn that she will call her in the morning. In the meantime, Jessalyn should go to bed.

"Good night, Mom! I love you."

In her car, she sees Jessalyn silhouetted in the doorway waving as Sophia drives away.

By the time Sophia returns to her apartment several miles away she has become increasingly upset. She'd thought that her mother was doing reasonably well until suddenly she'd begun saying such strange things about Whitey. Though there'd been a few times earlier when Jessalyn had seemed distracted as if someone (invisible) were close by and drawing her attention . . .

"I'm so worried—I think that my mother is having a nervous breakdown. She said the most astonishing things tonight. She'd never spoken like this in her life—she's always been a person who mainly *listens*. She seems to be turning into another person."

Alistair Means listens sympathetically. It has been illuminating to Sophia, how sympathetic her lover often is, even as he exerts upon her a steely sort of resolve: as willful (she thinks) as her father had been with her mother, and as (usually) low-keyed, unassertive.

"Is that bad, necessarily?"

"Yes! If my mother changes into another person, the rest of us won't know who we are."

A WIDOW WAKES TO FIND herself in unexpected places.

A large gathering. Music, flowers. Excited babble of voices.

(Costume party? No.)

(Wedding? Someone's daughter is being married—that must be it.)

"Mrs. McClaren! Hi."

"—get you a drink, Jessalyn?"

(Sparkling water. Thank you!)

No one can guess, the widow has pumped herself upright, very like pumping air into a flat balloon, otherwise she'd lie flat as a deflated balloon, just a skin on the floor.

No one can guess, the effort the widow has made. That morning hauling herself up as you'd haul a (sodden, limp) body out of a bog hand over hand pulling the rope, at last upright to stand on (shaky) legs. Panting with the effort and hair stuck to her sweaty forehead and skull. Migraine headache threatening, ache in both jaws. Cannot comprehend why (is he annoyed? about Leo Colwin?) in the night Whitey seemed to have abandoned her.

Waking so cold, her jaws were trembling. Teeth chattering.

The way a skeleton would "chatter"—if shaken.

"Whitey? Please."

Silence.

"I am so lonely, Whitey."

Silence. (This is not like Whitey!)

"I am so tired . . ."

(True, Whitey was often a man of moods. Not that he'd be angry with Jessalyn but anger would settle inside him, cause him to brood, lash out irritably. Jessalyn had known how to treat him, how cautiously, always respecting what she'd learned to call The Anger.)

Yet she has made the effort for the widow is one who *makes the effort.*

Wedding party, old friends of the family. Children grew up together, or nearly.

Daughter is Sophia's age. (Were they high school friends? Widow can't quite recall.)

Not sparkling water, white wine. She sees her hand take the glass.

In this bright-lit place amid music, uplifted voices and laughter, vertical mirrors on the walls reflecting the stark-white-haired widow too many times, the widow is one who *makes the effort.*

There she is, Whitey McClaren's wife. Widow.

Jesus! What is that woman doing here, alive?

Why isn't she with Whitey?

Should be ashamed of herself, still alive.

It is true, the widow is very ashamed of herself. The widow is one who has learned that survival is shame. *Alive* after so many months.

Wanting to protest—*But I have tried! I have tried to end this misery but Whitey would not let me.*

Hiding in a restroom. Toilet stall. No eyes can follow her here.

For this ignominy the widow has carefully groomed herself, tastefully dressed in black silk, black high-heeled shoes, thin pale silk scarf of no discernible color (gift of Whitey's) around her neck. Bloodred lipstick in a white-skinned face. Sharp cheekbones, she has lost weight. Most elegant of widows, beautifully dressed, look at that stark white hair falling to her shoulders. In hiding.

Still alive still alive still alive. Why?

"I HAVE A LICENSE FOR IT. It's not illegal."

Jessalyn is shocked to discover a gun in the glove compartment of Leo Colwin's car. He asked her to get out a cloth with which he could wipe off steam on his windshield and instead, Jessalyn put her hand on something steely and cold.

Seeing the expression in his companion's face Leo says defensively, "I can show you the license, Jessalyn, if you don't believe me. My gun is for my self-protection and the protection of my family and friends."

Jessalyn stares at the handgun in the glove compartment, too surprised to react. Your first thought is: Is it real?

Belatedly, as Leo continues to defend his gun ownership, Jessalyn shuts the compartment door.

". . . civic unrest. Drug dealers. Gangs. Remember Pitcairn Boulevard, where black hoodlums threw rocks down onto our cars. Jigaboos, my father used to call them."

Jessalyn is dismayed. "'Jiga-boos'—?"

"You know—'blacks.'"

Leo plumps out his lips to make them look fleshier. Jessalyn stares at him not understanding that he means to be "funny"—he expects her to laugh.

"*You* know—'Ne-groes.'"

"I don't think that's funny, Leo. Please."

"Well. I'm sorry but *I do.*"

Leo is flushed, frowning. It is their first disagreement.

He has had enough of her, Jessalyn thinks. As she has of him.

Leo presses his foot down on the gas pedal and propels the car forward. Boxy old Cadillac with plush powdery-gray interior like the interior of a casket. Jessalyn has forgotten where they are going—where she'd agreed to go with Leo Colwin—a dinner party, a reception, a fundraiser at a theater, or in a hotel ballroom where festive-colored balloons bob about on the ceiling high above and a syrupy-voiced blond woman conducts a "silent auction" as the widow's mind wanders through the vents and heating ducts in the walls seeking extinction and oblivion.

Whitey, where are you?

Can't bear this much longer.

Please let me come to you . . .

He will take pity on her soon. Is that the promise?

In Leo Colwin's company she is struck dumb, not a thing to say. Where usually Jessalyn McClaren can manage to say, in her warm comforting voice, *something.*

Leo is driving jaggedly. Indeed, he is very upset. This side of Leo Colwin, thin-skinned, defensive and indignant, has been hidden from Jessalyn, until now. How relieved she is! She is sure that Leo is, too.

He turns his vehicle into a driveway and brakes to a jolting stop and Jessalyn quickly opens the passenger's door to climb out. Almost gaily, giddily calling back to the astonished man: "Goodbye, Leo. And thank you."

NO MORE FLOWERS FROM LEO COLWIN. In relief Jessalyn throws out the previous week's bouquet scattering bruised, browned petals in a trail to the trash though she refrains from tossing out the scummy vase as well.

Instead she washes the vase thoroughly and hides it away in an obscure cupboard.

That's something I haven't seen before. That vase.

Feeling such a surge of energy, such a suffusion of happiness, she will begin sorting Whitey's clothes and shoes at last. In the morning.

PHONE RINGS, IT IS BEVERLY in an aggrieved voice.

Mom? What on earth have you done?

Mom? Pick up, please!

Poor Leo Colwin is very upset, you have treated him rudely.

This is not like you, Mom.

This is very upsetting to us, Mom.

Mom, will you pick up please?

Mom, will you pick up PLEASE?

"MRS. McCLAREN?"

"Yes. I am 'Mrs. McClaren.'"

He's a new deliveryman. Or rather, it's a new florist's van in the driveway—*Hercules Flowers & Floral Designs.*

For a moment the young Hispanic-looking deliveryman is doubtful. *Is* this the lady of the house?—at 99 Old Farm Road? Untidy white hair to her shoulders, slovenly slacks, shapeless gray pullover with soiled cuffs, no makeup, barefoot on the threshold of one of those dignified old stone houses?

He thinks you're the housekeeper, darling.

"I guarantee you, I am 'Mrs. McClaren.' Thank you!"

Not altogether sure that she wants to sign for more flowers, Jessalyn signs. Though (she guesses) these are not from Leo Colwin.

A single white lily, a calla lily. Beautiful waxy-white flower on a long slender pale green stalk, looking like something sculpted. In crackling cellophane paper Jessalyn unwraps it in the kitchen tenderly—

> *In appreciation,*
> *Your friend Hugo*

Hugo? She has no idea who this is.

Belated condolences from a friend of Whitey's, must be. Someone who has only just now learned of Whitey's *passing-away.*

(Except: why *in appreciation*? Jessalyn's mind just skims over this.)

Thinking that Hugo must be one of Whitey's countless friends, acquaintances, business associates. Someone whom Whitey's widow has surely met, has met more than once, should know, does know, would recognize if she saw him; if, for instance, she encounters this "Hugo" in a public place, one of those individuals who, sighting Jessalyn McClaren, come hurrying to her to clasp her hand and assure her how shocked they were to hear of Whitey's death, how much Whitey McClaren will be missed.

One of those. The widow wants to think.

JESSALYN PUTS THE THREE-FOOT SLENDER STALK in a tall crystal vase on a counter in the kitchen where she will see it frequently; for the widow lives mostly now in the (upstairs) bedroom, and in the (downstairs) kitchen of the house on Old Farm Road.

The calla lily must be very special. It exudes a faint, unspeakably fragrant odor like something recalled only dimly—a whisper, a caress.

"WHITEY? NO MORE."

In one of his jackets she leaves the house to descend the hill to the creek. She has not planned this, she observes herself from a little distance.

Surprising herself, the widow has become assertive. And not so weak-legged as she'd anticipated, in sensible boots striding through wet grasses, through a faint mist like breath.

It is a gusty morning in early April following a rain-lashed night. Though the air is very cold at this early hour the sky is lightening—pushing through heavy banks of cloud. Like egg-candling, she thinks. Nothing can remain opaque, all is transparent and exposed if light is strong enough.

From the creek cries of peepers!—tiny tree frogs. This is new, Jessalyn is certain that this is their first morning of life.

Crazy peeping things, I never once saw.

Jessalyn has pulled the hood of Whitey's jacket over her head. A strand of brittle white hair is caught in the zipper. She is not certain why she has come here, why she has made her way outside in these fierce-gusting winds.

Not a good night, the previous night. How the widow has grown to dread and to hate the first, tentative cries of birds, in the twilight before dawn!

The narrow stream at the foot of the hill is rushing with mud-colored water, that empties in a lake a quarter mile away. Something exuberant in its rolling, curling, churning, twisting—like silk threads being woven, shining—a lunatic joy to the frothy shifting waves.

Sees, or thinks she sees, a small sodden animal-body amid storm debris, rushing past. And gone.

"Whitey? I think it's time."

Can't expect her to endure the spring without him.

Winter she'd endured. Winter paralysis. Snow-numbing, comforting.

It feels like betrayal, that time has not ceased. Forsythia blooming along the fence she'd planted years ago, which Whitey had loved—how painful it is to her, to see it when Whitey can't.

She'd (somehow) not expected the snow to finally melt, icicles along the eaves to drip with such ferocity, and disappear. Daffodils, jonquils, hyacinth she'd planted, tulips lining the front walk, red-stabbing tulips that hurt the eye, she'd planted (she sees now) for *him*.

Cries of the peepers, that had once stirred her heart, now seem to her strident, annoying. It is all too much, too soon.

At the creek she stands uncertain. She has thrust her wind-chilled hands into the pockets of Whitey's jacket. Observing the mud-colored seething water in which small sodden nameless bodies are swept past, and lost.

When they'd first moved into the house on the Old Farm Road Whitey had built a small dock here. He'd had a rowboat and a canoe which he'd taken out infrequently, for he'd been too busy (he claimed) to make use of them; he'd taken Jessalyn out a few times onto the lake in both the rowboat and the canoe, though the canoe had frightened her for it seemed so precarious. (Just sit still, Jess!—Whitey had laughed at her. I promise, this canoe will not capsize.) Of the children it was Thom who most used the canoe, alone or with friends; he'd been eleven when he'd gone out alone onto the lake despite storm warnings, and had been on the lake, out of sight from the dock, when the storm broke. Whitey had gone out looking for Thom, tramping along the shore—"Thom! Thom!" In a trance of dread Jessalyn had followed her husband. Pelting rain, lightning. No visibility. Their terror was that the canoe had overturned and that Thom had drowned but—as it turned out—he'd made it to shore a mile away, managed to drag up the canoe, and was waiting out the storm beneath some trees.

Why hadn't he gone into someone's house to call home, to tell them that he was all right?—Whitey would demand afterward for of course they'd anticipated the worst, and had called 911 for help.

When Thom was finally brought home by emergency rescuers, soaking-wet and bedraggled Jessalyn had hugged him sobbing with relief while Whitey had scolded him for being careless and irresponsible.

(Of course, Whitey had been vastly relieved, too. And Whitey had hugged Thom, eventually. But it is the scolding that Jessalyn recalls most vividly, and Thom's stammered apology.)

How long ago this was! Jessalyn scarcely recalls herself at that age (early thirties) though she recalls vividly Whitey's scathing words and Thom's abashed and guilty face.

Sick to death with worry. What if you'd drowned . . .

It was a memory Whitey would not share with Jessalyn for it had been too painful for him.

In a hurricane not long afterward most of the dock had been swept away. Whitey had had it repaired, but another severe storm a few years later swept most of it away again, and again Whitey had had the dock repaired though by this time the children were older and not so interested in rowing or paddling out onto the lake.

God damn if I'm going to give in!—Whitey had laughed grimly.

Now the dock is battered-looking but (she hopes!) sturdy enough.

Tentatively Jessalyn walks out onto it, for the mud-colored water rushing beneath is very high.

In the distance the lake is shrouded in mist. It has been years since Whitey even thought of taking her out in the rowboat, still less the canoe, for a sunset on the lake.

How happy we were. Even in our fury and terror.

Loud, louder the rushing water in her ears. Drumming in her ears. There is a headache awaiting, she'd anticipated while still lying in bed in the paralysis of early-morning waking with a jolt in the dark only minutes (it seems) after she'd finally fallen asleep in Whitey's arms as in the most merciful of oblivions.

Lifting her head cautiously from the pillow damp with sweat taking care not to dislodge the sharp ice-slivers that had congealed in her brain overnight, cold melting water like uncongealing blood.

Darling, don't think of it. Step back.

Whitey is alert to the possibility before Jessalyn is.

The dock isn't safe. The boards are rotted. You could fall through, one of your legs could be pierced. You would suffer, you might bleed to death. No.

You don't want to harm yourself. The children need you. They are still our children. We all need you. Darling?

Yes, of course. She understands.

The headache is coming on. Waiting in the tall trees, the slow-lightening sky, clouds like a vise gripping her head. And the tiny tree frogs, a deafening din.

"Oh, why can't you let me go, Whitey! I am lost without you. There is no way without you."

Shielding her eyes, for the blinding pain has begun.

III.

Untitled: Widow

APRIL 2011–JUNE 2011

Mack the Knife

He was a squint-eyed tom. He was a veteran of the wars, scarred-eared and progenitor of 14,288 kittens.

His fur had once been sleek-obsidian black but was now matted and dull-dusty-black as if he'd been rolling with zestful abandon in the dirt. His thick stubby tail looked as if it had been broken at the tip. The whiskers sprouting from his ears were bristling-black but the whiskers sprouting from beneath his nose were bristling-white, broken and asymmetrical. His "good" eye, his left, was tawny and glowering. His tummy had begun to slacken into a fatty pouch contiguous with his crotch but his body overall was fit, firm, muscled, tough as rubber.

He was large, hefty, the size of a piglet, weighing near twenty pounds. His head and paws were disproportionately large for this body like his penis which when erect was several inches long and thick and (just slightly) prehensile, barbed at the tip with one hundred small protrusions like nails. Three of his thick-padded paws were white, the fourth was black. His claws were still sharp though some had been broken off at the quick. The tip of his tail was white. His tummy was dusty-white. He had a way of mewing silently, drawing back his lips from his stained, still-sharp teeth, that might be mistaken for a hiss. His alternative mew was percussive, startled-sounding, and interrogative—*Myrrgh? Myrrgh?* His snarl was ferocious as a lynx but his purr was a guttural thrumming music that rose from deep inside his being, his battered cat-soul.

This purr, astonishing to the woman when first she heard it. Not immediately grasping where the sound was coming from, and what it meant.

Craftily, with much patience the squint-eyed black tom was courted by the woman. Food was set out for him on the rear deck of the house in two bowls—fleshy-wet, chewy-dry—and water in a large plastic dish in which (if he wished) he could dip his paws, wash his whiskers and head with a strange daintiness for one so large. He was often very thirsty, for the blood of his (usual) prey was salty: his thirst vied with his caution. Of course he was not always hungry but ate as if ravenous until his tummy swelled for eating was instinctive with him and not a frivolous matter of choice.

Having eaten, drunk, washed his whiskers, head, and much of his fur he might withdraw to sleep a heavy, profound sleep in the underbrush beside the creek or, more boldly, in the bushes beside the house; in time he was observed sleeping on the deck near steps down which he could propel himself within seconds if he sensed danger, a footfall on the deck.

By degrees the squint-eyed tom allowed the woman to approach him. His manner was kingly, skeptical. He was not a skittish creature who "took fright" over trifles nor did he cower, bare his teeth, and hiss in warning. He advertised himself as fearless—tufts of fur at the nape of his neck lifted, to magnify his size. His tawny-glowing eye was alert, unyielding. There might come a low growling in his throat over which (it seemed) he had little control; yet often there came the silent mew instead. A switching of the stubby tail that might be interpreted (for so the woman chose to interpret it) as inquiring, not entirely hostile.

"Kitty! Here, kitty!"—the calm-murmurous voice awakened in him a dim memory of a time when he'd trusted beings like her. His burly body shivered, recalling a caressing hand. He was undecided, ambivalent. The woman knew not to alarm him with affection but exuded rather an air of respectful caution like his own.

Finally after weeks of courtship the squint-eyed tom allowed the woman to touch—very gently—his head. His body quivered, his tail switched, but he did not hiss. He did not snarl. He did not bare his stained teeth or slash out with his sharp claws. Bravely he held his ground, and did not bolt away.

Not then, but soon after, the guttural vibratory purr began. The woman was deeply moved. She would invite the squint-eyed tom into the house if she dared.

Mack the Knife. Was that his name?

The Teasing

Years ago when they'd been young and credulous he'd teased them saying that when he died—"Which will be a long long time from now, kids"—he would follow the example of the Great Houdini.

Of course they'd asked: What had Houdini done?

He told them that Houdini had promised that, if there was an after-life, he would escape from it and return to this world so that people would know that there is life-after-death.

And did he?—did Houdini return to this world? (They had to ask.)

Whitey had laughed at them. But not unkindly.

"Kids, no. Houdini did not 'return to this world.' He died, and that was that."

Only then they asked him: "Who was Houdini?"

The Anger

Grimly Beverly called her sister. *Fuck you pick up that fucking phone. I have serious news for you about our mother.*

A violent anger seethed in her like the agitation of the (God-damned) washing machine in the basement of her house. Bile rising in her mouth black and viscous.

Pressing both hands against the washer's warm white surface as it vibrated, shuddered with idiot energy. What she'd done, fuck she'd jammed too many sheets, towels, kids' filthy jeans into the machine and had made it off-balanced, its mechanism askew. This had happened before, you'd think she would have learned but God damn, she'd been impatient, eager to get the load of smelly laundry *in* so she could get it *out* soon again and into the dryer. God damn fucking washer, she hated every moment of her life.

Fuck you—"Dr. McClaren"! Who the fuck do you think you are not calling me back when I call you!

The words that tumbled from Beverly's mouth! Worse than her teenaged kids! Words that sizzled and popped and emitted a sharp stink, surprising to her, dazzling.

Who'd guessed the sweet-smiling suburban mom was so stopped-up with her own fury and disgust? Once you began it was easier to continue than to stop like trying to stop an explosion of diarrhea.

No way as the smart-ass kids would say.

Pouring herself another glass of wine. Fuck, she deserved it: Who better?

It was Thursday. Housemaids (young sisters, Guatemalan, scarcely understood English, in the hire of an older Guatemalan woman with savagely penciled-in eyebrows who collected their checks) were not due to return until Monday morning.

What a family *is,* is *laundry.* And the suburban mom was *fed up.*

The money Whitey'd left her, most of it was gone, or where she couldn't touch it—CDs at Steve's bank, he'd talked her into investing, a yield of 3.1 percent interest he'd claimed was "excellent."

Fuck him she'd wanted to use the money for the house that was collapsing practically around their heads. Repainting the exterior, remodeling the kitchen, bathrooms—it was *her money,* Whitey'd wanted her to have. Maybe she'd spend a little on herself: hair, face. (Botox? If it didn't hurt too much.) Yes, certainly, a good portion of the money should be invested, kids' college tuition, God knew how much that would add up to, like a vise gripping the heart. CDs at the Bank of Chautauqua—"certificates of deposit"—whatever the hell these were, Beverly wasn't sure. Brain just shut off when anyone began talking about money, math, interest rates—IRS, taxes.

Laughing at Jessalyn for not knowing how to activate a new credit card, Whitey'd had to do it for her, a simple telephone call. They'd laughed at Jessalyn fondly, tenderly—(all of them: even Beverly, who couldn't add up a column of numbers)—but no one laughed at Beverly in that way, the older kids were merciless and Steve just this side of sarcastic.

Mom, grow a brain will you? (Had one of her children actually dared to say this to her?)

This scared her: ending up like Jessalyn lost and forlorn since Whitey's death. A woman who'd been an ideal wife, a truly beloved wife and mother. Adored. Intelligent, totally sane. None of her children had ever once insulted Jessalyn or ceased to love her for a half-second. Not one! And now: not answering calls, not seeing friends or even her family, shockingly uninterested in her own grandchildren whom she'd always adored. Saying to Beverly apologetically *I guess I am tired, Beverly. I don't think that I can be Granma Jess right now, I hope you understand.*

Well, Beverly could not understand! Beverly had never heard of such a thing.

It wasn't natural, and it wasn't normal. A widow became more devoted than ever to her family, not less. Most women Jessalyn's age lived for their grandchildren, practically begged to be allowed to spend time with them, even if their husbands were still alive.

I guess I am tired. Scary to hear Jessalyn McClaren of all people say such a thing. When after Whitey'd died she'd been *so strong.*

Never spoke of herself in all the years Beverly could recall, in any complaining way. Not Mom!

"Fuck. Fuck *fuck.*"

Damn washing machine convulsed, squealed like something being strangled, shuddered to a stop. Still in the first cycle. If she opened up the lid she'd see warm soapy water slopping amid soggy clothing so God damn, she would not open the lid.

Her own grandchildren, Mom doesn't have time for any longer. Fuck she's "tired"—we are all fucking tired!

Not the cheap twelve-dollar wine Steve served to most guests but the more expensive French chardonnay he kept in a cabinet in the basement, that was what Beverly deserved.

Bastard. Had to laugh at how surprised he'd be, discovering several of the bottles missing.

Mad as hell, he'd suspect her (would he?) but if she denied it—what? *Think I don't know your lecherous heart, bastard.*

Since last October when Whitey passed away Beverly was becoming increasingly angry.

At first she'd been grief-stricken. Exhausted, could hardly get out of bed. Cried all the time. Then, irritable. People's fucking trivial problems made her furious.

In stores, waiting in line, hearing people complaining over shit—

she'd wanted to shout into their faces. *Are you serious? What the fuck do you know about life? You will learn, assholes.*

Snotty salesclerks at the mall looking like some cheap version of Britney Spears, these were the worst. Eyeing her, that crease in the crotch of her slacks.

Striking back at her kids who'd condescended to her quite enough.

Little bitch. You'd better watch your smart mouth.

Astonished by their mother, who'd been so long-suffering. No more Mister Nice Guy!—she wanted to jeer at them.

"Dad was a nice guy. A damned nice guy. And now he is dead."

(Had Whitey McClaren been a *nice guy*? Not all the time, and not with everyone. But mostly yes, fuck it *he had been*.)

(Stopping to help that Indian doctor, what was his name—"Murtha"? Stopping to prevent "Murtha" from being beaten by cops so he's beaten by cops himself, except worse. What happens to "nice guys.")

No wonder she was angry. Jesus!

Steve was becoming afraid of her. So long he'd been the one to make her feel inadequate, clumsy and unattractive, now it was—"Bev, what's wrong? Why are you angry with *me*?"

Bev. Hated that name, almost wasn't a name, insulting, insufferable.

Darling he'd used to call her. Now if it was *darling* you'd know he was being sarcastic.

She'd glared at him. She'd stood her ground. What a great question the husband has asked, why is the wife angry with *him*, well—"You know why, Steve." Her voice heavy with sarcasm.

Think I don't see the way you look at the young girls. Jesus! Mouth open, practically drooling. As if any female under thirty would give you a second glance, asshole. Unless you paid them.

That, Beverly did not want to consider. *Unless you paid them.*

Furious with her husband and the older kids. Building up for years. But the younger children were beginning to shrink from her too.

"Hey, sweethearts—Momma loves you." Stooping to kiss, still they shrank from her. (Smelling the wine on her breath? Was that it?)

Had enough of all of them, frankly. Pulling on her like baby monkeys, too many kids no wonder her breasts hang down like udders and her only thirty-six, or is it thirty-seven now—*not fucking old.*

Fuck he'd helped out around the house. *Not my bailiwick* he'd actually said, she'd had to ask what *bailiwick* meant. Fucking meek too many years. Now, the scales were fallen from her eyes.

But she was more angry with Thom. Another smug asshole like her husband. Superior-acting, bossy. He's going to sue the Hammond PD over their father's death? What about *her*? What about her opinion? Lawsuit, publicity, death threats, her kids in school, what would Whitey say about this?—*You know damned well what Whitey would say.*

He'd get the guilty cops fired, kicked out on their asses. But he wouldn't go to the media. He wouldn't sue. He'd work behind the scenes, he'd had connections. Thom wanted to make a public issue of it—"police brutality"—"racism"—not like Whitey who'd been practical-minded.

The lawsuit was progressing, Tom had told Beverly. Only just not as fast as he'd hoped.

First, they were filing criminal charges with the country prosecutor. Later, after the criminal case was adjudicated, they would file civil charges.

Meaning—what? Suing for how much? *Millions?*

That's right, Thom said grimly. You'd better believe it.

Beverly asked if the two cops who'd beaten and Tasered Whitey were still on the force and Thom answered evasively saying he wasn't sure.

Not sure? Couldn't you find out?

Thom hadn't liked that line of questioning. Thom didn't like being questioned at all.

Beverly had the idea that the cops hadn't been suspended. Probably hadn't even been disciplined. She'd given up looking in the paper for headlines—HAMMOND POLICE OFFICERS CHARGED IN McCLAREN BEATING, DEATH.

Dreaded seeing a photo of John Earle McClaren in the paper, on TV. How shocked everyone would be, what a scandal, that Whitey McClaren had been beaten by Hammond police officers who hadn't known who he was, or who he'd been.

Whitey had hated people who sued the city, made a big deal of being victims. *What the hell will a big settlement do for me, I'm dead and gone. And you kids don't need any more money.*

Riveting to Beverly, to hear Whitey's voice as if he were here in the room with her—almost.

"Daddy? Steve took my money from me. He forced me. CDs at his fucking bank. That was *my money.*"

Why'd you give in to him, honey? Should've just said no.

"Oh Daddy. It isn't so fucking *easy.*"

This was wrong. This was not right. In life Beverly would never have uttered *fuck* in Whitey's presence, he'd have been stunned.

In the presence of women, Whitey had been a gentleman in his speech. Never would Whitey have even muttered *fuck* in Jessalyn's presence.

That generation. Sinking away, falling. Whitey had joked about not troubling to learn much about computers, cell phones, "electronic gadgets," he'd been sure it was all just a fad, and wouldn't last.

Well, Beverly wasn't much better. Knew fuck-all about the new TV, damned remote controls, DVDs and such, even the young children snatched the gadget out of her fingers—*Mom-mee! Like this.*

So angry! Bile rising in the back of her mouth.

Hell with the fucking washer. Can't deal with it now.

Upstairs she rinsed her mouth, spat into the sink. Could've sworn something tarry-black came up.

Another glass of wine. Soothe her nerves.

Since Whitey, she'd been seeing a psychopharmacologist in Rochester. Prescribed a new antidepressant with "no side effects"—problem was, alcohol was prohibited.

Couldn't stop taking the pills, she'd be suicidal. Just lie in bed and cry and cry and when she did get up, overeat and pack on weight—she'd gained eight pounds in a single week, back in December. But she wasn't going to stop drinking: the taste of wine was a solace, not just the alcohol-effect.

First it was *I need this*. Then, *I deserve this*.

"Lorene? I need to speak with you. Call me."

Trying to remain calm. Upstairs in the bedroom, door shut. Sprawled on the bed, bottle on the bedside table and glass in hand, cell phone in hand. (How long until the kids came home from school? Couple of hours.)

What was infuriating was, Lorene never called back. Pretending she was God-damned busy.

She was planning a trip to Bali, after the school term was over. Already she'd bought a new car with some of the money Whitey'd left her, and was talking about a down payment on a condominium in that new high-rise overlooking the river. Nothing Lorene liked better than lording it over her teaching staff at the high school especially the older teachers she'd surpassed, being promoted to principal.

"Selfish bitch. *Selfish*."

Since they'd been girls together Lorene had been the *selfish one*.

Anything she could do to get the highest grades, flatter her teachers, plagiarize an idea, copy out of a book and "translate" into her own prose—Lorene would do. Homely as a fire hydrant (one of Beverly's boyfriends wittily observed) but that didn't seem to deter her: Lorene had guy friends as well as a cluster of girls vying for her (often sarcastic) attention. Despite her size she'd been a competitive athlete—captain of the girls' volleyball and field hockey teams. Vice president of her graduating class. With as much care as another girl would take to avoid contracting herpes or (worse yet) getting pregnant Lorene had steered her way through college and graduate school by avoiding, as she'd admitted, the more difficult and challenging professors who might've given her grades below A. Ending up, somehow, with a Ph.D. in something called educational psychology from the State University of New York at Albany.

Winced recalling how proud Whitey had been. *Do I get to call my little girl "doctor" now?*

As if conniving Lorene had ever been a *little girl.*

"Lorene? Please call me back or God damn you, I will drive over there and march into your office and expose 'Dr. McClaren' to the world as a hypocrite and negligent daughter. I will expose you as an utter phony as a fucking 'educator' who doesn't give a damn about her faculty, her students, or her fucking school."

There! Beverly's bare toes writhed in delight. Had to laugh imagining the expression in Lorene's pug-face when she hears this message.

Within minutes Lorene called back. For once hushed, concerned.

"Bev, what is wrong? You sound so—angry . . ."

"Fuck 'angry.' First words out of your mouth, attacking *me*—attacking the fucking *victim*."

So furious was Beverly, so stunned Lorene, for a moment neither could speak. Then Beverly said in a hissing voice: "I have been the victim long enough. All of my adult life. Trying to do the right thing, the decent thing, remembering birthdays, taking time to buy presents, having my share of family celebrations, or more than my share—while nobody else gives a damn. *You* can't be bothered—too busy. Sophia and Virgil can't be bothered—wouldn't even think of it. Thom's prissy wife goes through the motions every second or third year—gives a big party at Christmas for her friends and invites *us*. And we are supposed to be grateful. Why Brooke thinks she can look down on us, I have no idea. Who's *she*? Who's her family?"

"Excuse me, Bev? I'm in my office at school. I don't have much time. What exactly are you talking about?"

"Don't you fucking condescend to me, Lorene. I'm not one of your cowed teachers. I'm talking about our family responsibilities. I'm talking about you, Lorene. First you'd said you had to work extra hard to get a promotion—then you'd said you had to work extra hard because you got the fucking promotion. Since Dad passed away you are not doing your share in taking care of Mom."

"My impression is that Mom is doing pretty well. When I speak with her—"

"—on the fucking phone. But when do you see her?"

"I—I've seen Mom—not long ago . . . It's been hard to connect with her, she's been volunteering at the library. I think she said—"

Beverly laughed harshly. "No. Stop. Just fucking *stop.* Let me tell you what the situation is."

"What—what situation? What are you talking about?"

"Yesterday I drove to the house. Mom wasn't answering the phone, so I thought I'd better check up on her. It was shocking to see broken tree limbs and storm debris in the driveway—after that windstorm last week Mom hasn't had anything cleared away. Dad would've had it cleared away the next day—he might've done it himself. Remember, I told you—Mom isn't using Hilda anymore? After twenty years she says she wants to take care of the house herself—a house that size! Dad would be astonished, Mom was always so *reliable.*" Beverly paused. It was rare that Lorene shut up, and listened; Beverly meant to enjoy the situation. "So—I came into the house—let myself in—and called 'Mom? It's me, Beverly'—and there was no answer. All I heard were wind chimes, and wind—nothing else. And the house was cold—I couldn't stop shivering. The kitchen wasn't nearly as clean as Mom used to keep it—there were dishes in the rack that might've been rinsed, but not washed; the dishwasher was empty! (I checked.) (Why on earth would the dishwasher be *empty*?) There was a strange smell—sort of meaty, rank. And on the floor, on stained newspaper pages, plastic bowls for an animal to eat from, that weren't looking very clean."

"An *animal?* You mean a dog or a cat, Mom has adopted?"

"Just wait! I'll tell you." Beverly took time to pour more wine into her glass.

Lorene protested faintly: "She didn't tell us that she was even thinking of—"

"Mom didn't *adopt* this animal, it's a stray. A large ugly feral cat with one eye missing, that must weigh thirty pounds. It is huge, with matted black hair, and it *snarls*."

"Feral cats have all kinds of diseases. Oh, God."

"Actually, I didn't see the cat just yet. I was in the kitchen calling for Mom, and nobody answered. (I knew that Mom was home, both the cars were in the garage.) I was beginning to get scared thinking Mom might have collapsed or hurt herself so I went upstairs calling 'Mom?'—'Mom, it's me'—this terrible vision came to me of Jessalyn upstairs on the floor—in the bathroom—having overdosed with drugs, or—Jesus!—slashed her wrists . . ."

"That's ridiculous. Mom would not. Not ever. Not pills and certainly not slashing her wrists. You know Mom—she would *not ever* make a mess for anyone else to clean up."

"Yes. I mean no—that's right. Normally. But Mom might be losing control. She has said she is 'lost' without Whitey and I think she means it literally. Remember how rudely she behaved to poor Leo Colwin? He's still talking about it. He has complained to everyone. Ginny Colwin won't even speak to *me,* she's so insulted. So—I was in the upstairs hall calling for Mom, and this—this thing—came bounding at me out of nowhere. It was snarling and hissing—might've been a raccoon—a lynx—it came rushing at me as if it was going to attack me—I screamed and got out of its way but the thing wasn't actually attacking me, just rushing past me, to escape down the stairs. But I'd almost fainted, or had a heart attack. If it had collided with me I'm sure it would have raked me with its claws, and bitten me—it might be rabid . . ."

"Wait. What was it?"

"A feral cat. 'Mack the Knife.'"

"'Mack the Knife'—what's that?"

"That's the cat's name. Mom calls him 'Mackie.'"

"Beverly, I'm confused. Where'd Mom get that name from?"

"Where? Frankly—I think from Whitey." Beverly lowered her voice though there was no one within earshot to hear her.

"What do you mean, 'from Whitey'?"

"When I asked Mom about the cat's name she said, 'That's his name. It came to me.' I didn't want to press her but I got the impression that—well, 'Mack the Knife' is Whitey's name for the cat, because it's exactly the kind of name Whitey would think up, for exactly that cat."

"Dad wouldn't allow a wild, feral cat into the house! You know that."

"Mom said the cat 'just appeared'—at the back of the house, on the deck—in the snow. She said she started to leave food for it, and it has become 'tame.'"

"My God. Can we take it away from her?"

"'We'—? What's this 'we'? If anyone helps out Mom it's *me*—it isn't likely to be *we*. Fuck that!" Beverly spoke with renewed vehemence. She could hear Lorene's indrawn breath over the phone.

"Well, I—I hope Mom has taken it to a vet to have it checked . . ."

"All this about the God damn fucking cat came later. We didn't even talk about 'Mackie' right away. Because when I found Mom she was in the bedroom in that old cream-colored robe of hers, and her hair was tangled and matted, and her eyes were dilated and wild-looking, and she was actually panting like a wild animal. And she just stared at me blinking as if she didn't recognize me at first—'Oh, Beverly. Is it *you*.'"

Beverly paused, recalling. Her heart beat resentfully, she'd had to endure this terrible experience alone. "It was kind of a crazy scene—clothes in piles all over the floor."

"Well, finally! Whitey's clothes for Goodwill."

"No. Not Whitey's clothes. Mom's own clothes. She has yet to take Whitey's clothes out of the closet, in fact she's been putting Whitey's woolen things in mothballs. It's her own clothes she was sorting out for Goodwill. Can you believe it, Lorene?—Mom's beautiful dresses, her shoes and coats, the *mink coat*."

"What? The mink coat Daddy gave her?"

"All these beautiful things in heaps! On the floor! Jewelry, too.

Gloves! Cocktail dresses, black silk, red silk, the long mint-green gossamer gown she wore to the McCormick wedding, the white pleated dress, a bunch of high-heeled shoes—'My life is over. Whitey wanted "the best for his wife"—that was me. But now Whitey is gone. A fur coat is ridiculous—an abomination. I will never wear that abomination again.' I couldn't believe what I was hearing—from Jessalyn! 'My life is over.' In this sad, calm, matter-of-fact voice. In this voice that wasn't even self-pitying! I was pleading with her, 'Mom, you can't give away a *mink coat*.' And Mom said, 'I don't have any choice, Beverly. It's an abomination, I have to give it away.'"

"Jesus! If Whitey knew."

"We actually argued about it. Not just the mink coat but other coats, too. The only coat she was willing to keep is the black cashmere, that has got mud on it somehow—she hadn't even seemed to notice. It was very upsetting. How could Mom give her beautiful things away? And why? I don't think that I've ever argued with Mom about anything—just trivial things, when I was a kid. Nothing serious, and nothing ideological. She's gotten it into her head that fur is 'sinful'—must've been that God-damned Virgil talking to her. But also she kept saying that her life was over and she didn't need so many clothes any longer. The most distressing thing, Mom's body *smelled*—this animal smell. Her hair hadn't been washed in days. She has always been so clean and fastidious, remember she taught us to brush our teeth after absolutely every meal and to wash our hands *with soap* after using the bathroom . . . Oh, another thing Mom said was: 'I hate high-heeled shoes! I only wore them for Whitey.'"

Lorene was silent as if stricken. God damn her, Beverly thought, if she'd *hung up*.

But Lorene had not hung up. She'd been listening, and she'd become upset. Saying, "I hope you didn't, Bev. I am hoping to hell that you *did not*."

"'Did not'—what?"

"Take that coat for yourself. The mink coat Daddy gave Mom. Don't you tell me you took that gorgeous coat for yourself."

"I—I told Mom that—well, yes—if she didn't want it—"

"No! You will not take Mom's mink coat. Damn you, Beverly, that's why you called me—to tell me you've got your hands on Mom's mink. A coat that cost, how much, fifteen thousand dollars—don't tell me that Mom gave it to you. She did not *give it to you.* She isn't in her right mind and can't give consent. Damn you, Beverly—is that why you called me, to gloat about this?"

"N-No. It is not."

"It is! It's exactly why. You've taken all of Mom's good things, that's what you've done, her good clothes, her good jewelry, at least you can't fit your big feet into her shoes—at least." Now Lorene was furious, stammering.

Beverly protested: "Mom's things are in safekeeping with me."

"Is that what you call it—'safekeeping.' What a euphemism!"

Euphemism. Beverly had no idea what the fuck this meant except it was her hypocrite sister plying her pretentious vocabulary like nasty little missiles. She protested:

"I had to plead with Mom. She was becoming very emotional. She isn't the Jessalyn we know, or think we know—it's like something has infected her, some kind of madness. If I hadn't arrived just when I did, she would've dumped everything out at the curb in cardboard boxes. Right now, everything would be gone including the mink coat. Where the fuck were *you,* Lorene! Don't you dare judge *me.*"

This shut Lorene up. Beverly heard her sister breathing harshly at the other end of the line.

"And another thing: there were scratches on Mom's hands and arms. When I saw, she tried to hide them inside the sleeves of her robe. At first I was panicked thinking she'd slashed herself with a razor then I realized it had to be that disgusting animal. A dozen scratches and cuts at least, not fresh and bleeding but scabby, ugly. I asked her what on earth had happened to her and she backed away saying nothing, it was just an accident, and I said, 'An accident! How could anything like this be an accident! Wounds like these could become infected.' And Mom said in this sort of pleading voice, 'Oh, Beverly—it doesn't hurt at all. Please just leave me alone.' As if that was a sane, sensible answer!"

All this while Lorene had been listening, Beverly had supposed with mounting concern, for both their mother and for *her.* But now, Lorene said nothing.

Beverly listened. What was she hearing? In the background were voices, indecipherable words. Then Lorene's voice, addressed to someone else *Excuse me, will you—*

A sharper sound, as of a filing cabinet drawer being shoved shut. And Lorene on the line again, suddenly loud in Beverly's ear: "Sorry! Something has come up here. I've been listening but—have to hang up—what I'll do is, I promise I will stop by Mom's tonight on the way home. Problem is, we have a late meeting. The new guidelines from Albany are impossible—a battery of state-monitored tests—it's a crisis situation coming at just the wrong time . . ."

Beverly broke the connection. Tossed the cell phone down as if it were radioactive.

"Fuck fuck fuck *fuck you.*"

But she was feeling tired now. Deflated. The euphoria of rage had seeped out of her like air out of a balloon leaving her sprawling and fleshy-limp on the bed she hadn't troubled to make yet that day, a bed she shared with what's-his-name, the asshole who was betraying her (she knew) a dozen times a day in his head if not actually with his rubbery knob of a penis, well fuck him too—*fuck the husband.*

(Was she waiting for Lorene to call her back, apologize? Fuck no!)

(The cell phone had fallen onto the floor anyway. Fuck she had the energy to lean over, reach down and retrieve it. No fucking way.)

The wine was depleted. Her head was starting to ache.

Crying now. A blubbering sort of crying you wouldn't want anyone to overhear. Not sorrow for her dear widowed mother nor even for her dear, deceased father but for her own lost self, exiled from the house on Old Farm Road she had to realize now permanently.

Please just leave me alone.

The Wave

And then, one morning in early May she was herself (again). (Or nearly.)

Waves that had been lifting her, throwing her down, beating her against the tight-packed wet sand for months seemed to have receded. Dazed she lay scarcely daring to breathe. Was it over? The terrible malaise, the sickness like death, the widow's raw grief like a gnawed stump? *Was* she herself again? There came a starburst, dazzling light rippling across the earth. Chickadees and titmice at the feeder calling excitedly to one another.

New day! New new new day day.

And the squint-eyed black tomcat nudging his big head against her legs, purring loud as a defective motor *New day! Now! Feed me!*

Suffused with strength. Her old strength. Another time the tight-choking tourniquet thrown off and blood rushing in to reclaim what had been numbed, paralyzed in all of her limbs, her belly, throat, and heart.

That morning, she read a Dr. Seuss story to enthralled young children at the Huron branch library where she'd been a volunteer since before Whitey had been stricken; next day, she returned to her volunteer position at Hammond General Hospital, stepping into the hospital foyer like one walking on eggshells, herself fragile as eggshells—and she did not faint, she did not burst into tears, in wonderment she observed herself greeting her friends at the Information counter, accepting a hug or two, a smearing kiss on the cheek—*Thank you. I missed you, too. But I am very well now. And you?*

She took a deep breath. She called Thom, Beverly, Lorene, Sophia—left messages. *Just saying hello. I am feeling much better. Sorry to have been out of touch. I am catching up now—but slowly.*

Later that week she drove to visit an elderly, ailing relative in an assisted living care facility, whom she'd been neglecting since the previous October, and who had not been informed (to spare her being upset) that Whitey had died.

Forgive me please. Much has happened. I have been distracted.

TWO ITEMS SHE'D NOTED (for Jessalyn McClaren was one who perused public bulletin boards thoughtfully) on the hospital bulletin board: the Eleventh Annual Chautauqua Arts & Crafts Fair to be held on May 29, and a meeting that very night at the Hope Baptist Church (Armory Street) organized by the SaveOurLives Caucus open to "All Citizens Concerned with Hammond Police Department Racism, Brutality & Injustice."

It was possible that Virgil would have new work in the Chautauqua Arts & Crafts Fair, but Virgil would never tell her beforehand; she would have to drive there and see for herself. And the meeting at the Hope Baptist Church on Armory Street—this seemed to Jessalyn, in her state of renewed strength and purpose, in the rush of optimism that coursed through her veins like adrenaline, to be something she should attend as a concerned citizen.

(Should she call Thom? Would Thom want to attend with her? Jessalyn had the idea that the lawsuit against the Hammond police was not going well—at every turn the attorney for the defendants was "stalling"—"obstructing." Briefs were prepared and filed, hearings were scheduled in the Hammond County Courthouse and then postponed. To bring the subject up to Thom was to risk rousing him to fury.)

(Would Whitey be comfortable with her attending such a meeting, in inner-city Hammond? Jessalyn could not imagine that he would approve though her presence there would be solely because of him.)

And so, that evening a lone white woman appeared diffidently at the rear of the small redbrick church on Armory Street. She took a seat in the last pew. Already there were forty or more people in the front pews and in the center aisle, talking together with much animation. Everyone seemed to know everyone else: of course. The lone white woman understood that she was (perhaps) a curiosity to them: not only a white woman in a company of (mostly? entirely?) persons of color but a woman with a very white skin, a porcelain sort of pallor, and stark-white hair to her shoulders, of a length uncommon in women her age. And though this woman was dressed inconspicuously it was evident that her clothes were not inexpensive, and that her manner lacked the ease and camaraderie of whites accustomed to black activist occasions. This white-skinned woman smiled in greeting to anyone who acknowledged her but her smile was over-eager, timid.

She'd rehearsed the way in which she would identify herself should anyone ask. Not *Jessalyn McClaren*—(for the name *McClaren* might be recognized in ways she could not anticipate)—but *Jessalyn Sewell.* It would be a relief to her, yet a disappointment, when no one asked her name.

Alone in the last pew of the little church she listened to impassioned speeches from the pulpit with mounting alarm. She'd had no idea that so many unarmed and defenseless individuals in inner city Hammond, ranging in age from an eight-year-old boy to an eighty-six-year-old woman, had been shot by Hammond police officers within the past decade. So many deaths, and not a single conviction of any police officer! In fact, not a single indictment.

Not a single apology from the Hammond Police Department.

The minister of Hope Church spoke, gravely and with dignity. The head of a New York State youth training program spoke, vehemently. A young black lawyer spoke, his voice quavering with emotion. Mothers spoke, holding pictures of their murdered children. Some were tearful and tremulous and some were angry and resolute. Some could barely speak above a whisper and others raised their voices as if keening. Young dark-skinned men and boys had been assaulted by Hammond police in the greatest numbers but no one was exempt from police violence—women, girls, the elderly and even the disabled—a nineteen-year-old Iraqi war veteran in a wheelchair, shot dead by police officers for seeming to "brandish" a weapon; a twelve-year-old boy Tasered into unconsciousness by police officers for "suspicious behavior"—nothing more criminal than fleeing a police cruiser that braked to a stop in the street.

Jessalyn listened, appalled. She would have liked to add her voice to these voices but could not bring herself to speak.

She was not feeling so strong after all. There was such sorrow in this gathering, she could not add to it. Her own loss seemed not singular but rather one of many, unheralded.

Eyes on her were curious, inquisitive; not hostile if not (evidently) friendly. The minister smiled in her direction but rather stiffly, guardedly. *White lady? Why's she here?*

As it turned out there were several white or very-light-skinned individuals at the meeting. One of these was lanky-limbed with his hair tied back in a slovenly ponytail—for a moment Jessalyn thought this might be Virgil. (It wasn't.) Another was a tall gray-mustached man in a Stetson hat, wearing a dark-rose embroidered shirt and a black string tie, at whom Jessalyn found herself staring—felt her heart thud in her chest, and her hands jerk with a rush of blood.

Him. The man in the cemetery.

The man who'd found her glove. Called her "dear" . . .

But the tall mustached man was involved in an intense conversation with several others and took no notice of the (white) woman at the rear of the church.

A sharp-voiced white woman sporting a mane of ashy-blond hair, in gaudy quilt-like clothes, turned to stare at Jessalyn, and to glare at her;

here was a middle-aged Caucasian hippie-activist, contemptuous of the diffident white woman of a very different background.

This woman's companion at the gathering was a massive black woman with a stern Easter Island face, who turned to stare at Jessalyn with an air of outraged incredulity. She'd spoken from the pulpit in a fierce voice denouncing the "time-honored Christian tradition" of white racism and white indifference to black victims dating back to pre–Civil War times and here, as if to taunt her, was a representative of such racist-enabling Christians.

Jessalyn had never seen so large a woman in person, and she'd never seen anyone stare at her with such hostility. The woman was in her mid-forties perhaps, and must have weighed three hundred pounds; she was at least six feet tall, and wore a sack-like article of clothing that fell loosely over her bulk; her legs were columnar, and her (bare) arms were masses of slack, pocked flesh, enormous. Her face was massive as well, yet sharper-boned. Her eyes were accusing. "Yes? Ma'am? What d'you want with us, ma'am?"—in a mocking voice loud and assured as a bugle she called to Jessalyn at the rear of the church.

Jessalyn shrank away in embarrassment and unease. Why had she come to the Hope Baptist Church, to intrude upon these people who knew one another intimately, and had no need of *her*? Badly she wished she could escape but in a hoarse voice she managed to stammer that she'd wanted to contribute to SaveOurLives but her words were so faint no one seemed to hear.

Fortunately the massive woman with the Easter Island face and her ashy-blond-haired friend lost interest in Jessalyn almost immediately. Nor did anyone else take notice of Jessalyn except, out of politeness it seemed, the minister of Hope Church, who smiled worriedly in her direction, uncertain whether he should approach her, or take pity on her and ignore her.

How thoughtless and foolish she'd been, Jessalyn thought. An affluent white woman, a resident of suburban Old Farm Road, hoping to align herself with inner-city residents who'd suffered at the hands of white police officers, and through white indifference, not a single time but countless times: What had she been thinking? Lorene would charge her with *white-liberal condescension.* Beverly would charge her with lunatic recklessness. Thom would have been furious and Whitey would have been speechless, as deeply shocked by Jessalyn's behavior as if she'd set out deliberately to betray and upset him. Driving into the inner city, alone!—Jessalyn McClaren, of all people.

So utterly intimidated by the situation Jessalyn dared not even reveal that her husband had died as a result of Hammond police brutality, no one wanted such an offering from her, indeed they did not want anything from *her.*

Yet, the minister decided to come to speak with her. He had a wan, worn face, kindly eyes, his impatience with the awkward white woman vied with his natural courtliness. She saw that he was older than he'd appeared at the pulpit, Whitey's age at least. *Maybe he knew Whitey McClaren, when Whitey was mayor. Maybe they worked together and were friends.*

It was the most tenuous, the most pathetic of hopes. But she dared not suggest it. There seemed to her no words she could offer in the little redbrick church, no attitude that was not in some way condescending, or inadequate; ridiculous, self-serving and (unavoidably) racist. The massive stern-faced woman had peered into her white, shallow soul and annihilated her.

Vaguely Jessalyn had intended to donate money to SaveOurLives. For that purpose she'd brought along her checkbook. She had no idea how much money to give: $1,000? But she was thinking now that such a sum was too much, that it might surprise and offend these people; the massive woman would sneer at her, and the ashy-blond-haired woman would sneer at her, as a rich white woman who hoped to absolve herself of racial guilt by giving money. But was five hundred dollars too little? Was five hundred dollars both *too much* and *too little*?

In his will Whitey had left thousands of dollars to Hammond charitable organizations with ties to the black, inner-city community; he and Jessalyn had donated to these, as to the NAACP, for years. But the donations had been impersonal, mediated. Here, Jessalyn was exposed. Her generosity, or lack of generosity, could not be hidden. She wondered how much other visitors were giving—the mustached man in the Stetson hat, for instance.

The kindly minister stooped over Jessalyn, introduced himself and shook Jessalyn's hand. He did not ask her name but thanked her gravely for coming. He did ask if her car was parked near the church. Rapidly Jessalyn's mind was working: Should she make out a check for seven hundred dollars? (Not much, but nothing she could give would add up to much. The racial situation in the city seemed all but hopeless, during the very reign of the first black president of the United States.) Jessalyn wanted to apologize to the gentlemanly minister for having so little to give: her husband had limited the amount of money she received each quarter to prevent her being extravagant in giving money away to causes like SaveOurLives . . . But of course she couldn't give such an excuse: it would seem to be blaming Whitey, the most generous of men.

In the end, as the minister looked on with some embarrassment, Jessalyn hurriedly made out a check for $1,500 to SaveOurLives. It was more than she could afford this month but she couldn't explain that. Her face burned with shame, discomfort. "Ma'am, thank you!"—the minister smiled and blinked at her in genuine surprise, and shook her hand another time.

He had seemed to like her, at least. The others, at the front of the church, speaking intensely together, had forgotten her utterly.

The minister walked her to the door of the church. In some magical way, a click of his long deft fingers perhaps, he'd summoned a boy named Leander to "walk this lady to her car, please"—that happened to be in the parking lot of the Hammond Public Library three blocks away.

Tall spindly-limbed Leander was polite, taciturn with Jessalyn. He had not balked at the minister's request though he did not appear to be thrilled with it. As he escorted Jessalyn to her car she tried to make conversation with him but he replied in mumbles—*Yes'm. N'm.* The distressing thought came to her—*Should I give Leander something? But—of course not. I should not.*

At her car Jessalyn thanked Leander for his kindness and Leander muttered *Yes'm* and quickly edged away.

She could call after him—but she did not.

Of course, she *should not.*

Driving home she felt her heart pounding against her rib cage as if she'd narrowly avoided a terrible danger.

She might easily have given Leander a twenty-dollar bill—he would have appreciated it.

Yet, Leander might have been insulted by a tip. (He had acted out of kindness, not for a tip.) (She knew this: yet, knowing it, could she not in any case have given him a twenty-dollar bill as a sort of acknowledgment of his kindness, and *not a tip*?)

"But when is a tip not a tip? Is a tip always a tip? Is there no escaping—*tip*? If you are *white*?"

There was something debasing in the very word *tip*. Flippant, insulting. No one wants a *tip.*

The man in the Stetson hat, who'd seemed so much at home with the members of SaveOurLives, would know. Even if he laughed at Jessalyn he would not scorn her for asking.

By the time Jessalyn arrived at the house on Old Farm Road she was feeling very tired. Disgust and depression commingled in an ashy taste at the back of her mouth. The drive from Armory Street in downtown Hammond should have taken no more than twenty minutes but it required forty minutes for Jessalyn who stared through the windshield at the highway as if she'd never seen it before and who was assailed by panic that she might take the wrong exit, and become hopelessly lost in the city in which she'd lived most of her life. Rarely had she driven into Hammond, and virtually never in the night, returning home: Whitey had always driven.

If Whitey was in any vehicle, Whitey drove that vehicle. You would not want Whitey McClaren in the passenger's seat reacting to your driving with grunts of surprise, alarm, disapproval and amusement, and braking motions of his right foot against the floorboard.

And how dark Old Farm Road was, without streetlights! *Of course, it is a white enclave. Strangers are not welcome here after dark or before.*

Belatedly Jessalyn realized that the minister would recognize her name from the check: *McClaren.* She hadn't disguised herself after all; and if she had, to what purpose? Who could care in the slightest about her, or John Earle McClaren?

The strength that had coursed through her several days before and stirred such hope in her, such optimism, had now vanished utterly.

Her blood had turned leaden. Her eyes ached as if she'd been crying. A wave washed over her, of the most bitter grief.

What had she done?—Why had she done it? Driving so far from the house, behaving in a way of which Whitey would never approve, in fact in a way of which Whitey would have strenuously disapproved?

On shaky legs the widow entered the large darkened house from which (it seemed) she'd been gone a long time. The first shock was—she'd forgotten to lock the door: the knob turned too readily in her hand.

(How Whitey would scold her, leaving the damned door unlocked! She'd had this habit, careless, negligent, complacent for years that the house on Old Farm Road was inviolate. And since becoming a widow she was forgetting so much.)

Lights she switched on, in the kitchen. Was something wrong? What was wrong? Her vision wavered, she was close to fainting.

This sensation of blood beating in the ears. The widow's heartbeat.

The second shock was: Whitey had died. How could she have forgotten? A wave of filthy water rushed over her—*Whitey has died, and Whitey is dead. What are you doing, still alive!*

Unbelievable to her, she had forgotten this fact. She had been walking about as if her life had not collapsed and ended, how was that possible?

She would be punished. Must be punished. Possibly, the punishment had already begun.

"Oh, God. Help me. Whitey . . ."

Someone, something, was in the house. She could smell the rank animal odor. Her own perspiring body, and yet more than just her body—the body of another.

She had scarcely time to be terrified as a creature rushed at her, scuttling across the kitchen floor on its nails or claws—matted black fur, big block-head, tawny squint-eye, lips drawn back from sharp glistening teeth in a petulant *myrrgh*?—she gave a scream, and shrank away; but it was only the cat, the cat she'd taken in, Mack the Knife—"Mackie."

In her absence he'd devoured every particle of food in the cat bowls. He drunk all the water, or he'd caused it to spill by stepping in the plastic bowl.

She'd set a door ajar at the rear of the house, to allow the feral cat to come and go as he wished, for Mackie had grown demanding in the several weeks he'd come to live with her, and mewed loudly and persistently to be allowed *out,* and to be allowed *in;* and *out* again, and *in.* He did not like to be confined: he could not bear a shut door. If Jessalyn did not feed him promptly, he mewed in an aggrieved manner; if she did not feed him quite the (canned, moist) food he preferred, he nudged his head roughly against her legs hard enough to cause her to stagger. Sometimes, purring loudly and abrasively, Mackie kneaded his oversized paws against her legs, hands, or arms; sometimes, she hoped inadvertently, he raked his claws against her bare skin, and drew blood.

It was not enough to scold him: "Mackie, no! You must not hurt me, I am your friend." For Mackie only just stared and blinked at her with his single good eye as if he'd never encountered anyone so naive as to attempt to reason with a cat.

He was hungry now. He seemed not so sensitive to the widow's fraught nerves, her stricken face and air of desolation, defeat. As she managed to open a can of cat food he nudged against her legs, nearly capsizing her. By the time she emptied the fishy contents of the food into the bowl, Mackie had drawn blood on the backs of her hands, mewing querulously.

She staggered upstairs. The wave of grief was pounding at her now, near-suffocating. It was difficult to breathe. Beyond this, the pointlessness of breathing mocked her. Barely she was able to stagger into the bedroom where she fumbled to switch on a light, but there was no light—(had the bulb burnt out?); in a swoon of panic, despair she fell onto her bed.

Darling I've missed you. Don't leave me ever again.

IN THE MORNING she came very slowly to consciousness. Like one who has been washed onto shore scarcely alive.

Could not move, so exhausted. Too exhausted to have removed her clothing, even her shoes.

Through the night the wave had beaten against her. Pounding, pounding without mercy. She had difficulty opening her eyes, her eyelids were leaden. *Why did you think you could leave me? Betray me?*

Her nostrils pinched: somewhere close by was a sharp animal smell. The creature was in the room with her, in the night he'd leapt upon the bed. She had encouraged him to make a nest for himself at the foot of the bed and he was there now. She could hear his deep breathing, that was a kind of purring in his sleep. And in his sleep, his stubby tail twitched. All of his legs, his big paws, twitched with the thrill of the chase, the catch. He had brought with him into the bed the remains of something he had hunted in the night, a bloodied furry shank, a part of a rabbit's leg, or a part of its head.

Demon Rakshasa

He'd seen, in the rearview mirror of his car. He was sure.

The police cruiser surging near. Very near to touching his rear bumper.

We will run you off the road.

This time, we will finish what we started.

SO NERVOUS, he could not sleep. Could not lie still. Could not find a position in which to be comfortable.

Restless leg: something of a joke and yet not a joke. For the (left) leg was moving ceaselessly. The leg was running. Twitching. The foot was cramped. Each bone of the foot was aching, arching.

Sudden pain! Cramps in the leg, in the foot. Rousing him from his bed, he must walk, bring his feet down hard and flat on the floor. Bare feet. Though it was only "cramping" the pain was excruciating.

Sharp and fast like electricity. *Tasered.*

How he'd convulsed, on the ground at the side of the Expressway. Powerful bolts of electricity shot into his (unresisting, undefending) body prone on the littered pavement.

The (white) police officers' shouts, screams of fury, rage. For what, why, how could such a thing possibly happen to *him*—as confounding months later as it had been at the time of the assault.

Why do these strangers want to kill me. If it is to cover up their own mistake, I have no chance.

All that he could sweep from his mind during the day, at the hospital, in the busyness of his work, in the neediness of others and in the resolve of Dr. Azim Murthy to be available to all who required him, came flooding back to him at night.

At night, vulnerable as a skull that has been sawed open, the derma pierced, the moist gnarled brain laid bare. Vulnerable as a victim of third-degree burns. One whose immune system has collapsed to a pinpoint.

Eleven days without sleep is the medically recorded limit for human beings. Beyond that, hallucinations, dementia, and death.

Of course, Azim has not been entirely *sleepless*. What happens is that as soon as he falls asleep his dreams are so disturbing he is awakened immediately covered in sweat and his heart pounding like a small, trapped creature.

The terror he'd felt. That the (white) police officers were going to kill him.

That they had not killed him is the greater mystery. That they regret not having killed him when they'd had the chance has occurred to him many times.

In his head the reel winds, unwinds. Starting with the siren suddenly so close behind his vehicle on the Hennicott Expressway and then beside his vehicle on the driver's side.

Him? The police are forcing him off the road? Stopping *him*?

Out of the car. Out of the car. OUT OF THE CAR!

Your license. Your car registration. Keep your hands in sight! Keep your hands on your head! On the ground! ON THE GROUND!

No matter how he complied, how he protested, no matter how he groveled before the shouting men he could not avert the terrible beating to come and the guns from which sharp darts leapt and sank into his flesh and caused him to convulse like a violently shaken rag doll.

And through it all the conviction—*How could such things happen to* him?

Saved from a fatal beating (he is convinced) only by the white-haired stranger who'd dared to pull his vehicle off the roadway and intervene.

HIS CRIME, WHAT WAS HIS CRIME, is it a crime even now?—dusky-dark skin. Very dark hair, eyes.

It is a dusky-pale skin, in fact. It is, or was once, a smooth and unblemished skin, a healthy skin, not "dark" though (of course) not "white." At a glance you can see that Azim Murthy is *Indian,* from the great subcontinent of India.

Yet still seeing their victim close-up, realizing that he was not a thug, not a drug dealer, not even a drug user, the (white) police officers did not cease their assault.

Infuriated at their victim for being not what they'd hoped for, they'd become more violent.

And their violence had spilled over onto Azim's rescuer, who had bravely/recklessly intervened in the assault.

All this Azim Murthy will testify to the grand jury when he is summoned. He will not be intimidated, threatened.

He has promised the son of the deceased man—McClaren. He will not back down from this promise.

On the eve of the deposition in the office of the Hammond district attorney, Azim Murthy vows.

BUT THIS TERROR. It is familiar to him from long ago.

In the Bhagavathi temple in Kerala to which his parents had taken him and his sisters while visiting his father's family in Cochin. Seven-foot demon Rakshasa—fangs like monstrous sharp-gleaming buck teeth, glaring mad eyes, multiple arms like spider-legs, misshapen fat-bellied body. Unspeakably ugly, hideous—the seven-year-old Azim had wanted to hide his face, hide his eyes, but had been paralyzed with fear.

Worse, the demon was a cannibal. Rakshasa devours male, female, children, the elderly. He slobbers as he eats. He is insatiable, his stomach is bottomless. From his cupped hands he drinks blood. With his fat lips he sucks at a skull. His fingernails are talons. But he is a happy demon, it appears. Rakshasa is not raging, or scolding, as a parent might scold. This demon's joy is the misery of others, the cries and screams of his victims. For all whom the demon encounters are his victims. All, all are helpless before him. Piles of bones, skulls. Picked clean. Rakshasa is something of a scavenger as well, like a vulture, a hyena.

It is the *efficiency* of Rakshasa that most horrifies the child who is a practical-minded, bright child who scores high on all written tests and whose teachers in the United States praise him. An American child, indeed not "Indian"—the "Indianness" is only skin-deep (already at age seven Azim is sure).

Hands where we can see them! On the ground!

Drenched in sweat. Jolted awake. The creature has him in its fat taloned fingers.

AS A HINDU—(but Azim Murthy is hardly *Hindu:* he is thoroughly secular)—you discovered that the most hideous monsters are but incarnations of the single god who is the god of love. For how could it be otherwise when all is all, one is all, the deity inhabits all consciousness, *you are the deity yourself.*

To the adults the idols at Bhagavathi were "exotic"—not to be taken seriously. No more than, in their adopted country, Hallowe'en demons, witches, and vampires were to be taken seriously.

Of course, the idols in the Hindu temples were extraordinarily detailed. Carved, painted. Not like living persons but more magnificent than living persons because so much larger, so much more monstrous. The temple itself was frightening to a child with its heavy, heady smells of rotted things, stale urine. Incantatory chanting, long lines of pilgrims with glazed faces, eyes.

Why had the Murthys taken their children to such a place? To inoculate them? To infect them? To take pictures of their wide-eyed children gaping at the idols? They took pride in thinking of themselves as wholly secular, nonbelievers—"modern." Both had gone to universities in the United States and both exalted most things American.

Their dream for their son, which he has fulfilled. Medical school, M.D., resident physician at St. Vincent's Hospital for Children in Hammond, New York.

The residency in upstate New York had not been Azim's first choice. But it was not a shameful choice. It would do well, for his first job out of Columbia medical school.

Except in their souls the Murthys remain Indian. His fiancée and her family who live in the Buffalo suburb of Amherst, Indian. Struggle, hard work, but if you fail, passivity, fatedness. The way in which trapped in the viper's jaws the small furry creature ceases to struggle, its eyes glaze over in the ecstasy of oblivion.

Who is Lord Vishnu? Vishnu is all-in-all, each incarnation of Vishnu contains all incarnations.

Rakshasa is the demon that will never cease. The god hides inside the demon.

Why?—that is your answer.

Of his own volition Azim had sought out the McClaren son. He'd agreed to allow the son's lawyer Mr. Hawley to record his accusatory words. *I was the reason Mr. McClaren stopped by the side of the Expressway. He was protesting two police officers beating me. He was a very brave man, he saved my life. The police beat him savagely when he intervened. They knocked him down, and kicked him, and shot him repeatedly with stun guns despite his age, and his being no threat to them. Even after he was unconscious they kept on shooting him with the Tasers like maniacs—as if they wanted to kill him.*

He would swear. He was a witness. He'd suffered a terrible beating at their hands, and in the end they'd "dropped charges"—there had been no crime committed, all had been a ruse. He would seek justice for himself but more urgently, for the courageous John Earle McClaren who had died in protecting him.

The Hammond PD has issued only a terse statement that the "alleged assault" by police officers is "under investigation."

The officers being investigated have not been suspended by the force but report for "desk duty."

Their salaries have not been affected.

Azim Murthy will not be frightened by their threats. He will not be intimidated. He has filed a complaint with the Civilian Review Board. He will testify to the district attorney on behalf of the McClaren claim. He is much admiring of the McClaren son—Thomas. He has spoken with Thomas several times. He does not intend to betray Thomas. The McClaren loss is greater than his for he, Azim Murthy, had not died.

Next time we finish what we started.

HE IS AWARE: half his brain remains alert, wary while the other half sleeps. For half his brain is galvanized by fear that he will be murdered in his sleep if he dares sleep.

How has it happened, his chest is not a manly chest but thin-skinned, bony, the hairs that cover it are sparse and prematurely gray. What a sorry specimen Azim Murthy has become—and he'd been meant to be a *man*! Within six months he has become middle-aged. He is only twenty-nine, a part of his life has ended. Kicked, struck by their booted feet, Tasered. He has not told his fiancée. He has not told his family—of course. To explain his injuries, bruised face, limping, welt-marks from the Taser he'd concocted a far-fetched tale of tripping and falling on hospital stairs, hurrying down a flight of stairs when an elevator had malfunctioned. They had seemed to believe him. They revered him, of their several children he is the only son. Though they are secular Hindus yet they cannot help but revere the son above the daughters. How is that Azim's fault? It is not Azim's fault. He will not accept such fault. His parents do not interrogate him closely for they understand that his life as a rising young physician is beyond them to comprehend as it is beyond them to judge.

Impossible to tell them. If they learn what was done to him by the

Hammond police they would be terrified for his life. They know of religious riots, massacres swift as flash floods, temples cordoned off, trains barricaded, explosives, fires, automatic weapons. Primitive blood-wars masquerading as religious wars. Hindus, Sikh militants. You cannot trust the police—you cannot trust uniformed men. Incarnations of Rakshasa. The Murthys do not speak of such things. They hide their eyes at gunfire on TV. They are baffled and repelled by American movies. They would insist upon sending their prized doctor-son back to India to live with his father's brother who owns a radiology clinic in Cochin. Azim could be a doctor in the beautiful city of Cochin, his Columbia medical degree would be of great value. He would have a good life there. He will not have a good life in Hammond, New York.

In his misery he has no time to think of the future beyond the next week. Of course it is time to marry, his mother has insisted. He is not young: he must make amends for the delay. His fiancée must not know about the deposition. She is not much aware of the police assault, he has chosen not to confide in her. She is a young nervous woman. She is not so young, she is Azim's elder by nearly two years: for a female, old. She has a good job as a laboratory assistant at Squibb pharmaceuticals. She plucks her thick eyebrows to prevent them growing together across the bridge of her nose. Azim is not supposed to know how she swoons with envy and jealousy of the gorgeous Indian girls, the slender Indian-American teenagers, their astonishing beauty, perfect olive skin, peony mouths. All of them so petite—never weighing even one hundred pounds. Her name is Naya which is not an attractive name in her own ears. She would have wished a more American name: Susan, Sarah, Melanie, Brook. She is sick with worry, when her fiancé sees her without clothes he will not like her. She makes up her face very carefully. Her lips are purple grease. Her eyebrows are given a delicate arch. Her eyes are outlined in black ink. Her breasts are heavy. Her hips are heavy. She is (is she?) heavier than Azim, at 148 pounds—that is her secret, she is terrified he will discover.

Azim scarcely thinks of Naya without a pang of apprehension, regret. Guilt. He feels no desire for her. Cannot maintain desire, the jeering (white) faces intervene. The Taser voltage, terrible electric shocks convulsing his body more violently than any orgasm.

"A NEW CAR IS LIKE NEW HOPE."

A foolish saying, he isn't sure if it is specific to his family—(his father repeating a father's words)—or if it is very well known, belonging to "posterity."

New car, new hope. One must *hope*.

Of course, he has bought a new car. Soon after the outrage of the previous October he traded in the Honda Civic for another compact car, a Nissan. Where the Honda Civic was white, a foolish eye-catching hue, the Nissan is a discreet silvery-gray like so many other vehicles, intended to blend in with its surroundings like the camouflage of a prey animal.

His reasoning is the reasoning of a desperate, almost a superstitious man—*They will not recognize the new car so quickly.*

(But what of license plates? His old license plates are on the new car.)

The Hammond police officers will have no difficulty identifying Dr. Murthy's new-purchased car as *his*. Soon, a police cruiser will sideswipe his car. It is only a matter of time. When he leaves St. Vincent's, and enters the Expressway at Fourth Street, the cruiser comes up swiftly and unerringly behind him. No one will know, no one will be a witness. No one dares to give testimony against the Hammond police.

In the parking garage he has seen them on foot (he thinks). A single shot to the back of the head. A single shot into his face, fired from the cruiser as it glides past his vehicle. Who would know? Who would care? The Indian community is not large in Hammond, all are law-abiding citizens who shrink from publicity and are not to be associated with radical causes. Especially, they do not wish to be associated with Muslims.

Stray bullets in this part of Hammond. In what is called the *inner city*, that empties out rapidly by 6:00 P.M.

In the rearview mirror he sees the cruiser edging closer.

His eyes fill with moisture, he is so frightened. It is the very face of demon Rakshasa just visible through the cruiser windshield. In another second or so, the demon will nudge the bumper of his vehicle against the rear bumper of the Nissan . . .

Drenched with sweat Azim exits at Twenty-second Street. The cruiser does not follow.

Trembling badly Azim is grateful for slow-moving traffic on the ramp that moves, halts and jerks forward like a nightmare peristalsis.

IT IS THE EVE OF the deposition at Center Street. All day at the hospital his mind is fixed upon this fact. Staring at computer screens, decoding blood work. *Dr. Murthy? Excuse me?*

No. Wait. It is not yet the eve, that will be next week. Not yet, the grinning police officers will come to murder him.

For all of the Hammond police are his enemy. He is in their computers. Name, license plate number trapped in their computers like screaming prey in the mouth of demon Rakshasa.

Never will Azim arrive at 11 Center Street—he knows that now. He will not dare drive into the inner city on such a mission. Never arrive at the courthouse where he is expected at 9:00 A.M., May 11.

If Azim Murthy does not give his deposition, he may be subpoenaed. Will he be arrested? It is a lesser threat than the police threat of violence.

If he acknowledges that he saw nothing at the edge of the Hennicott Expressway, knows nothing and has nothing to testify, they will not harm him. That is the only way.

On the ground, fucker! ON THE GROUND.

Waking drenched in sweat. Another time.

IN THE BLEAK HOUR BEFORE DAWN staring at his ghost-image in the bathroom mirror he rehearses in the bright schoolboy voice he means to reclaim: "I think that I will return to medical school but in Buffalo.

I will specialize in blood cancers. I will broaden my training. There are too many internists. I am already in debt, it will not matter if I am more deeply in debt. My fiancée's family has promised that they will help. Certainly, they will help. Naya will see to that. She has all but sworn. There is much money in blood cancers. There is a rich future in blood cancers.

Recurring Dreams of the McClaren Children

After seven months still they dreamt of Whitey.

After seven months still each night was a rough journey from which they had no more protection than children trapped in a jolting cattle car.

Thom was saying how in his dream news had come that Whitey had been moved to another hospital—"In Buffalo, I think. The dream was about driving to Buffalo on the Turnpike but the drive was very complicated and tricky. And the vehicle I was driving was open—no roof. Something like a tractor, with huge tires. And the highway was under construction, or a bridge had collapsed, and I was stuck in traffic like the end of the world and it was dangerous—you needed to protect yourself with a weapon—a gun, a baseball bat. But I didn't have any weapon, and there was no roof to this vehicle I was driving. And I was bawling—like a big, helpless kid—I didn't know where the hell I was, what the hell was happening, why I was being punished, what I could do to get to Dad before it was too late . . ."

Lorene was saying she'd been having the same terrible dream essentially—"Dad is in a hospital in some other city. You have all left without me so I have to take a bus. A bus! I haven't taken a bus for years. And when I get off the bus I don't actually know where the hospital is. And when I finally get to the hospital it's enormous, like a huge train station, the size of a city block. I can't find the entrance, and keep walking around the outside trying to find a way in, and there are people coming up from some underground place like a subway station, with these blank, terrible faces and I'm confused thinking—'Is one of these supposed to be Dad? Or—who?' At the same time I'm supposed to be at school—there's an assembly, I have to make an announcement—the auditorium is filled and they're waiting but I have to see Dad first (in this other city, but I don't know the name of the city or how far it is from school) and I have to make sure Dad is all right because there's been some mistake in his treatment and none of you are around—not even Mom. And I'm feeling—just—so—awful . . ."

Beverly was saying her dream was like theirs but weirder and scarier because in it she was actually at the Hammond hospital except in Whitey's room there was a stranger who was supposed to be John Earle McClaren but was not—"His face was blurred but you could see, he wasn't Dad. He just wasn't! But I had to act as if he was Dad—the idea was, I couldn't insult this person if it turned out he actually was Dad—that was the crucial thing. Or, if it was Dad he had changed because he had *passed away* and it was up to us to keep him from finding out, because that would be crushing to him, just terrible. And Mom was there—(but it didn't really look like Mom)—pleading with us, 'Don't let him know! Don't let him know!' (So I guess you guys were there, also. But I couldn't see your faces clearly and you never said a word.) I had to go closer to the bed where the man was reaching out for me and trying to talk to me—like Dad tried, his mouth all twisted—and he touched me—my arm—and I was so frightened I couldn't scream— And next thing I know Steve is shaking me awake and sounding annoyed, I've wakened *him*."

Sophia was saying that she didn't dream at all. Her sleep was smooth as raked sand. But often she was at the bottom of a sand pit, and when she tried to climb out the sand-walls collapsed and cascaded down onto her and there was the danger of suffocation—"This was in place of a dream of Dad. Somehow, I was made to know this. A voice like a voice over a loudspeaker—'Because your father is not here, this is the dream in place of your father.' When I try to wake up it's the dream that cascades down over me like sand. But I can't wake up, so the dream never ends though it isn't—actually—a dream . . ."

Virgil was saying that personal dreams were of not much interest to him. A merely personal dream promises little of significance or worth to anyone apart from the dreamer trapped in the mire of the small soul.

Yet—(Virgil acknowledged)—since last October he'd been having dreams about Whitey, or more precisely the possibility of Whitey—"Set in some large building like a hospital, but not the Hammond hospital. And I am supposed to meet someone in this building, to 'report' to him. But I can't find the right floor. I don't know the right floor. I'm in an elevator, and pushing along an underground passageway where I can scarcely breathe, the air is so foul. And there are these people, strangers—in white hospital gowns, or death-shrouds—and each stranger's face is vivid to me as if I have met these people and know them—they are people important to my life—except I've never seen them before, I'm sure. And Dad is supposed to be among these people somewhere, but I never see him. Or if I do, I don't recognize him. I'm being knocked around, onto my knees, there are rough people here. But then I find a little hiding place like under some stairs. And there's a way out, if I crawl on my hands and knees—a way out to the daylight, and fresh air. And then I think—'He can't see me, either. He is not watching me.' And I get happier and happier like air blown into a balloon. Helium—laughing gas! And when I wake up I'm laughing and my face is wet with tears."

May Heat

Fury mounted in him like mercury in a thermometer in rising heat.

Hot red mercury, in Thom it was hot red blood.

Sometimes he wanted to kill. Murder with his own hands.

In his car driving the Expressway. CD turned up high. Deafening. Hot frantic pulsing beat of Metallica.

Thom please turn down that music, please Thom we have to speak.

Pretending to be concerned for him. Frightened for him, and frightened of him.

Soon, the wife wouldn't have to pretend.

IN HOT MAY. TOO SOON. Made him sick.

Like a girl you think is just a kid, young kid, twelve, younger than twelve, just a child then you learn *Holly has had her first period* and that is dismaying, and that is disgusting.

Not Thom's own daughter, but yes, one of Thom's nieces. Overheard Brooke and her sister Maxine talking about the girl who was only eleven and Christ!—he'd been shocked, dismayed. Next time he saw Holly couldn't take his eyes off her and she'd asked, What's wrong Uncle Thom? He wasn't smiling.

SORRY. *I'm afraid I will have to let you go.*

But that was an awkward way of speaking. What he meant was *Sorry. I'm afraid I have to let you go.*

Better yet: *Sorry. I have to let you go.*

Still better: *I'm letting you go. Three weeks' notice. Sorry.*

HE WASN'T, THOUGH. WASN'T SORRY.

Each day since Whitey had died and his remains had been consumed by flame at 1800 degrees Fahrenheit to a fine, gritty-powdery dust it had become increasingly hard for Thom to pretend to be *sorry, patient, forgiving, kind.*

He'd always been admired. Even as a boy. One of those tall husky frank-eyed boys whom adults trust on sight. He'd been what you'd call *stalwart.*

Now it was *fuck stalwart. Fuck Thom.*

These words like jolts of electricity coursing through his brain, he couldn't shake off.

Fuck every fucking thing, they killed our father.

Hearing on TV fatuous commentators discussing politics. Price of gasoline, a sports team, weather.

Weather! Jesus fucking Christ.

How the dead would love to complain about rain, snow. How the dead would love to complain about anything.

Hearing his kids bickering, whining. His wife Brooke. His sister Beverly leaving a message in her breathy-girl voice *Thom! Please call Mom tonight. Not that she will admit it but she is* so depressed! *And that horrible feral cat she has adopted—someone has to get rid of it . . .*

"Fuck you, Bev. Get rid of Mom's fucking cat yourself."

Laughing. In a fury deleting her message.

And Lorene annoyed him also. Sending cryptic emails inquiring after the suit against the Hammond PD—"What's the progress, or lack of? How much is this going to cost us?"

Thinking about the case roiled Thom's blood. He had to remind himself that he had not ever actually seen Whitey beaten by two cops young enough to be his sons, had not ever seen the cops discharge electrified darts from stun guns into his father's fallen body—this was the young Indian doctor's testimony. But the vision assailed Thom as if he'd been a witness himself. Haunted him, made him want to kill.

"With my own bare hands." (But why would a premeditated killer's hands be *bare*?)

As of early May the case was stalled. Thom was sleepless thinking about the department's attorney's claim that sixty-seven-year-old John Earle McClaren had had a medical record of high blood pressure and that he'd been a "walking time bomb" at the time of the (alleged) police attack in October.

How to prove that the cops were responsible for Whitey's death in the hospital? Whitey's collapse? In a civil suit the likelihood of convincing a jury or a judge that the cops were liable was high; in a criminal case, requiring a unanimous jury verdict, not so high. Except for Azim Murthy's testimony they had little to bring to the district attorney as evidence.

None of the others asked about the lawsuit. Not Jessalyn—of course. Beverly avoided the subject as one might avoid discussing a terminal illness. Sophia and Virgil would not have inquired even if they'd known much of Thom's plans.

See no evil, hear no evil, speak no evil. Wasn't this the monkey-mystic logic in which Virgil believed? Passivity of Eastern religion in which nothing matters except to overcome human desire that anything might matter.

Thom couldn't think of his brother without feeling a wave of disgust and disapproval. How it pissed him, their father had left Virgil exactly as much money as he'd left Thom, the father of children and Whitey's right-hand-man at the company. As *if he'd valued both his sons equally.*

Since Whitey had died, the sons had kept their distance from each other. Thom didn't think he'd seen Virgil since the disclosure of the will in the law office. In fact he hadn't seen Virgil there.

Lorene kept him informed: "Virgil has bought himself a fancy pickup truck. He'll probably purchase that farm for his commune friends."

"Fuck Virgil. What the hell do I care what he does with his money?"

"Because it's Dad's money. Or was."

Thom marveled how his sister could take time from her busy schedule at the high school to needle him on the subject of their younger brother, as on the lawsuit against the Hammond PD. Was this Lorene's break from work? Her recreation? Had she no friends, not even online companions in meanness? Beverly had told Thom that Lorene had feuds with certain of her faculty who feared and resented her and were waiting for her to misstep so they could agitate to bring about her fall.

Yet Lorene had confided in Thom in an unguarded moment that she missed Whitey—"Like, all the time. I miss Dad just *being*. He was so proud of me when I was promoted, and I try to think of that now he's gone." She'd paused, considering. "I mean, in the beginning it had seemed that Dad was just away somewhere, but he'd be back and we should keep things going as they were. But now it's sinking in, he isn't coming back. So that leaves us—where?"

— ∞ —

"Mr. McClaren—"

"Thom. Please call me Thom. There was only one 'Mr. McClaren.'"

"'T-Thom.'" The name sounded oddly in the woman's voice, like an echo in a small space.

Some of the staff at McClaren, Inc. knew Thom McClaren from when he'd been a boy. Newer employees knew him as Whitey's older, adult son, who'd taken over Searchlight Books and moved away to Rochester. Now, Thom had moved back to Hammond, and was bringing the (small, all-female) Searchlight staff back with him, as the new CEO of McClaren, Inc.

He'd hoped to hell, Whitey had said, that he'd outlive certain of his employees so that he could hire better replacements. Since he hadn't the heart to "downsize."

The new CEO wasn't going to have that problem. A week into his father's former quarters Thom was preparing his hit list.

Perusing the books. Whitey'd never shared with him.

Past quarter. Earnings, expenses. Operating costs at all-time high, projected costs expected to be higher. Insurance, building maintenance, employee benefits.

Staring at Whitey's old Dell computer that had needed replacing years ago. Slow-moving as (you'd imagine) one of those dinosaurs with very long tails and small heads—*Brontosaurus*. (In his room as a boy Thom had had model dinosaurs hanging from the ceiling from wires. Why'd he love dinosaurs so much? Even as an adult he'd been crushed to learn that the authenticity of *Brontosaurus* had been questioned by paleontologists and only somewhat mollified to learn that the skeptics had been mistaken, maybe.) Swivel in Whitey's old, creaking chair—the seat smoothed to fit Whitey's buttocks—to stare out the window in the direction of the Chautauqua River, barely visible beyond rooftops and rusted water tanks and a tangle of telephone wires. This was the *downtown scene* like a painting by Edward Hopper to which Thom's father had been so attached, he'd wanted never to leave.

Before even Whitey McClaren was born, McClaren Printing, Inc. had occupied a suite of rooms on the eleventh, top floor of the dignified old brownstone building locally known as The Brisbane. Originally built in 1926, The Brisbane had long been the most prestigious of Hammond office buildings as it had been the tallest. Now, many buildings in downtown Hammond were taller including a new Marriott of more than twenty floors, flashy and rude-seeming, blocking part of the view from McClaren, Inc.

When he'd taken over Searchlight Books Thom had insisted on moving the subsidiary company to Rochester; McClaren, Inc. had grown cramped in its quaint Edward Hopper quarters, and he'd had no interest in an office on a lower floor in the same building, in such proximity to Whitey who'd have wanted to have lunch with Thom five days a week and insist upon taking him to chamber of commerce meetings, business dinners with clients, receptions at the Marriott. It was pressure enough to get a call from Whitey once, sometimes twice a day, and to hear that air of scarcely disguised impatience, exasperation in his father's voice.

Worse, Whitey's habit of praising Thom as he praised everyone, lavishly, promiscuously, condescendingly—"Great work! Thanks."

Whitey's way of manipulating others, Thom knew. You soon caught on as one of Whitey's children.

Still, it did bring a thrill of a kind, those cheering words—"Great work. *Really* great work! Thanks."

Whitey had been impressed with Thom's work at Searchlight Books. He'd given Thom a good deal of responsibility rather quickly as if to see—(but surely Thom was imagining this)—if Thom would crack under the strain.

Had to be gratified, Whitey took the most pride in Thom. Expected the most from Thom.

Whitey had a sharp eye for flaws, typos, infelicities of design. Carefully he proofread each page, each paragraph of prose to be rendered into print by McClaren, Inc., from pamphlets of a few pages to handbooks of hundreds of pages—"The buck stops with the CEO," he'd liked to boast.

He'd always read the books Thom published, or read through them, even the breathless YA novels of Christian girls torn between boys who believed in Christ and boys who didn't (yet) believe in Christ. On shelves in his office he'd kept copies of Searchlight books in chronological order of publication and it was touching to Thom to see that they were displayed with pride.

Some of the school textbooks had bookmarks in them. When Thom opened these it was to discover poems that Whitey must have liked—excerpts from Carl Sandburg's *The People, Yes,* Robert Frost's "Stopping by Woods on a Snowy Evening" and "The Death of the Hired Man." In a high school anthology he'd marked an excerpt from Henry David Thoreau:

> Many men go fishing all of their lives without
> knowing that it is not fish they are after.

(What was it, then? What were they after? Thom hated riddles.)

(Not that Whitey knew much about fishing. From stories he'd told, he had been taken fishing by male relatives as a boy, black bass fishing in Lake Chippewa, but he'd never caught a single damned fish and that had included ice fishing as well.)

His father hadn't wanted Thom to move his family and relocate Searchlight Books in Rochester but he'd given in, finally. Whitey had been a shrewd businessman as well as a proprietary and somewhat possessive father and he'd seen that Searchlight Books could become a serious moneymaker if properly developed.

He'd been frankly surprised that Thom's subsidiary had done so well. Each quarter, profits rose. The YA novels were written to formula by earnest, middle-aged women writers who were eager to sign multi-book contracts for modest advances and royalties; the textbooks were edited by academics at small universities and community colleges, also eager to be published.

Whitey hadn't wanted to acknowledge that The Brisbane was no longer a prestigious address and that the building itself had become weatherworn, shabby. Why did it matter that the foyer downstairs was tiled in (now grimy) black-and-white octagons and the solid-oak doors to each suite were frosted glass? Why did it matter that the (sole) elevator moved with elephantine slowness? That there was (Thom recalled as a child, shivering at the sound) an actual *echo* if you called up the stairwell? Whitey thought of The Brisbane as a sort of vertical village populated with doctors, dentists, businessmen like himself: he'd always had a dread of being alone.

He hadn't wanted to acknowledge that Hammond was gradually emptying out like so many American cities ringed by white suburbs. He wouldn't consider relocating, he'd hated the look of blandly affluent, corporate-type office buildings in the Hammond suburbs, that lacked souls.

Souls. A curious usage for Whitey who'd prided himself on not being religious in any conventional way.

That joke he'd made about Houdini. Vowing to return from the dead to attest to the fact of an afterlife but—of course—Houdini had never returned.

The joke, if that was what it was, had made Whitey's children uneasy. How could it be funny, Daddy saying the terrible words *when I die?* Sophia, only five at the time, had looked as if she were about to cry.

None of them had known who Houdini was, very precisely. Lorene had thought he was some sort of famous sailor. Thom had known that he'd been a magician but had had no idea how famous and how ingenious his performances had been.

When he'd become a father Thom resolved that he would not ever make enigmatic remarks, still less unfunny jokes, about death, dying, anything to upset a child. *He would not.*

"MR. McCLAREN—"

"Please call me Thom. There was only one 'Mr. McClaren.'"

"'T-Thom . . .'"

Breathy voice. Streaked and strawlike hair. Staring wide-eyed at the new CEO in Whitey McClaren's old swivel chair as if hypnotized.

You know, "Tanya." You know what this is. Can't you make it easier for both of us?

These months Thom had become irritable, edgy. He hadn't broken down to weep for his father (or if he had, he couldn't recall; and no one saw him) but he came close to weeping for other reasons, frustration, dismay, despair. Fury. Felt as if he'd been locked in a box (precisely the size of Whitey's old office) and the oxygen was being pumped slowly out.

Seeing in the eyes of Whitey's faithful staff their unease with Thom whom they didn't trust, scarcely knew. He had yet to praise them as Whitey had, in Whitey's negligent kingly way—*Great work! Thank you.*

Fourteen full-time employees in the office, most of them long-term. Just a few were relatively new, young, digitally trained, skilled at computers and online salesmanship, Thom's age or younger.

These young employees Thom intended to promote, with substantial raises. They were the future of McClaren, Inc.

The eldest, who'd worked for Whitey McClaren for most of their lives, Thom hoped not to terminate, at least not within the year; but he planned to shift their responsibilities, assign them tasks of which they were capable. He would monitor their work closely. He would freeze their salaries.

(Time to retire? The oldest employee was seventy-one.)

(McClaren, Inc. had excellent retirement benefits in which Whitey had taken particular pride.)

One of the newer employees with whom Thom wasn't so impressed was a young woman named Tanya Gaylin, a graduate of the local community college with a degree in communication arts and graphic design. Tanya wore clothes to catch the (male) eye, very short skirts and low-cut blouses; she cast covert glances at Thom which (for the most part) he hadn't acknowledged. Her cubicle in the open office, small as a closet, was adorned with Day-Glo flowers and snapshots. Annoyed with her work which was frequently slapdash and sloppy as if quickly prepared, Thom had not criticized Gaylin in front of the others but invited her into his office to speak to her in private.

Each time, she'd seemed surprised, as if no one had ever found fault with her work before; each time, she quickly became silent and sullen. In her eyes was a look of disbelief and resentment as she was made to realize that Thom McClaren wasn't nearly so charmed by her as his father had been.

Following Thom's suggestions she'd revised her work, to a degree.

But in the end, more experienced coworkers would have to finish it.

Today, Thom invited Tanya Gaylin to speak with him in his office, in the late afternoon when most of the others had gone home. It would be her last day at McClaren, Inc., Thom was determined.

"Miss Gaylin. 'Tanya.' I'm afraid—I hope this isn't a surprise—I'm going to have to let you go."

Not at all what he'd rehearsed. Stilted, awkward. Made him feel like a dentist extracting a tooth with a pliers.

Wide-eyed Tanya seemed not to comprehend. *Have to let you go*—what did these words mean?

She smiled hard with sharp-defined crimson lips. She was not so young as she appeared in her short skirts and high-heeled shoes: in her mid-thirties. Her low-cut cotton-knit sweater fell forward to expose the tops of bulging breasts, from which Thom averted his eyes, frowning.

He had discovered to his surprise that, though Tanya Gaylin was a relatively new hire at McClaren, Inc., her salary was disproportionately high. As an assistant to the graphic designer she made nearly as much as the graphic designer did. Her mascara eyes glared at Thom and her breath came sharply.

"I—I—don't understand. Mr. McClaren—Whitey—your father—said he liked my work. He hired me himself, and he always praised my work. There was, like"—Tanya paused before plunging on—"an understanding between us."

"Was there? What kind of understanding?"—Thom was careful to speak politely.

"A—an—understanding. Between Whitey and me."

Whitey. Don't you dare call my father "Whitey."

"Yes, you've said. And what kind of understanding was this?"

Tanya licked her lips. Very carefully she said that sometimes, Whitey would ask her to stay after work in the office—"To go over a brochure design if there was, you know—a deadline for it." There was something suggestive in the phrasing *after work in the office* which Thom did not care to ponder.

"And—Whitey would say, 'I like your style of doing things, Tanya.'"

"Did he! Well."

"Just before your father got sick there was a rush order for the Squibb brochure—we were working on it together—and—when it got to be late," Tanya said, fluttering her eyes and daring to plunge forward, "Whitey said we should have dinner together, and so—at Lorenzo's . . ."

Tanya's voice trailed off inconclusively. Her eyes were fearful and defiant, fixed on Thom's face.

"That was just one example! Whitey took me to dinner more than once—he might give me a ride home. He always liked my work, from the start—my designs, and my copy. He'd have one of the copy editors go over my copy to fix up little mistakes but mostly he was never critical—he would say 'Great work, Tanya! I like your style.' He was a *gentleman*."

Thom let her speak. The more silent the man, the more the woman will speak, inanely, recklessly. Tanya's lavishly made-up eyes were damp. Not tears of hurt or alarm but (Thom guessed) tears of resentment, dislike.

Finally he had to speak:

"I'm afraid, Tanya, that I don't share my father's appreciation of your 'style.' I think that your work is substandard for McClaren, Inc. and you've had a long enough time to adjust to our standards. And so, as I've said—I have to let you go."

Still, Tanya was staring at Thom with a look of astonished hurt.

"You have three weeks' notice. But don't feel obliged to come into the office during this time."

Thom was not taking pleasure in this. He was not!

Go away now for God's sake. Please.

Tanya protested, as he'd known she would:

"But—Whitey was my friend. He wasn't just my boss, he was my friend. He cared about me. There was an understanding between us. He asked about my life—my divorce. He was really, really sweet and supportive. It was such a shock—when news came of him, in the hospital. I went to see him there. I brought him flowers—he used to bring me flowers here, sometimes—like, for Valentine's Day—just kind of joking—but beautiful flowers. He did! He was the most wonderful friend and I miss him so! My heart was just broken when I heard what—what happened. Your father would never, ever fire me the way you are doing—he would be very angry about this, if he knew—how you are treating me—you are not giving me a chance—'Thom'—your father would be so upset about this, he was such a gentleman and so kind about everyone, other people's feelings, he wouldn't like your behavior *at all*."

Thom resisted the impulse to shut his eyes. If the woman uttered the reproachful words *Your father* one more time he couldn't predict what he might do.

"I—I met your mother, once. She didn't know me—of course, she had no idea who I was. 'Jessalyn' would be surprised to meet me now, I think—if I went to visit her . . ."

Tanya was speaking boldly, recklessly. A crude flush had come into her face and she wasn't so attractive now.

"Is this a threat, Miss Gaylin? Is that how I should interpret what you're saying?"

Calmly Thom spoke. He was resolved, he would not lose his temper as so frequently lately, with his family, with strangers, he was doing.

"It's a—a—whatever you want to think it is! Whitey would be so, so upset—if he knew how you are treating me—"

"*Is* it a threat? You're suggesting that you intend to intrude upon my mother's privacy?"

"N-No. I didn't say that."

"But you suggested it. Didn't you?"

"I—I did not. No."

"Not trying to blackmail me, are you? 'If I visited your mother . . .'"

"No . . ."

"Well, good. That's good. Because if you ever try to see my mother, or communicate with my mother, if you ever speak of my father to my mother—you will regret it, Tanya. Do you understand?"

Tanya's lips were trembling. Yet, like a reckless child she persisted, "Why's *she* so special?—'Jessalyn.' Looking right through me like I didn't *exist*."

Seeing his face Tanya backed down. Here was a face from which defiant adolescent children quickly backed down.

"Well, I'm sorry. I guess! It's just that I miss your father so much.

There were some kinds of—you could call them 'promises'—Whitey had made to me . . . It isn't the same without Whitey, here. Everybody says so."

"You won't mind so much leaving, then."

Tanya was looking as if she might burst into tears. None of her stratagems had worked against Thom McClaren.

Was it possible, Thom wondered, that the woman had genuinely cared for Whitey? *Loved* him?

He'd hardened his heart against her. He would never forgive her for the things she'd said, especially about his mother.

"Good night. Goodbye."

He was on his feet. The conversation was over. He was trembling badly with a wish to grab hold of the woman and shake her until her teeth rattled and tears spilled down her cheeks powdered to an apricot sheen.

It was nearly 6:00 P.M. The outer office was deserted. Everyone had departed. Only Tanya Gaylin remained, and Thom McClaren. If Tanya lingered at her cubicle, wiping at her eyes, breathing harshly and muttering under her breath, half-sobbing, Thom kept his distance, and did not hear, and when finally he left his office a half hour later, to lock up, Tanya Gaylin was gone and the cheery crap with which she'd decorated her work space was gone.

He'd already hired a twenty-three-year-old graduate of the Newhouse School of Communications at Syracuse to take Tanya Gaylin's place. He would pay Donnie Huang nearly as much as Whitey had been paying Tanya Gaylin but he would expect more of Donnie Huang than anyone had expected of streaked-blond short-skirted Tanya.

AN UNDERSTANDING BETWEEN US. *Whitey and me.*

Met your mother. Why's she so special . . .

"I like your style."

Mixed with the car's air-conditioning fan, turned up high. Insinuating, insidious words he knew he had better make every effort to forget.

"PLEASE, THOM. NO."

"Daddy, *no*."

The wife did not want to move from Rochester to Hammond. The children did not want to move from Rochester to Hammond. The children had never lived in Hammond, and knew that they did not want to live in Hammond where their grandparents and cousins lived and where they visited a few times a year for family occasions. The river that ran through Hammond—the Chautauqua—was nothing like the fast-moving, turbulent river that ran through Rochester—the Genesee. The downtown buildings of Hammond were nothing like the downtown buildings of Rochester. The children were in high school, middle school. Their lives were their friends—how could you live without your *friends*? Their alarm could not have been greater than if their father had presented them with a perverse and inexplicable decision to relocate to Mars.

Pleasantly the Daddy said that he respected their wishes but he was now CEO of McClaren, Inc. and McClaren, Inc. headquarters were in Hammond. And headquarters were going to remain in Hammond. So Daddy was moving to Hammond, and they had the option of coming with him or remaining where they were.

Bravely Brooke hinted, maybe yes. Maybe they would remain in Rochester, for the time being at least.

(Did Brooke mean this? From the quivering mouth, the evasive eyes, the way in which her voice lifted like the soft, startled cry of an animal whose paw has been stepped-upon, not quite by accident—Thom guessed not.)

Telling her in his most pleasant Daddy-voice that certainly that was a possibility for her and for the children. For the time being at least.

"You can stay in Rochester but it will have to be in another, smaller place. I can't afford two houses. There's a property in Hammond that's just come on the market, on Stuyvesant Road, a few miles from my parents' house, that I'd like to consider. You can find a condominium, if you want to stay here. The kids won't need to transfer to new schools.

I can see you on weekends. We'll work something out. What's called 'visitations.'"

So affably Brooke's husband spoke, you would not be likely to detect the fury in his heart.

— ∞ —

And then, the most profound shock.

A call from Bud Hawley informing Thom that their witness Azim Murthy wasn't returning his calls or emails. The grand jury was in session and the district attorney had planned to present the McClarens' case the following week.

Thom was stunned, disbelieving. How was this possible? Murthy had come to *him,* to volunteer his testimony against the police officers. And Hawley had recorded it.

Hawley explained that the young Indian doctor—their sole "witness"—hadn't been under oath. There was no way to force him to cooperate. If a witness has second thoughts it usually means that someone has gotten to him, to intimidate him. That would be the Hammond police.

"We could insist upon a subpoena. But Murthy could claim he doesn't remember—he'd been injured by the police himself, his memory was affected. If he's been threatened by them there's no way we can prove it."

"But—can't we use his testimony? He came to us, because he knew about Whitey. He'd volunteered . . ."

"We can't use a witness's testimony if he recants. No."

"Why the hell not? There's only one reason the witness would recant, because he's been threatened. The district attorney knows this, he has heard the testimony. What do D.A.s do in these cases?"

"Offer police protection. But in this case, it's the police our witness needs to be protected against."

It was sickening to Thom, the irony of such an impasse. For there is a complacency in irony, the resignation to what is intolerable. Thom's heart beat quickly in revulsion.

Gleeson, Schultz. Thom knew their names well.

Murderers, racists. Still on the Hammond PD payroll, though not at the present time allowed to carry guns.

They'd never been arrested. They'd never had to account for their actions publicly. An internal review was "in progress." Through the department counsel they had issued their flat, lying statements: their actions against John Earle McClaren and Azim Murthy had not been excessive but warranted under the circumstances, for they'd feared for their own lives in an encounter with "violent" men they'd had reason to believe might be armed.

Nothing could shake them from this defense. Apart from Azim Murthy's testimony there were no witnesses. Whitey's remains having been cremated without an autopsy weakened their case, which had to be made on medical records and the cell phone pictures of his father that Thom had taken, which were open to disputed interpretations. Thom recalled how he'd pleaded with his mother to allow his father's body to be autopsied, but Jessalyn had become emotional and refused. He was dismayed by her, even now. His dear mother, acting out of a naive and unexamined sentimentality, had undercut their case, which was Whitey's case—why couldn't she have tried to understand, at least? But Thom supposed it was his own fault, he hadn't wanted to argue with her. He hadn't wanted to upset her any more than she'd been upset.

Hawley had warned him at the time, this would be a mistake. And Thom had known. Yet, he'd drawn back from confronting Jessalyn. He would not reproach his mother now, allowing her to know that the case had been sabotaged by her wifely scruples. If he discussed it with her, as he rarely did, he would tell her about Azim Murthy's defection. And that was true enough, and disappointing enough.

A lawsuit was like a quagmire, or rather *was* a quagmire: you might step into it of your own volition, but having stepped in, you lose your volition, you are drawn in, and down, and are trapped.

He'd known this, Thom was no fool. He'd been dealing with lawyers through his professional life. And Whitey had been involved with lawyers through his professional life. You could not run a business without being protected by a team of lawyers, and you could not retain a team of lawyers without paying their exorbitant fees.

Yet, Thom couldn't help but feel that the case would be presented to the grand jury, and that the grand jury, consisting of Hammond citizens, people like Whitey himself, would be sympathetic; they would vote to indict the murderers, and there would be a trial.

Beyond this, Thom couldn't bring himself to think. A part of his mind exulted in Gleeson and Schultz being found guilty of second-degree homicide, and sentenced to prison; another part of his mind, more sober, subdued, doubted that this would ever be.

The purpose of the criminal case was to secure a kind of posthumous justice for his father, and to expose and punish Hammond police brutality and racism. If there was a civil suit, its purpose wasn't to win a large settlement but to bring the Hammond PD to its knees.

"I don't want money, I want justice for Whitey."

How many times over the past several months had Thom uttered these words.

It had become an obsession with him, the case. Even at McClaren, Inc., in the midst of a crowded schedule, Thom found time to call Bud Hawley to ask how things were going.

"Reasonably well, Thom. As Whitey used to say, 'Things could be a lot better, and things could be a lot worse.'"

The most diplomatic of answers, intended to assuage concern without exactly answering it.

It became a desperate matter, Thom needed to speak to Azim Murthy. He couldn't believe that Murthy would betray them—betray Whitey. After how grateful he'd been, how adamant, in his belief that Whitey had saved his life.

But Hawley tried to dissuade Thom from trying to contact Murthy. Their relationship should remain mediated through him, Hawley said. It could be a terrible mistake to contact Murthy directly, and to get into some sort of quarrel with him.

"If he doesn't want to talk to you, don't force it. Don't pursue him."

Of course, Thom understood.

"He's been frightened. He's in fear of his life. It took extraordinary courage for him to come to you initially, but he was angry then, and feeling reckless, and now it's months later, and he has to live with what he'd done, and that isn't so easy. So don't, you know, *stalk him*."

Fuck you. Mind your own fucking business, it's what you are paid for.

Fury mounting in Thom like molten lead. Red-hot, pulsing.

After months of planning Thom was seeing victory about to be snatched from him. Badly he'd wanted a trial, a public forum in which his father would be alive again, in the minds and memories of those who'd known Whitey McClaren, and even those who had not known him. He'd been so certain that this would happen, must happen: the police officers were guilty, and Whitey had been such a good, decent, courageous man. And Dr. Murthy, a young doctor misidentified as a drug dealer, a sympathetic victim of police brutality and racism as well.

The more he thought of it, the more likely it seemed to Thom that this must happen, as he'd originally planned. Hawley must be mistaken, or had misunderstood: Murthy was *on their side*.

The vehemence with which the young Indian doctor had spoken, when they'd first met. His gratitude for Whitey's intervention. His rage at the Hammond cops . . . How could that not have been sincere? Thom had felt for Azim an almost physical yearning to embrace him as a brother.

But when Thom called the numbers he had for Azim Murthy, no one ever picked up. And when Thom left messages, no one ever called back. His emails flew like missiles into an ether of oblivion, never answered.

Finally, Thom tracked Dr. Murthy down at St. Vincent's Hospital.

Seeing Thom in the corridor, the young doctor visibly shrank back. He knew at once what Thom wanted, and waved his hands in a flutter of helplessness, stammering nervously that he couldn't talk now, he could not speak with Thom now, he was very busy—"Please excuse me, I cannot. I am sorry."

In his face an expression of guilt and sorrow. But determination as well. So Thom retreated, reasoning that he had no choice: if he caused a scene in St. Vincent's security officers would be called.

Instead, through a series of discreet calls, Thom determined what Azim Murthy's hospital schedule was, and the next evening positioned himself at the rear of the building, where Murthy was likely to pass on his way to the staff parking garage.

Was this "stalking"?—Thom didn't think so.

A stalker was an irrational person, mentally unbalanced. Most stalkers were thwarted lovers.

Seeing Thom, Murthy would have hurriedly retreated back into the hospital, but Thom adroitly out-maneuvered him so that both men were outside the revolving doors, at the rear of the hospital. It would have been very awkward for Murthy to try to press past Thom, and he did not try.

How could Azim go back on his word to Thom?—How could he betray Whitey? These were questions Thom asked frankly. He did not accuse Murthy of deceit; he spoke as if only just puzzled, and hoping for an explanation.

Evasively Murthy said it had all become very complicated. He'd had to realize that he wasn't sure any longer what he remembered, and what he had surmised, or invented, or dreamt. He could not swear that he'd actually seen Gleeson and Schultz beating and Tasering Thom's father—he could not swear with 100 percent certainty that the officers he'd seen at the edge of the highway were the very officers who would be in the courtroom as defendants. "You see, I was on the ground. My eyes were beaten, my head was beaten. My ears were beaten, one of my eardrums had burst and I could hardly hear. I had not seen the police officers' faces clearly. I could not pick them out of a crowd. If it comes to a court trial and I am questioned by their lawyer, he might force me to take a vision test which I would fail, for my eyes are nervous eyes—if I am agitated, my eyes water so badly, I really cannot see well, and I cannot read. It could all turn against me—I could be charged with perjury! I have looked up the law, there are terrible things that can happen. So you see, Thom, I am so very sorry—*I cannot testify after all.*"

Murthy spoke rapidly, chaotically. He was smiling at Thom as one might smile at a snarling dog in a futile hope of placating it even as the ghastly smile infuriates the snarling dog further.

"Azim, wait. Please, let's talk . . ."

"We have talked! We have talked but on a confused subject. I was not in full possession of the situation, of my impaired knowledge of it, as I am now. I am certain of this."

"Has someone threatened you? Is that it?"

Thom loomed tall over the slender young man, intimidating him without knowing what he did. Murthy's dark eyes were widened, shiny, showing white above the rim of the iris. Murthy was desperate to escape Thom, hurrying to his vehicle in the parking garage, all but running as Thom followed close behind him, trying to reason with him.

"If I could promise you that you would not be hurt—by anyone—that would make a difference, wouldn't it?"

"No! There could not be such a promise. Good night."

"Azim? Wait. You know that my father saved your life, don't you? How can you betray him, now? You would not really betray my father, would you? Azim?"

"I am telling you, please—*no.* And now I must leave, I cannot talk further. I have said everything that I can say, I have explained to Mr. Hawley—*no.*"

Very close, Thom loomed over the smaller man. His eyes swerved in their sockets, he felt such a powerful yearning—to seize hold of the man, to grip him intimately and punishingly as a brother, to shake him, to make him listen, to make him come to his senses. With a cry of fear Murthy pushed from Thom, losing his balance but managing to half-fall into the front seat of his car, causing the horn to sound.

"No no no *no.* I am telling you."

Murthy was terrified of him. Absurdly, of *him.*

No choice, Thom had to let Murthy go. The last thing he wanted was a physical confrontation, a public scene. Had to stand there fucking helpless as Azim Murthy, his sole witness, his brother who'd betrayed him, drove his dark-silver compact Nissan jerkily out of the St. Vincent's parking garage, and out of Thom McClaren's sight.

— ∞ —

"One thing I can do. I will do."

Rid his mother of the feral tomcat that had entered her life out of nowhere.

From his sisters Thom had been hearing for weeks of Jessalyn's adopted stray, mysteriously named Mackie. Thom had yet to have a confrontation with the tomcat, which was rarely in the house when he stopped by; only once, as he'd entered the kitchen, and called for Jessalyn, he'd been startled by a blurred shadowy shape rushing out of the room and he'd heard claws frantically striking the tile floor as the animal fled through a part-opened door at the rear of the house.

He'd smelled the cat, though. Unmistakably.

He'd seen the plastic food bowls set out for the cat, on newspaper on the kitchen floor. A water bowl in which the cat must have dipped a bloody snout, or dipped bloody paws.

What a pathetic sight! His mother setting out food and drink for the wild creature, like an offering at an altar.

Never before had there been anything like this in the kitchen of the beautiful old eighteenth-century house on Old Farm Road.

Of the sisters Beverly was the most incensed. She called Thom to complain that their mother had taken in an ugly, scarred, dangerous and probably diseased stray animal—"You know, feral cats have all kinds of diseases like feline leukemia, parasites, rabies. This one is psychotic as well! It looks at me with its evil yellow eye and I just *shudder.* It should be taken away and euthanized before it attacks Mom."

Lorene complained that the animal was hostile to her though she'd tried to befriend it—"I don't like cats much, so I've been making an effort with this one, for Mom's sake. But it's always baring its teeth at me, and hissing. Mom is afraid of it, I can tell. It has scratched her arms terribly. It should be taken away and euthanized before something tragic happens."

Both sisters wanted the tomcat euthanized but (Thom took note) neither was volunteering to take it to an animal shelter. That was for someone else to do.

Sophia told Thom that she'd been surprised to see a large black tomcat at their mother's house, part-feral and part-domesticated. So far as she could gather, the cat had appeared a few weeks before on the rear deck of the house, very hungry, and grateful for food Jessalyn set out for him.

"Mom hasn't had a pet since she'd been a girl, she says. Dad never wanted any pets. She has become very attached to Mackie even if—to us—he isn't very attractive, at least at first glance. He's large and stocky and not very graceful. One of his eyes is a scarred socket and the other is tawny yellow, and squinting. His fur is thick-matted black with white markings like dabs of paint. His purr is very loud—like a motor. When you first hear it you can't quite figure which direction it's coming from. I think that, most nights, Mackie sleeps with Mom, on the end of her bed, which maybe isn't such a good idea if he has some sort of feline disease. I've told Mom that he should be taken to a vet's as soon as possible and given shots. If he hasn't been neutered, he should be."

Thom waited for Sophia to suggest that the cat be euthanized, but she only added, as if Thom had already raised an objection, "Mackie seems to make Mom happy, and a little less lonely, and that's all that matters."

"Really? Couldn't Mom be 'happy and a little less lonely' with another, nicer cat? A normal-sized cat? Why a stray with only one eye and a habit of clawing her?"

"I don't think that Mackie has a habit of clawing Mom, exactly," Sophia objected. "He can be nervous if you touch his head the wrong way, or pet him at the very end of his spine, by the base of his tail, so he reacts, and sometimes with his claws—but he doesn't do it deliberately, you can tell. Lorene says he's vicious, and will never be housebroken, but I've seen him just a few times, and each time he has been better adjusted. He has obviously been an abandoned, stray cat for a long time, living a rough life. He might be younger than he appears—feral cats don't live nearly as long as house cats. But he does make Mom happy, and she was so sad before."

A debased sort of happiness, Thom thought. What if our mother contracts rabies!

When Thom asked Jessalyn about the cat Jessalyn said defensively that he'd come into her life by chance, and that must mean something.

Thom wasn't sure he'd heard correctly. *Must mean something?*—What was Jessalyn saying?

An ugly old stray tomcat wandering into his mother's life, allowing her to feed him, invested with *meaning*?

Thom thought, with a shudder—*Jesus! Is that pathetic.*

Just as well that Whitey couldn't know that his wife whom he'd loved so very much had succumbed to a morbid fixation upon an ugly tomcat missing one eye.

"Well. You should take him to a vet, to be examined, in any case. I could help you."

"No! Mackie would be very upset if anyone tried to put him into a carrying case. I don't think that's a possibility."

Jessalyn spoke excitedly. Her hands fluttered like wounded birds.

A vet would surely want to euthanize the feral cat, Thom supposed. Jessalyn must have been thinking that, too.

It fell to him to provide the solution, Thom thought. His mother wasn't able to think clearly on the subject of the cat, as on other subjects since Whitey's death, and it did no good to press her.

Quickly Thom formulated a plan: he would "euthanize" the cat himself, and no one would know.

So far as Jessalyn could know, the cat would have disappeared. As mysteriously as it had appeared in her life, it would disappear.

Thom determined when Jessalyn was going to be away for an evening, at an event at the Hammond Arts Council, and that evening he went to the house on Old Farm Road, which was darkened, and brought his baseball bat with him. He wore gloves, and he carried a burlap sack.

In stealth Thom entered the house in which he'd lived for so many years as a boy. He did not call "Mom?" as usual; instead, he called "Mackie?" in what seemed to him an affable and affectionate voice. "Kitty-kitty-kitty!" If the wily tomcat was in the house he did not come to this stranger calling him by name.

Calling "Kitty! Kitty! 'Mack-ie'!" Thom prowled through the downstairs rooms switching on lights. He might have gone upstairs but decided against this.

The spirit of his father brooded here. But more obviously upstairs than downstairs.

"Mackie? Kitty? Come here." Thom shook a small bag of dry cat food, to entice the cat; but still no cat appeared.

Jessalyn had happened to mention that she still left food for the cat outside, on the rear deck. There were times when the cat seemed fearful of entering the house, for no reason that Jessalyn could discern, and so she made sure that there was always plenty of food outside for him.

Quietly, Thom let himself out onto the rear deck. Since he no longer lived in this house, but recalled it intimately, there was a curious doubleness in his experience—he was both an inhabitant of the house, and a visitor; in this case, a surreptitious visitor. He was sure that, in all of his life, he'd never entered this house, or any other house, in such a way: invisibly.

Thrilling to him, such a state. His heart beat lightly in elation.

Overhead, a faint quarter moon. It was a predator's moon—not too bright, veiled, ideal for hunting. The day had been unpleasantly warm for May, rife with seeds and pollen, a smothering density to the air. But night was different.

A cat is a nocturnal predator, Thom thought. Of course "Mackie" would prowl by night.

Thom would hide in the shadows against the wall of the house, and wait for the tomcat to appear, to approach the bowls Jessalyn had left for him; he could linger here at least an hour, or a little longer. Jessalyn was attending a fund-raiser dinner that would last a minimum of two hours. He intended to be gone well before she returned.

Thom was noticing how, since Whitey's death, all things that Jessalyn did seemed but random acts, of no significance. If she attended the Arts Council dinner, or if she did not—it came to the same thing: *nothing.*

A widow is one to whom *things happen,* but randomly.

Jessalyn hadn't told Thom this. Not quite. For Jessalyn would never share such a terrible truth.

Fact is, if Whitey were alive, and had accompanied her to the event, it would have been a festive occasion, shimmering with significance.

For Jessalyn was one of several Hammond women being honored at the dinner, for their effort in overseeing the council's funding campaign, now nearing its (triumphant) end. She would be warmly applauded by the gathering. Her picture would appear in local papers. Whitey would have been enormously proud of her.

Without Whitey, however, the occasion meant nothing to Jessalyn. Words of praise and affection lavished onto her meant nothing, or suggested mockery. One more thing for the widow to endure.

Thom would rid her of the loathsome disease-bearing tomcat, at least. Though other matters in his life and in the life of his unhappy mother were not in his control, *that* he could manage to do.

Like a predator, Thom hid in shadows against the wall of the house. His gloves were on his hands, and his hands gripped his baseball bat. He was prepared to wait, and took pleasure in waiting; he had no doubt that the animal would appear, if he was patient enough. He would be patient.

Twenty minutes, twenty-five minutes . . . The faint quarter moon moved in the sky, in and out of a thin cloud-layer like an eye that is veiled, yet still vigilant. When he roused himself at last, hearing something close-by, at least forty minutes had passed.

He strained to see in the darkness, like a nocturnal creature himself. There it was—the husky tomcat: so quietly had it crept up the steps to the deck, and along the very edge of the deck, Thom had nearly missed it. And now, quivering with hunger, it began to eat from one of the plastic bowls.

Swiftly Thom acted, swinging the bat down onto its head. There came a shriek, horrific, hideous, as the creature tried frantically to escape, while Thom brought the bat down again, and again, shattering bone—vertebrae, skull—even as the terrified animal tried to crawl away on its belly; then it convulsed in an expulsion of blood from its gaping mouth, and ceased struggling.

The bat was slick with blood. The deck-slats were slick with blood. Thom wished he'd laid down burlap, or newspaper, to soak up the blood. What had he been thinking?

The creature lay lifeless, a mound of wet dark fur. Without looking at the body too closely Thom pushed it with the bat onto the strip of burlap, and wrapped it up securely, and shoved it into a garbage bag; he was panting, uncomfortably warm, beginning to feel regret for what he'd done. The tomcat was not nearly so large as it had seemed but rather diminished in death, pitiable. Thom was stricken with remorse. *The cat had only wanted to live. Now you have taken its life from it.*

He dragged the garbage bag around the house to his car in the driveway, and lifted it into the trunk—the creature's lifeless body was surprisingly heavy, like something sodden. In the trunk, the bundle lay unmoving; yet Thom imagined he could hear a faint, irregular breathing inside. For a full minute or more he stooped over the bundle, listening, not knowing if it was his own breathing he heard, or the tomcat's; finally, he decided that it was his own breathing, and not the cat's.

Next, he had to clean the deck, wipe it down with paper towels, with hot water, soap, disinfectant. He worried that Jessalyn would see that the roll of paper towels beside the kitchen sink was badly depleted; it was like Jessalyn to take note of such small household matters. ("Thom? Did you use up that entire box of Kleenex so soon? I just put it in your room last week.")

He was moving swiftly, yet numbly. He was feeling sick with regret. Ridding his mother's household of the diseased stray had seemed like a very good idea, a necessary idea, in fact it had been his sisters' idea, not Thom's; but now, he had changed his mind. The doomed cat had tried to live, desperately, valiantly—its cries had been terrible to hear, like the shrieks of a baby.

(Thom hoped to God that no neighbors had heard, and had called 911 reporting shrieks at the darkened McClaren house.)

(Of course, that was unlikely. No one would call 911 for such a reason: predator animals killed their prey frequently here in the country, in the night. Raccoons, owls, prowling cats, coyotes. This killing had been one of these.)

Thom wiped the dampened deck with a final swath of paper towels, and threw the befouled trash into the garbage bag with the animal corpse. There! A *fait accompli.*

By this time it was almost 9:00 P.M. He must escape!

On his way back to the apartment he was renting in North Hammond Thom deposited the garbage bag in a Dumpster behind a 7-Eleven.

"Never again! Jesus."

Felt like hell. His soul burnt and wizened like something moist that had been left out in the sun.

But then, he consoled himself: "Don't be ridiculous. You did the right thing."

(Was this so? Euthanizing the diseased, one-eyed cat?—the right thing?)

(If Jessalyn knew, she would never forgive him. But if Jessalyn truly knew how her son wished to protect her, she would certainly forgive him.)

Not that night but the following morning Thom called Jessalyn to ask about the Arts Council dinner. Surprisingly, she said nothing about

Mackie being gone. Thom was reluctant to ask her about the tomcat, and Jessalyn did not volunteer; instead she told him, with a rueful laugh, that, at the dinner, virtually no one had mentioned Whitey to her, though the last time she'd seen most of these people had been at Whitey's memorial.

"It's as if he has stepped off the earth. Just—gone."

Thom listened sympathetically. He could hardly tell his mother—*Yes, that is what Whitey has done. Stepped off the earth.*

They spoke for a while longer, but not about Whitey, and not about Mackie. By the time Thom broke the connection he'd sweated through his shirt.

Already he was at McClaren, Inc., in his office, early. But too late now to return to his apartment to take another shower and put on a fresh shirt.

Next day, guiltily, Thom called Lorene. He told her that he'd seen Jessalyn just before the Arts Council event but they'd spoken only casually. He said nothing about the feral cat, and he said nothing about the murder; and Lorene said nothing about a missing cat, if she'd heard about a missing cat.

Another day, and Thom called Beverly, who'd attended the Arts Council dinner and spoke at length about it, at much greater length than Thom wished; but Beverly had nothing to say about a missing cat.

Another day, and Thom could bear it no longer: he returned to see Jessalyn in the evening. His pretext was to speak with his mother about the court case, which Thom was determined not to give up, though he'd had a setback, and McClaren, Inc., the family business which seemed (to Thom) like a vehicle that had been moving along a roadway at a steady speed but had now begun to accelerate, to descend a near-imperceptible hill, moving ever faster, and faster, inadvertently, but irresistibly. How to jump off? *Should* he jump off?

But as soon as Thom stepped into the kitchen, before even calling for Jessalyn, he saw, to his horror, the squint-eyed black tomcat there before him, lapping water from its bowl on the floor.

"Jesus! You."

Unperturbed, Mackie lifted his head and fixed his single, tawny eye upon Thom. A defiant look seemed to pass from the cat to Thom—*Yes. Here I am. This is my home.*

Jessalyn hurried downstairs to greet Thom and saw that he was looking distracted, anxious. "Thom! Hello, dear. Please come in . . ."

Hugging him, tight. He could feel her ribs, the frailness of her being. No!

It was a delicious cold supper Jessalyn had prepared, served to Thom in the kitchen, which appeared to be the only downstairs room Jessalyn inhabited now. He'd brought a bottle of red wine which he drank entirely himself. Though Jessalyn called *Kitty-kitty! Mack-ie!* several times, wanting the tomcat to come and be petted by Thom, and demonstrate for Thom his remarkable purr, Mackie kept a wary distance, and did not purr; most of the evening he spent curled up on a chair in a corner of the kitchen, licking with surprising daintiness at his big forepaws and washing, in brisk circular motions with these paws, his big furry head.

Visions at Dutchtown

It is not a dream exactly, this conviction that her eyelids have been ripped from her eyes. So that she is awake continuously. Visions flood her brain.

"MA'AM? Anything I can help you with?"

Yes, probably. Soon.

No. Not ever again.

Shocked to see the face of someone she'd known, in that other lifetime. Saturday afternoons at the Dutchtown Farmers' Market across the county line in rural Herkimer County, a forty-minute drive from the house on Old Farm Road.

The woman, a farmer's wife, had grown gaunt and wizen-faced where once (as Jessalyn recalled) she'd been solid-bodied, flushed with health. She'd never hesitated to lift heavy packages to load into Jessalyn's car trunk, not stooping to lift the packages but bending her knees in a practiced motion, gripping with the crooks of both arms, unerring. She'd been very friendly, and may have seemed to the (older) McClaren children just slightly simple-minded, being so very friendly, and always asking their names, which she would never recall; always calling Jessalyn "ma'am" though she was older than Jessalyn by as many as twenty years.

Today, the farmer's wife wouldn't have been recognizable to Jessalyn if Jessalyn had met the woman elsewhere. Nor was Jessalyn, white-haired and alone, diminished in widowhood as a plant after the first frost of the season, recognizable to the farmer's wife.

And where was the farmer?—an older man even at that time, now certainly long retired, vanished.

Shawcross—that had been the name. Jessalyn knew better than to ask where Mr. Shawcross was.

"I'll take this. And this. Oh, this is beautiful—thank you . . ."

Lush, wet-bright-green romaine lettuce, red-leaf lettuce, spinach with veined and sand-flecked leaves, crinkled dark-green kale . . .

She was feeling giddy, selecting these greens. As she'd have felt if she were going to prepare a lavish meal that evening.

For if you have bought such beautiful fresh produce presumably you are planning to prepare it for others to eat, and if you are not planning to prepare it for others to eat, why have you bought it? Jessalyn supposed that she could drive by Beverly's house, and give the greens to Beverly; but this was risky, for her daughter would certainly insist that Jessalyn stay for dinner with the family, and Jessalyn preferred to be alone.

(In fact, there was nowhere Jessalyn felt more alone than at the Benders' where she was obliged to impersonate "Granma Jess" and where Beverly and Steve spoke cuttingly to each other as the children bickered at the dinner table until such time as they were released, to run upstairs to their rooms and beloved electronic gadgets.)

"Oh, you're lucky! Or very brave. No one in my family will eat kale. Especially not my husband."

At these airy playful words Jessalyn glanced around, and saw a woman smiling at her, a woman not unlike herself, casually dressed, yet tastefully dressed, a woman with glittering rings, blond-rinsed hair, manicured nails. The woman had spoken in such a way that Jessalyn might acknowledge her remark, or ignore it altogether, without being rude.

"*My* husband hates kale. He prefers iceberg lettuce to red-leaf."

Jessalyn heard herself speak lightly, entertainingly. It was to make the woman laugh, or at least smile; and the farmer's wife, gaunt and wizened Mrs. Shawcross, she too was invited to laugh, except preoccupied Mrs. Shawcross was putting the greens in bags, and may have been hard of hearing.

"My husband thinks there are just five dogs in our house but in fact there are nine."

What was this? Dogs? Jessalyn had no idea what the woman was saying and felt the need to move away, and move on.

"I should explain—we have a large house. The dogs are never in one room at a time."

"Oh yes. That's—good."

Jessalyn smiled vaguely, paid for her lavish, lush greens and edged away from the friendly woman with blond-rinsed hair and five dogs, or was it nine. The woman remained behind to engage hard-of-hearing Mrs. Shawcross in conversation, and to make purchases of her own.

Dutchtown Farmers' Market in the rain. A strange place to be alone.

There were not many customers at this hour, in the early afternoon. Jessalyn estimated that only about two-thirds of the usual number of farmers had set up their stands along the asphalt strip near Dutchtown Pike, Herkimer County. Bins of fresh produce and some meat (steaks, pork chops, chicken, turkey, beef sausage) protected by strips of rain-splattered tarpaulin, but not very well protected.

Why did you come to this dreary place, darling? What are you hoping to prove?

Feeling for a moment that she would faint! Recalling walking here with Whitey, on a sunny autumn day, hand in hand. Along the rows of farmers' stands. A purchase of fresh-cut flowers—those flowers with myriad curly petals, soft-pastel-colored, what was the name?—a hybrid chrysanthemum, Whitey had selected. She remembered Whitey striking up conversations with farmers and their wives, how amazing to her, how wonderful, that Whitey could talk to anyone, and enjoyed talking to anyone; like a politician, though Whitey hadn't (in fact) been a very adroit or ambitious politician, he'd remembered names, he'd remembered the names of children, where people were from, what their interests were. If you'd asked Whitey why, why on earth, why expend so much energy on strangers who did not overlap with your life, who had not the faintest idea who you were, Whitey would have said that was exactly why: to no purpose.

Jessalyn remembered chickens in large cages, for sale. White-feathered, red-feathered, gray-speckle-feathered. And smaller, beautifully feathered game chickens. Their excited clucks when they were fed seed. Now there were only dead, defeathered chickens for sale hanging upside down.

The smell of manure, Whitey had claimed to like. At a distance, like skunk.

Even in the rain, huddled beneath a tree, a half-dozen ponies were waiting to be ridden. But who would ride them in the rain? Jessalyn wondered. Who were the parents who would allow their children to ride ponies in even lightly falling rain?

The farmer who owned the ponies had had to herd them into his truck very early that morning, Jessalyn supposed. All of the farmers began their days very early, when everyone else was in bed. You had to have faith, if you had a stand at the Dutchtown Farmers' Market, that rain would lighten in time; if your competitors left early, or failed to come at all, you would persevere, for that was your life.

Beneath a dripping tarpaulin Jessalyn stood, watching the ponies.

Their slow-swishing tails, thick manes and somber eyes. Why does a pony or a horse seem so much more somber than (for instance) a cow, or a pig? These were compact, comely animals, not beautiful as horses are beautiful, their bones not so easily shattered. Or so Jessalyn thought.

The children had loved pony rides when they'd been young. A pony ride was so thrilling! Jessalyn recalled Sophia clutching at the mane of a palomino pony—but the child's face had been tense with fear. Jessalyn recalled Thom, seated in a saddle on a pony's back, lowering his toes to the ground, stretching his legs to demonstrate how tall he'd become.

The children hadn't seemed to mind swarms of flies tormenting the ponies, even the pony's eyes. Or possibly, the children hadn't noticed.

Thom had been the first to lose interest in ponies. The first to lose interest in coming with his mother to the Dutchtown Farmers' Market to buy fresh produce and flowers.

In those years Whitey hadn't time to accompany Jessalyn but he'd liked it that Jessalyn bought things at the farmers' market, not at local food stores like everyone else they knew. One more (small, significant) fact about his dear wife that made her special.

A birthday outing for Lorene, that was to begin with pony rides at the Dutchtown Farmers' Market and end at the Zider Zee Inn a mile away on a bluff overlooking Lake Ontario. Thom, Beverly, Virgil, Sophia—and Whitey had promised to join them at the inn for lunch.

Always Jessalyn would remember waiting for Whitey—the children waiting for Daddy—at the inn, at the special window table Whitey's secretary had reserved for them; the older children growing peevish, and especially Lorene whose (eleventh) birthday it was; and finally a call came for "Mrs. McClaren"—it was Whitey, apologizing for being unable to join them after all.

Jessalyn gave the phone to Lorene, who listened sullenly to Daddy's excuses. From Lorene the phone was passed to Beverly, to Virgil, to Sophia, to Thom, and to each of them Daddy apologized profusely, and made Daddy-jokes at which they laughed. (Though Lorene had not laughed.) And so back to Jessalyn who assured Whitey that no one was angry with him but yes, they were disappointed.

And Lorene said, smirking, "Listen to you, Mom! You never say anything you mean because you don't mean any damn thing you *say*."

So startling an outburst for a girl of eleven, Jessalyn could not think of a reply. Fumbling with the phone, which was a cordless phone brought to her by the Zider Zee hostess, as the other children looked on in embarrassment.

THAT FINAL TIME JESSALYN DROVE the children out to Herkimer County to buy pumpkins for Hallowe'en, in Whitey's new SUV in which five children including two teenagers could fit easily. No question of Whitey accompanying them on such an excursion any longer, his work at McClaren, Inc. had become far too pressing.

Family life had become the mother's province almost exclusively. The father's province was outside the home.

Of course, the older children were almost too old now for these drives into the countryside. Long sloping hills, cornfields, wheat, soybean, forests. Cows, horses, sheep grazing in fields, like creatures asleep and dreaming on their feet.

Billboards proclaiming "historic" Dutchtown (founded 1741)—"It's a sure sign that a place is totally boring," Lorene remarked dryly, "if it has to boast of being 'historic.'"

The mother laughed. For Lorene was witty, funny. The mother did not dare not laugh, for fear that her dislike of her middle daughter would become too evident.

Beverly said, in rebuke, "*You're* boring."

In the backseats the children squabbled. In the front seat, beside the mother, Sophia, the youngest, stared out the window silent and mesmerized. Especially, horses fascinated the child. It was like a fever to her, imagining their pounding *hooves*.

Sophia was the child the mother most loved. Was this obvious? The mother hoped not.

Hallowe'en. How quickly it came each fall! No sooner were the children back in school, and it was Hallowe'en.

The mother had not ever liked Hallowe'en. The most discomforting of holidays, if that was what it was.

All Hallows' Eve, but now just Hallowe'en. No one knew what it meant and so it meant nothing. Skeletons, witches, black cats, death. Filmy cobwebs strung across front porches, cloth-bodies hanging by their necks from trees like lynching victims.

As if children have the slightest notion of death! And if a child did have such a notion, it was to understand that death was not funny.

Jessalyn had lost her own mother when she'd been in high school. The brick facade of the school festooned with ghostly figures, bright orange pumpkin cutouts, plastic skulls with hollows for eyes.

She'd helped put up these childish decorations, for Jessalyn was one of the good girls, and there is solace in such goodness.

She lacked the courage not to be *good*. Not even Whitey knew that.

Thinking how Hallowe'en encouraged young children to imagine that something exciting was imminent but the excitement never materialized. Your masks and costumes were just silly. Looking through the eyeholes of your friends' masks were their eyes. You saw *them*.

She'd lost the memory of her mother. A woman's face, a presence, a voice—fading like a Polaroid photo.

Though sometimes a vise tightened around her heart, she could scarcely breathe for yearning, grief. *Don't be silly. You are the mother now. This is what has happened to you.* At such times praying that she would die before Whitey, for she could not bear such a loss another time.

Ah, Whitey! He had claimed her as his, he had made her his young bride, he had promised never to abandon her.

"It was a more innocent time, when no one put razor blades into apples to give to children."

At the pumpkin market telling the children about her memories of Hallowe'en when she'd been a child.

A more innocent time: Had it been? Was any time innocent, except in retrospect?

So many pumpkins, and some grotesquely misshapen like gigantic goiters. The largest pumpkin resembled an obese person, orangey flesh melted to a circumference of five or more feet, weighing beyond thirty—fifty?—pounds; someone had carved clownish eyes, nose, mouth into this monstrosity, at which the children stared with repugnance.

In mockery Thom whistled.

"Looks like some fat lady. Christ!"

There was a sexual overtone to Thom's whistle, the mother did not care to acknowledge. Beverly retorted: "It looks just as much like some fat *man*."

But no, the misshapen pumpkin more resembled a female than a male. At fourteen Beverly was particularly sensitive to remarks about fleshiness, breasts and hips. Jessalyn drifted away, so that the children would follow.

Virgil was asking anxiously why did people put razor blades in apples?—to cut the mouths of trick-or-treaters? *Why*?

"Because some people don't like trick-or-treaters. Or children," Lorene said.

"Yes, but—*why*?"

To Jessalyn Lorene said, "Mom, I don't think that ever happened, razor blades in apples. Someone just made that up."

"Of course it happened! We read about it."

"Yes, you read about it, but it was all invented."

"My goodness, why?"

"Why? Why's anything invented?" At twelve Lorene was easily exasperated by her sweetly naive mother. "To get attention. To get the attention of credulous people."

Beverly too was easily exasperated, by her sister, whose fancy words she resented: "*You're* 'credulous.'"

Thom pointed out that there were "copycats" every Hallowe'en. Once the razor blade story began to circulate.

"So if there are copycats, there have to be actual razor blades," Beverly said loudly. "That proves it."

"Oh, stupid! Proves *what*?"

Like knives in a drawer, knocking together. The older children did not seem to like one another yet could not resist one another, vying for the attention of a parent—the mother, the (usually absent) father.

She did not like them, though she loved them. She loved them, though she did not (much) like them. They were all actors in a script who inhabited distinctive roles, that could not change.

Well, this was hardly true of the youngest children. *They* would change, the mother was sure. In unpredictable ways.

The little girl nudged against the mother's thigh. In public places Sophia liked her hand held, as if she might become lost from her mother otherwise. A small soft pliant hand, and the little girl nudging against her leg, in a way that broke the mother's heart.

Virgil had chosen a subtly misshapen pumpkin without a carved face. "His name is Jimmy Fox."

"Oh, you're so silly, Vir-gil! Why *Jimmy Fox*?"

"'Cause that's his name."

Thom lifted a heavy pumpkin, that slipped from his grasp, and shattered on the ground. "Damn! I'm sorry."

How casually Thom murmured *damn!*—as his father would have done. Jessalyn did not entirely approve yet felt a kind of pride in her adolescent son, for whom adulthood would be not much more difficult than putting on a succession of new clothes.

Beverly winced, and made a fastidious face. The shattered pumpkin was like a shattered head, the spilled seeds like *brains*.

There followed then some discussion whether Jessalyn would pay for the pumpkin. The farmer assured her that it was all right, just an accident, she did not have to pay; Jessalyn insisted of course she would pay. Thom said again that he was sorry, and offered to pay for the shattered pumpkin himself. (Thom had an after-school job bagging groceries and was intent upon saving his money.)

Primly Lorene said: "I think Thom should pay. He's always lifting things, showing off how strong he is, and breaking things. He should learn responsibility."

Thom said, hurt, "I didn't do it *on purpose*. I was just going to put it on that cart."

"You were showing off. You always are."

"*I was not.* I was helping Mom."

Jessalyn had been watching several girl bicyclists walking their bicycles at the pumpkin market. Their faces were flushed from the bright, chilly October air and their physical exertion. In fact they were not girls but women in their late twenties or early thirties, attractive in colorful tight-fitting spandex that fitted their lean bodies like gloves, and on their heads were shiny safety helmets, straps beneath their chins. Their bicycles were sleek, Italian-made, with low handlebars and raised seats and behind each seat, a bottle of Evian water.

One of the young women wore fingerless gloves! Jessalyn had never quite understood fingerless gloves.

These were serious bicyclists on an outing of many miles in Herkimer County, very likely along the cliff at Lake Ontario where the beauty of the choppy dark-blue water as well as the perpetual wind could take your breath away.

Jessalyn stared, and smiled. She saw the bicyclists' eyes move over her and the children, with only mild interest.

She thought—*I could be one of you.*

She felt a surge of elation. Heedless, mindless, thrilling. So staring, Jessalyn could scarcely look away from the bicyclists, to pay attention to what Sophia was saying, tugging at her hand.

Wait. Wait for me . . .

But the bicyclists were moving away. Three of them, conferring together. No pumpkins for them, with their sleek lightweight bicycles, and no wire baskets, and no children to impede their motion.

She had married the man who'd loved her. She had rejoiced in the man's love, she had allowed herself to be adored as a woman who was someone other than herself, and this woman she had become, to please the man who loved her. What was wrong with that? What was the mistake in that? Otherwise, the children would not exist. Virgil with his "Jimmy Fox" pumpkin, little Sophia squeezing her hand. Thom with his wallet in his hand and a wounded expression on his face, seriously intending to pay for the pumpkin he'd dropped onto the ground as his sisters looked on, bemused, jeering.

"Don't be silly, Thom. I'll pay."

"THANK YOU."

"Thank *you*."

She'd bought so many things at the farmers' market, her arms ached pleasantly.

Fresh produce, fresh flowers, jars of honey—she hadn't been able to resist. At each farmer's stand she'd said she was having a "large, family dinner" that weekend. At one stand she said that she and her husband were celebrating their fortieth anniversary.

"Congratulations, ma'am! Forty years . . ."

Important to her too, to distribute money among the farmers on this rainy market day. Seeing in their faces when they thought no one was observing expressions of disappointment, tiredness.

She had outlived her life, she thought. She had not been a mother to children who really needed her for many years. When the last child, Sophia, had left home years ago she'd wept but also drawn a deep breath of relief, or resignation.

Her life had come to a halt. So long as Whitey had been alive, she had not realized.

Like cotton candy in the rain. Easily melting, sugary and silly, of no consequence. Her soul.

NOT AT THE ZIDER ZEE Inn but at the smaller Dutchtown Café she'd met Thom, without Whitey knowing, or Brooke knowing. For Thom had said he had to see her, it was crucial.

Thom was in his early thirties at this time. His hair was still a burnished red-brown rising thick from his forehead. He had the look of a boy who'd wakened to find himself a young husband, father. Speaking with Jessalyn he'd rubbed his knuckles against his eyes in a way he'd done for most of his life, that made Jessalyn cringe, and want to snatch his hands away from his face.

She didn't feel that she could do that, any longer. Reach out and touch any one of her children, now "grown up."

Gravely he was saying to her, he didn't think that he could do it. He wasn't the one. Whitey had other, more suitable relatives—nephews, cousins.

"I don't love the business the way Dad does. I tried but—I just can't."

"Don't tell him, Thom! That would break his heart."

Jessalyn remembered now, with a pang of guilt.

The tarpaulin coverings flapped in the wind. A sad sound as of weak applause.

"NINE DOGS. SHELTER DOGS. Each one is precious to me. Each one is a life I have saved."

The rinsed-blond woman was named Risa. Earnestly she spoke to Jessalyn as if (almost) she wanted to take Jessalyn's hand.

She'd called out to Jessalyn excitedly as Jessalyn was being led to a table in the Zider Zee Inn. For an instant Jessalyn had been tempted to turn away, pretend she hadn't heard; she'd asked the hostess if she might be seated out in the glassed-in porch where long ago she'd taken the children for Lorene's birthday, and where she and Whitey had sometimes dined. But Jessalyn was too polite to reject the rinsed-blond woman, who was looking so hopefully at her.

"Hel-lo! What a coincidence! Will you join me?"

Jessalyn smiled faintly. Of course.

"Or are you meeting someone?"

"I—I—I am meeting my husband, but not until later. He's working, in Hammond and is joining me later . . ."

"*My* husband isn't working, and he isn't 'joining me later.'"

The rinsed-blond woman laughed as if she'd said something witty, if obscure.

Risa Johnston. Jessalyn McClaren. As they introduced themselves

Jessalyn saw the woman frown slightly hearing "McClaren" as if (perhaps) she recognized it; but she said nothing which was both a relief to Jessalyn and a disappointment.

Risa was having a glass of wine. Would Jessalyn join her?

"I don't think so, thank you."

"Oh, come on! Our husbands won't know."

Jessalyn laughed, hesitantly. She could not escape the conviction that Whitey knew everything about her including much that she did not (yet) know herself.

It was Risa's second glass. Very dry white wine.

"I love this old inn. Didn't General Washington or some other patriot stay here, once? Or did the British have a garrison here? Also I love the farmers' market. I feel that those are real people, real Americans—like those poor whites in Walker Evans's photographs. And their fresh produce is so superior to anything we can get in Chautauqua Falls in a *store*."

Chautauqua Falls was an affluent suburban community not unlike North Hammond, nearer Rochester. Jessalyn had no choice but to remark that she lived in North Hammond.

"Oh, North Hammond! We'd almost bought a house there, on Highgate Road. D'you know it?"

"Yes . . . I think so."

"You must know—"

There followed some minutes during which the women sought to determine whom they knew in common, in their respective towns. Quite a few persons! Jessalyn lifted her wineglass to her lips but took only the smallest of sips. *Oh God help me. No.*

Badly she did not want to be here. She felt like a blundering moth that has become entangled in a spider's web, all smiling and unknowing. Yet she could not escape the cheerily animated Risa Johnston for such behavior would be not only impolite but also desperate.

Risa was telling Jessalyn how she'd started adopting shelter dogs a few years ago. Not when the last of her children had left home—*that* had been years earlier.

"Oh, what peace! Everyone said, 'Your house is so large, why do you need such a large house, don't you miss your children, it must be awfully lonely, that place is practically a *mausoleum*'—but I just laughed and said, 'I love my own space!—lots of it.'"

Jessalyn smiled, for she saw (to her relief) that the rinsed-blond woman meant to be entertaining, and not serious. And the lunch would not last beyond an hour or so, if Jessalyn hurried it along.

"There was an advertisement on television about abandoned dogs. Especially pit bulls. How most of them are euthanized because there are not enough homes for them. And pit bulls most of all—a misunderstood breed associated with drug dealers and dogfighting."

Jessalyn listened as Risa related (airily, laughingly) a complicated tale of bringing dogs home, and her husband's reaction—"'As long as you take care of them, and keep them away from me'—that was about it. Pike isn't the most observant of men." After several dogs the husband told Risa no more; but Risa (cleverly!) kept the dogs in separate parts of the house, so that the husband never quite realized how many dogs she had adopted.

Risa laughed, delighted. Jessalyn smiled, for in a way it was delightful.

"Our house is large—'French Normandy.' It *is* like a mausoleum on wet, dark days. The dogs have the entire third floor to themselves—and the rear lawn, which is about two acres, so they can run, and run. And sometimes I run with them, when Pike isn't around to observe."

Pike. Jessalyn assumed that this was the husband's name, uttered with a downward twist of Risa's crimson lips.

"Do you like dogs, Jessalyn? Do you have pets? They bring such happiness into our lives."

Jessalyn could not say the bleak words *Yes. I have a cat*.

"The relationship between a human being and an animal—(so-called: we are all 'animals' of course)—can be as profound as human relationships. And since human relationships are unreliable, and never fail to disappoint, relationships with animals can be more meaningful."

Risa had begun speaking pedantically, and ended almost vehemently. She signaled the waitress for another glass of wine.

"Maybe we should order lunch . . . It's very late, the kitchen will close."

"Nonsense. They should be grateful that they have any customers at all for lunch here on this dreary day, in this dreary place."

Jessalyn was thinking that it had been a mistake to come to the Zider Zee Inn for such a sentimental, futile reason. Her last visit here—Lorene's birthday lunch—hadn't even been a very enjoyable experience. But she had not eaten yet that day, and worried about being light-headed on the drive back alone to the house on Old Farm Road.

Her health, on the whole, did not worry her. Vaguely she felt a tug of guilt, that she had not sickened, collapsed, died long before now. For after all, Whitey had died: why was she (still) alive? (This question seemed to her reasonable, and she did not doubt that many others thought it reasonable, too. She did not doubt that most widows felt exactly this way.) A relatively mild attack of shingles had come and gone in November leaving only striations in the flesh of her upper back that sometimes quivered with pain like a zipper being rapidly unzipped; there were headaches, at unpredictable times; more often there was shortness of breath, an airy lightness in the brain that felt like a window shutter being rapidly opened and closed.

She'd been unpleasantly surprised, the historic old Zider Zee Inn must have been sold to new owners. The gray shingleboard exterior that had once looked romantically weathered as a barn in an Ansel Adams oil painting had been replaced with stark gray asphalt siding; the old lattice windows had been replaced with plate glass; crabgrass flourished along the meandering front walk of cracked paving stones. The building was attached to a windmill with painted pale-gray blades, and these creaked in the wind like arthritic limbs. The interior, that had once been decorated with nineteenth-century artifacts and old, sepia photographs of windmills, was now decorated in a bland, generic style, with full-color photographs of Disney-looking windmills.

Even the waitstaff seemed wrong somehow, too young, not so very well dressed (pullovers, jeans and khakis, even shorts) and at this hour of the afternoon (past two o'clock) clearly waiting for the few, straggling customers to leave.

Through a window Jessalyn could see the shadows of the windmill blades, haltingly moving on the scruffy grass. The sky was splotched with rain clouds like daubs of gray paint. One look at this Zider Zee "historic" Inn and Whitey would have rolled his eyes and said *OK, we're out of here.* Not even sentiment would have drawn Whitey back to their old favorite place in all of Herkimer County.

If they'd had a final meal here, Whitey would have been distracted by his cell phone. For Whitey was never not connected, as by an umbilical cord, with his office, with his work. Always there were crises at McClaren, Inc.—failed or unsatisfactory printings, deliveries, inexplicable behavior on the part of a client, financial urgencies of which Whitey, on an "outing" with his dear wife, did not care to speak.

Obliquely, Whitey might complain of Thom to Jessalyn. For he would not—ever—complain of his son to anyone at McClaren, Inc.

His heart just doesn't seem in it. He's making money, why isn't that enough? Does he ever talk to you, Jess?

Jessalyn was finding it difficult to pay attention to Risa's chatter which was having the effect upon her of hearing fingernails being tapped, rapidly against a tabletop.

"Do you have a family, Jesamine? Children?"

Jessalyn didn't trouble to correct the mispronunciation. What did it matter who she was, of course it did not matter.

"Yes. But they're all grown up." Trying for a flippant tone, to deflect this line of questioning.

"Well—I should hope so! At our age, we hardly want *children*."

Risa was being flattering, perhaps. For she must have been younger than Jessalyn by as many as ten years.

"Grandchildren?"

Jessalyn shook her head, *no*.

And now Granma Jess was denying her own grandchildren? Jessalyn could imagine Beverly's look of incredulity and disapproval at such a betrayal.

Oh but it was too much effort to speak of the grandchildren to a stranger, to register the proper enthusiasm and pride in them required on such occasions! That she might be spared seeing the grinning grandchildren of others, she did not proffer pictures of her own.

But Risa laughed, and lowered her voice. "Lucky you, Jesamine! My grandchildren are terribly boring, and expensive. One is a bossy little spoiled thing and the other is a bossy little spoiled thing. My daughters—(I have two, both have young children and one is missing a husband, and that *is* expensive)—seem to think that I owe them something, just for having babies." Risa paused, frowning. A glint in her eye announced an imminent witticism. "You'd think they were pandas, having babies is such a *feat*."

Jessalyn laughed, uncertainly. The rinsed-blond woman seemed eager to be entertaining, and Jessalyn had not the heart to withhold an animated response.

"I've been married for sixty-six years." Risa laughed, and shook her head. "I mean, it feels like sixty-six years." Like a stand-up comedian pausing for a beat to add: "To the same husband. You don't get prison sentences that long even for homicide, if you're white-skinned."

As if encouraged by Jessalyn's response Risa went on to confide in her that she and Pike had not made love—"in any identifiable way"—for the past eleven years; possibly longer, for Risa had not been "paying strict attention."

Jessalyn laughed, now giddily. It occurred to her that she had not laughed since the previous October.

For what is *laughter*? Without hope, there is none.

At last their food was brought. Cups of creamed asparagus soup, salads heaped high on plates. The meals were served by a smirking young waiter in sandals, bare feet. Young enough to be a son—no, young enough to be a grandson, or nearly.

Neither woman was eating with much appetite. Jessalyn regretted the thick, clotted asparagus soup that clung to the spoon like paste.

"Waiter? One more glass of wine, thank you."

"Yes, ma'am."

"Fuck *ma'am*. Just bring the wine—two glasses, in fact."

The smirking young waiter ceased smirking, and staggered away in shock. Jessalyn could not quite believe what she'd heard, and so decided that she had not heard it.

How had her wineglass *emptied*? That was unexpected.

Whitey had often complained, his dear wife so rarely drank. Not much fun to drink (at home) alone, was it?

No wonder they had to go out with others, who drank. Often.

Whitey would've winced, seeing his precious whiskeys, gins, bourbons poured down the sink. But the widow did not dare keep such lethal medication close at hand.

Handful of sleeping pills, several shot-glasses of whiskey. *We're out of here!*

Risa was making witty remarks about their rings. Jessalyn's, and her own.

"*Yours* are very beautiful, Jesamine. But mine aren't bad, either."

"No. Yes. Your rings are lovely."

Risa held out her left hand, that was slightly tremulous. Her engagement ring was a large square-cut diamond in an old-gold setting, that matched her wedding ring.

"It's the least we expect of rings, that they cost somebody something." Risa laughed, heartily. The skin on the back of her hand was blue-veined and creased with myriad small wrinkles.

When Jessalyn failed to laugh at this remark Risa leaned forward against the table, to peer at her.

"Jesamine? What did you say your husband does?"

"I—I didn't say."

"Well—what does he do?"

"He's—retired. He'd been in a family business for most of his life and—he—has decided to retire."

"Oh, that's a mistake! You shouldn't have let him retire. Without anyone to boss around, a man just *mopes*."

Jessalyn wanted to protest, her husband had not ever *bossed her around*. He had not ever *moped*.

"Did you say that your husband is coming here? Coming to meet you at the inn?"

"Coming to meet me?—no." Jessalyn couldn't recall what she'd told the rinsed-blond woman. "I mean—I think—I am going to meet him—soon . . ."

"He's coming to Dutchtown? Will you introduce us?"

"No! I mean—he won't be here for—a few hours . . . We're going to spend the night at the inn, it's an anniversary."

"That's very sweet. Which anniversary is it?"

"Our thirty-eighth."

"Thirty-*eighth*. That's tinfoil, I think. No—Styrofoam stuffing."

Jessalyn frowned at the other's mirth. Her wineglass was in her hand, and her hand was trembling.

"We're—we're waiting to hear—this afternoon—if I will be allowed to donate blood marrow. Bone marrow. If my husband is strong enough for the operation. If I am strong enough."

Jessalyn spoke softly, near-inaudibly. These breathless and totally unexpected words issued from her mouth with a taste of something dry and smarting.

Wide-eyed Risa stared at her. For the first time Jessalyn saw that the rinsed-blond woman had fine, near-invisible scars at her hairline, like commas. And her hair, sleekly blond against her head, was a dull, dim hue at the roots as if her soul were oozing out of her scalp.

"Ohhh. You must be very brave."

Quickly Jessalyn stammered: "Not—not brave at all. I guess—I am desperate . . ."

Laughing, for the wine had gone to her brain. Her laughter was the sound of something small, shattering into smaller bits.

(But why was this funny?) (It was not funny.)

Soberly Risa said: "I hope that the surgery turns out well, Jasmine. A bone marrow transplant can't be fun. And yes, to me you are brave. Desperation can make people brave and perhaps that is the sincerest kind of bravery."

What fantastical remarks! Why were they saying such things?

The very marrow in the widow's bones had turned to ice.

Risa persisted, with a cooing sound: "That is sooo generous of you, Jasmine. I would not have that kind of courage. And my husband, well"—the woman laughed, lowering her head—"he doesn't deserve it, maybe. He'd never do anything remotely so selfless for *me*."

"Oh but I'm sure that he would . . ."

"Really! *You're* sure? But you don't know my husband, Pike, and you don't know me."

Jessalyn knew herself rebuked. She was feeling stunned, distracted. She had very little idea what she and the rinsed-blond woman were talking about.

Thinking: in fact, her blood was (probably) not so good. Not hale, hearty. Iron deficiency anemia.

Sophia's friend Dr. Means had suggested this, gently. He'd run his fingertips over her nails when they'd shaken hands, and remarked that they seemed "brittle."

A rare occasion indeed, when Sophia allowed her mother to meet a male friend of hers. ("But you must not tell anyone especially Beverly and Lorene. Please, Mom! Promise.")

Alistair Means might have been twenty-five years Sophia's senior, a gentlemanly man with a distinctive Scots accent. He was not much taller than Sophia. He'd been very courteous to Jessalyn. He'd seemed somewhat ill at ease as Sophia's companion, perhaps because of the difference in age, and Sophia's oddly stiff, awkward manner with him in the presence of her mother.

Jessalyn had prepared a meal for the three of them. To a neutral observer she and Means might have been the staid parental couple, Sophia the schoolgirl daughter with shy eyes, wary smile.

SOPHIA HAD BEEN EMBARRASSED that her friend had been so forward with Jessalyn but Jessalyn had not minded at all—she'd been touched. The kind of forwardness that is protective, Whitey would have appreciated.

Blood work. Means had urged her to make an appointment with her physician, soon. For it seemed that Means was a doctor as well as a distinguished research scientist.

And Whitey hovered near. In the beating of her blood she could hear him, trying for a lighter tone.

Take care of yourself, darling! You are all I have.

The hostess at the Zider Zee was a stranger. Much too young to remember the couple, from years ago.

They had held hands. They had talked and murmured together, laughed together. (But what had they said? All lost.)

She'd worn a wide-brimmed hat made of a fabric like black lace, though thicker and more durable than lace. She'd worn a pearl-colored dress with thin black vertical stripes. Around her slender neck, a strand of perfect pearls. Her face, lovely and inconsequential, for it was a face that could not endure, was partly hidden by olive-tinted glasses. This had been a time when Jessalyn had looked chic, or what had passed for *chic*.

She must try not to laugh at herself, the innocent vanity of the young, thirty years later.

The lake was shimmering choppy water, an inland sea. Like molten flame at sunset. He'd said he was so happy, sometimes it scared him—like reaching to grasp a fallen wire, a wire through which electric current is flowing, that might kill you, but how can you resist?—you cannot.

My dearest wife. I will love you—forever! Into the next world. I swear.

Vaguely she'd thought, before Risa had called out to her, that she might take a room at the inn. As she and Whitey had fantasized they might but had not. Not once. She would lie on the unfamiliar four-poster bed, on a quilt. Fully dressed, for she would not have the energy to remove her clothing. Antique furniture, showing its age. A single window overlooking rain-pocked, choppy Lake Ontario, with sun-faded drapes. Would there be a storm? Lightning?

Hurricane lamps, musty-smelling embroidered pillows, horsehair mattress. On the walls silhouettes of long-ago women, pioneer women, gentlemen with white lace at their cuffs. In the eyes of the long-deceased, that look of shared bewilderment—*Who were we? Who did we imagine we were? What has become of us?*

All this while Risa was chattering. Or was that grating sound Risa's (crimson-polished, just slightly chipped) fingernails drumming against the tabletop.

Risa was impressed with Jessalyn, it seemed—the brave selfless wife eager to donate bone marrow for a sick husband. But Risa was becoming impatient with the wife's *goodness,* possibly.

She'd excused herself, to veer in the direction of a women's room. Jessalyn felt the relief of a brief respite, the rinsed-blond woman's (welcome) absence.

Thinking: you are not, strictly speaking, a "widow" at such times when your (theoretical) husband is not present. So long as the husband is (seemingly) elsewhere, his absence/non-existence is not detectable.

Rehearsing to say to Risa—*Oh but please don't worry! My husband is traveling in—Australia . . . He is not here but that does not mean he is not somewhere.*

Fact is, she'd betrayed the husband. Her desperate need to leave the house on Old Farm Road.

But then, once away from the house, her desperate need to hurry back.

Except: she'd been having trouble breathing. Increasingly in May, in premature heat. Whitey had no idea, he'd never had any idea, how he sucked up the oxygen in any space he inhabited.

She'd found herself desperate for air. Driving in the countryside away from Hammond. In motion, not yet where she is headed, the widow is undefined, like a face blurred by water.

The Dutchtown Farmers' Market had not been a bad idea except she'd bought too much. Wanting to make purchases, give away money, see faces lighten, that had been dimmed by Saturday rain.

Whitey had always liked to spend money, leave large tips. He'd quoted—was it Hemingway?—making people happy is easy to do, just leave large tips.

The Zider Zee Inn had been a mistake but an innocent mistake. Such beauty in the long rolling hills of northern Herkimer County. Derelict farmhouses, abandoned farm equipment, hulks of automobiles and pickup trucks in front yards. PRODUCE AUCTION—a billboard just outside Dutchtown. Newer houses with asphalt siding, "ranch" houses and A-frames. Mayflower Movers, Rent-a-Truck. Late May, the season for house sales and for moving. The effort of a new life, new furniture and Formica-topped kitchen counters, not-yet-scuffed hardwood floors—these filled the widow with despair.

Driving restlessly. Scarcely knowing, or caring, where she was headed. Goaded by impatient drivers behind her into accelerating her speed, taking turns above the speed limit. When she'd been alive the widow had never behaved in such a way.

Mom for God's sake, what are you doing so far from home . . .

What would Daddy say!

"All I really want is to avoid self-pity."

(To whom had she made this pronouncement? Herself? Whitey?)

It was at the Zider Zee Inn that Whitey had first told Jessalyn, elated, yet somewhat frightened, that his first full year at McClaren, Inc. had been profitable beyond even his own optimistic expectations.

(Of course, Whitey McClaren wasn't an optimist. If you knew Whitey, you knew that the man was a pessimist. His poker playing habits made this clear. But a pessimist can play at optimism better than any optimist, for a pessimist has no expectations to defeat him.)

By cutting back on their many small clients, cultivating just a few rich, prestigious clients, predominantly pharmaceutical companies, McClaren, Inc. would itself become rich, maybe. Looked like it. Maybe.

Like skiing down a steep slope expecting to fall on your ass, or break your neck, Whitey had said, gloating. But you don't. Instead, applause.

She'd wanted to protest no. Please no. We don't need to be rich—we need only to be happy.

(She'd had a suspicion that she was pregnant, on that very day. A big baby it would be, seven pounds, husky and hale, they would name Thom, for one of Whitey's beloved brothers who'd died a young and pointless death in Vietnam.)

"There is no door. There is not even a window. The wall is all there is."

(To whom had she said *this*? Not Whitey, for Whitey disliked pompous-sounding remarks.)

Everywhere the widow goes, *alone* accompanies her.

Creaking windmill blades. Paralytic limbs, barely moving.

Why had they ever thought this place charming? *Had* it been charming, once? Whitey wouldn't have consented to return, he had better things to do. His favorite restaurants were dark-paneled steak houses attached to upscale hotels where the best malt whiskey was served.

It was a posthumous life, this masquerade. She knew better.

She'd missed the opportunity to end it. The masquerade. That night at the creek, a rushing current in which she might have drowned, she'd been prepared but had lacked moral courage. Whitey had too easily dissuaded her.

An easy way of dying, a cowardly way, would be to simply cease eating. But she hadn't even the courage for that, probably. When she forgot to eat, or was nauseated at the thought, a headache began to take shape behind her eyes, like a metallic flower opening.

Symmetrical, beautiful, yet sharply metallic, opening inside her brain. An exquisite pain that, once begun, had to be allowed to open fully—it could not be stopped by Tylenol or aspirin.

No. If the widow tried to starve herself she would end up devouring anything edible she could get her hands on. Eating like an animal, shameless. Like Mack the Knife when she'd first put out food for him on the rear deck. Quivering animal, squint-eyed and his ribs protruding through his matted fur. That squinting yellow eye.

The rinsed-blond woman had returned to their table. There was a jut to her chin Jessalyn hadn't noticed before. Doggedly Risa would return to their subject as if she'd been rehearsing an argument in the women's room. But Jessalyn said:

"People do things you don't expect. Sometimes."

Hoping to encourage her companion who'd drained her second, unless it was her third, glass of wine—urging the woman to think generously of herself, in the matter of bone marrow transplants, organ donations. But Risa seemed to have lost her effervescence, or her capacity for humor. Almost, Jessalyn could smell her companion's soured breath.

"Real-ly! You think so, 'Jasm'en.'"

"Well—yes. I think so."

Jessalyn was sounding uncertain. Something about the other's wetly steely eye was disconcerting.

"What's wrong with your husband, exactly, Jasm'en?"

"What's wrong? I—I'm not sure—a rare kind of blood cancer, that attacks the marrow . . ."

"Something like lymphoma?"

"Y-Yes."

"But lymphoma attacks the lymph nodes. Maybe you mean myeloma?"

"I'm—not sure . . ."

"Could be leukemia."

"I think—yes. That's it."

"My first husband died of leukemia."

"Oh." Jessalyn was stunned. The vision came to her of one of her own children, very young, caught in a blatant lie.

"It was a generation ago, and more. He'd be the age of my son now, and he wouldn't cast a second glance at me. The bastard."

Jessalyn groped for something to say. “That’s—very sad. I’m so sorry to hear that.”

“Oh, don’t be! You’re too damned polite. What the hell do you care about my husband, if I don’t? Water under the bridge.”

Risa laughed, wiping at her mouth with a napkin, and leaving a rude lipstick smudge on the white linen. In a bemused, gravelly voice she continued: “Just on TV or in movies, or old-fashioned novels, where people donate blood, or bone marrow, or kidneys to one another. Hardly ever in real life where you see one another every damn day and run up against one another like damn bumper cars. And if you use the same bathroom, forget it”—Risa drew her finger swiftly across her throat.

Jessalyn seemed to consider this, respectfully. Her heart beat hard in opposition but she would not reply.

Daring to hope that this stressful and interminable lunch was ending, or had ended. She began to reach for her handbag as Risa spoke scornfully:

“Y’know—you think pretty highly of yourself, Jesamine, don’t you? Your husband you want to donate bone marrow for. Man, we are impressed!” Risa mimed applause, glancing about the near-emptied dining room. “Think he’d do the same for you?”

Jessalyn was baffled by the rinsed-blond woman’s sudden hostility.

“Y-Yes. He would.”

“You’re sure of that? *Love* rhymes with *smug*—don’t it?”

Jessalyn groped for her handbag—grasped it. Time to leave!

She’d come to wonder if Whitey had thrown away his life, possibly. For her. Traded his life for an ideal of himself, the man he’d wished his dear wife to admire. He had not been that man, perhaps. But he’d fashioned himself into that man, brave, reckless, so manly a man, daring to brake his vehicle to a stop on the Expressway, to confront two police officers young enough to be his sons, to halt a murderous rampage.

For you, darling. All that I did, I did for you.

He was not accusing her. Never would Whitey accuse *her.*

“Let me. Please.”

Desperate to escape she was appropriating the check. She would pay with a credit card, not even glancing at the bill. For it was like Whitey to appropriate restaurant bills. But Risa did not appreciate the gesture. "Think you're pretty damned superior, don't you. Every damn word you've uttered, boasting and gloating. Think I can't pay for my own fucking meal, I have more money at my disposal, Jez-lyn, than you—I bet! And know what?—You should cut your 'snowy-white' hair, you look like a hillbilly. You are *not chic*."

Quickly, fearfully, Jessalyn paid the bill. The hostess was staring at livid-faced Risa, and then trying not to stare, trying not to overhear.

But in the parking lot Jessalyn could not escape in time. The rinsed-blond woman pursued her, coming very close to her. Slurred words, accusations. Jessalyn was utterly astonished, frightened.

"You have no respect for other people, do you? People less 'blessed' than yourself. D'you know how it feels, hearing you boast about a husband you'd die for, and he'd die for you, bullshit, nobody dies for anybody else, d'you know how it feels to hear such bullshit, for other people? And who are *you*? Wait! Don't you walk away from me!"

Jessalyn was trembling badly. She had not—ever—been so confronted by another person in her life; certainly not in her adult life.

Her car keys were in her hand but the rinsed-blond woman drew near quick as a cat, and snatched them from her, and tossed them into a path of tall wet grasses with a little cry of malice.

Jessalyn had to search for the keys in the grass, trying not to break into tears. Risa stomped away, to her car.

On her knees in the sharp-bladed grass. The air was wet, a light rain continued to fall. Whitey had abandoned her after all, he was nowhere near.

A creaking sound of the windmill blades turning in the wind. The very sound of futility, vanity. And in the distance a raucous sound of crows. She was groping with outstretched fingers in what appeared to be marsh grass, for the car keys without which she could not return to her home.

Something black passed over her brain. A black-feathered wing, a flash of talons. Months ago she'd been frightened of going mad, of something in her brain cracking, shattering like glass: but that had not happened. At her most unhappy, she remained sane. Was that her punishment?—an irrevocable and implacable sanity.

ON HER HANDS AND KNEES, *groping for the keys.*

She slips, falls. She is so very tired. The keys are lost, she must abandon the keys. Retaining her life is all that matters.

Thick sinuous tendrils of mud. Mud like writhing snakes. In her throat, in her lungs. The lungs are a mysterious organ—organs. So suddenly, the lungs can collapse.

Can't breathe. Choking, suffocating—her mouth is parched with mud.

But Whitey is beside her, quick and capable. Whitey has never been away but Whitey has been observing.

He has a pocketknife—his Swiss Army knife, he'd had since he'd been a boy. With the sharp point of the knife he performs a tracheotomy on his dear helpless choking wife—(she recalls: he'd been an Eagle Scout, he'd learned first aid).

Blood spurts through the hole in her throat but it is therapeutic, it will save her.

You can breathe through this hole, darling *Whitey consoles her.* Just to make sure, I'll insert this.

An ordinary straw pushed into the little bloody hole, into her trachea. The wound is so small, the knife blade is so sharp, she hardly feels pain only just a comforting numbness like ether.

Within a few seconds the congestion thins. She is breathing, if barely.

Through this straw you can breathe. It is all that you need. Do not ask for more.

Keziahaya

In his bed uttering the name aloud—*Keziahaya.*

Marveling at the sound—*Keziahaya.*

Not a soft or a weak or a wishing-to-please sound but harsh strident singular syllables—*Keziahaya.*

Others at the farm called the boisterous six-foot-four young Nigerian *Amos* but that was a weak-seeming name, a biblical name. The true name was the African—*Keziahaya.*

Sleepless in his bed in the cabin with a tin roof hammering rain and in the most exquisite misery—*Keziahaya.*

In the anguish of muted love uttering the name aloud—*Keziahaya.*

"NEED ANY HELP?"—casually he'd asked the young black man with the scarred cheeks.

The answer had not been *yes* but it had not been unambiguously *no.*

Mumbling thanks, maybe later. *OK?*

It was a speech-habit of Keziahaya to amend virtually all his remarks with *OK.*

Could be a flat statement—*OK,* or a question—*OK?*

Like punctuation. A verbal tic. So that no remark of his was truly final but provisional.

And the broad quick smile that stretched the lower part of his face. The squinting gaze that puckered skin at the corners of his eyes.

Is he wary of me? Fearful of me? Because I am white? Because I am a stranger?—Virgil wondered.

That luxury of wonder the love-object evokes. Luxury of anticipation, anxiety. Luxury of dread, yearning. Luxury of not-knowing.

Virgil was offering to help others pack their things, to bring to the Chautauqua Arts & Crafts Fair in his Jeep pickup. It would not seem exceptional for Virgil to invite the Nigerian who was new to the sprawling farmhouse on Bear Mountain Road and whose first exhibit at the fair this would be.

It was Virgil McClaren's reputation locally, to be a friend to other artists. You did not have to like Virgil's work, nor did Virgil have to like your work, for him to befriend you in a common cause.

Some thought Virgil McClaren not a serious artist because he was (rumor had it) the heir of a well-to-do father, others thought him a serious artist because (rumor had it) he'd been disinherited by this father who'd been a wealthy businessman.

Some knew the name *McClaren*. Some knew how John Earle McClaren had died, or it had been charged he'd died, as a consequence of police brutality. Some knew that a lawsuit had been filed against the Hammond police by the McClaren family but no one could have said what had happened to this lawsuit, if it had been settled, or dismissed, or continued still in that subterranean way of lawsuits after their first spiking news in the media.

Not even Virgil's closest friends knew whether Virgil was involved in the McClaren lawsuit for Virgil rarely spoke of his family. It was a belief of his that the family is but the personal expression of the spirit, and it is only the impersonal expression that prevails.

So rarely did Virgil speak of his family, it was a surprise to some who knew him to realize that he had a (still living) mother, and several siblings.

Once or twice a younger sister came to visit Virgil in his cabin behind the farmhouse. But Virgil had not introduced this young woman to anyone and no one knew her name.

Several times a year as if in compliance with a mysterious algorithm Hammond County sheriff's deputies raided the farmhouse on Bear Mountain Road with a warrant empowering them to search for "controlled substances." Their claim was invariably that they'd received a tip from a confidential source but they had not yet found anything incriminating beyond a few marijuana cigarettes scattered amid some thirty or more residents. A virulent strain of crystal meth was rumored to be manufactured in the scrubby hills of the Chautauqua Mountains in derelict farmhouses resembling the farmhouse on Bear Mountain Road but no crystal meth, nor the paraphernalia involved in its manufacture, had ever been found in the farmhouse on Bear Mountain Road, or in the sparsely furnished cabin behind it.

Virgil feared that, if sheriff's deputies raided the farmhouse at the present time, they would single out the young Nigerian artist/teacher for particular harassment. Virgil had seen videos of (white) cops beating, Tasering, choking to death (black) men that filled him with dismay and outrage.

Virgil knew: Amos Keziahaya had been born in Lagos, Nigeria. His father had been a politician who'd come to a "bad end." Remnants of the family had fled the capital city of Abuja when Keziahaya was a child of two; they were Christian converts, and they were granted political asylum in the United States. Keziahaya had lived in various cities in northern New Jersey and had attended several colleges without graduating. He'd become a graffiti artist, so-called, in Paterson, New Jersey, who'd been one of the primary subjects of a PBS documentary on such artists. He was twenty-eight and looked both younger than this age and, in moments of repose, older. He could have no clear memory of Nigeria, Virgil supposed, yet, seeing him, Virgil felt a sweet, sinking sensation as if he were gazing into a past not his own.

So far as anyone knew Amos Keziahaya had no family in the vicinity of Hammond. He attended a local Christian church but he did not appear to be unusually religious. He'd had a New York State arts grant and taught printmaking and lithography at the State University at Hammond as an adjunct instructor with little possibility of a permanent job, like so many of the young instructors of Virgil's acquaintance.

Like Virgil McClaren, when Virgil had a job at all. Which wasn't often.

Keziahaya's skin was very dark, somewhat roughened, even pitted and scarred, whether from acne or some other more violent means wasn't evident. He had a big, blunt, affable face, thick-lashed protuberant eyes, a way of laughing that was hearty and explosive. His voice was a boy's voice, virtually a tenor, issuing strangely from that big body. He was shy, or shy-seeming. He could be loud, out of a kind of nervous excitement. He could be silent, sucking at his lips and watchful. He must have weighed at least 230 pounds and he stood a head taller than most of the residents in the sprawling farmhouse on Bear Mountain Road, and several inches taller than Virgil.

Strangely thrilling to Virgil, to be obliged to crane his neck and *look up* at Keziahaya.

To look elsewhere at Keziahaya, to allow his gaze to drift downward, past the muscled torso, in the area of the thighs and the groin, the imagined genitalia solid, heavy, smooth-skinned and darkly beautiful, was to risk feeling a sensation of weakness, faintness like a breath too swiftly exhaled.

"No. You will not."

So Virgil chided himself, lightly.

For there was still lightness in this—he had not yet acknowledged his desire, not another soul knew.

Alone of the residents of the farmhouse on Bear Mountain Road Keziahaya frequently wore white shirts, clean pressed khakis. He owned a navy blue blazer, and sometimes wore neckties.

Neckties! Virgil had not worn a necktie since high school graduation when ties for boys, and white shirts, had been obligatory. Even then, he'd had to borrow a tie from his father.

Keziahaya's dense-dark lusterless hair was trimmed short and shaved at the back and sides. His boy's smile was wide and yellow-tinctured.

On his left wrist, a digital watch with a stretch band and on his right wrist a bracelet that looked as if it were made of braided straw.

Keziahaya wore sandals, running shoes, hiking boots. His feet were of a remarkable size, like his neck, his hands, and his wrists.

Often, he wore a khaki-colored baseball cap bearing a logo incomprehensible to Virgil—(sports team? rock band?)—likely to be turned backward on his head.

"Amos! Can you give a hand?"—Virgil would hear someone call to Keziahaya and the vision came to him, Keziahaya extending his large strong dark-skinned hand for another to seize in gratitude.

At their first meeting in the most casual of circumstances in the sprawling farmhouse Virgil had experienced that sweet slipping-down sensation as if he wanted both to cry and to laugh; as if he wanted to fling himself forward, to grasp the other's hand, or to shrink away, to flee.

He'd been unhappy, then. In the aftermath of his father's death.

Kept a discreet distance from the other residents. As some residents, for instance his (former) friend Sabine, kept a discreet distance from him.

(Virgil wanted to protest, he had not meant to hurt Sabine. He never meant to hurt anyone. He was blundering, blind. He was clumsy, stupid, clueless. *Forgive me!*)

Even when he and Keziahaya shared meals at a long communal table Virgil took care not to appear over-eager to speak with the Nigerian as others did, or to linger after a meal in his company. Excused himself early, disappearing into his cabin behind the farmhouse.

It was the last thing Virgil wanted, to embarrass another person with the rawness of his emotions; especially, he did not want to embarrass Amos Keziahaya who was new to Hammond, and whom he scarcely knew.

Also, he feared making an utter fool of himself. That mocked, jeered-at, despised "effeminate" boy of middle school, high school whom he liked to think he had outgrown by an act of will.

All desire is ephemeral, rising and falling, fading, passing.

Of all desires carnal desire is the most treacherous for it is the serpent that sinks its poisonous teeth into its own being.

These were words of caution, wisdom. Virgil had given himself up to such wisdom and wished to feel that he was protected by it as a lead vest shields us from radiation.

It was true, Virgil's attraction for Keziahaya was not neutral. It was not Platonic though not (he told himself) physical, or carnal; he had not ever had a lover who was male, and (he told himself, hotly) he did not wish to have a (male) lover.

His feeling for Keziahaya was sheerly emotional. Sharply and crushingly emotional and not to be reasoned away in moments of calm.

Any damn freak, Virgil will fall for. Count on it!

So Whitey would say in disdain.

Or, rather Whitey would say in dismay of his younger son who had so disappointed him.

But Amos Keziahaya was no freak. Whitey would have been in awe of him if they'd ever met.

Anyway, the hell with Whitey. It was just Virgil now.

"**DON'T LET THOSE DEADBEATS TAKE** advantage of you, Virgil. You know how naive you are."

Deadbeats was his sister Beverly's word for persons unlike herself, whose standard of living was well below hers.

Naive was her word for *foolish, stupid*.

Virgil wanted to protest: his friends were not deadbeats but individuals, each unlike the others. In a loose and shifting commune they shared the sprawling farmhouse on Bear Mountain Road. Some of them were artists like Virgil, some farmed the property, a few were teachers and tutors. Their employment was likely to be part-time, seasonal. Their employment was not permanent, and did not provide medical or hospital coverage. The youngest was a college dropout of nineteen, the oldest an intermittently employed physical therapist, a woman, whose age hovered perennially just beneath forty. Who was involved with whom, which individuals were couples, or lovers, married, about-to-be-married, divorced—Virgil had no clear idea, and no actual interest, except in terms of Amos Keziahaya who lived alone and appeared to be unattached.

Keziahaya had come to stay in the farmhouse with friends originally, a married couple who'd taught at the college. Now this couple was gone, and Keziahaya had stayed.

How had it happened?—Virgil had become one of the longtime residents at Bear Mountain Road. He was thirty-one years old!

He'd assumed, when he'd first moved into the derelict cabin behind the farmhouse, and appropriated an even more derelict outbuilding for a studio, formerly a corncrib, that he would stay only a few months before "moving on."

Yet, that had not happened. Why, Virgil wasn't so sure.

(His older sisters were sure: Virgil was over-attached to their mother who, in turn, was over-attached to Virgil.)

(To a sibling, a sibling is "over-attached" to a parent if this "over-attachment" seems to exceed the "over-attachment" of the rival sibling.)

(Virgil did not dignify his older sisters' claims that he'd been "leeching"—or was it "mooching"—money from Jessalyn for years, without Whitey's knowledge. He did not attempt to rebuke his brother Thom's claim that he'd failed to grow up, *be a man* as Whitey had wished and [of course] Thom had done with such success.)

How furious his older siblings would be, if they knew how, with his inheritance from their father, Virgil had purchased a Jeep pickup which he made available to virtually anyone at the farm who needed it—a pack of *deadbeats*.

So long as the keys resided with Virgil, he could think of the vehicle as *his*.

Of course, few who used his truck filled the gas tank when they returned it to him. Often, the gas needle was delicately poised at just above *empty*—a kind of feat, Virgil had to admire.

At thirty-one he was magnanimous enough to understand: some individuals would exploit his generosity. He knew who they were beforehand, usually. And he'd allowed them to take advantage more than once. But he reasoned that he'd many times exploited others, including friends and lovers, including his parents, and so he could not reasonably object to being exploited himself.

Virgil paid more than his share for groceries and often did the shopping himself. He paid for upkeep on the property which was a rental property in which the (absentee) landlord had lost all interest.

He helped pay for a fellow resident's dental work, and he paid for another's emergency medical care following a tractor accident in one of the fields. He helped pay for, or indeed paid for, supplies for fellow artists including his (former) friend Sabine who now despised him. He'd even paid for what he assumed was a woman friend's abortion at a Rochester clinic. (Virgil hadn't asked questions, and he hadn't been provided with details.) He gave money to a local animal shelter, a wildlife sanctuary, a hospice. He volunteered hours each week at the animal shelter and at the hospice, bringing therapy dogs to be petted by the dying who sometimes mistook him for a son, a grandson, a brother or a husband.

Always it pierced Virgil to the heart, when one of these dying persons expressed surprise and hurt that he was leaving—"So soon? Oh, where are you going?"

Yet, he'd been avoiding his own family. His own mother whom (he would have said) he loved very much.

It was just that her widowhood was devastating to him. Her loneliness, the raw loss in her eyes, her face, the tremor of her touch—especially her effort to be cheerful, upbeat, "recovered" for his sake. He could not bear it, he was not that magnanimous.

And it was risky to him, how close he'd come several times to confessing to Jessalyn that he was the one who'd caused his father's death, not washing his hands adequately. Virgil, and the brutal Hammond cops . . .

Wanting to tell Jessalyn, but fearful of doing so. For she would forgive him—of course. He knew he did not deserve to be forgiven.

But one thing was clear: he hadn't ever accepted money from Jessalyn for himself. For others, but not for himself. He knew that his sisters were furious, that Jessalyn gave him money. He had too much pride to confront them, to deny this. They wouldn't have believed him anyway, they so resented him.

But now, with Whitey's money, he was set for (the remainder of his) life. He'd have liked to tell his family except here too, he had too much pride.

Squandering our parents' money. Deadbeat!

There were persons at the farm who had only to hint to Virgil that they were in need of financial help and he would give them, that's to say "lend" them, money. Family emergencies, college tuition, interest payments and mortgages, fines and fees . . . He was running through the money his father had left him, fascinated by its disappearing as he'd been fascinated as a boy by an hourglass in his father's office through which sand flowed very slowly, thinly—inexorably.

"The difference between an hourglass and an actual hour," Whitey had said, "is that you can set the hourglass upside down and repeat the flow of sand. An actual hour, you can never repeat."

Virgil had thought—*Good!*

Age twelve or thirteen you know you will live forever. Who could care about *reliving* an hour?

Virgil's volunteer work brought him no income, of course. From time to time he worked at about the minimum wage for local employers, or taught a course at the community college, as a way of forestalling the day when his inheritance would run out, inexorably.

He'd said to Sophia that maybe, just maybe, the money from Whitey had been meant to last his entire life and when it ran out, his life would run out, too.

Sophia had not laughed. Sophia had looked away from Virgil, upset by what he'd said.

He'd had to assure his sister, he wasn't serious.

Sophia had not seemed placated. Wiping irritably at her eyes saying the same terrible thought had occurred to her about her own inheritance but of course it was unthinkable.

Yes! Unthinkable.

Not serious.

Still, it was something to consider. For he'd caused his father's death, and no one knew.

Thinking such thoughts while driving the Jeep pickup. On the steep foothill road traversing Bear Mountain. Descending to the Chautauqua River. A sensation of weightlessness, elation. Imagining that the steering wheel and the brake pedal have been disconnected from the engine and there is no control over the speeding vehicle, you are in free fall . . .

In a dream Virgil wrenched at the steering wheel, pressed the brake pedal to the floor. Nothing happened, the vehicle careened and plunged off the road *but it was not Virgil's fault.*

Then, Amos Keziahaya entered Virgil's life and life became suddenly precious to him again.

SINCE HIS FATHER'S DEATH. This new self pushing through.

Like buried statuary of the ancient, Hellenic world. Shifting of earth, astonishing shapes of beauty and terror emerging out of the rubbled earth at Pergamon.

His newest work mimicked this emergent being. He'd modeled a waxen-white figure after the *Dying Gaul:* the dying self, bound with twine, wire, aluminum strips.

Suddenly then his sleep was haunted by heraldic art. Heroic art.

He'd driven to New York City to see classic Greek statues at the Metropolitan Museum, he'd felt his heart pierced and numbed by such beauty, and more than beauty. Transcendent art, so very different from his scrap-metal art . . . And mixed in with his feeling for the young Nigerian which was a kind of white-hot welder's tool, galvanizing, liquefying all that it touched.

A succession of bodies. Humanoid figures, scarecrows, mannequins overlaid with wax. Bound tightly as in a straitjacket. Faces obscured like something that has melted. (Male) genitalia obscured beneath bandage-like swaths of coarse white cloth.

His body: the white man.

The paradox: you do not know that you are "white" until you encounter the other—the "black."

Recalling the sculpted Greek hermaphrodite figure, a beautiful smooth female back, limbs; male genitalia visible from one side. Could he, Virgil, dare such a transgression, in Hammond, New York? To be displayed at the Chautauqua Arts & Crafts Fair?

He had to laugh. Ridiculous.

He had to laugh. The prospect was terrifying.

Many nights too excited to sleep. Lights in his studio, in his cabin, through the night. Blindly he worked, his vision was inward, inchoate. His previous work, junk-metal sculptures, collages of domestic utensils, clothes, images from popular culture of decades ago and many in the shapes of animals, affable to the eye, charming, saleable, now seemed to him childish, trivial.

Whitey's death, and the emergence of Amos Keziahaya into his life.

Never had Virgil encountered any presence like Keziahaya's—he could not have said why. Never anyone who so inspired him as an artist, whom he scarcely knew and often tried to avoid.

"Don't you like Amos, Virgil?"—a friend asked; and Virgil retorted, "Of course I like Amos, everyone likes Amos!"—coming very close to saying *Everyone loves Amos.*

So parched for life, for joy, for hope since Whitey's death! Sometimes Virgil's heart pounded with tachycardia, scarcely could he bear this happiness.

Observing Keziahaya leaving the farmhouse in the morning. Striding to his car. In cold weather, breath steaming. The tall big-bodied figure boyish in eagerness. Keziahaya resembled Muhammad Ali when Ali had been Cassius Clay—that young. A kind of young-male bravado in the reversed baseball cap as there was a kind of melancholy-adult formality in the navy blue blazer and necktie.

Was Virgil jealous when he saw Keziahaya speaking with others?—walking with others? Driving away with one or another individual in his car, headed for the state university campus?

Women were attracted to Keziahaya, of course.

A look of almost dazzlement in Keziahaya's face, confronted by a woman, or a girl.

Did Keziahaya see them as *white*? Virgil wondered. Or did he see them as *female,* and the color of their skin not relevant.

The issue of Keziahaya's sexuality. *Do not go there.*

Sometimes it did happen, to Virgil's embarrassment, that Keziahaya noticed Virgil and lifted a hand in greeting, and smiled, or grinned—if they were outdoors, and each headed for his vehicle.

How're you doing? OK?

OK. And you?

Virgil was the one to turn away. Trembling, and his jaws rigid with smiling.

Keziahaya went on, oblivious.

(Yet sometimes whistling to himself. Virgil strained himself to hear but could not identify the melody.)

Wondering: Did the young, six-foot-four Nigerian know that someone was likely to be observing him, much of the time? Did he know, and did he care? Did he bask in such knowledge, or did he shrink from it?—not visibly, of course. For Keziahaya comported himself with dignity, even a kind of stiffness.

It was a season in which, in a sudden reversal of mood, Virgil might destroy much of his work.

Because he had the energy, the insight. Because he was angry with himself, or disgusted. Because what ravished him for days in succession might suddenly repel him in the raw unsparing light of an early morning.

Not discarding but reshaping, recasting. Art is *tonal,* he was thinking.

Tonal, spiritual. The exterior of the artwork is but a means to the interior.

He wasn't sure what he would call it. *Work-in-progress* was often a title he used, a sort of useful non-title, but he had used it many times, and this work felt different.

Something to suggest mortality, and yet transformation; a title like *Metamorphosis,* but not so pretentious.

Seeing Virgil's new work his friends appeared baffled. They did not exactly recoil from it—not exactly. Mostly, they remained silent. One or another might murmur an uneasy *Wow.*

He didn't take offense. He wasn't easily wounded by those whose opinions he didn't much value as he was not easily flattered by these same people who (unfortunately, ironically) constituted most of the people Virgil knew.

Hoping that, if Keziahaya saw his work, he would like it. But even this, Virgil did not dare to expect.

AND NOW. AND AGAIN. And another time he will ask—*Need any help?*

Nothing more likely than Virgil helping the young Nigerian load his framed lithographs and paintings, some of them quite large, into the rear of Virgil's truck as he'd helped others bring their work to the Chautauqua Arts & Crafts Fair in the past. His work, like Virgil's, was to be exhibited in one of the larger tents, for which Virgil was an overseer. A scattering of crafts, photographs, sculpture and paintings.

Virgil has seen to it that Keziahaya is exhibiting in "his" tent.

You trust in chance, if you are fated to meet. But chance can be amplified. Chance can be accelerated.

OK?

Untitled: Widow

Flaps of the tent stirred in the wind. Rain had subsided, that was a blessing. And wooden planks laid down in the muddy grass, for visitors to the fair to use, awkwardly moving from tent to tent in gusts of surprisingly chilly wind.

Oh, here was Virgil's tent, and here was Virgil's exhibit.

Jessalyn stared in dismay. *What* was she seeing?

She'd come to the Chautauqua Arts & Crafts Fair alone as she went most places alone, not knowing how long she would want to stay. And how fortunate she hadn't come with a friend, or a relative, or one of her daughters, for Virgil's new sculptures were distressing, surprising—to say the least. No wonder he hadn't wanted to show her beforehand.

Mortality & The Stars was the title of the exhibit. The artist's name was just *Virgil.*

Virgil had long signed his artworks with only his first name, with a sort of innocent vanity, Jessalyn thought. As a boy he'd signed his Crayola drawings with a flourish—*Virgil.*

("Kid thinks he's Rembrandt," Whitey had observed wryly. At the time Whitey hadn't yet become annoyed with the *artiste.*)

She'd never gotten over her anxiety on his behalf. A mother's fear that her child will embarrass himself in public long after the child has grown up and has assured her many times that he didn't care in the slightest about a public reputation, let alone making money.

Still, it was noted by the McClarens that Virgil took quiet pride in his work, and in the fact that it did sell, at modest prices. You would never get him to admit this, of course.

Most of the sculptures in *Mortality & The Stars* were stunted humanoid figures shaped out of coarse material like burlap, mannequin parts, Styrofoam and wax dribblings, bound tight with twine, wire, and strips of aluminum; faces were minimal, lacking distinctive features. There was a succession of waxy-white figures, evidently male—(you could see male genitalia flattened beneath crude bandages); only the last figure in the sequence was free of its bondage, having risen to its knees, with an upturned, blank-minimalist face and a smooth bald eggshell head.

In a parallel series was a succession of black figures of the same approximate size, and the final figure was also on its knees with a similarly blank-minimalist expression and a smooth bald dark-eggshell head.

Jessalyn tried to comprehend the exhibit. *Mortality* she could see, yes—but *The Stars*? Were the kneeling figures gazing up at (invisible) stars?

"What do you make of this? Weird, in't?"

"Kind of, what's it—'prevert'-looking . . ."

"Maybe it's a race thing."

"It is, sure—some kind of 'race thing.'"

Jessalyn was relieved, these overheard remarks were more bemused than offended.

Others drifted by, staring. Teenagers smirked and giggled. A young child shrank away in fear—"Mom-*my!*"—and had to be gathered up in his mother's arms.

"This is Virgil McClaren's work? *This?*"

A tone of repugnance, disapproval. Obviously these individuals—both women of youthful middle age—were familiar with Virgil's more characteristic work, and were feeling betrayed.

"What'd you even *do* with something like this? Even for Hallowe'en you couldn't hang it out on the porch, it'd look just *weird*. Like something you'd see in an art museum like in New York or what's it—that 'Albright Gallery' in Buffalo."

"That place! Too weird."

The women glanced at Jessalyn with complicit smiles but Jessalyn pretended not to see. It was such a habit of hers, to concur with whatever another person was saying, to smile and nod in instinctive complicity, she had to force herself not to join forces with them against *weirdness*.

She was feeling sorry for Virgil. No one was going to buy these new pieces.

The main attractions at the fair were a children's puppet show, a local potter demonstrating his skill at the wheel, a weaver with a nineteenth-century Irish loom. Watercolors and paintings by local artists—landscapes, sunsets, reflections in water, children. Glazed pots, wall hangings, macramé planters, handmade jewelry, candlestick holders, every sort of knitted, crocheted, carved item. The most popular displays were in other tents, which Jessalyn could avoid.

It was her custom now—(she knew: people spoke critically of her)—to avoid being seen by people who knew her, who might call out happily—*Jessalyn!*—the effect was of a fishhook through the lip, trapping her and reeling her to shore.

And how are you? We have not seen much of you lately . . .

No. They had not seen much of Jessalyn McClaren lately. She could not explain why and was upset at being asked.

It was instructive for Jessalyn to examine *Mortality & The Stars* and try to comprehend how the artist was her *son*. Nothing in the stark anguished images suggested the Virgil whom she knew, or believed she knew. *Son* did not really identify this Virgil, which might have been upsetting to her, as (probably) it would have been upsetting to Whitey; but that was for the good, Jessalyn supposed.

We are all so much deeper than we know. Deep is where pain abides, and this is what we don't (always) want to know.

Virgil's previous works of art had been playful, even prankish. He had used bright colors to liven scrap metal. He had distorted the shapes of things in ways that had not offended the eye, or provoked the viewer to think. It had been on the whole a decorative art people could fit into their households—Jessalyn had fitted it into hers. But—these humanoid figures! It was painful simply to *see* them.

"Powerful"—you might say. "Original"—"striking"—"thought-provoking." Jessalyn rehearsed these words to describe Virgil's new work.

Whitey had not ever come to the Chautauqua arts fair, so far as Jessalyn knew. She'd invited him many times, pleaded with him to come see Virgil's exhibits at least; but Whitey had not ever had time. And just as well this year, for if Whitey had seen *Mortality & The Stars* he'd have been unsparing in scorn. And alarmed.

Prevert?

Sharing space in Virgil's tent with the more serious local artists was a Nigerian man of whom Jessalyn had never heard, with an unpronounceable name—"Keziahaya." His work was boldly colorful, abstract; he too had created odd, quirky sculptures, out of (African?) fabrics, not immediately identifiable as human, or animal. Visitors seemed to admire these exotic works, and were buying smaller pieces. His lithographs were densely detailed, resembling the dreamscapes of—was it Henri Rousseau? Jessalyn noted that "Amos Keziahaya" had been living in the Hammond area since 2009, and taught part-time art classes at the state university. She wondered if Virgil knew him.

Jessalyn wondered what could have brought Keziahaya to this obscure city in upstate New York. Whether he had friends here, or knew few people and was lonely.

Still. You could know many people and still be lonely.

She returned to Virgil's exhibit which was now deserted. She was feeling a mother's anxiety, that her son would be devastated not to sell a single work of art—not that Virgil would tell anyone of course.

Fortunately Virgil had included several smaller pieces, though they lacked the playfulness of his former work. His scrap-metal roosters, goats, oxen and horses painted in festive colors had been popular items at previous fairs; once, he'd displayed patchwork-quilt human figures with wings, that had sold briskly; charming birds, butterflies, bats, frogs and toads. Every friend of the McClarens owned at least one of these, displayed on lawns or garden walls. Of course, Jessalyn owned many. So very different from these corpse-like figures on their backs on the ground naked and vulnerable, tight-bound as in straitjackets. What could Virgil be thinking, forcing people to gaze upon such horrors?

His father's death had unmoored him. That was it. But—what could Jessalyn do about *that*? She was unmoored herself.

When she saw him Virgil often seemed excited—she didn't want to think manic. He'd spoken of being insomniac—but happily, for it allowed him to get more work done.

He'd gone on a spending spree—(for Virgil, who hadn't bought anything for years except at rummage sales and flea markets)—purchasing the Jeep and proper art supplies. He'd even made an appointment with a dentist.

(Did Virgil still have his old, ugly bicycle?—Jessalyn hadn't seen it in months.)

Jessalyn stooped to look closely at the tight-bound humanoid figures. If you took care, you could see that each figure was less tight-bound than the preceding; at the end, the bounds had loosened and fallen off, and the figure was "freed." Was that the point? Out of bondage, into a kind of shaky freedom? Their eyes lifted to the stars? The problem was, no one would want to purchase a single figure, which wouldn't make sense out of the sequence; and no one would want to purchase all of them—at least twenty figures. (Well, maybe a museum. But no museum had ever bought anything of Virgil's, and it was not likely that a museum would buy anything at this point.)

Jessalyn saw: the black figures, close behind the white figures, were meant to "shadow" them, perhaps.

Or was this a racist notion, of the kind only a white person might have?

Or—was it a satire of a racist notion, of the kind only a white person might have, but a black person might accept as a legitimate vision?

Apart from being freed of their cruel bindings the "freed" figures did not inspire much hope in the viewer. Each looked quite desolate on his knees, gazing away from the other and upward toward the ceiling of the tent, which had begun to drip. Jessalyn supposed that this was deliberate: what Virgil would call a "stratagem." He had deliberately not made the final figures obviously very different from those that preceded out of a fear of seeming sentimental, or too obvious. Since pubescence when he'd first encountered the phrase *art for art's sake* Virgil had expressed contempt for "happy" endings in art or in life.

If Whitey had been beside her Jessalyn would have shielded his eyes with her hand. Never mind, darling!

Jessalyn counted the cash in her wallet. It was always a surprise to her—she never knew what she might have. A few single-dollar bills, or much more. Thom had shown her how to withdraw cash from an ATM machine and this she did in modest allotments. She spent so little on herself, basically just food, and gas for her car which she used sparingly . . . If she wanted to buy something of Virgil's she would have to pay cash, reasoning that if she paid by check or credit card Virgil might discover who'd made the purchase; but she had to buy something, for it looked as if no one else would. To her surprise she discovered several twenty-dollar bills in her wallet, as well as a fifty-dollar bill.

On a shelf Jessalyn discovered a scrap metal sculpture of Virgil's painted oyster-white, about two feet in height, that was not so ugly or accusing as the newer work. *Flower Shock* resembled a daisy that looked, if you examined it from a certain angle, like a screaming mouth—but Jessalyn could avoid examining it from that angle.

Jessalyn had to search for a saleswoman. All were volunteers, and not always within earshot.

"Excuse me? Hello? How much is this flower?"

"'Flower'? That's what it is?"—a pretty young blond woman in a caftan and flaring white pajama-pants hurried over to peer at Virgil's sculpture. It seemed clear that she didn't think much of *Mortality & The Stars,* and was frankly surprised by Jessalyn's interest. "Oh gosh! Let me look at the label."

How like Virgil to scribble a price on in pencil, already faded so you couldn't figure out what it is.

"Maybe—fifteen dollars?"

"Oh, it must be more than fifteen dollars!" Jessalyn was shocked.

"Fifty?"

"Even fifty seems low, for such a—an—interesting piece."

Dubiously the young woman eyed *Flower Shock*. "I guess you could say it's 'interesting.' Not so depressing as these dummy-things lying on the floor, we were worried might cause the exhibit to be shut down—you know, if people complained they were 'obscene.'"

"Oh no—'obscene'? Really?"

"You didn't look too close at them, ma'am. Just as well."

Jessalyn ignored this remark, murmured in a lowered voice.

"The artist lives right here in Hammond. You'd think he's from some city where there's—you know—'race' issues . . ."

Quickly Jessalyn said that she had a tote bag, the clerk didn't have to wrap up the flower.

"You'd almost think, y'know, that this 'Virgil' is a black person—but I saw him install the exhibit, and he's *white*. But, like, a white 'hippie' or something—kind of weird, with a sweet, sad face, with long hair."

With Jessalyn's assistance the young woman set the unwieldy metal flower into a cloth bag imprinted with the words HAMMOND PUBLIC LIBRARY 50TH ANNIVERSARY GALA. The sculpture was surprisingly heavy and smelled strangely, like a sweaty coin.

Where could she put *Flower Shock,* that Virgil would never discover it? Or—should she allow Virgil to discover it, in a few months? Probably, Virgil would just laugh to see who'd bought one of his sculptures.

(But would Virgil laugh? He might be offended by his mother purchasing his work surreptitiously, as if he had to be humored like a child.)

Impulsively then, since her wallet was out and opened, Jessalyn decided to buy something by the Nigerian with the unpronounceable name. This, an egg-shaped curiosity constructed of layers of emerald-green fabric interwoven with white feathers, of about the size of a basketball, was more favored by the young woman clerk. "Now, this is pretty! You could use it as a throw pillow or a cushion, you know—on a bed, or a sofa. This artist *is* a black person—an African—I saw him. But he was wearing a white shirt, and spoke English like he really knew it. He was very polite."

The emerald-green egg had no name or title and was reasonably priced, Jessalyn thought, at thirty-five dollars which she paid with her credit card. Unlike *Flower Shock* it was very light to lift.

Jessalyn was feeling gay, giddy. How tempting it was to make other purchases at the fair—works of art that few customers would want. If only she had more money to spend!—spreading it among local artists to raise their spirits. And best to buy in secret, so that no one knew who their benefactor was.

Whitey would approve, she believed. Lately, Whitey had been approving of her more reckless behavior.

Proper and good, sweetheart. Though you are not happy yourself you can make others happy, that's what life is all about.

If only she'd gone home now. But, she had not.

Photography exhibits were in an adjoining tent. Here too the most popular sale items were of familiar images: smiling children, frisking dogs, sunsets and sunrises, blossoming trees, shadow-silhouettes on grass. Several of the photographers were locally known, and known to Jessalyn. But the major exhibit was titled *The Mourners* by a photographer named Hugo Martinez, of whom Jessalyn had never heard.

Amid the local photographers Martinez was clearly exceptional. You could see at a glance that his work was—well, "serious" was too weak a term. Beautiful, profound, captivating? Very professionally printed and mounted, the largest measuring at least four feet in length, three feet in height.

Martinez seemed to have traveled a good deal: here were photographs of a Tibetan "sky burial," brightly clad Indians bathing in the Ganges, corpses burning in a funeral pyre. Churchyards, funeral processions, black-clad mourners on a boulder-strewn island off the coast of Scotland. In a gaudy Mexican cemetery, a spirited celebration of the Day of the Dead; on a Greek island, solitary mourners, female, black-clad, kneeling at graves. Jessalyn was appalled to realize what she was seeing: Roman catacombs exposing skulls, bones amid rocks. So many!

The photographs were sharply focused, intimate and unsparing. Death has no dignity, the dead can have no privacy. How different from our way of life in the United States, Jessalyn thought, where death is terrifying, and shameful; people hide away to die, and are buried or burnt and their ashes buried. To the very end, and after, we must believe that we *matter.*

Wanting to protest—*Oh Whitey. I can't accept it, you are one of so many. Please no.*

Her husband's death was singular, Jessalyn must believe this. She could not surrender this belief. She could not even surrender the notion that he was (somehow) not really gone, not close beside her, aware of her every thought and fleeting emotion.

Whitey, help me! I know that it is ridiculous, I am ridiculous but I know that you are with me, you will never abandon me . . .

At the end of *The Mourners* were a number of less spectacular photographs, not so large, their colors muted, taken in the United States.

Jessalyn found herself staring at one of these, which she thought heartstoppingly beautiful, and made her want to cry—*Untitled: Widow.* Here was a woman in a black coat stooping above a grave, on which there was a small, meager marker, unlike larger gravestones on neighboring graves; the woman had her back to the camera, oblivious of the photographer's presence as if totally absorbed in grief. The photograph had been taken at dusk, the atmosphere was misty, dreamlike; it reminded Jessalyn of nineteenth-century photographs by Julia Cameron.

The widow's posture was awkward, as if supplicant; as if she were speaking to someone in the earth below, making an appeal. She was in profile, but not clearly; you could not see much of her face. Yet the sobriety of the photograph, its melancholy mood, was qualified by a swath of mud on the side of the woman's black coat, and (if you looked closely) on her legs. Jessalyn thought—*Oh! She has no idea.*

Other photographs of Martinez were similarly solemn but "flawed": a fat-bellied man in a dingy white clinician's coat, seated spread-legged outside a doorway marked EL DEPOSITO DE CADAVERS, and smoking a cigar; a glamorously made-up obese woman in a church pew, blowing her nose into a handkerchief; twin boys in twin suits beside a hearse, with identical crossed eyes; high-school-age girls giggling together, with bare midriffs, bare legs and bare feet in flip-flops, flirtatiously posing for the photographer in a cemetery. Jessalyn looked again at *Untitled: Widow* and recoiled with shock: "Why, that's me."

It was so. The widow of *Untitled: Widow* was Jessalyn McClaren.

For a very long time Jessalyn stared at the photograph without quite seeing it. She could feel blood draining out of her head, she was becoming faint, stunned.

But—how could this be? Jessalyn, in her black winter coat, at Whitey's grave . . .

One of the volunteer clerks approached her, smiling. Could she be of help?

Jessalyn stammered no, not at the moment.

Wanting to hide her face. Wanting to run away . . .

It must have been the man in the cemetery months ago, who'd helped her when she'd fallen—he'd taken her picture, secretly. Helped her wipe mud off her coat and legs, and helped her find Whitey's grave. He'd been an older man in a Stetson-like hat, a stranger. He'd had a mustache, a soft voice, he'd seemed calm and wise when Jessalyn had been agitated.

Had he been carrying a camera? He must have concealed it.

"Mrs. McClaren? Hello! I thought that was you. How are you?"—the smiling volunteer inquired.

Jessalyn could not meet the woman's eye. She murmured something polite and eased away.

A hot blush swept over her, that everyone who saw the photograph would recognize Jessalyn McClaren.

What a shock! She was feeling exposed, betrayed. By the stranger who'd seemed so kindly to her.

Had to escape. The fair was ruined for her now.

Poor, piteous Jessalyn in her mud-smeared clothes—exposed in *Untitled: Widow.*

On the drive home recalling the mysterious calla lily someone had sent her—she thought the name had been "Hugo." This had been months ago, probably after the cemetery encounter. Obviously, this had been the photographer who'd taken advantage of her—"Hugo Martinez."

He'd known who she was, evidently. From the grave marker—JOHN EARLE MCCLAREN.

Martinez must have looked up her address, in order to send her the calla lily. A gesture of reparation, perhaps. An acknowledgment of guilt.

She was hurt, and she was angry. Nothing like this had ever happened to her before. Had this "Hugo" dared to thank her, in his note? In a kitchen drawer she found it:

> *In appreciation,*
> *Your friend Hugo*

Your friend. How had he dared!

CAREFULLY VIRGIL SAID: "The photograph is a work of art. It isn't about *you.*"

And: "Even if it's about you, it's just a photograph—a 'likeness.' It's not like the photographer has stolen your soul."

Virgil was trying to speak in a comforting, cajoling voice. Though Jessalyn was sure she'd seen him wince when she pulled him by the sleeve to stand in front of *Untitled: Widow.*

So agitated by the photograph, so unable to expel it from her mind, Jessalyn had to seek out Virgil in his cabin on Bear Mountain Road.

She'd insisted that Virgil accompany her back to the fair that very evening.

It wasn't like Jessalyn to be so upset, Virgil thought. His usually mild-mannered mother, biting her lower lip to keep from crying, her eyes leaking tears of something like humiliation . . .

There were more visitors to the fair in the early evening. A sizable number drifted through the photography tent, and lingered at Hugo Martinez's more spectacular photographs. Virgil saw how Jessalyn cringed, in fear that they would see *Untitled: Widow* and discover the widow a few feet away, stricken.

"This awful man, this 'Hugo Ramirez'—"

"—'Martinez'—"

"—he must have been hiding in the cemetery to take pictures of people at graves—'mourners.' He must have seen me when I was visiting Whitey's grave. This was last November, I think. It wasn't a good time for me, I may have struck him as—unstable." Jessalyn had more to say but wasn't sure that she should continue. Virgil was looking at her with alarm, she'd spoken with such emotion.

How much was Martinez asking for *Untitled: Widow*? Unframed, a print measuring two feet by eighteen inches, one hundred fifty dollars which seemed to Virgil a reasonable price.

Even if Jessalyn bought the damned print to hide it away, or destroy it, there would be other prints. The photographer owned the original, the purchaser could own only a print.

"Is that the way I look to other people? Sort of—stooped, stunted? With mud on my coat and legs?"

It was her vanity that had been injured, perhaps. Her pride.

Your mourning is tragic to you but not to others.

Virgil was admiring Martinez's other photographs. His favorites were the Tibetan "sky burials"—thinly swathed corpses laid atop rock-pedestals—altars?—to be devoured by vultures. What a scene! You stared and stared, you could not look away. There was nothing in his own work, Virgil had to concede, that could compare.

"A photograph is a work of art, Mom. A photograph is *not life*. No work of art should be confused with *life*. This is a fleeting glimpse of something that looks familiar to you, but has no existence any longer. It ceased to exist within a moment. Certainly, the figure in the photograph isn't *you*."

But what did this mean? Was it meant to be mollifying? Was Virgil humoring her? Jessalyn could not be comforted so easily.

Virgil added, somewhat reluctantly, "I know him. Hugo Martinez."

"You know him? The photographer?"

"Many people know Hugo Martinez."

"Don't tell me he's a friend of yours!"

"No. But I've admired him, from a distance."

"Oh, why? Why would you admire *him*?"

"He's very talented but has trouble getting along with people. He'd had a professorship at the state university at one time. He's been Poet Laureate of Western New York. He's won awards with his photography—he's been involved in political protests. He's a 'local figure of some controversy'—like me, I guess. But more so." Virgil laughed.

Jessalyn was embarrassed to have never heard of this "local figure."

"Is he a—respected person? Did Whitey know him?"

"Yes, and no. He's respected if not universally liked. But no, Whitey wouldn't have known him."

"Is it like him to take a picture like this in stealth? Without asking permission?"

"He wasn't taking your picture, Mom. I've tried to explain."

"You're defending him? Against your own mother?"

Virgil was astonished, Jessalyn continued to be so upset. She was virtually beating her fists together. He had not seen his mother so agitated even at the time of his father's death.

"Mom, try to understand: this isn't a picture of anyone specific. It's a composition. A study in contrasts—light and dark, solid blocks of black, an almost complete absence of color, mist. The pale sliver of the woman's profile mimics a sliver of a moon, you can barely see through clouds. The miniature marker on the grave has a very faint color, like copper. So there is color in the photograph, though it looks like a black-and-white picture. You don't see that immediately—you have to wait. The photograph evokes mourning and it's very beautiful, actually. Though I agree, maybe the photographer shouldn't have taken it surreptitiously, I think with a long-distance lens."

"Can we ask him to take it down? Please?"

"Well—you could try."

"Would you try?"

"I—I—I don't think that I can, Mom. I wouldn't feel right. Hugo Martinez is a serious artist and I don't believe in censorship. The photograph is about a 'widow'—not about you."

"But that 'widow' is *me*."

"No. The figure in the composition is not *you*."

"But people don't think that way. The woman in the photograph is me—Jessalyn McClaren—I am the mourner, you can see it's me."

"No. Your face is turned away, Mom. There is no 'face' to the mourner. We don't own ourselves when we are in public places—you have no reasonable expectation of privacy when you are in a public place like a cemetery."

"But I know it's me, that's my coat, that's my leg, splattered with mud. Is the photographer laughing at me?"

"Of course not, Mom. The photographer is not laughing at you. He has created a work of art, that will outlive you and him both. That is what he has created."

Virgil spoke with such passion, Jessalyn was finally silenced. She felt so foolish, so diminished and so—left behind.

"I suppose it is beautiful. But it *hurts so*."

HERE WAS ANOTHER SURPRISE FOR VIRGIL: Jessalyn's purchase of the emerald-green fabric-and-feathers egg by Amos Keziahaya.

He'd come back to the house with her, for she'd seemed so upset he didn't want to leave her alone, and she brought the curious object out to show him. Turning it in his hands he'd laughed with pleasure and a little stab of something like pain. "What led you to buy this, Mom?"

"I—I don't know. It caught my eye. I thought it was—it is—unusual . . ."

"It is. All of Keziahaya's work is unusual."

"Oh, do you know him?"

Virgil considered. "No. Though he lives on Bear Mountain Road, in the farmhouse."

A brooding look came into Virgil's face that Jessalyn could not interpret.

"Do you think he's lonely, being from Nigeria? Or is he—does he—have many friends?"

"I don't know. I really don't—know much about him."

With a mother's instinct Jessalyn said impulsively, "Would you like to invite him to dinner sometime, at my house? I'd like that."

Virgil looked at her, startled. "Y-Yes. Maybe. Sometime."

"Well. Just let me know."

Jessalyn settled the emerald-green egg, woven with white feathers, onto a cushioned chair in the living room where it seemed to subtly rearrange the room, like a soft explosion.

Dear Hugo

June 9, 2011

Dear Hugo—

You don't remember me—probably. I am the "widow" in your photograph.

At first it was shocking to me, to see this photograph in a public place, and to be unprepared to see it. And to see the mud on the widow's coat, and the curious way she is standing as if her back is broken.

Then, I saw that the mud is why the photograph is strange and beautiful. The mourning is "flawed." The widow is self-absorbed though she is a mourner. She is staring at the earth at her feet, she is unaware of the photographer somewhere behind her who is a living person.

You were very kind to me when I was in need of kindness.

I was angry at you at first but now I see differently.

My son is an artist—he has explained to me the special beauty of your work.

You have brought a calm into my life. I am not sure why. The widow wants to live, it is not enough to mourn.

Your friend
Jessalyn

IV.

The Stars

JUNE 2011—DECEMBER 2011

Enemies

"Lorene-y? Come sit right here!"

Beside Daddy, that was. *Her.*

HER ALL-TIME FAVORITE FILM WAS *PATTON*.

Just a girl maybe ten or eleven when she'd first watched it in the basement TV room.

Daddy had said here's a great film, kids. Great performance by George C. Scott.

Seated close beside Daddy she'd watched enthralled. Whoever was sitting on her other side, quite possibly Beverly, maybe Thom, she didn't remember, just a blur. Wanting to think—maybe—it had been just her and Daddy, for a change. Not everybody else.

Five children in a family is too damn many. Ask anyone who's been there.

Ideal number?—Lorene would have said *Just one.*

But which *just one*?

Obviously, some parents stop having kids with *just one*. But that would have been her damn big bossy brother Thom, not her.

Some parents stop having kids after two. Especially if one's a boy and one's a girl. But that would've meant that her damn big bossy sister Beverly got born, not her.

Fact is, Lorene was number three. Two older siblings, two younger. (Not that the younger siblings counted for much, being younger.)

Still, Lorene felt like an only child. The center of gravity in the McClaren family.

An *only child* is likely to identify with parents and authority figures; younger children are likely to rebel. This was a popular psychology theory of the 1990s with which Lorene (who had a degree in psychology) did not agree.

Lorene identified with parental figures, particularly fathers. Particularly Daddy who was Whitey McClaren and no ordinary father.

As a girl she'd have said she wanted to be *him*—but since she couldn't be him, she could be what Daddy might've been if he'd been *her*.

(Did that make sense? It made plenty of sense to Lorene.)

He was the one who called her, at special times, *Lorene-y*.

No one else would ever call her, at any time, *Lorene-y*.

Six times she'd seen *Patton* since that first time squeezed close to Daddy on the sofa. Six times she'd been enthralled by the portrait of the great, eccentric general of the American forces in World War II, and had felt a thrill of satisfaction when he'd slapped the trembling young soldier in the army hospital as the medical staff looked on in horror.

Coward! Patton had recoiled with fury and revulsion; he'd threatened to shoot the young soldier for desertion, with his own pistol.

Lorene had wanted to clap. This was how *cowards* should be treated!

But Daddy had surprised her. Daddy had not liked this scene so much. He'd said it was shameful hitting a sick soldier like that who couldn't defend himself. And Patton a four-star general, a famous man, losing his judgment and behaving like a bully.

"General Patton just wants soldiers to be brave," Lorene had protested. "He wants them to be *men*."

"Sometimes men get sick, like anybody else," Whitey said. "Sometimes a man gets sick and tired and fed up with being a *man*."

Lorene laughed, thinking that Daddy meant to be funny. How was it possible, a man could get fed up with being a *man*?

Not Lorene. Not ever.

ON QUESTIONNAIRES SHE'D SOMETIMES CHECKED, half-consciously, *only child.*

"DR. McCLAREN? A call for you."

"Say I'm not in. Didn't I tell you!"

Like a soft-centered cake, collapsing. Found herself crying in her office. Not taking calls, canceling appointments. In her secretary's eyes, a look of surprise and alarm.

Principal at North Hammond High for nearly four years and in that time, in fact before that time, she'd scarcely had a week off and now she was thinking, since Whitey's death, since the money he'd left her, she must take a trip, she must travel, somewhere away from this place, and soon.

Not that she wasn't in excellent health. She was.

Certainly, she *was.*

Except no trips for her. She had work to do.

Instructing Iris to explain—*Dr. McClaren is involved in an urgent conference call. She will speak with you tomorrow morning.*

Respected, admired, feared.

And the greatest of these is fear.

IN THE BEGINNING she'd liked them. Well, maybe she hadn't *liked them,* exactly—but she hadn't *disliked them.*

Now, they'd become the enemy. Her enemy.

More than eight hundred adolescents enrolled in the suburban high school and in their midst, hidden and protected by their sheer number, the small, core group, names unknown to her, who constituted the threat to the principal's authority as the presence of a virulent strain of amoeba in the human gut is the threat to human life, erupting in bloody dysentery.

What exactly did these mutinous students do, to what did they conspire, smoking in lavatories which was forbidden, smuggling drugs into the school which was forbidden, "dealing" God knew what drugs—

marijuana, amphetamines, painkillers, cocaine? Heroin? Laughing at "Dr. McClaren"—"Principal McClaren"—behind her back. Challenging her authority. Graffiti on walls, sidewalks. Veiled allusions, insults in the school newspaper and online.

The most mortifying was Lorene's head atop a squat-pig Nazi body. *She-Gestapo McC___.*

Or maybe, the most mortifying was Lorene's head atop an actual sow-body, with flaccid, drooping dugs and hideously raw and reddened genitals.

It was shocking to her, who so little identified with *female,* to be reduced to *female* in the grossest of ways, in derision and mockery. Why, Lorene somewhat despised *female* herself, and far more readily identified with *male.*

Yet, it was male students who were her enemies, mostly. Though there were girls also—of course. *Bitches.*

She knew (she suspected) who they were. Knew their faces.

As in a fever dream their faces floated past her insolent and beautiful.

So young, they were likely to be beautiful and their beauty careless as milkweed seed blown in the wind, promiscuous as it was ubiquitous.

Having sex. She knew, that was what they were doing in defiance of her also, *having sex* crude and graceless as guzzling cans of beer on school property, behind the bleachers or in the parking lot which was forbidden as the dealing of drugs was forbidden, so much was forbidden that had been unleashed during the years she'd become the youngest principal in the history of North Hammond High.

From her office window in the school building, through part-drawn venetian blinds she observed them, the swarm of them, deadly in their very anonymity.

Social media, a new nightmare unknown to her parents' generation. Internet postings, anonymous websites, vile words, obscene images. Typing in the name LORENE MCCLAREN, PRINCIPAL NORTH HAMMOND HIGH had become an exercise in self-laceration akin to tearing off her skin with her teeth yet she could not resist in the hour before midnight and in the unhappy hours after midnight unable to sleep and so rising from her bed to return to her laptop determined to know who was taunting her, which of the vermin it was, the most vicious enemy, that must be extirpated.

She'd been assured by her allies among the faculty and staff that these (mutinous, monstrous) students/trolls at North Hammond were not really trying to destroy Lorene McClaren, their crude and cruel cyberbullying was hardly limited to her, best for her to ignore it.

We all have to deal with it, they'd claimed. *Just don't Google your name for God's sake.*

But she could not resist. How could she!—like trying to ignore amoebic dysentery as your bowels were being evacuated in the scalding-hot stench of shit.

And so, she was determined to track them down—*trolls.* Track them to their lairs. Pour poison into the lairs. Better yet, something flammable into their lairs and set afire.

Oh, she knew who some of her tormenters were! She was sure.

Never forget, and never forgive.

Within a few months in pursuit of these canny little bastards Lorene had acquired computer skills to put her into a league (almost) with the elite of Russian and Chinese hackers. She'd have liked to boast but boasting wasn't her (public) style.

Mostly senior boys, and mostly jocks. Arrogant kids, spoiled and stupid, even the smarter ones, even those whose grades were high enough for them to apply to first-rate universities with a reasonable expectation of being accepted, even—(Lorene was sure)—an honors student whose column in the school newspaper, brimming with sarcasm, so closely echoed phrases in certain of the online postings, Lorene had no difficulty identifying him as a principal troll. His name was appropriate: "Todd Price."

Lorene smiled. Price would pay the *price.*

Applications to Harvard, Princeton, Yale?—MIT, Caltech?—Cornell? The spoiled brats didn't suspect that they had to contend with a (female) principal so skilled in computer use, she had little difficulty altering their precious transcripts and letters of recommendation to assure rejection by any "competitive" university to which they applied.

Among the girl-trolls she'd been able to identify one just the other day. Bland pretty face, straight blond hair falling past her shoulders, yearbook co-editor, class officer, exactly the sort of girl of whom it is said *Oh but not Tiffany!—not her.* But Lorene, sharp-eyed, practiced in detecting subversion, had observed this sly little bitch whispering and giggling with a friend in the very first row of the auditorium as Lorene in her cranberry-colored gabardine pants suit took the podium at a school assembly with a bright welcoming smile.

Hello! How are you all on this beautiful morning in June?

And to Tiffany, silently gloating—*Bitch, you're dead. And you don't even know it.*

From the pitiless online-adolescent world Lorene had acquired a macho swagger that was contemptible to her and yet—perversely—intensely enjoyable. It was the atmosphere of the video game, she suspected, though (of course) she'd never glimpsed an actual video game, soundly condemned by educators of her generation as time-wasting, soul-abrading.

All that she knew of the adolescent soul was repugnant to her. Though she had to keep her knowledge safely hidden.

(Of course! That was the delight of it.)

Adolescents were devious, sex-obsessed, gross and *smelly.*

Sniffing the corridors of the school you could smell their monkey-stench. The boys *jacking off* (as they quaintly called it) and the girls *on the rag* (ugly).

Sperm, semen. Vaginal juices, menstrual blood.

No wonder they became druggies, many of them. Smoking dope had started for them in middle school, she'd just inherited the problem.

"Drug users" had no one's sympathy. All you needed to do was wait patiently for them to self-destruct: *over-dose.*

No matter what she said publicly, the principal of North Hammond High did not believe in rehabilitation for the young. It was too expensive, and its results were unreliable. Recidivism was high. Better to accept that with a few exceptions the young were an accursed generation, frontal lobes stunted from video games, cell phones, TV, sex-gratification by the hour. They had no sense of history and so could have no sense of the future. Equipped with state-of-the-art computers—(North Hammond was an affluent school district)—they had never to think for themselves, facts and pseudo-facts were at their fingertips, free, thus of little worth. Equipped with calculators they had never to add up a column of numbers, multiply or divide. They were volatile, impressionable. They had the scant memories of fruit flies and would have bred as promiscuously except they were canny enough to use condoms. (Condoms! High school! Excellent idea so that they didn't breed but how disgusting when you thought of it, and how hard not to think of it.) They cheated on their homework of course, and tried to cheat on their tests. They could not very easily cheat on state-mandated exams, though they tried. Can't trust them, and can't put anything past them. This generation!

Once adolescents got into drugs, that was the end for them. They had not the intelligence or the stamina or willpower to resist. Their lives went up in smoke—literally! Lorene wanted them out of the school, gone. Hosed out. Gone. No regrets. The ones identified as drug users did not merit leniency, mercy. How would General Patton have reacted? Lorene didn't believe in mollycoddling drug users any more than the great four-star general believed in mollycoddling the unfit and the "malingerers." Oh yes, Dr. McClaren was concerned when she spoke with the parents of such miserable offspring, sympathetic-seeming, encouraging them to send their addict-sons and -daughters to rehab clinics out of state—West Palm Beach, Florida, was a favored place, lately a notorious place, for several teenagers had died of overdoses there in the midst of being "rehabilitated."

Well, not on her watch. Not her responsibility. Caught with drugs on school property, a single marijuana cigarette or prescription pill for which the culprit had no prescription—out.

"Sorry. You have all been warned. Many times. North Hammond High is a zero-tolerance school. No drugs. No negotiations. No exceptions. Out."

It was an extreme position for a school principal to take in these over-therapized and mollycoddled times and there were those (her enemies among the faculty, whose names Lorene knew well) who were sure that it would precipitate the tyrannical woman's downfall, but no, Principal McClaren's "zero tolerance" stance was met with approval by an overwhelming majority of parents, taxpayers, and civic leaders. She was doing her job, she was "weeding-out" the unfit from the fit, casting the unfit into oblivion, preserving the stellar reputation of the school. It did not escape general notice that among the unfit were a disproportionately high number of "minority" students—that was how it was. In the affluent and career-obsessed suburban setting such law-and-order firmness was desired.

You could always find dark-skinned mothers to praise her. Hispanic parents, Asians. *This is what our children need. This is America.*

Driving the school's ranking up, upward. That was Lorene's obsession. When she'd begun as principal four years before, North Hammond High had been ranked thirty-sixth in all of New York State, out of more than 2,100 schools; through her effort, the school was most recently ranked twenty-eighth. In all of the United States, North Hammond High was ranked 416, up from 422, out of more than 23,000 public schools.

For this, and other accomplishments as an educator, Lorene had been awarded a Hammond Citizens' Award for 2011; deeply touching to her, for John Earle McClaren had received this same award in 1986.

At the awards ceremony it was observed that North Hammond High principal Lorene McClaren, that brisk dynamo of a "little woman," tough, laser-smart and no-nonsense, with a face sharp as something hacked out of stone and hair razor-cut short as a Marine's, had to fight back tears when the award presenter reminisced about "Whitey" McClaren and what *he'd* done as a Hammond citizen.

Liking to think that Whitey would have indeed been proud of her.

Liking to think that indeed she was weeding out her enemies at the high school. One by one and eventually none would remain to defy her.

Whitey had often said, mysteriously laying his finger alongside his nose like a sly Santa Claus—*Revenge is a dish best served with no witnesses.*

IT WAS TRUE, Lorene's clock ran fast. Like her heart.

A pulsebeat more rapid than normal. Quick darting thoughts like piranha fish. Since childhood she'd been a *schemer.*

"Mackie! Why, hel-*lo.*"

First damn thing you encountered at the house on Old Farm Road—the ugly squint-eye black tomcat standing squarely just inside the kitchen door like a guard dog, stubby tail erect, single tawny eye glaring. The creature drew back its lips to expose sharp yellowed teeth and discolored, dingy gums in a soundless hiss. Lorene was frightened, but held her ground. The thing was only a cat after all!

Why hadn't Thom solved the problem of the stray cat that was taking advantage of their soft-hearted mother? He'd promised that he would, and he had not.

She could not bring herself to murder the damned thing, Lorene thought. Even poison, a cowardly sort of murder, was not for her. And poor Jessalyn would be inconsolable from another loss.

Discreetly Lorene avoided the ugly tomcat. If the creature was spoiling for a fight, Lorene was too practiced in public-school-administration quasi-diplomacy to be suckered into a confrontation.

"Would you like to take a trip with me, Mom?"—Lorene heard herself asking.

"A trip—where?"

Jessalyn was sounding dubious. Seemed like each time you tried to talk to her about something serious that implied a future Jessalyn edged away, or changed the subject, or smiled at you with that sweet tense smile that all but begged—*No! Whatever you are asking of me, please don't.*

It was as Beverly complained, their mother who'd once been so social and so outgoing had become morbidly attached to the house; you had to pry her away just to go shopping at the mall.

(You would think—you would not want to think—that Whitey was still living here, somewhere upstairs.)

"I was thinking—Bali. Thailand. Somewhere far away, exotic." Not adding—*Where thoughts of Whitey can't follow you. Where Whitey has never been.*

"We've never traveled together, Mom. You've hardly traveled at all, and I haven't left North America in twelve years."

"Did you say—Bali? That's the far side of the world . . ."

"It's supposed to be very beautiful, and not so spoiled like other Pacific islands."

Practically pleading with her mother! Why?

Had Lorene no one else with whom she might travel? At her age of nearing-thirty-five? So—*alone*?

"I would make all the plans myself, Mom. Of course!"

Instead of greeting this remark with enthusiasm Jessalyn shivered. Lorene felt a stab of rage at her widowed mother clinging pathetically to her narrow safe life—*resolutely self-blindered, haut-bourgeois, massively-boring-suburban-hausfrau life* as Lorene thought it. More pointless now than it had been when Whitey had been alive.

Jessalyn said, "You used to say that you didn't 'believe' in vacations, Lorene. Even as a young girl. Just like your father—Whitey didn't 'believe' in vacations either . . ."

Lorene said, exasperated, "Well, I'm older now. I've been working damned hard and I think I deserve a break and even Daddy would concur. He used to say—'They will suck your blood and wring you dry if you don't keep up your guard.'"

"Whitey said *that*? When?"

"When I first started teaching. Public school. He knew what a rat race it is and how the young and idealistic burn out fast unless they can protect themselves."

"Really! Whitey said that?"

"He did, Mom. Maybe not to you, but to *me*."

"It doesn't sound like Whitey, somehow. *He* was the idealist, all his life."

"Not really. Daddy was no fool. He knew where the bodies are buried."

Jessalyn reacted with a startled look as if, indeed, real bodies had been buried, really. And Whitey had known where?

"To be a public school principal is like trying to keep order in a banana republic. Even your allies, the ones who owe you everything, can't be trusted; and your enemies are waiting to slit your throat."

"Oh, Lorene! You're being funny, I hope."

Jessalyn laughed, distractedly. Something strange tonight, Lorene thought: her mother seemed to be paying only partial attention to her as if her mind were elsewhere.

Even glancing about as if she expected to see—who? Lorene didn't want to think *She is missing Whitey.*

Usually on such occasions Jessalyn could be counted on to dote on Lorene's every word: grateful for her daughter's tales of incidents at North Hammond High, bad student behavior punished, faculty detractors and "ingrates" outmaneuvered at staff meetings. Budget crises invariably ended with Lorene triumphant for (as Lorene liked to boast) she'd made North Hammond the most "winning" school in the district and the superintendent of schools admired her—and maybe feared her.

In each of the tales Lorene was the pure, selfless, educator-warrior-woman who prevailed, triumphed against forces of ignorance and meanness. (Though Lorene spared her mother details of the ugly cyberbullying.) These exploits Lorene laid at her mother's feet like Mack the Knife bringing back mutilated prey with an expectation of praise.

"Well, I am very busy right now, Mom. These are frantic weeks, coming to the end of the school year—I feel that I am 'on' at least one hundred hours a week. That's why I've been thinking of a trip when it's all over. And taking you with me, Mom."

Thank God, graduation was next Monday. As principal Lorene was to preside over the commencement ceremony which would last approximately ninety minutes and which would be, except for those minutes when Lorene herself was speaking, the very quintessence of boredom.

Self-congratulations, praise. Earnest student speeches, the deafening student band with its thumping beat like a gargantuan beast waddling from side to side. The senior prom would have taken place the previous weekend—God knew what awful things would happen at, or after, this ghastly spring sex-ritual about which adults were not supposed to know, and Lorene had not the slightest interest in knowing. These several hectic days were the culmination of the school year that gathered momentum as the end approached like a train whose brakes have failed rushing down a steep grade.

Eight months since Whitey had died, and yet it seemed like eight years—so long.

It seemed like eight weeks. Eight days—still breathless.

The prospect of graduation, so many hands to be vigorously shaken, such a barrage of congratulations and farewells—Lorene was feeling drained of spirit beforehand, like a general walking a corpse-strewn battlefield in polished boots.

Worse, she had to pretend to *care*.

And if troubled parents engaged her in confidence amid the festivities, baffled and disappointed that their seemingly bright offspring had failed to get into their first-choice universities, Lorene would feign indignation on their account, and promise to *see what I can do*. (That's to say, *nothing*.)

About this at least, Lorene felt good. You had no need to confront the enemy openly when you could (secretly) cut them off at the knees, aged eighteen, and play the role of sympathizer, commiserator. Revenge had to be the best remedy for any sort of malaise.

"It would do you good, Mom. A change of scene."

"Oh but—why? Why would I want the scene—'changed'?" Jessalyn was looking stricken. "I—I couldn't go away and leave Mackie . . ."

"Of course you can go away and leave that cat! That's the most ridiculous thing I've ever heard you say, Mom."

"But who would take care of him?"

Lorene laughed, this was preposterous. The creature was a *feral cat* and could take care of itself.

"Maybe—Virgil? He'd be perfect. He loves animals and he has virtually nothing to do. If you could rely upon him to drop by the house, of course. That's a big 'if.'"

Midsentence, Lorene was casting doubt on the reliability of her brother. There was something like a knot in her brain, she sometimes thought. She could hear herself say these self-harmful things but could not always control herself. Fortunately, Jessalyn would never notice.

"Well—it's too soon. I wouldn't feel right."

"'Too soon'—meaning what?"

"After—you know . . ."

"No, Mom. You tell me."

"Well, I mean—it's hard to explain. Bali is so far away . . ."

"Yes, you've said. 'Far away' is the point."

"I'm not a good traveler. I never have been. There are reasons for me to stay here . . ."

"Really? What reasons?"

Jessalyn fell silent. Her eyes were lowered, evasive. Her mouth moved as if she were about to cry.

Lorene felt a wave of exasperation for her mother, and for herself. *For God's sake leave the poor woman alone. It's Whitey she can't leave, of course Bali is far away.*

NEXT MORNING a call came from Beverly, sounding agitated.

"Lorene! I know you're there, God damn *pick up*."

Lorene hesitated. It was not her usual custom to *pick up* when her excitable older sister called her, which was too frequently.

Lorene was preparing to leave for school and she did not want to speak with her sister particularly at this early, unspoiled hour of the day—that would be like starting a ski run in pristine-fresh snow a short distance above a tangle of rocks and underbrush.

"Lorene! Do you know that our mother is *seeing someone*?"

Lorene fumbled to pick up her phone. "'Seeing someone'? You mean—Leo Colwin?"

"No! For God's sake, that's been over for months. This is a new person—a stranger. But Virgil seems to know him, he has said. An *artiste*. And *Hispanic*."

"Wait. How do you mean, Mom is 'seeing' this person? I had dinner with her just last night, and she didn't tell *me*."

"Because she isn't telling us! Because she feels guilty! Because it has been only seven and a half months since Daddy passed away, and this is *too soon,* and the identity of the man is shameful to her—some sort of *Hispanic*."

Each time the word *Hispanic* rolled off Beverly's tongue the sound glittered with sarcasm like saliva.

Lorene was stunned. Jessalyn had behaved deceptively with *her*?

There was a small Hispanic population in the Hammond area, and virtually no overlapping with the "white" community except for house cleaners, lawn crews, service people. An ever-increasing number of Hispanic students at the high school but not one Hispanic faculty member.

Well, yes—there was an Hispanic custodian who greeted "Dr. McClaren" with exaggerated courtliness whenever they met in the corridor.

Beverly was saying, incensed: "Thom has had his suspicions, he told me. Last week he went over to visit Mom and said it was very upsetting, he could detect the presence of a stranger as soon as he stepped inside the door. He could practically smell this intruder, Thom said."

"Do you mean—someone is living there? A man? In our house?"

"No! That would be outrageous." Beverly paused, breathing audibly. "It hasn't come to that—yet. We don't think."

"But—who is this person?"

"His name is 'Hugo Ramirez'—or maybe it's 'Martinez'—he's a *Cuban.*"

Lorene listened in disbelief. Their mother, with a *Cuban*! The McClarens didn't know any *Cubans,* she was sure.

"How would Mom ever meet a *Cuban*? Our housemaids were Filipino and the lawn crew men are Mexicans, I think. This doesn't seem plausible."

"I told you, Virgil knows this person! He isn't a laborer! Mom must have met him at the Chautauqua arts fair. She hasn't said a word so far to *me.*"

"But how does Virgil know about this?"

"Who knows how Virgil knows? For God's sake, Lorene. That isn't the issue."

Beverly spoke rapidly, not very coherently. Lorene couldn't quite follow the nature of her sister's grievance but understood clearly—they'd all been *betrayed.*

For unmistakably, Jessalyn had deceived Lorene. Even if the relationship with the "Cuban" was utterly innocent, Jessalyn had certainly not informed her.

Wasn't omission a kind of deception? A failure to reveal the truth? Lorene tried to recall the evening: they'd had supper together in the kitchen, a favorite childhood meal (Spanish omelet, whole grain bread) which Jessalyn had happily prepared and Lorene had hungrily eaten. Lorene had discussed with Jessalyn, admittedly it had been a one-sided conversation, the possibility of Jessalyn accompanying her on a trip to Bali, or Thailand; just once, the phone had rung, and instead of ignoring it as she usually did, quietly Jessalyn had gone to check the caller ID, but had not picked up the phone. (Had the call been from the mysterious Cuban? If so, he hadn't left any message. Lorene had assumed that the call had been from a solicitor and Jessalyn hadn't said a word about the call.)

Over the course of the evening Lorene had confided in her mother that, since Whitey's death, in fact since Whitey's hospitalization, her sleep patterns had been "shot to hell"; she found herself weeping over trivial things, like a newspaper obituary for someone she didn't even know—"James Arness, remember? Daddy used to love him in *Gunsmoke*." She had not wanted to upset Jessalyn by telling her about her enemies at the high school, still less the lengths to which she was driven to defend herself against them.

"Oh Mom, what is this weird thing?"—Lorene had discovered, on a sofa, an odd, egg-shaped object made of bright green yarn and white feathers, that looked like a TV comic's parody of something "arty."

Embarrassed, Jessalyn identified it as a work of art created by a Nigerian artist living now in Hammond. Lorene asked how much it had cost, which was Lorene's usual query in such circumstances, and when Jessalyn told her, Lorene laughed heartily. "As P. T. Barnum said, Mom—'There's a sucker born every minute.'"

"Oh, but I think it's very—beautiful . . ."

"Well, it's *green*. And Mackie hasn't torn it to pieces just yet."

And what else? Had that been all? Had Jessalyn hinted at something further? Lorene did now remember her mother fussing more than ordinarily over a crystal vase filled with sharply sweet white flowers—lilies?—she'd positioned on the kitchen table between them, exactly in the middle.

The Dice

Whitey said, *Your life is in your hands, darling.*

And when she opened her hand, there on her palm was a pair of eyes.

She recoiled with horror and another time she looked, and saw—*Not eyes. Dice.*

THESE WERE OLD, IVORY DICE. Handed down through Whitey's family. She'd found them in his bureau drawer among cuff links, a very old wristwatch, nail scissors. The dice were discolored, the hue of jaundice. And grimy.

Whitey said, *Toss the dice, darling. Don't be afraid.*

She was hearing wind chimes at the back of the house. This was a comforting sound and yet a worrisome sound, like a smell of ether.

A wind had started in the night. Rain was flung against the part-opened windows of the bedroom. In the morning, the filmy curtains would be damp beneath her bare feet.

Something timid about bare feet. She walked mincingly, hesitantly.

She'd pleaded *no*. She did not want to toss the dice.

She wasn't that sort. She had never taken risks. Her marriage had been a large, gentle net that had caught her and Whitey together and held them fast and secure and would not ever release them except Whitey had vanished, she was left to struggle in the net, alone.

She did not want to toss the dice for the dice were her life now, and not his.

And so Whitey said, *Toss the dice, darling. It's your time.*

Dear Hugo

It is not enough to mourn.

She'd written him the letter which was a letter from the heart.

She'd written the letter and sent it and forgotten it.

In such haste she'd written, and the sheet of paper stippled with her tears.

It had not been calculated—*Dear Hugo*. There was nothing in it of deliberation, premeditation.

In the very writing, the forgetting.

IN LATE JUNE she glanced out an upstairs window of her house and saw, at the end of the driveway, a man on foot, seemingly a stranger, starting to push her large trash container on its wobbly rollers in the direction of the house.

Who was this? Not one of the county sanitation workers—there was no sanitation truck in sight, and in any case the workers never troubled to push emptied trash containers back to a house. Usually, they left the containers overturned on the road, like collapsed drunks on their backs.

Also, it was late afternoon. The weekly trash pickup was always in the morning.

Whoever this was, he was being very helpful. Jessalyn was uneasy, wondering *why*.

She'd been noticing how long the driveway was, and how impractical. Not a straight driveway—naturally, it had to curve, like a meandering stream; not paved, not covered in asphalt, but comprised of very small, pink-hued pebbles through which, in the absence of Whitey, miniature weeds had begun to sprout.

No longer regularly mowed, the lawn was reverting to tall grasses, and no longer *grass*. In season a marvel of yellow dandelions, thistles and "wildflowers."

Of course, the property at 99 Old Farm Road wouldn't be going entirely *to seed*. That was not going to happen. Included in the contract establishing the widow's trust was an allotment for ongoing property maintenance which Jessalyn was spared having to negotiate, as she was spared dealing with taxes on the property, fuel delivery in cold weather, the cleaning of roof gutters and other routine services. The late husband John Earle McClaren had seen to all that.

In addition, the widow's children kept a sharp eye on the property. That is, several sharp eyes. Beverly was always showing up unannounced to prowl through the house to see how it was being "kept." (Surprisingly, the house was looking very "well-kept": Jessalyn avoided most of the rooms.) Thom dropped by once a week to see how things were looking outside; after a windstorm, Thom ordered Whitey's old lawn crew to return, to haul away debris and remove damaged limbs. He saw to it that the irregularly tended lawn didn't turn into an uncouth field, that would dismay and infuriate residents on Old Farm Road who (so far) had been sympathetic with Jessalyn McClaren as a "despondent"—"mildly deranged"—widow. If and when the house needed major repairs, Thom would step in. Paying for the upkeep on the family property out of his own pocket was a sound investment, and Thom believed in sound investments.

Jessalyn was thinking that, with things so altered in their lives, Whitey himself might not care quite so much about appearances as he'd once cared.

What the hell, darling. Lighten it, eh?

Jessalyn was trying. She was!

For the worst had happened, after all. The husband had died, the wife had survived, if but barely. There was that: the worst was over.

But you have to try again, Jess. Just one more time.

Jessalyn could hear the rumbling, rattling sound of the trash container being pushed toward the house. If she hadn't been looking out the window she might have mistaken it for thunder.

Once every two weeks Jessalyn pushed the trash container out to the curb—she had very little trash, not nearly enough for a weekly pickup; she supposed the sanitation men felt sorry for her. When the McClarens had all lived in the house, two large trash containers were required a week, at least. Now, with just the widow, there was a scarcity of trash and the recycling was even more pitiable—these squat rubbery bins Jessalyn hauled out to the curb only once a month, green for paper products, yellow for bottles/cans. Her muscles ached, and her breath came short—the containers all wobbled on their wheels and seemed to resist her. For what is hauled out to the curb is the futility of our lives, that loops back upon itself, endless.

But the curbside bins were a reassuring sign to neighbors: *Yes, I am alive! I am still producing trash.*

As he drew nearer to the house the stranger so affably pushing the container began to look familiar: wide-brimmed hat that obscured much of his face, drooping gray mustache that obscured the rest of his face. A white shirt, sleeves folded neatly back to the elbow.

He wasn't young, you could see. An odd combination of dignified and just-slightly-shabby.

Tall and loose-limbed, even jaunty, pushing the container on its rattling rollers. It had not seemed to occur to this person that he might be trespassing on someone's property, and that his presence might be a cause of alarm.

Jessalyn felt a stab of hot blood in her face. *Him!*

The man in the cemetery—*Hugo.* The photographer who'd taken her picture without her permission.

She'd written to him—of course. A hasty letter sent to "Hugo Martinez" in care of the Chautauqua arts fair, she'd forgotten almost as soon as she'd mailed it.

Well, he'd sent her a single calla lily. She did remember that.

She'd seen him (she was reasonably sure) in the Hope Baptist Church on Armory Street but (she was reasonably sure, to her relief) he had not seen her.

What had Virgil said of Hugo Martinez?—Jessalyn tried to remember.

He respected Martinez. He admired Martinez's work, which he seemed to consider superior to his own. Virgil's honesty was such, he didn't spare himself such evaluations, as he did not spare others.

Not like he'd stolen your soul. Had Virgil said that?

The driveway curved off, and Martinez followed the driveway, not entering a small courtyard at the front of the house, and not approaching the front door; he was pushing the cumbersome container back where it belonged, almost as if he'd known where it belonged—out of sight, alongside the garage wall. Like a handyman!—Jessalyn thought. Or a husband.

HE'D SAID HE COULD HELP HER, if she needed help.

Being a widow. He figured, she could use help.

She opened her mouth to thank him, and to protest—she didn't need help. But her throat closed and she could not speak.

Somehow, she'd hurried downstairs. He had been about to leave. (Had he? She wasn't sure. Had he parked out on the road, out of sight of the house? But why?)

She'd been breathless, hurrying after Hugo Martinez. She'd steeled herself for a ringing doorbell, or a knock at the door—which she had not intended to answer; for he had no way of knowing if she was home, or, if home, if others were in the house with her. *He had no way of knowing anything about her, how vulnerable she was, how lonely, how badly she had been hoping he might come to her in a way like this though never would Jessalyn have imagined that he might come to her like this.*

Somehow, she heard herself inviting Hugo Martinez inside. And he was saying, Yes!—but first he had something to bring for her; awkwardly backing off, smiling in a way you'd have to call boisterous, the droopy gray mustache like Spanish moss getting in the way of his speech so that his words were blurred; Jessalyn stared after him not knowing what he was doing, if he was leaving her to return, or only just leaving; hurrying out to the road, actually half-running, but with a just-perceptible weakness in his left leg; but then returning at once in his car, a stately deep-purple Mercedes-Benz, but a badly weathered Mercedes-Benz missing chrome trim along its sides and with one mismatched tire; very carefully Martinez drove this vehicle along the pink-pebbled driveway stippled with weeds, and parked in front of the little courtyard where Jessalyn waited in a trance of apprehension not knowing what on earth she was doing, what terrible mistake she'd made, that might be irrevocable, for which her children would pity her, and grieve for her.

Out of the car Hugo Martinez emerged smiling—his smile, baring somewhat yellowed, uneven teeth, was really remarkable, triumphant. In one hand a bouquet of a dozen waxy-white flowers, Jessalyn knew to be calla lilies at a glance, even before she'd detected the exquisite, sickly-sweet odor, and in the other hand a bottle of wine she guessed to be red wine. And inside the house she took both the calla lilies and the bottle of wine from Hugo Martinez as if the visit were not a surprise, but had been expected and anticipated.

HE SAID, HE'D BEEN GRATEFUL to have her letter. It was a beautiful letter he'd read several times, and would always treasure.

He'd thought of her quite a bit. He could not say why. He had not intended to speak with her. He'd sent the lily—that was a kind of apology. But since he hadn't been *sorry,* it wasn't clear what he was apologizing for.

He had known her name from the grave marker, and indeed he knew the name *McClaren.* And so he'd made inquiries. It was not so difficult to discover where she lived. That was how he'd known where to send the flower.

He hadn't intended to seek her out, personally. He had not.

He'd hoped she wouldn't see the exhibit. Wouldn't see the photograph in the cemetery. Usually people didn't recognize themselves in the photographs of Hugo Martinez in which faces were turned aside and identities obscured.

It was startling to Jessalyn, to hear her visitor speak of himself in so formal a way—"Hugo Martinez." There was an innocent sort of vanity in this, like the vanity of a child.

His English was slightly stilted, self-conscious. Yet there was no discernible accent in his speech.

He'd come to apologize, he said. That she had recognized herself, and this recognition caused her pain. She had been so lost in the cemetery, he could not leave her.

Well—he'd left the cemetery to return to his car, he said; but then he'd gone back again. He'd found her glove on the path. He'd taken her picture surreptitiously. It was a failing of his, the habit of secrecy, the illicit and the taboo. He did not want to be "open" and "honest"—that was not his personality.

He'd been thinking about her, even before her letter. He had not wanted to think that he'd fallen in love with her, in just those few seconds in the cemetery.

Fallen in love!—Jessalyn wasn't sure she'd heard this. She began to laugh, startled and confused.

Well—why was it so funny? Hugo Martinez glared at her and demanded to know.

Quickly Jessalyn said it wasn't funny at all—really, not at all. It was a very serious thing—if he was serious.

Martinez said, huffily, that he was *always serious*.

She wasn't understanding, that was it.

He laughed and said, D'you have a corkscrew, dear? I'll open the wine.

NO! THANK YOU but she did not drink. Usually.

Is this—*usual*? He'd seemed curious to know.

Kindly eyes, but bemused. Inquisitive. A face once handsome but now creased, weatherworn like old leather, with odd comma-like dents in the forehead, and a long, elegant, flaring nose like a miniature horn.

The mustache was distracting. Too large, too lank. Graying-silver stiff hairs, different in texture from the softer, thinner silver-coppery hair of the man's head.

Smiling to see the hairs of the mustache stirring, with the man's breath. Oh but why would you want such an encumbrance on your face, drooping over your mouth?

As a girl Jessalyn had shuddered at the very idea of a mustache—all the girls she knew did. Imagine kissing *that*.

Of course, you didn't kiss the mustache. But the mustache was *there*.

And why was she smiling?—Hugo Martinez asked, curious.

Was she smiling?—she hadn't known. For a moment she'd been feeling giddy, unreal.

You seem happy, Jez'lyn. Much more than I remember. But, well—*El tiempo cura todas las heridas.*

Jessalyn laughed startled and uneasy as if, in the guise of saying something comforting in his courtly deep-baritone voice, her visitor had cursed her.

How to reply, she could not. A stammer began deep in her throat.

She'd understood exactly what Hugo Martinez had said. Not knowing a syllable of Spanish, yet she'd known.

It is the most banal truths that endure, Hugo Martinez said, gently. (Had he seen her stricken look? *Had* she revealed her emotions so transparently?) But you soon learn, dear, if you are of any age, that the most urgent truths are never not *banal.*

Jessalyn murmured a vague *yes*. She had no idea what they were talking about.

Recklessly she'd climbed into a small boat with this mustached stranger. She had no oar, he was the one who had the oar, who had called her *dear.*

There was an air of the buccaneer about Hugo Martinez, in fact. The rakish angle of his wide-brimmed straw hat which he'd politely removed, entering the house; his shirt, open nearly to mid-chest, revealing a dense clump of silvered hair; the straightness of his shoulders, that signaled a kind of male swagger. His hair was long enough to fall languidly over the collar of his shirt and his shirt was made of a fine, soft material like Egyptian linen, worn at the cuffs.

His trousers were badly wrinkled though also of a fine fabric.

On his feet, hand-tooled leather sandals, also worn. Jessalyn had not been able to resist glancing at his feet, appalled to see that the nails of both his big toes were badly discolored, thick as horn.

Old, black blood beneath the nails, Jessalyn knew. The nails of Thom's big toes had been identical when he'd been a teenager, from hiking boots.

Why are you crying, now, Jez'lyn?—Hugo Martinez stared at her in dismay. Please, I wish you would not.

ON OPPOSITE SIDES OF THE KITCHEN TABLE they sat breathless.

As if they'd climbed a great flight of steps and each ahead of the other calling *Hurry!*

In the center of the table Jessalyn set the calla lilies in a cut-crystal vase.

Their beauty was mesmerizing to her. Their sweet scent, sharp as a blade piercing her brain as the mustached man regarded her with bemused eyes.

Gray irises, shading to dark. Fine-burst capillaries, a faint yellowish tinge to the eyeballs as if Hugo Martinez had been ill recently, or had not slept well the previous night.

She was feeling just slightly faint: the man's nearness.

The chair in which she sat felt as if it were at the edge of an abyss. Dared not glance downward for fear she could not see any floor.

With delight and trepidation she'd brought wineglasses from a cupboard: very clean, spotless, for Jessalyn washed such delicate glassware by hand.

The most innocent and piteous of vanities: the widow's pride in cleanliness, order in her empty house.

With an air of zest and ceremony the mustached man poured wine into glasses for each of them. What was the celebration?—the man's hand was not quite steady.

Yet, it was a perfect moment. Hugo Martinez had imagined it so, and it was so, and Jessalyn would recall for the remainder of her life each moment of this evening with the magnified precision with which, using the smallest possible tweezers, you would pick tiny fragments of glass out of your skin.

A special sort of red wine, Hugo said, not expensive, not showy but very good, his favorite wine from the Douro Valley, Portugal.

Jessalyn had set out a hunk of Italian cheese with a tough, dried rind, a plate of Whitey's favorite rye crackers. A small bowl of olives (she hoped had not acquired mold from the refrigerator), and a large bowl of (seedless) black grapes just slightly past their prime.

Oh, and a container of "organic" hummus, that Virgil had brought over several weeks ago.

Smiling inside his mustache Hugo helped himself to the feast. Was her guest laughing at her?—Jessalyn wondered.

Then she saw, to her horror: she'd forgotten napkins! Never in her adult life had she forgotten napkins!

Discreetly, unobtrusively, Hugo Martinez removed a handkerchief from a pocket, on which to wipe his fingers. (Jessalyn's stunned brain managed to register that the handkerchief was cotton, and not mere paper tissue.)

Belatedly now Jessalyn went to fetch napkins from a drawer. Very handsome mauve linen napkins they were, one for Hugo Martinez and one for her.

So sorry! I don't know what I was thinking . . .

Courtly Hugo Martinez took no note of her self-consciousness, no more than he might have taken note of her nakedness if she'd appeared naked before him, in her confused state.

His manners were exquisite. Though he was eating with his fingers and cheese crumbs were accumulating in the silvery rifts of his mustache.

Next time, Hugo Martinez said, pointedly, he would take her out to dinner, for a proper meal.

Proper meal. What did that mean?

Jessalyn laughed. She was feeling giddy, unreal.

Boldly she picked up her wineglass. She knew, Hugo Martinez would be hurt if she failed to drink his favorite Portuguese wine: that was how men were.

Yet, she could not bring herself to drink. It was enough to touch her lips to the dark liquid, that seemed to give off a smoldering glow, an actual heat.

She thought—*I must not get drunk. That would be a terrible mistake.*

Long ago, years ago in another lifetime, wine had had a palpable effect upon her: eyelids drooping, a sensation of erotic yearning in the pit of her belly, slurred speech, inappropriate hilarity.

. . . a terrible mistake.

Staring at Hugo Martinez. The vulpine nose, the drooping mustache and stained teeth. Broken capillaries in his eyes. His breath sounded scratchy.

She was enthralled by him. She could not look away.

(An *artiste*. Whitey would laugh, in derision! Beverly would shake her head, in disgust.)

(But where was Whitey? Upstairs, in retreat?)

She was in dread of Hugo Martinez asking her about—Whitey.

She would shake her head, in silence. Nothing to say. Please.

But Hugo did not ask her about Whitey. Instead, he asked her about the house: D'you live in this enormous place by yourself?

Out of nowhere the question came, veering at her like a bat.

She could not duck. Her eyes blinked rapidly. Was this an accusation?—or just a curious question?

Murmuring *no,* not exactly alone. But—*yes.*

Recalling how she'd seen Hugo Martinez outside in the driveway, just for an instant, glancing up at the house, and at the horizontal sprawl of the house, a fleeting expression in his face of surprise, disapproval.

Don't hate me because I am rich. Please no.

Wanting to explain to him, really she wasn't rich! Her own family had not been rich. Her life was just something that had happened to her, virtually none of it had been her choice.

But she sat mute, abashed. Seeing that she was uncomfortable Hugo said it was a beautiful house, and must be quite old. Beautiful tall trees—he'd recognized black oaks. And tall grasses, unlike the "manicured" lawns of North Hammond.

His tone was more bemused now, and not accusatory. He did not (seem to) blame *her.*

But Jessalyn quite understood, how absurdly large the house was, even when Whitey had been alive, and even when the younger children had been still at home.

Hugo was asking if the house had a history?—Was it listed on the National Register?

N-No. It was not.

Properties in this area, on Old Farm Road, were Revolutionary War—wasn't that so? Hugo Martinez was asking, not unpleasantly.

He is a Marxist. A Maoist. He will hate you, and hurt you. Mom, think what you are doing!

(Was this Beverly? Why on earth was Jessalyn thinking of Beverly at such a time?)

In a voice determined not to sound defensive Jessalyn heard herself say yes, part of the house was said to date back to the 1770s but there had been many renovations and additions in all that time, so the house wasn't on the Register. Whitey had said—*We don't want to live in a museum!*

Whitey. Jessalyn hadn't intended to speak the name but suddenly and unexpectedly she'd spoken it, as matter-of-factly as if Whitey were in the next room.

There was a moment of silence. A crackling sort of silence it seemed, like electricity.

And then gravely Hugo Martinez nodded, and sighed such a great sigh, the hairs of his mustache stirred.

Indeed, my dear, you are correct—*We don't want to live in a museum.*

BETTER SEND THIS PERSON AWAY. *What are you thinking of, Mom!*

Are you so lonely? So desperate? Why aren't we enough for you?

What would Dad think?

Had not she promised the children that she would not invite anyone into the house whom she didn't know? Didn't know *well*?

Beverly was still marveling over how Jessalyn had invited back to the house *an actual homeless, destitute madman we were all God-damned lucky didn't rob and murder her and burn down the house—Mom, that's our house, too!*

(Strictly speaking, the house was not theirs. The property at 99 Old Farm Road belonged now exclusively to Jessalyn McClaren though under the terms of the trust, Jessalyn could not sell the house, nor "enter into any legal arrangement by which the house became a rental property" without the permission of the trust executor.)

(In Jessalyn's will the property was to be left to the five children, to do with what they wished: a prospect Jessalyn would no more allow herself to consider than she would have shoved her hand into the running garbage disposal.)

But Hugo Martinez, though a stranger to Jessalyn, was not a stranger to Virgil, and was a "known quantity" in the Hammond area—Jessalyn could have explained. Photographer, poet, "activist"—(what did that mean, exactly? Political?).

Virgil hadn't told Jessalyn anything crucial about Hugo, now that Jessalyn thought of it.

They were still hoping that Leo Colwin would return. Beverly never lost the opportunity to speak of Leo in the warmest terms—*A widower, a sweetheart, plenty of money of his own and not (so far as we know) yet incontinent or demented. Mom, come to your senses!*

(Had Beverly really said these words? Not quite yet. But soon, Jessalyn feared.)

In fact Leo continued to call Jessalyn. His voice mail messages had turned resentful, accusatory. He had not forgiven her for fleeing from his car, he'd been embarrassed by her abrupt departure from his life—*People ask about you, and what can I say?—I'd thought you were a gracious person, Jessalyn. I spent money and time on you and you led me to believe you returned my feelings. I thought you were a LADY.*

In one message, Leo had seemed to be weeping angrily, or choking back fury.

Jessalyn no longer listened to Leo's messages but deleted them as quickly as she discovered them. She was determined not to feel guilt—not to *feel guilty*. No.

DAMN! WHAT WAS *IT*?—a *cat*?

So quickly it happened, neither Jessalyn nor Hugo Martinez had seen the squint-eye tomcat creep up soundlessly beside Hugo, upend himself on hind legs and swat at Hugo's hand with unsheathed claws.

Nearly capsizing in his chair, spilling some of his wine, Hugo shoved the animal away. Red-faced in an instant he cursed in (what Jessalyn assumed to be) Spanish.

Oh Mackie!—how could you . . .

Appalled, Jessalyn tried to slap the tomcat away from Hugo Martinez, but Mackie paid not the slightest heed to her. He was on four legs now, back arched like a Hallowe'en cat and stubby tail erect, baring his teeth in a silent hiss.

No, Mackie! Stop that. Hugo is a—a friend . . .

(This was embarrassing. In the excitement Mackie seemed to be defying Jessalyn, too. Making menacing growls you could interpret as directed at *her.*)

Fairly quickly too, Hugo recovered from the attack. Seemed to recover. Flush-faced and laughing, wiping a streak of blood from the back of his hand onto his handkerchief.

That's some damn-big bastard-cat you have, Jez'lyn. Man!

Unexpectedly, Hugo was sounding admiring. Indeed, Mackie was an astonishing sight, considered purely as an animal: his fur was no longer matted but glossy-black from an improved diet and brushing with a hairbrush by Jessalyn, his single tawny-golden eye glared with something like animal intelligence, ferocity.

Hugo broke off a piece of the hard Italian cheese, and held it out to Mackie, who considered it for a moment before swatting it out of Hugo's fingers, and devouring it hungrily on the floor.

Within a moment the cheese-fragment was gone. Hugo broke off another, and after that another, each hungrily devoured by the tomcat—Jessalyn wanted to plead with her guest no, not a good idea to feed an animal from the table, especially not this animal who knew to take advantage of human weakness.

But Hugo Martinez and Mackie were rapidly becoming friends, it seemed. Hugo spoke to the cat in a low admiring voice—*Mi amigo,* a beautiful cat.

Jessalyn was astonished. No one who'd seen Mackie had had a good word to say about him, and her older children considered him a health hazard.

Jessalyn said that she supposed Mackie was beautiful, in his own way . . . His few white markings, lightning-shaped, were somehow *mitigating.*

Smiling Hugo dared to touch Mackie's hard head with his knuckles—Jessalyn held her breath, expecting the cat to rake the man with his nails, but Mackie, absorbed in eating, scarcely seemed to notice.

Hugo asked about the cat's name and Jessalyn said that his actual name was "Mack the Knife."

"Mack the Knife"—that is this big guy's *name*?

Jessalyn was at a loss to explain the name, which seemed to amuse Hugo Martinez. She could not recall where the name had come from, and had begun to think, in a way, that Mack the Knife was the cat's actual name—how she'd learned it, she could not recall.

Had he been wearing a collar, originally?—no . . .

Jessalyn explained that Mackie was a stray who'd showed up at the rear of the house a few months ago. At first she'd just left food for him outside, then in the cold months she began to let him spend more time inside, and now—he spent at least half his time indoors and most of that time asleep.

(She didn't want to add that Mackie sometimes slept at the foot of her bed, on her bed; that he sometimes nudged against her feet through the bedclothes. These were the happiest moments in her life now but she did not want to share such revealing information with a stranger even if the stranger had kindly eyes.)

She had asked neighbors along Old Farm Road if Mackie belonged to anyone. She had left flyers in mailboxes with his fierce, single-eyed picture clumsily photocopied. As the older children said disapprovingly, it was obvious that Mackie had been abandoned—*exiled*. Who would want such an ugly thing!

All this delighted Hugo Martinez. In the last several minutes he'd acquired a raucous sort of deep-chest laughter. He didn't seem to mind that Mackie had scratched him—he hadn't said a word about rabies, tetanus. The cat's roughness and size, even the single glaring eye, that so offended others, seemed to impress and amuse Hugo, and to have expanded his estimation of Jessalyn.

That she could handle a cat like Mackie? That she *could not handle* a cat like Mackie, but took tender care of him just the same?

Impulsively Jessalyn confided in Hugo Martinez that her older children hated Mackie—it was very distressing, they were always after her to take Mackie to the vet's and have him put to sleep.

Older children. Jessalyn hadn't meant to introduce this subject just yet.

Like *husband. Deceased husband.* Not yet.

Oh, why'd she say *older children.* Hugo would have a vision of overgrown stunted creatures, wizen-faced with age, hunchbacked, like dwarves in old Spanish paintings.

But he said nothing. He did not inquire.

He, too, must have—children? Adult children?

Hugo Martinez was Jessalyn's age, at least. His creased and leathery face suggested age yet the briskness and swagger of his manner suggested a younger man.

She wondered if he, too, despite his hearty laughter and the gusto with which he ate and drank, was living a posthumous life. A masquerade-life, like her own.

A life where nothing mattered, essentially. But there were accidents possible, like rips in a tent . . .

All this while Hugo was smiling, leaning over to rub his knuckles against Mackie's hard-boned head. (The black fur on the top of Mackie's head was thinner than elsewhere; you felt the bone of the cat-skull startlingly close.) Jessalyn would never have dared to rub Mackie's head so vigorously, he had a way of suddenly nipping. But he'd begun to purr loudly at Hugo's touch, like a slightly malfunctioning motor.

This purr delighted Hugo who dared to tickle Mackie beneath his chin, dangerously close to the sharp yellowed teeth.

Thoughtfully Hugo said, it was a good idea to take Mackie to the vet's. Y'know, Jez'lyn, a tomcat has a need for—(here Hugo made a vague snipping gesture toward his crotch, without the slightest hint of self-consciousness)—if he has not yet had it.

Jessalyn bit her lower lip. Of course, she knew—Mackie was a tomcat, and tomcats had to be *neutered.*

It was an embarrassing subject, or an awkward subject, or ought to have been, but Hugo didn't seem to notice unlike Whitey who (Jessalyn knew) wouldn't have been able to resist making a nervous joke.

Oh but Jessalyn had tried. She'd tried to take Mackie to a vet. After her children had nagged her. Tried to convince Mackie to get into a carrying cage, which she'd bought at a pet store at the mall for just that purpose, but Mackie fought desperately, and caterwauled as if he were being murdered, and would have clawed her badly except she'd had enough sense to wear gardening gloves. (Jessalyn didn't add the lurid detail that Mackie had sprayed much of the kitchen before running outside and staying away for forty-eight hours.) One of the problems was, the carrying cage was smaller than she'd thought it would be, and opened from the top, which gave the crazed Mackie an advantage.

Somberly Hugo Martinez announced he would do the task tomorrow.

He would do—what?

Assist her with the cat.

Assist her with the *cat*?

Jessalyn was stunned, Hugo spoke so familiarly. As if they were old friends, and he had every right to tell her what to do.

Hugo said: Since the spaying had to be done, and should have been done long ago, for the cat's sake, and for hers—he would assist her.

Jessalyn was stammering no, she didn't think . . .

Looking very pleased, Hugo poured another glass of wine for himself. He'd blotted all the blood from the back of his hand onto his handkerchief, and the scratches were no longer bleeding.

No trouble, dear. I will drop by tomorrow, I am busy but I will make time in the late morning—around noon.

Tomorrow! Hugo had not even left her house, and already he was planning the next visit.

Suddenly, Jessalyn was feeling very tired. Unwisely she'd swallowed a mouthful or two of wine and the effect was instantaneous—her eyelids were shutting.

Tried to protest to Hugo: Mackie wasn't hers, really. She had no authority over him—his cat-body. Though she had not been able to locate his owner, Mackie certainly had had an owner, and she couldn't interfere with him—"Mackie" wasn't even his name.

Hugo regarded her quizzically, as if she were saying something meant to be witty—but what?

Mackie was a "free spirit"—Jessalyn tried to explain. He happened to have taken up residence in this area, but he wasn't *hers.*

Jessalyn was speaking carefully and yet not clearly—she could hear her voice slurred, as if through water. Wine?

Hugo disagreed with whatever she'd struggled to say. Not true, he said. The tomcat was a creature who'd come to depend upon her. He was in her care now. Jessalyn must know that feral animals lived much shorter lives than house pets. Mackie was a "big, tough bastard" but he needed a vet's care, as he deserved to live a long time.

Like all of us, Hugo added, pointedly.

By this time Jessalyn was feeling very—strange. Badly she wanted this man, this stranger, to leave her house, it had been a mistake to invite him inside.

Oh, what had she done! She was crushed with shame, apprehension.

It happened often to her, in this new life. A wave of terrible contrition would sweep over her, scarcely could she breathe.

Ridiculous! Why are you still alive?

Well, then—breathe through this straw. If you must.

Hugo Martinez was regarding Jessalyn with a smile you'd want to call cunning. Inside the mustache, the man's mouth looked more *intimate* than it would have without a mustache—Jessalyn thought.

He'd been extolling—what? Something about the cat, his "wild spirit"—yet, he was insisting that Mackie be *neutered*. Had he been reciting a poem? First in Spanish, then in English. A poem by—Lock-a? *Lorca?*

She was remembering now, the man was a poet as well as a photographer. Somehow, she trusted a poet even less than she trusted a photographer.

For instance, in all this time Hugo Martinez had been careful not to say a word about his background. Not one word about his personal life—was he married? Or had he been married? (Of course, Hugo Martinez had been married. You could see at a glance that this was a man who'd had "relations" with women—girls—since the age of twelve. That kind.) He had avoided saying anything revealing about himself—all Jessalyn would recall afterward is that he'd boasted of being a "secretive" person—as if warning her, he didn't intend to be "open"—"honest" with her—for *that was not his personality.*

He'd drunk most of the bottle of Portuguese wine, and he'd eaten most of the Italian cheese, and left skid marks in the hummus from dipping with crackers. In front of him, and on the floor, were scattered crumbs; Mackie had discovered the floor-crumbs and was licking them up greedily with his pink tongue in a way that made Jessalyn want to laugh.

Time for Hugo Martinez to leave. He had sensed the shift in Jessalyn's mood, and knew he should not linger.

Perhaps he knew: a widow is exhausted easily. A widow is easily becalmed, lost at sea. Her sails are befouled, leaden.

Neatly Hugo folded his bloodstained handkerchief, to return to his pocket: he'd patted and dabbed at his mustache, fastidiously. Now folding up the sleeves of his shirt, deliberately. Jessalyn saw the dark, slanted hairs on his wrists, thick as a pelt on his forearms, and felt a sharp, indescribable sensation.

Yet wondering: Why is a man's hair such different hues, arms, chest, mustache, head? Whitey too had brandished a kind of *miscellany* of hues as if different parts of his body were different ages and the hair of his head the very whitest—the oldest, and the most sage.

Jez'lyn, dear—what is so funny?

So *funny*? Jessalyn was not laughing, was she?

Her eyelids had become so heavy, she could barely hold her head erect. The effort of speaking with this man, this aggressive stranger, the effort of listening to him, and feeling his presence so close to her, only a few feet away, was a strain like pushing a heavy trash container out to the curb, on faulty rollers.

Hugo Martinez rose to his full height—he had to be as tall as Thom. Jessalyn narrowed her eyes not wanting to look up at him but having no choice.

Here was the problem: the man took up too much space. He'd been encroaching on *her space.*

Since Whitey had left her Jessalyn had become accustomed to space around her in the house, no one crowding near, no one *looking at her in that way.*

Recalling how long ago Whitey McClaren, he'd been Johnny McClaren at the time, had looked at her—his eyes moving over her, startled and yearning, seeing a girl Jessalyn herself could not quite imagine, surely not the girl she saw in the mirror . . .

And now, Hugo Martinez was looking at her. Not quite so helplessly, for Hugo Martinez was much, much older than Johnny McClaren had been. And Jessalyn was much older than the girl she'd been.

He did seem very happy with her. Or because of her. His big stained teeth bared inside the drooping mustache—Jez'lyn, good night! My dear.

Jez'lyn. Dear.

He took up his dapper wide-brimmed straw hat, and positioned it on his head, just so. Jessalyn could see that, in his mind's eye, he was seeing his reflection in a familiar mirror and approving of what he saw.

At the door Hugo paused to take her hand, that was warm in his, like a living thing, and kissed the palm, lightly.

To the man's departing back she said, in a hoarse voice, she didn't think he should come back the next day . . .

Had he heard her?—Hugo Martinez turned, smiled and waved, and strode briskly to the deep-purple Mercedes-Benz parked in the driveway.

From the doorway she watched him drive away. Then, she shut the door and locked it.

Alone! Alone at last.

She was nearly fainting with relief, the man had gone. And she would not see him again.

"MACKIE! COME HERE. *PLEASE.*"

The damned cat was lingering downstairs in the hope that the loud-laughing male visitor who'd fed him bits of dried cheese and rubbed his head with his knuckles would return. Only late, at midnight, when Jessalyn had given up calling him, did Mackie come padding into the room with a querulous *Mew!* As if *he* was annoyed with *her.*

So tired! She'd fallen onto the bed with only her shoes kicked off.

The first sleep had washed over her like oily water. She was paddling with her arms to keep afloat.

Why hadn't Whitey let her go. The creek had been swollen from rain, rushing past the dock as if it wished to tear the dock into pieces, and yes, it was likely, the rotted timbers would have broken beneath her weight, her legs trapped, lacerated, just possibly a major artery severed, she would not have felt much pain, not as pain is measured, rather a mounting numbness, for the air had been cold, the water colder, the rushing water even colder, draining away the heat of her body she'd come to understand was life itself: *heat, life.*

Life is beating, pulsing, thrumming—*heat.*

Without *heat,* no *life.*

But she had failed to act. She had known exactly what to do, but she had not done it. And now.

Waking abruptly, at only 1:00 A.M.! The bedside lamp was on. Mackie was heavily asleep at the foot of her bed with a sawtooth sort of breathing that might have been mistaken for a faint human snoring. And the rest of the night ahead.

At least, she'd sent away that man, what was his name—*Hugo.*

She was frightened of him. She did not trust him. Hadn't he warned her?—he would steal her soul.

She had come close—too close. The abyss at her feet. But she'd sent the man away. She seemed to know, he would not return.

And if he returned, she would not let him into the house.

What would Whitey think! (What had Whitey been thinking, earlier?)

She would not unlock the door. She would not be anywhere in the vicinity of the door. She would flee.

(Why was Whitey so silent? Had not Whitey nudged her—*You have to try again, Jess. Just one more time.*)

Already Hugo Martinez was receding from her. The rushing creek at the foot of the McClaren property, bearing him away like debris.

Not good, if you live on a creek if after a storm you stand on the bank staring, for you will see, you will imagine you see, lifeless bodies rushing past, spinning in the current, faceless, human or merely animal, passing too swiftly for you to be certain.

Oh Whitey, take me with you.

But that was wrong: Whitey hadn't chosen to die.

Whitey had chosen *not to die.* He'd fought like hell. He'd never have given in. He'd had to *be killed.* That was the only way Whitey McClaren would die.

At 2:30 A.M. trying to read *The Sleepwalkers* . . . It would go on forever, this effort. Whitey had never finished the book, and Whitey's widow would never finish the book.

The dense paragraphs were like ether. She'd lost her place and couldn't determine if she was reading, or rereading. *She* was having a stroke, possibly.

How would you even know? If you were having a stroke? If you lived alone? If you opened your mouth and uttered gibberish—*Vreet vreet* were sounds Whitey had managed to speak, with effort; she had not known what *vreet* might mean. So earnestly he'd uttered this sound, a single yearning syllable—but no one had understood.

But she'd understood *H'yeh. (Hiya.) Jes'lin. L'vyeh. (Jessalyn. Loveya.)*

"Oh, Whitey. We all loved *you.*"

Also on Jessalyn's bedside table was a paperback copy of Richard Dawkins's *The Selfish Gene.* This book was more recent, and shorter. Whitey had (possibly) read all of it, one summer in the hammock.

Oh, she'd begun this, too! Years ago. *We are machines created by our genes. A successful gene survives through ruthless selfishness. Universal love does not make evolutionary sense.*

Who had to be told, to be *selfish*! The first law of humanity.

It was a gift, to be capable of selfishness. Whitey had lacked it—despite being a "successful" businessman. His widow lacked it, fatally.

If only her genes were more *selfish*! Everything she did was for someone else, or something else, and nothing she accomplished was of any significance.

At her feet the squint-eyed tomcat stirred in his sleep, mewing faintly, hungrily. Preparing to leap onto his fleeing prey.

— ∞ —

Next morning she was feeling much better. She had slept late, for her—nearly 8:00 A.M. Mackie had leapt down from the bed and vanished without waking her, sometime before dawn. Another time, it was as if a tourniquet were untied, freeing the pent-up blood in her veins.

Especially, her head felt clearer, lighter. The heaviness had vanished.

Carefully, shrewdly she planned: she would be nowhere near the house by the time Hugo Martinez arrived. (If he arrived at all.)

What had the man said—late morning? Noon?

She would be gone by 10:30 A.M. She had no intention of allowing a stranger to "assist" her in taking Mackie to the vet; she would take Mackie herself, another day.

She would stop by the library. Today was not one of Jessalyn's volunteer days but if someone had canceled, Jessalyn could take her place. Nothing was so comforting as volunteer work at the branch library—reading to children, shelving books and DVDs, straightening the newspaper and magazine racks that were always becoming disorganized. Everyone knew her—"H'lo, Mrs. McClaren!"—"Hi there, Jessalyn!"—and she knew everyone in turn.

Ma'am? Excuse me but I have to say—love your white hair.

Ma'am? That white hair is beautiful! I am going to let my hair go just like that, hell with people sayin I'm too old.

Got to think, ma'am, you were real good-looking when you were young.

Glowing-white hair, parted in the center of her head. Hair of the hue of radium.

For months she'd barely glanced into her clothes closet. She'd given away to Goodwill articles of clothing that had struck her as frivolous, vain, silly, sad, she knew she would never wear again. She'd given away most of her shoes. Only vaguely could she recall the frantic urgency with which she'd flung things onto the floor, how shocked Beverly had been to see her in such a state, and how Beverly had insisted upon taking away the most stylish, expensive items "for safekeeping . . ." Still, it was a surprise to see that most of the hangers were bare.

At the very rear of the closet Jessalyn found a pale yellow pleated dress like a Greek tunic, not worn in twenty years. It had been one of Whitey's favorite dresses of hers, she had not had the heart to give it away.

And with the tunic-dress, a necklace of amber beads that Whitey had given her, and amber earrings, in the shape of teardrops.

Brushing her hair until it sparked electricity.

Now—she must hurry! She had come so close to stumbling into the abyss.

But as she was preparing to leave the house at 10:20 A.M. there came the battered Mercedes-Benz up the curving driveway, and there came Hugo Martinez up the front walk with an eager step. He was carrying what appeared to be a large carrying cage for an animal.

Jessalyn was astonished. How had this happened? Hugo Martinez was *here*.

No choice but to open the door. The man's eye fell upon her in the pleated tunic-dress, with her brushed, very-white hair, with a look almost of alarm. On his head was the wide-brimmed hat at a rakish angle and again today he wore a shirt open at the throat, nearly to mid-chest. On his hands, trim-looking leather gloves.

How beautiful she was looking, Hugo Martinez said. In a quiet voice, not his ebullient voice, so that Jessalyn wanted to cry, she could not love any man again, that had been decided.

Well. Hugo was all-business. He'd come for Mackie as they'd planned. He'd brought a carrying cage large enough for a moderate-sized dog, and Mackie would fit inside easily.

Mackie! Mack-ie!—Hugo Martinez called for the cat in a falsetto voice, moving past Jessalyn into the kitchen, and into a hallway; Jessalyn was sure that the wily tomcat would not be deceived by such a false, ingratiating voice but there came Mackie at a trot, big head uplifted, stubby tail uplifted, suspecting nothing though the carrying cage was set in full view on the floor, its door flung wide open. Mackie did not hesitate but mewed an audible greeting to Hugo Martinez—*Myrrgh.*

Jessalyn was trying to explain to Hugo, apologetically: she had forgotten to call the vet, to make an appointment . . .

No problem, Hugo told her. He'd called a vet he knew, he'd made the appointment himself. They were expected by 11:00 A.M.

Stooping to rub the tomcat's head with his knuckles. And still, to Jessalyn's amazement, Mackie did not hiss and bolt away but purred loudly, and rubbed against the man's legs even as, with a little grunt, Hugo managed to pick the tomcat up, in his gloved hands, and swiftly urged him into the carrying cage, shutting and latching the door before the tomcat could grasp what was happening—all these moves executed with such precision, Jessalyn stared in awe.

At once Mackie began thrashing about inside the cage, enraged and caterwauling. Jessalyn could see his bristling whiskers and fur pushing through the wire—the single glaring-mad eye. *What have you done to me—you!*

Hugo spoke in a calming voice but Mackie continued to wail. He was clawing at the wire, so violently you feared he might tear his way out. Jessalyn pressed her hands over her ears—the creature's cries were heartbreaking. You would think the poor cat was being murdered . . .

Hugo just laughed. Mackie's furious shrieks and desperate thrashings did not daunt him. Gripping the cage handle in both hands Hugo lifted the cage and managed to stagger with it outside to the Mercedes where one of the rear doors had been shrewdly opened; carefully Hugo positioned the cage atop outspread newspaper pages. Despite his gloves, and the care with which Hugo set the cage down, furious Mackie managed to rake him with a single claw on the wrist, which began at once to bleed.

Diablo bastardo! Yet it was clear that Hugo felt very good about himself; and Jessalyn had no choice but to marvel to him, he'd executed a miracle . . .

Jessalyn dabbed a tissue against Hugo's bleeding wrist. It was startling how deep the single claw had sunk, so swiftly.

Hugo was boasting that it was the way you must be, with animals. You allow them to know who is master but you are always kind to them, they understand that you are their protector, even if they protest at first.

Jessalyn shook her head in wonderment. *She* could never have cajoled Mackie into any carrying cage, and she could certainly never have forced him. Bloody murder, that would have been.

And even if she'd managed to get the enraged animal into a cage, she could never have lifted the cage and carried it out to her car.

Well. That's why he was here, Hugo said, pleased at being praised.

And then, Jessalyn was seated in Hugo Martinez's car, in the passenger's seat. (In the rear, photography equipment. A lightweight rain jacket, a pair of hiking boots, scattered books, newspapers. Crumpled paper napkins and a faint smell of something like salami, sausage.) And Hugo was driving out the crushed-stone driveway and onto Old Farm Road, and onto Highgate Road, past familiar houses and landscapes that yielded by degrees to the less-familiar and less-cultivated, and finally to a quasi-rural scrubby area (not far from Bear Mountain Road, in fact) that abutted a rushing state highway where, since she'd become a widow, Jessalyn had not dared to drive. Here were melancholy little strip malls with FOR RENT signs in their windows, gas stations and fast-food restaurants and a tire franchise with red flags flapping in the wind. And in a stucco house with a coarse-graveled parking lot at the front, HAPPY VALLEY ANIMAL DOCTOR & SHELTER.

Inside, a big, burly woman in bib overalls greeted Hugo like an old friend with a handshake and a hug and a bold swiping of her lips across his mustache—this was "Doctor Gladys."

To Jessalyn, Dr. Gladys was very hearty. Her handshake was crushing.

Dr. Gladys then squatted, to peer into the carrying cage at the affronted Mackie. She whistled at the tomcat's size—big as a Maine coon, though he was a short-hair. How old?

Jessalyn said she had no idea. He'd come into her life out of nowhere—he was what's called a "stray."

Dr. Gladys said they would check for a microchip. To see if the cat could be identified and its owner contacted. Did Jessalyn imagine just an air of reproach in the animal doctor's tone, that Jessalyn had not succeeded in locating the cat's owner?

Carried into the veterinary by Hugo the tomcat had ceased wailing. He'd become strangely subdued; he was behaving now with a sort of animal stoicism, resignation. Jessalyn felt a pang of regret for what they were doing to Mackie, even if it was for his own good. De-sexing, demasculinizing—for a marauding tomcat, already battered and scarred, this had to be a good idea. She tried to comfort him by making a petting motion on the wire beside his glaring eye but Mackie only just stared at her as if he'd never seen her before. He hadn't even the spirit to swipe at her with a claw.

Prior to neutering, which required anesthesia, a cat must be kept from eating for at least twelve hours. It had to be assumed that Mackie had probably eaten not long before he'd been put into the carrying cage, for Mackie ate often, and so the surgery would have to be postponed until the next morning, for safety's sake.

Jessalyn was disappointed but Hugo said that was fine. In the interim Mackie would be thoroughly examined and given his shots.

While Dr. Gladys and Hugo Martinez talked and laughed together Jessalyn filled out forms at a receptionist's counter. She couldn't help but overhear the two speaking with such familiarity and intimacy, she felt a pang of envy as if a door had been flung open into a life very different from her own.

And was Hector *still in*—? Dr. Gladys asked; and Hugo said, with a heavy sigh, yes he was. Yes.

But Carlin was *out*. For the time being . . .

And how were Anita, and Yolanda, and Denis . . .

And Esme, and Luis . . .

Were these—children? Mutual friends? Spouses?

Jessalyn overheard what sounded like "Attica"—could this be the notorious maximum-security prison, a fifty-minute drive south and west of Hammond? She'd never heard of any person named "Attica."

Now in lowered voices Hugo Martinez and Dr. Gladys conferred together and Jessalyn could no longer make out what they were saying.

Except she heard, or believed she heard, the furtive words "hearing" . . . "probationary" . . .

Jessalyn asked the receptionist what the price of the examination, shots, and neutering would be; and if she could pay for it, next day, by check.

She was uncertain of the status of her credit card. In fact she had several credit cards and had discovered recently that one had expired months ago. Before Whitey's death she had never feared being overdrawn but now—"overdrawn" had become an obscure and continuous worry.

Well—the bill for Mackie would be quite high. Higher than she'd expected. Jessalyn could imagine Beverly's reaction—*That awful feral cat? You're throwing all that money away on—that? Oh, Mom.*

Also, a deposit of 20 percent was required, this very day.

Seeing that Jessalyn was looking dismayed Hugo came over quickly, and handed a credit card to the receptionist.

Jessalyn tried to protest but Hugo insisted.

She could pay him back at any time, Hugo said happily. No hurry!

Dr. Gladys said that they should return for their cat in approximately twenty-four hours. If there was an emergency, Jessalyn would be called.

Their cat. Jessalyn waited for Hugo to correct the doctor, but Hugo did not.

By this time Mackie had given up struggling inside the carrying cage. Even his stubby tail had ceased twitching. How sad, to see the tomcat's spirit so broken . . .

When a husky girl-assistant came to haul Mackie away he didn't give Jessalyn so much as a backward glance.

Outside, in Hugo Martinez's car, Jessalyn fought back tears. Why was she here, why *here* with this man who was a stranger to her, who had so intruded into her life!

As Hugo drove the deep-purple Mercedes at a fast clip along the state highway she did not meet his frequent glances at her, that seemed to her both affectionate and coercive; she only half-listened to his exultant talk that ranged over many subjects like a man lurching on stilts. What would Whitey think of all this! Driving south on Route 29 in a stranger's car, when she should have been at the branch library reading stories to pre-school children?

And Jessalyn was feeling a sick dread that she would never see Mackie again, she'd sent the poor cat to his death out of cowardice—she had not been able to withstand the overbearing will of Hugo Martinez.

The way he'd pushed the trash container along the driveway. Dared to position it along the side of the garage, exactly where it belonged. How had he known? Why had he taken such liberties?

She would not see the man again, after this. Tomorrow was unavoidable—she would see Hugo then. A final time. For she could not possibly carry the heavy cat into a car by herself.

But that would be the end. No more!

Yet Hugo Martinez was so very kind to her, so warmly sympathetic.

His handsome, ruined face. She could not bear to look at him, to see him looking at *her.*

Along the state highway he drove. The Mercedes rattled and vibrated like half-heard music. Jessalyn was watching the man's hands on the steering wheel. Large hands, with pale blue veins visible across the knuckles. At the wrists, coarse hairs so much darker than the hairs of his mustache or his head, she had to smile.

How old was Hugo Martinez? Jessalyn wondered. There were obvious ways of finding out which for some reason she'd avoided.

He was older than Jessalyn, surely. Might've been as much as ten years older. Or, he might have been younger.

She was no judge of others' ages. She tended to avoid speculation. She felt a kind of pain, when people said to her, meaning to be kind, Oh how young you look, for your age!

Jessalyn McClaren is always a lady. Jessalyn McClaren has such poise. For an older woman, Jessalyn McClaren is always beautifully groomed, gracious.

But where was Hugo driving now?—turning the elegantly shabby Mercedes onto Cayuga Road, that led through back-country hills in the vicinity of Bear Mountain.

(Bear Mountain was the highest peak in the Chautauqua range, at 3,200 feet—that's to say, not high. The highest peak in the Adirondacks was Mount Marcy, 5,344 feet.)

Jessalyn asked where Hugo was taking her?

Hugo assured her, he wasn't *taking her* anywhere. He was just driving.

Just—driving?

Well, in the direction of Old Farm Road. In the general direction of North Hammond.

It had to be a very general direction, Jessalyn thought. Judging from the distance to Bear Mountain they were five or six miles from 99 Old Farm Road in hilly countryside where shadows of high-scudding clouds flew before them like giant birds.

How beautiful it was here!—Jessalyn had had a fantasy since girlhood of being stranded in some unpopulated place like this, somehow on foot, alone, and yet—absurdly, improbably happy.

Yes but you would soon be terrified. Alone, you could not survive.

Desperate, you would climb into the first vehicle that came along . . .

The road was bumpy, unimproved. Though soon they were passing farmland, or what had once been farmland. Old, abandoned farmhouses dignified in dereliction, part-collapsed barns bearing the faintest trace of red paint, silos, tilted fences, pastures gone to seed. From time to time, fields in which animals grazed—cows, sheep like figures in a dream.

Hugo remarked how strange it was, Cayuga Road was less populated than it had been one hundred years ago.

Jessalyn said yes, it was strange. Sad.

This recession, Hugo said, sighing. Upstate New York, that is so beautiful.

Jessalyn thought—*But he lives here. He is taking me to his home.*

She asked Hugo if he lived on Cayuga Road?

Hugo said *yes.* He supposed he did.

He laughed uneasily, as if Jessalyn had caught him out in some trickery.

Well. He didn't live *alone,* Hugo said. He lived with—a family.

Adding, not what you'd call a usual family.

Jessalyn took *usual family* to mean a wife, children. But Hugo Martinez was too old for children to be living at home, in any case.

She wanted to ask him who this family was. What his life was. Had he been married, was he married now. Though Hugo was a spirited and indefatigable talker he'd said very little that was specific about his life.

Jessalyn supposed he was waiting for her to ask him, would he take her to his home? Would he show her how he lived?—introduce her to his "family"? Badly she wanted to ask, yet she could not. The words would not come.

Hugo Martinez appeared to be enjoying himself: he was a man who liked to drive his car, and he was a man who liked to display himself to a woman, ideally a woman seated close beside him in his car, properly belted-in.

He did not seem to mind that his passenger was reticent, uneasy. Though (probably) he took note of her nervously glancing into the distance, hoping to get her bearings in this unfamiliar place.

She was not in any danger, Hugo said, amused. *Por favor, saber que!*

And what did that mean? She could guess.

Jessalyn smiled. A steely sort of smile. Her hands were loose on her knees, not tight-clasped. Her palms sweated just slightly, against the pale-yellow pleats of her skirt.

She told Hugo Martinez, she did not think she was in danger of course. She was just slightly apprehensive—about Mackie, and about where they were headed.

But they were not *headed* anywhere, Hugo protested.

Did she think that he was kidnapping her?—or, "abducting"? He laughed heartily.

But almost, Hugo was beginning to sound hurt. Deflated. A buccaneer who has been misunderstood; a gentleman whose courtliness has not been appreciated.

Jessalyn assured him, she was very grateful for his help. Bringing Mackie to Dr. Gladys—that had been very kind of him.

Did this mollify Hugo Martinez?—he did not reply at first, concentrating upon the bumpy road. Jessalyn had the impression that he was chewing his mustache.

Terrible habit! She could not imagine intimacy with a *mustached man.*

Tell me one thing about yourself, dear—Hugo said, hoping to restore some measure of control.

Jessalyn considered. What to say? *One* thing? The paradox of life was that there is no *one thing,* there are only *many things* strung together like a cobweb. You can't extract *one* from *many* without misrepresenting both . . .

Finally she told Hugo Martinez that the one thing in life, she believed, was love.

Really!—Hugo Martinez shook his head, ponderously.

Yes . . .

Jessalyn was hurt, annoyed. Was he laughing at her?—she asked.

No, no! Of course he was not laughing at her . . .

Obviously yes, Hugo was laughing at Jessalyn. Yet he was delighted in her, she could see.

(And what did he see? Jessalyn wondered. The rich man's widow who dared not dress other than elegantly, even to drive to the branch library, or to the vet's; the starkly-white-haired woman who was, to herself, a stuttering girl-child, a prude, a puritan, self-condemning, self-doubting and yet vain, a cowardly heart yet yearning to be bold, even reckless; not knowing what to say that was not banal and self-exposing, for these were the perimeters of her soul?)

Hugo said, he'd meant that she should tell *one thing* about herself that was a fact. Something actually *about herself.*

I—I—I am—I am a . . .

But what she was, Jessalyn could not utter.

The *one thing* about a widow's life is that it is a widow's life, a posthumous life; a left-over life, you could say. Yet, saying this, putting such a melancholy truth into words, made it sound exalted and profound somehow, when in fact the widow's condition was a diminishment, like a wizened pea or a crumpled napkin, contemptible, of no worth.

But even to say this was to hope to inflate the diminishment, and in this hope there was folly.

As if he were reading her mind, the cruel whiplash of her thoughts, Hugo said, gently—Here is one thing about me, a simple fact: I was born on April 11, 1952, in Newark, New Jersey.

He was fifty-nine! Five years younger than Jessalyn.

And twelve years younger than Whitey would have been, were Whitey alive.

Hugo was teasing, that hadn't been difficult—had it? Now, Jessalyn should please tell him *one thing* she thought he should know about her—something that would be helpful for him to know if he was, as he believed he was, falling in love with her. Could she?

Falling in love. Jessalyn's face went hot as if he'd slapped it. What did the man mean, saying such things to her. He was joking, she supposed. Yet it was cruel to joke with her, she would never have joked with another, in such a way.

Rapidly her eyes darted about—the wild thought came to her, she could open the car door, escape. Hugo was driving slowly enough over the rutted country road.

Hey, no!—Hugo laughed, reaching over to seize Jessalyn's hand, as if he'd been reading her mind.

Jessalyn laughed. Tried to laugh. Though her heart was beating rapidly, at the man's touch.

Jessalyn said, she wished that Hugo would not say such things . . .

Gaily Hugo replied—he should not "say" such things, or he should not "feel" such things?

But this too was teasing. This too, Jessalyn could not take seriously.

Of course, the man was not sincere. He was a poet, an artist, a photographer. He arranged words, and he arranged pictures. He dealt in artifice, exaggeration. He'd dared to take her picture without her permission, without even her awareness. Hadn't he warned her, he was not to be trusted.

A sexually aggressive male. A certain sort of *male*. A woman could have no doubt but that such a man might desire her, as such a man might desire virtually any woman. But a woman could not place much trust in such desire.

Heard herself saying that the *one thing* about her was that though she lived in a pre–Revolutionary War house on Old Farm Road she really didn't have much money. Her expenses had been pared back, she lived as frugally as she could. Mackie's surgery would be a "splurge."

Coolly then Jessalyn repeated, so that the ardent male could not possibly misunderstand, that, despite what people might think she was not—(Jessalyn took a deep breath, the word was so awkward)—*rich.*

But Hugo Martinez's response was unexpected. Or maybe she should have expected—laughter.

So? Not rich? *Yo tampoco.*

By the man's jovial tone Jessalyn guessed these words meant *Me, neither.*

HE DID MAKE HER LAUGH. A startled laughter, like a small bird fluttering up.

Since Whitey, she had rarely laughed. (Whitey had made her laugh, often.)

Was it a betrayal of Whitey, to laugh at the whimsical remarks of another man? Of whom Whitey would not have approved?

How long had it been since Jessalyn had been *happy.*

How long, since she'd been *angry.*

Emotions had lost their buoyancy. It's as if she'd left part-deflated balloons in the driveway and carelessly she'd run them over with her car. Glancing out to see in the pink-graveled drive a scattering of broken flattened balloons and scarcely caring what they'd been.

Yet, she was angry now.

The voice on the phone inquiring—Ma'am? Are you still on the line?

No. Yes—of course.

Anxiously she'd snatched up the receiver. Usually not coming anywhere near a ringing phone (for there was no good news the phone could bring to a widow, only just the memory of bad news endlessly echoing) but this time she'd checked to see the caller ID was HAPPY VALLEY ANIMAL HOSPITAL.

It was late afternoon, the same day. Mackie had been at the animal hospital for several hours by that time.

And here was a person informing her that, after having examined Mackie thoroughly, Dr. Gladys was not recommending that the cat have neutering surgery and shots after all but that he be *put down.*

Excuse me? What?—through a roaring in her ears Jessalyn wasn't hearing clearly.

The voice repeated its words. Flat, unfeeling. But what was this?—*put down?*

Jessalyn fought back tears. Oh, where was Hugo?

He'd driven her back home as he'd promised he would do. She had not invited him to come inside.

She'd been relieved, sending Hugo Martinez away. He had promised to return the next day, to drive her to the vet's to retrieve Mackie.

Now with maddening calm the voice continued. Had to be an assistant of Dr. Gladys notifying her that the examination had "not gone well."

Her cat had mites, and parasites (two distinct types, both intestinal), and a respiratory condition, and a blood deficiency condition, and he was mean-tempered, and blind in one eye, and he "wasn't a young cat"—

Jessalyn interrupted: Of course she knew that Mackie was blind in one eye, and that he wasn't a young cat. She knew! But—

The voice continued: It seemed that the cat did not have a microchip embedded beneath his skin. There was no way of knowing who his owner had been, and there was no way of knowing his age. Of course Dr. Gladys would be happy to proceed with the surgery and shots but it was her policy to notify pet owners of their pets' medical conditions so that there could be "no ambiguity" at a later date.

Also, with his many health problems, Mackie would require more medical treatment than they'd anticipated. What the final bill would be, Dr. Gladys could not say.

Jessalyn said that did not matter. Whatever it cost—she would pay.

Finally, Dr. Gladys wanted Jessalyn to know that a homeless stray like Mackie was not considered a "good risk" as a house pet, especially when so many more suitable cats and kittens were available for adoption at Happy Valley.

Her voice shaking Jessalyn said she didn't want a "more suitable" cat, she wanted the cat that had come to her back door.

PUT DOWN. The words were blunt, insulting.

Jessalyn was too upset to tell Hugo Martinez about the phone call from Happy Valley. All she told him when he returned the next day was that she'd had a call from Dr. Gladys's assistant and that the surgery had gone forward as planned.

No further calls had come. Jessalyn had steeled herself for a call announcing Mackie's death, under the anesthetic.

At the vet's they were made to wait until Mackie was ready to be taken out of his veterinary cage and transferred to his private cage. They were told that Mackie's surgery had "gone well" and that he was "resting"—unusual for an animal recovering from surgery, he'd even been able to eat a "small breakfast."

In one of the examination rooms Dr. Gladys showed Jessalyn and Hugo Martinez, on a magnified, full-color photograph, precisely how a male cat is neutered. With a ballpoint pen she pointed at the small organ that was the "penis" and the saclike organ that was the "scrotum" containing the "testicles" to be removed—an operation that required but two minutes.

Jessalyn half-shut her eyes, with a shudder. But Hugo Martinez looked on with a stoic smile.

There would be little recovery time, Dr. Gladys said. The anesthetic had not totally worn off yet and the cat would be groggy for the rest of the day but soon his full appetite would return and by evening he would be himself again, or nearly.

Jessalyn felt a flood of compassion for Mackie. She was grateful to be told that despite his blind eye, battered ears and broken tail, and his myriad medical problems, he was actually in "remarkably good condition" for an outdoor cat; he did not have feline leukemia, for instance. Or feline AIDS. And he was probably younger than he appeared, Dr. Gladys said. Possibly, as young as five years.

Five! Jessalyn laughed. There was a good chance then she'd have Mackie for the rest of her life.

Hugo Martinez looked at Jessalyn, shocked by this remark. *Only five years?* Jessalyn expected not to live even *five years*? What was she thinking?

Shrewdly the animal doctor had seen, Jessalyn supposed, that despite his personality flaws and his medical problems the squint-eyed black tomcat was beloved, and so Dr. Gladys was saying only positive, encouraging things about him now. No more suggestions about *putting him down*.

It's good to be loyal to your kitty, Dr. Gladys said, with a throaty chuckle. Even if your *kitty* isn't going to win any cat shows.

Kitty. An incongruous word, applied to Mackie.

Jessalyn steeled herself for the bill. But to her chagrin Hugo appropriated the bill—It's OK, dear. No problem.

Explaining that this past spring he'd made more money selling photographs than he'd expected. Jessalyn could repay him whenever it was convenient.

Jessalyn protested, she'd brought a checkbook! Really, she could afford to pay for her own cat . . .

You could not argue with Hugo Martinez, not easily. Like throwing yourself against a stone wall, that would not yield.

He is impossible. He is domineering. This is wrong. He has no right.

When the vet's assistant brought Mackie out in his carrying cage the neutered tomcat glared at them with his single tawny eye as if he understood very well that something essential was missing in his life. He was groggy, subdued. His tomcat-spirit seemed to have been broken in this place of torture and confinement. He even looked smaller. Sprawled on the bottom of the cage scarcely lifting his big tomcat head.

They leaned over Mackie's cage, murmuring to him. He ignored them. Risking a sudden swift claw in their flesh they stuck fingers through the wire to touch him. Hugo managed to stroke the top of his head, and after a sullen moment Mackie began to purr a loud, harsh, crackling purr. You could hear the joy of recognition and relief in such a purr, and the desperation.

Jessalyn brushed tears of relief from her eyes, so grateful the squint-eyed tomcat had been returned to her alive.

He knows you—that you saved his life, Jessalyn.

You saved his life, Hugo.

Together, Jessalyn and Hugo Martinez brought Mackie back to the house on Old Farm Road.

The Hornets

On the underside of the drainpipe of the old farmhouse on Bear Mountain Road, a hornets' nest of the size and shape of a pineapple.

Buzzing with hornets in a furious rant.

Danger! Hornets protecting their nest like crazed warriors.

Other hornets, farther from the hive, drifting wayward and random like bomber pilots considering where to attack . . .

No need to destroy the hive, was Virgil's logic. The hornets were living creatures, not dangerous to human beings except when human beings interfered in their hornet-lives.

Among the residents on Bear Mountain Road were those who disappointed Virgil, wanting to destroy hornets' nests as if hornets were enemies of humankind.

Just avoid the nest, Virgil suggested. Take another route to the barn. Avoid that side of the house. Hornets will not pursue you.

(Usually, this was true. Though perhaps there were exceptions.)

"A hornets' nest is a beautiful construct, considered as architecture. Since the hornets are related, you could say that a hive is a *family home*."

In his sweetly disarming way, that some found persuasive and others found exasperating, Virgil managed to protect the hornets against those residents of the household who wanted to destroy the hive and any other hive in the vicinity.

Adding, reasonably: "No toxic sprays are allowed on this property, so the hive can't be sprayed. And I don't recommend trying to douse it with gasoline and setting it on fire—the house will catch fire too and burn down and the insurer won't pay. And getting near enough to knock the hive down with a hoe will take some courage."

Among those who listened was the tall boyish-faced Nigerian whom Virgil particularly hoped to impress and for whose sake Virgil uttered such pronouncements, modestly and yet forcibly.

"*Me,* I'm not about to do it. Good night!"

Virgil strolled off. They would not band in opposition to him, he believed; they would disband, disperse.

Listening with the others had been the six-foot-four Nigerian—Amos Keziahaya. His height, his roughened cheeks and stark-white eyes drew Virgil's attention like a magnet; it was all Virgil could do not to stare openly at him as if no one else were present.

Keziahaya did not say anything but nodded as Virgil spoke and smiled in approval. That quick flitting smile of his, gone before you can reciprocate.

Yes. Good. I agree. I am on your side. OK!

Often it happened, Keziahaya was *on his side*. So Virgil thought.

Amos Keziahaya was the only dark-skinned resident in the house on Bear Mountain Road. He appeared to be the only foreign-born resident, and he was certainly the only one from Africa. Some controversy rippled about him—Virgil didn't quite know what it was.

People were drawn to Amos Keziahaya. But not always could Keziahaya reciprocate their interest.

Out of this, resentment. Sexual jealousy, anxiety. Dislike.

Women were attracted to Keziahaya, that was clear. But also men. Unavoidably.

Uneasily, Virgil knew this. He took care to befriend Keziahaya in the most casual, the least intense of ways.

They'd been friendly at the time of the Chautauqua arts fair. Virgil had helped Keziahaya display his work, and he'd helped him dismantle what remained unsold and load it into the rear of Virgil's truck and bring it back to Keziahaya's studio at the farm. Keziahaya had sold much more work than Virgil had sold, and had been in boyish good spirits as a consequence.

But since then, the two had had few exchanges. You wouldn't say that Keziahaya avoided Virgil. But he hadn't gone out of his way to spend time with him.

It was agony, Virgil thought. And ridiculous.

He was now—what?—thirty-two years old. *Thirty-two.*

In high school, he'd been immune to the tumultuous emotions of his classmates. Their desperate/ridiculous infatuations with one another. He'd been Virgil, and superior. But now.

Waiting for a knock at the door of his cabin. Still possible, after Virgil had walked away with a wave of his hand, that the strikingly tall very dark-skinned Nigerian would follow him down behind the house to knock lightly at the (opened) door.

And Virgil would glance up, frowning. *Yes?*

HE HAD NOT EVER BEEN *in love* with a man, Virgil was sure.

Rarely had he been *in love* with any woman—not really.

He'd been attracted to individuals, he'd felt emotional attachments—he was sure.

As a younger man he'd traveled and met persons—young women, girls—with whom he had become involved, to a degree; he'd had a pleasurably guilty sense that they expected more of him than he was capable of giving. *Like a rolling stone. No direction known.* It had been his custom to leave without saying goodbye—not a backward glance.

Even his parents had not seemed altogether real to Virgil, in those years. He was fully capable of forgetting them for days at a stretch, as if they'd never existed.

What are your people like?—a girl had asked him once in some faraway place like Wyoming, Oregon, Idaho; and Virgil had laughed and said he had no idea—he didn't even understand the question. *My people?*

Well. You seem like a kind of, I don't know—guy with money.

Virgil had been astonished, insulted. His clothing, his way of life, his obvious frugality—what could possibly lead a stranger to think he'd come from a background with money?

He had not ever, not once, called home to ask for money; he'd supported himself with part-time work.

You just don't seem that worried, I guess. Like even if you don't have money right now, it's somewhere you could get to.

That wasn't true!—Virgil had wanted to protest.

Now that he was older, he felt differently. To a degree.

He'd been deeply affected by Whitey's death, which had been unexpected. He dreamt often of Whitey, who appeared in his dreams as a blurred figure of some menace, like Francis Bacon's "screaming popes" series.

He loved Jessalyn deeply. Did not want to think how very deeply, especially since Whitey's death.

His feelings for Amos Keziahaya were inchoate, unclear. He didn't think (he told himself) that it was anything so simple or as simply satisfied as sexual attraction.

Though he felt a visceral jolt when he saw Keziahaya unexpectedly. A current of yearning, of sheer desire, that made him feel faint, and his mouth dry. For always, seeing Keziahaya he was taken by surprise. Like a tightrope walker he felt, gripping his long pole for balance, and suddenly there comes a gust of wind rendering him helpless.

Amos. Hey look: I think I am in love with you.

I know, it's ridiculous—I know you don't feel anything for me.

I don't even mind that you don't feel anything for me! Really.

I would not expect. I could not hope. I can only . . .

Amos? Jesus! I am so, so sorry.

Please forgive me if these words disgust you.

Or better yet—please forget if these words disgust you.

Back to zero? Forget? OK?

OK.

GAY, SAME-SEX, HOMOSEXUAL—these were cultural taboos/crimes in Keziahaya's native Nigeria, punishable by as many as fourteen years in prison. Punishable by extrajudicial violence.

Back to zero. Forget.

FURIOUS BUZZ OF HORNETS. Close in Virgil's ears.

Demanding *Virgil? It's gotten worse—Mom and that awful man.*

"Awful man?"—who?

A man. A Cuban! A Communist!

Cuban? Communist?

He's after her money, just as we'd thought. It's shameful!

But—who—

A friend of yours—isn't he?

No. I don't think—

Did you introduce them, Virgil? Is that what you did?

N-No . . .

He's Hispanic. Maybe not Cuban but definitely Hispanic, everybody says he's practically black.

In Hammond? There aren't many—

Yes! There are! If you look closely, they're all over. Like Koreans—every damn grocery store. And Pakistanis—every damn gas station. Everywhere you look—Asians and Hispanics. And Indians.

Our mother has every right to—

She does not! She's not in her right mind. People are seeing them all the time—in public. More than one person has called. And I've spoken with Mom—or tried to.

Has something in particular happened? We knew—

How can you sound so calm, Virgil? When you've caused this—the destruction of our family! And it's so—shameful!

But—why?

Because they're after her money—I mean, he's after her money! Dad's money! Our money! The estate! Our estate!

Wait. Who are we—

This is our mother, Virgil. This is—Jessalyn! Our lovely, beautiful, perfect mother! What has happened to her? She doesn't have time for her own grandchildren any longer—they're asking "Where is Granma Jess" and I don't know how to answer them, I am so embarrassed.

Mom would have forgotten Daisy's birthday—except I called her the day before. Can you imagine!

You *forget our birthdays, too. But nobody expects* you *to remember.*

It's your fault, Virgil. You have never had a shred of respect for our family. The family. Normal life not—twisted and perverted . . .

It's like revenge on our father—on the family . . .

It will probably turn out that you brought some filthy germ into Dad's hospital room, Virgil. Caused that infection that killed him, living on that filthy manure-stinking place of yours with all the flies, Sophia told us, even Sophia was disgusted, just what Dad might have predicted since you didn't—ever—wash your God-damned hands even as a boy, you selfish, selfish—

The cell phone slipped through Virgil's numbed fingers and clattered to the floor. Just dimly Virgil heard the word *prick* in the vicinity of his feet.

So shocked by his sister's words, and the venom in the words, the very sister who'd so seemed to adore him when he'd been a little boy, Virgil would not remember most of what Beverly said afterward. An amnesiac balm would spare him.

Soon after, the second furious sister called, with more words to sting Virgil's eardrums, but this time Virgil knew better than to speak with her.

Virgil? Hello?

Virgil? God damn you!

It's me—Lorene. You'd better call me back! This is an emergency.

I need to know what do you know about this—this—"artiste"-friend of yours who's practically living with our mother? Beverly says he's a Cuban . . .

We are all—stunned. We are sick with worry . . .

Could be Cuban, or Puerto Rican. Could be Mexican. There are Hispanics at our school—every fall, more.

Bad enough they are everywhere and having babies at five times the rate of white people—more babies than black people . . .

Virgil—God damn you. You'd better call me back.

Oh it's awful. Just—obscene . . .

Poor Mom. They say the two are holding hands—*in public . . . They've gone to the movies together! Where anyone can see. So shameful!*

Mom won't listen to us, Virgil. She is obviously having a nervous breakdown—she hasn't been herself since Dad died.

I've tried to reach out to her. I have. Tried to get her to travel with me. Even with the trust, Mom has plenty of money. We could have had a wonderful, fantastic trip—to some place exotic—but Mom refused. Like she couldn't bring herself to leave Dad. And now, this awful man—a stranger . . .

We hope you're satisfied with yourself, Virgil. Your disgusting hippie friends! Now they're moving right in our house.

You were always the weak link—Dad knew. Trying to break up our family. Always playing at being a—provocateur!

Oh Jesus, it makes me sick to think of another man, a stranger, and a Hispanic, in our house—with our mother who doesn't have a clue about life . . .

Virgil? I'm warning you—you'd better call me back.

What would Dad think, how you and Mom have betrayed him!

Soon after the furious sister, a furious brother. The first time Virgil could recall his brother calling him on the phone, ever.

Was it possible? In all of their lives?

Thom could barely speak, he was so angry. Virgil shrank listening to his percussive deep-throated voice and imagining how Thom would put his hands on him, if he could.

God damn you, Virgil. Introducing our mother to an ex-convict Hispanic. You never took this seriously and now Bev and Lorene are telling me they are practically living together. And I've had calls from friends. Jesus! Enough to make me puke.

One of your fucking artist-friends. Lives on that fucking commune with you. I asked around and turns out, this "Hugo" who is seeing our mother was arrested in 1991, in Hammond.

Disturbing the peace. Aggravated assault.

Probably drugs. Dealing drugs. "Latino."

He was in Hammond County Detention! He has a criminal record . . .

He's younger than Mom, and he's after her money. We have got to stop him before it's too late . . .

Thank God, Dad left her money in a trust. It's like Dad could see into the future . . .

His heart would be broken now.

Fuck you, Virgil. Just—fuck you . . .

If you actually had anything to do with this, I will break your sorry ass . . .

We've tried to speak with Mom and she just will not listen.

You'd better go over there, right now. She'll listen to you.

Not in her right mind. Jesus!

What if they get married? What if they are already married?

A trust can be broken. But even if it isn't broken, if she's his wife he'll find a way to get his hands on that money. And the house. That's our house!

Oh Christ. What would Dad think!

Virgil was stunned. He'd assumed that Jessalyn had seen Hugo Martinez just casually, just a few times, but now—*Practically living together. Married?*

He recalled how intense Jessalyn had been, asking him about Martinez. How uncharacteristically emotional she'd been, that Martinez had dared to take her photograph without her permission.

Officially Virgil had not heard a word from her about Martinez, or about the photograph. He did not think that it was his right to interfere with his mother's private life—but then, he hadn't realized that Jessalyn and Hugo Martinez had become so involved.

He kept in contact with Jessalyn, as he did with Sophia, but not with the others, who seemed to despise him.

It had intensified since Whitey's death, this dislike of Virgil. Since the will. Bitterly his elder siblings resented it, that Whitey had left Virgil exactly as much as he'd left them.

But their dislike of Virgil had begun when he'd been a young child. He'd been too "special"—too much fuss was made over him by adults. Beverly and Lorene had adored him initially, then they'd become jealous, resentful. Beyond the age of seven or eight he'd become too clever for them. He had not needed them.

He'd feared for his life, when his big brother Thom had advanced upon him glowering with dislike.

Couldn't remember. If Thom had actually roughed him up, or just threatened him. How many times? Thom had never injured Virgil so that their parents could see, that was certain.

He was a dangerous person, Thom. No one knew but Virgil. No one else would ever believe how murderous Thom could be, especially not their mother.

Yet, Virgil had admired Thom when he was growing up. At a distance, he'd been proud of his tall handsome so-virile brother . . .

Recalling how he'd mortified Thom by asking him point-blank, just once, *Why do you hate me? What have I done?* Thom had backed off with a look of disgust.

The faggot kid-brother. Disgusting.

What Virgil knew of Hugo Martinez, he'd been a political activist as well as an artist and a poet. Their paths had not often crossed though they'd both taught, at different times, at Hammond Community College. Virgil was sure that Martinez had children, whom Virgil might have met—the name "Martinez" was familiar. Hugo was a hugely charming older man with a drooping mustache, long wavy hair, a flamboyant manner. He was also an excellent photographer.

Why was it being said that Hugo was after Jessalyn's money? That was insulting to both Hugo and Jessalyn.

It was not at all unlikely that a man might be attracted to Jessalyn.

Less likely, that Jessalyn might be attracted to a man . . .

Virgil was certain that the relationship, if there was one, was being misinterpreted. On the phone his sisters said the most astonishing and irresponsible things. They seemed to have gotten more accusatory, more profane, more reckless since their father's death. Beverly was certainly drinking more than she'd ever drunk. And Thom as well. Unraveling.

Without Whitey, a kind of fixture had slipped. A lynchpin. Things were veering out of control.

The sisters had whipped Thom into a frenzy. He was living in Hammond for part of the week and in Rochester on weekends. His marriage was falling apart. He was distracted by the responsibilities of McClaren, Inc. like a burning tire around his neck and he was distracted by the lawsuit he'd initiated against the Hammond Police Department, that moved with glacial slowness. He'd fired Bud Hawley and he'd hired a new lawyer. The most recent news of the lawsuit Virgil had heard, the young Indian physician who'd been the (sole) witness to Whitey's beating by the police officers had lodged a complaint against Thom for stalking and threatening him and he'd filed for an injunction to keep Thom from contacting him. Worse, the Hammond police officers named in the suit had countered with a lawsuit of their own against Thom McClaren, charging reckless defamation.

Virgil had tried to reason with Thom in the matter of the lawsuit. Naively he'd tried to explain to him the wisdom of Buddhism: not pessimism or optimism but resignation in the face of the vicissitudes of the world. *Of course* there was injustice. *Of course* the police would not admit to any wrongdoing. *Of course* the current mayor of Hammond and his police chief would be shocked to learn what had happened to Whitey McClaren who was one of their own but they would not try to rectify the wrong publicly; they would suppress evidence, protract and prolong, obfuscate, try to bury the case with every ruse of the law at their disposal—exactly as Whitey would have done.

For all Virgil knew, Whitey himself had done such things. Whitey had certainly not protested against police misconduct, publicly. He'd had to work with the Hammond PD which meant accommodating what was now called "white racism"—in previous decades, keeping residents of the inner city "in their place" so that they were no threat to the white majority.

Why Whitey had quit politics, Virgil assumed. Too many moral compromises. Too much corruption. You could not be both a politician and an idealist. Most governing bodies were criminal enterprises. You could make your way through muck without getting entirely covered in it—that was the hope. When the muck begins to cover your mouth, and to get into your mouth, that is the end. From his Buddhist distance, Virgil understood.

Not that Virgil would have judged Whitey harshly. He did not judge anyone, really. Except maybe (hard to resist!) himself.

Thom had been drinking. His breath had smelled sweetly of whiskey. His voice had been slurred. His face that had once been startlingly handsome had been ruddy, coarsened. Scarcely had he listened to Virgil. He'd interrupted to say that "money was no object"—he would "spare no expense" in the lawsuit. What ominous words! Virgil shuddered.

And Thom had no doubt—"Whitey will win."

All of the money Whitey had left Thom was going into the lawsuit.

Virgil's most recent visit with Jessalyn had been twelve days before. She had not seemed secretive or evasive with him but had rather seemed calm, happy. She'd been spending time in her garden, she'd said. A friend had come bringing her a rosebush—a mature, sprawling bloodred climber rose planted beside the garage. In retrospect, Virgil wondered about the rosebush. Which friend, and why? Why a mature bush, which would be difficult to plant? At the time he'd scarcely listened and had had not the slightest curiosity. Jessalyn had dragged him out into the bright blinding heat of midsummer to stare at the straggly rosebush she was trying to support against a trellis beside the garage. "Isn't it beautiful? The roses are so *perfect*."

All he'd really noticed was that she was smiling, often. Possibly, too often. Her fingers were thin, her rings were loose; but that was nothing new. If anything, Jessalyn had regained some of the weight she'd lost in the weeks following Whitey's death. Her face wasn't so drawn. Her skin wasn't sallow with fatigue.

She'd said nothing about having met Hugo Martinez. Neither she nor Virgil had brought up the subject of the surreptitiously taken photograph at Whitey's gravesite.

"How are you doing, Mom?"

"Oh Virgil, you know—'One breath at a time.'"

He hadn't known. *One breath at a time.* Exactly, the wisdom of Buddhism.

They'd prepared a meal together. From the farm on Bear Mountain Road Virgil had brought an armload of produce he'd grown himself: mammoth leaves of dark kale, sprigs of broccoli, beefsteak tomatoes, carrots. (They'd laughed at the carrots, which were far too ugly to be sold commercially: spindly, like aborted fetuses with roots like coarse hairs, obscene to the touch.)

During the dinner the squint-eyed black tomcat had entered the room, silently on his soft thick pads. His stubby tail switched. His single eye glared yellow. Mackie leapt with surprising agility onto Jessalyn's lap. She told Virgil that the cat had had surgery and had made a very good recovery. He would prowl less, and he would certainly fight less. Spared the rigors of reproducing his kind, he would live a longer life. Already, his fur was looking glossier and he purred more readily. Jessalyn encouraged Virgil to lean over and stroke the cat's big, hard-boned head, and for an anxious moment the cat stiffened and growled deep in its throat, as if it were considering clawing Virgil's hand; but it had not, and had purred instead.

"Mackie likes you, now. You are his friend."

Was he! Virgil had to laugh.

He had very little interest in the damned cat, as the cat clearly had very little interest in Virgil.

Maybe, Virgil thought, his hysterical sisters were confusing Mackie with a man. An "Hispanic"—"Latino"—who'd come to take Whitey's place in their mother's life.

THE INVITATION HAD BEEN CASUAL—*Virgil! Please come to our Fourth of July barbecue & bring a companion.*

Not sure why he'd accepted. He scarcely knew the hosts—they were "friends of the arts." He didn't really like large parties—though he didn't much like small parties either.

Also, he had no companion.

Driving alone in his Jeep across the Chautauqua River into rural Herkimer County. There was a Fourth of July gathering in a hillside park in Pittsfield, there would be fireworks above the river at dark. In the sky just before sunset, a rackety biplane trailing a banner advertisement for a local winery—PITTS WINES.

Rural Herkimer County evoked nostalgic memories: drives into the countryside with his mother, years ago.

Of course, Virgil hadn't been alone with Jessalyn. Sophia had been there, and—the others.

Until those others had grown too old, and lost interest in driving over to the market at Dutchtown and having lunch along the river in the windmill restaurant . . . All of the windows of the Jeep were down, crazed hot air rushed about his head.

Lovesick Virgil, though wanting to think otherwise.

At thirty-two he'd become a kind of vagrant in the familial lives of others. So lonely, even working on his sculptures couldn't assuage his conviction of being in the wrong place at the wrong time.

Where Keziahaya might be on this festive national holiday, Virgil had no idea. A celebration that consisted mostly of brainless loud-cracking noises, flares and simulated explosions could not have much appeal for one who'd narrowly escaped death as a boy in civil war.

Virgil had praised Keziahaya's paintings and sculptures, sincerely.

But Keziahaya only just seemed embarrassed. Murmuring—*OK, man. Good. You, too.*

Virgil knew from his own experience that when people praised his work, no matter how sincere they seemed, he felt uneasy, manipulated.

Especially by women. A certain sort of woman. Eager, alone. Not young.

Strange. He'd rarely felt lonely before in his life. Maybe it wasn't Amos Keziahaya for whom he yearned but someone else.

Shut his eyes and what did he see—(it had come to haunt him recently, bizarrely)—a smudged figure like one of Francis Bacon's "screaming popes."

In Whitey's frigid hospital room. It had begun then. The slipping-down, sick sensation.

All his life he'd imagined himself indifferent to his father. But in the hospital room he'd been suddenly anxious as a child. Baffled by what was happening to his father which he could not control with the fantasies inside his head.

Just the word *stroke*. Virgil had never quite been able to speak it aloud.

Poor Whitey shrunken inside his body. Staring at Virgil as if trying to recognize him.

When you realize: as the life goes out in another, it is your own life that shrivels and expires.

Dad—don't die. Don't leave me. No.

Whitey had seemed to hear. Though Virgil had not spoken aloud.

At least, Whitey had responded to Virgil's flute-playing. Virgil was grateful for that.

He'd never quite recovered from Whitey's death, that was the mystery. Shut his eyes and there was a nightmare "screaming pope" staring him in the face.

(Virgil didn't even know the work of Francis Bacon well. He'd never seen a Bacon painting on the wall, in person. What he knew, he didn't greatly admire. Art to make your head ache like migraine. Art like a sharp stick in the eye.)

Not yet dusk but idiot firecrackers were being set off by boys in the riverside park, running with their hands over their ears. Cracking noises in mimicry of gunfire.

Each bullet seeking a target. Why was there such exulting in bullets, noise? Was it purely a masculine activity? Was it *supremely* a masculine activity? Virgil felt nothing but repugnance for such displays of war.

Driving through Pittstown, an enervated old mill town on the Chautauqua River, it came to Virgil with the force of a sequence of firecrackers that maybe he should extinguish himself, while there was still time. Before he became older, middle-aged and beyond. Before the *stroke* rendered him helpless.

When he ran through the money Whitey had left him. Which, seeing that his income was so modest, somewhere below the "poverty level," would be fairly soon.

Or no: better before he ran through the money. He could prepare a handmade will, typing it himself and having his signature witnessed by a notary public.

Virgil's favorite charities. He'd wanted to double-tithe but had procrastinated.

The thought of *extinguishing himself,* which sounds so much loftier than merely *killing himself,* was cheering, and just in time.

At the barbecue Virgil's first instinct was to flee before anyone recognized him. The place was a self-styled "ranch"—a sprawling homestead on the Chautauqua River amid acres of pastureland. Many vehicles were parked in a field. Teenaged boys were offering to "valet park." Virgil parked his own vehicle and hiked to the loose crowd of guests at the rear of the residence, to get a cold beer. Someone cried, "Virgil McClaren! So good you could come." His hand was clasped in triumph by a lively taffy-blond woman whom he recognized as one of the local art patrons who often bought his scrap-metal sculptures.

Later, Virgil would see sleek marmoreal sculptures on the lawn, Henry Moore–influenced. Had to smile ruefully, nothing of his was in sight.

Drifted with others to admire llamas and ostriches in a pasture. (The creatures kept their distance, aloof. All were somewhat mud-splattered from beneath.) There were miniature horses, goats and sheep. Farther on, a flock of guinea fowl pecking in the dirt.

Virgil did know some people here. Virgil did shake some hands. He saw at a little distance a slender woman with very white hair worn in a plait between her shoulder blades, and with her a man in a wide straw-brimmed hat, raspberry-colored shirt, khaki shorts. The man was not a young man but his dark-skinned legs were knotted with muscle. His hair was gunmetal-gray, beneath the wide-brimmed hat. It was notable how the man loomed over the woman, considerably taller than she was. The couple was very affectionate: Virgil saw the man clasp the woman's hand and the two leaned together, whispering and laughing.

Virgil stared. His vision blurred with moisture.

Was it—Jessalyn? It was.

For a moment Virgil stood paralyzed. Stunned. Never could he have predicted such an emotional reaction—in an instant he'd become a hurt, aggrieved son.

Without thinking he backed away. Edged away. Overcome with chagrin.

If she'd seen *him*. He could not bear facing her, confronting her—in the company of a stranger, a man.

How swiftly things turn random, bizarre. For in his blind eagerness to escape his mother and her companion Virgil found himself on a collision course with a young woman in a wheelchair, being pushed along a walkway—a young woman who closely resembled his former friend Sabine—(*was* she Sabine?—Virgil didn't dare look too closely)—and here too, Virgil had to back off hurriedly.

A pert frizz-haired young woman in floral-print pants that hid her thin, wasted legs, wheeled along by a person whom Virgil did not recognize, possibly male, possibly female. He wasn't about to linger to find out.

What a coincidence! What bad timing! At least, neither Sabine (if it was Sabine) nor Jessalyn seemed to have seen him.

Virgil's romance with Sabine—if that's what it had been—had long ago imploded. There had been misunderstandings between them which (Virgil was certain) were not his fault—entirely.

The upshot was: Sabine might not have loved Virgil but she'd perceived in him a person who might adore *her*—it had been a bitter disappointment to her, that Virgil hadn't been that person.

Officially, the two were on fairly good terms. They never spoke harshly of each other to mutual acquaintances—at least, Virgil did not speak harshly of Sabine and if Sabine spoke harshly of him, Virgil was spared the knowledge.

He could not bear to encounter Sabine in his agitated state, in any case. Could not bear to hear her thin mocking drawl—*Oh Vir-gil! Is that you? Don't run away scared, I won't bite.*

Amid a tight knot of people Virgil moved to a position on the flagstone terrace where he could observe the white-plaited woman and her flamboyantly dressed companion a short distance away. His mother Jessalyn, and Hugo Martinez.

It was true, the lurid rumors his sisters had hissed into his ear. That Thom had fumed about. Their mother and Hugo Martinez!

Virgil's face was hot, heavy with blood. Dazedly he turned and walked stumbling away.

Someone called after him—"Virgil! You aren't leaving, are you? Have you had any ribs?"

What a bizarre question, Virgil thought. *Have you had any ribs.*

It was not tolerable. His mother with another man.

So soon. Too soon. Oh God! If Whitey could know . . .

Virgil felt it keenly, his father's mortification. You did not really expect Jessalyn to recover from Whitey's death. Theirs had been so special a marriage . . .

Vaguely Virgil had hoped that Jessalyn might one day remarry—what's-his-name—Colwin?—the mild-mannered widower-friend who was so deeply boring, his presence was a kind of sedative. As Beverly had said, the two were of the exact same "social class"—no one had to worry about Colwin marrying Jessalyn for her money. Whitey had sneered at Colwin, but not unkindly. Whitey would (possibly) have approved of Colwin as a companion for Jessalyn, if necessary. But Hugo Martinez—*no.*

Virgil half-ran to the Jeep. Eager to escape. God damn! The valet-parking boys were staring frankly at him. Fortunately Jessalyn hadn't seen him and he would be prepared to avoid her in the future if she was in the company of Hugo Martinez.

But maybe, Virgil was mistaken. Sitting in the Jeep, having turned on the ignition, behind the wheel he wondered.

Possibly Jessalyn and Hugo Martinez had just met at the party. Or, they were not a couple, just friends. Hugo had taken Jessalyn's photograph, as Virgil recalled, without her permission . . .

Rapidly Virgil's brain clattered—what? Why? Thoughts without contents came swiftly by like empty freight cars.

Every notion Virgil had, every instinct, every "hunch"—usually, he was wrong. He'd liked to think that Amos Keziahaya was (secretly, intensely) aware of him, and preparing to approach him openly, sometime soon—but Virgil had been cultivating this fantasy for months, since he'd first set eyes on the tall scarred-faced Nigerian and shaken his hand . . .

Well, possibly he was mistaken now. How cowardly a son, to refuse to greet his own mother.

Turned off the ignition, and hiked back to the party. Hoping that the taffy-haired smiling hostess wouldn't greet him a second time, clasping his hand in hers and lifting it to her heart.

This time, Virgil made his way directly to Jessalyn.

"Hey Mom? Hello."

Bounded up to his mother with a wide smile. Ignored Hugo Martinez as if he didn't know that the two were a couple—(for how would he know that the two were a couple?).

"Virgil! We thought that was you, running away."

Jessalyn laughed, happily. They were embracing, greeting each other as a son and a mother might greet each other on such an unexpected occasion, Virgil felt his face burn, both Jessalyn and Hugo Martinez were laughing at him and yet not unkindly. Virgil had an impression of Jessalyn's smooth-plaited white hair, never had he seen his mother with her hair parted in the center of her head like this, and plaited down her back, with an artificial, white silk gardenia affixed to the braid; never had he seen his mother wearing what appeared to be, at first glance, a Latin American peasant's costume—a short-sleeved blouse of some ultra-crisp, crimped white fabric covered in embroidered butterflies and flowers, and pajama-like pants in a similar, yellow fabric.

Virgil stared and stared, smelling a faint lavender scent that rose from his mother's hair. In his agitation he could barely make out what they were saying—what he himself was saying.

"Virgil! Hello, my friend."

Hugo Martinez came forward to shake Virgil's hand. His manner was warm, gregarious, proprietorial.

Virgil thought: the man's face was too broad—his skin too burnished, aglow. It was almost aggressive, how he exuded *happiness*. The dark bemused eyes were kindly, crinkled with humor as if he knew exactly what Virgil was thinking.

Hugo had brought one of his cameras to the party, hanging from a strap around his neck. A heavy, expensive camera, Virgil knew it to be.

Hugo had questions to put to Virgil—friendly, fellow-artist questions which Virgil might answer without stammering. For he was very distracted by Hugo, Hugo could see.

But Virgil could feign an interest in Hugo's fancy camera—there is nothing photographers like better than to boast of their "lenses."

He was traveling to Morocco soon, Hugo told Virgil. From there, to Egypt and Jordan. Just three weeks which was much too short.

Virgil asked if Hugo had been to that part of the world before and Hugo said yes, just once in the late 1980s. He was afraid that Marrakesh had changed a good deal. And his favorite Moroccan city—Fez.

Virgil said he'd have liked to travel more, too—but his life hadn't turned out that way . . .

"We could go together!—the three of us."

Virgil was taken by surprise. Jessalyn laughed uneasily.

It was wonderful, unless it was overbearing, how spontaneously Hugo Martinez spoke. A kind of entrepreneurial manner, hyper-enthusiastic, innocently coercive.

The man resembled Whitey, in that way. The father, the head of a family, not a bully and not exactly coercive unless you opposed him. The nicest person you would ever want to meet, the most generous, kindly, persuasive—unless you opposed him, then you saw the steel-glittering eyes, the tightness at the jaws.

In other ways, Hugo Martinez was nothing like Whitey McClaren. Imagine Whitey wearing khaki shorts and a raspberry-colored shirt at an evening social gathering, open-toed sandals, hair to his shoulders and an outsized mustache . . . Whitey would have stared at Hugo Martinez with scarcely disguised dislike, disapproval.

Hugo was talking enthusiastically of northern Africa where he hoped to travel by himself—like a nomad.

Virgil knew from his photographs that Hugo Martinez had traveled a good deal, to parts of the world beyond Europe. He recalled reading travel poems of Hugo's, that had been published in a local literary magazine; long-lined, zigzagging and incantatory poems in the style of Allen Ginsberg, Gary Snyder, Jack Hirschman. Hugo had taught at the community college until he'd been fired—a mild scandal, Virgil remembered. He'd been Poet Laureate of Western New York—until he'd been asked to resign, or had resigned out of principle. The kind of person whom Virgil admired, to a degree—activist, self-proclaimed anarchist, showy, self-aggrandizing. But talented, and good-hearted. Or so Virgil thought.

He was feeling a stirring of envy. He'd purposefully lived a frugal life, in resistance to his father's wishes for him. He'd avoided acquiring too many possessions, responsibilities. He'd wanted to live a life close to the bone, like the Buddha, an "empty" life—no ambition, no desire. Even with the money he'd inherited from Whitey, Virgil wouldn't have felt comfortable spending it on himself, on travel.

But now, in Hugo Martinez's presence, Virgil was feeling a lesser person, incomplete. There was only pride in renunciation if there was someone to register your sacrifice. He wondered what Jessalyn had told Hugo of him, if anything.

Jessalyn said, "Hugo loves to travel. I will miss him for three weeks."

Jessalyn spoke with an air of regret, though (possibly) it was a feigned sort of regret for Hugo Martinez's benefit. Virgil wondered if in fact his mother would be relieved that Hugo was gone—the man was so exuberant, so vocal and expansive.

Gallantly Hugo said, "I will miss *you*."

It happened then, though he'd certainly intended to leave the barbecue, Virgil remained to have supper with Jessalyn and Hugo, seated on lawn chairs on the flagstone terrace. Hardly to be believed, Virgil thought. What would Whitey say!

Even as the two spoke together companionably, even as he saw how Hugo smiled at Jessalyn, and Jessalyn smiled at Hugo, with Hugo hurrying off to get a cold drink for Jessalyn, and Jessalyn deferring to Hugo when he interrupted her, indeed it was obvious that they were a couple; not a long-married couple but a couple in the early, enthralled stages of getting to know each other.

Hugo said, "I'm trying to talk your mother into traveling with me later in the year, in the Galápagos," and Jessalyn said, in a voice that sounded pleading to Virgil, "No. Don't listen to him, Virgil. That's ridiculous." There was a flirtatious sort of tug-of-war between them; clearly this was not a new subject.

Virgil thought yes, it was ridiculous. Jessalyn in the Galápagos!

Whitey would have laughed heartily. His dear wife, totally unsuited for rough travel, primitive settings.

Virgil saw how Jessalyn glanced at him, from time to time. She was smiling in the way of a mother who knows that her child is not entirely happy, and it is her fault.

Virgil! I am sorry.

Mom, it's OK. No problem.

But I mean—I am sorry to have surprised—shocked you . . .

OK, Mom. I'll deal with it.

But, Virgil . . .

Damned if Virgil would be judging his mother, as his sisters and Thom did. Yes it was a surprise, something of a shock, but Jessalyn's life was her own, not his.

Indeed it did seem too soon, as his sisters had charged. Too soon after Dad. Too soon for Jessalyn to be fully recovered. As everyone liked to say—*herself again*.

Virgil wondered: Is a widow ever *herself again*?

Illogical to think so. Cruel to expect so. Losing Whitey had been like losing a limb, Virgil supposed. Bad enough for Virgil, surely worse for his mother.

No, he couldn't judge her. No business of *his*.

(Still: couldn't help wondering if Jessalyn and Hugo were—what's called *intimate*.)

(*Sleeping together.* Not possible!)

The likelihood did fill Virgil with distaste, repugnance. He would not allow himself to speculate—*no*.

That his mother could smile and laugh and seem to be enjoying herself at a Fourth of July barbecue, eight months after Whitey's death, with big blustery Hugo Martinez: Was this commendable, or was this pathetic? Admirable, or desperate?

That she no longer looked so thin, bereft, destitute but (almost) beautiful again, with her white hair brushed and gleaming, in a plait between her shoulder blades; not in the fashionable black she'd been wearing, but in what looked like a dramatic peasant costume—how could anyone judge her?

Virgil wanted to murmur—*Hey Mom. You're great. I love you.*

Jessalyn asked if Virgil had seen his sisters lately—and Virgil shook his head truthfully, *no*.

"They're not so happy with me, I'm afraid. And Thom, also."

Virgil shrugged. He knew nothing about it! His older siblings rarely confided in him, you might deduce.

"They don't approve of Hugo, I think. On the phone they've been difficult to speak with and I—I don't think—it's time just yet to introduce them to him." Jessalyn spoke bravely, wistfully. Hugo, smiling to himself, as if he weren't intently listening to each word of Jessalyn's, was devouring barbecued ribs with a pretense of delicacy.

Hugo was a handsome man with a somewhat ravaged face. Virgil knew him to be a few years younger than his mother but (to Virgil's eye at least) he looked older. His smile exposed uneven teeth, of the hue of weak tea. His manner was just slightly abrasive, aggressive. The wide-brimmed straw hat was worn at a jaunty angle that suggested assurance, arrogance. The drooping mustache had to be an affectation, large enough to cover much of the man's mouth. His hair too was an affectation: shoulder-length like Virgil's but more obviously brushed, tended-to. (Virgil did nothing with his hair except, not very often, wash it. Consequently his hair was drying and fading like straw in midsummer. He would have considered it vanity to have done much more.) The raspberry-colored shirt was (it seemed likely) a companion to Jessalyn's crisp white blouse, probably bought at the same Mexican market by Hugo Martinez. On Hugo's big-knuckled fingers were several rings including a large dull-silver ring in the shape of a star. He wore a silver bracelet. His belt had a silver buckle. His shirt was open to mid-chest, to show a snaggle of silver-gray hairs. The khaki shorts were hiker's shorts with many pockets and zippers and (Virgil saw with satisfaction) freshly stained with barbecue sauce.

Jessalyn had noticed the small stain, Virgil saw. But Jessalyn said not a word. As she'd have noticed Whitey with a stain on his clothing in a public place but would not have said a word.

It was dusk. Fireworks over the river, a mile away at Pittstown.

Hugo had adjusted his camera to take pictures of the nighttime sky. Exploding colors, like multifoliate roses, juxtaposed with a wan quarter moon, a filigree of clouds. Dark foliage overhead framing the view.

Beauty of the most obvious flashy kind, Virgil thought. A crowd will *oooh* and *ahhh* predictably, if not required to think.

Whitey had liked fireworks well enough though he'd remarked that you got the point pretty soon and the rest was just repetition.

Hugo wandered off with his camera, in the direction of the river. Taking photographs of the fireworks wholly absorbed him. You felt the relief—as least Virgil did—of the man's fierce attention deflected elsewhere.

"How long have you known Hugo, Mom?"

"I—I'm not sure. It happened so—unexpectedly."

Jessalyn spoke evasively. Virgil could see that she was embarrassed, wishing that Hugo had not left her alone with him.

Maybe she didn't know what had happened, Virgil thought. Maybe there were no adequate words to explain. And she was determined not to apologize.

Virgil was remembering that Hugo Martinez had been one of the local activists involved in unionizing Hammond civic workers in the late 1980s, when Whitey had been mayor of Hammond. The workers had included public school and community college teachers, county government staff, even cafeteria workers and custodians at City Hall. Hugo Martinez had been the chairman of the art department at the college and he'd angered the administration by leading the strike in which, eventually, Whitey McClaren had had to intervene. Virgil recalled the excitement of classes being disrupted at school. Each night on TV there was footage of workers "striking"—a week of picket lines, arrests by police, denunciations on both sides, accusations, even vandalism. Whitey—their Dad!—had been on TV sounding harsh, unhappy but resolute. *Will not tolerate anarchy. Will not give in to blackmail.* So far as Virgil knew there had not been any violence against individual strikers—at least, no incidents had been broadcast by the media.

The youthful Hugo Martinez, dark-haired at the time, fiery and provocative and roundly denounced as a *hippie-anarchist,* had received a good deal of attention in the media, most of it highly critical. His Hispanic identity had drawn racial slurs and accusations of being a Communist. Yet glamor had accrued to him as well for he resembled no one so much as the revolutionary Che Guevara. In front of City Hall he'd shouted through a bullhorn—*The Hammond city government is not going to cajole us with phony compromises, crooked dealings and slave-wage contracts any more than they are going to intimidate us with their "show of force" . . .*

Eventually Hugo was arrested by Hammond police, along with fellow demonstrators. In handcuffs they'd been taken to the Hammond men's house of detention in a police van. This must have been what Thom was fuming about in his phone message: their mother involved with a *Communist, ex-convict.*

Soon, the strike ended. The city allowed the civic workers to join the union but concessions were limited and contracts were not what strike leaders had demanded. Several persons had to be sacrificed so that a new coalition could be formed; extremists like Hugo Martinez were ousted from their positions or forced to resign.

Virgil wondered how much Jessalyn knew about this. He had no doubt that Hugo Martinez knew very well whose wife Jessalyn was.

Hugo had remained in the Hammond area. He'd continued to work as an artist and to involve himself in various activist causes, some of which overlapped with Virgil's, though the two had never picketed or demonstrated together. Each community has such a "rebel" figure—admired and disliked in about equal measure.

Like other artist-friends, Virgil had always admired Hugo Martinez's work. Virgil had even heard Hugo give poetry readings at the community college to which, eventually, he'd been invited back, under the auspices of a new administration. Possibly, somewhere in his haphazardly stored possessions, Virgil had a signed copy of one of Hugo's books.

And yes—more recently Hugo was involved with "exonerating"—"freeing"—prison inmates "wrongfully convicted." A local activist organization of which Virgil had been hearing, with a vague intention of aligning himself . . .

At least now, if he wished, Virgil could *donate.* A worthy cause, a moral impulse—never a mistake to *donate.*

Whitey would approve. Whitey had always been outraged by injustice. Hadn't Whitey sacrificed his life in a (possibly futile) gesture of outrage against injustice?

"Oh! Look . . ."

There came a final paroxysm of fireworks, explosions of riotous color in rapid succession. Cries of excitement. How annoying fireworks are, Virgil thought, demanding to be admired!

It was dark by the time Hugo returned to Jessalyn and Virgil; Virgil began to sense that Jessalyn was becoming uneasy, wondering where her companion was. Their hosts had lit lanterns, and were urging people not to leave just yet. But the barbecue was dissolving, guests were drifting away. Virgil was half-hoping that Hugo and Jessalyn would ask him to join them, wherever they were headed next, but when Hugo did make a suggestion of this kind, with seeming sincerity, and a squeezing grip on Virgil's forearm, Virgil quickly demurred.

Time to get home!—he wanted to get up early the next morning, and work.

Indeed, he was eager to leave before Hugo and Jessalyn left. He didn't want to see them walk off together hand in hand—drive away in a vehicle together—presumably, Hugo's.

Didn't want to speculate if Hugo would stay with Jessalyn that night, in Jessalyn's house which was (Virgil didn't want to think!) *his house.* It did not seem likely that Jessalyn would stay with Hugo in his house, wherever that was.

Possibly, neither stayed with the other. It was low-minded to speculate about such matters, that were none of Virgil's business.

Jessalyn kissed Virgil good night. In a wistful voice she asked if he would have dinner with them, soon—"Before Hugo goes away?"

Virgil murmured *yes*. He'd like that.

"I'll call you tomorrow, dear. We can set a date."

"Better if I call you, Mom. My cell phone doesn't always work on the farm."

"Well, all right. Call me tomorrow. Promise!"

Backing away Virgil promised.

Before Hugo goes away—the wistful words lingered in Virgil's ears for a long time afterward.

CLUTCHING AT EACH OTHER.

And you—a coward.

— ∞ —

In early August it happened, at last.

So long he'd anticipated. So long unable to sleep, yet he'd dreamt.

And then swiftly, as if without preparation, after Virgil helped Amos Keziahaya dismantle a small exhibit of his work in a local gallery, and loaded this work, along with his own, onto a truck to bring back to Bear Mountain Road; after he and Keziahaya stopped for a meal at a tavern, to celebrate, as Virgil insisted, Keziahaya's having sold several lithographs and sculptures, for more than two thousand dollars in all—(Virgil had sold fewer, for less than nine hundred dollars); after Keziahaya accepted Virgil's invitation to come to his cabin for a drink and the men talked for nearly two hours mostly about Keziahaya's experiences in the United States, his bemusement and alarm at American life—"the not-so-hidden racism"—"the optimism like children's balloons"; after Virgil may have had one beer too many, mistaking the young Nigerian's exuberance and gaiety for something more personal between them, trembling with excitement, filled with happiness and hope (for at the back of Virgil's mind was the vivid memory of his mother and Hugo Martinez bravely clasping hands) he found himself walking with Keziahaya to the door of his cabin and impulsively daring to bring his lips against Keziahaya's startled, parted lips with a near-inaudible murmur—*Good night, Amos!*

It had not been a forcible kiss. It had not been a passionate kiss. It had been light as the touch of a moth's wings. A laughing kiss, a mere caress with the lips. Not a *kiss*.

So Virgil would protest, afterward. If only to himself.

But Amos Keziahaya was taken by surprise by the gesture, and recoiled with a look of genuine shock—as if a hornet had stung him. However warmly he'd been talking and laughing with Virgil for much of the evening, however relaxed he'd appeared to be in Virgil's company, he had clearly not expected this conclusion to the visit, and he had not wanted it.

Quickly departing without looking at Virgil, very embarrassed, possibly repelled, muttering something inaudible in which the only word Virgil could hear clearly was *no*.

Black Rush

Of course she was *all right.*

Of course she'd *had a good week.*

God damn beginning to resent these stupid questions.

If her health insurance didn't cover twelve sessions with (aptly named) Dr. Foote she'd never have started.

Waste of time. Asinine insipid inane and inept.

Nothing wrong with me. Ridiculous!

AT FIRST her father's death was a point of the size of a period at the end of a sentence: .

At first just a single, singular hair, or (possibly) several hairs in succession pulled individually from her head. Hardly conscious of tugging at the hairs at her right temple as she worked at her computer long after every other adult (faculty, staff) had gone home for the day without a backward glance.

(Though possibly they'd registered some mild anxiety registering her steel-colored vehicle with its grim military look in the parking space reserved for PRINCIPAL which was closest to the rear entrance of the building's east wing.)

(What a shrewd idea, to move her office to the rear of the school! Not the front where you'd expect the principal's office to be.)

(The bland-beige facade of North Hammond High overlooked just a bland-grassy front lawn, walkways and street.)

(Rumor was, Dr. McClaren behind the [usually drawn] venetian blinds of her office was keen to take note which of the faculty left at which time. How early? How late? Walking alone or—with whom?)

(If walking with another person or persons, surely talking about *her*. Conspiring, collaborating.)

(By which *take note* was meant literally.)

Twisting hairs around her fingers, tugging. Gently.

Oh, gently! At first.

Exerting pressure—gentle, subtle pressure!—on the roots, embedded in the scalp. And what a stab of satisfaction, relief, a little jolt of electricity-pain to wake her from the stupor of her work, like a shot of caffeine to the heart.

Oh God.

Like scratching mosquito bites or rashes until they really, really hurt and have begun to bleed. Like that.

Not knowing what she was doing, or only one-tenth knowing. And that was the pleasure of it, the not-knowing when the sudden sweet pain would strike her (sensitive, sensual) scalp.

Oh. God.

In fact she'd stared at the short, stubby, dark hairs on her desktop not recognizing initially what they were. If a hair drifted onto her computer keyboard she blew it away like dust.

No clear memory of how, when it had begun. Pulling God-damned hairs out of her God-damned head.

Except had to have something to do that smothered the black rush that had swept over her at the time of the call from the hospital from Thom—*Lorene, bad news. Dad didn't make it.*

"Oh my God. What—"

"Can you get here? Can you call Bev? I'll call Sophie."

Fuck she'd give up precious time calling Beverly.

Soon after that terrible hour. After the cremation, and the gathering at the house where to her chagrin Lorene had had too much to drink (which wasn't like her—everyone agreed).

She'd returned to work very soon. But the black rush in her lungs had poisoned her. Lungs, cavity surrounding her heart.

So it had begun in late October possibly. Without her quite realizing. At work, at the computer, alone, in her office at the rear of the school or in her home-office where she had an identical computer. Her fingers seeking out a single, singular hair to tug, just to ease the tension but then, when that wasn't quite enough, hairs.

The advantage of the single hair is that there is a tiny *pop!* when the hair-root is yanked from the scalp. Maybe you can't hear it but you can feel it.

The advantage of several hairs is not just the grip is easier but the *frisson* of pain is more profound.

Lorene? Just come. I'm hanging up now.

She'd realized belatedly that she had truly believed that Whitey would recover. Somehow, she hadn't taken the stroke, the neurological impairment, even the infection that seriously. Daddy was tough, resilient, stoic, never complained and never (so far as they knew) worried.

A surprise of the kind when you misstep on steps. Something very startling about it, a visceral disbelief.

She'd felt just slightly—only *just slightly*—a tinge of what you'd have to call annoyance. Vexation. As if the fact of the death hadn't sunk in just yet but oh! what an inconvenient time the call from Thom came, a workday, meeting with faculty scheduled for that afternoon, stacks of paperwork on her desk, online registrations and forms to fill out, *could not come at a worse time.*

A call that changed all of their lives. You don't know, reaching innocently for the phone.

So swiftly it had happened. Yet irrevocable.

The entry to a black hole? Is that what it is?

"DR. McCLAREN? DID YOU—HURT YOURSELF?"

"Hurt myself? How?"

With a flutter of her fingers Iris made an awkward gesture toward her own hairline. Deeply embarrassed to be speaking in so intimate a way to Dr. McClaren who stared at her coldly for a moment without seeming to know what Iris meant then, turning away, saying in an undertone, "It's nothing. Some sort of skin allergy. Take no notice, please."

A penny-sized pale spot on her scalp, just above the right temple, oozing droplets of blood. Startling to see in the mirror, and to realize that she hadn't been aware of it until now.

(Had others, like Iris, seen? What had they been thinking?)

How the brain corrects the eye. Seeing what the brain is prepared to see and not what the eye reports.

Except: *she* was not a weak person. *She* wasn't going to succumb to a neurotic tic.

Yet: not long afterward while working at the computer she happened to notice on her desktop several short, stubby hairs oozing blood at the roots.

(But when had this happened? Had *she* done this?)

She'd been commending herself for having behaved so responsibly since Whitey's death. Keeping in contact with her mother by calling nearly every day at a fixed time (easier that way: like most administrators Lorene lived by her schedule) and taking care not to become emotional in her mother's presence (unlike her exhibitionist-sister Beverly who burst into tears at the slightest provocation, bawling and moaning like a sick cow).

Lorene wasn't what you'd call an *emotional* person, frankly.

Not sure she'd cried when Whitey died. Couldn't recall when she'd cried last, or why.

Anyway: "raw emotion" wasn't for her. Only made things worse for poor Jessalyn as for anyone else who preferred to mourn with a modicum of dignity.

A strong will is a strong backbone. Not sure who'd said that, possibly General Patton. Possibly Whitey.

She did not indulge weakness in herself, any more than she did in others.

Hardest on herself, she liked to think.

No more pulling out hairs from her head!—"That will stop, immediately."

Yet: shopping at the mall despite the risk of encountering North Hammond students (unavoidably, she needed a new cranberry-colored pants suit) she happened to see, in a three-way mirror in a clothing store, the (right) side of her head where there seemed to be a bald spot of the size of a nickel . . . "Oh. My God. What is *that*."

The saleswoman pretended not to notice but Lorene was so demoralized she left the store without making a purchase.

"My enemies are winning. Thank God they don't *know*."

Difficult to stop pulling God-damned hairs out of her head since Lorene was (mostly) not conscious of pulling them out. How could you *consciously* stop doing something of which you were *not conscious*?

Worse, she was beginning to find clumps of hair in bed.

Wearing a cap indoors? Would that prevent hair-pulling?

Yet somehow, her restless fingers easily pushed beneath the cap, as soon as her mind was elsewhere.

Wearing gloves at the computer? Thick enough so that her straying fingers couldn't get a grip on hairs?

To Lorene's horror then, larger clumps of hairs began to appear on the desktop and in her bedsheets. Somehow she'd been able to get a grip on a strand of hair even wearing gloves.

Patchy bald spots of the size of quarters began to appear on her head.

The gloves were useless. But mittens—impossible, she could not type wearing God-damned *mittens*.

Reluctantly Lorene began to let her hair grow slightly longer. Now she would look more conventional—like an ordinary woman. But it was easier to hide the bald spots with longer hair which she could comb over, flatten.

Determined to overcome the habit. A *very bad habit* for one of her stature and sense of self-worth.

Indeed there was a name for it—*trichotillomania*. (Not to be confused with the yet more repulsive *trichinosis*.) Certain of the young, silly girl students at North Hammond pulled out their hair, or cut themselves with razors, or starved themselves until they resembled barely-living skeletons, or gorged themselves and vomited in the restrooms so frequently that some of the sinks were stopped up—("At least," Lorene fumed to her staff, "they could throw up in the *toilets*").

"Lorene? What on *earth*?"—Beverly stared at the dwarf knitted hat Lorene had begun to wear in the presence of others, outdoors and in, that covered her entire head like a swimming cap.

Flushed with annoyance Lorene told her sister that she only had some sort of skin rash on her scalp, like eczema—"Nothing worth discussing."

"Maybe a head scarf would be better," Beverly said. "Something like a turban."

"I am not going to wear a God-damned *turban*."

"What about a baseball cap? A Hammond High cap scarlet-and-gold? The kids would love it."

"I don't care to pander to high school students, Beverly. Please can we change the subject?"

Beverly laughed. The *She-Gestapo* of Hammond High in one of those little, pathetic knitted caps worn by cancer patients undergoing chemotherapy.

The sisters had met for a hurried lunch with the intention of discussing what to do about Jessalyn and "that terrible man, the Communist-Cuban"—since Jessalyn was continuing to see Hugo Martinez, and to be seen with him in public places, despite her adult children's strongly reiterated disapproval.

"I said to Mom, 'People are talking about you!'—'People are saying "What would Whitey say!"' and she was just—just so *quiet*. And I said, 'Mom? Are you still there?'—(I'd thought she had hung up the phone)—and Mom said finally, in this small sad voice like someone trying not to cry, 'How I live my life is my own business, Beverly. Good-bye.'"

Lorene shook her head. She'd had something of the same experience calling Jessalyn recently. So *frustrating*. And so *unlike the mother they'd always known*.

"What will be unbearable is if this awful person *moves in*. Into *our house*!"

"D'you think he stays there? Overnight?"

"I can't think about it at all. Please."

"You don't think that—Mom *loves* him, do you?"

"Oh, you know how Mom is—she *likes* too many people, and they take advantage of her."

The sisters were silent, considering. But the very possibility of their sixty-one-year-old mother—(or was Jessalyn now sixty-two?)—*making love* with any man was repellent, repugnant.

As adolescents they'd been deeply embarrassed to come upon Jessalyn and Whitey kissing, even holding hands. The notion of their parents *making love/having sex* had made them shudder.

"Really I think that Mom is—is not—you know—'sexually inclined.' Any longer."

"Jesus, Beverly! I've asked you to please stop."

"One thing they do is *hiking*. Can you imagine, our mother—*hiking!*"

"No, frankly. Are you serious?"

"In Pierpont Park, up on the cliff, they were seen. This *older couple*."

"Dad would be so surprised! The only walking he did was on the golf course."

"No. Daddy walked downtown. He liked to walk at lunchtime, he said. But alone. He'd never have wanted to *hike*."

The sisters were silent, considering. The thinnest of cobwebs passed over their brains, and was gone.

"Thom hasn't been any help so far," Beverly said grimly, "—he hasn't even gotten rid of that diseased tomcat."

"That damned cat! That was the beginning, we can see now."

"I'm thinking of asking Thom to do something drastic—meet with that man and offer him money to go away and leave our mother alone. What do you think?"

"Actually—Steve thought of that. I'm not sure if he was serious or joking but he knows how we are all feeling . . ."

Beverly's voice trailed off. In fact her husband joked harshly about her preoccupation with her family which he believed to be both morbid and futile.

"We would need Thom to do it. Not us. This Rodriguez is a 'Latino'—they are very macho, and don't respect women." Lorene had poked two fingers up inside the knitted cap at her temple and was absentmindedly tugging at hairs. "What do you think we should offer him? Five thousand dollars?"

"*Five* thousand? If he thinks that Mom has millions of dollars, five thousand isn't much."

"*Ten* thousand? *Twenty?*"

"He might just get insulted, and that will make things worse. If he tells Mom . . ."

"Thom will have a better idea how to go about it. He's a canny businessman. He knows about *deals*."

"Well. It could backfire. Paying off the man is a kind of blackmail and he might take the money but then demand more. Doesn't blackmail always *escalate*?"

"Oh, for God's sake! You are always *so negative*. Don't you realize—*we have to do something to save Mom*."

All this while Beverly had been gazing at Lorene with widened quizzical eyes in a way that made Lorene distinctly uncomfortable. At last Lorene asked irritably what was wrong and Beverly said, hesitantly, "Your eyes, Lorene. I mean—your eyelashes. You don't seem to have any."

—∞—

Her fifth year as principal at North Hammond High. It would be her most triumphant, she vowed.

Major (public) goal: to raise the school's ranking to twenty-fifth place in New York State (or better).

Major (private) goal: to receive the Distinguished Educator Award from the National Council of Public School Administrators, which had never been awarded to any public school administrator in Hammond and vicinity and for which (Lorene had reason to know) she'd been nominated the previous year.

The first academic year since Whitey's death, however. And nearing the anniversary of that death soon.

Plucking out hairs from her (stinging, smarting) scalp. Plucking out eyelashes. Experiencing small flashes of emptiness, panic. Even bouts of nausea. Oh, what was happening to her!

No. You can do it, dear. Don't give in like I did.

"DR. McCLAREN—"

"Please, Mark. 'Lorene.'"

Utterly friendly she was being to him. Utterly warm, guileless. *He* would never believe the vicious things whispered of Dr. McClaren as a consequence. *He* would always defend her, staunchly.

It was Lorene's strategy each fall to select younger teachers to favor among her faculty. Usually, though not always, these were young men in their twenties or early thirties whom she found particularly attractive, respectful and admiring of her.

Usually, though not always, they were unmarried. So far as Lorene could determine, unattached.

In all there were 109 classroom teachers at North Hammond, as well as a sizable staff, under the principal's direction.

Of these, Lorene calculated that she needed at least ten individuals resolutely, unswervingly, fanatically (but not obviously) *on her side*.

Most of the (older) faculty she'd inherited, of course. Belonging to the teachers' union they could not be "terminated"—not readily. On a master list Lorene marked (evident) supporters of her with flower-asterisks and (evident) detractors with tiny daggers. It did not escape her notice that individuals in one category (supporters) might shift to the other category (detractors) but it was rare indeed that the reverse was true.

Uncanny, too, how the protégés of one season lost ground, faltered and slipped and became the outcasts, if not the enemies, of another season. Like any skilled administrator Lorene played her underlings like cards, to trump one another. A mere, single vote against a policy Dr. McClaren was pushing might be enough to result in a teacher being tossed into the discard pile; many more votes in support of Dr. McClaren would be required to get out of the discard pile. "If you are dissatisfied here, I will be happy to write you a strong recommendation to transfer elsewhere"—with seeming sincerity Dr. McClaren uttered these words to individuals perceived as disgruntled, never failing to produce a chilling effect.

But the younger instructors, all of them Lorene's personal hires, began their careers at North Hammond High grateful to her, and eager to please her; especially since they were in competition with one another, and dependent upon the principal's evaluations. Their loyalty was fiercely vertical, to Lorene; they could not afford to be generous with rival colleagues.

She was coming to feel like a captain at the prow of a ship, braving winds and high seas. A pitching deck, and all hands on board to do her bidding—if she never let them out of her sight.

"So, Mark—I'm hoping that you will say yes."

"I—I would be very honored, Dr. McClar—I mean, 'Lorene . . .'"

"Good. I will send the program chairman your name. I think it will be very exciting for you—and a great challenge—to represent all of the English teachers at North Hammond in just your second year with us."

The young man was looking somewhat stunned. Smiling, but dazedly, as if Lorene had invited him into the inner sanctum of the principal's office with its (usually) part-closed blinds overlooking the parking lot, to inform him that his contract would not be renewed for the next year.

Instead, she'd asked him to participate in a panel at the New York State Conference of Teachers of High School English, to meet in Albany in November, titled "The Future of the Printed Word in Our Public Schools: Does It Have One?"

Lorene would attend the conference also. Possibly, she could ride with Mark Svenson who would drive to Albany.

Mark was in his late twenties and North Hammond wasn't his first teaching position. He had a B.A. degree from SUNY Buffalo and a master's degree in English education from SUNY Binghamton. A pert, upright, sharp-eyed but deferential wirehaired terrier with an affable face, good manners. A tail of thumping enthusiasm. Not a particularly handsome young man but Lorene hadn't much interest in "good looks"—she'd learned from experience that the more attractive a man, the less you could trust him. Also, she disliked men who were ironic, acerbic, over-informed and verbose, know-it-alls, like herself. She didn't like short men both on principle, because they were short, and because they were likely to gravitate toward her *simply because she was short*. She'd always stiff-armed these guys, cutting them off at mixers, cocktail parties, life. She admired tall men, and she admired (some) tall women, except she was likely to be jealous of tall women if they were attractive, and contemptuous of them if they were not.

Her own height was five feet three. Taller than Lorene was *too tall*. Shorter than Lorene was *too short*. Unofficially, with not a soul taking notice, or so Lorene believed, she'd ceased hiring attractive women altogether. Especially not Hispanic women: they tended to be too good-looking, glamorously well-groomed, nails always polished and hair always "dramatic"—*Carmen* can't be serious. And they wear high heels. Can't help it, they make (most) other women look unattractive.

For any job opening, of course Lorene favored men (white-skinned, dark-skinned—no matter); but she was restrained from always, and obviously, favoring men, for there were guidelines in her profession which she could not violate. Publicly, Lorene McClaren espoused "political correctness"—"diversity in all its forms." But it wasn't difficult to reject better-looking women judging by just their application photos and, in some quarters, might've been lauded as a kind of affirmative action hiring, plain-faced women, overweight women, blemished-complexion women, to Dr. McClaren's credit. As long as they were good teachers and there was a plentiful supply of "good teachers" seeking jobs.

It might have been, a good part of Lorene's motive in favoring Mark Svenson was to dis-favor another, more senior English teacher with whom Lorene had had an (unspoken, elliptical) alliance for several years, until recently. Though married, R.W. (as she thought of him now: she did not like to acknowledge his full name) had been a protégé and a strong supporter of Principal McClaren until things had gone wrong between them, irremediably, like a shifting in tectonic plates in the earth. R.W. had often accompanied Lorene to professional conferences including, the previous fall, a conference of English and drama teachers in Washington, D.C.; yet, inexplicably, R.W. betrayed Lorene soon afterward by voting against a crucial proposal of hers at a faculty meeting, and siding with one of Lorene's longtime adversaries on a trivial but life-shattering curriculum matter. And later by the purest chance Lorene had seen R.W. with colleagues in an Italian restaurant near the school, persons who were decidedly not *pro-McClaren,* all of them celebrating what looked like someone's birthday. Unforgivable!

Of course, R.W. had tenure at North Hammond. R.W. was a popular English teacher who also advised the Drama Club, and directed plays—the most Herculean of efforts in the profession, along with coaching losing sports teams. Even if Lorene had been able to terminate his contract she wouldn't have wanted to lose R.W., for a teacher of such quality could not easily be replaced. Still, she disliked him, and conspired to get revenge against him: one of the suspected trolls whose transcript she'd sabotaged the previous spring had been a star student of R.W.

There'd been rumors of a gala birthday party for one of the math teachers to which Dr. McClaren hadn't been invited. Rumors of other parties, celebrations, from which she'd been excluded though R.W. had been involved . . . It was too complicated, too demeaning and degrading, no wonder she felt a compulsion to pluck at her hair, her eyelashes, to tug at the soft crepey skin beneath her eyes . . .

Suddenly she was feeling tired. It had been a singularly long and hazardous day and she had more work to do in her office, at her computer.

Mark Svenson was on his feet preparing to leave the office. His dazzling good luck had produced a glow in his face. There was indeed something reassuringly terrier-like about the young man's affable manner; almost, Lorene would have liked to stroke his wavy, sandy-colored hair and see if he would lick her hand.

Not a tall man, no more than five feet eight. R.W. was taller, at least six feet. Arrogant, vain. But why think of *him*.

"I was thinking of an early dinner, at the Italian restaurant"—Lorene heard herself say impulsively—"if you happened to be free . . ."

Taken by surprise Mark Svenson stammered that no, he wasn't, not that night. In his face a look not just of surprise but of regret, Lorene saw.

It had been the most casual of invitations. Hardly an invitation, just a remark. Readily forgotten.

"Well. Thank you, Dr. McClaren—I mean, 'Lorene.' I hope I won't disappoint you on the panel."

"Yes. I hope you won't disappoint me, either."

Heartily Lorene laughed, to indicate that this was a joke.

The departing Mark Svenson laughed also, not so heartily.

NOT LONG AFTERWARD, the first of the "incidents."

Returning at dusk from a meeting in downtown Hammond in the steel-colored Saab she'd purchased with a portion of the money Whitey had left for her. A fine mist had spread over the flotilla of headlights with an enthralling beauty Lorene had never seen before and at the entrance to the Hennicott Expressway she heard a soft voice close beside her—*Close your eyes, Lorene-y. You've earned a rest.*

Next thing she knew her car was drifting onto the shoulder of the highway, that was littered with broken glass and debris. Her numbed foot groping for the correct pedal, not that one, not this, no it was the other, it was the *brake* she sought in desperation to save herself.

Jolting, thumping. Pulling up just inches short of a retaining wall.

Something struck her wetly between the eyes on that broad flat bone between the eyes that would swell and bruise to a lurid purple like a third, abscessed eye.

Could have wept with gratitude, the mercy shown Lorene McClaren she'd so rarely shown anyone in her life. Mist obscuring graffiti on the wall and making of oncoming headlights mild ghostly eyes lacking sight.

She was alive, she hadn't been seriously injured. Just the blow between the eyes. Just the constriction in the lungs. Just the lightning-flash of pain in the spine. Just the dryness of the throat, like the fine-granulated dirt of the grave.

Oh Daddy. Why did you call to me and then leave me!

WHAT GAVE HER PLEASURE, no one could guess.

Not of the body. For Lorene, there was no pleasure *of the body* for all sensation *of the body* was demeaning, and shameful, and finite.

Revenge is a dish best served with no witnesses.

Lying awake thinking with great pleasure of the student-trolls' transcripts she'd "hacked"—graduates of North Hammond who'd come to believe themselves entitled and privileged and marked for success but abruptly dog-eared, marked for second- or third-rate lives.

No one could have guessed the link between the half-dozen student-trolls for it existed in a pure realm of untraceable non-being: Lorene McClaren's mind.

Recalling how R.W. had come to speak with her troubled and mystified that one of his very best students had been rejected by most of the colleges to which he'd applied. Lorene had been surprised—why on earth would R.W., or any teacher, *care*?

Not that R.W. had the slightest suspicion that the principal of North Hammond High was to blame for who in his right mind could imagine that a high school principal would sabotage students at her own school?—no one.

Naive, trusting, a large shaggy sheepdog with shortsighted eyes, R.W. hadn't seemed to have grasped that Dr. McClaren no longer favored him. One of those dogs you'd have to kick more than once, to make them realize they are *not liked*. That something had gone irrevocably wrong, some small trigger had been pulled in Lorene's (inscrutable) brain. It was over between them, that had never been named or acknowledged.

You had your chance, my friend. You blew it.

The best sex, Lorene had come to think, was balked sex.

A woman stirred in a man—(not any man: the man did have to be someone special)—a sensation of sexual interest, even excitement; but the woman did not satisfy this sensation, only just kept it dimly aflame, over as long a period of time as she could manage. Eventually, the flame died out. Or, the woman lost interest in the project. But whose fault was that?

At the midpoint of her thirties Lorene appeared to be of no discernible age. She might have been thirty, she might have been fifty. You could not easily imagine her as a girl. You could not easily imagine her as *female*. Her uniform-like pants suits obscured her figure which was flat, hipless, sinewy-tough. Her legs were short, and tight with muscle. Her eyes were sly, silvery and quick-darting as piranha. Her mouth was a slash in her lower face which she'd smeared with her characteristic red lipstick, that glared out of her pale face. At the time of her confrontation with R.W., before Whitey, before the *trichotillomania,* her dark hair had been ultra-short, razor-cut, with no patchy spots to betray weakness. R.W. had gazed at her—(so Lorene would recall)—with something like puzzled wistfulness, as a man might gaze at something he has already lost.

Of course, between R.W. and Lorene there'd been (in the strictest, most clinical sense) *nothing*. They had not even touched except for brisk handshakes that left each grinning and breathless.

It was bewildering to him, R.W. told Lorene, that his "most promising student in years" had been rejected by the colleges he'd most wanted to attend, which were the very colleges R.W. had recommended for him, when his grades and SAT scores were higher than those of other students who'd been admitted to the colleges, and his letters of recommendation had to be stronger.

Lorene had been sympathetic at once. Yes, it was very sad. Very mysterious. No one could understand it.

She'd wondered also, she said. Though she knew little of cyberbullying, cybercrime (she said), she wondered if someone from North Hammond, a rival classmate of the boy's, had sabotaged his records.

R.W. had not thought of this. "'Hacked'—you mean? Someone might have 'hacked' into the school computer?"

"If that's the expression—'hacked.' You know, I am practically computer illiterate myself so I don't keep up with slang terms."

For reasons of her own Lorene promulgated the fiction that she was an old-fashioned "hands-on" sort of administrator who knew little about the arcane use of computers. Her reputation was of one so diligent, so resistant of electronic gadgets, she took careful notes by hand at meetings.

Earnestly Lorene said: "We could hire a computer expert of some kind. We could supply the names of 'suspicious parties' for him to investigate. There were several in last year's graduating class . . . If there was a cybercrime in our school, and your student was victimized, it should be detected."

R.W. looked at her in alarm. Clearly, he hadn't expected Lorene to respond in this way. "But—we wouldn't want innocent persons to be targeted. 'Naming names' is always risky. In the age of the Internet a rumor can spread like wildfire."

"Well. I suppose you are right. I don't know much about the Internet either, I'm afraid."

"The Internet can be hell for young people. Bad enough for adults but kids can be driven to suicide."

Lorene shook her head mutely. Suicide! Terrible thing.

R.W. spoke sadly of his student "Reg Pryce" who'd been stricken with lymphoma in tenth grade but who was in remission now, who'd given so much of his time to the Drama Club . . .

Pryce was he saying, or—*Price*?

Guiltily Lorene couldn't recall which had been the troll who'd tormented her—*Pryce, Price*. Possibly, she'd confused the two.

Well, too bad! There was little she could do about it now.

She told R.W. that he might ask the boy to meet with her. And his parents might accompany him. Possibly, if some actual injustice had been done, Lorene could make an appeal to the colleges . . . She spoke with a pretense of concern and naivete for (of course) no admissions office would pay the slightest attention to a high school principal trying to appeal a rejection of one of her students.

R.W. winced at the suggestion. Intervening in such a way might do more harm than good, he said, casting a shadow over future North Hammond applicants at the colleges. Also, if Reg hoped to transfer after his freshman year . . .

Lorene let R.W. talk. Utterly baffling to her that he should care so much about another man's son. *She* didn't care at all.

R.W. was a very good teacher, everyone said. The kids admired him, respected him. Almost, she felt sorry for him. That shaggy sheepdog look, mournful eyes. Good-hearted, foolish. Maybe she should erase the ill-feeling between them, and start anew.

But no. Too late.

Never forget, and never forgive.

When she looked up, R.W. was gone. Must've left her office quietly, and she hadn't noticed.

EVE OF DADDY'S DEATH. Eve of that telephone call from Thom, and the black rush that seeped into her lungs like cancer.

"Dr. McClaren?—please forgive me—I was not eavesdropping outside your office, I swear!—but I have been hearing—you are f-feeling bad, I think?"—moon-faced faux-blond Iris spoke hesitantly, in a lowered voice, as Lorene glared at her secretarial assistant uncomprehending at first. (Had Lorene been *crying*? Audibly? In this quasi-public place, her office at North Hammond High?)

Her face flushed with dismay. Something like shame. Had anyone else overheard her? Had Iris, her secretarial assistant, talked of her to others? And what did they say about the stupid knitted cap Dr. McClaren felt obliged to wear ever more frequently, as her hair disappeared in quarter-sized patches?—(oh God: she hoped no one was speculating that she was losing her hair from chemotherapy).

But Lorene did not lash out at her assistant as she might've done ordinarily for she was feeling less sure of herself lately, more dependent upon her support staff at the school to facilitate her work and her well-being; it was kind of Iris to be concerned for her though just slightly presumptuous of a secretarial assistant to dare suggest to a high school principal a therapist with the improbable name *Foote*.

Politely, coolly Lorene thanked the silly woman for her solicitude. Saw no reason to explain that it was natural for a daughter to "feel sad" given the circumstances (father, death, anniversary) of the date and that no therapist was required, certainly not a therapist named *Foote*.

SOMETHING OF A JOKE, WAS IT? Seeing a therapist—*Lorene McClaren* of all people?

Only because her health insurance covered twelve sessions with an accredited therapist, as it covered twelve sessions of physical therapy at an accredited physical therapy clinic. *That is the only reason I am seeing you, Doctor. I want to be honest.*

Early Friday evening. The only time she could fit an hour into her weekday schedule. (Dr. Foote did not see patients on the weekend.)

And is it "Doctor"?—as in "medical doctor"? Or—"Doctor" as in Ph.D. in clinical therapy?

Eager that no one in the family should know. What shame!

Especially not Beverly who would gloat and especially not Jessalyn who would be stricken with worry. And not Thom who would think less of her, or prissy Sophia whose business it was not, or Virgil whose business it certainly *was not.*

At least, Whitey could not know.

NEXT SHE KNEW—the beautiful shining new car drifting.

Shoulder of highway littered with broken glass, debris.

Damned numbed foot groping for the petal, what the hell—*petal*—but she didn't mean *petal* she meant—what?

Brake she meant. God-damned *brake.*

Jolted awake. Oh God!

Flung forward forty miles an hour. Head in the (stupid, shameful) knitted cap flung forward but stopped within inches of a concrete wall covered in filthy teenage graffiti.

Daddy, please no. I am so afraid.

AT FIRST, JUST CURIOUS. Just—well, wondering!

When Mark Svenson left the school building in the late afternoon, and with whom. Sometimes (it pleased her to see) the popular young wavy-sandy-haired English teacher walked briskly by himself in khaki jacket, neatly pressed chinos, running shoes to his car parked at the rear of the lot. Sometimes (pleasing her less) he walked with a student or two, chance encounters, as likely boys as girls, no (evident) design to it, their backs to Lorene peering through the slats of the venetian blind, faces unseen. But sometimes (pleasing Lorene not at all) he was seen with another young teacher named Audrey Rabineau, who taught ninth- and tenth-grade history, not walking but what you'd call *strolling.*

Buck-toothed Audrey, with dewy-doe eyes. Too tall for Mark, wasn't she?—his height almost precisely.

When it began, must've been sometime in early October. Not the sort of thing Lorene McClaren would *take note of.*

Not spying on her damned faculty. What the hell did she care.

To her face they were friendly enough—of course! H'lo Dr. McClaren. G'night Dr. McClaren. See you tomorrow Dr. McClaren!

Well, some of them were sincere. Dr. McClaren's hires. Like puppies eating from her hand at the interviews. They'd have groveled at her feet, tails thumping. Doggy eyes adoring, begging. *Love me love me do not be cruel to me. I am so deserving.*

Ironic, she'd taken a liking to Audrey Rabineau from the start. One of those homely-gawky-sweet girls, the more closely you looked, the more likable. Reminded Lorene of a more benign, less sharp-witted version of herself, with buck teeth and soft brown eyes. Nor did it hurt, Audrey Rabineau obviously admired *her.*

Of course, each new teacher hired at North Hammond High was as outstanding a candidate as the district could afford. Dr. McClaren's personal criteria narrowed the ranks, which made selection easier.

But there remained the cadre of older teachers pickled in spite like actual pickles marinated in brine. Most of them resented Lorene just for *existing.* A few, she'd managed to win over with the equivalent of doggie treats but the rest had ceased trying to please her or even to pretend to her face that they did not fear and hate her.

Their faces when they saw her revealed all—*We do not trust you, and we do not like you. But we must live with you. Have a good day!*

But Mark Svenson!—she'd trusted *him.*

Peering through the venetian-blind slats as he and the young woman teacher walked—lingeringly—to their vehicles in the parking lot. Glimpsing in the faculty dining room the two together at a table talking, laughing. A tweezers clamped onto her heart.

But no. She'd hardly noticed. Pride was like chloroform sweetly inhaled.

OF COURSE SHE WAS *all right.*

Of course she'd *had a good week.*

Yes! She was feeling *reasonably hopeful.*

Already by the third session beginning to resent the therapist's insipid questions.

Vowing this would be the last visit to Foote, even if she had eight more free sessions on her health insurance.

Yet: Wouldn't she be losing money, if she quit prematurely?

Whitey would be surprised, if he'd known. His favorite daughter—his favorite child, the one most like himself—*seeing a therapist.*

Well, it wasn't anything serious. Not like seeing a *psychiatrist.*

Absolutely forbidden in Foote's office: touching her hair, her face, her eyelashes, her fingernails grown raw and reddened from "picking" without knowing what she was doing.

Absolutely forbidden: telling this nosy woman anything too private, that might be used against her: falling asleep at the wheel of her car, spying on the young English teacher, brooding over R.W. and her many enemies among the faculty, sleepless nights, obsessive thoughts.

Gently Foote said: "Would you like to remove your cap, Lorene? Just while you're here in my office."

Unambiguously Lorene said: "No."

The horse-faced female! Lorene pitied her.

"You might feel more comfortable, Lorene. We should discuss the *trichotillomania* more openly and what we might try to help you overcome it."

"Well. It isn't so repulsive as *trichinosis,* at least"—Lorene laughed harshly.

Foote smiled, just barely. "Yes. You've made that joke twice now, Lorene."

"And you've called me 'Lorene' thrice now, Dr. Foote."

Infuriating to Lorene, that this horse-faced female dared to call her by her first name, as if they were friends or peers.

"I'm sorry. You would like to be called—'Dr. McClaren'?"

"Since I respect you by calling you 'Dr. Foote,' and not by your first name, I think that you should respect me by calling me 'Dr. McClaren' and not 'Lorene.'"

Foote mumbled an apology that sounded, to Lorene's suspicious ear, more bemused than sincere.

"After all, I am not a child, or a servant, or a relative of yours."

Behind her desk, zombie-Foote did not dispute this.

"I am not a friend of yours. At least not yet."

That put the shoe on Foote, Lorene thought with a small thrill of satisfaction.

Almost, she might enjoy this bullshit.

NOW SHE WAS SEEING Audrey Rabineau too often.

By *too often* meant a few times a week, usually by chance.

Rabineau laughed too loudly, exposed her gums. She'd had her lank limp mud-brown hair cut and styled in an effort to look "glamorous"—a failure. She wore clunky jewelry. Since she was tall, she wore flat-heeled shoes. Her manner was overly sweet, insipid. Her hips were wider than her torso. At faculty meetings she laughed at stupid jokes to ingratiate herself with her elders. Worse, she made a show of seeming *interested*—a transparent ruse.

Wearing lipstick! Well, that was a failure too, like makeup on a horse.

Seeing Rabineau walking in the hall with several (girl) students, deep in conversation, aroused the principal's suspicion: *What are they talking about?*

But far worse, seeing Mark Svenson walking with Rabineau in the late afternoon, out to the parking lot. Seeing how they stood together, near Rabineau's car, talking earnestly. *What plans are they making?*

Should acquire a pair of binoculars, Lorene thought miserably. Some sort of "bug" to pick up voices at a distance.

Not that she gave a damn. Not *her.*

CALL CAME, BEVERLY.

One of Beverly's quiet-hysterical messages which Lorene has no intention of answering.

Lorene! Yesterday they went out in Dad's canoe.

Our canoe!

Out on the lake, in our canoe.

Just the two of them together.

Imagine—Mom in that canoe!

(Pause. Beverly's breathing, amplified.)

Neighbors saw them on the lake. I am so embarrassed!

Minnie Haldron called—"Beverly, it looks like your mother is out on the lake in a canoe with one of the lawn service men and we thought you would want to know. And she is wearing her hair in a new way—like an Indian squaw, braided down her back."

HERE WAS A SURPRISE: Mark Svenson was indeed driving to the teachers' conference in Albany, in November, to participate in a panel titled "The Future of the Printed Word in Our Public Schools: Does It Have One?" but when Lorene casually brought up the subject of the conference, hinting that she hadn't yet decided what her transportation would be, Mark said (disingenuously?) that several colleagues were coming with him, he hoped his car could hold them all.

Lorene heard her voice sounding startled, disappointed—"Oh. Who?"

(Why did she ask? Why would Lorene McClaren *care*?)

Just colleagues, fellow English teachers. Lorene knew them all of course and had no comment to make other than a vague murmur of enthusiasm—*Very good, professional conferences are important for your career.*

She went away, smiling. Really, it was a relief—what would she have found to talk about with a junior faculty member, alone in his car for several hours on the New York Thruway?

I THINK THAT I AM JUST—bored. No one to love who is worth loving who would love me in return.

ITCHY SCALP. ITCHY EYELIDS. Itchy cuticles.

Late-night. Brain hyperactive.

Resolutely not-thinking about Mark Svenson.

Not-thinking about Rabineau. (Who, if she was Mark's lover, would probably attend the conference in Albany, to sit in the audience at his panel to gaze at him with admiring eyes; meaning, Rabineau would be riding in Mark's car with him, squeezed in with the others. *But Lorene cannot ask, it is all so petty.*)

Decided to skip the conference, herself. Not crucial for a principal to attend. One of the lesser conferences, in fact.

Not-thinking about having a drink. Of the elder McClaren sisters *she is the one who does not drink.*

HI, THOM?—I haven't heard from you in a while. How's the lawsuit going? Or maybe—I shouldn't ask. (Pause) *And what about meeting with what's-his-name—Ramirez? Did you ever set that up? Trying to talk to him, making a deal with him to stay away from our pathetic mother?* (Pause) *I guess not. Since you've never mentioned it.* (Pause) *Since you've never mentioned it, I guess not.* (Pause) *Bev called the other day, says Mom and Ramirez have been sighted by neighbors out on the lake in our canoe . . . At least I assume it was the Communist Cuban, the neighbor thought he was one of the lawn service workers.* (Pause) *And she is wearing her hair like an Indian squaw, braided down her back.* (Pause)

Oh God, Thom. What would Daddy think!

TERRIBLE NEWS! Buckshot to the heart.

The New York State Department of Education released its new rankings based on 2010–2011 evaluations: North Hammond High School was now ranked thirty-third in the state, where previously it had been twenty-eight.

How was it possible?—*thirty-third.* North Hammond had not risen despite Lorene's heroic efforts but *dropped.*

Lorene was stunned. Hid in her office and shut down her computer with a directive to her assistant that she did not want to be disturbed until further notice.

Thinking—*Could it be, the trolls didn't get into good schools? Bringing our reputation down?*

No. Of course not. That was minor. Minuscule. Could not possibly be the reason.

But if so, Lorene's own fault.

You have sabotaged your own school. Your own reputation.

At least no one could know. No one could guess. It would not happen again. She'd ceased typing *Principal Lorene McClaren, North Hammond High* on her computer, ceased being appalled and sickened by what she saw there, like overturning a rock and seeing, among the scuttling beetles and worms, a tiny hairless creature bearing your own face in miniature.

SHE'D BEEN PREPARED TO SNEER but once inside the Chautauqua Guerrilla Arts Gallery had to admit she was impressed by the photographs by "Hugo Martinez" displayed on the not-very-clean white walls.

She'd researched Martinez online. Her mother's Hispanic lover.

(Except: *Were* the two actually, literally lovers? Or just romantic friends? The distinction was urgent, crucial in Lorene's mind.)

She'd been surprised to discover that Martinez seemed to be something of an accomplished person, poet, photographer, teacher, "social activist" (whatever that meant) born in Newark, New Jersey, in 1952, consequently a U.S. citizen.

Not Cuban! Lorene was feeling cheated, somehow.

Hugo Martinez's father had emigrated to the United States from San Juan, Puerto Rico. His mother had been a U.S. citizen. They had lived variously in New York City and in New Jersey and were now both deceased. Lorene was surprised to discover how *normal*—how *civilized*—Hugo Martinez's background was though the man had a considerable list of titles to his credit: poems, magazine publications, books. He'd had a number of photography exhibits through the state.

He'd been Poet Laureate of Western New York State, 1998–1999. He'd had teaching positions including a residency at Cornell. Awards, grants. Co-founder of the Chautauqua Guerrilla Arts Gallery (ridiculous name—"Guerrilla"!) and of something called Liberation Ministries.

Most of the photographs were street portraits in black and white, taken in foreign cities. There were too many close-ups of soulful faces, unique and individual faces, complex signifiers of clothing, background architecture—Lorene had not time to absorb so much. In her edgy state she moved swiftly through the exhibit in the windowless space of the gallery. It was her primary resolve not to sneakily push fingers beneath her knitted cap and seek hair to tug and this resolve was distracting. She saw that the photographs were priced at three hundred dollars each which seemed to her insultingly high. Rehearsing words she would utter scornfully to Beverly, Thom: *He thinks pretty well of himself, this Martinez. Overpriced!* At the end she studied a photograph of Martinez who did not look at all like the person she'd expected. (Vaguely she'd supposed he would resemble Whitey's long-time lawn service man Marco, not Hispanic but Italian, whose surname escaped her.)

This Martinez had intense very dark eyes, warm coffee-colored skin, a strong-boned Indian face with a long aquiline nose, lined cheeks and creases bracketing his eyes. His hair, thick at the time of the photograph, had been brushed back from his forehead like a rooster's comb. He wore what appeared to be a peasant's shirt, white, of a thin fabric like muslin, opened to mid-chest. Around his neck, a gold chain. His eyes were swimmingly dark. Again Lorene wanted to sneer but could not, quite.

There was a sexual presence here, an unrepentant display of *maleness*.

Was this man her mother's lover? Astonishing to think so.

Oh, what would Whitey *think*! His soul would be stunned, obliterated by the fact of Hugo Martinez.

If Jessalyn and Martinez were married, Lorene thought, with a sensation of something like dread, Hugo Martinez would be her *stepfather.*

The Chautauqua Guerrilla Arts Gallery occupied a former convenience store in a no-man's-land on Hammond's East Side. The area was neither urban nor suburban but derelict, quasi-abandoned, near a boarded-up train depot. Thistles grew through cracks in the sidewalk. Yet there were children playing noisily nearby—the rear of a daycare center. Hugo Martinez had co-founded *this*? Not quite the stature of McClaren Printing, Inc. The gallery owner was a woman of about Lorene's age with long, streaked-purple hair to her hips, in an Indian-looking shift to her ankles. There were small silver rings in her nose, left eyebrow. Her scrawny arms clattered with jewelry. She seemed grateful for Lorene's presence in the otherwise deserted place and for Lorene's offhanded remark that the exhibit was "very interesting."

"Oh yes. Hugo Martinez is very 'interesting.' And much more."

"D'you know the photographer? Personally?"

The woman laughed. Lorene could have sworn, a faint blush rose in her weathered face.

"Oh, everyone knows Hugo."

"And what do they know about him?"

"That he is—he is—*Hugo.*"

"He is respected? Well-liked?"

"Oh yes, of course. Hugo is one of our most successful photographers in Hammond. He has an international reputation—almost . . ."

Lorene would certainly quote this: *He has an international reputation—almost . . .*

"But I see that not much in this exhibit has been sold. Those little red dots . . ." (Indeed, only six photographs out of approximately thirty had been sold.)

"Well! Hugo has sold prints of these same photos elsewhere, I'm sure. This isn't absolutely new work. We're just a small local co-op . . . we don't get many customers."

The streaked-purple woman was beginning to look at Lorene with something less than pleasure though, Lorene was sure, she had not betrayed the slightest edge of hostility or mockery in her demeanor.

"Are you from around here, ma'am? I'd have thought you might have heard of Hugo Martinez, if you are."

"Around *here*? No. I am not."

"Are you a reporter, ma'am? Some sort of critic?"

"No. Just a curious observer."

"Curious about photography?"

Lorene considered. To say *yes* was to risk having to purchase something here; to say *no* would terminate the conversation.

"I am curious about art, generally." Lorene paused, feeling a surge of something like defiance, hope. "I am curious about *life*."

In the gallery lingering as if she were trying to decide which of several photographs by Hugo Martinez to buy. Asking the purple-streaked woman if she would take a credit card?—and the woman said yes, certainly. But then, Lorene discovered that she didn't have a credit card in her wallet; and she didn't have three hundred dollars in cash—at least, not to spend in such a way.

"Sorry! Another time, perhaps."

Leaving the gallery, smiling. Feeling uplifted for the remainder of the day.

HE REMINDS ME OF CHE GUEVARA. *This Martinez person Mom is seeing.*

"Chay"—who?

Che Guevara. The man our mother is seeing.

The Cuban?

Actually, no. Puerto Rican.

Is there much difference? Aren't they all—Caribbean?

He looks like Guevara, the Communist revolutionary—is what I am saying.

Who looks like—who?

Beverly, for Christ's sake! Have you never heard of Che Guevara, the famous Argentine Marxist revolutionary hero?

Argentine? Like, from Argentina? Is he from there, too?

*I told you—*Puerto Rico. *It's an American territory, actually.*

What's this got to do with—whoever you were talking about . . .

I was trying to tell you Mom's friend Martinez looks like Che Guevara except his mustache is bigger, and he's older—I mean, older than pictures you see of Che Guevara.

Lorene? You met him—?

No! Jesus. I did not say that. Are you sober, Bev?

Are you *sober? Why'd you call me at this time of night, to start a God-damn fight?*

I'm returning your call, in fact. There're half a dozen messages from you, I'm trying to be polite.

Fuck you polite.

Bev, please. I'm trying to talk to you . . .

Like poison ivy, talking to you. *I come away and afterward there's these rashes.*

Well. Martinez isn't what we expected. He might be after Mom's money—or her social position—but he actually has a career of his own. A reputation.

You met him?

No! I just told you.

You saw him? In person?

I went to a photography exhibit of his on the East Side. I saw some photographs of his in this run-down old gallery—"Guerrilla Arts."

What were you doing there?

I told you—I went to see Martinez's exhibit. Can you turn down that damned TV?

Lorene, did you ever find out—are they lovers? Literally?

I've asked Virgil. He's the only one who might know and God damn him, he refuses to discuss Mom at all.

He's a friend of Monterez . . .

Martinez. They aren't actually "friends." We could just go over there and ask her point-blank what the hell is going on . . .

But—what if he's there?

Well—that would be good. We need to meet him . . .

No. I'm not ready for that. Not just yet.

Don't be ridiculous. We should talk to Mom. I mean—really talk.

Wasn't Thom going to talk to Monterez? Offer him money to go away?

Oh, the hell with Thom. He promised he would look into it—you know Thom: "I'll look into it"—but never got back to me.

But—oh God, Lorene. I can't bring myself to ask Mom such a question.

You could more easily than I could, you're married . . .

What the hell's that got to do with it?

I don't know—you both had babies . . .

Jesus! That makes no sense at all.

Look, I could never just ask Mom—anything, really. That would upset her.

Well, me either.

She needs to know—we just want her to be happy . . .

Do we? Is that it?

Isn't it?

NEXT THING SHE KNOWS the shining steel-colored Saab is skidding across three lanes of the Hennicott Expressway amid a cacophony of horns like *Götterdämmerung* . . .

NO! NOT YET.

First was Bali. New Zealand. *Pacific Cruiseways.*

Had to get away. Desperate.

Overwork. Stress. Unrelieved pressure.

Even Foote agreed, Lorene deserved a vacation from North Hammond High. (Part of the relief of a trip would be getting away from *her.*)

What happened in Lorene's office had not been planned. By chance she'd summoned the sandy-wavy-haired young English teacher to see her, to congratulate him on the panel: "Mark! My sources have told me very good things about you in Albany. 'Bright, articulate, persuasive'—'the audience loved him.'"

Flushing with boyish pleasure Mark Svenson thanked Lorene. Saying again how honored he'd been that she had selected him for this—honor.

For a few minutes they talked together, companionably. Lorene was skilled at exuding an air, to favored persons, that they were equals of hers, or nearly; her manner was forthright and friendly, no one would ever have thought *But the woman is deceiving you! It is all a ruse.*

Like all administrators Lorene understood that it was good to congratulate a subordinate if circumstances warranted it, no matter how insignificant the accomplishment was, and how foolishly vain the recipient of such banal praise might be, like this young man who wished to believe that his participation in a panel at a gathering of high school English teachers was an accomplishment of some order of magnitude.

Gratitude in the damp doggy eyes spilled over like sunshine, or gold coins. Speaking so generously to Mark Svenson, Lorene felt herself a generous and good-hearted person, not mean-spirited, anxious, and miserable. (Resolved: to keep her restless fingers out of her hair. No digging at cuticles with her short-trimmed nails. No surreptitious scratching at rashes in the tender inside of her elbow.)

Hears herself speaking as if impulsively.

"Mark! The strangest thing—coincidence—an old friend of mine and I have been planning a trip to Bali and New Zealand—at Christmas break—and my friend has had to cancel. She can't get a refund for her plane ticket and the cruise but—if someone else were interested—at a discount . . . Do you know of anyone?"

Waiting. Warm shining terrier eyes lifted to her face. Oh, Lorene's heart is pounding absurdly!

"I—I don't know, Dr. McClaren. I mean, I would have to . . ."

Evasive. Embarrassed. Eyes shifting.

What am I doing. Oh Daddy, dear God help me.

". . . would have to ask. I could do that . . ."

"Well." A pause. And then, "I don't suppose you might be—interested in the cruise yourself? I think you could get a reduced rate—a discount—Bali is astonishingly beautiful, and New Zealand . . . at that time of year, when it's so cold here. In fact, summer there. I have Cruiseways website on my computer, if you'd like to look."

Mark Svenson is sitting very still and is very quiet. Lorene can see him breathing—his nostrils widening, contracting, widening. She can sense his mounting discomfort. An awkward smile, not boyish so much as childlike. He'd dropped by Lorene's office as she had requested at the end of the teaching day; he has a brief break before he meets with the yearbook staff, for which he is a faculty advisor.

It is clear, Mark Svenson is not exactly elated at the prospect of the trip to Bali, as Lorene had supposed he might be.

He doesn't want to travel with you. Why would he want to travel with you!

What are you thinking? He is twenty-seven. You are thirty-six. You are not even a woman to him—you are Dr. McClaren, his supervisor. How can you abase yourself like this?

Mark repeats, he will have to think about it. He will see if he can come up with someone . . .

Speaking so vacantly, it's clear that he has been shocked, disoriented by Lorene's proposition.

Has he misinterpreted it as a *sexual proposition*? Lorene is appalled, outraged to think so.

Abruptly she tells him good night. Bares her teeth at him in a dismissive smile. As he flees the office she calls after him, like a fly fisherman casting a line, unerringly: "And again, Mark—congratulations!"

After he has gone she makes a horrific discovery: somehow there is a short strand of hair wound about two of her fingers, oozing blood at the roots. A new spot on her scalp tingles, throbs.

WANTING TO PROTEST: every fact of grief she'd encountered inside or outside her own rattling head was a cliché. Her own death someday, no doubt she'd be bored by its perimeters. Limited primer vocabulary.

"I can't love anyone. I'm so *bored*."

OF COURSE SHE WAS *ALL RIGHT.*

Of course she'd *had a good week.*

Nothing to report. Nooo.

Well—her news was, she'd decided to book a cruise for Bali, New Zealand over winter break.

Yes she was going alone.

No she had not asked anyone to accompany her.

Except her mother who'd been behaving strangely since her father's death . . .

Yes Lorene and her mother were "very close"—though not "overclose."

Yes Lorene had a "very good" relationship with her mother.

Yes Lorene had had a "very good" relationship with her father.

No she *was not crying.*

Surreptitiously digging at a thumbnail. Hands in her lap so that Foote could not observe.

"My sister and my brother and I are worried about our mother. We are worried that, out of loneliness, she might do something rash to hurt herself and—others."

"Such as?"

"Well—she is 'seeing' a man no one knows, a man no one has met, not in her and Daddy's circle. Naturally, we're concerned about that."

"Does your mother know how you feel?"

"Oh, yes. I'm sure that she does. But she doesn't *care*."

"What is your principal objection to this man?"

"He—he's—not her type, as I just said. He's of another ethnicity—Hispanic."

"Hispanic!" (Was Foote laughing at her? It was all Lorene could do to keep from glaring at the therapist.)

"His background is somewhat lower class. Working class. We're concerned that he is after our mother's money."

"Does he know of your feelings? Have you spoken with him?"

"Of course not! We haven't wanted to acknowledge him, I think. We've been hoping he will just go away."

"And your mother knows how you feel?"

"Well, I can't be sure. Our mother is not a realistic person, I think."

"How do you mean?"

"Mom seems to see only the best in people. Or, she refuses to see anything else. She's very *kind*. It has been exasperating to us, over the years, to see how people take advantage of her kindness."

"Such as?"

Lorene bit her lower lip. Beverly was always accusing Lorene of taking advantage of their mother's kindness. But Beverly was a worse offender, and Virgil was the worst of all.

"I'd rather not discuss my mother right now, Dr. Foote. It's a painful subject."

"I can see that it's painful. You are looking—pained . . ."

"Well, we are concerned that Mom might be having a nervous breakdown. There's a matter of her mental competence, her 'power of attorney' . . ."

"That would be a painful issue, indeed. How old is your mother?"

"Maybe—sixty-five."

"Sixty-five? But sixty-five is hardly *old*."

"But she's very frail emotionally. And physically. My brother is particularly concerned—if this man-friend of our mother's manages to inveigle himself into her life . . ."

"You are concerned about your mother's 'power of attorney' . . ."

"Excuse me, I've said that I don't want to discuss my mother right now. She was raised to be—well, gracious. Intensely feminine. A woman to be married—*loved*. Our personalities are antithetical. She is all-forgiving, and I—I am not. I am trying to uphold standards." Lorene paused, breathing harshly. She'd managed to keep from digging at the raw thumbnail cuticle only just barely.

"These are—moral standards? Professional?"

"Last week you asked me to think about myself in terms of relationships with others, Dr. Foote. I did—I spent a good deal of time thinking—and I've come to the conclusion that my problem has been that I am a—perfectionist."

There. She'd said it. At last.

But Foote being Foote, literal-minded like all horse-faced therapists, scarcely took time to absorb this before asking Lorene to please "amplify" the statement.

Amplify. Impossible! That would require an accounting of Lorene's entire life.

Please try, Foote urged.

Lorene was drawing a blank. Lorene heard herself say, not very convincingly, "I am considerate of others even when they are not considerate of me. I'd always been the 'responsible' child in the family though I was not the oldest but the third-born. More was expected of me because I was the smartest, which my father eventually acknowledged. 'I love your brothers and sisters, Lorene-y. But you are special in my heart, as I think you know.'"

Wiping tears from her eyes. Oh what was Foote staring at!

"And how do you perceive yourself as a 'perfectionist' with your faculty at North Hammond?"

"I—I—expect the very best from them, as I do from—myself . . ."

Her voice was faltering. Badly she wanted to run out of the room and never return.

"It's just been like a curse. Never satisfied with what I've done because it—it is not—perfect."

In a faux-kindly voice Foote said, "You have heard the adage, Lorene: 'perfect is the enemy of good.'"

Perfect is the enemy of good. Lorene had never heard this so-called adage before in her life.

"Sounds like a fortune cookie."

"Yes. There is that Zen-simplicity to it, that hides the deepest wisdom."

"Except it also sounds like criticism. Of me."

"Of you, Lorene? However could any criticism be of *you*?"

Foote was speaking from the heart, with utter sincerity, or with shocking irony. Lorene had no idea.

"Excuse me. I am 'Dr. McClaren' to you—I've explained. Not 'Lorene.' As I respect you by addressing you as 'Dr. Foote,' so I request that you respect me by calling me 'Dr. McClaren.'"

"Of course. I am so sorry—'Dr. McClaren.'"

(Was Foote stifling laughter? Lorene was sure she saw the woman's shoulders shaking.)

"I—I think this will be my last session, Doctor."

"Will it!"—Foote contrived to look surprised.

"Yes. I've been here eight times. I think that is more than enough."

Foote did not (probably) pluck her eyelashes but the lashes were scanty, the gray-owl eyes naked and unsparing. "I am sorry to hear that, Lorene. I mean—Dr. McClaren. I think we've been making some definite progress."

"Well, I don't."

"You don't? Really? Isn't the *trichotillomania* more under control? The 'obsessive' thoughts?"

"Who told you about 'obsessive thoughts'? I don't have 'obsessive thoughts.'"

To this hotly articulated remark Foote had no ready reply. Lorene perceived that the therapist was at least more somber now, confronted with her client's extreme dissatisfaction.

"I don't agree that the *trichotillomania* is more under control. The impulse has shifted elsewhere, to other parts of my body." Lorene paused, to let this accusation sink in. Then, "I never thought there was much wrong with me to begin with. I only came here because"—

Lorene ransacked her brain to come up with the perfect riposte—"my health insurance covers twelve sessions of therapy."

Though (surely) hurt Foote was smiling. A hurt-Foote smile. Lorene's heart was beating hard, like a trapped frog. Almost, she would miss her weekly, Friday evening sessions with Foote, boring and fruitless as they were.

"My father, John Earle McClaren, was a very self-sufficient person. He would be shocked—mortified—to learn that his daughter, the one most like himself, was reduced to seeing a—a—"—Lorene searched for the proper word like one searching through a Dumpster, with a look both fastidious and repelled—"*mental health clinician.*"

"I see."

"Daddy taught us to be independent. Daddy instilled in us qualities of resilience, stoicism. The very opposite of self-pity. And what is therapy but a kind of self-pity."

"That is a way of seeing it, I suppose. Yes."

It was a strategy of Foote's, to seem to be considering more than one side of an issue, like a parody of a reasonable person.

"What is therapy but a kind of *wallowing* . . ."

"Perhaps you are correct, Dr. McClaren. 'Wallowing' is not for everyone."

Lorene laughed. This was so transparent on Foote's part!

Yet Foote had become, by default, a kind of friend. Not an intimate friend, rather more the concept of a friend, against whom one might lash out in hatred or despair.

Oh Daddy. Why'd you take everything with you.

Time to leave. Time to escape. Lorene snatched up her handbag, pivoted on her heel, considered saying *Goodbye and good riddance!* but instead heard the most astonishing words spilling from her mouth.

"What I think is—by dying the way he did, so suddenly, it's like my father consented to die. As if he'd opened a door. And now, the door is still open. He's waiting there to welcome any of us who steps through."

. . . . **REAR OF THE SAAB *FISHTAILED,*** fender crumpled against a concrete retaining wall, sudden jolt and her head felt as if it were being flung forward. An explosion (she'd thought was the windshield, in fact the air bag) amid a smell of hot singed air and acid. *Oh oh oh!*—she'd held herself very still wondering if all of her bones had been smashed. Wondering if she was alive. And why.

SENT HIM AN EMAIL. Just to be clear.

> *Hi Mark. Just to clarify: turns out I do have a friend who will purchase the cruise ticket to Bali etc. after all. So there is no need for you to ask around as you'd kindly offered. Thanks!*
>
> *Sincerely,*
> *Lorene McC.*

Thinking, this will be the end of it. No more!

EXCEPT: IN THE DAYS, WEEKS to follow she seemed to see, without wishing to see, everywhere she looked, or almost, Mark Svenson and the Rabineau woman.

Not just at school. Not just in the parking lot, or in the faculty dining room, or (most annoying!) whispering together in the aisle before Friday morning assembly, as their home room students trooped into the auditorium, but elsewhere, off-campus, at a café in North Hammond, at the North Gate Shopping Mall, or waiting in line together at the CineMax . . . Most of the time the couple, focused upon each other, had no idea that Lorene had sighted them; once, noticing her, at the mall, they'd both smiled and waved, which had seemed to Lorene an astonishing sort of effrontery—"Hiya, Dr. McClaren!" She was sure they'd laughed together, as soon as she passed by.

What did he see in *her*! Rabineau was tall, slump-shouldered, gawky and plain. Often she wore no lipstick, her bloodless mouth had the shape of a slug.

She will diminish you, Mark. I'm afraid that she has already.

What would students think! They would be shocked, demoralized.

Online, the trolls would be merciless. Their singular subject was sex, its deformities and absurdities. And in older persons like their teachers—obscene and unforgivable.

"Men are stupid. Men think with their genitals. Even the smart ones." (Who had said this? Lorene wondered if, in a bleak unsparing mood, she had said it herself.)

And so, she could not resist. Summoned Mark Svenson to her office another time.

The young teacher was looking wary now, like a hunted creature. His formerly boyish smile seemed to have shrunken. With a small stab of satisfaction Lorene saw that his forehead was just slightly blemished and his khaki trousers were rumpled. Though rumors continued to come to the principal's ears that "Mr. Svenson" was a very popular teacher and an enthusiastic advisor for the yearbook staff Lorene was beginning to have her doubts about her young colleague's good judgment and that elusive element—"character."

She'd given Mark Svenson a high evaluation the previous year. This year, she wasn't so sure how she would assess him though she had no doubt how she would assess Rabineau. In fact, though it was months before an evaluation was due, Lorene had already drafted a brisk, pitiless paragraph on the insolent young history teacher.

Began by saying, in a solemn voice, not chiding, not censorious, but concerned as a friend might be concerned, that probably Mark knew why she'd asked him to come see her?—and when Mark shook his head, no he did not, Lorene said, "This is very awkward for me, Mark. Indeed, I am reluctant to bring up the subject. But I'm afraid that I've been hearing from a number of sources that you and a certain young woman history teacher have been seen together quite a bit in a way that has made some persons uncomfortable. They—colleagues of ours—have expressed the concern, which I am inclined to share, that students have noticed you and your woman-friend also, and have begun to 'make comments'—I think you can guess the kind of comments we've discovered. Our students can be crude about sexual matters, and they can be very mean." Lorene lowered her quavering voice in confidence.

Mark Svenson looked as if Lorene had leaned over her desk to slap him in the face. Almost, Lorene felt sorry for him.

"But—who is saying—what? About Audrey and me?"

"Evidently, quite a few people. Your colleagues, and your students."

"I—I don't know what to think. My God . . ."

"It isn't good policy to be dating a coworker. It doesn't look good. Of course people will talk about you. Make jokes."

"Make *jokes*? Why? Audrey and I are . . ."

"As I said, it doesn't look good when coworkers are dating. It's really poor judgment on your part, and on hers. And frankly, Mark, some of our colleagues are saying that you are diminished by Audrey Rabineau—she doesn't seem to be your 'type.'"

"What? That's outrageous!"

"Nonetheless, it is what people are saying. People whose opinions you respect, since they are your colleagues and have your best interests at heart."

"Who would say that about Audrey? She's a lovely person—everyone likes her. There can't be anything wrong in being friends with her—going out with her—"

"Well. Are you having sex with her?"

Mark stared at Lorene, for a moment speechless.

"That is what everyone assumes, Mark. Especially, you know, *adolescents*."

So taken by surprise, Mark could not think how to respond except to stammer that he thought he'd better leave now, the conversation was very upsetting to him . . .

Hotly Lorene said, "Yes! It is upsetting. *I find it upsetting, too*—which is why I have called you here."

"A question like that—I think—I think it is not allowed, Dr. McClaren. It is my private life, you have no right to—"

"For your own good, Mark. I am bringing up this ugly situation for your own good, since you seem to be blinded by—some sort of sex-infatuation with that woman."

"That's ridiculous. There is nothing wrong with Audrey and me seeing each other in any way we choose . . ."

"Use your common sense, please. You are two years older than Rabineau. Your relationship might be considered coercive."

"'Coercive'—how? Audrey isn't my student or a staff worker—she's a full-time teacher, like me—there is no way that I could coerce her into anything. She is my dear *friend*."

The piteous way in which the young man uttered *my dear friend* was particularly annoying to Lorene. Had he no pride?

"Mark, it is simply poor judgment, carrying on the way you two do, in public. Adolescents can't be fooled, they see everything."

"But—what is there to *see*? Audrey and I—"

"'Audrey and I'—there you go. That's the issue."

"Dr. McClaren, I just don't understand. I do see Audrey quite a bit but mostly away from school. We spend our evenings together, usually. I'm sure that no one is watching us . . ."

"Yes! You are a pair of exhibitionists, practically. Many people are watching you, and many people are not happy at what they see."

"But—really? You are not serious, Dr. McClaren, are you?"

"Not serious? Try me."

Lorene slammed her hand on her desk. In an instant she was furious with Mark Svenson, in his pretense of naivete.

Yet the young man persevered, flushed with indignation, saying that there were two pairs of married couples on the faculty, what about them? He and Audrey Rabineau were not married but—possibly—might soon become engaged.

Engaged. That was unacceptable. Rapidly Lorene's brain worked: both their contracts would be terminated.

Or rather: she would suggest to Mark Svenson that, if he continued to see Rabineau, his contract would be terminated. Rabineau's contract would be terminated in any case.

Pathetically, Mark was trying to defend himself by pointing out that there were two married couples on the North Hammond faculty. No one had seemed to object to them.

"Oh, no one cares in the slightest about them," Lorene said irritably. "They're middle-aged, older than the kids' parents. As the kids would say—*bor-ing.* No one would have sex fantasies about *them.*"

"Look, I can't be responsible for other people's *sex fantasies.* That is ridiculous."

"You make yourself ridiculous, Mark, with an unsuitable woman. In the hothouse atmosphere of a high school, you should certainly know better."

Mark ran his hands over his hot face. Lorene could see that the agitated young man wanted to defend himself further, perhaps he wanted to utter something self-righteous and irrevocable to her, but was thinking better of it. Instead he conceded that he and Audrey could—maybe—try to avoid each other at school, if seeing them together really was upsetting people; but they were certainly not going to break up for such a ludicrous reason.

"You don't really mean to suggest that you 'love' this person?—she is not of your stature, Mark. You should know."

Almost, a neutral question put to the hot-flushed young teacher, as if Lorene truly wanted to know.

On his feet now, indignant. So furious, Lorene felt a thrill of dread, that he might hit her; but of course, Mark Svenson was too clever to behave in such a way, and bring about immediate dismissal, an arrest for assault.

Stammering that he was leaving Lorene's office—"Before I say too much and regret it."

Coldly Lorene said, "You have already said too much, Mark. And you will regret it."

WAKING TO A NOVEMBER MORNING of pelting rain, sleet.

Tiny ice-pellets slamming against the windows.

Waking to the most profound sense of—worthlessness . . .

That black rush in the lungs, coursing through all of her veins.

Aren't you ashamed. What have you done. What would Daddy say.

Why don't you do something for someone else, instead of just for yourself.

In the steel-colored Saab, entering the Expressway. Visibility poor. Windshield steaming up. Foot on the gas pedal, foot on the brake. Driving while braking. Slippery-icy pavement. Streams of agitated water cascading over the windshield, tiny ice-pellets clattering against the glass and the roof of the car.

Instead of the far Pacific you are going nowhere.

Suddenly, skidding across three lanes of traffic. Crazed horns, fury of strangers. Her head slammed against something very solid—might've been the steering wheel. Because she was not a tall person the air bag slammed terribly into her upper chest with such violence it felt at first as if the bone had been crushed. Torso, neck, shoulders and arms—a solid bruise.

Was she alive, or—? Not-alive?

Mouth filling with blood. Black rancid-rot in the marrow of her bones. The steel-colored door was bent in such a way impossible to open if she had had the strength to open it.

But she was alive. That seemed to be so. A voice was calling to her—*Ma'am. Ma'am!* Traffic slowed, flowed past. Rain, hailstones continued. In the eyes of these others she was a crumpled vehicle, a slumped body of indeterminate sex, age, skin color. Still some drivers sounded their horns, as in a display of pettish derision.

Oh Daddy. Why did you call me—again—if you didn't want me.

The Handshake

He'd told no one. He had no one to tell.

No one he trusted. No one he wished to trust.

Not his wife: he was estranged from his wife. And even before their estrangement he wouldn't have entrusted Brooke with such a secret.

No one in his family. Not even his sisters who'd goaded him to this act for they talked too much, and too vehemently. There could be no secrets entrusted to them.

And not his mother. Of course.

Only his father, since his father's death, seemed close to Thom, and not *estranged*.

For often he was confiding in Whitey these days. Living by himself, working at the office in the evening. Sitting at Whitey's old desk.

He'd discovered that he liked staying late to work in the office. After everyone else had gone home. (Discovered too that he wasn't able to terminate any of the older employees he'd inherited from Whitey, as he'd planned. The older the employee, hired by Whitey decades ago, the less possible it was for Thom to "terminate." He took a grim hope that retirement, indeed termination, would come naturally, inevitably.)

But sometimes it wasn't McClaren, Inc. work that absorbed him. There was the lawsuit, that gripped him like a vampire bat with fangs sunk into his throat . . . There was the problem of Hugo Martinez, that might be more readily solved.

CALLED MARTINEZ, AND IDENTIFIED HIMSELF: "Thom McClaren. Jessalyn's older son."

In a voice that was level, matter-of-fact, even genial: "I think you know why I am calling you, 'Hugo.' Why I think we should meet."

Hugo. Just a hint of irony in the enunciation of the name. Not hostility, not contempt. Not quite.

Hugo Martinez was sounding surprised, puzzled.

No, really, he did not know . . .

Thom ignored this reply saying that it would be good to meet in a "neutral" place. He named a tavern on the Chautauqua River which he had not frequented for years, where no one would recognize him, a ten-minute drive from The Brisbane.

The tavern had an outdoor deck, Thom recalled.

After a pause Hugo Martinez agreed. (How long a drive would it be for him?—Thom wondered. He'd done a little research and learned that Martinez lived in East Hammond township in an area of derelict farms, uncultivated fields, a trailer park or two, but among these a scattering of still-operating farms and dense-wooded acreage where individuals wanting privacy had built houses not visible from the road and festooned their property with NO TRESPASSING signs.)

A time was set: 8:00 P.M.

At that time Thom arrived promptly to discover a man who had to be Hugo Martinez already seated at a table on the outside deck, overlooking the river that rippled with lights from both shores. As Thom approached the table Hugo Martinez half-rose with a look of cordial welcome and extended his hand for a handshake even as Thom gestured that he had no need to stand, please stay seated, in such a way that he was able to ignore Martinez's offer of a handshake.

Thinking—*So, you know how it is. You get it.*

If a flush rose into Hugo Martinez's face, of surprise, hurt, indignation, if Hugo Martinez's jaws tightened with the resolve not to smile as it was his instinct to smile at persons with whom he was speaking, Thom took no heed. He was brisk, no-nonsense, in control here. Pulling back a chair from the table with some force, seating himself, and calling for a waiter.

Whiskey for Thom, a beer for Hugo Martinez.

Thom had had a drink before meeting Hugo Martinez. It was his habit to stop for a drink at a cocktail lounge near The Brisbane where they knew him as the son of Whitey McClaren who'd taken over Whitey's business.

Frankly, not very politely Thom considered Hugo Martinez with unsmiling eyes. So this was the man who was *seeing his mother.*

(Thom did not want to consider precisely what *seeing* meant. His feeling for Jessalyn was so highly charged, so fraught with emotion, often he could not bring himself to think about her at all.)

Martinez looked to be in his late fifties or early sixties. Tall, broad-shouldered and straight-backed, with a youthful manner, that irritated Thom, as the thick mustache irritated Thom, and the loose, wavy hair to Martinez's shoulders that was dark brown threaded with silver. Very dark eyes, thick eyebrows, a somewhat coarse skin, not so dark as Thom had anticipated. His facial features were as likely *Native American* as *Hispanic*.

As if in mimicry of Thom, Martinez was wearing a long-sleeved white shirt, with cuff links. Yet there was something wrong with the shirt: no collar. What kind of asshole wears a shirt with no collar that is otherwise a good-looking, expensive white cotton shirt!—with cuff links! As Thom approached the table Martinez had removed a wide-brimmed fedora from his head, setting it on the table at his elbow, and this too annoyed Thom, as if Martinez had brazenly set a shoe on the table, or a damned boot, taking up more than his own share of the table.

Whiskey helped. That scimitar-flame of comfort, solace in his throat, in the region of his heart and in his gut—knew he could depend upon it, a surge of strength and well-being.

No point in small talk. Ever more frequently now, Thom eschewed small talk.

Bluntly saying, "We think you're not good for our mother. We think that you should stop seeing her."

The look in Hugo Martinez's face!—as if Thom had reached over and yanked at that ridiculous mustache.

Managing to recover enough to ask, in a stammer, who "we" was?

"*We*. My sisters. My brother. All of our relatives."

In fact, this was so. Thom was certain. All of the McClarens who knew about it, all of Jessalyn's side of the family—had to be, they all disapproved and were concerned for her.

"Well. I am—I am sorry to hear that . . ."

Hugo Martinez did appear sorry, to a degree. Yet it was an effort for the man not to smile nervously at his blunt brash aggressive adversary who was as tall and fit as he but much younger.

"But not surprised, 'Hugo.' You are not surprised, are you?"—Thom spoke with barely concealed hostility.

More upset than he'd anticipated. He had not rehearsed this encounter quite enough, had not imagined the adversary's reaction or his words, only his own. A sensation of nausea stirred in his gut, he could taste bile at the back of his mouth.

"In fact, we think you are after our mother's money. 'Hugo.'"

Hugo was uttered in contempt. *Hugo* caused Thom's lips to quiver as if he were tasting something very bitter.

How did Martinez defend himself against this charge?—only just staring at Thom, in offended silence.

"Her money. *Our* money. *Our* house. That's what we think!"

Thom went on to tell the silent man that, as he'd discovered by now, Jessalyn McClaren was a very special person. She had loved her husband deeply, and had not recovered from his death the previous October. It had not yet been a year. It was *too soon* for another relationship. Jessalyn wasn't responsible for making decisions, she was too emotionally fragile.

"What do you say, 'Hugo'? Are you after our mother's money?"

Thom kept his voice low, controlled. The tables closest to them were not occupied. A light wind had come up on the river, a sharp melancholy odor as of impending rain.

So absorbed was Thom in Hugo Martinez, he'd more or less forgotten his surroundings. He was watching the adversary's mouth, inside the drooping mustache, with the intensity of a lip reader.

Stiffly Hugo Martinez said: "I—I think that your question is—too insulting to answer . . ."

"Well, then—don't answer it. We wouldn't want to insult you."

It was an adolescent sort of sarcasm. But Thom felt a thrill of vindication, his adversary could not even defend himself.

Both men were breathing quickly. Thom had struck the first blow, and the second—the other was blocked from advancing, and was (perhaps) about to retreat.

A matter of degrees, Thom knew. Such confrontations. Whoever raised his voice to speak excitedly or to betray emotion would be in retreat. *He* would stand his ground.

Martinez was stammering: "I—I think—this conversation has ended. You don't have your mother's best interests at heart. You—"

"Excuse me, Martinez. Don't you tell me what to think about my mother."

Warning you. Take care, you sorry son of a bitch.

Thom had finished his whiskey, and ordered another. This was not going badly, he thought. Whitey would be impressed.

In Thom's SUV, in the rear, the baseball bat. He had not gripped it in both his hands since the night he'd hunted the stray tomcat at the house, intending to batter in its ugly head; he had failed ignominiously at that, but no one had known. He'd dirtied the damned bat killing an innocent racoon (?), however, and had not been able to wash away the worst of the stains.

"I think—I will leave now."

"*You will not leave just yet,* Martinez."

Now Thom had raised his voice. Deepened his voice. The situation was stressful. Like high-altitude hiking. If Martinez made a sudden move Thom was prepared to attack.

"I—will not be talking about your mother to you . . . But you have no right to, to—talk like this to *me*."

"I have every right to talk to you, Martinez. You—you have intruded in my—our—lives . . . We have to get something straight."

These were prepared words, most of them. He'd acted in a high school play just once. The girls had cajoled him into it, Thom McClaren was such a good-looking guy like—had it been Tom Cruise? Brad Pitt?—he'd had to try at least once, and the drama coach had allowed it but he'd had stage fright—grasping at "dialogue" as a drowning man might grasp desperately at sticks floating in the water, anything to save him.

"What I've brought, Hugo, is a checkbook. I am going to reach into my pocket for it, Hugo—that's all I am reaching for. It's what you were expecting, isn't it?"

"Expecting—what? N-No . . ."

"Well. I am prepared to write out a check for you, for 'Hugo Martinez.' I am prepared to do that. But the understanding will be, you will not see my mother again. Is that agreed?"

"A check for—how much?" Hugo Martinez spoke warily.

"Ah. How much."

This was better. No more bullshit between them.

Thom drained his glass. The sensation was warm, delicious. He was feeling much better. He was like a man who has been teetering and swaying but now he has begun to walk steadily because the floor beneath his feet that had been tilting was now steady.

"Fifteen thousand, 'Hugo.'"

With a scornful shake of his head Martinez vetoed fifteen thousand. *No.*

"Twenty thousand."

This was quite a leap. Thom hadn't been prepared to leap so far, so quickly. Hugo Martinez too seemed to be taken by surprise.

Still, Martinez shook his head. *No.*

Insufferable, the man's pretensions of superiority. Some sort of Mexican-peasant-nobility like—who had it been? Zapata?

Marlon Brando as Zapata. The dark mustache, that look of infuriating smugness.

Coldly Thom countered: "Twenty-five thousand." He was the *gringo* with money, the dark-skinned peasant bastard had the cards.

Adding, when Martinez said nothing, as if it were the purest form of contempt: "Twenty-*six*."

Still Martinez sat silent. His only betrayal of unease was his stroking of the mustache and an evasiveness about his eyes.

"All right: thirty thousand. That's my last offer."

"Thirty-*five*." It was the first that Martinez had spoken since the bargaining had begun.

Thom gave the impression of considering this. By now both men were regarding each other with mutual contempt.

"Thirty-*five*. We have a deal."

To this, Hugo Martinez conceded. His face was a mask of disdain, dislike.

"And you promise then not to contact Jessalyn again? Just—to break it off with her? Whatever it has been?"

Thom spoke less certainly now. He did not want to hear anything frank or in any way intimate from this man's lips, any remark that might violate his mother's privacy. Fortunately, Martinez just shrugged in agreement.

"All right. We have a deal. I would like you to call my mother just one final time—tonight—and tell her you're going away—traveling. And you won't be seeing her again when you return."

"In fact, I am going away. I have already told your mother."

"Good. That's very—good . . ."

As Thom made out the check his hands were shaking. It was a self-conscious gesture, writing the check as Hugo Martinez looked on, with that sneering part-smile.

Well, this had gone exactly as he'd planned. Though perhaps he had not expected to go as high as thirty-five thousand dollars.

There was a ringing in his ears. In a way, he could not quite believe that the agreement had been made, and Hugo Martinez would disappear from their lives.

Martinez was gazing at him, not so embarrassed as Thom would have anticipated, but rather defiant.

Carefully Thom made out the check to *Hugo Vincent Martinez*. He'd looked up the adversary's full name, he did not intend to make any mistakes with this transaction.

The check would be drawn on Thom's personal account. It would not involve McClaren, Inc. of course. It would not involve his sisters for the transaction was between him and Martinez exclusively, as Whitey would have wished it.

Thom handed Hugo the check—*Thirty thousand dollars and no cents payable to Hugo Martinez.*

Martinez frowned at the check. "It was to be thirty-*five* thousand."

Of course: thirty-*five*. Though well-to-do and superior in all ways the *gringo* had made a misstep.

Feeling his face beat with blood, Thom tore up the check and made out another, this time yet more carefully—*Thirty-five thousand dollars and no cents.*

Martinez took the check from him, read it carefully, folded it in two and slipped it into an envelope. He fumbled for his beer, drank from the bottle and wiped his damp mustache with the edge of his hand. Coldly he said:

"I won't be cashing this. I will keep this—it is a memento. If you or anyone else in your family approaches me, tries to threaten me, intimidate me, I will show this check to Jessalyn, and tell her about your 'deal.' It will reveal to her your callow heart and that you do not love her or respect her—you do not even know her. It will reveal much that you do not wish to be revealed so I suggest that you never, ever try anything like this again."

Calmly, with dignity, Hugo Martinez rose to his feet. Tossed a bill onto the table, snatched up his fedora hat and turned and strode away as Thom stared after him too surprised to comprehend what the man had said.

The Braid

Loved the braid. Feeling the weight between her shoulder blades like a consoling hand.

MOM WHAT ON EARTH HAVE YOU DONE *with your hair? It's—it's like some hippie or Indian—it isn't* you.

JESSALYN, *let me touch your hair! Is it—real? That color?*

YOUR HAIR IS SO BEAUTIFUL, *Mrs. McClaren! Such a pure shade of* white.

No choice but to smile at such compliments, which she often received in this new phase of her life. Wondering why *white* is so precious, and who cares if *white* is *pure*?

So soft, too. I love how it's braided, you never see a woman your age with hair in a braid, or almost never . . . Very sweetly the nurse spoke to Jessalyn shivering in the dark green cotton smock that tied loosely in the front. Hoping to sound in this place of refrigerated dread genuinely uplifting, enthusiastic.

But realizing belatedly she'd made a blunder, maybe. Alluding to Jessalyn's age.

Jessalyn laughed and murmured *Thanks!*

Though embarrassed. Self-conscious. Through her life she'd learned to politely deflect compliments about her appearance, her poise, her clothes, all that was visible about her, as if most people who encountered her felt obliged to issue some sort of assessment. *Why?*

If you are female, if you'd been a particularly pretty little girl, inescapable the compliments, the praise, the smiling attention, smothering and suffocating like a hand over your mouth. *Be still. Listen. We will tell you who you are.*

Can't disagree, that would be hostile, rude. But neither can you seem to agree, that would be vanity.

Do you braid this yourself, Mrs. McClaren? Looks like it'd be kind of hard to reach behind your head . . .

Heard herself say quietly *My husband braids it.*

The words came out without her intention. No idea why she'd said such a thing.

Well, she could not have said *My lover braids it*—the word *lover* would strike the wrong note, and make the middle-aged radiology nurse Stacey uncomfortable.

A woman of Jessalyn's age would have a husband, not a lover. A husband of many years.

The nurse marveled at this fact, also. A husband! She had never heard of a man braiding anyone's hair let alone a *husband.*

Unusual, yes. Jessalyn agreed. Something small stirred within her, a memory of something like pride.

Seems like your husband must be a very nice man.

Yes. He is.

Positioning Jessalyn at the X-ray machine that loomed above her like something in a science-fiction movie. Now brisk and no-nonsense and the harmless flattery about her hair and her husband dropped as the nurse steadied Jessalyn by her left shoulder, instructing her to open the smock, urging her to lean forward into the machine, farther forward, not to stiffen but relax, deep breath and exhale and relax, like this, shoulder down, left hand here, fingers outstretched, elbow here, elbow down, cup her breast from below, hold and don't move, a little higher, hold still, elbow a little farther down, chin up, head back, shoulder a little farther down, hold still, this will pinch a little, hold it, hold breath, don't move please, *hold breath.*

Excruciating pain as the soft white breast was flattened between clamps like bread dough. Each time she'd had a mammogram the despairing voice had screamed at her—*No. Never again. Can't endure this again.*

But each time she succeeded in forgetting. Each year she returned for her annual mammogram for that is what a responsible woman does.

Shutting her eyes as the machine emitted its whirring sound.

Shutting her eyes as the nurse reiterated instructions.

Shutting her eyes as the pain came—again . . .

Oh! Oh God.

Almost over, Mrs. McClaren. Just one more X-ray.

Thinking of Hugo braiding her hair. Brushing her hair.

Surprising gentleness, the man's large fingers. Deft and skilled for (of course) (but she couldn't inquire) he had braided hair like this before.

She'd shampooed her hair and combed it out and it was drying and he'd said tenderly *Let me braid your hair, dear.* She'd been shocked, disapproving. So intimate a gesture, and they were yet strangers. So inappropriately intimate a gesture, she'd wanted to cry *No, no thank you* laughing embarrassed as so frequently she did when Hugo Martinez suggested something strange, disconcerting, extravagant—but somehow she'd said *Yes, good.* Intending to say how ridiculous, people will laugh at me, I don't want my hair in a big thick braid like an Indian woman in a painting by what was his name—Remington. I have not had my hair in anything resembling braids since I was five years old. Intending to say you are a kind man, you are a most exceptional man, but I don't want to be touched by any man not even you, and certainly I don't want my hair brushed and braided. But she did not say anything like this, instead she inclined her head meekly, in delight saying *Yes. Please.*

There followed then an extraordinary interlude. She was very still, she did not resist, her blood beat calmly and evenly even as stray hairs caught now and then in calluses on the palms of his hands.

Grateful to the man, he said nothing. Deep in concentration, he did not even hum his tuneless melodies as often he did. His large fingers stroking her hair. The slow and languorous brushing with her tortoiseshell brush. And with a comb then, picking out snarls. Especially at the nape of her neck where the hair was thickest, where heat gathered on her skin and he lifted the hair and kissed her there, very gently, in the way that one might kiss without expecting or even wishing a reciprocal gesture. And she'd shivered, biting her lower lip and holding herself very still. And so the moment passed. And he did begin to hum, just audibly. With the brush carefully lifting her hair from her forehead and brushing it back so that it seemed fuller than it was, as if she had not suffered a catastrophe.

By this time, months later, her hair was no longer so thin as it had been soon after Whitey's death when she'd been dismayed to see hairs in the shower, clumps of hair, and her scalp seeming to smart, to hurt, as if this were a kind of weeping, a shedding of tears. And later, her hair began to grow again, not lushly, but restored to her as the hair of a cancer patient might be restored to the afflicted, altered in texture, not so wavy as it had been, rather more fine, and of an astonishing white hue, as Whitey's hair had been, and she recalled a grandmother's hair, a great many years ago when she'd been a child beloved and kissed by elderly adults who had gazed at her with something like rapture, her mother's mother who'd smelled of something flowery and whose pale skin had seemed impossibly soft, impossibly thin, a somber staring child could see the tracery of pale blue veins beneath.

Oh never, never! Never that old.

The tortoiseshell hand mirror he lifted with the sweeping gesture of a magician so that in the large bright-lit mirror she could see her reflection more clearly, the back of her head framed in the smaller mirror, the tight taut precisely braided white hair, several strands coiled into a single thick braid, and she'd laughed at how unlike herself she looked, how strong, how capable, how smiling and assured and loved—*Hugo, thank you!*

Rummaging in a drawer he came out with a white silk gardenia, a favor of some long-forgotten dinner or gala in some long-forgotten lifetime, and this he affixed to the braid, at the nape of Jessalyn's neck, with a long sharp hatpin.

Voilà! What did I tell you?—beautiful.

"MRS. McCLAREN? I'm afraid we need to bring you back for a few more 'diagnostic' X-rays . . ."

In a subdued voice the radiology nurse spoke to the shivering patient still in the dark green smock with the ties in front now neatly tied shut. In this practiced voice intended to assuage alarm, anxiety.

"Oh." Jessalyn was suddenly too weak to speak more emphatically.

Thinking—*Has it begun? My death.*

THERE WOULD BE A WAIT. More X-rays, and a wait for the radiologist.

Possibly then, no further X-rays and she could go home.

Or, more X-rays and she could go home for the day.

(An acute ear will hear—*For the day.*)

An ideal radiology patient: older female, docile, unalarmed (-seeming), not overly questioning and in no way hostile or aggressive.

SHE THOUGHT—*I will accept it. This time.*

She'd gone without eating that morning and possibly that had been a mistake. Soon she would be feeling faint, light-headed. She had not told anyone where she was going this morning for it was, or had been, a routine mammogram at the medical center.

Later that day, that evening, Hugo was coming to the house for an early supper. Of course, Jessalyn had not told *him.*

Since the false positive of seventeen years before she'd dreaded mammograms. Not just the intense pain, and the grotesquerie of breasts so flattened you would expect their soft contents to spill out under the pressure, but the fear of a "node-sized shadow" in the X-ray.

So many women she knew had had breast cancer, over the years. With dread she'd checked boxes in the questionnaire she'd been given in the waiting room, family members who'd had cancer.

But now she felt a strange calm. If the X-ray came back "positive" Whitey would be spared knowing.

Recalling his fear when he'd thought that Jessalyn might have cancer. His face that was usually so solid, strong-boned, had seemed to dissolve in panic. She had seen how he loved her—with a love deep-rooted as a child's love for a parent—and she'd felt sick with guilt, that she might betray this love by falling ill.

Waiting for the radiologist Jessalyn was not thinking clearly. This was *widow-think,* a random firing of neurons. For almost it would be a relief if, assuming she'd had to be diagnosed with cancer, it was happening now and had not happened when Whitey had been alive.

Well. In any case Whitey would never know, not even that she'd been called back for more X-rays. And if indeed the X-rays indicated a need for a biopsy, and if the biopsy indicated a need for surgery, Whitey would never know.

Her feeling for Hugo Martinez was shallow like the roots of a flowering shrub that have not yet taken hold in the earth. Like the red climber rosebush he'd planted in the spring. To yank such roots out of the earth would not require much effort. To yank out a mature bush would be very difficult and even so, much of the hair-thin capillary roots would remain in the soil.

Widow-think was a barely controlled panic of neurons crazily firing but *widow-think* was incapable of being sustained for long and so Jessalyn found herself thinking about Hugo Martinez who must have noticed that one of the climbing roses by the garage had died for one spring day he drove to the house unbidden, unannounced, bringing with him a large, somewhat sprawling rosebush to take its place.

The nerve of the man! Without even ringing the doorbell to alert Jessalyn, let alone secure her permission, he'd only just removed the bush from the rear of his truck, hauling it around the garage to plant in the soil. Jessalyn stood at an upstairs window where she could observe the man without his knowing. A khaki jacket, a wide-brimmed hat at a cocky angle, a way of pushing his booted foot against the shovel to drive it into the earth with a percussive force—she'd looked down at him mesmerized by the deftness and certainty of his movements, unable to see his face. How deeply absorbed the man was in digging out the old bush, replacing it with the new.

He is making his claim here. Why can't you stop him? What is wrong with you?

She resolved not to go outside, not to speak with him. Certainly, not to thank him.

Yet, as minutes passed, Jessalyn worried that Hugo Martinez would depart without knocking at the door. Anxiously she watched him, from the upstairs window. At one point he let the shovel fall, and drew a red handkerchief out of his pocket, and wiped his forehead in a gesture that seemed to her primeval, ancient; for a moment the man was revealed as tired, somewhat winded, not so young, sweating in hot sunshine. And in a mirror she caught a glimpse of herself, that look of pathos and hope, a not-young face, though still what you would call an attractive face. It was like seeing herself suddenly naked, stricken with shame at the rawness of her need, as if she were a stranger, to be pitied and not condemned; for she would not have condemned a stranger so alone and so yearning, as she might have condemned herself.

Quickly she descended the stairs and went outside, shading her eyes. She would thank him. She would be very gracious, thanking the man. Meaning to explain to him that she was grateful for the rosebush. She was grateful for his friendship, his kindness and generosity, but—*I have no feelings for anyone, any longer. Please understand.*

Instead, as soon as Hugo saw her, and called out happily to her, and Jessalyn came to inspect the new, red climber rosebush, that had been positioned against the stucco wall of the garage so that it was already vertical and upright, it occurred to her that she would bring a sprinkling pail to water the bush; and soon after she and Hugo Martinez began talking, and laughing together; and whatever she'd meant to tell him, she would postpone for another time.

MOM, PLEASE. *You must know that man is only after your money.*

He's younger than you are! He's of a much lower class . . .

Some artist-friend of Virgil's. A hippie—at that age . . .

You are not thinking clearly. It's too soon after Daddy. You must not make any sudden decisions.

Has he asked you for money? A loan?

He has been arrested, you know. He could be dangerous.

Don't let him wander in the house by himself. Keep close to him.

You know, there are beautiful things in our house and once they are gone, they will be gone forever.

Oh Mom! What would Daddy think!

SHE WAS NOT CRYING. NO.

She was not crying for it is pointless to cry.

In an adjacent cubicle a woman was indeed crying. Impossible not to hear.

At first Jessalyn had thought that the (invisible) woman had been speaking on a cell phone in a low laughing voice (distracting to hear in this place) but soon it became clear that she was crying. Jessalyn thought, One of my daughters. Oh, where was her mother to comfort her!

A dozen curtained cubicles here, each with its own (somewhat mocking) mirror, and a little bench on which to sit, and wait to be summoned by a radiology nurse with a clipboard. Of these, it wasn't clear how many cubicles were occupied.

Jessalyn had been told it would be "just a few minutes" before the next X-rays. That had been some minutes ago. With trembling fingers she'd tied shut the front of the coarse cotton smock.

Naked from the waist up, inside the smock. Soft aching breasts just small enough to present particular problems for a clear mammogram.

She couldn't bear it, hearing the woman cry in the next cubicle. Pulling back the curtain of her cubicle partway she called out uncertainly, "Excuse me? Is something wrong?"—a foolish thing to say in these circumstances.

The woman was young, Sophia's age. She was very small, the size of a child, her eyes large, owlish, shadowed. She whispered to Jessalyn, "I'm pregnant. I am eight weeks pregnant. They are going to do a biopsy in the morning." Her voice was so plaintive, her fear so palpable, Jessalyn could only come to her, and hold her.

The girl—(Jessalyn could only think of her as a girl)—hugged Jessalyn tight, sobbing harder. "It will be all right. Please don't cry. Crying doesn't help"—Jessalyn spoke falteringly, not knowing what to say but only that something has to be said, some words of comfort however inadequate. Her words were banal and useless and yet the girl shivered in her arms, and seemed to be grateful. "All right. All right. I think I will be all right. Thank you."

Jessalyn asked if she should call someone for her?—"A husband? Your—mother?"

But this was not the right thing to say, it seemed. For the girl flinched, and turned abruptly away. In the mirror her face was tight, waxen. She would be all right, she said.

Still Jessalyn stood uncertainly, not knowing what to do; but after a beat realizing that she'd been dismissed, and so returned to her own cubicle.

The sobbing did cease. Soon then the girl was summoned by the radiology nurse and led away without a glance in Jessalyn's direction. (Like a repentant mother Jessalyn had not drawn the curtain to her cubicle quite shut. You give them a chance to make up with you, but you also give them a chance to snub you. Had to smile, remembering.)

If the diagnostic X-rays came back "positive" she would call Sophia first, she supposed. For Sophia had medical knowledge and was not likely to over-react.

Then, with the assumption that she wouldn't be able to speak directly with Lorene, who would certainly never answer a personal call at this hour of the day, she would call Lorene, and leave a message.

Then, Beverly. They were not on such good terms lately, because of Hugo. But Beverly loved her very much and would cry at once—*Oh Mom! I'll be right over, what can I do for you?*

Beyond that—Thom, Virgil—she did not want to think just yet.

Hugo. She would not think just yet.

EACH TIME HE'D GONE AWAY she assumed he would not be coming back. Yet, Hugo came back.

She could not discourage him, it seemed. Once she'd laughed at some particularly preposterous suggestion of his—(a canoe ride? on the lake? by moonlight?)—and he'd smiled at her and said, Good he could make her laugh. At least.

Jessalyn protested, she wasn't laughing at *him*.

Well. Laughing at something, he guessed.

Hugo was good-natured, amused. He had not taken offense though he'd been (it seemed) just slightly hurt at Jessalyn's stiffness when he'd kissed her.

Telling her, of course he knew how she must feel. Her life had been ruptured.

When his father had died (young: fifty-one) his mother had seemed to lose her will to live. She'd entered a kind of tunnel of the soul—she'd become remote to her family even when she was in their presence.

Astonishing Jessalyn by reciting, solemnly, the words to a Protestant hymn Jessalyn was sure she hadn't heard since she'd been a teenager:

"Jesus walked this lonesome valley.
He had to walk it by himself.
O, nobody else could walk it for him.

He had to walk it by himself.
We must walk this lonesome valley.
We have to walk it by ourselves.
O, nobody else can walk it for us,
We have to walk it by ourselves . . ."

He wasn't religious, Hugo said. But the hymn was beautiful, and true. You didn't need to believe in Jesus as the son of God to know that it was true.

Oh yes, Jessalyn said quickly. She was deeply moved by Hugo's solemnity which was not like him, in her presence. Even as she thought, it wasn't true. Not altogether.

Another person can walk with you, a good part of the way. Taking your hand, and his hand in yours. This too was true.

HIS SECRETS WERE MANY, she supposed.

Having to do too with death. Deaths.

A man Hugo Martinez's age, it hadn't just been parents and grandparents who'd died but others close to him. She would learn in time, Jessalyn supposed.

If she cared to know. If she persevered in knowing.

For instance: why he'd been in the cemetery that evening when they'd first met.

Hugo said, somewhat evasively, it had been the sheerest chance. He'd been photographing visitors to the cemetery but had put his camera away when . . .

Seeing in his face an expression of pain and melancholy Jessalyn touched his wrist, and asked what was wrong?—and after a pause Hugo said, Well—also he'd been visiting the grave of someone he knew. Had known.

Jessalyn thought—*He doesn't want to tell me. I must respect his privacy.*

And so she didn't ask. Recalling how her children had been exasperated with her excessive politeness. *Mom for God's sake—you didn't ask? What is wrong with you?*

After dinner her guest wandered (uninvited, inquisitive) into another part of the house, which Jessalyn hadn't quite wanted him to see. Through the long living room that was unlighted, and into a smaller room beyond to which Whitey had given the name *Jess's drawing room.*

Whitey hadn't felt comfortable in the room which was furnished with things Jessalyn had inherited. Lamps, cushioned chairs, satin pillows, a plush dark-red sofa. Cedar bookcases filled with books (mostly by women) to which Sophia had contributed some of her college paperbacks when she'd moved out of the house.

Jessalyn hadn't been in these rooms for weeks. Months? A widow rarely ventures out of essential rooms and so part of the house like part of her brain had become a no-man's-land, uncharted and benumbed.

Nor did she think much about the house except when someone well-intentioned if not frankly rude asked if she was going to sell the house? When would she be selling the house?

Her children did not want her to sell the house which was *their house*. Even Virgil who scorned material things grew anxious when the subject came up.

Thom said Mom couldn't sell the house!—they were each planning secretly to move back in an emergency.

It wasn't clear if Thom was joking and Jessalyn felt a pang of yearning. *Yes please!*

But no. That was not likely to happen, and should not happen.

Hugo Martinez marveled at the size of Jessalyn's house. His tone may have been ironic but it was not disrespectful, she thought.

Apologetically Jessalyn said, Well—we were a large family. Five children.

How unreal it sounded! *Five children. Were.* Jessalyn had not the energy to raise a single child now, even little Sophia.

Reading her thoughts Hugo laughed, it is all pretty preposterous, isn't it? Our children come through us, and beyond us. You never feel so like a *vessel* when you see them grown up, like strangers, utterly beyond you.

This was so. Jessalyn had always imagined that Sophia was most like her yet the Sophia whom she knew now, who seemed to be living with the much older Alistair Means, and had become secretive about her life, did not much resemble Jessalyn at all.

And Thom, seemingly separated from his family in Rochester. When Jessalyn asked him about this Thom smiled vaguely past her shoulder as if catching the eye of someone else in the room, to whom he hardly needed to explain himself.

Reluctantly Jessalyn switched on lights in this part of the house. In the drawing room, stained-glass lamps. These were beautiful, antique—Tiffany lamps that exuded rich, warm light. Hugo examined them, closely.

He'd never seen a Tiffany lamp outside a museum, he said.

Jessalyn said the lamps were not so uncommon, really. She hesitated to say that she knew several people who owned Tiffany lamps in their homes.

Jessalyn saw Hugo draw a forefinger across the Tiffany glass, leaving a faint trace in the dust. Embarrassing!

And there was Jessalyn's piano, a Steinway baby grand which no one had played seriously in years.

Hugo marveled at the piano, also: fantastic! Hugo was very enthusiastic about the piano.

His melancholy air of a few minutes before had vanished totally. How like a child he was, Jessalyn thought. He lived in the moment, the very essence of *mercurial*.

Hugo switched on a floor lamp behind the piano, opened the keyboard, struck several keys. There was such beauty in these isolated notes, Jessalyn felt a thrill of happiness.

Her guest seated himself at the piano running strong deft fingers up and down the keyboard. Jessalyn steeled herself to hear a flat or a sharp note. She'd neglected to have the piano tuner come to the house since Whitey's death as she had been neglecting so much.

Had to admire the man's boldness, seating himself uninvited and at once adjusting the stool. The way parking valets and auto mechanics adjust the driver's seat of any car in which they find themselves, making their claim.

You would be able to hear this piano played in the farthest upstairs rooms of the house, Jessalyn thought.

Hugo was leafing through sheets of music atop the piano. For the years she'd taken piano lessons Sophia had dutifully photocopied the easier/slower compositions of Bach, Mozart, Chopin, John Field. Erik Satie, Béla Bartók. Like her mother Sophia had played a competent schoolgirl sort of music, earnest rather than inspired, essentially timid, groping—the result of much practice and a wish to please a piano instructor.

Ten years, Jessalyn had taken lessons. Sophia had been allowed to quit after just six.

Hugo Martinez played piano with the brash confidence of one who'd never had formal lessons, thus had never disappointed an instructor. He played by ear, evidently—hit or miss, with much showy energy. Large hands, fingers spread, he delighted in a massive assault upon the keyboard, playing something Jessalyn couldn't recognize at first—a loose-jointed, mangled Liszt, perhaps. *Transcendental Études?*

Or was it the Spanish composer de Falla. Long ago Jessalyn had tried to play some of de Falla's spirited music . . .

She listened to Hugo's piano music, mesmerized. It made her want to laugh, it was so—capricious. How cautious her own piano-playing had been! She'd concentrated on not striking wrong notes, there had never been much pleasure in the effort.

Hugo didn't seem to mind striking wrong notes. Some of them were dead notes—dead keys. Like any naturally gifted musician he knew to keep moving swiftly, never to acknowledge a mistake, never pause to correct a note or a chord as a dutiful student might; never to hesitate. Amid a flash of notes like a cascading waterfall most dazzled listeners would not detect mistakes.

There, you see. He is the one. Beyond any wish of yours.

Ridiculous to think in such a way! Jessalyn knew better, she did not believe in fate or even circumstances. No.

Yet a strange lethargy overcame her. For forty minutes standing beside Hugo as he played with gusto the neglected and out-of-tune Steinway it had seemed almost criminal of her to keep, in this house where no one played it any longer, and probably would not again, ever.

Fascinated by his hands on the keyboard that seemed both too large and clumsy, yet assured.

Strange, Jessalyn didn't care to sit down a few feet away, and listen. Instead she was drawn to stand close beside Hugo, absorbed in the actions of the large long fingers bounding boldly up and down the keyboard.

That night, Hugo would stay with Jessalyn for the first time.

IN THE MORNING Hugo would confide in Jessalyn that he'd been in the cemetery the evening they'd first met to visit the grave of his son Miguel, who'd died at the age of eleven, in an accident—Miguel had been bicycling on a steep hill, on Waterman Street, and at the intersection at the foot of the hill a cement truck had barreled through a stop sign and killed him instantaneously.

Twenty-one years ago, Hugo said. That very day.

Tears welled in his eyes. His eyelids trembled. Wordlessly, Jessalyn held the trembling man in her arms.

The one. The only one. Save yourself, darling!

"MRS. McCLAREN? You can bring your handbag with you."

Another time Jessalyn was called into the X-ray room. Another time, untying and opening the coarse cotton smock. Positioning herself, her poor bare aching breasts, before the dreadful machine.

But this time the nurse was a brisk young black woman who did not comment on Jessalyn's white-braided hair that fell to the middle of her back but noted that she was shaking with cold or with fear and told her brusquely *Ma'am you have got to relax. Or else the X-rays won't come out clear.*

HE'D BEEN MARRIED OF COURSE, that was hardly a surprise to Jessalyn. That he'd been divorced for so long (twelve years) was something of a surprise for Hugo Martinez had the look of a man so comfortable with women, so *husbandly* in his manner, you'd have thought he'd spent most of his adult life married and not, as he'd said, *loose and lonely*.

Jessalyn had thought it must be a joke—*loose and lonely*. But Hugo sounded quite solemn telling her.

His ex-wife Marta lived in Port Oriskany, a few hours away. She had remarried but not happily. He sent her money when she needed it. She had left *him*. (In case Jessalyn was wondering.) The blame for their son's death had somehow fallen onto Hugo, who'd bought the boy that particular bike, and who hadn't done his share (the wife accused) of overseeing him, where he went on the bike, which roads he traveled. Possibly too, the marriage had been shaky at the time. Possibly, Hugo hadn't been living with the boy's mother and possibly, the boy had been on his way to see his father at the time of the accident . . . Hearing Hugo speak in a way that was heated, anxious, so very different from the way in which Hugo usually chose to present himself to her, Jessalyn saw how complicated it was, a terribly snarled knot. Hugo had exhausted himself years ago struggling to untie the knot and so had done the only sensible thing: walked away.

Saved himself, and walked away.

But yes, he had living children. Adult children.

She would meet them soon, Hugo said. If she wished.

Well, said Jessalyn. What do you wish, Hugo?

Yes. That you will meet. Soon.

Purposefully, *soon* was kept vague.

And vague too was Jessalyn's intention to introduce Hugo to her older children, who hadn't yet met him. (She'd had Virgil and Sophia to dinner, with Hugo; they had all gotten along very well though Hugo had talked with more than his usual exuberance and Sophia had stared at him through much of the evening as if she'd never seen anyone quite like Hugo Martinez in that house, at that dining room table.) Jessalyn hadn't told Hugo how hostile Thom, Beverly, and Lorene were to the very idea of him, nor had Hugo asked.

He had many friends, Hugo said. But no one to whom he was really close, any longer.

Some of his friends were former prisoners. Not *ex-convicts* for these were men who'd been wrongfully, unjustly convicted of crimes they had not committed.

One day, Hugo brought Jessalyn to his house in East Hammond, where he was scheduled to photograph two of these former prisoners, for the newsletter published by the non-profit Liberators Ministry.

Hugo lived on the ground floor of a large faded redbrick house set in a grassy lot bordering a marshland/landfill. The three-story house needed repair but exuded an air of dignity, austerity. Railroad tracks ran nearby: freight trains were infrequent but very noisy. Jessalyn was intrigued to see that the property was an untidy checkerboard of grapevines, brambles, black-eyed Susans, phlox, goldenrod and sunflowers; someone had been enterprising enough to plant tomatoes, green beans, sweet corn; especially, the tomato plants had grown lushly, spreading their tendrils for yards. And there was a melancholy-looking scarecrow amid the cornstalks, tilted on its crossbars like a drunken Christ, in a plaid jacket, satin gym shorts of the kind Thom used to wear, weather-worn straw hat that had to have belonged to Hugo Martinez.

How wonderful, Hugo's residence! *Seedy, run-down. Wild, overgrown, and welcoming.*

There were a number of vehicles in the rutted driveway. The front door, while not quite open, was not quite shut, either. It seemed that Hugo owned the house and five-acre property but it wasn't clear whether other tenants in the house paid rent, or were Hugo's relatives, friends, guests.

Within an hour Jessalyn was to meet or to glimpse a considerable number of people of varying ages, types, skin-tones, each of whom was introduced to *My dear friend Jessalyn*.

It was clear, painfully clear or thrillingly clear, that Hugo had very strong feelings about her. Introducing her with his arm about her shoulders, or slung about her waist, to suggest (unmistakably) their relationship.

At least, some representation of their relationship.

He would uplift her soul, she thought. As a cork is lifted by water, through no effort of its own.

Did it matter that she could not love him? She could not be *in love* with him?

At the rear of the house was Hugo's work-studio, which he'd converted "with his own hands" from an outdoor porch; the space was filled with photographs (Hugo's own, and others), art books, art magazines and journals. On the plank floor were gorgeously bright Mexican rugs and affixed to the ceiling were Calder-like mobiles (Hugo's own, inexpensively assembled). He'd once had a darkroom, he told Jessalyn, but now his photography was exclusively digital, he worked with a computer and a printer.

Jessalyn was dismayed to see how relatively little of Hugo Martinez's work was displayed, or even visible; most of it was stored haphazardly in corners, or stacked against walls. Even his books—even those slender books with *Hugo Martinez* stamped on their spines—were stacked on the floor, gathering dust-whorls.

Several times Jessalyn had asked if she could purchase photographs of his but Hugo had frowned and said no, certainly not—he intended to give her a selection of "special" photographs as a gift, soon.

On a particular occasion he would make this gift to her, Hugo added. It was to be hoped.

Particular occasion—Jessalyn wondered what that might mean.

Yet he'd procrastinated. Soon, soon!—he promised airily.

When they'd first become acquainted Hugo had inscribed for her one of his early books of poetry, *After Moonrise*. Jessalyn had read the book avidly if with not full comprehension; she'd recognized in the poet's long buoyant jazzy lines a clear influence of Ginsberg, Whitman, Williams (W. C.). But he'd more or less stopped writing poetry, Hugo told her. He'd never been satisfied with anything he'd written.

Why not?—Jessalyn had asked; and Hugo said because poetry is infinite and has no natural completion, to be truthful to the vagaries of life one could never *end* a poem, only just *continue*.

Also, words were just too frail, too easily smudged or deleted. Words were too easily misunderstood.

It was photography that gripped him now—visual images, actual things people could see. And people.

Especially, people's faces. He could devote the remainder of his life to photographing faces and never come to the end of his fascination.

Against a backdrop of a large white seamless sheet of paper Hugo photographed two ex-prisoners that afternoon, of several that had been released from incarceration recently through the efforts of Liberators Ministry.

Both were male, and African-American. More than 90 percent of the prisoners the Liberators had freed in twenty years were persons of color, Hugo remarked; all but one had been male and she had been a Haitian-American woman who'd been misidentified in a police lineup in Detroit.

Carlin Milner was forty-one years old, and had been incarcerated in a Pennsylvania maximum security prison for twenty-two years, for a robbery-homicide in Philadelphia which he had not committed; one night he'd been picked up by police on a South Philadelphia street, taken to a station house and threatened, beaten, coerced into a confession; he'd been sentenced to life in prison, and had only been freed by legal activists after years of appeals and litigation at a cost of more than two hundred thousand dollars.

Even so, Hugo told Jessalyn, Carlin wasn't altogether in the clear. Prosecutors were still pondering whether to re-charge and retry him though the "witnesses" they'd had in 1989 were dead or vanished.

Yet Carlin was studying to be a minister. His manner was guarded but friendly. When he shook Jessalyn's hand he avoided looking her in the face but his smile was engaging and he did not seem embittered or angry. She thought—*He sees a white-skinned woman. That is all he sees.*

It occurred to Jessalyn to ask if Carlin Milner was associated with the Hope Baptist Church on Armory Street—(that was the only African-American church she knew)—but she realized how naive this was, how possibly offensive.

She'd sent a second check, for seven hundred dollars, to SaveOurLives in care of the Hope Baptist Church but wasn't sure if the check had ever been cashed.

Hugo's second subject Hector Cavazos was thirty-nine years old. He'd spent eighteen years in the maximum security prison at Attica for a particularly brutal rape-murder (in Buffalo) which he had not committed; DNA evidence had eventually freed him, but only after years of obfuscation and hostility on the part of the Buffalo prosecutors who were now planning to retry him for the homicide, though their only evidence was the police-informant "eyewitness" who'd originally testified against him.

At thirty-nine Cavazos was a handsome man despite his scarred face and bloodshot eyes, the result of prison beatings. He had a severe stutter which had infuriated Buffalo police at the time of his arrest, and now he did not speak much if he could avoid it, and then in a low, near-audible voice. He'd been released from Attica with no education, no training, no one willing to take him in except a distant relative in Buffalo who was himself on public assistance; the Liberators Ministry was providing a residence for him and helping him find employment. More than three hundred thousand dollars had been spent to free Cavazos and more expenses lay ahead.

Lawsuits were pending against the respective police departments and municipalities that were responsible for such gross miscarriages of justice. Seven million dollars, twelve million dollars. Litigation would drag on, in both cases, for years.

Jessalyn felt a pang of sorrow for the men whose youthful lives had been taken from them so cruelly. They'd been fortunate just to survive in the maximum security prisons, Hugo said, where they'd received very poor medical care, if any.

Yet they were not bitter, at least not in the presence of Hugo Martinez and his white-skinned woman friend. Not much point to anger, Milner said. Just eats up your heart for nothing.

You could see why the man wanted to be a Christian minister, Jessalyn thought. Bringing *good news* to the world that so yearned to hear it.

It was touching to Jessalyn, to hear how warmly and matter-of-factly Hugo spoke with the ex-prisoners; how genuinely interested he was in their lives, and the care he took with their portraits. Hugo's casual manner did not extend to his photography; there, he was a perfectionist. Observing the men, from a short distance, Jessalyn felt both privileged and ashamed; she had suffered so little in her life, set beside Carlin Milner and Hector Cavazos, and others unjustly incarcerated for long periods of time; she knew nothing of such stoicism. She, a widow who'd believed that she had suffered greatly by losing her husband . . . Even from suffering she'd been shielded by her class, her money. Her marriage to a man who had loved and protected her.

Domestic life had blinded her to the real sorrows of the world. Happiness had blinded her.

She was feeling very warm, light-headed and disoriented. The weight of the braid falling between her shoulder blades had become mildly distressing like a mocking pat on the back.

If she were a good, generous person, Jessalyn thought, she would open her house to individuals like these. Her house on Old Farm Road was a fortress, and a sanctuary: she could not dwell in such a place alone, for very long.

Mom, don't be ridiculous. They all want to exploit you.

They know who you are. They have targeted you. How can you be so foolish!

Your lover is a Communist agitator. He has been in prison himself. He wants your money. He will discard you.

Later that evening when they were alone together Hugo mentioned to Jessalyn that he'd been jailed himself as a younger man, in the 1980s, though just briefly, in the Hammond Men's Detention Facility. Maybe one of her children had told her?

Jessalyn's reply was vague. Well, no—not exactly.

(Of course, Jessalyn was embarrassed that Hugo must certainly have guessed by now how her older children maligned him, to her. How they suspected him, and what terrible things they said about him.)

In a light-hearted tone Hugo reminisced of having been "pretty roughly" handled by police officers, indeed pepper-sprayed and struck with batons, but without serious or permanent injuries. A black eye, but not an eye *out*.

A sprained ankle but not a *broken leg*.

He'd been arrested with other striking protesters in front of the Hammond City Hall for "trespassing" and "disturbing the peace"—"failure to obey law enforcement officers' orders"—twenty-six years ago. The City of Hammond had forbidden employees to unionize, and Hugo and one or two others were leading a strike of teachers, municipal workers, township employees for higher wages and benefits. An unruly crowd had gathered in front of City Hall both *for* and *against* the strike. Traffic had been stalled, fistfights had broken out. TV crews had come to broadcast the excitement and had instigated more confusion.

At the time Hugo had headed the art department at the community college—his first, as it was to be his last, administrative position. He and several other strike organizers had been arrested, handcuffed, dragged into police vans and detained in the detention facility for forty-eight hours. They'd all been beaten but they had not been intimidated or terrified. The Hammond police had not used firearms. There had not been a SWAT team to disperse the crowd as there might have been in another city or in Hammond itself at an earlier time. In jail they'd felt energized, thrilled. Their supporters had rallied around them and some, if not much of the publicity was favorable to them; they'd received death threats, but also messages of sympathy and donations to the strike fund.

Indeed, the strike had been mostly successful. The union had been voted in, and new contracts negotiated with the city. Unfortunately, Hugo and the other organizers had lost their jobs and were sued by the city for various violations of the law, which had come to nothing, eventually—the lawsuits, that is. But definitely, they'd been fired.

Jessalyn had the uneasy feeling that Whitey might have been mayor of Hammond at this time.

She did recall that "outside agitators" had been blamed for acts of vandalism. She wondered if she'd seen Hugo Martinez's picture in the paper. UNLAWFUL PROTESTERS ARRESTED, JAILED.

If she'd seen his picture, and took note. *This man! One day, you will fall in love with him.*

How improbable, when she'd been in love with Whitey at the time. Long married to Whitey McClaren at the time.

Jessalyn told Hugo that he'd been brave to lead a strike. Someone had to stand up for underpaid and exploited workers.

Well, Hugo said. It hadn't quite been Tiananmen Square.

Jessalyn knew little of Tiananmen Square. Chinese students had protested, and the Chinese army had fired upon them? Hugo said yes, essentially that had been it. Protesters demanding more freedom had been cut down by gunfire, tanks, in 1989. The suppression had been brutal, terrible. Hundreds had been killed, possibly thousands. The wounds of Tiananmen Square had been still fresh when Hugo had traveled to China several times in the past twelve years.

They were driving in Hugo's vehicle along the Cayuga Road. It is very easy to feel like a couple in a moving vehicle, one behind the wheel and the other in the passenger's seat. It is not even necessary to speak, to feel like a couple in such circumstances.

Bringing the vehicle to a stop, getting out, walking—into what? where?—that is more problematic.

Jessalyn wanted to tell Hugo that her husband, too, had been injured by police officers. It had not been altogether clear what had happened to him but he'd been beaten, the police had used Taser guns on him, he'd had a stroke, two weeks later he'd died . . . But she had not yet been able to speak of Whitey to Hugo, except in the most abstract of ways.

No. She could not. It would be a violation of her deep and inviolable love for her husband, she could never reveal this to Hugo Martinez.

As Hugo turned onto Old Farm Road Jessalyn felt a quickening of dread, like one who is entering a tunnel. The vast world was rapidly narrowing, she was coming *home.*

Not alone, coming *home* with Hugo Martinez. But *home* was where she had lived with Whitey for most of her adult life, and where, if anywhere, Whitey yet dwelled.

By the time Hugo pulled into the driveway at 99 Old Farm Road Jessalyn had become overwhelmed by a sensation of vertigo, nausea. She could not ask him to come inside, she said. Not just now. She was feeling unwell. She was feeling very depressed. It had come over her suddenly like a great dark net . . .

Hugo was astonished. Hugo was hurt. Hugo stammered—but what was wrong? Clearly he'd expected to stay the night with her. He'd brought some things—toiletries, a fresh shirt. He didn't understand . . .

Jessalyn had to flee from the car. She had to be alone. No, she could not bear being touched by any man but Whitey.

Leaving this man in his vehicle, in the driveway. Not daring to look back at him. Sick with revulsion for him, and for herself with him. How had she dared? What had she been thinking?

That ridiculous mustache! His fatuous smile, so *happy*! The silly peasant braid halfway down her back!

Oh Whitey. Forgive me. I am so ashamed.

— ∞ —

"Mrs. McClaren? The X-ray looks good."

Jessalyn stared at the nurse with such startled disbelief that the woman was obliged to repeat what she'd said adding, "Must've been you moved, or breathed at the wrong time, the first time."

What was this? Good news?

So stoically she'd been preparing for different news. A biopsy, at least . . .

In a daze she left Radiology. Could not quite believe that she had been spared a second time.

She'd decided to call Beverly, only. No need to worry the others if it wasn't necessary. Something about the possibility of breast cancer terrified men in particular—husbands, sons. No need.

Certainly no need to tell Hugo Martinez. She'd agreed to see him that evening for the final time. Whatever had been between them, a small brushfire among dried, desiccated grasses, she'd beaten down.

No need to share such intimate news with *him*.

Her heart beat rapidly, almost in anger—thinking of *him*.

Though she recalled, Virgil had mentioned to her, there was a photography exhibit in a new wing of the hospital in which both he and Hugo Martinez had photographs, and so on her way to the parking lot Jessalyn sought out the display titled *Healing by Nature*.

Quickly seeking Virgil's photographs, which were landscape scenes probably taken along the Chautauqua River, and Hugo's, which were more complicated and problematic—three starkly black-and-white photographs of Moroccan children being bathed in some sort of open ditch or stream by a dark-skinned woman. Jessalyn felt a stab of dismay: it was like Hugo Martinez to expect too much of the viewer. You had to think too much, and you had to feel too much, and even then you didn't know what you were supposed to think and to feel. Other photographs in the exhibit including Virgil's were much more accessible, familiar and consoling.

And then, headed for an elevator to take her down to the first-floor lobby, Jessalyn saw, or thought she saw, Hugo Martinez striding before her, along a corridor. Like a kick in the heart it was, seeing Hugo when she hadn't been prepared.

Almost, she was feeling faint. She had determined to cease thinking of Hugo Martinez, essentially. And yet, there he was.

Had to be Hugo, wearing one of his wide-brimmed hats, and a very pale peach-colored, muslin-thin shirt she was sure she recognized, and cargo shorts though it wasn't a warm day; and the straightness of his back, that seemed exaggerated (though Hugo had told her why: as a boy he'd been horrified by an older male relative who'd developed curvature of the spine in old age); and the way he moved, that was both light-footed and aggressive, seemed to Jessalyn identical with the way Hugo moved when walking swiftly and not obliged to keep a slower pace with another person. For instance, her.

This person Jessalyn followed along the wide white corridor just far enough behind him so that if he turned suddenly to enter a room, or to turn onto another corridor, he couldn't easily have glanced back and seen her. Forced to walk so quickly Jessalyn felt the braid lightly slapping against her back.

At Oncology, he pushed through swinging doors. Jessalyn stopped in her tracks.

Yet, through a plate-glass window she could see Hugo, or the person she believed to be Hugo Martinez, back to her, leaning over a check-in desk. Blood work? Infusion?

Over the years Jessalyn had accompanied relatives who'd come to the hospital for infusions, chemotherapy. Chemicals so toxic dripping into their veins, nurses wore special gloves to prepare the medication and to administer it through an IV tube.

Jessalyn wondered: Was Hugo having chemotherapy? Or—another sort of infusion? Possibly, a transfusion?

He had not told her. He was fiercely private while seeming very open, frank. Any sort of flaw in himself, as he'd perceive it, he'd been sure to hide.

In that instant Jessalyn felt weak with love for the man, anxious for him. If that was indeed Hugo Martinez—(now walking away from her, toward the farther end of the waiting room)—he would need her, then. As Whitey had needed her, and she had failed to save him. Hugo too would need someone, and she would be the one. If he would have her.

The Last Will & Testament of Virgil McClaren

My earthly goods, I bequeath to Amos Keziahaya. "The rest is silence."

How exalted it sounded! Laughable.

Yet utterly sincere. If/when Virgil McClaren died, to leave his "estate" to a virtual stranger—in this way confirming his older siblings' conviction, he was hopeless beyond redemption.

How scandalized they would be! Especially Beverly.

Oh my God—his heir is a black man! How could Virgil do such a thing to us!

Not even American but what-is-it—Nigerian.

COUNTLESS TIMES he'd relived the scene in his cabin.

What had he been thinking! *Had* he been thinking?

Excruciating embarrassment. Not shame, not exactly, for (in fact) Virgil wasn't *ashamed* of being attracted to Amos Keziahaya; but indeed he was embarrassed because Amos had been embarrassed, and had fled from him.

Like a Möbius strip, having to see-again, live-again what he'd done: daring to approach the tall young man, daring to touch his shoulders, lift himself (just slightly, he'd hoped unobtrusively) on his toes in order to kiss Amos's lips . . .

Those lips: thick, very dark, startled, astonished and affrighted.

How had Virgil, who lived so much inside his head, who so carefully plotted, calculated, calibrated his moves with others, like a child prodigy–chess champ, how had he done such an impulsive thing, made such a mistake, been so foolish!

Of course, Keziahaya now avoided Virgil. Out of tact, Virgil avoided him, too.

Well, not just tact. Better to avoid altogether than to *stalk.*

AMOS: I AM SO SORRY. *I did not mean it. I acted stupidly. I'd had too much to drink—I should not drink. Ever.*

Amos: I am so sorry. Please forgive me. A kind of fever came over me. And I should not drink. I hope—I hope—I hope that we can be friends . . .

Amos: I am not sorry at all. I am not ashamed or even much embarrassed for having kissed you. Fact is, I think—(do I mean "think"?)—(trying now for once in my stunted life not to be circumspect, i.e., a coward)—that I LOVE YOU.

At least, Whitey would never know.

"GOD DAMN."

Had he been stung by a hornet? So swiftly, and a tiny red mark in the skin of his upper arm swelling, throbbing pain.

Had to laugh. Served him right. He'd defended the hornets building their nest beneath the barn eaves, a hive now metropolis-sized.

Well, no time now to treat the sting. In his Jeep and on his way.

Almost mid-September and still very hot. Airless-hot. Cicadas screaming by day as by night so his head rang with their desperate cries anticipating their deaths and he'd been too excited most nights to sleep thinking of Amos Keziahaya and when not thinking of Amos thinking of how he was not thinking of Amos, how stoic and resolute, how *good:* for that *good straight heterosexual son* his father would have respected if not loved.

Too excited to lie horizontal. Alone.

Something crackling racing through his veins. Shut his eyes and saw himself a bionic man, transparent skin, arteries, nerves, bones, musculature illuminated for teaching purposes.

Fact is, to be alone is to be incomplete. To be rebuffed by the other is to be eviscerated. Unbearable!

When Whitey died, Jessalyn had lost her will to live. If death had been a doorway, and the door open, possibly she'd have stepped through. Her children who loved her had known yet none of them could speak of it. Now their mother had no need of them, she'd found her own way back and her children had had nothing to do with it.

Entrusting yourself to another, as Virgil had never been able to do. Giving your hand to another, *hand being held*. If he didn't succeed in killing himself, if this too turned out to be another Virgil-fiasco, he felt a stir of excitement envisioning a sequence of sculpted figures, transparent-skinned, hand-holding.

At the Chautauqua River at Dutchtown. Wasn't sure what he would do though it would involve water.

Three hundred thousand six hundred dollars he would be leaving to Amos Keziahaya for that was what remained of Whitey's bequest. Plus the Jeep, odds and ends in the cabin. Plus Virgil's unsold artworks of which there were at least thirty in his studio or stored in the barn or in a scattering of galleries awaiting purchase.

Last Will & Testament of Virgil McClaren he'd prepared from an abbreviated form online. Scorned the idea of going to a lawyer, squandering money that might better go to an heir. He had not warned Amos—of course. He hoped that it would not be an unpleasant surprise for his friend, to be notified out of nowhere—*Amos Keziahaya? You are the sole beneficiary of Virgil McClaren's estate.*

To simplify matters (at least Virgil thought this would simplify matters) Virgil had also named Amos Keziahaya the executor of his estate. He had considered for a short time the notion of leaving some of his artwork to people who admired it—Jessalyn, Sophia, Beverly among others—but decided that that involved too much complication.

Feeling grandiloquent, transfixed. Lines of a favorite Yeats poem came to him as he braked the Jeep to a bucking halt.

And twenty minutes more or less
It seemed, so great my happiness,
That I was blessed and could bless.

IN HOT SUN ON THE BANK of the Chautauqua River. Would think it was the peak of summer except for curled and discolored leaves underfoot.

Feeling reckless, manic. But *happy.*

Wanting to squeeze Amos's hand. *Don't feel sorry for me, my friend. Don't feel guilty! In fact I am happy. Never quite realized—happy.*

Sad, never to have squeezed Amos's hand. He would have been so honored, to have squeezed Amos's hand.

Sad, Amos wasn't with him right now. Why wasn't Amos with Virgil *right now*?

How did men reach out to one another? Virgil had known the script, awkward as it was, for relating to girls and women who'd meet you halfway, or more than halfway for they knew the script too. But another man—even in this era of gay liberation, gay consciousness, he could not quite imagine.

Striding along the embankment of the river outside Dutchtown. No one knew he was here, or anywhere. And when the news came to them they would say—*Oh but why was Virgil* there?

Had to be an accident. Otherwise, unthinkable.

Hadn't left a note. Only just *Last Will & Testament of Virgil McClaren* on his worktable which you could interpret in any way you wished.

Virgil had signed the document in the proper places, and dated it. He'd asked friends at the farm to witness his signature. What is this we're signing, Virgil, they'd asked, looks like a contract; and Virgil said just a form he'd downloaded from the Internet, nothing important or of significance to their lives.

They'd signed, without further questions. Which was why he'd asked Conner and Jake and not someone else.

It was the kind of glaring-white day you might toss away your life like a handful of pebbles. Out into the shining water.

Well, the Chautauqua River might appear shining, at a little distance. Closer up, the water was murky like muddied thinking.

Swaths of the river had actually burst into flame forty years before, downriver from Hammond industry. Power plant, chemical plants. Nitrogen. Local TV news had played and replayed the astonishing sights. Too young for the spectacle, Virgil had collected photographs of it in high school for one of his science-art projects.

Long ago. Lonely kid he'd been. Arrogant, secretive.

If guys had jeered *faggot* at him, he had not heard. And if he'd heard, something in him deflected the insult as a superhero deflects a lethal blow with a negligent gesture of his superhero hand.

Along the riverbank was a faint path among rushes, cattails, detritus which he found himself following for the first/last time in his life. There was novelty in this!

Amos: If we could do all things for the last time even as we did them for the first time, what joy.

On the farther shore was a makeshift beach where children appeared to be playing. Virgil shaded his eyes: too far to see.

Too far for them to see *him.*

By slow degrees making a deep-guttural throbbing sound, a barge from downriver. On the path Virgil stood staring, waiting for the words to come to him.

Swim to that barge. Grab hold, and be hauled to freedom.

First time/last time. Hurry!

An absurd idea, Virgil thought. The last thing any sane person would want to do.

Pulling off his shirt, kicking off his sandals. Good that he was wearing shorts, not his khakis.

Walking now swiftly along the embankment. Couldn't remember

when he'd bathed last and so he smelled to himself like a goat. But he was happy! Damned happy.

Virgil McClaren happy at last.

And then he was wading in the murky water at the shore. Always a surprise to step into water, its unexpected stolidity, coarseness where there should be transparency and airiness. Its surface was seed-flecked, oily. Beneath, almost cold.

Surprised too at the soft-mud bottom beneath his bare feet. And how vulnerable the soles of his feet. Taking a deep breath (for he was beginning to shiver) and boldly pushing himself out and beginning to swim trying not to be wounded by Thom's scorn *Jesus! Call that swimming that's dog-paddling.*

His intention had been to throw himself bravely into the water but he had not anticipated the river's swift current. Rough fingers grabbing at him not knowing *him* and how special he was in the universe.

Don't give up don't despair

I will come to you

I am coming to you

I will save you

Frantic swimming. Desperate. Swallowing mouthfuls of water.

No one saw. No one was aware. His cruel older brother stared in silence, appalled.

The enormous barge was passing at a distance of about twelve feet. Waves swept over him, rocking his weakened body. Was he in danger of being caught up in an engine?—the vibrating noise had become deafening. But there was a cable dragging in the water behind the barge, thick, coarse, badly frayed, made of some synthetic material like needles tearing at the flesh of his grasping hands. With bizarre clarity as if his skull had been sawed open to admit the most intense light Virgil thought—*I can hang on. This is the right way.* Thinking he would hang on to the cable until the barge pulled him downriver to oblivion but then, the pain was excruciating, he could not hold on to the damned cable long enough to be drowned in the barge's wake, that had been a blunder. Whatever he'd meant to do, fact is he had no clear idea what he'd meant to do, thinking he would simply act, he would *plunge in* and give himself up to chance. He owed Whitey that, to give himself up to chance. But his hands were being torn raw and he had to release the cable choking and sputtering in waves behind the barge like rollicking laughter.

He'd been hauled beneath the bridge. He may have screamed for help. Here the river was narrower, shallower—broken concrete and rusted iron rods had been dumped in the water, near the shore. Scarcely conscious of what he did he managed to grab hold of a massive chunk of concrete with his bleeding hands.

At last, he crawled onto the shore too exhausted to stand. The folly of his swimming to the barge, being dragged by the razor-sharp cable, had not lasted beyond twelve minutes but it would require many more minutes to recover.

"Hey man? You OK?"—someone called to him from the path above.

Young guys, bare-chested. Staring at Virgil in amazement he was still alive.

Mumbled he was all right but the guy on the path came closer. Saying, "You don't look good, man. Maybe we should call 911?"

But no, Virgil was all right. Managed to sit up, choking and spitting out filthy water.

He was able to talk the kids out of calling 911 to summon an ambulance. No, no! Last thing he wanted was an emergency room.

In crazy triumph his heart beat—*Well—you are still alive. Amos won't know. No one will know.*

Allowed them to help him up the embankment. Help him back to his Jeep. Didn't fend them off when a girl provided him with wads of tissue for his bleeding hands.

"Hey, man—here." One of the boys tossed Virgil's shirt and sandals at him, which he'd left on the embankment some distance away.

Returned to the farmhouse on Bear Mountain Road where (of course) no one had the slightest awareness he'd even been gone. Exhausted, nauseated, sunburnt but no one would see. His shorts stank of river water. His matted hair stank. But there was *Last Will & Testament of Virgil McClaren* where he'd left it on his worktable.

He'd drowned, but not died. Died, but was still here.

Was that the best? The *better*? He would see.

Warning

Coming up close behind her car, startlingly close in the rearview mirror, a vehicle driven by a man whom she couldn't see clearly and suddenly she was frightened, was this aggressive person going to strike the rear of her car, was she going too slowly along Old Farm Road where the speed limit was forty-five miles an hour except at curves where twenty miles an hour was posted, was the (male) driver angry with her, was she in danger from his anger?—pressing on the gas pedal to accelerate, to appease whoever it was behind her, give him room to pass her if he wished, she had no intention of making an impatient driver more impatient by keeping her speed down in this quasi-rural area where there was little traffic at this hour of the day; and within seconds hearing the wail of a siren, for the vehicle close behind her was a police cruiser, possibly unmarked, she hadn't seen, would not see in her alarm and confusion.

Sophia braked the car to a stop. She could not imagine what she'd done wrong. A beige-uniformed officer was leaning close to her window saying in a loud voice, "Ma'am, lower your window."

Then, "Turn off your engine, ma'am."

Rapidly his eyes ran over Sophia. He was beefy-faced, heavyset, though relatively young, in his mid-thirties perhaps. He wore a brass badge, leather belt, holster. He identified himself as an officer with the North Hammond Police Department. His manner was both hostile and bemused as if he hadn't been aware that the driver of the car he'd stopped was an attractive young woman and this was an additional surprise, a kind of bonus.

"In a kind of hurry, ma'am, weren't you? Speed limit is twenty and you were doing thirty-two."

Sophia tried to explain: she'd accelerated her car because he'd come up so close behind her, she'd been afraid that his vehicle would hit her, she hadn't realized that he was a police officer . . .

"Right, ma'am. You didn't 'realize.'"

"But I—"

"Twelve miles over the speed limit, ma'am. Also your vehicle was weaving."

Weaving? Sophia had no idea what that meant.

"I've been following you for a mile or more and you've been all over the road, ma'am. Erratic driving plus speeding." By this time it was clear that the police officer's enunciation of *ma'am* was derisive, jeering.

"License please, ma'am."

"Y-Yes, officer."

Sophia's heart was beating rapidly. She had not ever in her life been pulled over for any traffic violation. She had not even been ticketed for a parking violation.

Speeding, weaving, erratic driving—these charges could not be right. She'd been driving no differently than she always drove on Old Farm Road which was so familiar to her she might have driven it in her sleep anticipating every driveway and neighbor's house, every intersection with another road, every curve posted at twenty miles an hour.

Later she would recall that she'd seen the police vehicle in her rear-view mirror since she'd left Jessalyn's house ten minutes before. She'd had no reason to think at the time—*That person is following me.*

"'McClaren'—eh? That's your name?"

"Yes . . ."

The officer was looking from the photo ID to Sophia's face with an exaggerated suspicion, or the pretense of suspicion. In a flurry of uncertainty Sophia wondered if her driver's license had lapsed, if she'd unwittingly violated another law.

"'McClaren'—and you live at . . ." Squinting at the address on the driver's license. "Not on Old Farm Road."

"No. I don't live on Old Farm Road . . ."

"But you were coming from 99 Old Farm Road."

"Yes, I was visiting my—my mother . . ."

"Your mother? You were visiting your mother."

The officer's voice was flat, derisive. Why was he asking her such a question? Did he know her?—the name "McClaren"?

Sophia explained that she didn't live at 99 Old Farm Road any longer but she'd used to live there, until she'd moved away; it was her family address, she'd been visiting her mother . . . Heard herself speaking rapidly, anxiously.

"Car registration please, 'Soph-ia.'"

"Yes, officer."

Yes officer. How craven she sounded. How *feminine.*

Exactly how Jessalyn would act in such a situation: courteous, deferential, frightened but taking care not to show it. *Feminine.*

From the glove compartment Sophia removed a folder presumably containing auto registration, insurance. She had not so much as glanced into the glove compartment in months. Her fingers had gone cold, her hands had begun to shake.

"Who's this? 'John Earle McClaren.' Not you."

Sophia explained: the car had been given to her by her father, a few years before. He'd bought a new car for himself, an SUV or rather—this car had been her mother's, and her father had given her mother the car he'd been driving when he'd bought a new car . . . In her own ears this tangle of words sounded suspicious, unconvincing.

"It needs to be in your name, 'Soph-ia.' You are driving a vehicle registered in the name of another person." (Had he been about to say *a deceased person*? Sophia wondered.)

"Is that against the law, officer? I—"

"If you are driving this vehicle, if it is in your possession, you need to have title to the vehicle. You can request transfer of title at the motor vehicle division."

"But—is it against the law to drive someone else's car? If they have lent it to you?"

"Gave it to you, you'd said."

"Well—they just sort of gave me the keys. My own car had worn out, and instead of getting it repaired . . . I don't actually know if it was a 'gift,'" Sophia said, weakly, "—it might have been more of a loan . . . within the family . . ."

"Ma'am, step out of the car please. Leave the keys in the ignition."

"Step out of the *car*? But—why?"

"I've told you, ma'am. Step out of the car now. Right now."

The police officer was speaking loudly. As if on the verge of anger.

Sophia would recall later this (male) *anger* just barely held in abeyance, which it was her responsibility as a detainee and a woman to forestall.

She was trembling badly. There were no witnesses along this stretch of Old Farm Road. The police officer could do virtually anything to her he wanted to do, she could not prevent it.

McClaren. 99 Old Farm Road. The officer had been stationed there, waiting for her. For someone who lived at that house to turn out of the driveway.

Surely he knew the names: *John Earle McClaren, Thom McClaren.*

"Pop the trunk. Now."

Sophia obeyed. Was a warrant required, to search a car? She could not think. There was nothing in the trunk that violated any law—was there? A spare tire, recycled grocery bags? A pair of muddied hiking shoes she'd forgotten to bring into the house after a recent hike with Alistair at Weeping Rock . . .

Awkwardly like one at attention Sophia stood beside her car staring straight ahead. She did not dare look around. She could hear the squawk of a police radio. She could hear the officer rummaging in the trunk, forcing something open. But only the spare tire was beneath the panel . . .

"'Soph-ia'—what's this?"

Swaggering back to stand close beside her the officer held out to show her, on the palm of his hand, several dried, part-shredded yellow leaves.

"I—I don't know. Leaves . . ."

"What kind of 'leaves'?"

"From a—tree? Something that blew into the trunk when it was open . . ."

"'Blew into the trunk when it was open'—eh?"

Were these—oak leaves? White oak? Sophia had taken botany as an undergraduate, she should have known. But this was so ridiculous! In the agitation of the moment, the uniformed man looming over her, nearly touching her, in fact brushing against her, she could not think clearly.

He was sniffing at the leaves. Crumpled the leaves in his fist to further pulverize them, and sniffed noisily. Held out his hand for Sophia to sniff, also.

"What's it smell like, Soph-ia?"

"I d-don't know . . . Nothing."

"'Nothing'—eh? That's how you'd identify this?"

"I think those are just oak leaves . . ."

"How'd they get in your trunk, again?"

"They must have blown in, from—from a tree . . ."

So frightened Sophia was stammering like a child. Brain flailing for words.

He was laughing at her. Teasing, tormenting.

He could not be serious about this—could he?

Yet, Sophia was in terror that the officer would handcuff her.

Suspicion of—narcotics? That was not implausible.

And what did police officers do next, after handcuffing?—if the suspect "resisted" he would have the right to throw her down onto the hood of her car, or onto the ground. He would have the right to overpower her, press his knee into the small of her back, make her scream with pain. She knew, she knew very well, since Whitey's death all of the McClarens knew, far more than they wished to know of the virtually unchecked behavior of local law enforcement.

(At last a car passed, slowing and then accelerating, and out of sight around a curve. Sophia had not a glimpse of who was driving, if it might be someone who lived nearby, who might recognize her, and help her.)

(But help her—how? Why? Anyone glancing at a young woman standing beside her car, a beige-uniformed police officer questioning her, would probably glance quickly away, and depart. Exactly what Sophia herself would do in such circumstances.)

Trying to calm herself. What law or laws had she violated? Was speeding on this rural stretch of Old Farm Road so serious a violation, she might be arrested? *Was* she arrested now, without realizing? Being ordered to get out of her car—was that the prelude to an arrest?

Thinking—*At least my skin is white.* She could not imagine this situation if she were a person of color, a woman of her age, alone in her vehicle on Old Farm Road, vulnerable to the white police officer.

At least too, Sophia was tastefully dressed. Her clothes were quite ordinary, and did not fit her body tightly. No ear- or face-studs, no tattoos. She'd seen the man's eyes move rudely upon her, down to her feet and up again, legs, hips, breasts, face. The expression in his face suggested that he was not so impressed, he'd seen better.

"Stay right there, 'Soph-ia.' I'll be right back."

In his mouth *Soph-ia* sounded salacious, dirty.

Very still Sophia stood beside her car. Her mouth had gone dry. She did not dare look after the swaggering man now calling in to his precinct. That static-y squawk of a radio. A sound of derisive laughter. She was feeling weak, helpless. Tears of frustration stung her eyes. And how ironic: in recent weeks she'd come to think of herself as regaining some of her strength, that had drained from her at the time of Whitey's death.

Though he'd (evidently) found nothing illegal in her car the officer was making a show of investigating the driver. Checking her ID, auto registration. Perhaps the pretense was that the vehicle might be stolen. Or, Sophia McClaren had warrants against her name. Or, "Sophia McClaren" was not the person she claimed to be but an imposter.

If he wished the officer could plant narcotics in her vehicle. In her handbag. It had become a running subject in local media, the corruption of local police departments, their intimidation of persons of color and of women, rape of juveniles taken into custody, brutality and threats of murder. The victims were almost exclusively persons of color, white-skinned citizens were rarely targeted and could not imagine what *all the fuss* was over.

She'd been surprised, Jessalyn had told her about attending a meeting of SaveOurLives. In a black church in inner-city Hammond—her mother!

Never less than once a week Sophia drove to her mother's house. She didn't feel comfortable with Jessalyn coming to see her in the rented house in Yardley where Alistair Means stayed with her when he could, in the final, melancholy stage of an acrimonious divorce.

When she was away from Alistair, Sophia was sure that she loved him. When she was with him, or rather when he was with her, distracted, not so affectionate as he'd been at the start of their relationship, she found herself thinking *I have been biding my time. Until I am stronger.*

Still, she loved him. She had never loved any man (apart from her father) so much as she'd loved Alistair Means.

He was the only person to whom Sophia had spoken of what was most crucial in her life. The only person to whom she'd confessed that her childhood, her family life, her relationship with her mother in particular had been so intense for her, so happy, it was difficult for her to adjust to an adult life.

(Even a sexual adult life. But Sophia hadn't told Alistair that.)

He'd said, she should count herself most fortunate. But maybe Sophia wasn't remembering everything of her early life.

Yes of course!—she'd readily agreed. (Sophia was a scientist: she knew just enough about the human brain to know that very little could be known, and what was "memory" was largely fictitious. But still.) But when she was feeling helpless, hopeless, her thoughts turned inexorably homeward. She could not, somehow, break the spell.

He'd laughed, slightly offended.

Tactlessly adding that he had a daughter almost Sophia's age who hadn't had much difficulty breaking the *daughter-spell* with him.

Ironic too, driving on Old Farm Road less than a half hour before, hopeful about the prospect of (at last) completing her Ph.D. and entering medical school at Cornell. She'd discussed medical school with Alistair who had not very enthusiastically recommended it for her. (Not wanting Sophia to move away, perhaps. But Cornell was less than a two-hour drive from Hammond, they could see each other as frequently as they did now.)

He wanted her to stay with him. He'd been unmoored by the divorce though he had initiated it himself. He'd been speaking wistfully of another chance, another life. Another child.

Another child! Sophia wasn't sure she'd heard this.

"Ma'am? Here."

Roughly the uniformed officer handed back Sophia's driver's license, auto registration. An air of manly-aggrieved fury radiated from him.

"Thank you, officer . . ."

"Fuck you *thank you*. Cunt."

So quickly the words lashed at her, like a whip striking her exposed skin and lifting away almost in the same gesture. Sophia was too surprised, too shocked, to react; she could not have said what she'd heard, not with certainty.

Blinking back tears she lifted her eyes to his flushed face. His skin was coarse, clay-colored. The olive-dark lenses, behind which the man's eyes glared.

Why was he so angry with her? Why did he hate her?

Had to be the lawsuit. Had to be the name *McClaren*. But, Sophia wanted to protest, her family wasn't suing *him*.

A man had died. Her father had died. The police had to be held accountable. *He* should want that, too . . .

What happened next Sophia could not clearly recall afterward. So shaken by his words she scarcely registered as the police officer seized her hand, yanked her hand down to his groin and against his groin, telling her there was a way she could "make it good"—but Sophia reacted so violently to this, with such panic, pulling frantically away from him, crying as a child might cry, desperately, helplessly, the officer stepped away in dismay, disgust: "Ma'am, shut up. Nobody's touched you, ma'am."

It was a fact, Sophia had surprised him, too. Her childlike wail, her utter loss of composure were fearful to him.

"What I could do, ma'am, is issue you a ticket. Thirty-two miles an hour in a twenty-mile-per-hour zone. Erratic driving, 'weaving.' I could issue you a ticket but what I'm going to do, ma'am, is issue you a warning."

He was red-faced, furious. But something seemed to have been decided, he did not hate her quite so much. Almost, Sophia would think afterward, he'd felt sorry for her.

"This time, ma'am. A warning."

Turning from her, with that air of manly disgust. In a daze of relief Sophia climbed back into her car.

Fumbling as she turned the keys in the ignition. A wave of faintness came over her, nausea. In the rearview mirror she saw the cruiser back away, make a U-turn in the narrow road, and swiftly depart.

She'd been spared. This time.

Shaken with fury. Yet relief. So very *tired*.

Exhaustion swept over her. This sensation of extreme fatigue, a weakness in her very bones, she recalled from the days just after Whitey died—first the shock, which includes something like disbelief, denial, and then the weariness.

Could not bring herself to drive forty minutes to Yardley where Alistair was to join her that evening. Instead, returned home. That is, the McClaren home.

Entering the house through the kitchen, the very doorway through which she'd left scarcely an hour before, with a kiss from Jessalyn and an airy goodbye *OK, Mom, love you. I'll call you.*

And there was Jessalyn startled at the sight of her, and Sophia moving into her mother's arms sobbing, she'd been so frightened, so lost control of herself and so *cowardly,* and Jessalyn said, "Sophie dear, what on earth has happened to you? Sophie, you are breaking my heart"—for Sophia could not bring herself to tell Jessalyn what had happened, the police officer, the threat, the warning; it would be too upsetting for Jessalyn, and could not possibly do any good; if Sophia told anyone, it would be Thom.

Explaining to Jessalyn that she'd been under strain lately. Hadn't wanted to worry her. Yes, it had to do with Alistair—but no, he hadn't precipitated this, it wasn't his fault, only Sophia's *fault.* She could not return to Yardley that night.

Of course, Sophia was welcome to stay with her mother. Though it was now meant to be a guest room her old room remained more or less unchanged—bookshelves crammed with her girlhood books, a scattering of college texts. She would call Alistair when he arrived in Yardley. She would explain to him that she did not think that she could remain with him . . . She would move to Ithaca. She would make the break, to medical school. She could afford the cost now, without taking out loans or asking Jessalyn for help. Or Alistair.

This call lasted some time. And after it ended, soon then the phone rang again, and it was Alistair in an agitated state wanting to talk further, and wanting to see her, and Sophia said yes, but not just then. "Not tonight. Not now. But soon." And, "I am so sorry, Alistair. Please understand."

He would understand, she knew. Eventually, it would come to seem to him, as to her, inevitable.

From the start their relationship had been asymmetrical: his strength, her weakness. And Sophia's weakness in time the greater strength, exerting its gravitational pull.

She would always love him, she told him. She would always be grateful for how he'd helped her, this past year . . .

After she hung up Jessalyn knocked at the door, very gently.

"Sophie? What has happened? Have you been talking with Alistair?"

Sophia came to her mother, to be comforted. Her face was dissolving like wet tissue.

"Are you breaking up with him, dear? What has happened?"

Breaking up sounded odd, awkward out of Jessalyn's mouth, as if she were quoting from a language not her own.

Sophia nodded yes, in such a way that indicated she didn't want to talk about it just now. Jessalyn would respect her wishes and would not question her.

Later, Sophia woke to hear voices in the corridor outside her room. Not close, at a little distance. Jessalyn's voice, and a male voice, conferring.

Was this Hugo Martinez? A comfort in this, the adult voices. Speaking about her. Concerned for *her.*

That night in the old house Sophia slept, not a dreamless sleep, but a sleep of great relief after exhaustion, and waking from time to time in the night taking solace in immediately knowing which bed this was, where she was.

The Murderous Heart

Incredible! Was this—malpractice? Foote declaring she was giving her client Lorene McClaren *the boot.*

Saying in that voice of prissy adult reasonableness, "I don't think that we can continue our sessions, Dr. McClaren. If you persist in this intensity of hostility."

Intensity of hostility. Seated across from the therapist on a sofa that appeared cushioned but was in fact haunch-hard as rawhide, Lorene leaned forward, disbelieving. This was—unfair! Unjust! Unprecedented! Unprofessional—Lorene was sure.

"Dr. Foote, this is very surprising—and very disappointing. You are being paid—very well-paid—to offer 'therapy' to persons who need your help. I—I—I don't understand, I'd thought we were making p-progress . . ."

Calmly Lorene had begun this statement yet midway her voice began to falter and crumble like shoddy caulking.

"I'd thought—I mean, isn't this the tacit promise—that, even if a patient is impossible, the therapist is obliged to tolerate her?—I mean, to continue to treat her?—as in a—a—as in a . . ." Lorene's voice trailed off weakly.

Grudgingly Foote supplied the elusive word: "'Family'—? Is that what you are trying to say, Dr. McClaren?"

"I—I'm not sure . . . Did I say 'family'? Or—I think—well, look!—you were the one, Dr. Foote. *You* said 'family.'"

Suffused with triumph like a shot of adrenaline to the heart Lorene reared to her feet and (of her own volition: not because she'd been insulted) left Foote's office.

Not slammed but forcibly shut the door.

Not coming back. No.

RIDICULOUS! *Family.*

Lorene already had a sister, thank you. In fact, two of them which was more than one too many.

Already had a *family*. One was enough.

What was Foote thinking? *Did* the therapist think, or did pseudo-clever paradoxical remarks issue from that pike mouth like robo-calls? Client utters X, therapist replies Y. There was probably an online course for therapists with columns of these rote replies.

In any case, Lorene wasn't returning to Foote. Months of therapy and money wasted. Enough.

A close call, too: What if someone in the family, nosy Beverly for instance, had found out? And, if he'd been alive to be embarrassed by his favorite daughter, Whitey.

NOT AN *ACCIDENT*, EXACTLY. *Incident.*

The blame wasn't Lorene dozing off at the wheel but weather.

Eruption of rain, heavy draperies of rain, and suddenly then hailstones tumbling, bouncing, frolicking like crazed mothballs on the hood of the Saab, reducing her visibility to scarcely the length of that hood, and then, even as she drew breath to scream, the handsome steel-colored Saab purchased with Whitey's bequest skidded out of its lane and across pavement like a loosed bumper-car in an amusement park as horns blared with murderous intent . . . *Oh Daddy! Help me.*

Covered in bruises from the God-damned air bag that had detonated in the driver's seat, aching for weeks, with a lump on her forehead and acid burns on her hands, half-choking in her effort to cough up the black phlegm that had coagulated in her lungs, she'd felt a (desperate, craven) need to see Foote twice a week: Fridays, but also Tuesdays. She'd used up her twelve insured sessions with Foote by the time of the accident—that is, *incident*—and was now, pitiable expression, *paying out of pocket.*

Paying by check, $215 per session, to this person who called herself *M. L. Foote, PsyD.*

(And Foote was cashing the checks, too. Lorene, who had a minor obsession about balancing her bank accounts precisely, keeping records both online and on paper, saw how the therapist never failed to endorse those checks!)

Would've walked away from this ridiculous charade months ago. Except—somehow—if but inadvertently—Foote did manage to say, or to suggest, or to prod Lorene into thinking, enough sensible things each session to make the therapy seem, if not worthwhile, the only alternative to what Lorene had come to think of as the *quagmire of her life.*

Well, she hadn't managed to kill herself on the Hennicott Expressway, at least. These close calls would be a secret from the rest of the McClarens, too.

Oh but her poor, plucked head—one of those meek hen's heads from which other hens have pecked all her feathers preparatory to pecking her to death! So ashamed.

The *trichotillomania* had not cleared up, despite Foote. For a while it had seemed to be getting less severe, less compulsive, and she and Foote had been (naively) optimistic, but then Mark Svenson had behaved so astonishingly badly, at about the time of the accident, which had been at about the time of North Hammond's revised-lowered ranking in New York State, and shortly after the first anniversary of Whitey's hospitalization, that Lorene had succumbed anew to her affliction though the hairs on her head were now so piteously short, and so sparse, and her fingernails so bitten, it was difficult to get hold, to yank.

Add to this, bleeding cuticles. Grinding molars in the night that left her jaws aching by day. Chronic constipation of both bowels and brain! Couldn't Foote see, her client was approaching a *crisis*?

Personal, professional. Spiritual.

Foote could not kick her out now! Abandon her now!

AFTER WEEKS OF HESITATION, DENIAL, she'd told the therapist in excruciating detail of Mark Svenson's deceit. She'd told Foote about the shameless slut Rabineau. Loyals vs. rebels. Friends vs. foes. How she lay in bed grinding her back teeth tallying up sides, furious and exhausted. Could not trust anyone! Young ingrates in their twenties whom Principal McClaren had hired now slandering her behind her back, siding with senior-faculty adversaries, posting cruel innuendos and insults on the Internet.

Tried to explain to Foote: she could no longer trust anyone at North Hammond. Once it had been a nasty little knot of students who'd opposed her authority (*She-Gestapo*—felt like nostalgia now)—now it was many in the faculty, a honeycomb of rot.

Recording her on their iPhones. Surreptitiously taking (unflattering) pictures to be posted online.

Could not bring herself to contemplate the filthy and actionable things said of her. It was hell, a living hell. It was *a parallel universe,* the Internet. And it never went away.

All this, she had to make Foote realize. Desperate to make Foote realize.

Wisps of hair, with bloody roots, sent in an envelope to Foote with an advance check for December. *Look Foote what you made me do.*

Except she'd typed wrongly: *Look what we made me do.*

AS SHE'D THOUGHT, FOOTE AGREED to take her back. Of course!

"We will think of it as probationary, Dr. McClaren. But you *must not bring hostility into our sessions.*"

AND THEN, STUNNING NEWS. Full-time North Hammond faculty dared to stage a rebellion: met in secret, after-hours, off-campus, to cast a *vote of no confidence* in their principal.

The results were emailed to Lorene in so cunning a way, through an anonymous server, she received the news with no warning, seated at 6:00 A.M. at her home computer about to scroll through the schedule of her upcoming day.

Dear Dr. McClaren. We, the full-time faculty of North Hammond High School, have not felt free to express our dissatisfaction with the several repressive, undemocratic, and unprogressive decisions you have forced upon us in recent months. Therefore, we have felt ourselves forced to . . .

What? What? *What?* Lorene stared in disbelief. Skimmed the lengthy document, began to reread, then in a fury deleted the entire thing, an obscenity flung into TRASH.

EXPLAINING TO FOOTE WHY her eyes leaked tears though she was not crying.

She knew, she told Foote, that Mark Svenson was one of those behind this collective stab in the back. Young ingrate spreading lies about her, slandering her, the very person who'd advanced his career.

First, he'd come often to see Lorene in her office on the pretext of having a question for her, an idea for his classroom. Shamelessly he'd fawned, flirted, offered to drive her to a professional conference in Albany. Next, hearing of a trip Lorene was, at that time, only just considering, he'd strongly hinted that he would like to travel with her to Bali. He could "help carry luggage"—he'd said. Then later, when he'd become involved with the slut Rabineau, and the two of them were sneaking into empty classrooms and closets to have sex, he'd pretended that he hadn't led Lorene on, there'd been a "misunderstanding" between them.

Too-literal-minded Foote interrupted to ask: Had Lorene begun to book for the trip? Bought plane tickets yet?

No! With a savage grimace Lorene indicated to the therapist that that wasn't the point she was making. The point was *betrayal.*

Also, *age.*

Like a flashing comet Lorene's (thirty-fifth) birthday had come and gone. No one had remembered it (except her mother, which was sweet of Jessalyn, but tedious) and already she was plunging into her thirty-sixth year. Beyond that, forty. Beyond that, the grave.

At this, Foote, on the farther side of whatever murky hinterland lay between late forties and early sixties, frowned.

Good! Any reaction at all was good, in zombie-face.

But Foote ruined the moment by asking, in that faux-reasonable way of hers that so provoked Lorene: "Aren't you exaggerating all this, Lorene?—I mean, Dr. McClaren. Forty is hardly so very proximate to the *grave*."

Patiently Lorene tried to explain: age was not the subject, like booking tickets for Bali. The crisis in her life—that was the subject.

She'd come to think that it was related to the fall/winter season. Pitiless shortening of each day's light. Summertime she'd been fine—more or less. But as dread October melted into murky November and next was the promise of December like an eyedropper of anthrax in a woodland spring, the winter solstice and the shortest day of the year.

"Dr. Foote, I am afraid that—that—d'you know that little black dog of Goya, that's about to slip over the edge of the world?—*that is me, in the dark winter.* I'm so afraid."

Foote seemed contrite, to see her obstinate client so humbled.

Pushed a box of tissues in Lorene's direction, tactfully averting her eyes as Lorene wept noisily into a Kleenex.

THIS NEW COMPULSION, OH DAMN!—grinding her molars in the night in her bed until her jaws ached with fatigue as if she'd been berating her ungrateful faculty in some dank subterranean place throbbing with furnace heat. And there came a hand to touch her cheek, to console.

Daddy?

Yes, Lorene-y. But you have got to stop, you know.

Stop what, Daddy? Tell me.

Your murderous heart.

FOOTE HAD ADVISED HER to write down her dreams, at least fragments of dreams, that made an impression on her.

Fuck Foote! Who had time for such garbage?—Lorene was livid to think the woman imagined her so idle, so replete with time to squander, she could sit on the edge of her bed like a bourgeois neurotic in a Woody Allen film jotting down "dream-fragments" of no more significance or value than puff-balls of dust under a bed. So she hadn't. Hadn't had time. Until now.

Murderous heart.

Oh, what did Whitey mean?

"**DR. McCLAREN?** Call from Dr. Langley."

Not good news. Notably, Iris averted her eyes.

Summoned to meet with the superintendent of Hammond public schools all the way downtown at the Schools Building.

Not like the first time Lorene had been so summoned, a celebratory mood when she'd learned of her promotion. *Lorene, this is coming a few years early. But not, we think, prematurely.*

God-damned *no-confidence vote.* Must be it.

Defiant en route to the meeting but, in person, seeing the expression of disappointment, concern, something like pity in the man's face as he registered the knitted cap on her head, suddenly tearful, apologetic.

No! She had absolutely no idea why her faculty had voted against her in such a blind self-destructive way.

It was not encouraging, Langley had a folder opened before him on his desktop at which he glanced frowning. Quite a stack of papers there. Had those treacherous sons of bitches provided him with a transcript of their illicit meeting? Had they given him statements, depositions? Nor was it encouraging, an attorney for the public schools was also present. Lorene scarcely glanced at this person, and forgot his name at once.

Questions were asked of Lorene. Words were exchanged. Though she'd broken out in an actual cold sweat—(why did life so frequently, so stupidly, confirm every cliché?)—she was thinking she'd defended herself impressively, convincingly.

What a shock then, low blow to the gut, when Langley said it might be "politic" if Lorene took a leave of absence from North Hammond—"Effective immediately."

Effective immediately. So stunned, Lorene felt the floor tilt beneath her feet.

Grudgingly then seeing the look in her face Langley amended, "Well. A leave of absence in the spring term?"

Leave of absence. Sliver of ice in the heart.

With as much dignity as she could summon Lorene stammered it would be devastating to her—"Everyone would know."

"Know what, Lorene? A half-year off, after you've been working so hard, would not be so unusual."

"I think it would be viewed as a punishment, Dr. Langley." Lorene paused, swallowing. "A humiliation."

"'Viewed'—by whom?"

"My faculty. My staff."

"Why do you care what they think, Lorene? You've indicated your contempt for them."

"I—I have? My contempt?"

"Certainly. It's written all over your face."

Written all over your face. Another crude, clumsy cliché. Lorene did indeed feel contempt now, for this fat-faced apparatchik who'd once been her friend and supporter but was now abandoning her.

"You don't take much care to disguise your contempt, 'Dr. McClaren.' We can see."

We. Was this the royal *we*?

"In fact you seem to be smirking at me, 'Dr. McClaren.' Is something wrong? Do you find this discussion disagreeable?"

Smirking. But Lorene was not!

Trying to explain to him, and to the rudely staring attorney, that if she took a leave of absence so soon, before one was scheduled for her to take, it would seem obvious that she was being punished. Her faculty had voted "no confidence" in her out of spite because she insisted upon excellence, unlike her predecessor.

"But numerous 'excellent' teachers signed the letter. How would you explain that?"

"Collusion with the others. Jealousy, spite."

"But you've seen their list of grievances? Some of these are quite convincing."

Lorene had not seen the list of grievances. She had deleted the lengthy email after a few lines.

"Out of one hundred nine teachers at North Hammond, ninety-four signed this letter to me, and seven wished to indicate that they were 'abstaining.'"

Eight teachers were supporting her! She would learn their names, they'd become precious to her and she would never forget them.

Stiffly she said: "They want me transferred to another school. That's their agenda."

"Would you consent to a transfer, Lorene? Would you prefer that to a leave of absence?"

"No! North Hammond is the outstanding high school in the county, because of my efforts. I refuse to be driven away."

"A transfer might be in everyone's interests. There will be an opening for an assistant principal at Yardley High School next fall. I think you would be ideal."

Assistant principal. A demotion. Lorene did indeed feel the floor tilt beneath her feet.

Soon then, the meeting ended. Lorene had much more to say but could not draw breath to speak and found herself, panting, on the verge of hyperventilating, in the corridor outside Langley's office.

And that man had been a friend of Whitey's, in the old days! God damn, she would never forgive him.

FINGERS NUMB, could hardly locate hairs to pluck inside the pathetic skullcap.

Cement in her guts shifting to scalding-hot lava demanding to be evacuated. At once.

PANICKED CALLING FOOTE IN THE NIGHT. Knowing the therapist wouldn't answer her phone yet had to call for she'd been wakened from sleep by Whitey touching her face another time, sternly rebuking her *murderous heart*.

Emergency session with Foote scheduled just a few hours later. The therapist seemed now to be regarding her difficult client with concerned eyes.

Worried that Lorene might commit suicide? Worried that it might reflect upon *her*?

". . . not normal. These dreams in which Daddy appears. It just isn't like him. If you knew him—you'd know. *It is not*." Pause.

". . . once said, 'Forgiveness is beside the point. Anyone you've hurt will never forgive *you*.' But now Daddy seems to be feeling differently. Now—Daddy seems to be chiding me." Pause.

". . . not jealous, Doctor. Not a jealous bone in my body. If Mark Svenson and that woman have no more dignity than to make themselves an object of lurid gossip, that's their concern." Pause.

". . . worried about my mother, though. Since my father's death she has become emotionally fragile. She has a 'man friend'—(I know, I've told you about this 'Hugo,' Doctor—he doesn't go away)—who coerces her into doing things she'd never have done when Daddy was alive. This awful man has actually braided her hair! She looks like an Indian squaw half her age. She never wears nice clothes any longer, only jeans and sweaters and 'native costumes' when they go out—to 'art' movies. Daddy *hated* 'art' movies. This Hugo reputedly makes Mom go on hikes with him. They were seen in Pierpont Park, and at Weeping Rock. He has taken her to a sports store and made her buy hiking boots. My mother! —*hiking boots*. Mom made a pathetic joke of it, telling me how her friend forces her to lace up her own boots, which requires some skill, and he only helps her if she becomes hopelessly confused. Sometimes they even hike in the rain! Hugo has taken her out in our canoe, on the lake near our house. *Our mother has always been scared to death of boats.* He thinks it's 'good for Jessalyn' to drive a car when they're together. *Daddy never let Mom or anyone else drive any car he was in.* To Daddy, Mom was like a princess, or an invalid. It was a kind of foot-binding, I suppose. Their marriage. Not for me, but some women prefer such relationships. As there are women who support female genital mutilation." Pause.

(Lorene was breathing quickly, incensed. Not certain if she was incensed by Hugo Martinez's hold over their mother or by foot-binding, about which she knew just enough to be appalled and contemptuous at females who let themselves be so mutilated.)

(Glancing over at Foote who was looking grim. Most women at the thought of female genital mutilation feel nauseated or faintness but zombie-Foote seemed to be taking this in stride.)

". . . definitely, Mom isn't herself. Daddy would scarcely recognize her. He'd have made her color her hair—he wouldn't have wanted a wife who looked her age. He'd be just sickened by this Hugo—looking like Che Guevara. *Daddy hated Communists.* If we were a Mafia family we'd know what to do. We wouldn't be wringing our hands and sniveling. My brother Thom was supposed to talk to Hugo, put pressure on him, offer him money to go away but seems like Thom has lost interest, he's obsessed with this futile lawsuit . . ." Pause.

(Had Lorene told Foote about the lawsuit against the Hammond PD? Maybe not. Maybe now wasn't the time. Lorene's therapy was supposed to be focused on *her.*)

". . . nightmare since Daddy died. Nothing has been right. The family is broken into pieces like the big bang—flying away from one another at the speed of light. Now 'Hugo' is in our lives trying to marry our mother and take her from us. He's always traveling to places like China, India, Africa, something terrible could happen to her there and

Hugo would inherit half the property if they are married—that's the law in New York State. Well, good luck to 'Hugo' budging our mother from that house!" Pause.

". . . not jealous, Doctor. Why are you looking at me like that?"

THERE CAME A SHIMMERING PRESENCE she'd been given to believe would be Langley, the schools' superintendent who'd had a change of mind, and had totally reinstated her; yet, when she could see his face more clearly, it was Whitey.

Want to help you, Lorene-y. All the time in the world to help you now. I regret I didn't see where you were headed while I was—well, you know, alive.

You were not a mean-spirited little girl. I don't think so. There was a wrong turn, maybe I was to blame. I remember your mother gripping my hands one day, you couldn't have been more than eleven years old, and Jessalyn was trying not to cry saying Whitey, I have a bad feeling about our middle daughter. I think something has gone very wrong.

So I think, dear, it is time for your murderous heart to—stop . . .

HER FATHER WANTED HER TO DIE.

Her father wanted her to come to him, to join him—in this way Lorene (whom he'd loved most) would be the first, of the McClaren children.

By the cobwebbed logic of night this seemed self-evident. By day, light hurting her eyes, as if she were a moist-white mollusk shivering inside a shell, and that shell pried open to let in a knife-blade of light, it did not seem so self-evident.

"Dr. Foote? I n-need to speak with you." (When had she begun *stammering*? All so ridiculous.) "I—I—I am becoming afraid of—what might happen . . ."

Soon after this frantic call at seven o'clock in the morning, in Foote's office, shoehorned into a slot between two other clients (whose faces Lorene would resolutely not-see when she arrived and departed, in the hope that they would tactfully not-see hers), Lorene found herself speaking to the therapist in a way that might be called *pleading* though (Lorene was sure) she had never *pleaded* with anyone in her life.

Really, she didn't want to kill herself, she explained to the stiff-faced therapist. No! Really, not! Yet, she understood that it might be better if she did.

And why was that?—Foote inquired.

Because her father had rebuked her. Because her father was disappointed in her. Because her father did not, it seemed, approve of her life any longer, as he'd once had.

And Lorene believed that her "father" in the dream was—actually—in some way—her *father*?—politely Foote inquired as if in the presence, not of a deranged person, but a fully rational person who in her professional life was the youngest-ever principal at North Hammond High School.

Well, no. But, well—yes . . . I—I—think so . . .

Fingers of Lorene's right hand creeping surreptitiously up inside the snug-fitting knit cap until a stern look from Foote put an abrupt stop to the creeping.

No. Not here. *Do not touch your head, face, fingernails. Do not scratch any itch. Breathe, and remain calm.*

Behind her desk Foote was sitting with hands clasped over a small hard drum of a belly like a Buddha in mohair vest-sweater, white linen shirt, corduroy trousers. Some sort of Jungian horn-amulet around her neck on a black leather thong. M. L. Foote's face was long and horsey and grave and yet (Lorene saw for the first time) not an unattractive face; and her hair (Lorene also saw for the first time) was clipped nearly as short as Lorene's hair had once been in the prime of her life only a year or two ago, like new-mown hay, the hue of scorch laced with white.

Foote was saying that she did not customarily speak in a dogmatic way to clients. Or to anyone, in fact. She did not preach, sermonize, or moralize. But she believed that she could "solve" Lorene's problem in this way: "You can redeem your 'murderous heart' by acting as if you are a good, kind, generous person, Dr. McClaren. You don't have to be that person to behave in a way your father might have approved. He is instructing you to give up a way of living, not to give up your life."

Lorene was struck by these words. Unspeakably banal, trite, maudlin, even silly. And yet—to her, thrilling as a door flung open showing the way out of an airless and suffocating interior.

"But, Doctor—"

"No. Don't say a word. Words are not good for people like you, Dr. McClaren. Just *do*."

"'Do'—what?"

"You will know. *Go*."

Though the hour was not quite over Foote gestured for Lorene to depart.

— ∞ —

Now then, shivering with excitement and apprehension, fired by the wisdom of Buddhist-Foote, the first hour of the remainder of Lorene's life:

Mark,

It is not easy to write this. I am very sorry that I have behaved as I did these past months. I cannot explain except (perhaps) a kind of sickness of the soul came over me.

I will write to Audrey Rabineau to apologize to her as well. I know, I have caused you both distress and I wish to make amends. Your friendship is none of my concern of course except now I would like to reiterate that I wish you well and not ill.

I will write strong evaluations of you both for the academic year and I will write strong letters of recommendation for you if you wish to transfer to another school as I hope you will not feel you would wish to do. Your performances here at North Hammond have been outstanding.

It is possible that I will be the one to transfer to another school in the district. I do apologize for my unprofessional behavior.

I do not blame you if you don't feel comfortable here and I do not blame you if you cannot find it in your heart to accept this apology or even believe it as I have difficulty (in rereading) believing it myself!

However, it is sincere.

Very best wishes,
Lorene McClaren, Ph.D.

Dr. Langley—

I am very sorry to have put you in an awkward position these past several months. After your early support of my career it is particularly disappointing to you, I realize. My professional behavior has been a kind of sickness for which I am being treated at present by an excellent therapist who has very positive hopes for my recovery.

Though I am surprised at the depth (and breadth) of hostility expressed toward me by my faculty, I am not surprised (I suppose) that there is hostility, and that it has been expressed in such a way.

Accordingly, I am willing to accept your proposal of a leave of absence and/or a transfer to another school district. I understand the (unspoken) wish that I resign my position at North Hammond and I will not oppose this if I am correct in this supposition.

I am writing to my faculty today as well to express apologies for my behavior and a plea for forgiveness if not for understanding, for it is hard to understand such behavior which (I concede) I would not understand or perhaps forgive in another!

I would not claim it is a result of my dear father's death but perhaps it was precipitated by that loss. I believe that Whitey would concur in my apologies and he would wish perhaps that I make amends by doing something constructive for my school like (for instance) endowing a scholarship for an economically disadvantaged student.

But <u>I am sorry</u> in any case for there can be no excuse for murderousness of heart and for those whom I have hurt.

Sincerely,
Lorene McClaren, Ph.D.
Principal, North Hammond High School

Dear Mom—

I have behaved very badly toward you these past months. I am sickened to think how I misjudged your friend without knowing him and so misjudged you. I can't explain, it is something that happened to me like black bile rising in my mouth.

It is not my business or anyone's business how you live your life and with whom. You are a brave woman, I love you (though I guess I can acknowledge that I don't really know you!) and hope you will forgive me. I am not a good daughter even to Daddy who would be ashamed of me now.

It is almost too late now, I think. But I am trying. I hope to be a loving part of your (new) life and your happiness with Hugo if that is possible.

Love
Your daughter Lorene

DETERMINED TO MAKE AMENDS! Very excited now.

Checking in with Foote every hour: *Yes. You can do it, Lorene. Have faith.*

Long-delayed physical checkup. Cardiologist. Running panting on treadmill. Thought/half-hoped the murderous heart would burst. Then EKG lying flat in refrigerated room in white paper gown, electrodes taped to bony-flat chest.

Oh Daddy! I am so ashamed.

Oh Daddy! I wanted you to be proud of me.

She would endow not one scholarship in his name but two. Three!

All that money, she'd intended to spend selfishly on herself.

John Earle McClaren Scholarship Fund. North Hammond High.

Thought of making amends for last year's seniors whose college applications she'd sabotaged and for other hard-core student-enemies she'd revenged herself upon over the years but no, maybe not.

Doing good while not *being good* had its statute of limitations.

"Dr. McClaren—you have a slight heart murmur. But you've always had this, yes?"

Did she? Had she? For years Lorene had been avoiding doctors especially gynecologist, cardiologist.

No pelvic exam for her! No Pap smear, mammogram. No thank you.

Likewise, no cardiologist. Better not to know.

Yes maybe . . . Maybe she did recall—*heart murmur.*

Examined in this office years ago when she'd been college-age, by another cardiologist, now retired. On bitter-cold windy days she'd had attacks of breathlessness on the hilly campus at Binghamton, rapid heartbeat, fainting. Wanting to tell no one. A physical weakness of which she did not wish to speak even to her parents. Even to Jessalyn.

". . . not an abnormal heart condition, only just a 'murmur' . . . Otherwise you are . . ."

Oh. She *was*?

Icy fingertips. Fatuous smile. Sudden twitch in right eye and moisture flooding both eyes.

Had not expected this news, evidently. Had expected very different news.

"Thank you, Doctor. That—that is good to hear . . ."

Shaking hands with Dr. Yi in parting. The cardiologist knew that Lorene was a high school principal, may have been impressed. In the ordinary course of her life in Hammond, many were. Quizzically Yi glanced at the knitted cap on Lorene's head as possibly he'd noticed her lashless eyes and bitten-down nails but was not about to inquire. Asian tact.

In her car in the parking lot immediately called Foote on her cell phone. Good news to share—*I guess I will live for a while yet, Doctor!*

This dark wintry snow-dusted day she returned home and discovered, on a windowsill in her study, a line of hairs.

In all, twenty-one hairs. Short, stubby. Unmistakably her own.

Oh God. Who'd put them there? And what did it mean?

RETURNED TO FOOTE FOR THE final time.

At least, Lorene wanted to believe it would be the final time.

Thanking Foote for "all you've done for me." And Foote grimacing in a kind of abashed smile.

She'd brought a bottle of wine, Lorene said. To celebrate.

Celebrate?—Foote was looking skeptical.

She'd solved the problem of her life, Lorene said. Like a knotty Zen koan. Or rather, Dr. Foote had solved it for her.

"My father would have wanted me to be a good person, and do good things; though I can't actually be a 'good' person, I can do 'good things.' And I have."

Endowed college scholarships, and (possibly) an endowed sabbatical leave for a teacher at North Hammond—what wonderful ideas, everyone was saying, you could see that they were impressed with Lorene's sudden generosity if surprised. Best of all, these endowments would be in the name of John Earle McClaren.

"Daddy would have liked that. He wasn't a vain man but he didn't believe in false modesty."

Foote agreed, these were very generous decisions to have made. It is always better to err on the side of generosity than not.

Lorene caught the qualification: *err.* No idea what that meant.

"Maybe I'll add the NAACP. That's a good cause."

Foote agreed, the NAACP was a very good cause indeed. But Lorene should realize, she was not making out her will.

Making out my will. I am not.

There came an awkward pause. Lorene could not remember what she'd been telling the therapist, that had raised her to such heights. A high-bobbing glittering fountain, now beginning to ebb.

"This doesn't need to be our last session, Dr. McClaren. I seem to think that you are thinking so, but I am not clear why."

Because—because I am cured. That's why!

There was another awkward pause. Lorene was feeling a powerful sensation of grief.

Foote saw, or seemed to see. Discreetly changing the subject: "What about your trip to Bali, Dr. McClaren? Are you leaving soon?"

"N-No. I am not."

"You've changed your plans?"

"I never exactly had plans. It was all—speculation." Lorene paused, smirking. "Fantasy." Pause again, rubbing roughly at her nose with the edge of her hand. "Please call me 'Lorene,' Dr. Foote. I wish you would."

"Well—'Lorene.' And you can call me 'Mildred' if you wish."

"'Mildred.'" Lorene spoke wonderingly, uncertainly.

M. L. Foote. Mildred. So that had been it, all along.

"Where had you considered traveling, Lorene?"

"Apart from Bali, probably Bora-Bora. Indonesia. Possibly Thailand." Her eyes filled with tears.

All seemed so far-fetched now. Vain, futile. No one to accompany her not even her widowed mother. (Lorene had returned to Jessalyn, to plead with her mother to come with her. She'd been certain that, seeing Lorene's desperation, Jessalyn would give in, as she nearly always did with her children's requests, but no. Jessalyn had smiled apologetically, and kissed her, and said *Lorene, I'm sorry. I just can't.*)

"You weren't planning to travel with anyone, I think you'd said, Lorene?"

"No. I didn't *say*. I—I hadn't gotten that far in planning."

There was a pause. Foote smiled, just barely.

Around her neck the therapist was wearing the Jungian-looking amulet on a leather thong. A stone-colored cable-knit cardigan over a white linen shirt with long tight-buttoned sleeves. Black corduroy trousers. On a big-knuckled hand she turned a large dull-silver ring with an opal stone.

"I don't like to travel with groups, myself. No cruises."

"No! No cruises."

"But alone is, well—often too solitary."

"Yes. Alone is—too solitary."

"Well." Foote paused, turning the opal ring around her finger. "I could join you, Lorene. I suppose. For part of the way, at least."

"J-Join me?"

"For part of the way. Depending on your schedule. Usually I take three weeks off at Christmas, and that part of the Pacific has always intrigued me."

Just enough of an edge to Foote's voice signaling to Lorene that, willful as Lorene was, domineering, bossy, and difficult, Mildred Foote was all of these, and more.

"Three weeks is—good for me, too. Thank you." Lorene heard an odd girlish voice issuing from her throat.

"No *thank you* is required, Lorene. No one is doing anyone favors." Foote smiled, barely.

Out of her deep leather bag Lorene brought the bottle of wine to set on Foote's desk. The last of Whitey's bottles. From the cellar of the old house, not entirely clean of cobwebs and smelling of damp, grit, stone, dust.

Red wine, that didn't require cooling. And a corkscrew too, if Foote didn't have one in her office.

Justice

Almost shamefully, reluctantly she confessed to him: I was threatened, I think.

Not sure. Could not prove it.

What I'm going to do, issue you a warning.

On Old Farm Road it had happened. A lone police officer in a vehicle she'd thought might have been unmarked. Later she would wonder if he'd been off-duty, a Hammond police officer out of his jurisdiction in North Hammond but the man had certainly been in uniform, a beige uniform, wearing a badge and speaking in the bullying voice of law enforcement.

Gliding up close behind her car. Suddenly she'd seen him in the rearview mirror. Panicked that his vehicle would strike hers and force her off the road.

Happened so quickly, couldn't think. Her reaction was to press down on the gas pedal to get away from him but then she was "speeding"—thirty-two miles an hour in a twenty-mile zone.

So, he stopped her. Put on the siren, pulled her over. Looked as if he was going to give her a ticket, at first.

She'd also been "weaving"—"driving erratically"—he'd claimed. She was sure that this wasn't true but how could she prove it?

Alone in her car. No one to witness.

If a man is angry, a woman feels she must be to blame.

If a uniformed man, guilty.

Confessing to her older brother Thom whom she'd idolized through childhood: Didn't know if I should tell you. How you would react. If maybe I'd imagined it, some of it. I mean, that he'd threatened me. Issued a "warning"—knowing who I was.

Whitey McClaren's daughter. Thom McClaren's sister.

She'd played and replayed the encounter in her head. Was it the lawsuit? Had the police officer recognized the name on her driver's license? Or had he been waiting by the house to follow her, guessing she would be a McClaren?

The way he looked at me—the way he spoke to me. How angry he was and how that—really scared me . . .

Thinking then, maybe it hadn't been deliberate but just chance.

Maybe this was the way he got his quota of issuing tickets, driving up close behind people who looked vulnerable, for instance women, women driving alone, to goad them into speeding so he could stop them . . .

Possibly he wouldn't have done it, dared to do it, if the driver had been male, or someone else had been in the car . . .

Sophia was normally so soft-spoken and unassertive, so rarely emotional, it was crucial that Thom not be impatient with her, and not interrupt.

He had no doubt, Sophia hadn't been stopped by chance on Old Farm Road. Thom had been followed by police cruisers since his lawyer had first filed the lawsuit, at least a dozen times he'd seen Hammond PD vehicles gliding up close behind him at fifty-five miles an hour on the Expressway but he'd held his ground, had not panicked and had not been goaded into speeding up or driving "erratically."

Fuckers. Bastards. He'd have liked to murder them with his bare hands and they knew it.

A matter of time, he'd supposed. Before they harassed him more forcibly as they'd done Azim Murthy.

But Thom McClaren was tougher than the Indian doctor. The tactics they'd used against Murthy would not work against Thom.

Had she told anyone else?—Thom asked.

No. Not anyone.

Not her friend Alistair. Not Virgil. Especially, Sophia didn't want to frighten their mother.

Good, Thom said. No point in frightening Jessalyn.

Now she was afraid of driving on Old Farm Road, Sophia said. At least, driving alone.

Thom asked, Did he say or do anything else to you?

N-No.

You're sure? Nothing more than the warning?

No. I mean yes. I'm sure . . .

Eyes averted, and that look of shame. Thom could not bear to interrogate his sister further.

Had to have been something sexually threatening in such an encounter. But—how to prove? Even if the bastard had dared to touch her, her word against his.

Eleven years between Thom and Sophia, Thom was of another, older generation. He'd felt protective of his youngest sister—his "baby sister"—but scarcely knew her. Virtually never alone with her, or with Virgil. That was the way of growing up in a large family.

Siblings form alliances with one another that are both permanent and shifting. Disagreements, disappointments, feuds, temporary and expedient bonds, shared resentments—over all Thom had been the sibling with whom the others had most often wished to align themselves. But he and Sophia had never bonded even temporarily. That had never happened. And now, Sophia did not seem quite comfortable with him as if she suspected (wrongly) that he was judging her.

So, after their conversation, that evening Thom called Sophia to ask her a few more questions about the encounter with the police officer. More calmly then they spoke, and Sophia told him about her intention to go to medical school (Cornell) and her breakup with Alistair Means whom Thom had met only once and had not seemed to much like (perhaps because Means was older than Thom by several years) though he'd been impressed by the man's professional reputation. Thom didn't know how to react to this news except with a murmured expression of sympathy. (Brooke would have known. Women know when to sympathize and when to say *Good for you!*)

Sophia was saying she was afraid for Jessalyn, out there on Old Farm Road. Jessalyn's friend Hugo was with her some of the time but not all of the time for (Sophia gathered) Hugo Martinez led a busy life and was often traveling and many days Jessalyn was alone and might be driving her car alone and what happened to Sophia might happen to her or worse yet, a vindictive cop might run her off the road.

Sophia was speaking now rapidly, nervously. Thom assured her, he would protect Jessalyn, and he would protect her.

But how?—Sophia asked.

Thom assured his sister, Trust me.

CALLED THE NEW LAWYER (whose name was Edelstein) and told him that "after due consideration and discussion among the McClarens" he was dropping the lawsuit.

What? Why?—Edelstein asked, astonished.

Because he was afraid for his sister who'd been harassed by a Hammond cop. Because he was afraid for his mother. For his family.

Not for himself, he wasn't afraid. Fucking police didn't scare *him.*

But for his family, which included children as well as their mother Jessalyn who lived alone on Old Farm Road and who was sixty-one years old and vulnerable to intimidation, harassment, threats. The lawsuit wasn't worth the risk.

Thom spoke flatly, bitterly. A fact was a fact. The bastards had won, Whitey had lost.

Edelstein was confounded. The McClaren family (i.e., Thom McClaren) had initially filed criminal charges against the Hammond Police Department but this move had come to nothing for their sole witness had refused to cooperate and so, following the advice of Thom's previous attorney, they'd decided to file a civil suit where the likelihood of a decision in their favor was much higher. In itself this had been an admission of defeat, Thom believed. Yet not total defeat. Not yet!

In their relationship of just a few months it had been Edelstein who'd warned Thom that the civil case was "winnable" but could drag on for years and never be resolved as Thom wanted. City of Hammond attorneys would postpone and procrastinate and lose documents and at last offer a (low, insultingly inadequate) cash settlement but no public apology or disciplinary measures against the defendants Schultz and Gleeson; he had warned Thom, and had not even needed to suggest how much this was costing Thom (who was paying the legal fees himself), and yet Thom had insisted upon continuing, persevering. He wouldn't give the bastards the satisfaction of quitting, Thom said. Liked to think that Schultz and Gleeson were at least preoccupied by the lawsuit, might fantasize being found guilty of manslaughter, malfeasance of duty, misconduct, their faces blazoned in the media as corrupt cops even as John Earle McClaren's face was highlighted as a former Hammond civic leader who'd been a victim of police brutality.

These months, Thom had insisted. And now, Thom had changed his mind.

Repeating, he couldn't risk it. Once the police were your enemies it was finished. If you won, you lost. Eventually.

Thom told Edelstein how in the rearview mirror of any vehicle he drove there was often a close-trailing police cruiser. Or could be an unmarked police vehicle. You never knew, and you could not know. Of hundreds of local police officers there might be a small cadre of less than a dozen out to get you. *A few bad apples* was the preferred metaphor. But it required only a very few, only one or two, to precipitate disaster.

Many times Thom had wanted to pull his vehicle onto the side of the Expressway and to engage with whoever was following him. He'd wanted to confront the enemy. His heart beat hard in fury. But he knew better than to fall into the trap of playing their game, daring to defy armed officers who were trained in beatings and choke holds, overpowering their adversaries within seconds. He would win in the courtroom, Thom believed. If he persevered.

In fact, interest in Thom McClaren waxed, waned. The Hammond PD had other enemies and these included recently disruptive black activists and a few leftist politicians. They had become police targets, more consistently than the McClarens.

Edelstein was asking Thom if Hammond cops had openly threatened his sister and Thom said, Openly? How openly d'you want? The bastard didn't shove a gun in her face. No.

Only one cop. Might've been a Hammond cop out of his jurisdiction.

For all Thom knew, the cop who'd given his sister a "warning" could have been Gleeson or Schultz. Could have been a relative of either man. Generations of cop families in the Hammond PD, that protected one another's backs and never but never informed on one another.

Yes, Thom had spoken with the Hammond chief of police. He'd spoken with the Hammond mayor. He'd spoken with city politicians. These men and their cohorts were respectful to Thom and respectful of Whitey's memory and clearly troubled by what had happened to Whitey but they were not in positions to antagonize the powerful police union that was a perpetual adversary when contracts were negotiated. Threat of a police strike kept city officials in line.

Edelstein advised, wait a few weeks. There might be a development. Thom?

Wait a few weeks. Thom considered.

Then, OK. Three weeks I will wait. And if anybody gets killed you're the one who gets sued.

Jesus, Thom! What a—

Thom broke the connection. No need to hear the startled lawyer chide—*What a thing to say.*

AFTER A FEW DRINKS at the Holland Street bar near the riverfront where no one knew him he called Jessalyn on his cell phone to tell her it was over.

At first Jessalyn hadn't seemed to know what Thom meant. Or had not heard him clearly amid the noise at the bar.

Over—?

Suing the police department. The city. You know—for what they did to Dad.

Do you mean—they've offered a settlement? Or—

No. I mean *over.*

There was a pause. Hesitantly Jessalyn said, Well, Thom. Maybe it's for the best . . .

For the best. He'd steeled himself to hear these words in his mother's hesitant voice.

Not sure, Mom. Maybe there's no *best.*

Thom?—I can't hear you . . .

Nothing, Mom. It's OK.

Where are you, dear?

I am not your dear. I am no one's dear. No.

Must've sounded to Jessalyn in the stillness of the house on Old Farm Road like a convivial and festive scene here, in a bar perhaps, predominantly male voices, laughter. A place in which words were slurred, muffled, not-heard and soon forgotten.

Easy for Thom to lie to Jessalyn who would believe virtually anything her children told her: Not sure where I am, Mom. Someplace I dropped into on the way home.

PLEASURABLE TO THOM, if strange and disorienting—he had no actual *home.*

No one to whom he could explain this unexpected pleasure, and no one to whom he wished to explain.

Fact is: a man who sleeps alone is a man who needs no one. The most elemental truth, Thom was beginning only now to appreciate in his thirty-ninth year.

How bizarre it seemed to him, willingly he'd surrendered his freedom, his privacy, his very identity to a wife, and then to children, for so many years. The wife had wanted him to be a better person than he was. For too long, he'd wanted that too.

Sex he might find elsewhere, and not in his bed that was *his*.

Not in his apartment he'd rented, that was *his*.

So far as his family knew he was living in downtown Hammond in "temporary" quarters in a high-rise apartment building, one-bedroom, furnished, overlooking the river from the sixteenth floor. Less than a mile from The Brisbane so that he could walk if he wished.

No. No one else.

Then—why?

Could not speak. Could not explain. *Why?*

Brooke was astonished, deeply wounded. This news her husband had broken to her in a voice of terrifying matter-of-factness was the most shocking of her life.

Like an ugly bruise it would spread, beneath the skin. Though the surface of the skin had not been broken.

Why am I leaving you and our life together? Because it is time.

In fact, it was more than time. Ten years at least.

But he couldn't tell her that. In the exultation of his freedom he did not want to hurt another.

Brooke had been an ideal wife. A very attractive woman, very kind, intelligent and reasonable, good-hearted, and a good mother. A good sense of humor!

Good, good—the word was numbing, toxic. Thom had had enough of *goodness* for the rest of his life.

All he could tell her, faltering, evasive—Think I just need to be alone for a while . . . Nothing to do with you or with the children.

It was deliberate: *you, the children.*

In this way allowing the woman to know that he felt nothing for her any longer that related to her *womanliness*. She was wife, mother, as the children were children, not *his children* but *the children.*

Of course, he loved them. (He said.)

Of course, he would remain in constant contact with them. (He said.)

Of course, it was all "temporary." (He said.)

Family you loved but did not particularly want to spend the rest of your life with. Especially not intimate precious hours when you'd rather be drinking (alone). You did not want to listen to them and especially you did not want to be obliged to reply to them. You did not want to be a witness to their tears and their protestations of hurt, sorrow, indignation, bafflement.

Pleading with him, and furious with him.

Furious with him, and pleading with him.

Would he see a marriage therapist with her?—that was the least he could do.

In fact, it was the most Thom could do. But politely he spoke saying he did not see why not.

He did not see—*why not*?

Well, yes. He would. Of course. If she wished.

Thom knew, it was well-known, marriage therapy was to assuage the wounded pride of the rejected spouse. The spouse who wants to extricate himself from the marriage has made his decision long before he has announced this decision to the spouse who will be left behind, thus the tearful exchange is a sentimental gesture, futile. The rejected spouse, in this case the wife, perhaps in most cases the wife, must not be allowed to realize that nothing about her matters to the spouse who has made up his mind to leave her. Not her goodwill, not her anger, not her longtime fidelity; not her cheeriness, not her reproachful tears, not her threats, not her forced equanimity, her hope to appear reasonable, rational, sane and not vindictive. She must not know that her very being has the attraction to the restless spouse of wet wadded tissues.

He'd married too young, Thom might tell Jessalyn. Though (in fact) he had not married especially young.

Too long under the spell of his parents' marriage. The idyll of domestic life. It had all looked so easy, and it had looked inevitable.

So too with Beverly. Rabid to be married, scarcely graduated from college. No doubt, Steve Bender had married her so hurriedly because she'd been pregnant.

Their supple young bodies had been crazed for each other, for a spell. Their minds had had to hurry to catch up.

(Thom sometimes saw Steve with young women, in downtown Hammond. Once, at the Pierpont, on the farther side of a feathery waterfall in the hotel lobby, one hand at the small of a girl's half-naked back, the other jauntily lifted to his brother-in-law Thom. *H'lo!*)

Too much attention since high school. Too many admiring girls, women. It had caused a kind of blindness in Thom. He'd basked in his sexuality, in the avidity with which girls were drawn to him. Then, abruptly, in his mid-twenties he'd become self-disgusted, wary. He'd gone through a period of intense fear of AIDS, venereal disease, when he'd had his blood tested every six months and had been faint with relief when the report came back *negative*.

In one of these intervals of extreme relief he'd become engaged to Brooke. She'd adored him without question, and she'd adored his family. A bright beautiful young woman who was yet self-effacing, unobtrusive and unassertive, soft-spoken, kindly and gracious—like his mother.

And Jessalyn had adored Brooke. The two might have been of the same generation, Jessalyn an older sister. Brooke had said to Thom, meaning to flatter him—*I could marry you just for Jessalyn. The most wonderful mother-in-law.*

Oh, he'd been flattered! At the time.

Except, you don't really want to marry your mother. No.

Renegade thoughts in the therapist's office. Made an effort to listen politely. The women's voices (therapist, Brooke) were difficult to distinguish.

Earnestness: an overrated attribute.

Cheery, upbeat, reasonable, fair-minded, earnest—no more.

Therapist's name was Dr. Moody. Not an appropriate name for a therapist, Thom thought. (Also, reminded him of Dr. Murthy and how badly that had turned out.)

They were waiting for him to speak. But his mind had drifted off.

The husband had no serious stake in the game, that was the problem. He'd tossed out pennies, the wheel was spinning slowly, it was a pretense to care who won.

She could win. Thom would be generous: Brooke could have the house in Rochester. Child support, alimony. Furnishings, jointly owned possessions. Wouldn't begrudge her anything. Custody of the children. No contest.

But wait: this was marriage therapy. The hope/pretext was, the marriage could be *saved*.

Don't love them, at least? Our children?

Yes of course. Of course Thom loved the children.

"What will we tell them? What—what is wrong with you?"

Weekends, he would see them. If their schedules worked out.

"You've said, you have a one-bedroom apartment, Thom. Why only one bedroom? What were you thinking?"

Truth was, Thom loved the children when he was with them but he did not think of them often when he was away from them. Except with a sick, sliding sensation of profound grief and guilt. *As if their daddy has died, and vanished. And they are fatherless like me.*

In the early hours of the morning when he could not sleep it was not of his family he thought. Obsessively, with the zest of one prodding an open wound with a finger, he thought of the men who'd murdered his father and who'd walked away, unscathed.

Gleeson, Schultz. Whom he intended to murder. If/when he had the opportunity.

The baseball bat, rolled in canvas in the backseat of his vehicle.

Gloves, on the seat beside the bat.

Also, he'd called Tanya. One evening, no reason, her number was still online, just an impulse that excited him.

Hello. Who? Oh—you.

(She'd recognized his voice. No mistaking what that meant.)

Well, yes. Daddy had seen the surprise, hurt, fear in the children's eyes and he'd felt, guess you could say, sorry about that. Sad.

Maybe guilty. Yes.

The thing is, a five-year-old can't grasp Daddy going away without grasping too that it is his fault.

That is, it is *not his fault.*

"Thom, are you listening to any of this? You'd never explained: Why only one bedroom? If you want the children to stay with you where will they sleep? On a sofa in the living room? Will you sleep on the sofa? Do you expect Matthew to sleep on the floor? All of them—all of you—in one bed? What were you thinking?"

Not about you. Sorry.

Truly, he was sorry. But now Whitey was gone, fuck sorry.

Fuck guilty. Fuck Daddy Thom.

He'd told Tanya, maybe I was unfair to you. Maybe I didn't give you a chance.

Chance for what?—Tanya laughed.

Sexual assurance in the woman she hadn't seemed to possess in Thom's office when he'd intimidated her, scared her. A new man in her life probably, and a new job. Possibly.

They'd met for a drink at the Pierpont. Thom was surprised, he found Tanya attractive—though hardly his type. Though he could see now why Whitey might've liked her.

Considered whether to rehire Tanya at McClaren, Inc. Not a good idea?

Whitey's old staff, Thom had mostly retained after all. His intention had been to clear away the old, dead wood in the *family-owned business* but when he came to know the old, dead wood personally—he hadn't the heart.

Like a geriatric ward, Whitey's senior staff.

Thom had been hiring junior staff, however. Expanding the YA division. Could use another graphic artist. Maybe he'd been too severe on Tanya.

Whether to see the woman again? (No wedding ring. But plenty of other rings glittering on her fingers.)

Obviously, not a good idea. She saw his assessing eyes. Saying, "You really are one, aren't you?" And he'd leaned his head toward her as if he hadn't heard clearly, "One—what?" And she'd cut her eyes at him—"One bastard."

Had to laugh. Tanya laughed. Much more attractive than he recalled, streaked-blond hair spilling over her shoulders like a girl in a cheap sexy advertisement, breasts straining against the fabric of a black ribbed sweater threaded with gold braid. And on her throat just below her left ear, a tattoo of what appeared to be a juicy-ripe strawberry Thom hadn't noticed previously—*Jesus!* Took his breath away.

Tanya was (probably) expecting one thing from her former boss and so Thom surprised her with another: handed her a check for one thousand dollars, already made out to *Tanya Gaylin.* "What's this?"—stunned, the derisive smile faded from her mouth.

Well, she'd merited a higher severance pay than he'd given her, Thom said frankly.

(Was this true? Could be.)

One thousand dollars wasn't much to McClaren, Inc., but to Tanya, a lot.

Enough so that, another time, Thom might see her again if he wished.

Confused by the check. Fumbling to fold it, put it inside her handbag so that (she might've been thinking) Thom couldn't change his mind and take it back.

"Well. Thank you, Mr. McClaren . . ."

"*Thom.* Thank you, *Thom.*"

Making a joke of it. Sudden hilarity. Why not?

But he hadn't touched her. Might've tapped her wrist, her arm—(he could imagine Whitey making this gesture, basking in the young woman's attentiveness)—but he did not. Nor did he indicate to Tanya that he'd like to see her again.

Later, in a unisex restroom in the lounge, Thom found a tube of lipstick abandoned on the sink. Plastic tube, and inside a stubby dark-plum lipstick. Not Tanya's lipstick (which was unsubtle strawberry-red) but Thom slipped the dark-plum lipstick into a pocket, smiling.

Would he call Tanya? Sometime?

No. Better not.

Well—possibly.

"And what do you think, Thom?—is that reasonable?" Earnestly Dr. Moody addressed the problematic husband, whose mind (he could see) had begun to drift.

If you are the one who has wronged another, it is you who must be courted. Your very *wrongness,* the outrage and injustice of your *wrongness,* gives you the moral advantage.

Reasonable words were uttered and exchanged. The husband did not (visibly) embarrass himself.

The wife smiled, steelily. So strangely seated beside the husband on the therapist's sofa but at opposite ends of the sofa with a lone cushion between them.

Yet, the problem-husband's mind drifted. He did not care enough about what was *here.*

The *family-owned business*!

Trying to swim in the Chautauqua with a tire around his neck.

Whitey looking over his shoulder. *Good, Thom! Not so good, Thom! Can do better, Thom!*

Every few weeks it comes to him like a shot of adrenaline to the heart: Christ's sake *sell*. What're you waiting for?

(But Jessalyn would be upset, and the others. What of Dad's *legacy*?) Or, bring in others in the family, young relatives, a cousin of Thom's he'd always liked, smart kid graduate from the Wharton School, and his uncle Martin Sewell, his mother's brother semi-retired and with money to invest, who'd expressed an interest in expanding Whitey's line of science textbooks to break into the college market . . .

Maybe that was it. Not sell but bring in others and in a few years step down as CEO.

Then he could move away from Hammond. In fact. Sizable income from the business, Whitey had left him much the majority shareholder. Soon to be forty years old. Could live in New York: high-rise overlooking the Hudson within walking distance of Central Park.

Or, maybe farther downtown. South of the High Line with a view of the Statue of Liberty holding her scepter—or was it a torch?—aloft.

ANIMATION IN THE HUSBAND'S EYES. A good feeling!

Dr. Moody was looking hopeful: Will next Wednesday, same time, work for both of you?

Shaking hands with Moody. Next Wednesday, sure.

Uncertain how to say goodbye to the wife crinkle-eyed with smiling. Gazing at the husband with that expression he'd come to see in her face you might call *drowning hope.*

What could the wife have failed to realize? The husband had not touched her body in ___ months. Years?

(And Beverly, too. His poor, dear sister! Imagining her husband's deepest, most private self had anything to do with *her.*)

(Felt sorry for the women, yes. But you had to harden your heart against *sorry.*)

Outside the therapist's office in the street it was strange, yes: separate cars.

Almost, Thom felt the wrongness of it, that Brooke wasn't walking beside him to get into their car together but hesitating on the sidewalk, alone-looking. Still that crinkled smile, waiting. For there was (obviously) so much for them to say to each other, that Thom had absolutely no interest in saying.

Impatient to leave, to get back to—wherever.

Hadn't told Brooke about dropping the lawsuit. Hadn't wanted to share his anxiety with her and hoped she wouldn't hear from Jessalyn, or one of his sisters, it was a topic Thom hoped to consider closed.

Like the topic of Hugo Martinez, he'd made the mistake of sharing with Brooke all too often during the past several months. So Brooke too called Jessalyn, tried to determine what the situation was, taking an interest that Thom now regretted for he'd more or less decided not to oppose Hugo in his mother's life, he'd come to respect the man, if grudgingly.

Brooke was saying, risking so much, would Thom like to have lunch with her, at least? Just to talk about . . . Or maybe— (seeing the expression in his face)—not to talk about their situation at all, or the children, but just—anything . . . Any subject that wasn't personal.

What Brooke was not saying was *Thom, please. Don't do this. Don't push me away.*

Not pleading, and not begging. He was grateful for that.

Very much he'd have liked to have lunch with her, Thom said, but he had an appointment back at the office. Next time, OK?

Enormous relief just walking away. And Brooke in her own car after all.

Walked up the street whistling. The man is the long-legged one to walk up the street whistling.

Not looking back. Not seeing the solitary woman in her car, leaning over the steering wheel, hiding her face, wracked with sobs . . . No.

Thinking how when Whitey had been alive none of this could have happened. Leaving the wife. Leaving the marriage. Sylvan Woods in Rochester! The mortgage was paid off, the wife and children would not have to move. Now, such freedom was Thom's solace.

Like a gold coin sighted in the mud. Have to position yourself carefully, bending over in just the right way to snatch it up without soiling your fingers.

—∞—

Jesus. Here was pleasure.

Gripping the baseball bat with both hands.

Raised above his head, with both hands. And the swift unerring swing *down*.

A sexual pang. Rushed sex-stirring. In a delirium of anticipation wakened from an intense sleep to feel his head throbbing, jaws clenched tight, penis blood-engorged, hard-swollen.

THREE WEEKS. BUT NO HURRY. *Take time. One breath at a time.*

At the Holland Street bar where no one knew him. Where (in fact) he looked not so much like Thom McClaren.

Nights in succession in the dark cold fall/winter 2011. When Thom left the office late, returned to the rental apartment, changed clothes.

Only beer. Nothing stronger. At the bar, on his feet which felt good to him: standing. Seeing how, amid men, Thom was (still) one of the taller.

Through high school, that good feeling. Knowing that he could be soft-spoken, calm and unharried because unthreatened. One of the *nice jocks*.

The place was a police hangout. Thom had learned. Also COs from county detention. Burly-beefy loud (white) guys. Mostly in good spirits because drinking but if drunk, watch out. They all seemed to know one another. And Gleeson among them, often.

Rarely Schultz. Rumor was, Schultz was retiring.

They didn't know Thom. No one knew Thom. In an old worn windbreaker, soiled workman's hat pulled low on his forehead. Hunched shoulders. Eyes downlooking and averted, brooding.

Could've been a trucker. Could've been a factory worker. Someone local, in the neighborhood. Or maybe not.

A dark-skinned man would have attracted attention. Not Thom.

Whitey's windbreaker. Just about fitted Thom, slightly short in the arms.

Whitey hadn't liked to throw anything away. Old elbow-worn sweaters, shirts with missing buttons. This windbreaker at the back of a storage closet Thom had discovered, Jessalyn would burst into tears if she'd seen. *Oh Whitey! I thought I'd thrown that away.*

On the television above the bar, local news. Street crime: black suspects. A businessman's crimes are not *street crimes* and you don't get arrested in such a way.

Lipstick smile on TV, blond teased hair, might've been a younger sister of Tanya Gaylin reading off weather report. *Brrr! Central New York cold and colder!*

Weird to be standing at the bar with Gleeson only a few feet away oblivious.

Never did Thom actually look at Gleeson. Just the initial glance, the identification. And keeping him then in the corner of Thom's eye, unwavering.

He'd been tracking them for months. Even if the God-damned lawsuit would (eventually) be resolved in his favor Thom did not intend to let off easily the men who'd killed his father.

Unless they were charged with crimes, found guilty and incarcerated, which (obviously) wasn't going to happen.

He'd have a few beers. Use the lavatory. Return to the SUV where the bat lay in readiness.

Whitey was waiting. Whitey had all the time in the world.

Initially, after the lawsuit had been filed by Budd Hawley, both the cops were assigned by their precinct captain to "desk duty." Charges had been made by the plaintiff, made and denied, but the Hammond PD had made a conciliatory gesture by reassigning them.

Officially, in the media pertaining to the McClaren case it would be tersely stated *pending an internal investigation by the Hammond Police Department.*

It was a joke. Bad joke. Every time he'd asked Budd Hawley, more recently Arnie Edelstein, the reply was *ongoing investigation.*

Before October 2010 Gleeson had been several times cited for "excessive force"; there were civilian complaints against him, some of these by (alleged) prostitutes/drug addicts whom he'd sexually abused, threatened. He'd been passed over for promotion several times. Still, he'd been reinstated as an on-duty cop after six months on desk duty.

Gleeson had received a raise this year of $12,000 bringing his yearly salary, exclusive of overtime, to $82,000.

Schultz, older than Gleeson by several years, had been allowed to retire from the force with a medical disability. He'd had a similar record of civilian complaints and like Gleeson had several times been passed over for promotion.

Gleeson was thirty-six, Schultz forty-one.

Thom knew where Gleeson lived, he'd followed Gleeson home and subsequently driven past the shingled duplex on South Ninth Street on several occasions.

Not clear if Gleeson was married. Sometimes a female in the duplex, but lately not. Trash cans accumulated at the curb, lately toppled over. Thom hadn't wanted to make inquiries among the neighbors out of a fear of being identified later, after he'd battered in Gleeson's head.

About Schultz he knew relatively little.

One at a time. One target.

If the two happened to be in the Holland Street tavern at the same time they made no effort to speak to each other. (So Thom had noted.) Probably sick of each other. What memories cops shared: people they'd arrested together, handcuffed together, struck down together, shot with their stun guns together, caused to die.

Maybe nothing. Maybe they didn't remember. Maybe it was all forgotten in a cop's life, episodes of excessive force, like blood- or vomit-splattered walls hosed down.

My client denies any recollection of.

No memory of the white-haired older man named John Earle McClaren they'd struck down on a shoulder of the Hennicott Expressway, caused to die now more than a year ago?

My client denies all culpability.

Never more than a few beers, then he'd leave. Toss bills onto the bar. No one took notice. Not a glance. On the TV, smoldering rubble in a place called Kabul, another "suicide bomber."

That night, or another. Thom would take his time. Thom would make no mistakes. When a cop is killed, especially a cop with a record like Gleeson's, it would be assumed that his death had something to do with his life as a cop; but Thom would see to it, no suspicion would be directed his way.

He was sure. He owed that much to Whitey.

NOW WAS THE TIME! *He was prepared. Gleeson pulling into the narrow driveway at his house. Very late, houses darkened. Swift and unerring Thom climbs out of his vehicle and overtakes the (drunk, unsteady) Gleeson at the side door of the house, swings the bat, there's a grunt and the man staggers but does not fall and again Thom lifts the bat for another powerful blow, this time Gleeson slips on blood-slick ice, falls heavily. Labored intake of breath like a stunned steer and on the rippled-icy pavement lies shuddering on his back his head sprouting blood and yet another time Thom lifts the bat and brings it down onto the blood-matted head, and again until the skull is crushed, soft.*

Fucker!—now you know what it's like.

No haste. Must remove the wallet from inside the fallen man's tight-fitting trousers, the gun from a holster inside his jacket. Loose coins from his pocket fall onto the icy ground.

Might've been a robbery. Someone who knows Gleeson, who'd followed him home from Holland Street where he'd been since 9:20 this Friday evening.

Quickly walking away. Quick to his vehicle at the curb.

Undisturbed, the darkened houses. No movement at any window. If the dying man has a wife or a woman inside she has not been waiting up for him.

In no haste drives by the Charter Street bridge. Infrequent headlights at this hour but he takes pleasure in passing a Hammond PD cruiser coming off the bridge.

Throws the bloodstained bat into the river, weighted with heavy cords.

Bloodstained gloves, he will cut into pieces and dispose of in a Dumpster miles away . . .

Wakened abruptly by a phone ringing beside his head.

Landline phone in the apartment, virtually no one has this number, not Brooke, not Jessalyn, no one at the office. A new number he'd meant to reserve for particular persons though he'd given it to Arnie Edelstein in case something urgent came up and Thom's cell phone wasn't charged.

In fact it was Edelstein. Sounding excited.

Telling Thom he had good news, at least he believed it was good news: the Hammond PD and the City of Hammond were offering to settle the McClarens' claim after months of stalling. They were offering just under one million dollars but with the stipulation that the plaintiffs could not discuss the case publicly.

Thom swung his legs off the bed. Sat up. Mouth so dry! Wasn't sure he'd heard this correctly. Offer to *settle*? Hadn't he told Edelstein to drop the case?

Edelstein said, "I told you something was about to develop, Thom. I told you let's wait a week. Two weeks. I thought I'd had a heads-up on this. But I couldn't be sure which is why I didn't tell you more specifically."

"I don't understand," Thom said. "I thought the case had been dropped . . ."

"Look, there's an offer on the table. Not what we asked but we'd started high. Are you surprised?"

"Jesus!"—Thom whistled. "Yes. I am."

Hadn't expected this. Had reconciled himself to losing. But now.

Edelstein was saying it was more than just a token: nine hundred nine thousand ninety-nine dollars.

Thom laughed. "Ninety-nine cents, too?"

"No. Just dollars."

"What about Gleeson and Schultz? What happens to them?"

"Essentially, nothing. That we'll be allowed to know."

"They will just walk free?"—Thom heard the hurt, the wistfulness in his voice. Something that Thom might say, at such a time, that Edelstein would recall.

Walk free. Walk free.

Edelstein spoke at length. By nature he was an ebullient and contentious person who took seriously the litigator's charge to convince his client to accept a deal snatched from the jaws of utter loss, humiliation, oblivion. There had been little likelihood that Gleeson and Schultz would be charged with any actual crimes, still less that they'd be indicted and found guilty of manslaughter. Thom must have known that. But the lawsuit had been a worthy one and this offer was substantial.

"As I said, Thom: not just a token. The defendants are admitting responsibility."

Thom lay back onto the rumpled bed, shutting his eyes. Walls, floor and ceiling swung around him, not unpleasurably. But with his eyes shut tight he wouldn't be obliged to see.

"Thom? Are you there? Is something wrong?"—the voice over the phone was sounding concerned.

Thom said, "No. No one here."

"Thom? What?"

Couldn't trust himself to speak. Tears spilled from his eyes.

Thank God he was alone. If Jessalyn had been there, she'd have wrapped him in her arms, her tall sad son. Mourning Whitey they'd have cried and cried.

The Kiss

Amos Keziahaya has already rebuffed him, and Virgil has already drowned in a polluted river. What's the worst that could happen to Virgil now?

In his journal noting *Just because I give myself to my art doesn't mean that the sacrifice is worth it. Fact is, I have nothing and no one else to give myself to.*

A silly way to have died, dragged along by a barge cable in the murky Chautauqua River! Virgil is very grateful to have been spared.

Died but not-dead. Recalled with a smile.

Even before his lacerated hands are fully healed, before the bandages are removed, Virgil has returned to work. His vision is hands gripping hands. His vision is human figures tense with yearning.

So vividly Virgil *sees*! It has something to do, he thinks, with the muck-despair of the river, that almost sucked him down. Washing his eyes clear.

Not a high price to pay, his hands badly torn. His pride.

New work! Life-sized figures made of a transparent glazed plastic. Male, female. Both. Neither.

One of the figures is on his toes, like a dancer. Presenting his blank (yearning) face to kiss another. The other, head uplifted, mouth out of reach of the kiss. Title *The Kiss.*

The root of all sorrow is sex. The root of all joy.

BELATEDLY THE NEWS COMES TO VIRGIL: the McClaren lawsuit against the Hammond Police Department has been "settled."

Thom isn't the one to inform Virgil. It is Sophia who calls him, to share what she considers good news.

"Evidently Thom gave the lawyer an ultimatum—wind it up in three weeks." Sophia pauses, uncertain. "Not that anything is 'settled'—really."

Yes. Whitey is still gone from us.

Virgil asks what Thom intends to do with the money and Sophia says she doesn't know. What would Whitey have wished?

Give the money away. Blood money. Get rid of it. Quick!

"I'm sure that Thom will. That's what Dad would have wanted."

Would have wanted. All is past tense now for Whitey.

Virgil feels a pang of loss. While the lawsuit was pending there was the possibility of "justice"—however vague, ambiguous. An effort being made for an abstract principle as well as for the memory of their wronged father. Now, all is permanently "settled."

Virgil thinks, You can love a person but not regret his absence. That is a hard fact.

He has learned to accept this. His freedom to be who he truly is, the result of his father's death.

Not that Virgil would tell anyone: no. Certainly none of the McClarens.

They would not understand. Some truths can't be uttered. Not even Sophia would have been sympathetic, she'd have stared at Virgil in shock and disapproval.

Yes I miss Dad but no, I don't miss his presence. His judgment.

Without Dad in the world I can breathe. Forgive me!

Maybe one day he will tell Amos. Maybe Amos will say, *Yes. Same with me. My father.*

IN THE GUERRILLA GALLERY in East Hammond, by chance Virgil encounters Amos Keziahaya.

It is mid-November. It has been months since the awkward incident in Virgil's studio and sometime during that interval, without Virgil quite realizing at the time, Keziahaya left Bear Mountain Road to live elsewhere.

Where, Virgil doesn't know. Has not wanted to ask.

For a moment the two men freeze. Virgil dreads a grimace baring white teeth—*You! Get the hell away, I am not your friend.*

But no, it is not that at all, indeed the tall young Nigerian smiles at Virgil almost shyly—*Hello.*

Or, maybe—*Hello, Virgil.*

The exchange is brief, friendly. Just slightly dazed Virgil will recall how friendly.

Asking Amos how he's been and Amos shrugs and says in his laconic way *OK.*

So tall! Absurdly beautiful, with even his mysteriously scarred or pitted skin. With even his slightly stained teeth.

Afterward Virgil is proud of himself for not having lingered in the Gallery, not having tried to engage Amos in conversation. Whatever clumsy stratagem of the lovesick so painfully transparent to the loved one—thank God, he has spared the young man. Since the non-drowning in the Chautauqua River Virgil has been resolved not to embarrass Amos Keziahaya any more than he has already embarrassed him.

After all, Virgil is the *elder.*

Wondering—would friends have shaken hands? After not seeing each other for some time? Women friends would have hugged, kissed. Women are not so afraid of putting their hands on one another.

Or—is Virgil making too much of the casual encounter, as usual?

The artist is one who makes "too much" of things.

After all this time Virgil has not altered his impulsive hand-wrought will. If indeed it is a "will" and would carry legal authority. *All my earthly goods I bestow to my friend & fellow artist Amos Keziahaya. "The rest is silence."*

NEXT MORNING, feeling unaccountably happy.

Sometime in the night, in his sleep, deciding what the hell, what's to lose?

With eager clumsy fingers manages to text on the ridiculously small keyboard of his cell phone this terse invitation to Amos Keziahaya—

Amos: come by here, tomorrow 7 P.M.?

—to which after several suspenseful hours there comes a thrilled vibratory hum from Virgil's phone and the yet terser reply

OK

Gone

Felt like raking her face with her nails. Worry over her mother and *that man Hugo.* The latest was, what if they were secretly married, could such a marriage be annulled, undone. Could the heirs prove that a fraud had been perpetrated upon their mother. If money or property were appropriated by *that man* could they retrieve it. In the midst of Beverly's tirade on the phone (speaking with whom? which relative, friend?) heedless Brianna came in, bounding up the stairs in jeans so tight-fitting slender legs, thighs, buttocks you could wonder (her mother wonders!) how in hell the girl can breathe, ponytail bouncing sassily behind her, of course Beverly lowered her voice so the girl wouldn't hear, certain that the girl could not hear, and some minutes later there came Brianna in reverse, out of her room and down the stairs thudding on her heels with the arrogance of one who weighs two hundred pounds and not one hundred, and again Beverly lowered her voice out of maternal discretion just as Brianna halted at the foot of the stairs and turned to her, twisting at the waist like a dancer in a brilliantly tortured posture, young face livid with indignation: "For God's sake, Mom! Grandpa Whitey is *gone*."

Bounding then out of the house with a final sneer, and gone.

Thanksgiving 2011

Errands. What is the housewife's life but.

First, pick up the divorce papers. Then, Thanksgiving turkey, groceries, wine and soda.

On the way home bakery, florist, drugstore (Ambien), dry cleaner's (Steve's God-damned suit, he'd forgotten [again]).

"NO. IT'S TOO LATE."

Or, more eloquently: "In my heart I feel nothing for you any longer."

(But was that true? She felt *rage* for him! Betraying her! Humiliating her! Years of lying to her! Simmering water in a pan on the stove suddenly boiling, foaming over the rim of the pan, into the blue gas flames, onto the floor—*that was how she felt.*)

DIVORCE DOCUMENT PREPARED by a (female, junior) lawyer at Barron, Mills & McGee she'd brought home and reread in the secrecy of a (locked) room in awe of the razor-sharp precision of the legal terms and the look and feel of the law firm's stationery with its understated gilt letterhead.

Matter-of-factly the lawyer had asked Mrs. Bender if this was to be a *no-fault divorce,* or—?

No. Indeed no. Not *no-fault.*

Telling the woman there was plenty of *fault*. Enough *fault* to fill a Dumpster, a dump truck.

Enough *fault* to fill a God-damned landfill.

Very tactfully, the woman smiled in appreciation of her client's wit. Beverly wondered how much that half-inch smile would cost her but whatever, it would be worth it.

Saying, "In my heart I feel nothing for that man any longer. He has been unfaithful to me, and he has lied about it. Emotionally, he has not been there for me, for years."

Been there for me. Daytime TV! (Which, except when she was feeling really depressed, restless, bored or anyone else was in the house, Beverly never watched.)

It was not entirely true, perhaps. In the matter of the children she and Steve were usually allies, and he did not undercut her authority with them. (Of course, Steve was often not home to interfere. He'd left the essential *parenting* to her.)

Flattering to Beverly, how assiduously the lawyer was taking notes on a laptop. Long, polished nails, short skirt riding up a silky thigh, of an indeterminate age (early or mid-thirties) and (obviously) smart. You did not want a nice lawyer, a gracious lawyer, a ladylike lawyer, you wanted *smart*.

Suggesting to Beverly that she freeze all joint financial accounts before she gave her husband the divorce papers. Before he heard the very word *divorce*. Speak with their investment officer, accountant. Preparation was crucial. Surprise was to her advantage.

"You must protect yourself financially. A divorce can quickly turn mean."

But Beverly wasn't so sure she wanted to do this. It seemed dishonest, tricky. The husband was the dishonest and tricky spouse in this case, not the wife.

Financial issues were at the crux of most divorce negotiations, the lawyer explained. Whatever the wife might want, the husband would (almost certainly) offer less. In households in which the husband's income was high there was also the possibility of bank accounts of which the wife was unaware.

Really! Beverly was uneasy recalling that Whitey had had several bank accounts under his own name, about which Jessalyn had evidently known nothing.

Of course, in Whitey's case, there had been no intention to defraud Jessalyn.

(But why had Whitey done this, in such secrecy? No one had any idea.)

Husbands were usually reliable with child support, the lawyer continued. Especially if they were earning high salaries and were not in debt. And they loved their children.

Good to know, Beverly said with an effort at exuberance, buoyancy. *Very* good to know.

THE SHARPEST-EYED OF THE CHILDREN NOTED—"Mom, is something wrong? You're so kind of *happy* lately."

Though also, less flatteringly—"Mom, is something wrong? You keep *dropping things*."

HOW STUNNED THE HUSBAND WOULD BE to learn that the wife was filing for divorce. After seventeen years!

After the family Thanksgiving dinner which would be the last of the family dinners (for him) in this house. After the damned football game sprawling through the afternoon with its inane screeching like the cries of frenzied chimpanzees. Steve and the others (male, varying ages) would watch the game enthralled as the women cleaned up in the dining room and kitchen. Every year Thanksgiving was bifurcated: the meal, the game; the women, the men.

What was the connection?—there was none.

Post-game were replays of the game they'd just watched. On other TV channels were replays of other games. No end to *games*!

After the last of the guests left Steve was likely to remain in his leather recliner, TV remote in hand. His eyes would have grown heavy-lidded, his mouth slack. Exhausted, sated. Beer, salted peanuts. After he'd stuffed himself at the dining room table. Quietly Beverly would emerge from the kitchen and say in her calmest voice: "Here is something for you, Steve. I think now is a good time."

She would lay the folder on the table beside him. She would say nothing further but go upstairs to a private place.

Waiting then some minutes later for him to call after her—*Beverly?*

Waiting then for him to stumble upstairs after her—*Beverly for God's sake you can't mean this.*

She would not quarrel with him. She would speak to him in the calm and measured way she'd rehearsed for weeks. She would not allow him to precipitate raised voices, emotion. No more tears! No more weakness on her part.

He would be hurt, and he would be angry. Like a goaded pit bull *lashing out.*

But no. The wife would be prepared, poised. The wife would never again *lash out.*

She would help him pack. For he must leave immediately.

He would be stunned. He would be disbelieving. Please, one more night, he would beg but the wife would be unyielding, vehement. "No. There have been too many nights and now it's too late."

Standing a little apart from the husband, on the far side of their bed perhaps, so that he could not (easily) touch her. For his hands on her, in the past, had so weakened her, she could not defend herself. But that would not happen again.

In a voice of dignity and not the hurtful grating self-lacerating voice she had come to recognize with repugnance as her own:

"In my heart I feel nothing for you any longer."

IT HAD BEEN A DISPIRITING DISCOVERY, so banal. Of course she'd suspected. For years, she'd *known.*

So many evenings away. *At the office. Business dinner. Work.*

Conferences to which spouses had not been invited. (Suspicious, she'd checked the Honolulu conference. Why yes in fact, spouses had been invited, only just not Steve Bender's *spouse*.) (And why *Honolulu*? The very name suggested frivolity, drunken excess. Gaudy-colored leis around the necks of slobbering white-skinned men in newly purchased Hawaiian shirts.) The left-behind spouse was furious but said nothing. Not then. The deceitful husband would only lie, and she could not bear his lies delivered with the sneering confidence of a twelve-year-old bully.

Beverly, what the hell? What is wrong with you?

Hysterical. Jesus! Exaggerate everything.

And then, she'd managed to find her way into Steve's email account. Brianna had mentioned scornfully that most people (by which she meant most adults) knew so little about technology that they used their birth dates as passwords, or a pet's name, or a sequence of stupid numbers—*1 2 3 4 5*.

Steve's password was in fact his birth date. The email record was damning. Over the months *Toni* yielded to *Steffi,* but then *Steffi* yielded to *Mira*.

She had not confronted him, just yet. She had known she must be prepared, she must not rush at the husband in a maelstrom of accusations, tears and indeed yes, hysteria.

She'd spent much time thinking of it. How to proceed. If the marriage was over (as it certainly seemed to be over from Steve's perspective at least) then it was over for her as well—she could not love a man who did not love her!

Could not love a man who didn't respect her.

Rarely even listened to her. Spent time with her.

Especially if Beverly was—well, the word was *nagging*.

(Did men *nag*? No men did not. *Nag* is a female word, a *nag* is a used-up old mare. No word for used-up old stallion except *stallion*.)

She'd spent time away from the house. Walking, brooding. In the cemetery where Whitey's ashes were buried, which she had not (to her shame) visited in months.

It was November. Again. Wetted leaves blown against grave markers, a cobwebby sensation to the air. You dreaded to breathe. How she hated the approaching winter solstice, shortest day/longest night of the year.

John Earle McClaren. Beloved husband, father.

What to do? Separation, divorce? *Divorce* made her mouth dry but caused her heart to trip with something like actual excitement, anticipation of the kind she'd once felt, eighteen years before, when she saw Steve Bender approaching her with that smile.

Divorce meant failure. No way around that.

Whitey admonished—*Don't act rashly, Beverly! Steve is a good guy.*

But was this so? More like an *OK* guy, barely.

Great guy, in fact. As guys go. Lots of laughs.

Shouldn't you expect more from a husband than laughs?

More sternly Whitey warned—*It's like a door you step through, that locks behind you. I'd be careful if I were you, dear.*

How like Whitey to joke—*Look what happened to me! Damn door sure locked behind me.*

In the cemetery, at Whitey's grave. So dazed, she had to lean against the grave marker.

Make her way out of the cemetery haltingly. Out of earshot of Daddy calling after her—*Take care, Beverly! There are so few who love us.*

Another day she drove to Old Farm Road. Parked her car in the driveway but no one was home. (Oh, shouldn't Jessalyn be *home*? And if Jessalyn wasn't *home,* where was she? With *that man*?) Walked down to the creek, stood staring at the dark water grown sluggish with autumnal cold. Recalling how as a girl, a teenager, she'd had little interest in anything to do with the creek or the lake a quarter mile away. How boring, the out-of-doors.

Probably, the last year or two she'd lived in the house, in this beautiful setting, Beverly hadn't hiked down to the creek once. The last time she'd consented to getting into the canoe with Thom, she'd been thirteen.

What had her adolescent life been? A kaleidoscope of bright faces, endless phone calls, lurid and utterly absorbing sex-thoughts. Though she hadn't yet met Steve Bender there'd been numerous other boys/men to populate her fantasies.

And where had those lurid fantasies brought her?

Found herself sitting on the dock, weak-kneed. Water swirling past her bearing rotted leaves. In scrawny leafless trees, black-feathered birds shrugging their wings, cawing. And there was Jessalyn standing over her looking concerned, and a few feet behind her on the creek bank *that man* Hugo Martinez.

Embarrassing! Beverly's face was wet with tears.

Jessalyn and her friend had returned to the house, and seen someone, a stranger perhaps, on the dock at the foot of the hill. In her haze of self-pity Beverly hadn't noticed the couple approaching her.

Tactfully Hugo Martinez retreated. Jessalyn remained to comfort her.

Crying to her mother that Steve didn't love her anymore. Her life was over!

Jessalyn cradled Beverly in her arms, as best she could. Saying it was all right, everything would be all right, Steve loved her of course, it was all a misunderstanding probably . . .

No. Not a misunderstanding. After so long, an *understanding*. There was no pretense any longer.

In her mother's arms Beverly wept. How shameful, at Beverly's age. Did you never grow up? Did you never outgrow a need for your mother? Beverly would have been mortified if anyone had known—Lorene, Thom, Steve. Whitey.

Back at the house Hugo awaited. Seeing Beverly's distress he was soft-spoken, unobtrusive. By nature an inquisitive person he took care now not to intrude. Stroking his mustache, that covered virtually the lower half of his face.

He would prepare a meal for them, he said. He hoped Beverly would stay.

She could not! No.

Well. Hugo understood of course, if she didn't feel comfortable staying. Looking to Jessalyn, in appeal.

Please stay!—Jessalyn said. Lacing her fingers through Beverly's fingers, that felt thick and clumsy.

And so, Beverly stayed. So strange to be eating in the kitchen of her family home, with her mother, a meal prepared by a stranger!

Delicious food, slightly too spicy for her. Eggplant casserole, onions, tomatoes, goat cheese, chilies.

Red wine helped dilute the taste, also provided by Hugo Rodriguez.

It was touching to overhear her mother conferring with Hugo about her, almost out of earshot. Did Hugo Martinez, a stranger, an enemy, care for Beverly?—or rather, for Jessalyn's emotionally wrought middle-aged daughter?

Lorene had compared Hugo Martinez to Che Guevara. Possibly she'd been sarcastic, you never knew with Lorene who'd spent her adult life in the company of sarcastic adolescents. Still, Beverly could see the resemblance: handsome Latino males, self-regarding, manipulative.

Sexually aggressive, dangerous. Could not trust.

He was a very friendly man, Hugo Martinez. You might say over-friendly. Beverly wanted to take hold of his hands, press them against her face. In a weak moment, she'd come close to abasing herself to her mother's Hispanic lover.

Having to remind herself she wasn't a child, a young girl. She was herself a wife and a mother, nearing forty years old.

A glass or two of red wine, Beverly became very sleepy. Jessalyn drove her home in Beverly's car, and Hugo followed in his. The last Beverly saw of Jessalyn and Hugo, Jessalyn was climbing into his car, and Hugo was driving away.

A wink of red lights, and gone.

DIVORCE PAPERS IN THE (PLAIN) FOLDER provided by Barron, Mills & McGee. Sixteen-pound, four-ounce turkey in the oven and roasting by 11:00 A.M. of Thanksgiving Day.

No one knew that Beverly had gone to a lawyer. Not even Jessalyn.

And Beverly had a new prescription drug, an antidepressant with the hopeful name Luxor. To counteract the grogginess caused by her nightly sleeping pill which had begun to last well into late morning like a fog slow to lift.

Unlike most antidepressants Luxor was said to be almost immediately effective. Small white pills, five milligrams each day. Strongly advised not to take with alcohol. No driving or operating of heavy machinery.

It was rare, Beverly operated *heavy machinery*. So that part of it was no trouble.

"Mom, is something wrong? You're just standing there."

How long had she been *standing there*?—Beverly woke to find her eyes already open in the kitchen bright-lit as an operating room.

"Well. I am standing here *thinking*."

"Oh Mom. *Ugh*."

Brianna was staring at the sixteen-pound, four-ounce "organic" turkey as if it were a human cadaver. So bred that its breast was enlarged, its body misshapen. Thanksgiving turkeys were now so grotesquely bred for American consumers who preferred white meat, the poor creatures had difficulty walking and the largest, at twenty pounds, could not walk at all.

Clammy-white-puckered skin, made both Brianna and Beverly shudder to touch.

And that smell. Wet, dead meat. Flesh once living and now, not.

Eviscerated creature, its guts and genitals removed, that a very fancy stuffing (chestnuts, Portobello mushrooms, celery, sage and marjoram, salt and pepper, bread cubes drizzled with butter) might be shoveled into the cavity. What an odd tradition, Beverly thought. She'd never quite realized before.

A sixteen-pound turkey requires approximately three and a half hours to roast. Ugly thing, headless. Beverly struggled to fit it into the baking pan, one of the legs kept pressing outward as if in the grip of rigor mortis.

Sophia was helping in the kitchen. Lorene had promised to help but had been delayed. (How surprising was this? When it was a matter of helping her sister in the kitchen Lorene was always *delayed*.) And Jessalyn had come early of course, bringing her delicious sweet potato soufflé.

As many as seventeen guests were expected. Beverly had lost count. Virgil was coming, possibly with a "new" friend. Several of Steve's relatives (including his older brother Zack) were coming—"For the dinner and for the game." There were children, a shifting number that this year would not include Thom's children to the disappointment of their Bender cousins. (Brianna's reaction: "Kevin's not coming? Shit.") The table had been enlarged, chairs dragged into the dining room. Water goblets? Place cards? Matching napkins? Candlestick holders? Was the centerpiece too obtrusive? And which tablecloth? Each Thanksgiving Beverly impressed her family and guests with her hospitality, her energy, her excellent food. It had always been her particular hope to impress the elder McClarens, whose hospitality had been so admired for decades.

Whitey's face had fairly glowed with pleasure, when he'd hosted such dinners. For a while Steve had tried to emulate his charismatic father-in-law but had fallen behind in recent years.

And what had it all added up to, Whitey McClaren's many dinners? Parties?

A voice consoled her—*This will be the last Thanksgiving. No more husband for Thanksgiving!*

Was this what Beverly wanted? No husband for Thanksgiving? She'd poured a half-glass of wine without noticing. Her hand trembled.

The previous year they'd hardly celebrated Thanksgiving. A turkey half the size of this year's turkey, no elaborate meal. Only just family. No enlarged table. Jessalyn without Whitey, looking forlorn, lost.

No one had eaten much. Except Steve who'd helped himself to platters of turkey, mashed potatoes, cranberry sauce, sweet potato soufflé oblivious of how the others regarded him.

Beverly had wanted to defend her husband. He wasn't unfeeling, just—shallow-minded, you could say.

If in the future the children wanted to have Thanksgiving with their father they could make their own arrangements. *She* was finished.

This year they would celebrate Whitey's life. Too much emphasis had been placed on Whitey's death, and the injustice of his death, now they must celebrate his life. It was a relief that the lawsuit had been settled, which they chose to interpret as an acknowledgment by the Hammond Police Department of the injustice of Whitey's death and so a victory for Whitey.

Still, Thom had been very quiet about the settlement. As others expressed relief that it was over Thom said nothing. Observing her taciturn brother Beverly thought, with a little shiver—*Thom is planning his own kind of settlement.*

Nor did Thom seem much inclined to speak of Brooke and his children who were having Thanksgiving this year with Brooke's family in Rochester. When Beverly took Thom aside to ask him what was happening he told her that nothing had been decided, no one was (yet) speaking of divorce, he saw the kids each weekend, sometimes more often.

"But you're living *alone*? In an apartment—*alone*?"

"Yes. For now."

"You don't seem very upset, considering."

"Should I be?"

"Well—shouldn't you?"

"You tell me, Bev. You seem to know so much about it."

Beverly felt the rebuke like a jab in the ribs, delivered by a bullying older brother.

"It's just that I miss your family. Your great children."

Pointedly, Beverly hadn't said *Brooke.*

Tempted to tell Thom about the surprise waiting for Steve. *He* was not the only McClaren to declare his independence.

But Thom didn't seem eager to exchange intimate remarks with

Beverly. To her chagrin she saw him heading downstairs to join Steve and some others, watching ESPN on the wide flat-screen TV Steve had spent a small fortune having installed in the basement.

Of the men only Hugo had no interest in watching football. No interest in sports, he said—"Even soccer."

Even soccer. Was this a joke?

Of course, Hugo Martinez had come to Beverly's Thanksgiving dinner. Impossible to avoid the man!—Beverly tried to explain to Lorene and Thom, who expressed astonishment, disapproval. Lorene whispered in Beverly's ear: "You could poison 'Hugo.' Who'd know?" and Beverly retorted, "What do you mean, 'who'd know'?—he's probably told all his friends that he's coming here for dinner. And Jessalyn would know." Lorene said, laughing, "For God's sake, Bev. I was *joking.*"

How like Lorene this was! Maddening. To make a crude joke, and then to insist that was a joke, as if Beverly were too slow-witted and flat-footed to understand her wit.

When Beverly first spoke to Jessalyn about Thanksgiving she had not dared to tell her mother that Hugo was *not invited*. She had not dared partly because if she had, Jessalyn would surely have not come herself, and that would have been disastrous.

In his typically aggressive way Hugo insisted upon providing some of the wine for the meal, as well as pumpkin pies for dessert which he intended to make himself.

"That isn't necessary, Hugo," Beverly said weakly, on the phone, "—really. We always have too much food, especially desserts."

"Yes. I will bring wine and pies. Thank you for having me."

"But, Hugo . . ."

How had it happened, Beverly was calling this stranger *Hugo*. Trying to reason with Hugo as if he were one of the family. *Her mother's lover.*

The world was becoming surreal to Beverly. None of this made sense.

Oh, if Whitey could know! Sliding his hand around hers to comfort, console. *You'll be all right, Bev. You know I am always with you.*

She knew. She would not forget.

Since Beverly had eaten Hugo's eggplant casserole she'd been feeling indebted to him. It was not a comfortable feeling. She dreaded Lorene and Thom finding out through a casual remark of their mother's. Worse yet, a few days later Jessalyn called back to ask if Hugo could bring a friend with him to Thanksgiving, and Beverly was taken aback by the nerve—her own mother! Conspiring to bring an unknown person to the Benders' dinner table. And that unknown person her Hispanic lover! (Though Beverly reserved the right to doubt that, in fact, her mother and Hugo Martinez were *lovers*. That did not seem possible.)

In fact there'd been a McClaren tradition, as the children were growing up, of Whitey inviting people to Thanksgiving whom he called, not quite accurately, "lame ducks"—"left-behinds." Some of these individuals had been total strangers to the family, even to Whitey himself. Where he ran into them, no one knew. Some had been quite eccentric, indeed. Some had been "foreign." How had Jessalyn felt, as the beleaguered hostess? Beverly never remembered her mother as anything less than delighted to welcome Whitey's guests into their home.

Your mother is a saint. So people said.

Jessalyn was explaining to Beverly that Hugo's friend was alone at Thanksgiving, with no family. He'd recently had surgery and was convalescing. He was very nice—"Very quiet, thoughtful." They would bring him to Beverly's for just an hour or so, and then move on, to another Thanksgiving gathering, that had been scheduled weeks ago, which Hugo was obliged to attend, so really he wouldn't be staying long . . . In the confusion of the moment Beverly hadn't heard all this. Her heart pounded in resentment of Hugo Martinez's audacity, and his malevolent influence on her mother.

She felt that they were losing Jessalyn, she told Lorene. First, they'd lost Whitey. But they could not lose their dear mother!

When, on Thanksgiving Day, this mystery person appeared at the door with Jessalyn and Hugo, Beverly was the more astonished to see that he was an African-American, a diminutive man of about forty in an ill-fitting three-piece suit and shiny embossed necktie. Both suit and necktie looked like something from a bin at Goodwill. His name, Beverly was told by Hugo Martinez, was "Caesar Jones."

Caesar Jones! No choice but to shake the man's hand which felt overwarm in Beverly's hand, and which she dropped quickly.

(So far as Beverly could recall, she had never shaken the hand of an African-American man. Not that this meant anything, of course it did not.)

Even worse, Caesar Jones turned out to be, in Hugo's surprisingly frank words, a *formerly incarcerated person.*

Beverly managed to draw Jessalyn aside, that no one might overhear her alarm and indignation. What on earth was this!—an *ex-convict* in her house, invited to a meal with the family! With *children.*

Jessalyn told her that Caesar Jones had been "wrongly convicted"—"recently freed"—"exonerated"—after twenty-three years in Attica, for a crime he had not committed. He had no home at the present time and so was living in Hugo's house.

"Living in Hugo's house? But why?"

"Because—I've said—he has no other home right now."

"But—why Hugo's home?"

"Because Hugo has taken him in. He feels sorry for Caesar, and wants to help him adjust to the outside world."

This information was intriguing to Beverly who'd naturally assumed that Hugo Martinez was a deceitful or at any rate a disreputable person. Wanting to *help others*?

"Does Hugo have a large enough house?"

"Yes. It's quite large."

"As large as—this house?" Beverly was disbelieving, incredulous.

Jessalyn had to be exaggerating.

"I think so, yes."

This too was disconcerting. Hugo Martinez whom they'd vaguely assumed to be penniless, even homeless—owning a house as large as Beverly's own?

"Well, but—what was the crime he was convicted of? Not murder, I hope."

"Manslaughter. But—"

"Man-*slaughter*. But that is murder, Mom!"

"No. Caesar did not commit 'manslaughter'—he is innocent of the charge and was falsely convicted."

"For God's sake, Mom—don't they all claim to be innocent?"

"No. They do not. Caesar Jones is truly innocent. His sentence was not commuted but overturned by an appeals court."

"But—how would you know if he was 'innocent' or not? If he'd been found guilty . . ."

"Juries make mistakes. Police officers lie—as we know. Prosecutors hide exculpatory evidence. Caesar Jones has been a victim and not a criminal—he'd been a college student, an education major, when he was arrested . . ."

Beverly was astonished to hear her mother, usually so soft-spoken, speak so vehemently. Barely, Beverly knew what *exculpatory evidence* was. (She would not have trusted herself to enunciate the phrase aloud.) The influence of Hugo Martinez on Jessalyn was more profound and more insidious than any of her children could have guessed.

At least, Jessalyn was wearing her snowy-white hair loose to her shoulders, not braided like a peasant woman's hair. And she was wearing tasteful dark clothes, not some peasant blouse or smock that Hugo had given her, though around her neck were chunky amber beads that Beverly was sure she'd never seen before, and had to have come from Hugo.

Sharp-eared Hugo Martinez came over quickly to join Jessalyn. You could see (Beverly could see) that he'd been eavesdropping.

Caesar Jones was left to stand by himself in a doorway glancing about with lowered eyes, like a nocturnal creature in a brightly-lit place. He was smiling faintly, bravely. To Beverly's dismay she saw Brianna sidle up to him to say hello.

Hugo told Beverly, "Caesar is a gentle person. We won't let him out of our sight."

Beverly felt her cheeks flush. Was Hugo making fun of her?

He would tell Beverly more about Caesar some other time, if she was interested, Hugo said.

Of course she was not interested!—Beverly wanted to retort.

Stiffly she said yes, some other time—"Thank you."

(What were Caesar Jones and sixteen-year-old Brianna talking about? Shyly the black man smiled, revealing now broken and stained teeth. What would have repelled Brianna in another person seemed to have no effect upon her, in Hugo's ex-convict friend.)

More guests were arriving. Beverly hurried to greet them. The younger children had been entrusted to pass around appetizers—Beverly would have to oversee them. There came exclamations of surprise—an elderly McClaren aunt and her middle-aged son arrived, whom Beverly had not expected to come to dinner; in fact, Beverly could not recall having invited these two.

How like a great wheel rolling at you, a dinner party. If you did not get out of its way it would roll over you, crushing you in the mud. But if you did get out of its way you could imagine yourself its master, smiling and laughing. *Oh how good to see you!—and you . . .*

At last Lorene arrived, carrying a Styrofoam package from a food store—Lorene's customary contribution to Beverly's Thanksgiving dinner. A quart of greasy cold green beans, or dyed-looking beets, or fruit salad whose colors had faded. For the occasion Lorene wore one of her cranberry-colored pants suits and odd-colored rawhide boots. Her signature buzz-cut hair, which had given her such a unique authoritarian look, had been replaced by a rainbow-colored cap of the sort (Beverly thought) that might have been knitted by a handicapped person, for a handicapped person. Lorene's eyebrows were invisible and her eyes were lashless and blinking, touchingly naked.

"Here, Bev. Sorry I'm late."

"You're not late, Lorene. We hadn't even noticed."

This was so rude, and yet so innocently-sisterly rude, Lorene laughed; and Beverly laughed with her.

The last Thanksgiving. Just get through it!

As guests were taking their seats at the dining room table, Virgil arrived through the kitchen door. His absence Beverly had indeed noticed, and had been feeling an admixture of apprehension and hope. She'd had the impression that Virgil would come for her dinner, that he would not disappoint her (again). And here he was alone, and breathless. To her chagrin he explained that he could not stay for dinner after all, he was very sorry.

"What do you mean—'very sorry'? Why aren't you staying? Mom is here, and—your friend Hugo. And your nieces and nephews who haven't seen you in ages."

Virgil was carrying a half-bushel of apples from the farm on Bear Mountain Road, which he set on a table—not an appropriate place. At a glance Beverly could see that the apples were bruised and beginning to rot; they gave off a strong, cold, pungent aroma.

"Is this for me? Us? Well, thanks! You are very thoughtful as always, Virgil." As if Beverly's sarcasm could register with her self-centered and deeply annoying brother.

There was something strange about Virgil as well as annoying. His dirty-blond hair had been combed and brushed; not tied back in a straggly ponytail but spread out onto his shoulders, crackling with static electricity. Beverly stared. Was this—*Virgil*? Her hippie brother was clean-shaven for once, handsome. Or, if not handsome exactly, with that earnest, bony face, not nearly so plain and dour as she recalled. Like an *artiste* he was wearing a loose-fitting shirt of some crude fabric like congealed oatmeal, paint-flecked khaki trousers, sandals with red woolen socks. On his left wrist, some sort of beaded leather twine.

"Didn't you say you were bringing a friend? Where is she?"

"Did I say 'she'? Well—she isn't here. And I have to leave, Beverly, I'm sorry."

"Damn you, Virgil! You knew this was an important Thanksgiving—our first real Thanksgiving since Dad died. You're always 'sorry.'"

Beverly spoke heatedly but not so that anyone apart from Virgil could hear. She'd snatched up the half-bushel of apples, to shove back into Virgil's arms, but Jessalyn appeared in the doorway, to greet Virgil with a hug, and there came swarmy Hugo to shake hands, so Beverly had no choice but to retreat, carrying the God-damned unwanted apples into the kitchen, better yet into the garage, which was cold as a refrigerator. In the morning she could toss the grimy basket and its contents into the trash.

There came Lorene following after Beverly, with a disingenuous smile. "I'd meant to tell you, Bev—I saw Virgil last week at the farm market with his 'new friend.' His companion. I think that's what he is."

"What who is? What?"

"Virgil's new friend. An African-looking young man, years younger than Virgil, with skin so dark it's kind of purple—iridescent—like an eggplant. He looks like one of those seven-foot runners from Kenya, that win all the marathons. His eyes are bulging-white! His legs are knotted with muscle—he was wearing shorts. They were both wearing shorts. I was so surprised, I just stared at them. I don't think Virgil saw me. Or he pretended not to see me. I was—well, surprised."

"But what do you mean, Lorene? Why were you so—surprised?"

"Because almost, Virgil and this young African man were holding hands. I mean, not actually, but as if they'd have liked to. Walking close together, as men usually don't. And talking, and laughing. And Virgil's hair was loose like it is now and he was looking positively luminous."

Beverly stared at her pug-faced sister uncomprehendingly. "I don't know what you are saying, Lorene. I really don't. And this isn't the time for it, at Thanksgiving."

"Well, maybe by Christmas it will sink in. You can invite him—them—for Christmas Eve."

Lorene laughed with much pleasure, ducking away as a younger sister might duck to escape a cuff from an older sister, though in this case Beverly was too distracted to react.

When Beverly returned to the dining room Virgil was on his way out. He'd greeted everyone he knew, he'd introduced himself to Caesar Jones, he and Sophia had had a brief intense exchange, politely he'd declined Steve's invitation to sit down for just a few minutes, to have some turkey. To hell with him.

But Beverly hurried after Virgil, to shut the door behind him.

Calling after—"Next time give me some notice that you 'can't make it,' God damn you. *I hate you.*"

Bounding to his Jeep that was parked on the road Virgil seemed scarcely to hear. A fierce November wind blew Beverly's heartfelt words away like desiccated leaves.

At the head of the table Steve was carving the turkey as he usually did on such family occasions. He'd had several drinks hurriedly and his aim was slightly askew, or perhaps the carving knife had become dull, for the misshapen breast quickly became ravaged, pieces fell onto the platter in shreds. Beverly saw that her husband was affably drunk, his gaze unfocussed and benign. His hair, lank and long combed across the crown of his skull, trimmed shorter at the sides, once vivid-brown, had become the hue of dishwater, like Beverly's own if she'd neglected having it "rinsed" at the beauty salon. He wore a pink-striped shirt meant to be festive that gave him the air of a slightly dissolute croupier.

"Damn!"—Steve cursed mildly and held out the knife for someone to take from him. "Is there a doctor here? Surgeon? I think I'm retiring from the task."

Hugo Martinez, quick to descry an opportunity, rose from his seat beside Jessalyn, and came to seize the knife from Steve's hand.

"I will do it. *Gracias.*"

Beverly cast Steve a sidelong look of muted rage. What on earth did he mean, *retiring*?

Her deceitful husband had been in an obscure mood for days. Usually Steve was ebullient to a fault, cheerful and remote as an FM radio station almost out of earshot but playing great music. You could see that he thought well of himself, he was secretly pleased about something, but you had no idea what, only that it excluded you. But just recently, Steve was not so happy and seemed not so distant but annoyingly *near.*

Money problems? (Did bankers have money problems?)

Women problems? (Had *Steffi,* or *Siri,* or *Mira* deleted him from her in-box?)

Since that first, traumatic day Beverly had not returned to Steve's emails. Too upsetting, and a waste of her rapidly depleting energy.

With a flourish, like a pirate brandishing a scimitar, Hugo Martinez took over the carving of the sixteen-pound turkey. Within minutes, with an expert flashing of the blade, the immense bird was reduced to a carcass. Beverly had to concede, Hugo knew what he was doing. The boastful man had carved many a roast—turkey, suckling pig, goat. (Did Cubans roast goats? Or what was Hugo—Puerto Rican?) And he was damned happy, and pleased with himself, in a white peasant-looking shirt with no collar, of some fabric like linen, sleeves rolled to his elbows. His forearms were hard with muscle, matted with swarthy hairs. His skin was not smooth, but a warm rich taffy hue. His eyebrows and mustache were heavy, tangled. Like Virgil he'd brushed his hair smooth to his shoulders, coarse dark brown threaded with silver. As he carved the turkey and lay slices of meat carefully on a platter he cast smiling glances at Jessalyn at the farther end of the table.

Of course, they will be married. Nothing any of you can do to stop them!

"You're a poet, Mr. Martinez?"—Brianna spoke up boldly. It was clear that she was impressed with her grandmother's glamorous friend. "Can you say a poem for us, then? *Por favor.*"

Where did this come from? Beverly exchanged startled glances with Lorene and Thom. She'd forgotten that Brianna was taking first-year Spanish, if she'd ever known. *Had someone primed Brianna to make this request?*

"Brianna, that's rude. Maybe Hugo doesn't want to 'say a poem.'"

Hated to hear herself pronounce the name so familiarly—*Hugo.*

What the hell was this, *Hugo* at the Benders' dining room table? And Steve had unhesitatingly handed over the carving knife to the man, and announced he was *retiring* from turkey-carving?

But of course Hugo Martinez was not embarrassed by the insolently coquettish young white girl's request. Positively, Hugo was *thrilled.*

"Here is my favorite poem for 'quietude'—the poem that comes to me in the night, like a hand on my shoulder. And for Thanksgiving too, for which we give deepest thanks on all days of the year." Hugo spoke with much emotion, whether genuine or fraudulent, like one who is translating from another language, not quite easily into English. How deceitful he was!—Beverly wanted to leap up from her place at the table, grab her mother's hand and run out of the room.

In a beautifully modulated voice Hugo stood before them, reciting "A Clear Midnight"—by "your greatest American poet Walt Whitman":

"This is thy hour, O Soul, thy free flight into the wordless,
Away from books, away from art, the day erased, the lesson done,
Thee fully forth emerging, silent, gazing, pondering the themes thou lovest best.
Night, sleep, death and the stars."

There was a pause. Everyone was deeply moved, or nearly everyone. Lorene fussed with her napkin and Thom stared down at his plate. Sophia was looking rapt, and Jessalyn was looking radiant. Brianna clapped—"Awesome!" Steve's brother Zack lifted a bottle of Molson's ale to his lips and drank thirstily. Moisture glistened in Caesar Jones's somber eyes and threatened to run down his drawn cheeks. Beverly was so furious she hadn't heard most of the poem, had a vague idea that Hugo Martinez had written it, and resented such exhibitionism—nothing like Whitey telling his lengthy, funny jokes at the table, that most of them knew by heart and could anticipate. Why would you recite a poem on an occasion meant to be festive and happy, with such words as *night, death, stars*!

But soon after, to Beverly's chagrin, Hugo rose from his place at the table, and Jessalyn as well, and Caesar Jones who was seated beside her—for it seemed, after scarcely forty minutes at the table, these three were leaving for another Thanksgiving gathering some miles away in Harbourton.

"But—so soon? You haven't had anything to eat—or almost anything." Beverly was dismayed that her mother should be abandoning her at such a time, and could not recall that Jessalyn had warned her beforehand; or, if she recalled, she could not quite believe that she would actually leave so soon. "Why don't Hugo and his friend go to the other party, and you stay with us, Mom?—we never see you anymore . . ."

But Jessalyn was leaving with Hugo and Caesar Jones. There was no pleading with her, no shaming her into staying with her family, at the door she hugged Beverly and said again that she was sorry but plans for this event had been made months before—"It's a fund-raiser, it's for a really worthy cause. Hugo would be disappointed if—if I didn't come with him."

"And what about your family, Mom? Don't you care that we are disappointed, you aren't staying with us?"

What would Dad say? Beverly did not quite utter these damning words.

Yet, unbelievably—Jessalyn departed. With Hugo Martinez, and the African-American ex-convict who had the decency (at least) to appear embarrassed by Jessalyn's rudeness to her own daughter.

ANOTHER LUXOR, and another glass of wine. And pleasure in this exquisite Thanksgiving, a beautifully prepared meal at a beautiful table.

Except she was noticing, Brianna wasn't eating the turkey on her plate. Pushing it around, with a fastidious wrinkling of her nose.

"Brianna, is something wrong?"

Brianna shrugged, looking away.

Pleasantly Beverly observed that Brianna wasn't eating.

"I am eating, Mom! Jeez."

"But not turkey. Don't tell me you are suddenly a vegetarian."

Still Beverly spoke pleasantly, almost gaily. Others were listening, with hesitant smiles.

"Well, yes. Kind of, I think I am."

"Really! Since when?"

"Since out in the kitchen, Mom. Seeing that poor turkey so kind of *helpless* on its back. And the raw-meat smell."

Brianna shuddered. There was nothing mischievous-malicious in the girl's manner, for once she seemed utterly sincere.

"Who has been influencing you? Virgil?"

"N-No. Is Uncle Virgil a vegetarian? I didn't even know that."

"I think he probably is," Beverly said, laughing irritably. "Or if he isn't, he's the type that should be."

The other children at the table were alert, listening. Brianna's younger sister had a habit of emulating her, and Beverly was hoping to hell this vegetarianism fad wasn't contagious.

Brianna said, "Actually, I would like to be a *vegan*. I've been reading about eating animals and dairy products and how disgusting it is. Wasteful and unethical and *old*."

"What on earth is 'veg-an'?"

"'*Vee*-gan,' Mom. It's not eating any animals or animal products like milk. It's *respecting* other forms of life."

Could this be more bizarre?—at a Thanksgiving dinner? Whitey would be exasperated, impatient. He'd been disapproving as hell when Beverly came to the dinner table as a teenager reluctant to eat because she'd been on a diet; he'd seemed to be personally affronted.

Beverly didn't intend to be baited. Not on this special day. Turning her attention away from Brianna, to the person on her left: Steve's brother Zack who was talking earnestly with a McClaren relative about the upcoming football game.

Oh, how boring! She hated football, and she hated *men*.

There was Steve at the farther end of the table looking flush-faced, distracted. In his early forties, with a receding hairline and a thickening lower face, Steve still managed to be a "handsome" man—women seemed to find him so. (Women who weren't obliged to see him in the early morning unshaven, disheveled, shambling and not very coordinated, distinctly not in a smiling mood.) Beverly disliked her husband's drinking but could not reasonably complain since she was drinking too, except (she was sure) not so conspicuously.

Seeing her eyes on him Steve unexpectedly smiled; the smile he'd sometimes cast her across a room, his wife, the mother of children who were also, however astonishingly, *his;* the message was—*Jesus! How'd we get into this? Us two?* Now lifting his thumb in a jaunty gesture of approval that managed to be both congratulatory and condescending. *Great meal, darling! Great wife and mother! Terrific as usual.*

The wife was *meals,* other women were *sex.* Beverly could not easily forgive him, he had wounded her so deeply.

Well, she would wound *him.* No thought gave her a keener pleasure except (possibly) an acknowledgment from her sister Lorene finally that yes, Beverly's wife/mother life was superior in all ways to Lorene's unmarried/childless/career life.

But it was worrisome, Steve speaking of *retiring.* Of course he'd tried to give the remark a jokey cast. Like an unhappy boy turning his lips inside-out, to repel sympathy. But shouldn't the head of a household take pride in carving meat at his table? Feeding guests, displaying his bounty? As if the husband sensed how his life in this household was coming to an end. How that very evening, the wife he so smugly took for granted would serve him divorce papers.

Steve. There is something here for you to look at.

I will leave these with you, Steve. In this folder.

(But would Beverly actually do such a thing? *Could* she? The divorce lawyer with the chic polished nails had advised her to protect herself financially before telling her husband of her plans, yet she'd made no effort to do this; perhaps then, this meant that Beverly had no real intention of giving Steve the papers. Uttering the dread word *divorce*—could she?)

(She needed to talk about such a decision with Jessalyn, more than she had. Surprising to her, disconcerting, that Jessalyn hadn't tried harder to dissuade her, as Whitey would have.)

Wine? Yes please. One of the guests had taken up the bottle of chilled white wine that Hugo Martinez had brought, a very tart northern Italian wine. (Beverly would ask Steve to look up its price online. Though she supposed that canny Hugo acquired bottles like these at a discount.)

Dry-mouthed, from the medication (probably). But no one knew. No one's business. Wine (alcohol) dehydrates as well but water left her feeling nauseated.

For an hour or more she'd been eating in surges. Not hungry now but still eating. So many hours of preparation!—she had a right to extract as much pleasure from the lengthy meal as possible, as she sensed others felt they must, too. Thom's plate heaped with food, for the second, or was it the third time; yet Thom was probably not very hungry either, estranged from his family at Thanksgiving.

(Thom did miss his family, Beverly was sure. His wife whom everyone liked, to a degree; his children who were, on the whole, better-behaved and nicer children, Beverly had to concede, than hers. It was *not natural* for Thom not to miss them at Thanksgiving!)

Sophia was being asked about medical school. What would be her field of specialization? (Neurology.) When would she begin? (Early in January.) Would she commute to Ithaca, or live there? (Live there.)

Vaguely it was supposed by friends of the McClaren family that Sophia had a Ph.D. in something obscure like neuroscience, or molecular biology; but Beverly knew that Sophia had never finished her doctorate. She'd had some sort of crisis, she'd returned home to Hammond to be near her parents. (No one had ever explained it in those terms, but that was so.) She'd worked as a technician of some kind at that fancy research center—Memorial Park. There, she'd been involved with a married man, a scientist of distinction, Beverly had heard; he was her laboratory supervisor, also an M.D. Of course, Sophia had never shared such intimate information with Beverly, the sisters were not close. Beverly felt hurt that Sophia didn't seem comfortable around her, as Sophia wasn't comfortable around Lorene; which made the older sisters less inclined to be nice to Sophia.

This was a fact: never would Sophia have dared to have an affair with a married man, and a much older man, if their father had been alive.

Whitey would've been livid with disapproval. Jessalyn couldn't have been thrilled, either.

But the affair was over, evidently. Beverly was spared having to have an opinion. Sophia had come to the Benders' alone but didn't seem particularly lonely or aggrieved, talking and laughing with her nieces and nephews. Even talking with Lorene, who usually sneered at Sophia's earnestness. And Thom had spent time talking with Sophia in a corner of the living room, as if he hadn't wanted anyone else to hear; Beverly would have liked to eavesdrop. In a family of five siblings you felt anxiety seeing two or three of them together, out of earshot.

It was unsettling: though you could not really take younger siblings seriously yet with the passage of time they seemed to be gaining on you. When had Sophia ceased being a *virgin*? And Virgil? What sort of emotional/sexual experiences did Virgil have, with his exasperating faux-Buddhism? It was not believable, Virgil could be *gay*. No. Even with Whitey gone, Virgil wouldn't *dare*.

"Well, it's debatable whether consciousness, or 'mind,' precedes matter, or the brain," Sophia was saying, in response to someone's question, "—though it isn't very likely that consciousness drifts about like a cloud seeking neurons to slide into."

There was a startled silence. For a moment no one spoke. Then, eleven-year-old Tige asked suddenly, "Could it be like a radio? Radio waves? Some kind of frequency?"

It was unlike Tige to speak in the presence of adults. Of the Bender children he was the quietest, the most inward. Beverly was amazed, the boy had been listening to Sophia, and seemed to have understood her.

"Tige" was an abbreviation of "Tiger"—the family's pet name for Taylor. Whatever he'd asked, his aunt Sophia was taking the question seriously for Sophia did not condescend to children as most adults did. And so she shook her head gravely, no. She didn't think so. Not like radio waves.

Tige seemed disappointed. He'd wanted to impress his scientist-aunt, Beverly saw with a pang of jealousy.

None of the children ever wanted to impress *her.* Oh, what did they care, Beverly was only their *mom.*

Steve said, "What the hell, Sophie? Each word I can understand but how they fit together, I can't."

It was an awkward attempt at humor. Every exchange between Steve and Beverly's attractive younger sister that Beverly had ever observed was awkward. Sophia laughed, embarrassed. Clearly she didn't want to continue with this line of inquiry for everyone was looking at her now, with uncomprehending smiles. Why did people think that the obscurities of science were somehow *funny*? Beverly didn't.

Her calm young coolly beautiful sister was the medical specialist who studied your CAT scan and saw that you were doomed. Very carefully this woman with the schoolgirl face and mouth unsoftened by lipstick would choose the precise scientific terms in which to express this doom.

Thom said, with an edge of impatience, as if he'd been hoping not to become involved, "Wait. You're claiming, Sophie, that our personalities are just wisps of—cloud?—molecules?—coming out of nowhere and going nowhere? That's what you're saying?"

Sophia shifted uncomfortably. "I'm not 'claiming' anything, really. These are just theories of mind, I don't understand myself. I am not a researcher."

In Sophia's world, the highest calling was "researcher." Beverly knew this without quite understanding what "researcher" meant.

Thom protested: "Our personalities feel so strong. Maybe not from inside all the time but from the outside. Think of Dad—Whitey McClaren. Everyone who ever met him will always remember *him*. There was only one 'Whitey' and he certainly wasn't any wisp of cloud."

Others agreed, vehemently. There was an air of just slightly aggressive elation around the table. Steve said *Hell yes*, and Steve's brother Zack said *You said it!* Brianna said *Ohh, I miss Grandpa Whitey!* You wanted to glance about the table to see where Whitey was sitting, drink in hand.

(Yet: Was it true? Beverly recalled that when Whitey had been in the hospital following his stroke, sometimes he'd said very strange things. He'd been hallucinating. Some crucial part of his brain had been impaired, he could not enunciate words, he had lost the sensation in half his face. Once, Beverly had entered the hospital room and Jessalyn had come quickly to her, to pull her out into the corridor begging her *Not just now, please not now, dear. Dad isn't himself right now.*)

Sophia was looking relieved that attention had shifted from her to Thom, and beyond. Men took up combative conversation like football: the ball had to be passed about, but not meekly. No one waited his turn to speak. Beverly ceased listening, she was calculating when to begin clearing dishes, bringing out dessert. Much of the turkey white meat had been eaten, a good deal of the dark meat. The fancy stuffing had been popular, too. The damned brussels sprouts with slivered almonds that Lorene had brought in the Styrofoam container, stone cold, just perceptibly withered, had scarcely been touched; Beverly would repackage them to hand back to Lorene—*Here. Thanks!*

Or maybe Beverly would say, with a sisterly smirk—*Keep refrigerated, you can recycle next Thanksgiving.*

As always Jessalyn's sweet potato soufflé had been a favorite, the serving bowl was nearly empty. (Jessalyn's secret ingredient: marshmallows.) Each year Beverly vowed she wouldn't have a small spoonful of the soufflé but each year she had a large portion.

And there was Steve, emptying a bottle of wine into his own glass. Again regarding her. Guiltily? He'd just returned to the table. More than once in the past hour (Beverly had noted) he'd excused himself from the table, left the dining room, (possibly) slipped out of the house. Smoking out-of-doors (though he wasn't supposed to be smoking at all), or making a call on his God-damned cell phone.

I know about you, Steve.

Yes? What do you know?

I know what you do. What you think. Where your mind is. What your secret life is.

And what is that, darling?

It had been at least three years, Beverly had appealed to her husband to draw up a will. She would arrange for hers, and he would arrange for his. They would go together to Barron, Mills & McGee. They must not procrastinate any longer. They owed it to their children and to each other not to die intestate. (*Intestate* was a term Beverly had mastered, to be uttered carefully, to intimidate poor Steve who could not help but hear *testes* in it, and to feel imperiled.) Steve had agreed in theory that they should draw up their wills but each time Beverly made an appointment with the law firm Steve found an excuse to cancel. Pityingly she thought—*He thinks he will never die.*

A woman thinks otherwise. A woman knows otherwise.

Women are familiar with their bodies in ways men are not.

Each month, bleeding. You understand the body's propensity for dissolution. But also, the body's propensity to endure.

After dinner, after the football game, when everyone had gone home and the children were in bed, she would leave the folder with Steve and he would think the papers had something to do with the will.

Until he began reading. And then he would realize.

Too late. Yes I love you too—or I did love you. But now—too late.

What was Lorene boasting of?—her plan to endow scholarships at the high school, in Whitey's name. This was a new scheme of Lorene's, which Beverly resented. Her sister hoping to curry favor with the community and the family and with their (deceased) father in such an obvious way.

John Earle McClaren Scholarship Fund. It did sound noble, rather wonderful.

"You're also going on quite an ambitious trip, aren't you, Lorene? At Christmas?"

"Yes. I am. I deserve a break, I think."

"Public school teachers don't have summer-long 'breaks'? Really?"

"Administrators are not 'teachers.' We work on a different schedule—full-time."

"And you're 'on leave' for the spring term? No schedule at all? That will be a considerable break." Trying to speak sincerely but it felt as if mischievous red ants were running up Beverly's sides tickling. "And you are being 'transferred' after that—to another school."

"Yes."

Why not say it—demoted. You are being demoted to assistant principal at an inferior school.

Gritting her teeth (in rage? shame?) Lorene ignored her sister's taunts to tell the table that most of the money Whitey had left to her was to be passed on to the community—"Dad wanted us to be generous. He was a model to us, to think of others besides ourselves." In the tone of a high school principal addressing an audience of credulous parents, mildly hectoring but kindly, idealistic. What a charade! Even in her generosity Lorene was stingy, calculating. Beverly saw through the facade as you'd examine an X-ray. Especially, Beverly resented her sister's "philanthropy" for it meant that Beverly would have to be philanthropic, too.

Of Whitey's bequest she'd spent about one-third and most of that on house repairs, upkeep. New roof, repaving the driveway. Too weak-minded not to give in to Steve, who'd put pressure on her to provide money for one damn thing or another including a new SUV (for Steve). But she'd saved a portion for herself. Needed to hide it away in a special account in any bank but the Bank of Chautauqua where her deceitful husband could not find it.

One day, she would disappear. Fly away. A trip like Lorene's to an exotic island, or closer to home, maybe New York City where (she believed) she had a few friends from college, still. Sorority sisters. A circle of friends awaited her—somewhere. When the children were older and not so dependent upon her. When the last of them left for college which would be—when?—her brain went blank, the years shimmered out of sight.

Heard herself saying: "Yes, Dad did expect us to be generous. I don't think I've told anyone—yet—I've arranged to endow a space at the library—downtown . . . *The John Earle McClaren Reading Circle* for special groups, students, senior citizens, immigrants needing help with English . . . It will be in one of those rooms on the first floor with the glass walls, just behind the circulation desk."

Steve was looking quizzically at Beverly but others at the table were impressed. Several clapped, and Zack lifted his bottle of ale in a salute. Thom and Sophia were quizzical too but (it seemed) approving while Lorene stared coldly at Beverly as if to accuse—*Liar! What bullshit.*

(It was so, Beverly hadn't exactly spoken with anyone at the library yet. Whitey had left the library a considerable amount of money in his will and so Beverly's idea was not so very original, yet it had come to her in a flash, and had had to be uttered at this moment, before the dinner guests were dispersed. But she would call the development officer at the library whom she knew, and would drive down on Monday with a check.)

Beverly's philanthropy would be noted in the local press, she was sure. If she acted swiftly, before Lorene's "scholarship endowments" were noted.

At last there came dessert. Fruit tarts, vanilla sponge cake with strawberry frosting, Hugo's pumpkin pies (coarse crusts, too much allspice, otherwise decent), several flavors of ice cream. Buttercrunch cookies, oatmeal cookies. Chocolates in gaudy gilt wrappers.

Football preliminaries had begun on TV. Half the table departed noisily to watch downstairs.

Thom too rose with the other males but (it would turn out) did not accompany them downstairs, simply slipped away from the house without saying goodbye to anyone but taking time soon afterward to send Beverly a hurried and perfunctory email from his cell phone thanking her for inviting him and for *such a great dinner as usual.*

The elderly McClaren relative who'd come with her middle-aged son had a bout of dizziness trying to rise from the table. There were cries of distress. Beverly felt her heart sink—*Oh shit is somebody going to die, too*?—but practical-minded Sophia intervened, helping the woman to lower her head to her knees, to restore blood to her brain, and the crisis passed.

"Sophia will make a great doctor"—inevitably, this was said.

Soon then, they were clearing the table. Nothing so messy as the remains of a Thanksgiving dinner. The kitchen looked as if a whirlwind had blown through it leaving at its center a grotesque turkey cadaver on an enormous grease-streaked platter but Beverly only laughed—her heartiest laugh—had to hand it to her *Beverly doesn't let anything faze her, always in a good mood.*

Another little white pill washed down with tart white wine helping her to see the bright side of things, unless it was the absurdity of all things: husband downstairs avidly watching a *game with a ball* on TV, wife upstairs vigorously scraping and rinsing plates, running the garbage disposal so that it was threatening to explode even as the marriage was unraveling like a cheap synthetic-knit sweater.

Handing Lorene the Styrofoam container into which she'd spooned leftover brussels sprouts. Sweet-sisterly *Thanks, Lorene! As usual.*

Lorene had carried a few plates into the kitchen with the air of one to whom such women's work was a novelty, not entirely disagreeable but out of character; it was Lorene's strategy to keep at the margins of heavy lifting, plate-scraping, pan-scouring and anything involving garbage, leaving others who were more qualified ("women") to do such work. Though her dominant mode was sarcasm Lorene was curiously tone-deaf and rarely recognized sarcasm in another, accepting the uneaten brussels sprouts from her sister with equanimity—"Good! These were not cheap, and I can eat them tomorrow."

Sophia was the last of the McClarens to leave. Hugging Beverly impulsively as she'd rarely done and thanking her for being such a "wonderful sister"—(had the wine gone to Sophia's head?—these words made Beverly want to cry).

Then adding, hesitantly, riskily: "But I think, Beverly, if I were you, I wouldn't make Mom feel guilty about her friend Hugo. She is trying hard, you know, just to—keep going."

Beverly protested: "I—I wasn't trying—to make Mom feel guilty . . . I just—I don't think—"

"But it's Mom's life, Beverly. Not yours. Try to be happy for her."

"But it's wrong for Mom to be happy—isn't it?"

Not knowing what the hell she was saying. God damn Sophia for provoking her and now yes, Beverly was crying, angry-crying, as Sophia hurried out the walk buttoning her coat as she fled.

Wanting to call after Sophia—*I am not making Mom feel guilty, Mom is guilty!*

IT WAS 10:30 P.M. The football game was long over. Of the raucous fans only Steve remained in the TV room sprawled in his recliner, TV remote in hand and staring bleary-eyed at the television screen. Preparing herself for the mess of the TV room after hours of male occupancy Beverly entered with a steely smile carrying the folder from Barron, Mills & McGee which she set on the table beside her husband with a neutral, not-unfriendly remark: "Here is something for you to peruse."

Peruse. She'd decided on this canny word, an oblique word. The precise word for this occasion.

Steve blinked and squinted at the folder, shuddering. "Oh God. Is it the will?"

"There is no 'the' will. There is your will, and there is my will."

In her neutral voice Beverly spoke, calmly. Though her heart was beating rapidly with sympathy for the man who was looking so apprehensive.

"Jesus, why now? I mean—Thanksgiving night . . ."

How tired the husband was sounding! Hours of TV football had drained him of his youth.

Even now Beverly was tempted to touch him. Wrist, shoulder. Just a fleeting touch. And Steve might grasp her hand as he sometimes did, and kiss it. A casual and yet touching gesture that cost him very little and meant a good deal to Beverly.

She'd meant to bring him a bottle of club soda, as she often did at such times when he'd been watching TV sports intensely. In danger of dehydration. Even now, she might return upstairs to get a bottle from the refrigerator for him . . . He would appreciate that.

But Steve's gaze drifted back to the TV screen as if drawn by an irresistible gravity. Nothing there except an advertisement and so he switched channels. Another advertisement and so he switched again.

The air in the basement was stale, stuffy. Masculine odors. An atmosphere of depletion. Excitement that had plummeted to fatigue. Chairs had been dragged in front of the large flat-screen TV mounted on the wall and unwanted cushions had been tossed about. The children's stacks of DVDs had been pushed aside. On a cabinet shelf, leaving a ring on the maple wood, was a tall emptied Molson's bottle. The husband was in no hurry to rouse himself from the recliner and come upstairs. He'd loosened the top buttons of his shirt, and undone his belt. Kicked off his shoes. Drunk, or in the lethargic aftermath of drunk.

Beverly picked up scattered beer cans, bottles, plates bearing sticky remnants of desserts. Crumpled napkins on the carpet.

The last time. No more.

Steve made no move to open the folder. Cartoon laughter blared from the TV.

Politely Beverly asked, "How was the game?"

Steve shrugged, making a grunting noise—*Ughh.*

Who'd won, who'd lost was a matter of zero interest to Beverly but her principle had always been, regarding men/boys and games: be polite. Don't sneer. Sympathize, for it seems to mean much to them.

"Your team didn't win?"

"No-ooo. 'My team' did not win."

It was Steve who was sneering now, turning back to the TV.

For a moment Beverly waited. Would he say nothing about the Thanksgiving dinner? The food, the look of the table? The effort?

As she was about to leave he called after her: "Hon, that was great. The dinner. Really great." Pausing, and adding, "Could you bring me a club soda? If there's any left? Thanks!"

UPSTAIRS, SHE WAITED.

Lying on her bed positioning her head on pillows trying not to provoke a headache. Between the folds of her brain were slivers of glass. Take care! She'd had too much to drink, and too much to eat. She'd meant to loosen her belt but discovered she was not wearing a belt. The waistband of her black silk slacks was cutting cruelly into her (soft, flaccid) flesh.

The little white antidepressants had failed to dissolve into her bloodstream and were floating there now like phosphorescent globs of detergent in a stream.

Mom! Why are you just standing there?

What is wrong with Mom? Half the time we come into the house she's just—standing there like a zombie . . .

For God's sake, Mom. What is wrong with you?

She'd liked *Mommy.* She'd been a young *Mommy.*

But *Mom* was something else. *Mom* meant you are not yourself but a part of someone else. Belonging to someone else.

You had to be *My Mom, Our Mom.* You could not be just *Mom.*

It would not be said *A Mom was awarded the highest honor of the nation yesterday at a president's reception in Washington, D.C.* It would not be said *A platoon of Moms marched into and massacred a border village yesterday.* It would not be said *A gathering of Moms unveiled a stunning new medical arts center.* Nor would it be said *Mom Arrested on Rape Charge. Mom Indicted.*

Now that Whitey had gone away nothing was certain. The sky had opened. Like venetian blinds yanked open. What was beyond the blinds you hadn't seen before, could be just another wall. Or a corner of sky.

"What? Who is—" Wakened with a start. She'd thought that someone had entered the room to check on her where she'd fallen asleep in so awkward a way, her neck was aching badly. And her bladder aching badly.

Nearly midnight. Thank God Thanksgiving Day 2011 was ended.

Went into the bathroom to use the toilet. Not walking very steadily. Over-bright lights. Beyond the glare she could not see her face clearly which was a blessing. *Mom, for God's sake. That lipstick is not flattering.*

Suddenly she remembered: Steve!

She'd left him downstairs in the TV room. In the recliner.

If he fell asleep watching TV she would wait for him to come upstairs but if he failed to come, she would sigh and go downstairs, two flights of stairs, to wake him, and bring him back upstairs. It was cruel to let the husband sleep in the TV room and crueler still to pretend that you were not aware that the husband was sleeping in the TV room in the recliner that would cause his neck and his spine to ache.

Two flights of stairs she descended, and there was Steve on his recliner in the TV room as she'd left him, now asleep and breathing laboriously through his mouth. Reflected light from the TV played on his face that was slack in repose and looking years older than his age. Gently she extricated the TV remote from his fingers and switched off the TV.

How welcome, the sudden silence! For a moment she feared that Steve would waken. But he did not.

She saw, he had not opened the folder. Of course, he had not touched the folder. He'd drunk two-thirds of the club soda and had set the bottle on top of the folder where it left a ring. One of his legs had slipped from the recliner and lay at an odd angle like a broken or paralyzed leg.

"Steve. It's me."

And, "Steve? It's not too late."

Great annoyance she felt for the sleeping husband, yet sympathy as well. His neck would surely ache, and his spine. He would need help on the stairs. He would be embarrassed, needing his wife to help him out of the recliner and onto his feet and up two flights of stairs. He was not old, even if his back ached and his legs felt weak!—he was far from *old*. The wife would disguise the awkwardness of the occasion by counting *One-two-three! Up!*—as you'd joke with a young child.

Discreetly the wife took up the folder, beneath her arm. She would hide it away in a drawer in the bedroom. She would hide it from the husband until another, more appropriate time.

Wind Chimes

In the night. In the wind. A sound of distant voices, laughter.

She is not certain if she has been awake, or is waking only now. The room is lightless in a way that presses against her eyeballs, like invisible thumbs.

Fumbling for the bedside lamp but her fingers grope in the dark, in vain.

Or perhaps she is in another bed. In another room for she has been expelled from this room, in which she had slept for so many years with her beloved husband.

He is sleeping now in the earth, the husband. It is lightless there, moist and cold though not freezing for the earth is protective of those who lay beneath it.

Snow lies thinly over the grave markers, the tall grasses behind the darkened house. In the fast-running creek, snow melts without a trace.

She has removed the stack of books from beside her bed. Dog-eared at page 111 *The Sleepwalkers* has been returned to Whitey's bookshelf in another part of the house.

There are other books here now, on her bedside table. Slender books of poetry, a book of black-and-white photographs.

It is the eve of her wedding. Not to Whitey but to another—his face is obscured.

Yet, Whitey observes. Whitey has not ever ceased observing.

Toss the dice, darling. Be brave!

She is apprehensive for she is going to be married, she is going to be a bride (again).

Is she expected to wear white? A long white gown, a white veil? She has no white shoes, she is undecided what to do. In the end, she supposes she must go without shoes, barefoot.

The white bridal gown will be a sheet wrapped about her. Her arms crossed over her chest, for warmth.

Wind chimes!—that is what she has been hearing.

Close behind the house, wind chimes above the deck, in the lowermost limbs of trees. Who had placed them there? Possibly Jessalyn herself, years ago. In this bed Whitey had lain with his arms behind his head and Jessalyn beside him utterly content listening to rain, wind, the sweet sonorous chimes from somewhere beyond the darkened room.

So beautiful. It's like heaven here. I love you.

V.

Galápagos

JANUARY 2012

Her head! Such pain. Excruciating like nails driven into her brain.

And shortness of breath, and extreme fatigue. So that the thought comes to her almost as a relief that she has died in this strange breathless place in the mountains, she has *passed away.*

A man whose face she can't see is asking with some urgency: Darling? Can you open your eyes?

Gripping her hand as if to steady her. For the way down is steep, two hundred stone steps. Yet, she is lying very still in this unfamiliar place—atop a bed with a hard mattress—struggling to breathe. What an effort it is to open her eyes for the mildest light makes her cry out in pain.

Church bells, nearby. Exuberant, over-loud as deranged wind chimes.

It is a fairy-tale place. A fairy tale gone wrong.

What you deserve. How dare you imagine you can leave us.

Outside the windows of the beautiful old Quito Hotel, Quito, Ecuador. In the historic center of the old Incan city in the Andes, on a high hill amid rooftops of many colors. A nightmare of crammed-together dwellings, narrow passageways, crimson *bougainvillea*—a tropical flower unknown in the northern state in which Jessalyn has lived her entire life.

Wanting to show her beauty, he has said. The beauty of the world.

She'd only just glimpsed the church steeple rising out of the hillside, the previous day. Before the headache worsened. The sharp clear blade-like church bells tolling the hour had not tormented her, yet.

How beautiful! But how thin the air, in this place.

Her companion, to whom she is not married, speaking rapidly in a language she doesn't know, speaking and laughing with the taxi driver who'd brought them from the airport, the hotel manager, hotel staff. All are charmed with him, the swarthy-skinned visitor from the United States who speaks their language like a native. And she, the white-skinned American woman beside him, smiling mute and foolish, hopeful.

You don't have to go through with it, Mom. You can tell Hugo you don't want to go with him. Ecuador is so far—what if something happens to you?

We will be worrying about you, Mom. All of us.

The plan this morning is to visit a very old church, within walking distance of the Quito Hotel, then to climb two hundred rock-steps in a hillside behind the church to an abandoned stone chapel from which (it is promised) they will have a *muy espectacular* view of the city. But through the interminable breathless night Jessalyn has become increasingly ill.

Altitude sickness! Quito is more than nine thousand feet above sea level. (Hammond, New York, is approximately five hundred feet.)

Can't breathe, can't think clearly. Eyes aching. Where is she?

Wanting badly to cover her head with a pillow, to muffle the aggressive church bells. But too weak for even such minimal exertion.

He is very concerned for her, the man. Speaking to her in urgent words she can't comprehend. Too much effort to listen, still more to reply to him.

Hugo has closed shutters over the windows to keep out the bright-glaring sun. How vivid, how relentless the sun is in Ecuador, fifteen miles south of the Equator! They'd left an opaque gray January sky in Hammond, New York, to travel through much of the previous day to this glaring-blue sky in the Southern Hemisphere. Five degrees Fahrenheit there, seventy-two degrees here. Their plan is to spend three days on the mainland of Ecuador, then fly to the Galápagos Islands where they will stay for nine days. In Quito, Hugo has rented a car and a driver to take them to the equatorial monument at La Mitad del Mundo—"The Middle of the World"—and beyond that into the highlands of the Andes, to the town of Ibarra, where they are to spend a day and a night before returning to Quito, and from there to the Galápagos.

But Jessalyn is short of breath, paralyzed by headache pain of a kind she has never experienced before. Is her brain swelling?—pressing against her skull? Almost, she can feel the terrible pressure, increasing by slow degrees as her body flushes and sweats.

Fear of dying. In this remote place. Three thousand miles from home.

Hugo, that canny traveler, familiar with high-altitude travel, has taken care to provide Jessalyn with ibuprofen tablets and (bottled) water. (Of course, all drinking water must be bottled here. And beware of ice cubes!) Before leaving Hammond he'd acquired prescription medication for Jessalyn and himself: one capsule (Diamox) to be taken before leaving Hammond, another to be taken when they arrived in Quito, this morning a third (which Jessalyn could barely bring herself to swallow).

Fearful of vomiting, soiling the bedsheets. In this beautiful suite! The hotel staff has provided other remedies for Hugo to bring to the stricken *señora:* a dusky-tasting tea prepared from cocoa leaves, a dark, bitter chocolate bar.

Nothing seems to help. The dusky-tasting tea runs down her chin, impossible to swallow. Just the smell of the dark, bitter chocolate bar makes her nauseated.

So sorry! So very sorry.

She has disappointed Hugo, she knows. Though Hugo insists that this isn't so.

Jessalyn tells him, Please go without me. I will be all right.

She can remain in the hotel room, in bed. In the darkened room which is in fact a very comfortable room. (Except for the damned church bells! But these will cease at night, at least.) Hugo can travel into the mountains as they'd planned, to Ibarra, and stay the night at the hotel there. She will be safe here alone, she is sure. (Personal safety doesn't concern Jessalyn just now, she is so sick.) When Hugo returns in a day and a half surely she will be feeling better, and in any case they can fly to the Galápagos as they'd planned, which will bring them to sea level.

Difficult for Jessalyn to explain this. Her tongue is numb, words come slow and confused. But Hugo interrupts to say no, not a good idea. He can't leave her, so sick.

But please, Jessalyn pleads. You have come so far, you will be disappointed . . .

Hugo insists, no. He is not such a child to be *disappointed*.

Hugo has traveled in South America, Tibet, China, Nepal, at high altitudes, and has several times experienced altitude sickness, but at much greater heights—beyond twelve thousand feet. He'd taken a variety of medications including local, herbal medicines, he'd managed always to keep going. To Hugo, Quito is not so very high; he had not anticipated that Jessalyn might be so severely stricken.

She is probably dehydrated, he tells her. If only she would try to drink the bottled water he has brought her!

Gamely, she tries. But begins to cough, gag.

Church bells are tolling (again). Is it a death, a funeral?—Jessalyn wonders.

Never an end. An infinity of funerals.

The bells bring no comfort as wind chimes bring comfort. It is her punishment to have traveled so far to this strange place in the Andes.

How short of breath she is! Half-recalling, she'd run up a flight of stairs. (Had she? No: the elevator had ascended slowly, an ornamental gilt cage.) Still, she is breathless from the effort.

The room is darkened like a cave. Her eyes are damp with moisture, the pupils dilated like the eyes of a trapped animal. Meaning to comfort her the man half-lies on the bed beside her. Tall, large, ungainly, heavy pressing against her. They are not married yet he is husbandly, or would be husbandly. This is the role a husband would play, such solicitude, such care. Except the bed sinks beneath his weight which is jarring to her, and makes her head hurt. He is stroking her forehead, her hair that has become damp and matted.

His hand, a heavy hand, too warm. Calloused fingers catch in her fine hair and in a haze of pain she is not always sure whose hand it is. Oh, she wishes he would not touch her! But she cannot bring herself to push the hand away.

Maybe shut her eyes and try to sleep. A cold, damp cloth over her eyes. Would that help?

He is returning from the bathroom with a damp cloth. Not cold but lukewarm. Again, she steels herself for the sudden sinking of the bed on his side. Wincing in pain—*Oh!*

If she doesn't begin to recover soon, Hugo says. They will have to alter their plans.

Forget about driving into the Andes. Forget about Ibarra which is as high as Quito. If he can book a flight they can fly to the coastal town of Guayaquil where the altitude will be sea level. If he can book a hotel there, at this popular time of the year.

Jessalyn protests: she does not want him to change his plans. He has come so far, he has brought his photographic equipment . . . Two expensive cameras of which one is quite heavy. A tripod, in a backpack.

Jessalyn will be all right by herself, she is sure. If she can stay very still and not move her head, eyes shut. Without having to see or speak with anyone. A terrible malaise like filthy water washing into her mouth, filling her lungs, making her want to vomit up her guts, her very life. This malaise of which she cannot speak to her companion, it is her secret from him as (she is sure) he has secrets from her. But she is hopeful that the malaise will begin to lighten, if she is totally alone, and gives herself up to it unresisting.

It is a malaise that has something to do with the cemetery, that evening. The grave marker—JOHN EARLE MCCLAREN. How desperate the widow had been, seeking the lost husband in a wet cold place with no name.

Hugo insists, he can't leave her! Ridiculous.

His voice is too loud in the darkened room. It makes her head ache more sharply, it makes her sweat. So exhausted is Jessalyn, the very thought of staggering into the bathroom, to attempt to take a shower, leaves her weak with fatigue.

The bedsheets, crisp-laundered white cotton when they'd arrived the previous day, have become clammy-damp, smelly. Smelling of her (sick, fevered) body. She is ashamed, the man who has said he loves her is close beside her, on the bed, grasping her hand to comfort her when it is not comfort she deserves but pain, and the oblivion of pain.

What now? What is he saying? An edge of exasperation in his voice.

He wants her to eat! To try to eat. He has dared to bring food into the room, on a tray. But Jessalyn is not hungry, the thought of food is repulsive to her. The smell, sickening.

So tired, she only wants to be alone.

It is her fault. It is what she deserves. That she is here in this hotel, in the old "colonial" quarter of Quito, Ecuador. She has come here with a man who is not her husband, who has said that he loves her even if she does not (entirely) love him, a man of whom her family disapproves. Never in her life has Jessalyn done anything so reckless, so improvident.

Whitey had said—*Toss the dice, darling. Do it!*

She'd postponed immunizations (typhoid, yellow fever, hepatitis A, malaria) until two weeks before the trip, and some of these (probably) have had adverse effects, mild fever, nausea. The Hammond doctor had said to her, surprised, why, Jessalyn, where on earth are you going?—for Jessalyn had been Dr. Rothfeld's patient for years, as Whitey had been.

Where on earth. With whom. Why.

Haltingly she told him. Perhaps, just slightly proudly she told him. Travel to Ecuador? The Galápagos? Staring at Jessalyn as if he'd never seen her before. This white-haired woman, Whitey McClaren's widow? So recently a widow?

Must have been that Rothfeld knew no rumors of the widow's Hispanic lover for he'd asked if Jessalyn was going on a cruise with friends and in the awkwardness of the moment Jessalyn allowed him to think yes, a cruise ship, the *Esmeralda*. Smiling to think that the doctor was imagining a luxury cruise ship of *widows*.

Hugo seems offended, hurt. That Jessalyn would ask him to go away and leave her. That she thought no more of him than that, a man who would abandon a sick friend in a country new and strange to her, whose language she could not speak.

Would Jessalyn's husband have done such a thing? Abandon her? No? Then why would she think that he, Hugo, would abandon her? It is the first time in their relationship that Hugo speaks sharply to Jessalyn.

She has ruined everything now, she thinks, crushed. She has deeply insulted Hugo, she has destroyed his feeling for her that has been precious.

Her brain hurts so, it's as if a plate has been smashed inside her skull. Sharp pieces of glass, cutting into her brain.

Oh I am so sorry, Hugo! Forgive me.

Too weak to cry. The black rushing malaise sweeps over her.

And where has Hugo gone? Barely Jessalyn can open her eyes to see, the room seems to be empty.

But it is a relief, to be alone. The man's presence has been too much for her in this weakened state, she has felt oppressed, obliterated. Not enough oxygen in the room, Hugo has sucked it all up.

Especially, she has feared Hugo draining away her sorrow, her grief. Her loneliness, that has become precious to her.

Only in times of utter quiet does her loneliness return, as a kind of balm.

Though she is feeling devastated, she has driven the man away, insulted. (And if he doesn't return? What will she do then? She is helpless without him in this distant place.)

Thinking now, of course Whitey would never have left her in the hotel dazed and sick, as she has urged Hugo to leave her. Not for a moment would Whitey have thought of such a thing.

Yet, Jessalyn had left *him*.

In the misery of this illness realizing that she had betrayed her husband, unwittingly. Poor Whitey had died—"passed away"—when Jessalyn hadn't been at his bedside, to hold his hand and comfort him. She had been in the hospital and yet, by the time she'd been allowed to come to him, it was too late: his fever had spiked at 104.1 degrees Fahrenheit and his heart had failed. Jessalyn had not ever seen him alive again.

When she entered the room it was all over—the struggle of her husband to live. Medics had begun the preparation of his body for death. Tubes, needles had been removed from his exhausted veins. Machines monitoring his vital organs had been turned off. His life had ended so abruptly, Jessalyn hadn't had the opportunity to say goodbye.

Had Whitey's soul departed his body? Had Whitey's soul remained in the room, lost, confused, waiting for Jessalyn to speak to him?

Oh God. What have I done.

Waves of horror wash over her. In her husband's hour of need she had abandoned him.

It is her punishment, this illness. Why she has been brought here.

The church bells have ceased for the time being. It is past noon. The sun is fierce against the shuttered windows, a January sun at the Equator. Atop the bed with the hard mattress Jessalyn lies without moving, listening to the cries of birds. She wonders if they are bright-feathered, exotic birds—parrots? Cockatoos?

She has driven the man away, who'd loved her. Something reckless and greedy in her, terrible to acknowledge.

A small boat drifting. The canoe behind the house, at the creek. *Whitey? Where are you?* Sees her hand reach out for his, in a shadowy place.

She is in the canoe, this is a surprise. Always, she has feared canoes! A sudden move, a loss of balance, the canoe could capsize—easily.

Yet, her children had taken out the canoe, as well as the rowboat. Whitey had told her don't look, don't look out the window and don't be ridiculous, the boys can handle that canoe as well as I can. Whitey had spent much of their marriage laughing at Jessalyn, tenderly.

Here is the situation: if Whitey can securely grasp her hand, and if Jessalyn can grip the inside of the canoe, he could tug her toward him in the water. It would not be easy, it would require patience and very often Whitey has been impatient.

Here is a narrow cave into which dark water laps. She has to lower her head in order to enter it.

Jessalyn? I didn't expect to find you here. This far from home.

It is! It is far from home!—(her voice is gay, to disguise the fear she feels)—*I didn't realize it was so far. But I am here now.*

Darling! Give me your hand.

There is a bedside lamp with a stained glass shade. It must be later. The same day, interminable.

The stained glass light is muted but still hurts her eyes.

Jessalyn?—suddenly close beside her, he calls to her. Wake up. Give me your hand—the man is stooped over her.

More roughly than she would wish, the man is helping her out of the dank smelly bed. Explaining where they are going, how they must hurry.

How is it possible, Hugo hasn't left her? Had she failed to understand?

Her instincts bridle, it is wrong to put on clothes as she is doing, not-clean clothing, and her body slick and smelly with fever. And her hair unbrushed, matted. Dried mucus in the corners of her eyes. Surprising to her, the man is not repelled by her as she is repelled by herself.

Somehow, Hugo has managed to get Jessalyn dressed, and shoes on her feet. He has managed to get her on her feet and able to move as he supports her with his arm around her waist.

Descending by slow creaking degrees in the gilt cage elevator. Suitcases, Hugo's backpack, a hotel porter speaking rapidly to them in Spanish.

Interior of a taxi. Hugo is helping her inside. Less than twenty-four hours ago they'd come from the airport in a taxi very like this, now they are departing Quito.

Almost, Jessalyn feels a pang of regret. Somewhere behind her and lost to her now, the shadowy cave where Whitey had awaited her. Yet, it has not happened that way.

Obscuring half her face, a pair of dark-lensed sunglasses that Hugo has secured on her, to shield her eyes from the white-glaring sun.

On this bumpy ride they are being taken in the taxi to the airport outside town. Descending a long winding hill past lush vegetation.

Hugo has been telling her laughingly no, of course he hadn't left her. Only to make travel arrangements. Only to take a half-dozen quick photographs in the street. The taxi brings them to the airport which is a few hundred feet lower than Quito, miraculously the pain in Jessalyn's head begins to lessen.

She is not so nauseated now. Hugo insists that she try to drink bottled water, in small mouthfuls.

The small plane taxis along the runway like a frantic shorebird. It does not seem believable to Jessalyn that the plane will ascend into the air, rattling terribly, one of its wings dipping lower than the other, and yet within minutes they are rattling/humming aloft, and the glamorous air flight attendants are on their feet in the aisle, bravely smiling. And here the miracle increases, for the air pressure in the cabin allows her to breathe once again. Almost, she can feel the tight-tangled blood vessels in her brain begin to untangle.

The plane lurches!—at once, murmurs of alarm, and amusement at the alarm, ripple through the cabin.

Flying west, to the coastal city of Guayaquil. A quick flight, within an hour Jessalyn's headache has faded. In the resort city she is able to walk leaning on Hugo's arm, along the sun-splotched quay. Here are palm trees, crimson and purple bougainvillea. Paradise! To her surprise Jessalyn is very hungry.

Hugo is relieved that Jessalyn has recovered so swiftly. Several times he stops her to kiss her eyelids, her hair.

So worried about you, darling! Sick with worry.

Jessalyn perceives in Hugo a man who has been a husband and a father: a protector. She had not witnessed him *sick with worry* in the past.

She is giddy with love for him. Slipping her arms around him, in this public place. Kissing his mouth, the silly mustache. Love for the tall startled smiling man who'd brought her to a terrible place but has now saved her from it.

"MARRY ME, DARLING! TODAY."

It is not the first time that Hugo has suggested marriage. And Jessalyn has not known how to reply.

But—I am already married. I thought you understood . . .

But today is different. Laughing together at lunch on the quay, in the open air. Both are very hungry, in fact ravenous. Jessalyn has never been so hungry in her life.

Awaiting their food, tearing at crusts of thick dark bread.

Hears herself say yes of course, she will marry him.

It is very sudden. It is not at all sudden, it has been prepared with the fanatic care with which a small garden is tilled, seeded, planted.

"But do you love me?"—wistfully Hugo asks her.

"Of course I love you. Yes."

Hugo is astounded. But Hugo is tugging at his mustache, smiling.

"Oh, Jessalyn! Your family won't approve. You had better consult them, darling."

"No." Jessalyn laughs, wildly—"I had *better not* consult them."

A half-glass of wine has gone to her head. Indeed, her brain had almost killed her. Yet, her brain *had not killed her.* Whichever words she utters to this man gazing at her with adoration will become miraculously true.

It is so, Hugo Martinez has become precious to Jessalyn. Sometimes she feels that she has known him a very long time. That he has been waiting for her for a very long time.

And there is the prospect, of which Jessalyn doesn't want to think, of Hugo one day becoming ill, being hospitalized. And if so, Jessalyn must be *the wife*.

For there are places where if you are not a spouse or a relative, if there is not a legal contract defining your relationship, you may not be allowed at the bedside of your stricken companion even if you are all that he has.

Even now in the sun-splotched restaurant on the quay she is thinking of Whitey marooned in a hospital room, white walls, white sheets, shut doors, in the middle of the night no one there to hold him, comfort him.

It will not happen again. Not another time, her husband will die alone and not in her arms.

Not altogether seriously at first Hugo makes inquiries at the U.S. consulate on the Avenue Rodriguez Bonin near their hotel. The consulate is housed in a handsome old brick colonial town house set back in a meticulously landscaped park and surrounded by a five-foot wrought iron fence. Broad avenues lined with royal palms and bougainvillea, opulent rose gardens, stucco mansions with orange-tiled roofs, expensive vehicles parked conspicuously at the curbs—this is a wealthy part of Guayaquil where everything resembles an advertisement in a glossy magazine.

Not Hugo's kind of place, actually. Nothing that excites him to photograph. Yet, it is where he finds himself on this quest to be married.

(And how many times has Hugo Martinez been married? Jessalyn knows at least once, very likely twice. Beyond that?—she has not inquired, and she has not been told.)

All they need are their U.S. passports, they are informed by a smiling young receptionist in the consulate. The waiting time is twenty-four hours.

And so, twenty-four hours later Jessalyn and Hugo return to be married by the deputy chief of mission in his sun-filled office at the consulate. *Do you, Jessalyn Sewell McClaren, take this man, Hugo Vincent Martinez, to be your lawful wedded husband . . . And do you, Hugo Vincent Martinez, take this woman . . .* It is so vivid a scene, the deputy chief's midwestern voice so warmly enthusiastic, the crimson stripes of the American flag so neon-bright, cries of tropical birds (parrots?) outside the window so piercing-sweet, Jessalyn has to instruct herself—*But it is real! It is really happening.*

Like the second, or was it the third, mammogram. Hold breath, hold breath, don't release breath, continue to hold breath—*Now. Relax.*

Returned again to breathing. As she and Hugo manage to push rings (newly purchased, plain silver matching bands) onto each other's finger and Hugo stoops to kiss her happily on the lips.

(Jessalyn has moved her older rings to her right hand. Practical, pragmatic, an act of betrayal? Yet, it is accomplished.)

"Don Bankwell"—deputy chief of mission at the U.S. consulate at Guayaquil—is an exceptionally friendly fellow American specially empowered to conduct marriage ceremonies for U.S. citizens as well as to perform other legal services for Americans abroad, which he clearly enjoys, and why would he not enjoy such an enviable job, in this sunlit residence on Avenue Rodriguez Bonin, far from the howling-cold January American Midwest; not likely to be an ambassador, or even a consul general, but rather a trusted assistant, one day (perhaps) to serve in a great capital city like Paris, London, Rome, if he remains well-liked by his superiors at the State Department, and praised by Americans traveling abroad who are likely to be from time to time well-to-do and influential Americans, with friends in the State Department to whom they might report impressions of "Don Bankwell." And so Bankwell is eager to flatter Hugo and Jessalyn, and to introduce them to his administrative assistant, a dazzlingly beautiful young Ecuadorian woman who prepares the wedding documents and is a witness to the signatures.

Does it happen frequently, that Americans are married in the consulate at Guayaquil?

"Not what you'd call frequently," Don Bankwell says, "but yes, from time to time. Americans traveling abroad may suddenly have a strong desire to get married. Especially in tropical places. Nearing the Equator we start to feel that things are losing their reality. For the Equator itself hardly exists, it's more of a sensation. You begin to think, maybe nothing is real. But marriage, the actual thing—that will seem to most people real, permanent." So the deputy chief of mission declares, in his broad midwestern accent.

Jessalyn and Hugo are impressed. Marriage will seem, to most people, *real, permanent.* Yes. Yes of course, that must be so.

All things come to an end and melt into the stream. Husband and wife may vanish but their marriage is a permanent historical record.

Here is a remarkable coincidence: on a wall in the consulate reception area are several prints of photographs by Hugo taken years before in the Amazonian rain forest and given an exhibit, with other photographs of the Amazon, in the Whitney Museum, New York City, 1989. Hugo is astonished to recognize the several framed prints on the wall, and the deputy chief of mission is thrilled.

"*You* are this photographer? Martinez?"

It is such a pleasant surprise, staff workers are called to see. Too bad, the consul general isn't in his office! They have all been admiring these photographs, it seems, for months, if not years; and here, the handsome mustached photographer, in white cord suit, blue-striped shirt, sharp-creased trousers and open-toed sandals, stands smiling before them, accepting compliments and congratulations like a king, or a bridegroom.

So friendly, the deputy chief insists upon taking the newly married couple, and the gorgeous Margarita, around the corner to an outdoor restaurant for champagne.

"It isn't every day that I marry a great artist," the mission chief says gravely. "And such a beautiful gracious *señora*."

Margarita keeps a close eye on the deputy mission chief as if she fears that the American diplomat, middle-aged, going to fat, clearly and hopelessly in love with her, is in a tremulous state this morning.

Champagne!—a second round of toasts.

Even before the champagne Jessalyn has been feeling light-headed. A wave of vertigo.

If she were to shut her eyes and then open them, would she have any idea where she was?

Oh, Whitey! Where have you sent me.

Staring at her (new) husband: in his cord suit, striped shirt open at the throat. Very dashing, handsome. Is he a (Hispanic) film star just slightly past his prime? Or, rather—a world-renowned artist? His warm coffee-colored skin is flushed with pleasure, his dark eyes very bright. In moments of agitation he has a habit of plucking at his mustache. A wife will (eventually) try to discourage this habit, but not quite yet.

Jessalyn has made this man happy, has she?—perhaps then, Hugo will make Jessalyn happy in turn.

He'd insisted upon buying a dress for Jessalyn that morning, for her to be married in. White linen with short sleeves and a scooped neckline, the better to show off the bottle-blue glass beads he also purchased for her at a boutique on the avenue, where they'd picked up the matching silver rings. And an exquisite white lace shawl draped over her shoulders, as a bridal veil.

Poor Whitey had not known what to buy Jessalyn for birthdays and special occasions. A sort of shyness had paralyzed him. How very different Hugo Martinez who has given Jessalyn dozens of gifts during the relatively short time he has known her—handcrafted jewelry, scarves and shawls, hats, even dresses. Even a pair of "hiking sandals"—rubberized sandals with closed-in toes, very ugly but practical, ideal for the Galápagos. (How did Hugo know her size? He'd taken one of her shoes to the sporting equipment store.) Nothing shy about Hugo whose confidence in his own good taste is considerable.

Hugo examines the wedding certificate with its gilt seal of the

United States of America—*Jessalyn Sewell McClaren, Hugo Vincent Martinez*. The date of the marriage is January 11, 2012.

Hugo asks the mission chief, is this actually legal? Will it be recognized in the United States?—Bankwell assures him yes of course, it will be.

Shaking hands in parting. Don Bankwell is flushed with drink, moved nearly to tears. Beautiful Margarita will guide him back to the consulate, brew black coffee to sober him up. *Gracias! God bless you.*

After the champagne celebration Jessalyn purchases postcards in the hotel lobby. She will write home to her family at once. She has no intention of deceiving them.

To each of the children, a separate card. Though the message is identical:

> *Hugo and I were married this morning in the U.S. consulate at Guayaquil, Ecuador. Please be happy for us!*

AND WHAT HAVE THEY FORGOTTEN? Hugo suddenly realizes.

"We need prenuptial contracts. You are too trusting, dear."

Prenuptial contracts! Jessalyn wonders if this is one of Hugo's jokes, for Hugo has a whimsical sense of humor; but she sees that he has spoken gravely. In response, Jessalyn can only laugh nervously.

Hugo persists: "It's the first thing your children will ask about, Jessalyn. Especially your older children who are suspicious of me enough as it is."

Jessalyn tries to protest but her voice falters. Weakly she says, "But it's too late now, anyway. We are already married . . ."

In fact no, it is not too late. A prenuptial contract executed after a wedding has no less legal standing than one executed before. And the date is still January 11, 2012.

Hugo insists upon returning to the consulate before it closes that afternoon, to borrow the services of a secretary/typist and a notary public. It isn't required for them to see one of the diplomatic staff, or Don

Bankwell, only just the friendly Ecuadorian receptionist who recognizes the newly married couple and is willing to provide them with a secretary and a notary for a small fee.

Jessalyn is embarrassed at the prospect of such a contract. But Hugo says it's good for both of them, for instance she can't claim his house as shared property in the event that they are divorced, or any of his estate until the present day, and he can't claim hers.

Jessalyn sees that Hugo is joking. The (awkward) humor must lie in the fact, if it is a fact, that Hugo Martinez's estate is worth much less than Jessalyn's estate, but Jessalyn wonders if that's so. Surely Hugo's photographs are worth a great deal?

But Jessalyn understands Hugo's seriousness. He wants to show not Jessalyn, but her family, that he isn't after her money.

He isn't after the house on Old Farm Road. Or Jessalyn's shares of McClaren, Inc. Or whatever wealth her deceased husband has left her, bound up in a trust, or scattered among investments.

And so she agrees. What's the harm in signing a prenuptial?—there is no harm.

Basically, you are saying that all of your life previous to this marriage is walled-off from the new spouse. He/she cannot plunder it unless by a subsequent decision of your own you alter the terms.

Jessalyn could rewrite her will making Hugo a prominent heir. Hugo could rewrite his will. Jessalyn feels a shudder of dismay, thinking of such matters. Whitey's will!—in the near-catatonia of her initial grief she'd envisioned her husband's will as an oversized formal document and had searched for it in Whitey's desk drawers in vain, tears spilling from her eyes; when Thom searched he found the will within minutes, correctly filed in one of Whitey's drawers: a document of stapled pages of ordinary size.

Hugo dictates the prenuptial contract, stark in its simplicity, less than a page in length, and the secretary types it. The notary public will affix her seal.

"*Señora?*—please sign."

A new document to sign. Jessalyn obeys. It is all very formal, very proper and "legal"—though financial matters, and the talk that surrounds them, are the death of the soul and she is feeling just slightly dispirited, on this day when she should be so happy.

Out on the avenue Jessalyn tells Hugo in sudden passion that she hopes they live a long, long time together and that they die at exactly the same moment, so neither will have to deal with the other's estate.

Hugo laughs, startled. "Don't think of such morbid things, darling. That isn't like you."

"But I always think of such things," Jessalyn says, slipping her arm through his, "—don't you know me at all?"

NEXT MORNING in their airy white hotel room overlooking the Pacific Ocean Hugo plaits her hair: "For the first time, darling Jessalyn, as your husband."

Brushing the shoulder-length white hair, parting it in the center of her head, carefully braiding the strands together. Hugo is utterly absorbed, as in a trance of oblivion. Jessalyn leans her forehead against his shoulder feeling too weak, too deeply moved to speak. If Hugo plaits the hair too tight, Jessalyn does not register the fleeting pain.

"*Mi hermosa esposa,* I love so much."

"My dear husband, I love *so much.*"

They cannot possibly survive, Jessalyn thinks. Almost, she can envision the high white ceiling of the hotel cracking, collapsing. An earthquake?—does Guayaquil have earthquakes?

Expecting then, for such is Jessalyn's morbidity, that something terrible will happen to them on the drive to the airport or if not then, on the seven-hundred-mile flight west to Galápagos Islands National Park in the Pacific Ocean.

To the airstrip at Baltra Island where with other "eco-travelers" they board the *Esmeralda,* a brilliantly white cruise ship holding one hundred passengers.

Eight days in the Galápagos! It will be the adventure of Jessalyn's life.

For weeks Jessalyn has been reading books Hugo has provided her with such titles as *Galápagos: Enchanted Islands* and *Galápagos: Endangered Species* but she is still not fully prepared for the beauty and rawness of the region, or the physical arduousness required of tourists; she is dismayed by the wave-rocked dinghies that bear passengers from the *Esmeralda* to the islands in the Gulf of Chiriquí early each morning, and often involve "wet" landings—jumping out of the dinghy into the surf.

Nearly turning an ankle on one of her leaps onto a rock-strewn beach with other dinghy passengers. *Oh!*—the shock runs through her body, unaccustomed to such physical exertion.

Absorbed in his camera settings Hugo has gone ahead up the beach and another American tourist helps her regain her balance.

Ma'am? Are you all right?

Yes thank you. I am—all right.

Didn't sprain your ankle, did you? You're sure?

Oh yes. I am sure!

In a bulky orange life vest, in a long-sleeved white mosquito-resistant shirt, khaki shorts to the knee, the rubberized hiking sandals that tug like weights on her feet. In dark glasses and a wide-brimmed straw hat without which she would be blinded and helpless as a mollusk in the blinding tropical sun. Her neatly and practicably plaited hair will not be a distraction in the wind and she wears a backpack that Hugo has purchased for her. Hugo insists that she carry her own bottle of water on the island excursions, as he will carry his.

Hugo has a way of scolding her, if affectionately. Tugging at her braid. "Remember to drink plenty of water, *mi esposa*. I can't always be watching you."

Each morning they awaken early in their small spartan cabin in the *Esmeralda*. Each morning Jessalyn raises the blind to stare out the single horizontal window at darkened waters overtaken within minutes by an explosion of astonishing light, of indescribable hues. Always the ship is rocking, off-balance. Jessalyn has taken seasickness pills, that seem to have had some effect. At breakfast she has little appetite but is impressed to see how Hugo eats, with much zest.

Her heart is suffused with tenderness for the man who reaches for her in the night, in his sleep. Slipping his heavy warm arm over her as if to secure her. Though it is difficult to sleep beside him, he sleeps so deeply, his breathing is so deep and sonorous, while Jessalyn feels as if she is floating like froth on the surface of sleep, easily awakened.

Hugo buries his face in her neck. He calls her *dear, darling.* He calls her *mi amada esposa—my loving wife.* Jessalyn wonders if, in his deepest sleep, her husband knows who she is; if he confuses her with other women, as he might confuse himself with the other, younger man he'd once been.

How we sift through ourselves, with others. Clasping at hands that turn transparent, that dissolve in our touch. Crying out *No! Wait! Don't leave me, I can't live without you*—and in the next instant they are gone, and we remain, alive.

There is no housekeeping for their cabin—no maids to clean. Jessalyn who cannot abide messiness takes care to straighten the bedclothes, hang up Hugo's clothes flung across the bed, left atop a bureau. She takes care to hang damp towels neatly in the bathroom the size of a telephone booth, a narrow stall crudely hidden behind strips of translucent plastic. She cleans out the sink with wadded tissues and cleans the mirror, which Hugo never fails to leave splattered. It is awkward, such intimacy. In a weak moment Jessalyn thinks—*But why did I want to get married again? I was learning to be happy, alone.*

In the cabin they are always in each other's way! Hugo says, laughing, "I thought you were over there, darling, and here you are—*here.*"

Jessalyn says, "Are you sure there isn't more than one of you? Every time I turn around you are *looming.*"

And always the ship is rocking, night and day. Always seeming about to settle, then rising again, lifting and lowering, off-balance. Except that it varies in its force and rhythms the ceaseless motion would be comforting.

Hugo seems scarcely to notice even the rougher rocking. Jessalyn is aware of little else.

It is the adventure of my life. What remains of my life.

Of course—I am happy. I am alive.

Each morning passengers disembark from the *Esmeralda* in wave-buffeted dinghies quaintly named for Galápagos creatures—*Sea Lion, Tortoise, Dolphin, Iguana, Frigate, Albatross, Pelican, Cormorant, Howler Monkey, Boobie*. Like children at camp, or inmates in an institution, they line up dutifully to be issued safety vests and walking sticks. In the water the dinghies lurch, careen drunkenly. Suddenly you can't see the sky, for the choppy sea surrounds you. Passengers clutch at the edges of the dinghy with white-knuckled fists hoping not to look terrified. Jessalyn tries to laugh, she is so—breathless! Telling herself that there is no actual danger, Hugo would not have brought her to a place of danger, for he adores her.

Those fins in the water?—the tour guide points, and the dinghy passengers stare at the waves, trying to discern quick-darting dark fins.

Sharks. But probably baby sharks.

Some lift their cameras and cell phones, to take pictures. Baby sharks!

Are there often fatal accidents in the Galápagos, on these expeditions?—one of the more assertive passengers asks the tour guide; and the guide, a dark-skinned man in his early forties, looking as if he were part Indian and part Asian, says with a courteous smile that there are few accidents and virtually none that are fatal, if people follow safety rules.

None. If.

It is an ambiguous answer, Jessalyn thinks. But no one else seems to notice. For them, the answer is simply *none*.

PREDATOR, PREY. SURVIVAL, EXTINCTION. "Genetic memory."

In the Galápagos such divisions are stark. You are a predator, or you are prey. If you fail to survive, you become extinct. You do not exercise what is called, in some quarters, "free will"—rather, you behave by instinct, guided by something called "genetic memory."

If you survive, it is at the expense of others, who fail to survive. But if you survive, your survival is only temporary in any case.

Indeed, the islands are monuments to death. The bodies of animals are left where they have fallen, for no one in the park service will touch any of the animals. Bones stipple the landscape. In trees there are skeletons of birds, feathered wings trapped in branches. If you look closely on the rocky beaches you see the decaying, desiccated, or skeletal remains of creatures—sea lions, fur seals, turtles, iguanas, shorebirds. On the wind, over-ripe smells of corruption mixed with fresher, cooler air from the open sea.

Jessalyn thinks, dismayed—*But what a place he has brought us to, on our honeymoon!*

Yet each morning Jessalyn is exhilarated, hopeful. Each morning an astonishing dawn. Each morning new islands, and each island distinct from the others.

She finds herself thinking of the squint-eyed feral cat Mackie. In the Galápagos Mackie would have managed to survive, this is the predator's landscape.

Missing Mackie, as she misses her faraway home. A perverse nostalgia of which Jessalyn could never speak to another person, certainly not dear Hugo, for those nights of utter misery when the widow took comfort in a feral cat purring in a little nest at the foot of her bed, washing his whiskers clean of the clotted blood of some small devoured creature.

She smiles, recalling. Sophia is overseeing the house in her absence—will Mackie shift his affection to her? Jessalyn feels a pang of loss . . .

"Come along, darling. D'you need a hand?"

It is not altogether like Hugo, to be so solicitous. Usually, Hugo encourages Jessalyn to blunder along as best she can in such rough circumstances; he is a firm believer in what he calls *women's emancipation*—the emancipation from femininity, which is weakness and dependency upon men, which is a trap.

"Thank you, Hugo! I'm fine."

Not entirely true but uttering *fine* provides a certain small measure of satisfaction in this inhospitable place.

Jessalyn and Hugo have been assigned to the *Frigate* dinghy, which is one of the earliest to depart from the *Esmeralda*. At an hour of the morning when the air is still porous with mist and the tropical sun is just burning through layers of luminous cloud. And always there is wind.

Sixteen passengers in the dinghy. And the tour guide, who introduces himself as Hector—(his surname, Jessalyn cannot quite hear)—who has been a guide in the Galápagos National Park for nineteen years.

Hector is terse in his manner though friendly-seeming, courteous; carrying himself with a sort of military bearing, in the khaki Galápagos Park uniform: long-sleeved shirt, shorts to the knee, hiking boots. He informs the group that he is of Kuna Indian descent from the Kuna Yala archipelago, with a degree in evolutionary biology from the University of Ecuador; his particular interest is the ecology of coastal plant communities in the islands.

From her reading Jessalyn knows that their guide must be a descendant of Spanish holocaust survivors. A surpassingly ugly history, the ways in which the sixteenth-century Spanish conquistadores plundered the continent that would come to be called Latin America, wiping out most of the indigenous tribes of Central America in the name of religion—Roman Catholicism. It is striking, it is ironic, that their guide is himself a survivor of a massive near-extinction, a man-caused genocide.

Jessalyn wonders if Hector thinks of himself in those terms. And what does he think of his Caucasian-American charges?

A trip to the Galápagos for eight days is not inexpensive. Hugo has paid for the trip, over Jessalyn's protests. Even so, it is probable that her older children believe that she is paying for most, or all, of the trip.

Hector tells them of the fragility of ecosystems, that what appears to be solid and permanent is vulnerable to profound change. Introduce a new species of animal, insect, or plant to the Galápagos, and the results can be catastrophic. If plant communities are damaged, insects may be threatened, and creatures (like lava lizards) that prey upon insects may be damaged. Only recently did park authorities rid the islands of several devastatingly intrusive species—cats, rats, goats—at an expense of millions of dollars. European sailors had introduced these animals to the Galápagos in the nineteenth century, and their numbers had multiplied enormously, threatening indigenous species like giant tortoises, penguins, birds.

But how did you get rid of these cats, rats, goats?—Hector is asked by one of the tourists, who sounds startled.

Hector says that the information is included in the guidebook they'd all been issued, if they are interested in details. He assures them, "humane means" were used wherever possible.

However, the Galápagos environment is naturally pitiless. On the average of every four to seven years as many as 60 percent of Galápagos species die of starvation, despite the nutrient-rich nature of this part of the Pacific Ocean.

Overall, as many as 90 percent of all species that have ever lived have become extinct.

Jessalyn is stunned by such statistics. *Sixty percent? Ninety percent?* It does not seem possible.

She has never been a religious person. Casually, her family had seemed to believe in "God"—a Christian god, benign and abstract, in no way interfering with actual life. The question of "creation" had not engaged her intellectually but she sees now, in the wildly rocking dinghy approaching a rock-strewn shore in the Galápagos, in the Indian guide's matter-of-fact recitation, how absurd, how pitiful, for human beings to have imagined a special destiny, and a promise of immortality for believers, just for them.

One's own existence, so small. One's grief, happiness, love or failure to love—of so little consequence.

In this place in which suicide is a redundancy: a joke.

Beside her, Hugo is peering at his camera, adjusting the lens, with some difficulty in the rocking boat.

Jessalyn kisses the man's creased cheek. Jessalyn presses beside him, for warmth. Jessalyn asks if he finds the Galápagos overwhelming, or—inspiring?

"Overwhelming," says Hugo, after a moment. "And inspiring."

Does he think that human life is so inconsequential, as it appears to be here?

Again Hugo doesn't answer at once. He is adjusting something on his camera, Jessalyn's queries are distracting.

"Yes. Or, no."

"Yes and no?"

"No. But yes."

Peering into his viewfinder. Adjusting the viewfinder. For the photographer, the viewfinder puts all things that matter into scale.

"*SEÑORA*? BE CAREFUL, PLEASE."

What is it?—Jessalyn draws back in alarm.

She'd been about to step on what appears to be a miniature dragon. Seeing the creature suddenly, so camouflaged by its dull-glittering scales it is virtually indistinguishable from the coils of calcified lava beneath it.

On the paths around her, tourists are taking pictures of these large, slow-moving lizards—*iguanas*. On his long impatient legs Hugo has gone ahead, farther up one of the trails. It is midday, thrummingly warm. They have disembarked upon a volcanic-lava island with minimal, stunted vegetation, overrun with iguanas, smaller lizards, slow-scuttling red crabs. On higher ground, on cliffs overlooking the beach, vividly feathered shorebirds—blue-footed boobies, cormorants, gulls and pelicans.

The terrain of the island is astonishing. Very hilly, sculpted-looking, the calcified lava resembling coiled intestines of the hue of coal. At first glance the landscape looks dead but when you look closely you see that it is covered in iguanas that are near-invisible, camouflaged amid the coils of rock.

So many! Hundreds, thousands? Jessalyn feels a thrill of horror.

The prehistoric-looking creatures are of varying sizes, strewn across the terrain. Warming themselves in the January sun oblivious of lizards and crabs scuttling over them. Their hinged mouths are slightly agape, their tongues flick like raw nerves. They are dense-bodied, armored in scales, the largest the size of a Jack Russell terrier. They have survived hundreds of thousands of years and will very likely outlive *Homo sapiens*, Hector says. Hector seems somewhat bemused by the iguanas, describing their mating rituals. He passes his hand over the eyes of the iguana that Jessalyn has almost stepped on and the creature scarcely blinks.

A rudimentary consciousness, when not aroused to sexual excitement or fighting with another male. The island iguanas appear "tame" but it is misleading to call them "tame"—"They behave as they do because they have no genetic memory of human predators."

Hector explains that with the exception of the giant tortoises, which will retract their heads into their shells quickly if you approach them, all of the creatures in the Galápagos are indifferent to the presence of human beings, because they have no "genetic memories" of human predators—sea lions, penguins, shorebirds, pelicans.

Jessalyn asks if human beings have "genetic memories" of other human beings, as predators?—and Hector says, with a barking laugh, "But of course, *señora*. It is hardwired into our brains—what is called 'xenophobia.' The Neanderthals lacked such an instinct, and *Homo sapiens* destroyed them."

Was this so? Or did the Neanderthals die of other causes also? Jessalyn has only a vague memory from long ago, when she'd been an undergraduate fascinated by natural history, as she'd been fascinated by poetry and philosophy; a long-ago life, scarcely a fossil-memory now, before love, marriage, motherhood had grasped her in their snug comforting coils.

But what a curious world, the Galápagos!—Jessalyn thinks. Like the looking-glass world in which the child Alice wandered into a forest where no creatures had names and where, as a consequence, wild animals like fawns didn't know that human beings might be their enemies.

Someone in Jessalyn's group asks if man is the predominant predator of all predators and Hector says no, actually not, in biological terms *Homo sapiens* is an omnivore, and not a carnivore, capable of living without eating meat if necessary.

In terms other than biological—?

"Well, *Homo sapiens* is very aggressive. War-making. In that way, predatory."

Adding then, as if this is a personal, quirky notion and not a statement of the Galápagos Park authority, "And man is a being that looks upward. Always, upward."

Jessalyn, who has been feeling overwhelmed by the Galápagos environment, feels heartened by this remark. The mere word *upward* in this barren place is stirring and uplifting to her.

Of course, the Galápagos is hardly a barren place. It is ignorant, short-sighted to think so.

Teeming with life. In the swirling dark waters, teeming with microscopic life. In the sculpted-intestine lava rock, teeming with lizards, hideous scuttling red crabs.

Everywhere you look, shorebirds shrugging their wide wings, quivering with appetite.

Life *is* appetite.

But is appetite *life*?

But where is Hugo?—Jessalyn is missing her photographer-husband.

Like several others in the group he doesn't stay within Hector's earshot. He is an experienced hiker, the trails are not difficult for Hugo. He is not often beside Jessalyn on a trail for long, for he becomes impatient with the slow pace of the group, and with the often-inane questions put to the tour guide by the other tourists.

Some of these are families, with quite young children. All are earnestly taking pictures, and have to be reprimanded by Hector, from time to time, for drifting off the trail and coming too close to living things.

Jessalyn shades her eyes, peers ahead. Hugo has been hiking up the trail, which has turned steep, and is out of sight. (Not recommended, Hector has warned. Please keep in my sight at all times!) Naively Jessalyn has imagined that she and Hugo would spend time together in the Galápagos, perhaps walking hand in hand—she sees now that this is unlikely.

They are together on the *Esmeralda,* in their cramped cabin almost too much together, and in the dinghy Hugo sits close beside her, but as soon as the tour group sets out on an island trail, led by Hector, Hugo and a few others (male, of varying ages) are eager to slip ahead, to set their own pace; Hector doesn't try to rein them in, for they would likely rebel against him.

Of course, Hector respects Hugo: the two men have a rapport of sorts, recognizing each other in a way that circumnavigates the Caucasian-Americans among them. If they wished, they could communicate in rapid-fire Spanish. For a man of his age Hugo is very fit: his shoulders, arms and legs are ropey with muscle, he has been hiking (as he has said) for most of his life, and is usually brimming with energy. He rarely becomes out of breath, he rarely leans on his walking stick. Taking photographs excites him as a hawk is excited by sighting prey on the ground below—he simply must get to it!

But Jessalyn knows, Hugo can become very tired, suddenly; in her arms, he is capable of falling asleep within seconds, as a small child sleeps; a sleep so profound it feels exhausted, stunned. But when he awakens, he is suffused with energy, you might say with *himself.*

Jessalyn smiles, thinking of Hugo as a sexual being. He is very affectionate, very easily aroused, and very easily satisfied.

And how happy he has been, in this desolate place! Nothing more thrilling to Hugo than to rise early, clamber about on the decks of the *Esmeralda* to take photographs of the mist-shrouded ocean dawn, as the extraordinary Pacific sky lightens, and climb to the highest peaks of islands to take photographs in places few others would dare to venture.

Jessalyn is exasperated with Hugo, and Jessalyn is very proud of Hugo. She loves him, for Hugo is the most loveable of men, but she is not *in love* with him. She doesn't think so.

Or maybe yes, in fact she is. Maybe she has become, these last few days, since the wedding ceremony in the consulate, *in love* with Hugo Martinez.

As Whitey is less present in her life, Hugo is more present. Whitey is a sun, but a waning sun. Hugo is the new, luminous moon, coming into its fullness.

Without him, where would I be?

Without him to love me, who would I be?

But more, she would have no one to love. Tenderness stirs in her, like life itself. So long as Jessalyn is alive, she must have someone to love and to care for.

She respects women who live alone, who have renounced even the yearning for another. But she is not so strong, she does not want to be a *brave widow.*

Hugo has forced her to inhabit her body more fully. He has said, a woman must be as fit as a man. More than any man, for a woman will wind up taking care of a man. (This is a joke.) Your soul is not cotton candy to melt in the lightest rain but something beautiful and resilient like silk, he has said extravagantly. But Whitey hadn't liked seeing his wife struggling with a task, shoveling in the garden for instance, dragging a heavy chair, hadn't liked his beautiful slender wife panting with effort. Whitey had strolled about the lawn, declining to drag away fallen tree limbs—"That's why we hire a lawn crew," he'd said. "That's why we pay them good money. That's why we have more money than they do—to hire them, and shift money to them."

Whitey had meant to be funny, Jessalyn supposed. Now, his words didn't seem so funny.

Penguins, shorebirds, gulls. Continuous chattering, squawking. Everywhere on the rocks are glaring-white bird droppings. And animation in the air. Swift changes of course, feathered creatures diving into the water to spear prey in their beaks. All is food hunting, food consumption. Life begetting life. It is a blunt depressing fact or (perhaps) it is a beautiful fact, to be contemplated intellectually.

Jessalyn recalls—*Life is a comedy to those who think, a tragedy to those who feel.* Yet in time, comedy yields to tragedy. And tragedy to forgetfulness and oblivion.

Hector is leading his group in another direction. Trying not to think about Hugo, dear Hugo who has been out of sight for at least a half hour, Jessalyn is drawn to the remarkable penguins, so seemingly tame, and blue-footed boobies feeding their noisy young, on their white-streaked boulders above the sea. And cormorants whose bodies have grown too heavy for their limbs to lift.

Beautiful birds, wind rippling their feathers. Some are asleep on one leg, the other drawn up gracefully beneath their bellies. Such peace despite the animation in the air, eyes shut.

The previous day they'd hiked on an island inhabited by sea lions and their young. Not so much like lions as walruses, though smaller than walruses, fattish, graceless, with large black eyes that seem almost human. A pack of sea lions barking, braying, moaning, groaning and grunting. And yet in the midst of these, some were sleeping. And cubs were nursing. As in the interstices of lichen-covered rocks a decaying sea-lion corpse of massive proportions overlooked the inlet of living sea lions like a not-fully-banished deity.

It was Hugo who'd made that observation—*not-fully-banished deity*. Squatting to take photographs of the corpse amid the rocks, in juxtaposition to sea lions sleeping, nursing, playing on the beach oblivious of the death of an elder in such proximity.

Jessalyn shrank away, repelled by the rotting stench. But for the photographer, all is material. Young life, death. Beauty, decay. Beauty in decay. Wistfully Jessalyn observed the man who is her new husband, from a little distance.

Recalling how, at the start of their knowing each other, she'd been merely a figure in a composition to him—*widow.*

And that figure, in that composition, *Untitled: Widow* which Hugo Martinez has gone on to print and reprint, to exhibit and to sell, will outlive her.

Of course, *Untitled: Widow* will outlive the photographer, too.

In the midst of remarks by Hector on plant communities on the island—the relationship between the sea lions and crucial vegetation—suddenly there is a rainstorm: Jessalyn and some others huddle beneath a spindly-limbed tree as the sky bursts into rain like hot spit, rapid-fire and percussive.

Fortunately, Hugo has insisted that Jessalyn wear a rain jacket on the excursions, lightweight plastic with a hood; it is not much effort for her to pull the hood over her head, and wait out the rain.

Steam rises from wet-gleaming rocks, boulders. Cries of shorebirds seem amplified. A fresh smell of bird droppings is very sharp.

Hillsides of iguanas scarcely move, glittering now in the sun as sunlight returns with an eye-aching acuity.

Somewhere not too far away, Hugo is taking photographs. And these will be (Jessalyn knows) beautiful, striking. And yet, back home, in the house on Cayuga Road, there are hundreds, thousands?—of beautiful and striking photographs by Hugo Martinez, many of which he has not yet gotten around to filing, let alone framing. In the console computer in his studio, attached to a state-of-the-art printer, are even more photographs in digital storage, not yet printed out because (as Hugo says with comic despair) he is years behind. Jessalyn has wondered if he will ever catch up?

To Jessalyn's dismay Hector is summoning his *Frigate* group, to return to the dinghy and embark for another island. Like clockwork: as one dinghy arrives, another departs. Jessalyn hurries to search for Hugo whom she has not seen in—has it been an hour now? Asking people she meets on the trail if they have seen a "tall, older man with a mustache"—"carrying a camera"—trying not to show her alarm.

For Hugo will be annoyed with her, or embarrassed, if he knows that she is looking for him, and that she is worried about him.

Vaguely she is told that he is farther up the trail. Older man with a mustache, hair to his shoulders, carrying a camera?—and is he also *Hispanic*?

Seeing the not-quite-disguised surprise, or suggestion of surprise, in the faces of those to whom she has appealed, that a so-very-white American woman would be in the company of a Hispanic male.

Jessalyn hurries up the trail, which is rocky, and steep. In terror of turning an ankle at such a crucial time. It is difficult to breathe in the humid over-bright air.

In Quito, the air was too thin. Here at sea level, the tropical air is too thick.

When she finds Hugo at the very top of the trail she sees that he is seated on a rock-ledge, dabbing at a bleeding knee with a wad of tissues another hiker has given him. Sighting Jessalyn he calls out smilingly to her, to assure her that he's fine; just a little fall, no bones broken, he's been resting before he started back down. Jessalyn feels faint at the sight of the bright blood.

The other hiker who has remained with Hugo, a younger man, offers to help Hugo to his feet but Hugo waves him away with thanks. Of course—Hugo is *fine*.

Jessalyn kneels before Hugo and examines his knee. He'd fallen hard, it seems: already the knee is swollen and discolored. If the knee-cap is fractured or broken—! But Hugo insists that it is not, repeats that he'd just been resting, regaining his strength before starting back down.

Jessalyn sees that Hugo is quite upset. And that Hugo is determined to appear to be calm, even bemused.

To Hugo's embarrassment the Indian guide has followed Jessalyn up the trail, and insists now upon helping Hugo to his feet. Hector is kindly and yet forceful. He tells Hugo that their dinghy must leave soon, and he, Hugo, cannot be left behind.

Hugo is apologetic, his face flushed, abashed. He has been deeply mortified. He would have liked the guide not to see him like this and he would like very much to decline Hector's help, but he needs it; he would not be able to descend the trail unassisted. Heaving himself to his feet with a sharp intake of breath, as Hector and Jessalyn come to help him, slipping their arms around his waist. How warm Hugo is, sweating through his shirt! Normally graceful on his feet Hugo now staggers, and is uncertain. When he leans his weight on his right leg, he winces. Jessalyn bites her lower lip to keep from crying.

There is the danger, if Jessalyn begins crying over this trifle, she will not be able to stop.

From the foot of the trail the guide's young assistant comes running, to help as well. By this time people are observing poor Hugo, making his way painstakingly downhill, leaning on Hector and Jessalyn.

The tall mustached handsome man with the camera!—in the dinghy Hugo had always seemed so much at ease, so practiced and unconcerned about buffeting waves, shark fins circling the boat.

At the dinghy Hugo is red-faced and panting but insists upon climbing in by himself. He is using his walking stick as a cane. His body trembles with the strain of keeping his body erect without putting weight on his injured knee.

Discreetly, Hector keeps away. He has seen too many affluent North American male tourists turn nasty when they have needed his assistance; better to allow them to limp leaning on their wives, who can be despised but then forgiven.

Once settled inside the dinghy Hugo seems to feel better. Tries to joke to his fellow *Frigates* about being clumsy, taking a chance on a rock that turned out to be loose, most stupid mistake a hiker can make. Another time he checks his camera—thank God it wasn't broken.

Jessalyn's heart is suffused with sympathy for Hugo, the experienced hiker who has had an accident, the swaggering (aging?) male who has lost his balance and his composure in front of witnesses. From her shoulder bag she takes fresh tissues, to press against the wound, a series of abrasions just below the knee that continue bleeding, though not so profusely as before.

A stream of blood down Hugo's leg, glistening in the thick dark hairs of his leg, seeping into his rubberized hiking sandals.

Poor Hugo!—Jessalyn would embrace him, weep over him, but he would be mortified by such a display, and she dares not become emotional in such a public place.

The dinghy will drop Hector and the others on the island of Puerto Ayora but continue on to the *Esmeralda,* so that the ship's doctor can examine the afflicted man. Hugo exclaims wonderingly—it happened so quickly! A rock had come loose on the trail, his attention was distracted, he'd lost his balance and, in falling, tried to prevent the camera from being smashed . . . Yes, I know, Jessalyn murmurs, holding his hand as one might hold a boy's hand. (Which boy? Bold brash Thom, of course.) Hugo is disappointed to have cut the day short yet relieved that he has been brought back to the *Esmeralda*—he wouldn't have been able to continue in the condition he's in.

Back at the *Esmeralda* Hugo makes an effort to be good-natured, stoic. He allows the ship's doctor to sterilize and bandage the wounds, that are shallow; he allows Jessalyn to fuss over him, kiss him. She assures him, as others had: the rocks were slippery from the rain, the trail was steep. She assures him: she loves him, he has made her so very happy.

Drowsy with painkillers Hugo drifts off to sleep in the semi-darkened cabin. Soon he is snoring, in uneven gasps. Jessalyn sits on the edge of the lumpy bed, holding his hand; her fingers through his, though he is unaware of her. They are wearing matching wedding bands! How strange this seems, somehow reassuring. There is this bond between them, then—is there? Neither would abandon the other on a volcanic-lava island in the Pacific.

The Ecuadorian silver rings are quite elegant in their simplicity. Hers is just slightly loose, Hugo's fits snugly. It would not surprise Jessalyn to learn that Hugo has a wedding band or two in a drawer somewhere at his house.

Jessalyn wonders about the tact of wearing her old rings on her right hand. Surely, someone will notice, and comment dryly? But the rings are too precious to her to put away. The engagement ring with its small square-cut diamond which Whitey had purchased for her, at an age much younger than their youngest son is now . . .

Jessalyn thinks, she cannot bear another loss. Hugo had only slipped and fallen, bruised and battered a knee, indeed it is nothing serious (the doctor has said) but she remains badly shaken. Her heart is beating erratically, as it had beat (she recalls now) when the news had come, Whitey had been hospitalized with a (suspected) stroke.

If something happens to Hugo she will swallow all the pills she can acquire, as soon as she can. As she'd failed to do when Whitey had died, out of cowardice and confusion.

She had failed to save Whitey. Failed to keep Whitey from dying. With this man, she must not fail.

This man is so precious to her, it's as if her beating heart were exposed to the air. She has not felt so vulnerable since the children were very young. Each baby, so vulnerable! The soft spots on the infant's head, how terrifying! She'd been afflicted by horrific fantasies of the newest baby falling and by some bizarre fluke striking a soft spot of the skull, piercing the thin bone . . . *Fontanelle*. The very word had been frightening to her, she can hardly bring herself to recall it now.

But the babies had not fallen, in quite that way. Numerous falls over the years but none lethal. In fact, the babies had done very well for themselves, considering their *fontanelle*-vulnerable beginnings. Even Virgil, the most accident-prone of the children, had never seriously injured himself. And the mother had forgotten, in time. The mother had simply forgotten. Blessed forgetfulness, that wipes away the fears that so cripple us.

BEAUTIFUL!—the melting-red tropical sun is beginning to sink beyond the horizon, that seems very distant, thousands of miles away.

With the sinking of the sun there emerges an astonishing luminosity of clouds, minute cloud patterns that appear sculpted. Those dream-images that rush beneath our eyelids in the early stage of sleep and leave us hypnotized.

Since Hugo's fall that morning he has been unusually quiet. He is abashed, chagrined. Wants to laugh at himself—wounded macho pride. Indeed, wounded Hispanic-male macho pride.

Slept for two hours (sweaty, twitchy sleep) then dragged himself to the ship's library, leaning on a walking stick. (Of course, Jessalyn accompanied him.) Since the fall Hugo breathes more audibly than usual, wincing as he walks. But he insists that the pain is abating, it's mostly a swelling, a lurid bruise the size of a tennis ball his fingers can't resist touching, stroking.

The ship's doctor was reasonably sure that there is no actual break or fracture in the complicated bones of his knee: Hugo will know definitely when they leave the Galápagos and return to civilization, to a medical center where he can have the knee X-rayed. Until then it is only reasonable to stay off the leg as much as possible, to walk sparingly and always with a cane, in fact two canes.

Not "canes"—walking sticks, Hugo insists. There is a distinction!

Gloomily Hugo says, "A premonition of the future."

It is not quite the accurate term, is it?—*premonition*? Poor Hugo, Jessalyn squeezes his hand, to indicate that he is exaggerating, it is really nothing, cheer up!

So the wife will *cheer up* the gloomy husband. As the husband will *cheer up* the gloomy wife.

(But no: Jessalyn is resolved never to be *gloomy*. Or to give that impression, for who wants a *gloomy wife*?)

Since the wedding they have been discussing where they will live when they return to Hammond. Hugo believes (strongly) that it would be best for them to acquire a new residence, a new property, to sell their old houses (maybe) and start a new household together; for always in Jessalyn's house on Old Farm Road he would be a visitor, a guest; he would not feel at ease, and she would not be able to think of him as her *husband*. Still less is it likely that they could live in Hugo's ramshackle house on Cayuga Road, with the shifting population of tenants and the offices of Liberation Ministries; except of course, Hugo's studio is there, and he does not want to move his studio.

Jessalyn says, of course she understands. Hugo has had that studio for decades, he should not move if he does not want to move.

Jessalyn does not want to move out of her house, not just yet. Jessalyn feels just a slight prick of panic at this possibility—*No! Whitey would not understand.*

It is Whitey she would be leaving behind. Hugo is quite right, to understand that the deceased husband prevails in the house, and will never fade away. Yet, Hugo can't bring himself to utter this claim.

The house on Old Farm Road is so large, very reasonably others could live there, with Jessalyn (and with Hugo). A *halfway house* it could be. Not all of the house but part of the downstairs. There are eight or nine bedrooms. Certainly there is space for at least one of the unjustly incarcerated men freed by the Liberators, ideal for this purpose would be a guest suite with a door opening at the rear of the house . . . When Jessalyn first mentions this possibility to Hugo he says it's a very good idea, very generous of her, but in the next breath he adds, "Your children will be upset, however. They will never allow it." Jessalyn tries not to be annoyed by Hugo's conflation—*your children*. He should know very well by now that only the elder three are prejudiced against him, the youngest two are fond of him and are surely happy that he and Jessalyn have married.

"Sophie and Virgil won't object. I don't think so. Virgil might even want to be involved. I'm sure he's sympathetic with the Liberators."

And Whitey, what would Whitey think? God damn he'd have been surprised, indeed shocked, initially disapproving but in time, knowing Whitey, his generosity, his affable resignation to what he'd called expediency, political or financial expediency, a fancy way of saying whatever the hell came next, essentially Whitey would have been impressed that his wife, his widow, dear sweet unassertive Jessalyn, has so extended the perimeters of her life, as she has dared to travel to a part of the world he'd never seen, nor would have imagined seeing; as she has dared to remarry, and to keep herself alive. He'd have been happy for her, that his spirit might prevail in the house—*Think the best of me, Jessalyn. I tried to be the best person I could be and if I was not, I can be that person now. If you love me remember me in that way.*

IN THE SKY AT DUSK, a new moon of the delicate pale-orange hue of a cut melon. So beautiful!

It is a full moon glimpsed through skeins of slow-moving clouds, dimpled with shadow, luminous. Difficult to think of such glowering light as merely reflected, lacking its own life.

They have dragged deck chairs close together so that they can sit hand in hand, bathed in this strange pale-orange moonlight. Between them, two glasses of delicious dark red Ecuadorian wine.

Wanting to be alone they have ascended surreptitiously to the third level of the *Esmeralda*. Some areas of the ship are popular, others near-deserted. This is an area that is totally deserted though the view of the sunset has been spectacular.

Many *Esmeralda* passengers gather at the prow of the ship where there is a cocktail bar, guitarists playing festive Latin music. Others gather downstairs in a large bar, adjacent to the enormous dining room, where American pop-rock music plays continuously, grating to the ear.

Hugo especially wants to be alone with his wife, just for now. Away from the unwanted solicitude of others. He has purchased a glass of wine for each of them with the assumption that, if Jessalyn doesn't finish hers, he will be welcome to finish it as usual.

Jessalyn laughs, wine goes quickly to her head. She wonders at the wisdom of drinking, after an exhausting day in the Galápagos.

Hugo has been limping more noticeably when he doesn't think that anyone is watching. He has gripped the stairway railing, to haul himself up to the third deck. Jessalyn pretends she has not seen.

It is like sighting Hugo in the hospital, in the Oncology ward. Or someone who resembled Hugo. Best to pretend you do not see.

Drinking makes Hugo melancholy but also elated, prone to laughter.

What a joke it is!—on his honeymoon, his God-damned knee is *ruined*.

Well, not *ruined*—not exactly.

Jessalyn laughs at him. Why does he exaggerate so much?

In his photographs Hugo does not exaggerate at all. A deeper and more profound Hugo emerges in the photographs, not always evident in the man.

The artist is fearless, Jessalyn thinks. The man, not always.

In the main dining room of the cruise ship it has become known (somehow) that Jessalyn and Hugo are newlyweds. (Did Hugo tell someone? Jessalyn certainly did not.) The very term *newlyweds* is quaint, touching. Strangers smile at them affectionately. A beautiful brave "older" couple. But now Hugo, who never fails to dress for dinner (long-sleeved, embroidered white shirts open at the throat, with cuff links, sometimes a sport coat) seems to be limping. Oh, did Hugo hurt himself?—on one of those trails? Perfect strangers are sympathetic.

Coming down a steep path too fast. His own God-damned fault, Hugo will say. As *own God-damned fault* needs to be acknowledged.

Hugo insists upon sitting at different tables for most meals. There are no assigned tables on the cruise, fortunately, so no one is stuck with anyone else. Of course, Jessalyn would return to the same table, to the same people with whom they'd struck up a previous mealtime conversation, out of courtesy, or a wish not to hurt feelings, for she recalls the painful choices of middle school and high school, when she'd felt obliged to sit with girls less popular than her friends and herself, out of a dread of hurting feelings; but Hugo is shockingly indifferent to the feelings of their fellow passengers, including even people with whom (Jessalyn had thought) he had gotten along very well. Hugo's philosophy is that there are always more interesting persons somewhere close by, it is up to Hugo to seek them out—among the *Esmeralda* passengers are biologists, specialists in endangered species and global warming, research scientists, mathematicians, university professors and public school teachers, teenaged science prodigies, many amateur photographers, even an animal trainer. In his handsome clothes, his silver-streaked hair brushed back from his forehead, Hugo Martinez is a popular figure on the cruise ship; Jessalyn, beside him, is the gracious wife.

It is dusk now. On the open deck Jessalyn shivers. Over her shoulders, the white-lace shawl Hugo purchased for her as a bridal veil. But the shawl isn't very warm or practical.

Each day in the tropics the air is altered as soon as the sun disappears beneath the horizon. There is a particular sort of visceral anguish—foolish, involuntary—one feels as the glowing-red sun perceptibly sinks away. There arises then a prevailing wind with an undercurrent of cold.

Cheered and enlivened by the delicious dark-red wine, Hugo is talking about the Galápagos—this place of wonders! How he'd wanted to come here for much of his life but had never quite made it until now. For a while, he'd hoped to come with his son who'd died. But they'd never quite made it.

Hugo is not so cheerful now. He is a man of moods, Jessalyn has discovered. She must learn to accept these moods as they come, and to prepare herself (she suspects) for darker moods, hidden from her so far. She guesses that there are numerous painful losses in Hugo's life in addition to the loss of his son but he speaks only of his son.

For a man so seemingly extroverted, so curious about others' lives, Hugo is in fact quite reticent about his own. Jessalyn has casually asked him about his health and Hugo has said he is fine.

Really? He is *fine*?

Absolutely *fine*—"Don't I look good? For my age, at least? And what about you, dear Jessalyn? You look lovely but—how is your health?"

Teasing her. Expecting her to laugh.

If she'd asked him about the hospital, had he an appointment in the infusion room, Hugo would have deflected the question with a joke. *But that wasn't me, Jessalyn.*

And—*Of course, it wasn't me.*

But there is no one like you, Hugo. I would not mistake you for anyone.

I think you must have mistaken me, dear. For someone else.

If you are ill—please tell me. I want to know.

Not ill. Not now. Or if I am, I am in remission.

In remission? What do you mean?

Kiss me!

Shortly before they'd left for Ecuador Jessalyn happened to notice a tight adhesive bandage around Hugo's upper arm; when she'd asked what it was Hugo said he'd donated blood that day, at the medical center.

Oh! Was it a custom of Hugo's, to donate blood? He had not mentioned it . . .

With a gesture Hugo ripped off the adhesive bandage. Needle tracks beneath, not inflamed or reddened. He hadn't liked being questioned and had declined to explain further.

Of course, Jessalyn had never told Hugo about the false-positive mammogram. If she'd had a malignancy she would have tried not to tell him. There are many things in her personal life she has not told Hugo. Such as—*I am your wife but I am another man's widow. A widow who remarries is a widow who remarries. Please understand!*

Hugo would understand. You don't reach the age of almost-sixty without enduring losses of your own.

The older, the more secrets. And the fewer you wanted to share, if they were disturbing. Why would you?

Life too short. Sorrow too long. *Kiss me!*

Holding hands, peering at the moon. Clouds blowing across the moon like stray thoughts. Appear, disappear. So swiftly.

Trying not to think that they will be, must be, punished for their happiness; it does not seem just, that they will be allowed even a modicum of happiness. Surely it was a mistake to travel so far with a man she scarcely knows—though now, astonishingly, this man is her husband. *I will never return home. They will bury me here at sea. That is what I deserve.* The widow feels that she must accept this fate though it would be a terrible fate—devoured by sea creatures.

Jessalyn would hope to be dead, at least. They wouldn't toss her body overboard without determining that she was really dead—would they?

Hugo has been watching her. He asks what she has been thinking about?—"*Mi hermosa esposa,* you're looking so *grim.*"

Jessalyn laughs nervously. Trying to sound amusing as she tells him, "I've been wondering, if a person dies at sea, do they lower him—or her—overboard? Is there 'burial at sea'? The expense of shipping a body back to North America would be so high . . ."

Hugo laughs, startled. "Jesus! Nobody is going to die and be tossed overboard, this isn't a pirate or a slave ship. Lighten up, darling!"

Hugo is startled, taken aback as Whitey would have been. Jessalyn relents at once.

"Oh, of course. What am I saying. Don't listen to me, Hugo."

Laughing together. Jessalyn recalls how the children used to laugh at her, their sweet silly mother who said the most unexpected things.

Dusk is deepening. In the windy air laced with an actual chill there is a smell of something like flowers.

Don't listen. Nothing that I say matters.

Nothing that any of us says matters.

Amid a vast expanse of rolling, rocking waves. Occasionally there comes ocean spray like cold spit against their faces.

What do they matter, such miniature lives? The wisdom of the Galápagos is brute survival, for a time. But only for a time. And beyond that, death and extinction. There is comfort in this, that individuals matter so little, and yet are gripping each other's hand so tightly.

Oh, Jessalyn will. She promises! She will *lighten up*.

The beautiful white-braided hair is stirred by the wind. Her eyes are moist from the wind.

Roiling, rocking waves in which the luminous moon is reflected like a mad face. Mesmerizing how, with each passing second, light reflected from this mad face breaks and ripples in the waves, forming new designs, like the murmurations of flocking birds, fleeting, dazzling, and gone. With each heartbeat all is changed, altered. That warm strong hand grasping yours to the point of pain.

Never let me go! I love you.

Hugo is excited by something he has just noticed. At the horizon, where the sun disappeared just a few minutes ago, there is something like an after-sun, a kind of post-sunset of muted light—"See? There? Or maybe it's an optical illusion . . . D'you see it?"

"Y-Yes . . ."

Though Jessalyn isn't sure what she is seeing, if anything. Her eyes blink away moisture in the chill wind.

For this fleeting moment you have (almost) forgotten the man's name though you understand that he is your husband. Your hands are clasped together tight, this is a comfort on the rocking ship. It has happened, you have been (re)married, he is the husband who adores you and will protect you until that moment in the rush of time to come when he cannot any longer adore you and protect you and he will release your hand, and you his; it is that faint haze at the horizon lifting from the sea like a glimmer of hope, where moonlight ripples in the roiling dark water at which you stare and stare.